First Edition

(Acts)

EMPIRE

EMPIRE

BY

GORE VIDAL

ANDRE DEUTSCH

First published in Great Britain 1987
by André Deutsch Limited
105–106 Great Russell Street London WC1B 3LJ

Copyright © 1987 by Gore Vidal
All rights reserved

A signed first edition of this book has
been privately printed by The Franklin Library

ISBN 0 233 98152 7

Printed in Great Britain by
St Edmundsbury Press, Bury St Edmunds, Suffolk

1

"The war ended last night, Caroline. Help me with these flowers."
Elizabeth Cameron stood in the open French window, holding a
large blue-and-white china vase filled with roses, somewhat show-
ily past their prime. Caroline helped her hostess carry the heavy
vase into the long cool dim drawing room.

At forty, Mrs. Cameron was, to Caroline's youthful eye, very old
indeed; nevertheless, she was easily the handsomest of America's
great ladies and certainly the most serenely efficient, able to
arrange a platoon of flower vases before breakfast with the same
ease and briskness that her uncle, General Sherman, had devastated Georgia.

"One must always be up at dawn in August." Mrs. Cameron
sounded to Caroline rather like Julius Caesar, reporting home.
"Servants—like flowers—tend to wilt. We shall be thirty-seven for
lunch. Do you intend to marry Del?"

"I don't think I shall every marry anyone." Caroline frowned with pleasure at Mrs. Cameron's directness. Although Caroline thought of herself as American, she had actually lived most of her life in Paris and so had had little contact with women like Elizabeth Sherman Cameron, the perfect modern American lady—thus, earth's latest, highest product, as Henry James had not too ironically proclaimed. When Del asked Caroline to join the house-party at Surrenden Dering, deep in the English countryside, she had not even pretended to give the matter thought. She had come straight on from Paris, with a single night at Brown's Hotel in London. That was Friday, and the United States and Spain had been at war for three exciting months. Now, apparently, the war was over. She tried to recall the date. Was it August 12 or August 13, 1898?

"Mr. Hay says that the President agreed to an armistice yesterday afternoon. Which was last night for us." She frowned. "Those roses look rather awful, don't they?"

"They're a bit . . . dusty. I suppose from all that heat."

"Heat!" Mrs. Cameron laughed, a fairly pleasant sound so unlike the stylized staccato screech of a Paris lady. 'You should try Pennsylvania this time of year! My husband has two places. Each hotter than the other, with mosquitoes and gnats and something very small and vile that burrows like a mole under your skin and raises a welt. You would make a good wife for Del."

"But would he make a good husband for me?" Through the tall windows Caroline could see her co-host, Don Cameron, on the grassy lower terrace. He was driving a buggy, drawn by a pair of American trotting-horses. Senator Cameron was a red-faced, heavily moustached but modestly bearded man, older by a quarter century than his wife. As she could not abide him, she treated him with exquisite courtesy and deference; just as she treated in a rather cool and offhanded way Caroline's other co-host, the equally ancient Henry Adams, who entirely adored her as she entirely accepted him. According to Del, the trio had struck Henry James, who lived a few miles away at Rye, as "maddeningly romantic." When Del had repeated this to Caroline, both agreed that although antiquity might indeed be instructive, exotic, even touching, no couple so aged could ever be romantic, maddeningly or otherwise. But then the celebrated expatriate Mr. James was like some highly taut musical string of feline gut, constantly attuned to vibrations unheard by cruder ears.

Yet old as Mrs. Cameron was, Caroline could not help but admire the slender waist, which seemed unstayed; also, the heat had so flushed her cheeks that she looked—Caroline finally capitulated—beautiful, at least this morning, with naturally waved, old-gold hair, cat-like blue eyes, straight nose and straight mouth, framed by the square jaw of her celebrated uncle. Had Caroline not been so recently and so arduously finished at Mlle. Souvestre's Allenswood School she might have offered herself as an apprentice to Mrs. Cameron: "Because I want to live forever in America, now that Father's dead." Caroline heard herself say rather more than she had intended.

"Forever is a long time. But if I had forever to spend somewhere it wouldn't be there, let me tell you. It would be Paris."

"Well, since I've spent most of my life—so far—in Paris, home looks all the greener, I suppose."

"May you find it so," said Mrs. Cameron vaguely, her attention now distracted by the cook, an elderly woman who was at the door, with the day's menus to be discussed. "Oh, Cook! What a triumph last night! Senator Cameron admired—and couldn't stop eating—the sweet potatoes."

"Impossible things he gives me to prepare." In a long white dress, the cook looked like an abbess in a novel by Scott.

Mrs. Cameron laughed without much joy. "We must do our best to please. All of us. My husband," she turned to Caroline, just as Don Cameron made a second appearance on the lower terrace, waving a whip, his trotting-horses busily trotting, "hates English food. So he sends home to Pennsylvania for everything we eat. Tonight we shall have corn."

"But which is it, ma'am?" The cook looked desperate; the abbey besieged.

3

"It is green and cylindrical and should be shucked of its covering and boiled, but not too long. We'll have the watermelon with the other fruits. I trust you with the rest, dear Cook."

"But . . ." The abbess wailed, and fled.

Mrs. Cameron sat on a sofa beneath a Millais portrait of a lady of the previous generation; and looked, in her yellowy-white lace, as if she, too, belonged to that earlier time, before the new era of loud clattering railroads, sinister silent telegraphs, garish electric lights. Caroline noticed a delicate line of perspiration on her hostess's upper lip while a vein at the forehead's center pulsed. Caroline thought of goddesses as she gazed upon Mrs. Cameron; thought of Demeter's long search for her daughter Persephone in hell; thought of herself as Persephone and Mrs. Cameron as the mother that might have been. On the other hand, was she herself in any sense in hell? And if she was, would Mrs. Cameron rescue her? But Caroline was quite aware that she had never really known anything except her life just as it was; yet she also knew enough of metaphysics to realize that it is often a condition of hell *not* to suspect the existence of any alternative to one's life. Caroline had gone from nuns to a freethinkers' school. From one concentric ring of hell, she now decided, to another. Yes, she was in hell—or Hades, at least, and though regnant over the dead, she eagerly awaited the earth-mother goddess to free her from Death's embrace and restore—oh, the glamor of Greek myth!—springtime to all the frozen world above.

A shaft of bright morning light suddenly made Mrs. Cameron's face glow like pink Parian marble, made the hair gold fire, prompted the goddess to turn her glittering blue gaze on Caroline and say—now for the oracle! thought Caroline, the next thing she says to me will change my life, liberate me from the underworld: "I allow the servants exactly eight percent for graft. But not a penny more." Demeter radiated earthly light. "As there is no reforming them—or anyone else—I believe in keeping graft to an agreed-upon but never mentioned figure. That is how my husband

4

governs Pennsylvania." Well, I have the message, thought Caroline; now I must interpret it.

Caroline answered in kind. "My father could never bear the commissions servants take. But then he never got used to France."

In fact, Colonel Sanford had refused, on what he claimed to be moral grounds, ever to speak French. He thought the French indecent and their language an intricate trap laid for American innocence. During the Colonel's long widowhood, a series of intensely moral English, Swiss and German ladies had interpreted for him, pale successors to Caroline's mother, Emma, alleged by all to have been vivid; she had died not long after Caroline's birth; she had been dark. For Caroline, Emma was not even a memory, only a portrait in the main salon of their chateau, Saint-Cloud-le-Duc.

Mrs. Cameron was now ablaze with August light. "Why did he exile himself?" Mrs. Cameron was suddenly almost personal; as opposed to inquisitive.

"I've never known." But of course Caroline and her half-brother, Blaise, had their suspicions, not to be voiced even to an earth-goddess. "It was after he married my mother. You see, she was really French. I mean, she was born in Italy, but her first husband was French."

"She was born a Schermerhorn Schuyler." Mrs. Cameron was prompt. Everyone knew everyone else's connections in the grand American world, so unlike Paris, where only a few deranged spinsters in the Faubourg Saint-Germain busied themselves with genealogy. "Your mother was a bit before my time, of course. But people still talked of her when I was young."

Actually, Caroline knew that Mrs. Cameron had married the Senator in the obviously astounding year of her own birth and Emma's death, 1878: a silver box on a console gave the wedding date, a gift from Mrs. Cameron's other famous uncle, a longtime senator who had been, until that spring, President McKinley's secretary of state. The great career had been brought to an abrupt and ignominious end when Secretary Sherman had had a lapse of memory while talking to the Austrian minister at Washington, no bad thing in itself but when it developed that he thought that *he* was the Austrian minister and lapsed into German, which he did not know, President McKinley was obliged, sadly, to let him depart. Mrs. Cameron was still upset. "After all, Uncle John signed my passport," she would say.

Now Mrs. Cameron wanted to know what would become of the Colonel's celebrated place at Saint-Cloud. Caroline said, truthfully, that she did not know. "Everything has been left to Blaise and me. But the will hasn't been properly—what is the word?"

"Probated," said the goddess brightly. "Let us hope the division will be equal."

"Oh, I'm sure it probably is." But Caroline had her doubts. Over the years, Colonel Sanford had progressed from pronounced eccentricity to the edge of madness, obliging the butler to double as taster at mealtimes: the Colonel feared poison. In the warm weather, the Colonel preferred daughter to son; then, just as the leaves started to turn, he preferred son to daughter. During alternating equinoxes, new wills would be drawn. As luck would have it, he had died in cold weather, when the horse he was riding across the railroad track at Saint-Cloud shied, and threw him in the path of the Blue Train itself. Death was swift. That was a year ago; and the lawyers in New York were still unravelling the various wills. In September, Caroline and Blaise would know who had got what. Fortunately, the Sanford estate was supposed to be large enough for two. The "house" at Saint-Cloud was a palace built by one of Louis XV's less able—and so enormously wealthy—finance ministers. In Caroline's youth there had never been fewer than forty servants in the chateau while two villages on the estate provided farm labor. But as madness began to claim the Colonel, potential murderers were summarily dismissed until there was hardly anyone left to keep up the splendor paid for by Sanford Encaustic Tiles (made in Lowell, Massachusetts) as well as the Cincinnati-Atlanta Railroad, a profitable postwar invention, built to replace the railroad that Mrs. Cameron's Uncle Cump (William

Tecumseh Sherman—hence, Cump) had smashed to bits on his
exuberant march to the sea.

Six children now filled the room as if they were twelve. There
were two nieces of Mrs. Cameron, her stolid twelve-year-old
daughter, Martha, one Curzon girl, two small Herbert boys, and
Clarence, the plain young brother of Adelbert Hay and son of the
house celebrity, John Hay, American ambassador to the Court of
St. James's. Mrs. Cameron now directed their revels with brisk
authority. "You are to go outside, girls. To the stables. There's a
cart. And Mr. Adams—Uncle Dordie—has got you two ponies.
Boys, there is lawn tennis in Pluckley . . ."

"We've won the war, Mrs. Cameron," said Clarence, in a voice
that kept cracking. "On Father's terms, too. Cuba's forever free,"
he suddenly boomed, as the voice dropped an octave, to everyone's
delight. "But we get to keep Puerto Rico. For ourselves."

"The question, actually," said the grave Herbert child, all nose
and high color, "is the matter of the Philippines. You Americans
must really keep them, you know. In all of this—"

"We shall decide the Philippines at lunch," said Mrs. Cameron;
and dismissed the lot.

Caroline had now moved to the great table between the terrace
windows. Cameron stationery, Surrenden Dering stationery,
United States embassy stationery were scattered over the worn
pear-wood surface. Blaise must be written: her hand hovered over
the table. Although it was tempting to write on embassy paper,
she decided that that might be misrepresenting herself, and so she
reached for the pale gray Surrenden Dering writing paper. As she
did, she saw a small stock of old-ivory note-paper, each sheet
emblazoned with five small Chinese-red hearts, arranged like those
of a playing card.

"What is this, Mrs. Cameron?" Caroline held up one of the
sheets.

"What's what?" Mrs. Cameron shut the door after the last of
the children.

"Writing-paper. With," Caroline looked down at the tiny scarlet hearts, "the Five . . ."

". . . of Hearts." Mrs. Cameron took the stationery from Caroline. "I can't think who left them here. I would appreciate it if you said nothing about it."

"A secret society?" Caroline was intrigued.

"Something of a secret, yes. And something of a society, too."

"But what . . . *who* are the Five of Hearts?"

Mrs. Cameron smiled with no great evident joy. "You must guess. Besides, there are only four now. Like those ladies-in-waiting to Mary Queen of Scots."

"*They* were four to begin with."

"Well, these were five. But like the old ballad, where once there were five, there were then four, where four three. . . ." Mrs. Cameron suddenly swallowed very hard. 'In time, there will be none."

"Are *you* one?"

'Oh, no! I am not so good as that." Mrs. Cameron was gone, the mystery clutched in her long capable hand.

Caroline was halfway through her letter to Blaise when Del Hay came in from the terrace. He was very like his mother, Clara Hay, a heavy, large-boned, handsome woman who had produced an equally heavy, rather broad-hipped son, with more face below the eyes than above, the reverse of Caroline, whose face tended to the triangular and broad-browed. "We've won the war," said Del.

"As a general greeting, I prefer good-morning." Caroline was cool. "So far, today, everyone's told me that we've won the war, and no one's mentioned the weather. Besides, *I* haven't won the war. You and your father have."

"You, too. You're an American. Oh, it's a great day for all of us."

"A very hot day. I'm writing your former classmate. Any message?"

"Tell him *he* should be happy. At least his employer should be.

The *New York Journal* must be frothing at the mouth, like some rabid . . ."

"Eagle. May I write him on your father's stationery?"

"Why not? This is the summer embassy." A young man with hair parted neatly in the middle looked into the room. "Have you seen the Ambassador?"

"He's in the library, Mr. Eddy. Did you just come down from London?"

"I was here last night for dinner." Mr. Eddy was reproachful. "Of course, there were so many people."

"I'm sorry," said Del. "But there *were* so many. What's the latest news?"

"I don't know. The telegraph office in the village has either broken down or just shut down. They've never had so much work, they say. But Mr. White's on his way from London. He'll have the latest news." Mr. Eddy left the room to Caroline and Del, who left the room altogether. Caroline held on to Del's arm as they stepped out onto the stone terrace with its long view of the Weald of Kent. Although Caroline did not know just what a weald was, she assumed that it must contain green woods and distant hills—the vista before them, in fact. They moved toward the one end of the terrace that was in shade, from a giant gnarled diseased oak. The soft green English countryside was beginning to shimmer as the before-noon sun burned a hole in a sky that ought to have been pale blue but instead was white from heat.

"You should be more interested in our war." Del teased her as they sauntered decorously in the shade, gravel crunching beneath their feet. Below them, on a grassy terrace, a somber peacock glared, and unfurled a far too brilliant tail. Everywhere, the bright, if dusty, overblown roses grew in remarkably ill-tended plots. But then Caroline had spent her life seeing to gardens and houses. "She will make some fine lord a splendid hostess," said her father's last but one "translator," a Miss Verlop from The Hague. "Or," said Blaise maliciously, "some fine capitalist a good factory boss." But Caroline had no intention of being either a hostess or a wife, though a factory boss sounded interesting. Of course, she had had no desire to be a daughter or a half-sister, either. But she had dutifully served her time as the first—and duly matriculated; as for the second, Blaise was good company; and she quite liked him, so long as he did not steal her share of the estate.

"Why should he?" Del stopped beneath a vast—again dusty—rhododendron.

Del looked as surprised as Caroline felt: she had not realized that she had spoken aloud. Was this madness? she wondered. The Sanford family was full of eccentricity, to put the matter politely, which is how they put it to one another, quite aware that a number of them, including her father, enjoyed the homely modifier "mad as a hatter."

"What did I say just now?" Caroline was determined to be scientific; if she was to be like the other Sanfords, she wanted to know every phase of her descent. She would be like M. Charcot, clinical.

"You said you didn't care if anyone were ever to remember the *Maine* again . . ."

"True. Then?"

"You said you thought Mr. Hearst and Blaise probably sank it together."

"Oh, dear. But at least I tell the truth in my delirium."

"Are you ill?"

"No. No. Not yet, anyway. Not that I know of. How did I get from the *Maine* to my father's will?"

"You said . . . Are you making fun of me?" The small gray eyes in the large face were kind, with a tendency to absorb rather than reflect the now intense August light.

"Oh, Del!" Caroline seldom used a young man's first name. After all, her first language was French, with its elaborately gauged and deployed second person. On the subtle shift from intimate "you" to formal "you" an entire civilization had been built. Although Caroline had never been in love (if one did not count a fourteen-year-old's crush on one of her teachers at Allenswood), she knew from the theater and books and the conversation of old ladies what love must be like and she fancied herself best as Phaedra, consumed with lust for an indifferent stepson; worst, as a loving wife to a good man like Adelbert Hay, whose father, the celebrated John Hay, was once private secretary to Abraham Lincoln, and now ambassador to the Court of St. James's. John Hay was himself not only civilized to the extent that any native American could be (Caroline was never quite sure just how deep the veneer could ever be of any of her countrymen) but wealthy as a result of his marriage to one Clara Stone, an heiress of Cleveland, who had borne him two sons and two daughters. As luck insisted on having it, the eldest son had been at Yale with Caroline's half-brother, Blaise Delacroix Sanford; and Caroline had met young Mr. Hay twice in New Haven and once in Paris; and now they were houseguests in Kent, contemplating the question she had allowed herself to ask, quite unaware that she was literally speaking her mind, something not encouraged outside the bluestocking academy of the grand Mlle. Souvestre: "Will Blaise try to take all my money now that he's sunk the *Maine?*"

Caroline did her best to pretend that she had been joking— about the money if not the *Maine*; and so she managed to convince Del that she was not joking. He shut his eyes a moment. Two tiny lines formed a sort of steeple between his brows, filial imitation of the Ambassador's deep lines. "Blaise is very—fierce," said Del. The peacock shouted harsh agreement beneath them. "But he is also a gentleman." Del opened his eyes: the matter was, for him, satisfactorily resolved.

"You mean he went to Yale?" Caroline had a truly French distaste for the Anglo-American word—not to mention romantic concept—"gentleman."

"Of course, he didn't graduate. But even so . . . ."

"He is half a gentleman. And, of course, he's only half my brother. I wish I were a man. A man," Caroline repeated, "*not* a gentleman."

"But you would be both. Anyway, why be either?" Del sat on a bench carved from dull local stone. Caroline arranged herself, at an angle, beside him. How pleased, she thought, Sanfords and Hays would be to see so inevitable a young couple merging like fragments of mercury into the silvery whole of marriage. Del would one day be as huge—no other word—as his mother, Clara. But then Caroline knew that she could very well become as huge as the Colonel, who, at the end, gave up going to the theater because he could no longer fit in any seat, and refused to arrange for a special chair to be placed in a box as his one-time friend the even more enormous Prince of Wales did.

"We could be fat together," murmured Caroline, wondering if she had revealed herself in a *murmured* aside about Blaise, or had the voice been normal? Normal, she decided, when the puzzled Del asked her to repeat herself. She asked, "What is your impression of his character?"

"I don't know any more. I haven't seen him since he quit Yale and went to work for the *Morning Journal*."

"Even so, you were his classmate. You know him better than I do. I'm just the half-sister, back home in France. You're the—contemporary in America."

"I think Blaise wanted to get his life started earlier than most of us do. That's all. He was—he is—in a hurry."

"To do what?" Caroline was genuinely curious about her brother.

"To live it all, I suppose."

"And you're not?"

Del smiled; the teeth were like a child's first set, small irregular pearls; he also had dimples and a turned-up nose. "I'm lazy. Like my father says *he* is, but isn't. I don't know what I shall do with myself. But Blaise knows just what he wants."

Caroline was surprised. "Last year he wanted to study law. Then he quit Yale and went to work for a newspaper, of all things. And what a newspaper!" Caroline had yet to hear anything good of the *Journal* or its proprietor, the wealthy young Californian

William Randolph Hearst, whose mother had recently inherited a fortune from his near-illiterate father, Senator George Hearst, a crude discoverer of gold and silver mines in the West. It was the Senator who had set up his cherished only son as a newspaper proprietor, first with the *Daily Examiner* in San Francisco and then with the *Morning Journal* in New York, where young Hearst had spectacularly succeeded, through a form of sensational journalism known as "yellow" (fires, alarums, scandals), in surpassing Mr. Pulitzer's original "Yellow" *New York World*. The *Journal* was now, in its own words, "the most popular newspaper on EARTH." "And Blaise delights in Mr. Hearst," said Caroline. "And I delight in hearing about Mr. Hearst."

"But you've never met him?"

"No. No. He is not to be met, I gather. He goes to Rector's with actresses. *Two* very young actresses, I am told. Sisters."

"He is a cad." Del said the final word; there would be no appeal. "So why does Blaise want to work for him?"

This time Del's smile was more grown-up and knowing: the baby teeth unrevealed by smooth lips. "Oh, Miss Sanford, has no one told you yet about power?"

"I read Julius Caesar's handbook in school. I know all about it. You start at first light and then, by forced marches, you surprise the enemy and kill them. Then you write a book about what you've done."

"Well, the newspapers are now the book you write. Blaise has simply taken a shortcut. He has gone straight to the end-result."

"But isn't it better—if that's what you want—to win a war first?"

"But that's exactly what Mr. Hearst has done, or thinks he's done. All those stories of his about how the Spanish blew up our battleship."

"Didn't they?"

"Probably not, according to Father. But it's the way that things are made to look that matters now. Anyway, Blaise is in the midst of it. He wants to be powerful. We all noticed that."

"Don't you?"

"I'm far too easy-going. I'd rather marry, and be happy, like my father."

"But the Ambassador has always been at the center of—forced marches at first light."

Del laughed. "It was the others who got up early to do the marching. Father just wrote the book."

"Ten volumes, in fact." Caroline had yet to meet anyone who had been able to read all the way through the ten-volume life of Abraham Lincoln by John Hay and his fellow secretary to the President, J. G. Nicolay. Caroline had not even made the attempt. The Civil War had no interest for her, while Lincoln himself seemed as remote as Queen Elizabeth, and rather less interesting. But then she had been brought up on Saint-Simon, in whose bright pages there were no saints with stovepipe hats making sententious appeals to the Almighty, only a king who was compared, quite rightly, to the sun, in bed and out.

Mrs. Cameron appeared on the terrace. "Del!" she called. "Your father wants you. He's in the library." She went inside.

"What," asked Caroline, as they returned to the house, "are the Five of Hearts?"

"Where did you hear about that?"

"I saw some letter-paper. I asked Mrs. Cameron. She was mysterious."

"Well, don't mention the subject to Mr. Adams, ever."

"Then he must be a Heart?"

"It was long ago," was all that Del said.

Caroline returned to her room; and dressed for lunch. She had come to Kent without a maid; old Marguerite had gone to Vichy to take the waters. In the past, Caroline had always travelled with a mademoiselle, who was half governess and half maid. But now, in her twenty-first year, Caroline was an orphan; and she could do as she pleased. The problem was that she was not certain where pleasure for her might ultimately lie. In any case, until the Sanford estate was settled, she was in limbo. And so she had chosen to spend August with Del and his family at the "summer embassy," presided over by the Camerons and the *Porcupinus Angelicus*, their name for Henry Adams, who was indeed prickly as a porcupine if not always much like an angel.

But, happily, Adams was now in a celestial mood, at least with Caroline, who found him alone in the yellow drawing room, so called because, with age, the frayed green damask on the walls had turned a sickly yellow, made even sicklier by the contrast with the heavily gilded—and dusty—furniture. Was dusty to be emblematic of the state of an English August, or merely her own state of mind?

Henry Adams was shorter than Caroline; and she was less than Amazonian. At sixty, Adams, grandson and great-grandson of presidents, as he was inexorably identified, possessed a full white beard, carefully barbered to a point, a full moustache, a high, pink, shining bald head—the Adams's birthright, he liked to say—and a full paunch held ever so slightly forward in order to balance properly the small round figure that existed only to support the large round brain-crammed head of America's great historian, wit, dispenser of gloom—not to mention lover of Lizzie Cameron. But were they, actually, lovers? wondered Caroline, realizing that the country of her father was not that of her own birth and education, and as the chronicler, Adams, was no Saint-Simon, there were no rogue bastards to occupy his pen, though such things did exist in American history, but hidden from view, like the old story that her own grandfather, Charles Schermerhorn Schuyler, was the bastard son of that dark son of the American republican Aaron Burr, who had, so tremendously, like Lucifer, fallen.

"Dear Miss Sanford." Henry Adams's old bright eyes were very alert; but the smile was curiously tentative for one so venerable. "You do illuminate at least one sexagenarian's summer." The accent was British. But then Adams had matured in England, as his father's secretary when that dour and gelid statesman had been President Lincoln's minister at London during the Civil War. Like so many entirely Anglicized Americans, Adams affected to despise the British. "They are impenetrably stupid," he would say, with quiet delight, when confronted with some new demonstration of British dimness.

"Mr. Adams." Caroline mocked a reverent curtsey. "Is the war concluded to your satisfaction?"

"Well, it is all over, which satisfies me. But then for two years the Cuban business drove me so wild that there was a movement to confine me to the Washington Zoo. At the mention of 'Cuba Libre,' I would howl—like a wolf at the full moon." Adams bared his teeth; looked to Caroline not unlike a wolf at noon. "But then I always lose my head when others are calm. The moment they get off *their* heads, *I* am calm. Once the war began, I was serene. I knew we had our man of destiny securely in place."

"Commodore Dewey?"

"Oh, infant! Commodores are simply playthings in war-time."

"But he took Manila, and defeated the Spanish fleet, and now everyone wants us to stay, at least the English do."

Adams tugged the tip of his pointed beard with, she noted, a small rosy hand that was more like a baby's than that of an old man. He cocked his head to one side. "We students of history—no matter how dull—like to know just who it was who put an admiral, like a chess piece, in Far Eastern waters—soon to be called Far Western, as what's west to us is what's true west."

"My brother Blaise says it was Mr. Roosevelt, when he was at the Navy Department. Blaise says he did it without telling his superiors."

Adams nodded approvingly. "You are getting closer. Our young bumptious friend Theodore—a student of *my* young bumptious brother Brooks—deserves more credit, certainly, than the knight—admiral, that is—I think in chess terms—that checkmated Spain. But whose hand directed our castle Theodore?"

A flight of children, led by Martha, filled up the room. All the girls surrounded Uncle Dordie, a name Martha had invented for Mr. Adams, whose pockets turned out to be filled with hard candies, that were promptly and ruthlessly suppressed by Mrs.

Cameron. "Not before mealtimes, Dor!" she announced, confiscating whatever she could pry loose from clenched fists.

Other houseguests were now entering the drawing room, without announcement, to the butler's sorrow. But Mrs. Cameron's word was final at the summer embassy. Only officialdom was proclaimed. The rest came pell-mell.

To Caroline's surprise, Adams turned back to her and resumed their conversation where it had broken off. "In those affairs where the balance of power in the world suddenly shifts, there must be a consummate player, who calculates his moves. This player puts Theodore at the Navy Department so that he will put the Admiral at Manila; he then responds to the sinking of the *Maine* with a series of moves that lead to a near-bloodless war, and the end of Spain as a world-player, and the beginning of the United States as an Asiatic power . . ."

"I am in suspense, Mr. Adams! Who is the consummate player?"

"Our first man of destiny since Mr. Lincoln—the President, who else? The Major himself. Mr. McKinley. Don't laugh!" Adams frowned severely. "I know he is supposed to be a creature of Mark Hanna and all the other bosses, but it's plain to me that they are *his* creatures. They find him money—a useful art—so that he can delivery us an empire, which he has! The timing is exquisite, too. Just as weak England begins to loosen her grip on the world, just as Germany and Russia and Japan are jostling one another to take England's place, the Major preempts them all, and the Pacific Ocean is ours! Or soon will be, and the new poles of power will be Russia on the eastern landmass and the United States on the west, with England, ours at last, in between! Oh, to be your age, Miss Sanford, and to see the coming wonders of our Augustan age!"

"In Paris, Mr. Adams, you once told me that you were a lifelong pessimist."

"That was on earth. I am now in Heaven, dear Miss Sanford, and so my pessimism ended with my earthly life. Up here, I am not even a porcupine." The moustache twitched at the corners as

17

he looked up at her—how small he was, she thought, angelic and diabolic.

They were joined by Don Cameron, who smelled of whiskey, and by the stout, bald, bearded figure of Henry James, who had just arrived from his house at Rye. When Caroline was very young, the novelist had been brought to Saint-Cloud by the Paul Bourgets. She had been impressed when James had spoken to her entirely in unaccented French; she had also been intrigued by an American whose two Christian names were affixed to no family name— Henry James What? she asked her father. The Colonel neither knew nor cared. He disliked literary men, except for Paul Bourget, whose aggressive snobbism gave Sanford quiet pleasure: "Can't read his books. But he knows *le monde de la famille*." When the Colonel did use a French phrase, it was always eerily mispronounced; yet the Colonel had a good ear; and loved music if not musicians. He had even written an opera about Marie de' Medici, which no one would put on unless he himself paid for the production. But as he was the sort of man who would never spend a penny that might give himself pleasure, there was no production of the opera in his lifetime; no life, either. Caroline vowed that she would not make the same mistake.

Don Cameron's voice was slow, rumbling, hoarse. "Well, you could at least try it out."

"But, my dear Senator, I am already so beautifully *machined*. At Lamb House, I am fitted out like the latest, most modern manufactory, geared for the most intense production, with a chief engineer who is *hopelessly* wedded to that intricate, fine-grinding mill that he performs upon with a positively virtuoso's touch . . ." Henry James spoke in a low, deep resonant voice, well-produced by a huge barrel of a chest that contained a singer's lungs, thought Caroline, for his breath never gave out, no matter how long and intricate the sentence.

Cameron was persistent. 'You'll never regret trying it out. I know. I tried it out. I'm no writer but it could change your life."

"Ah, *that!*" began James.

Adams broke in. "What is *it?*"

"I already showed you." The small, red, suspicious eyes turned toward Caroline now. "I'm selling the thing—the rights, that is—for Europe. Exclusive rights."

"Our senatorial friend," Caroline noted that Henry James had taken a very deep breath before he spoke; thanks to the Colonel, she knew rather a lot about the tricks of opera singers as well as opera, "has now in his exile . . . no, his highly thoughtful refuge from the clamorous Senate House, turned the full ripeness of his attention onto a commercial object which he quite rightly suspects is, to me, of all people here, at least, of poignant importance—and interest, although whether or not the Senator, as emptor—or tempter—will make on Miss Sanford the same profound effect that he has made on me, with his description—ever so lucid, so compelling, even—of that commercial object of which you, my dear Henry, now inquire the identity, I cannot, at hazard, guess. *Mais en tout cas*, Mademoiselle Sanford, I cannot think that you, as the chatelaine of the great palace of Saint-Cloud-le-Duc, would even find Senator Cameron's utensil of any intrinsic—or even extrinsic, I am impelled to add—interest save . . ."

"What . . . what is *it?*" cried Henry Adams, as the sentences slowly looped around them, verbal equivalents of Laocoön's serpent.

"It's this typewriter I've been promoting," said Senator Cameron.

"For an instant, I thought it was some sort of home guillotine," said Caroline.

"*Homely* utensil?" Adams asked; then answered his own question. "Well, why not? We could certainly use one in Lafayette Square."

"Now if Mr. James would just give us an endorsement," began Senator Cameron.

"But I am wedded, Senator, to another. I am—let me pronounce once and for all the honorable name—*united* to the Remington typewriter-machine, and have been for close to two wonderfully contented and happy years."

19

"You manipulate it yourself?" Caroline could not visualize the ponderous Mr. James confronting a metal machine, stubby fingers tapping.

"No," said Henry Adams. "He paces about the garden room of his house and unfurls his sentences into the ear of a typewriter-machinist who turns them into Remingtonese."

"Which is, at its best, so like English," added Henry James, eyes sparkling. Caroline vowed that she must one day really read him. Except for *Daisy Miller*, required reading for every American girl in Europe, Caroline had always steered clear of the books of the man that so many knowing Americans in Paris referred to as the Master.

"I'll bring it over to your place anyway." Cameron was dogged. "Get your man to try it out. There's a fortune in these new gadgets. Where's Lizzie?"

No one knew. She was not in the room. As Cameron made his way through a group of children to the hallway, Mr. Eddy bowed low to the statesman, who did not see him.

"Our good Don is persistent," said Henry Adams; and though the tone was agreeable, the expression of the face was not. Caroline saw that James had noticed, too.

"It must be very hard, no longer being in the Senate, after so many years, at the center." James was uncharacteristically tentative.

"Oh, I think he has a good enough time. He's rich, after all. He's got the place in South Carolina to worry about . . ."

"It must be even harder for La Dona, as you, not I, call her." James was studying Adams's face with acute interest.

"She has not been well." Adams was neutral; flat. "That's why Don and I formed our syndicate, to take this place for the summer, to unite us all."

"She is thriving then?"

But Henry Adams was saved from answering by the butler, who was at last permitted to come into his brilliant own. The long cadaverous figure of Mr. Beech stood very straight in the doorway, as his basso voice ecstatically proclaimed, "His Excellency, the Ambassador of the United States of America, and Mrs. John Hay."

"I shall now say 'hurrah' three times, I think," said Henry James, "and very loud, too."

"Don't," said Adams.

The Hays were a curious-looking couple. He was small, slender, bearded, with, at a distance, a boy's face that, close up, was like a delicate much-wrinkled beige chamois skin. Hay wore a pointed beard, like all the others; his full head of hair was parted in the middle and dyed the same dull chestnut color as the hair of his tall, fleshy, large-faced wife, who looked even larger and more formidable than she was when standing beside her husband. Caroline could see Del's face peering out of Clara's; but except for the turned-up nose, saw no resemblance to Del at all in Hay, who came toward them, hand outstretched to greet Henry James. They were old friends.

"In fact," said James, more to Caroline than to anyone, "when I needed employment on this side of the water, Mr. Hay—this was a quarter-century ago, and the world was younger, as were we, to strike the Dickensian note of spacious redundancy—Mr. Hay, as an editor of the *New York Tribune*, persuaded, with who knows what wiles, that worthy paper to take me on as its inadequate Paris correspondent."

"Easily the wisest thing I ever did." Hay's voice was low and precise and, that rare thing to Caroline's critical ear, agreeably American. "Now you are become so great that I have your bust in my library, along with Cicero's. Adams often compares the two of you—the originals, that is, not the busts. Every day he thinks up something new to say, when he pays me a call." Del had told Caroline a good deal about the curious Hay-Adams living arrangements at Washington.

Ever since the Civil War, Hay and Adams had been friends; the wives, too, had liked each other, a source of amazement to Caroline, who said as much, amazing Del, who was innocent. When the Hays at last abandoned Cleveland, Ohio, where Hay had first worked for—and then with—Mrs. Hay's father, they had come to Washington to live, largely because Henry Adams lived there; and *he* lived there because, as he had told Caroline, it is a law of nature that Adamses gravitate to capitals. Since he would never be president like his two ancestors, he could at least live opposite the White House, where each Adams had, so disastrously, presided; and thus, close to "home," he could write, think, and even make—through backstage maneuvering—history.

In due course, Hay and Adams had built a double house in Lafayette Square, a red brick Romanesque affair, whose outside Caroline already knew from photographs and whose inside Del intended for her to get to know. But though the two houses were physically joined, there was no connecting inner door. In this joint house, Hay had finished his interminable life of Lincoln while Adams had written much of his long account of the administrations of Jefferson and Madison, demonstrating, as Del had observed, how the Adamses, though seldom mentioned in the text, had almost never been wrong—unlike their opponents, Jefferson and Madison and the terrible Andrew Jackson, whose statue at the center of Lafayette Park was daily visible to Henry Adams, who, daily, chose not to look at this ungainly reminder of his grandfather's political ruin, not to mention that of the republic. For was it not with Jackson that the age of political corruption which now flourished began? But despite the city's ever-present mephitic corruption, the two wealthy historians lived contentedly side by side, influencing events through various chosen instruments, among them Senator Don Cameron, hereditary czar of Pennsylvania. When Lincoln wondered if Don's father, Simon Cameron, would steal once he was secretary of war, a Pennsylvania colleague observed that, well, he would probably *not* steal a red-hot stove. When Simon had heard this, he demanded an apology. The congressman complied, with the words, "Believe me, I did *not* say that you would not steal a red-hot stove."

Hay's career had seemed at an end when he moved into the Romanesque fortress opposite the White House. But then, as the political dice were again cast and Ohio, yet again, was about to produce a president, the obvious candidate was the state's governor, one William McKinley, known as the Major—pronounced Majah. A Civil War veteran and longtime member of the House of Representatives, the Mayor had sworn eternal loyalty to the tariff, the creed of the higher Republicans, and so gained the attention and loyalty of the party's leaders, the merchant princes. For them, McKinley was immaculate. He was poor—hence, honest; eloquent but without ideas—hence, not dangerous; devoted to his wife, an epileptic who always sat next to him at table so that when she went into convulsions, he could tactfully throw a napkin over her head and continue his conversation as though nothing had happened; when the convulsions ceased, he would remove the napkin and she would continue her dinner. Although Mrs. McKinley was not entirely an asset as a potential first lady, the fact that she was an "invalid" (and he deeply devoted to her) counted for a great deal in the republic's numerous sentimental quarters.

Unfortunately, McKinley went bankrupt at the start of the campaign. Out of friendship, he had signed his name to a note, which the friend in question could not redeem, to the amount of $140,000. The McKinley campaign was about to end before it started, giving the election to the so-called boy-orator of the Platte, that fire-breathing populist and enemy of the rich, William Jennings Bryan. As blood would obscure the moon for a generation if Bryan should prevail, McKinley's campaign manager, a wealthy grocer named Mark Hanna, appealed to a number of other wealthy men, among them Hay, to pay off the note and save the moon from a sanguinary fate. The Major was grateful. Hay, who had been passed over for high diplomatic office by an earlier president because "there was just no politics in appointing him," now found himself in high favor with the latest Ohio management across the road.

The Major appointed Hay ambassador to the Court of St. James's; and Hay had arrived in London the year before, accompanied by Henry Adams, whose father, grandfather, and great-grandfather had each held the same post. The ambassadorial party had been met at Southampton by Henry James, who was never seen anywhere near the world of politics or near-politics or even plain celebrity. But there he most loyally was at the customs house, crushed by the international press. After observing Hay's dextrous handling of the thorny flower of the British press, James had whispered to Hay, in a voice audible to more than a few, "What impression does it make on your mind to have those insects creeping about and saying things to you?"

"I do not know this man," Hay said with mock severity, getting into his carriage.

"Anyway," Del had told Caroline, summing up, "the firm of Hay and Adams prospered from the day they moved into their joint house."

But Caroline had been conscious of an omission. "Weren't there, to begin with, *two* couples who were friends?"

"Yes. My father and mother. And Mr. and Mrs. Adams."

"What became of Mrs. Adams?"

"She died before they could move into the house. She was small and plain. That's all I remember. People say she was brilliant, even witty, for a woman. She took photographs, and developed them herself. She was very talented. Her name was Marian, but everyone called her Clover."

"How did she die?"

Del had looked at her, as if uncertain whether or not she was to be trusted—but trusted with what? Caroline had wondered. Surely he knew nothing that others did not know. "She killed herself. She drank some sort of chemical that you use to develop pictures. Mr. Adams found her on the floor. It was a painful death."

"Why did she do it?" Caroline had asked, but there had been no answer.

As the lunch party began to drift toward the dining room, with its southern exposure of quantities of Kentish Weald, Mrs. Cameron hurried toward John Hay. "He's come! He says you invited him . . ."

"Who?" asked Hay.

"Mr. Austin. Our neighbor. Your admirer."

24

"Oh, God," murmured Hay. "He thinks I'm a poet, too."

"But so triumphantly you *were*—" began James.

"Tell Mr. Austin there's been a mistake . . ."

But there was no telling Mr. Beech, who was now declaiming, "The Poet Laureate of All England and Mrs. Alfred Austin!"

"What joy!" Hay exclaimed so that all could hear and relish. Then he hurried to greet what many believed was the dullest poet in all England.

Caroline sat at table between Del and Henry James. The dining room was easily the most agreeable of the old house's state apartments, and here Mrs. Cameron presided efficiently over children, young adults, statesmen and—now—a dim poet, wreathed in courtly laurel. "Mr. Austin is under the impression that our friend Hay is the American poet laureate," said James, doing justice to a quantity of turbot in fresh cream. Across the table a very small Curzon girl sniffled next to a nanny who had apparently invoked an unfair prohibition.

"Father keeps telling Mr. Austin that he hasn't written a line since . . ."

Like the low rumbling note of an organ the voice of Henry James began, through a last mouthful of turbot, to intone.

> "And I think that saving a little child,
>   And fetching him to his own,
> Is a derned sight better business
>   Than loafing around The Throne."

At the quatrain's end, half the table applauded: Mr. James's voice was unusually sonorous and compelling.

"I always find that part the most moving," said the Laureate, "if not theologically tactful."

"I hate it," said Hay, who looked most embarrassed.

"I am sure that Dante must have felt the same whenever the *Inferno* was quoted." Adams was most amused.

"What on earth *is* it?" Caroline whispered to Del, but Henry James's ear was sharp.

"'Little Breeches,'" he boomed, "the poignant narrative—nay, epic—of a four-year-old boy saved from the wreckage of some sort of rustic conveyance that was drawn, most perilously, as it proved, by horses, the sort of conveyance, ill-defined, I fear, and of vague utility, what one might term . . ."

"A wagon?" Caroline contributed.

"Precisely." James was enjoying himself. The first of several roast fowls had now appeared, further brightening his mood. "The small boy—hardly more than what Adams would call an infant, except to Adams an infant is any unmarried maiden who might be his niece, and this child—Little Breeches," again the name vibrated in the air and Caroline could see Hay cringe, and even Del cleared his throat, preparatory to drowning out James's inexorable voice, "—apparently, this small untended rustic person fell from the moving conveyance and was saved by a rustic hero, who deliberately sacrificed his own life for this pair of, as it were, small trousers, or, rather, its contents, and for this noble act, despite a terrestrial life of some untidiness—even sin—he was translated to Paradise."

"The churches still complain about Father's poem." Del was more than ready to change the subject.

"But it sold, as a pamphlet, in the untold millions," said James, dislodging with a forefinger a morsel of chicken from between his two front teeth. "Like the later and, perhaps, more profound 'Jim Bludso,' your father's most celebrated ballad, the hero of which gave *his* life to save those of his passengers aboard a—this time nautical—conveyance, the *Prairie Belle*. Mr. Hay's fascination with the hazards of American travel was very much the spirit of the seventies. In any event, this steam-propelled barque explodes, if memory serves, in some wild American river, enabling the paragon to give his life for innumerable little breeches, not to mention other garments, including maidenly costumes, all the passengers in short, thus ensuring himself a direct passage to Paradise on the demo-

cratic ground—highest of all grounds—that 'Christ ain't going to
be too hard on a man who died for men.'" But this time James
dropped his voice dramatically and no one but Caroline heard. To
her left, Del was talking to Abigail Adams, one of Henry's actual
nieces, a large plain girl, recently broken out of a Paris convent.

As boiled beef relentlessly followed fowl, and the conversation in
the dining room grew both louder and slower, Henry James said
that, yes, indeed he had met Caroline's grandfather. "It was in
'76." He was suddenly precise. "I had decided to make my . . .
deliberate removal to Europe, like Charles Schermerhorn Schuyler,
who had made his thirty years earlier. He had always intrigued
me, and I had noticed, most favorably, for *The Nation*, his *Paris
Under the Communards*. I can still see him in bright summer Hudson
riparian light, on a lawn at river-side, somewhere north of Rhine-
cliff, a Livingston house behind us, all white columns and cinna-
mon stucco, and we spoke of the necessity, for some, of living on
this side of the Atlantic, some distance from our newspapered
democracy."

"Was my mother with him?"

James cast her a sidelong glance; and helped himself to horse-
radish sauce. "Oh, she was there, so very much there! Madame la
Princesse d'Agrigente. Who can forget her? You are very like her,
as I told you at Saint-Cloud . . ."

"But not so dark?"

"No. Not so dark." James was then drawn by his other table
partner, Alice Hay, who resembled her father—small, shrewd,
quick-witted; also, pretty. Although Caroline had not found either
of Del's sisters particularly sympathetic, she did not in the least
mind their company, particularly that of Helen, who sat across the
table, next to Spencer Eddy, who seemed infatuated with Helen's
precociously middle-aged radiance. She was like her mother, large-
bodied, with glowing eyes and quantities of glossy hair, all her
own.

Suddenly, Senator Cameron shouted, "What's this?" He sat at
the head of the table, as befitted the married co-host. In one hand

27

he held a silver serving-spoon from which hung a gelatinous mass, rather like a jellyfish, thought Caroline.

"A surprise," said Mrs. Cameron, from her end of the table. The Curzon child promptly burst into tears; the word "surprise" had not a happy association.

"What *is* this?" Senator Cameron turned his small fierce eyes upon the butler.

"It is the . . . corn, sir. From America, sir."

"This is not corn. What is this mess?"

From behind the coromandel screen that hid pantry from dining room, the cook appeared, like an actress who had been waiting in the wings for her cue. "It *is* the corn, sir. As you said to make it. Boiled, sir. Should I have left the seeds in it?"

"Oh, Don!" Mrs. Cameron laughed, a most genuine sound in that often dramatically charged household. "It's the watermelon. She mistook it for the corn." In the general laughter, not shared by Cameron, the cook vanished.

"Father thinks now that we shall keep all the Philippines," said Del. "The Major has come round, he says. But it hasn't been easy. All those people who didn't want us to take on Hawaii last summer are at it again. I can't think why. If we don't take up where England's left off—or just given up—who will?"

"Does it make so much difference?" Although Caroline had been delighted by the war's excitement, she could not see that there had been any earthly point to it. Why drive poor weak old Spain out of the Caribbean and the Pacific? Why take on far-off colonies? Why boast so much? It was not like Napoleon, who did appeal to her because he had, himself, wanted the world, which Mr. McKinley did not seem to want to be bothered with, unlike that friend of her hosts, a man to whom they all referred, with an inadvertent baring of teeth, as Thee-oh-dore, who had managed, under fire, to lead some of his friends to the top of a small hill in Cuba, without once breaking his pince-nez. The fuss in the newspapers over Colonel Theodore Roosevelt and his so-called Rough Riders was as great as the fuss over Admiral Dewey, who had actually defeated Spain's

Pacific fleet and occupied Manila. For reasons obscure to Caroline, the newspapers thought "Teddy" the greater of the two heroes. Therefore: "Does it make so much difference?" was not idly posed.

Del told her of all the dangers that might befall the world if the German kaiser—whose fleet was even now in Philippine waters— were to acquire that rich archipelago in order to carry out the current dream of every European power, not to mention Japan, the carving up of the collapsed Chinese empire. "We had no choice, really. As for allowing Spain to stay on in our hemisphere, that was an anachronism. We must be the masters in our own house."

"Is all the western hemisphere, even Tierra del Fuego, a part of *our* house?"

"You're making fun of me. Let's talk about the theater in Paris . . ."

"Let's talk about men and women." Caroline felt suddenly as if she had had a revelation about these two hostile races. The differences between the two sexes were known to her in a way that they could never be known to an American young lady. Although American girls were given a social freedom unknown in France, they were astonishingly sheltered in other crucial ways, their ignorance nurtured by anxious mothers, themselves more innocent than not of the on-going plan of Eden's serpent. Del looked at her, startled. "But what shall we say about—about men and women?" Del's flush was not entirely from the August heat and the heavy meal.

"I've thought of one difference. At least between American men and women. Mr. James called the United States 'the newspapered democracy.'"

"Mr. Jefferson said that if he had to choose between a government without a press and a press without a government, he would choose a press without a—"

"How stupid he must have been!" But when Caroline saw Del's hurt expression—plainly, he had identified himself with the sage of Monticello—she modified: "I mean, *he* was not stupid. He just thought that the people he was talking to were stupid. After all, *they* were journalists, weren't they? I mean if they weren't journalists of some sort, how would we know what he said—or might have said, or didn't say? Anyway, back to men and women. We women are criticized, quite rightly, for thinking and, worse, talking about marriage and children and the ordinary people we have to deal with every day and the lives we have to make for our husbands or families or whatever, and this means that as we get older, we get duller and duller because we have, at the end, nothing left but ourselves to think about and talk about and so we become perfect— if we're not already to begin with—bores," Caroline concluded in triumph.

Del looked at her, quite bewildered. "So if *you* are—like that, then men are . . . what?"

"Different. Boring in a different way. Because of the newspapers. Don't you see?"

"You mean men read them and women don't?"

"Exactly. Most of the men we know, that is, read them, and most of the women we know don't. At least, not the news—what a funny word!—of politics or wars. So when men talk to one another for hours about what they have all read that morning about China and Cuba and . . . Tierra del Fuego, about politics and money, we are left out because we haven't read those particular bits of news."

"But you could, so easily, read them . . ."

"But we don't want to. We have our boredom and you have yours. But yours is truly sinister. Blaise says that practically nothing Mr. Hearst prints is ever true, including the story about how the Spaniards blew up the *Maine*. But you men who read the *Journal*, or something like it, will act as if what you read is true or, worse, as if, true or not, it was all that really mattered. So *we* are excluded, entirely. Because we know that none of it matters—to us."

"Well, I agree newspapers are not always true, but if . . . foolish men think they are true—or perhaps true—then it *does* matter to everyone because that is how governments are run, in response to the news."

"Then worse luck for foolish men—and women, too."

Del laughed at last. "So what would you do if you could alter things?"

"Read the *Morning Journal*." Caroline was prompt. "Every word."

"And believe it?"

"Of course not. But at least I could talk to men about Tierra del Fuego and the Balance of Power."

"I prefer to talk about the theater in Paris . . . and marriage." Del's lower larger face reddened; the small forehead remained pale ivory.

"You'll be the woman? I'll be the man?" Caroline smiled. "No. That's not allowed. Because we are divided at birth by those terrible newspapers that tell you what to think and us what to wear and when to wear it. We cannot, ever, truly meet."

"But you can. There is, after all, the high middle ground," said Henry James, who had been listening, the ruins of an elaborate pudding before him.

"Where—*what* is that?" Caroline turned her full gaze on that great head with the gleaming all-intelligent eyes. "Why, *that* is art, dear Miss Sanford. It is a kind of Heaven open to us all, and not just Jim Bludso and his creator."

"But art is not for everyone, Mr. James." Del was respectful.

"Then there is something not unlike it, if more rare, yet a higher stage, a meeting ground for all true—hearts."

On the word "hearts," Caroline felt a sudden premonitory chill. Did he mean the specific mysterious five or did he mean just what he said? Apparently, he meant just that, because when she asked what this higher stage was, Henry James said, simply, for him: "Dare one say *that* human intercourse which transcends politics and war and, yes, even love itself? I mean, of course, friendship. There—you have it."

31

In wicker chairs, placed side by side on the stone terrace, John Hay and Henry Adams presided over the Kentish Weald, as the summer light yielded, slowly, very slowly, to darkness.

"In Sweden, in summer, the sun shines all night long." Henry Adams lit a cigar. "One never thinks of England being almost as far to the north as Sweden. But look! It's after dinner, and it's light yet."

"I suppose we like to think of England as being closer to us than it really is." Carefully, John Hay pressed his lower back against the hard cushion that Clara had placed behind him. For some months the pain had been fairly constant, a dull aching that seemed to extend from the small of the back down into the pelvis, but, of course, ominously, the doctors said that it was the other way around. In some mysterious fashion the cushion stopped the pain from exploding into one of its sudden borealises, as Hay tended to think of those excruciating flare-ups when his whole body would be electrified by jolts of pain—originating in the atrophied—if not worse—prostate gland, whose dictatorship ordered his life, obliging him to pass water or, painfully, not to pass water, a dozen times during the night, accompanied by a burning sensation reminiscent of his youth when he had briefly contracted in war-time Washington a minor but highly popular venereal infection.

"Are you all right?" Although Adams was not looking at him, Hay knew that his old friend was highly attuned to his physical state.

"No, I'm not."

"Good. You're better. When you're really in pain, you boast of rude health. How pretty Del's girl is."

Hay looked across the terrace to the stone bench where his son

32

and Caroline had combined to make a romantic picture, suitable for
Gibson's pen, while the remaining houseguests—it was Monday—
floated like sub-aquatic creatures in the watery half-light. The
children had been removed, to Hay's delight, Adams's sorrow. "Do
you recall her mother, Enrique?" Hay had a number of variations of
Henry's name, playful tribute to his friend's absolute unprotean
nature.

"The darkly beautiful Princesse d'Agrigente was not easy, once
seen, ever to forget. I knew her back in the seventies, the beautiful
decade, after our unbeautiful war was won. Did you know
Sanford?"

Hay nodded. The pain which had started to radiate from the
lumbar region suddenly surrendered to the pillow's pressure. "He
was on McDowell's staff early in the war. I think he wanted to
marry Kate Chase . . ."

"Surely he was not alone in this madness?" Hay sensed the
Porcupine's smile beneath the beard, pale blue in the ghostly light.

"We were many, it's true. Kate was the Helen of Troy of E
Street. But Sprague got her. And Sanford got Emma d'Agrigente."

"Money?"

"What else?" Hay thought of his own good luck. He had never
thought that he could ever make a living. For a young man from
Warsaw, Illinois, who liked to read and write, who had gone east
to college, and graduated from Brown, there were only two careers.
One was the law, which bored him; the other, the ministry, which
intrigued him, despite a near-perfect absence of faith. Even so, he
had been wooed by various ministers of a variety of denominations.
But he had said no, finally, to the lot, for, as he wrote his lawyer
uncle, Milton: "I would not do for a Methodist preacher, for I am
a poor horseman. I would not suit the Baptists, for I would dislike
water. I would fail as an Episcopalian, for I am no ladies' man."
This last was disingenuous. Hay had always been more than
usually susceptible to women and they to him. But as he had
looked, at the age of twenty-two, no more than twelve years old,

neither in Warsaw nor, later, in Springfield, was he in any great demand as a ladies' man.

Instead, Hay had grimly gone into his uncle's law office; got to know his uncle's friend, a railroad lawyer named Abraham Lincoln; helped Mr. Lincoln in the political campaign that made him president; and then boarded the train with the President-elect to go to Washington for five years, one month and two weeks. Hay had been present in the squalid boardinghouse when the murdered President had stopped breathing, on a mattress soaked with blood.

Hay had then gone to Paris, as secretary to the American legation. Later, he had served, as a diplomat, in Vienna and Madrid. He wrote verse, books of travel; was editor of the *New York Tribune*. He lectured on Lincoln. He wrote folksy poems, and his ballads of Pike County sold in the millions. But there was still no real money until the twenty-four-year-old Cleveland heiress Clara Stone asked him to marry her; and he had gratefully united himself with a woman nearly a head taller than he with an innate tendency to be as fat as it was his to be lean.

At thirty-six Hay was saved from poverty. He moved to Cleveland; worked for his father-in-law—railroads, mines, oil, Western Union Telegraph; found that he, too, had a gift for making money once he had money. He served, briefly, as assistant secretary of state; and wrote, anonymously, a best-selling novel, *The Bread-Winners*, in which he expressed his amiable creed that although men of property were the best situated to administer and regulate America's wealth and that labor agitators were a constant threat to the system, the ruling class of a city in the Western Reserve (Cleveland was never named) was hopelessly narrow, vulgar, opinionated. Henry Adams had called him a snob; he had agreed. Both agreed that it was a good idea that he had published the book anonymously; otherwise, the Major could not have offered him the all-important embassy at London. Had the Senate suspected that Hay did not admire all things American, he would not have been confirmed.

"Money makes the difference." Hay took a deep puff of his

34

Havana cigar: what on earth, he suddenly wondered, were they to *do* with Cuba? Then, aware not only of the vapidity of what he had said but also of the thin blue smile beneath the thick blue beard in the chair beside him, he added, "Not that gilded porcupines would know—except by hearsay—what it is like to be poor and struggling."

"You wrench my heart." Adams was sardonic. "Also, my quills were not heavily gilded at birth. I have acquired just enough shekels to creep through life, serving the odd breakfast to a friend . . ."

"Perhaps you might have been less angelic if you'd had to throw yourself into . . ."

". . . wealthy matrimony?"

A spasm of pain forced Hay to cough. He pretended it was cigar smoke inhaled, as he maneuvered his spine against the pillow. "Into the real world. Business, which is actually rather easy. Politics, which, for us, is not."

"Well, you've done well, thanks to a rich wife. So has Whitelaw Reid. So has William Whitney. So would have Clarence King had he had your luck—all right, good sense—to marry wealthily and well."

Below the terrace, in the dark woods, owls called to one another. Why, Hay wondered, was the Surrenden nightingale silent? "Why has he never married?" asked Hay: their constant question to one another. Of the three friends, King was the most brilliant, the handsomest, the best talker; also, athlete, explorer, geologist. In the eighties all three had been at Washington, and, thanks largely to King's brilliance, Adams's old house became the first salon, as the newspapers liked to say, of the republic.

"He has no luck," said Hay. "And we have had too much."

"Do you see it that way?" Adams turned his pale blue head toward Hay. The voice was suddenly cold. Inadvertently, Hay had approached the forbidden door. The only one in their long friendship to which Hay had not the key. In the thirteen years since Adams had found his dead wife on the floor, he had not mentioned her to Hay—or to anyone that Hay knew of. Adams had simply locked the door; and that was that.

But Hay was experiencing vivid pain; and so was less than his usual tactful self. "Compared to King, we have lived in Paradise, you and I."

A tall, tentative figure appeared on the terrace. Hay was relieved at the diversion. "Here I am, White," he called out to the embassy's first secretary, just arrived from London.

White pulled up a chair; refused a cigar. "I have a telegram," he said. "It's a bit crumpled. The paper is so flimsy." He gave the telegram to Hay, who said, "Am I expected, as a director of Western Union, to defend the quality of the paper we use?"

"Oh, no. No!" White frowned, and Hay was suddenly put on his guard by his colleague's nervousness: it was part of White's charm to laugh at pleasantries that were neither funny nor pleasant. "I can't read in the dark," said Hay. "Unlike the owl . . . and the porcupine." Adams had taken the telegram from Hay; now he held it very close to his eyes, deciphering it in the long day's waning light.

"My God," said Adams softly. He put down the telegram. He stared at Hay.

"The German fleet has opened fire in Cavite Bay." This had been Hay's fear ever since the fall of Manila.

"No, no." Adams gave the telegram to Hay, who put it in his pocket. "Perhaps you should go inside and read it. Alone."

"Who's it from?" Hay turned to White.

"The President, sir. He has appointed you . . . ah . . . has offered to appoint you . . ."

"Secretary of state," Adams finished. "*The* great office of state is now upon offer, to you."

"Everything comes to me either too late or too soon," said Hay. He was unprepared for his own response, which was closer to somber regret than joy. Certainly, he could not pretend to be surprised. He had known all along that the current secretary, Judge Day, was only a temporary appointment. The Judge wanted a judgeship and he had agreed to fill in, temporarily, at the State Department as a courtesy to his old friend the Major. Hay was also aware that the Major thought highly of his own performance, in which he had handled a number of delicate situations in a fashion that had enhanced the President's reputation. Now, in John Hay's sixtieth year, actual power was offered him, on a yellow sheet of Western Union's notoriously cheap paper.

Hay was conscious of the two men's intent gaze, like a pair of predatory night birds in the forest. "Well," said Hay, "late or soon, this is the bolt from the blue, isn't it?"

"Surely," said Adams, "you have something more memorable to say at such a time."

A sudden spasm of pain made Hay gasp the word "Yes." Then: "I could. But won't." But inside his head an aria began: Because, if I were to tell the truth I would have to confess that I have somehow managed to mislay my life. Through carelessness, I have lost track of time and now time is losing, rapidly, all track of me. Therefore, I cannot accept this longed-for honor because, oh, isn't it plain to all of you, my friends and foes, that I am dying?

White was speaking through Hay's pain: ". . . he would like you to be in Washington by the first of September so that Judge Day can then go to Paris for the peace conference with Spain."

"I see," said Hay distractedly. "Yes. Yes."

"*Is* it too late?" Adams had read his mind.

"Of course it's too late." Hay managed to laugh; he got to his feet. Suddenly, the pain was gone: an omen. "Well, White, we have work to do. When in doubt about anything, Mr. Lincoln always wrote two briefs, one in favor, one opposed. Then he'd compare the two and the better argument carried the day, or so we liked to think. Now we're going to write my refusal of this honor. Then we're going to write my acceptance."

Henry Adams stood up. "Remember," he said, "if you don't accept—and I think you shouldn't, considering your age—our age—and health, you will have to resign as ambassador."

"On the ground . . . ?" Hay knew what Adams would say.

37

And Adams said it. "If you were just an office-seeker, it would make no difference either way. But you are *in* office. You are a man of state; and you are serious. As such, you may not refuse the President. One cannot accept a favor and then, when truly needed, refuse a service."

Thus, the Adamses—and the old republic. Hay nodded; and went inside. All deaths are the same, he thought. But some are Roman; and virtuous.

– 3 –

Caroline had escaped what was left of the house-party in order to explore, alone, the woods below the house. As always, she was impressed by the stillness. No breeze stirred as she made her way between huge rhododendrons, their white flowers wilting, long past their season—dusty flowers, she thought, and wondered yet again why dust and its connotations, decay, should be so much on her mind just as she was about to spread her own wings at last and begin her flight through the long-awaited life that she had dreamed of. It must be her European childhood, she decided, that was ending, dustily, so that she, the oldest child on earth, might now become, brilliantly, the youngest woman.

A deer metamorphosed in a clearing at whose center was an attractive—to the deer at least—muddy pond. Caroline stood very still; hoped that the animal would come toward her; but the dark brown eyes blinked suddenly and where the deer had been there was now only green.

The problem of Del, she began to herself, contentedly. But the problem of Del was promptly replaced, like a magic lantern slide, by the problem of Blaise. Moodily, she sat on a log near the mud pond; was it England or Ireland that had no snakes?

When she had written Blaise that she was staying at Surrenden Dering, he had answered that he was more impressed than not;

although Del Hay was "perfectly suitable," a condescending fraternal phrase, she ought to meet a few more men first. He then filled a page with admiring references to "the Chief," Mr. Hearst, and Caroline wondered if the actress-loving Mr. Hearst, still in his thirties and unmarried, might be Blaise's candidate for her valuable hand. But then Blaise had suggested that after England she go back to Saint-Cloud and look after the old place until he was properly settled in New York. At the moment he was living in the Fifth Avenue Hotel, and that was hardly a proper home for a *jeune fille de la famille*. The rest of the letter was in French, rather the way their conversations tended to be; thoughts, too. He reminded her that the will was still making its leisurely way through probate and nothing would be decided before the first of the year. Meanwhile, although he hoped that she was enjoying her new status as an orphan in Paris, he recommended that she take on one or another of the numerous d'Agrigente old maids or widows as a duenna. "Appearances count for everything in this world," he wrote, reverting to sententious English. But then Blaise should know. As a journalist, he was now a creator, an inventor of appearances.

"Caroline!" Del's voice recalled her to the house. Del was standing on the lower terrace, waving a paper at her. "A telegram!" Suddenly, he was no longer standing on the terrace; he was sliding down it on his ample backside. "Damn!" he said, standing up. "Damn," he repeated, looking at the grass stains on his handsome tweed. "Sorry," he said; and smiled. He *was* attractive, she decided. If only a bit of the smooth fleshy lower face could be moved above the eyebrows; and the eyes themselves, perhaps, enlarged.

Caroline opened the telegram. It was from her cousin, and lawyer, John Apgar Sanford. Shortly before Colonel Sanford's death, John had come to Saint-Cloud and he had said to Caroline, apropos nothing at all, "If anything should ever happen to your father, you'll need a lawyer. An American lawyer."

"You?"

"If you like." At the time Caroline thought the possibility of her father's death remote: Sanfords lived forever, enjoying to the full ill-health. But when the Blue Train had so abruptly transported Colonel Sanford prematurely to another plane, Caroline had written to John Apgar Sanford, to Blaise's disgust: "Everything was all set. All arranged. Now you've gone and complicated things." When Blaise had written her that the probate would not be settled until January, she had felt guilty. Plainly, she *had* complicated things. Now John Apgar Sanford urged: "Come to New York fastest will to be probated September fifteen don't worry."

"What is it?"

"I've been told not to worry—about something. I suppose that means I should be very worried."

"Are you?"

Caroline put the telegram inside her reticule; and chose not to answer Del. "That poor telegraph lady in Pluckley. How busy we've all kept her!"

"She has asked Her Majesty's Government for help. Otherwise, she says she will shut down." Del smiled. "Come on. Uncle Dor's brother, Brooks, has just arrived. He is something to see. And hear."

Caroline took Del's arm. "Can the embassy get me on a ship, to New York?"

"Of course. I'll tell Eddy. When?"

"Tomorrow evening, if possible. Or the next day."

"What's happened?"

"Nothing. That is—nothing yet. It's just business," she added lightly, and paused for fear of stammering before the "b", something she was prone to do when nervous.

Brooks Adams was holding court—no, she thought, more like a papal conclave—on the upper terrace. Brother Henry had so curled himself in a chair that he looked like a spineless porcupine, at bay. Henry James leaned against the nearby balustrade and studied the papal Adams with narrowed eyes. A plain little woman, Mrs. Brooks Adams, sat next to Mrs. Cameron, just out of range of her husband's eccentric orbit; and it was an orbit that he was

making as he waltzed excitedly . . . a pope with St. Vitus' dance
. . . about his seated older brother; yet of the two, Brooks, white of
head and beard, looked the older. "Here they are," the thin
cultivated voice was inexorable, "the best of France, the military
elite, brought into court, bullied, badgered, humiliated by a gang
of dirty Jews."

"Oh, no!" Caroline could not face another discussion of the case
of Captain Dreyfus that had divided France for so long, boring her
to death in the process. Even Mlle. Souvestre had lost her classical
serenity when she defended the hapless Dreyfus to her students.

"Oh, yes," murmured Del. "Mr. Adams's rabid on the subject.
So is Uncle Dor, but he's less monotonous."

Brooks Adams looked at the newcomers without interest. Then
he included them in his moving orbit. He resumed his crooked
circumnavigation of the chair that held his brother. "Now you may
say, suppose Captain Dreyfus is innocent of giving secrets to the
enemy?"

"I should never *say* such a thing," murmured Henry Adams.

Brooks ignored his brother. "To which *I* say, if he is innocent,
so much the worse for France, for the West, to allow the Jew—the
commercial interest—to bring to a halt—for nothing—a great
power. England and the United States, the one decadent, and the
other ignorant but educable—our task—to side with the Jew-
interest, which, simultaneously, may save us in the coming struggle
between America and Europe, which I have calculated should
start no later than 1914, because there are only two possible
victors—the United States, now the greatest world sea-power, and
Russia, the greatest world land-power. Germany—too small for
world power—will be crushed, and France and England will
become irrelevant, and so that leaves us, facing vast ignorant
Russia, dominated by a handful of Germans and Jews. But can
Russia withstand us in her present state of development or non-
development? I think not."

Brooks Adams's irregular ellipse now brought him face to face
with his brother. "Russia must either expand drastically, into Asia,

or undergo an internal revolution. In either case, this gives us our advantage. This is why we must pray for war *now*. Not the great coming war between the hemispheres." Brooks's odd circuit brought him to Henry James, who gazed like a benign bearded Buddha upon the febrile little man. "But the war to secure us all Asia. McKinley has made a superb beginning. He is our Alexander. Our Caesar. Our Lincoln reborn. But he must understand *why* he is doing what he is doing, and that is where you, Henry, and I and Admiral Mahan must explain to him the nature of history, as we know it . . ."

"I know absolutely nothing," said Henry Adams, abruptly sitting up. "Except that I want my drive."

"To Rye. With me," said Henry James, moving away from the balustrade. "I go home," he said to Mrs. Cameron. "I've invited your Henry—ah, and mine, too—for tea. We shall travel in a hired electrical-motor conveyance of local provenance."

Henry Adams was calling. "Hitty! Hitty! Where are you?"

But Hitty, the niece Abigail, was not to be found. And so it was that in the interminable confusion of Henry James's farewell, Henry Adams took Caroline's arm. "I must have a niece of some sort with me, at all times. It is the law. You are chosen."

"I am honored. But . . ."

There were no buts, as Henry Adams fled his brother Brooks, Caroline in tow, to be thrown, she thought, like dinner to wolves if Brooks were to draw too close to James's rented troika or, to be precise, and James was nothing but that, electrical-motor car. At the last moment Del was included. Yet even in the driveway, to the astonishment of Mr. Beech, Brooks continued to hold forth as the uniformed chauffeur got the two Henrys, the one Del and the one Caroline into their high motor car.

"War is the natural state of man. But for what? For energy . . ."

"Oh, for energy!" simultaneously shouted Henry Adams, as the ungainly electrical-motor car, driven by the uniformed chauffeur, glided through the park, to the further astonishment of Mr.

Beech—and of the deer. In the back seat Caroline and Adams faced Del and Henry James.

"I have never heard Brooks in such good and, may I say, *abundant* voice." Henry James smiled the mischievous small smile that Caroline had come to find enchanting; although he missed nothing, he seemed never, as far as she could tell, to sit in judgment.

"He wears me out," Adams sighed. "He is a genius, you know. Unfortunately, I am the genius's hard-working older brother. So he comes to . . . to *mine* me, like an ore of gold, or more likely, lead. You see, I have a number of cloudy theories, which he makes into iron-bound laws."

"Are there really laws to history?" asked Del, suddenly curious.

"If there were not, I wouldn't have spent my life trying to be a historian." Adams was tart; then he sighed again. "The only thing is—I can't work them out properly. But Brooks can—to a point."

"Well, what are they?" Yes, Del was genuinely curious, thought Caroline, and she was pleased because she was enough of a French-woman to take pleasure, no matter how cursorily, in the elegant generality made flesh by the specific.

"Brooks's law is as follows." Adams stared off into the middle distance where, invisible for the moment, stood Hever Castle, which he had already shown Caroline and a raft of nieces. She thought of Anne Boleyn, who had lived there, and wondered if, when Henry VIII cut off her head, he was obeying a law of history which said, Energy requires that you now start the Reformation: or did he, simply, want a new wife, and a son?

"All civilization is centralization. That is the first unarguable law. All centralization is economy. That is the second—resources must be adequate to sustain the civilization, and give it its energy. *Therefore* all civilization is the survival of the most economical system . . ."

"What," asked Del, "does most economical mean?"

"The cheapest," said Adams curtly. "Brooks thinks that there is now a race between America and Europe to control the vast coal mines of China, because whichever power has the most and the cheapest energy will dominate the world."

"But we have so much coal and oil at home." Del was puzzled. "So much more than we know what to do with. Why go to China?"

"To keep others from going. But your instinct is right. If Brooks's law holds, we shall have got—and won—everything."

"Is this—dare one ask?—a *good* thing?" James was tentative.

"A law of nature is neither good nor ill; it simply is. If not us, Russia? Superstitious, barbaric Russia? No. If not us, Germany? A race given to frenzy—and poetry? No."

"What then are *we* given to, that is so immeasurably superior?" James was staring, Caroline noticed, directly into Adams's face— something he, with his endless tact, seldom did. He appeared to be reading Adams's face, like a book.

"We are given to Anglo-Saxon freedom and the common law and . . ." Adams paused.

"And we are—extraordinarily and absolutely . . . we." James smiled, without, Caroline thought, much pleasure.

"Surely in your love for England," Adams delicately pricked his expatriate friend, "you must have found qualities here that you think superior to those of every other country—and you could have chosen to live anywhere, including our own turbulent republic. Well; then think of the United States as an extension of this country, which you do love and trust. So think of us as simply taking up the Anglo-Saxon radical task, shouldering it for these islands as they begin to lose their—economy."

James spread his hands placatingly. "You speak of laws of history, and I am no lawyer. But I confess to misgivings. How can we, who cannot honestly govern ourselves, take up the task of governing others? Are we to govern the Philippines from Tammany Hall? Will we insist that our oriental colonies be run by bosses? Will we insist that our Spanish possessions be administered by the caucus which has made our politics so vile that every good American—and bad, too, let me hasten to add—cringes when he hears our present system mentioned?"

Adams frowned, not pleased. "We are in a bad way, it is true. But the England of Walpole was far more corrupt and narrow and provincial . . ."

"True. But the acquisition of an empire civilized the English. That may not be a law but it is a fact." Henry James looked at Adams very hard. "But what civilized them might very well demoralize us even further."

Adams did not answer. Del looked worried. "Have you talked like this to Father?"

James's voice lightened. "No, no. Poor man. He has the weight of the world on him as it is. I think him noble beyond description to offer himself, at his age and in such—wintry health, on the altar of public service."

Suddenly, James began to intone, the great organ notes quite filling the village through which they were passing. "'He seen his duty, a dead sure thing. And went for it thar and then.'"

"What," asked Caroline, alarmed, "is that?"

"From 'Jim Bludso,'" said Del. "Father does hate to hear it."

"Well, 'Father' is not here, and I do like the roll of it. What might he not have made, in his marvelously rhythmical chronicles, dedicated to the hazards of transportation, out of a runaway—let us say—electrical-motor car in which an historian and giver of immutable laws is saved from extinction by the swift strong arm of a mere storyteller from Albany, New York, but currently domiciled at Rye . . ."

By the time that James had finished elaborating on this mock-Hay ballad, even Henry Adams was laughing.

Lamb House proved to be a miniature stone manor house with a garden in disarray, all weeds and, yes, dust, thought Caroline obsessively. At the door a man and woman greeted them.

"The Smiths," said Henry James, with uncharacteristic brevity.

Joyously, the Master and his guests were greeted by the Smiths, who dropped his baggage repeatedly, as they hurried, swinging from side to side, into the house's small drawing room.

"The Smiths are a legend," whispered Del, as Henry James

seated Henry Adams in an armchair next to the empty fireplace.

"Why?"

As if challenged to dramatize the legend, Mrs. Smith began to sink slowly, almost gracefully, to the floor, a gentle smile on her lips.

"Mr. Smith." Henry James's voice betrayed no agitation, as Mr. Smith, thus summoned, fell into the doorway from the hall. "Sir?" his voice rang out.

"It would appear that Mrs. Smith's siesta, interrupted by the excitement of our arrival, has been resumed upon the drugget."

"Ah, poor woman!" Smith shook his head. "It is the new medicine the village doctor gives her, not at all what she's used to in London, in Harley Street." During this, Smith had pulled his smiling unconscious wife to her feet, and sleep-walked her to the door. "Hers," Smith declared proudly, "is . . . a highly sensitive sort of organism." They were gone. Henry Adams had succeeded in not laughing but the tip of his neat beard was twitching. Henry James looked endlessly melancholy, even Byronic, thought Caroline, who said, "But surely, Mr. James . . ."

There was a terrible crash at the back of the house: plainly, both Smiths had surrendered to gravity's stern law. "They are indeed, surely, as you put it, to put it finely, the Smiths, a couple richly experienced in domestic matters, but prone in the wastes, as it were, of unfamiliar country life to exceed—go past, even the earliest of warning signals . . ."

"Drunk!" Henry Adams's laugh was so startlingly loud and uninhibited that Caroline could not stop herself; nor could Del.

The Master, however, was a study in polite anguish. "I'm sorry," he said, "that your introduction to Lamb House should be so spoiled by the Dionysian—no, Bacchic—transports of the loyal good Smiths whose transference from their native London to the unfamiliar countryside has tended to overstimulate them, in every sense . . ." The sound of crockery crashing caused James's large smooth brow delicately to furrow.

But Henry Adams then took the lead; and the Smiths, as a

subject, were banished; as a fact, however, they did produce a respectable tea, and Mr. Smith, having got a second wind, served efficiently.

Adams was curious about the neighborhood. Was there sufficient company? "As you prefer solitude to company, this means that you must have some very good company nearby so that *not* seeing them will be all the more agreeable and inspiring."

"Well, there is the Poet Laureate." James passed a plate of heavy cakes to Caroline, who refused; to Del, who took two. "I find that every day that I don't see him is a pleasure. In fact, I see no one here. I did join the golf club, for the tea that they serve, not for the curious lonely game that precedes it, and though unanimously elected as vice-president of the cricket club, I declined the election, as the game is even more incomprehensible to me than golf, and no tea is served. I thought to embrace my solitude this summer little realizing that the Camerons, the Hays, the Adamses should all descend upon me, like a . . . like a . . . ."

"I cannot wait to hear what he will say *we're* like," said Adams to Caroline, who rather wished the windows onto the garden were open: the room was close, and flies circled the cakes.

"I am torn," said James, "between the image of a shower of gold and the lurid details of a passion play. In any case, were it not for you passionate visitors, I would be chained to my desk, writing . . . ."

"Dictating . . . ."

"The image is the same. I am chained to Mr. McAlpine, who is chained to his Remington, while I copiously dictate book reviews for *Literature*, a biography of William Wetmore Story . . . ."

"That crushing bore?"

"You have put in a single phrase what I must make a book of. But as the heirs have paid me a useful sum to memorialize our old and, yes, boring friend, I must do the work to pay for these sticks and stones that compose the first—the last—house I shall ever own."

Del asked James if he had met Stephen Crane, the young American journalist who was said to be living nearby. James nodded. "He is at Brede Place. He came to call before he went to Cuba, to describe the war. He is most talented, with a wife who . . ." James glanced at Caroline, and she realized that whatever the wife might be she, as a virginal girl of American provenance, was not about to be told. ". . . once kept an establishment in Jacksonville, Florida, I believe, named, most evocatively, the Hotel de Dream. Poor young Mr. Crane is also chained to *his* desk, only his desk is now in Havana—where he writes for a newspaper . . ."

"For the *Journal*," said Caroline. Blaise had told her how Hearst had managed to get Crane away from the *World*, where he had described, tactlessly, the cowardice of the 71st New York Volunteers. In a series of headlines, Hearst had denounced the *World* for insulting the valor of America's brave fighting men; then he hired the author of the canard to write for him.

Henry Adams wondered how someone who had never seen a battle could have written such a fine war novel as *The Red Badge of Courage.* James reminded him that "the titanic Tolstoi" had, after all, not been alive during Napoleon's invasion of Russia, yet he could imagine that War as well as Peace, to which Caroline felt mischievously obliged to add, "Although Mr. Crane has never been a girl of any kind, much less one of the streets, he did create for us Maggie."

"Dear, dear!" Henry Adams looked more than ever like an uncle. "You are not supposed to know of such things. Mlle. Souvestre has been lax."

"But Miss Sanford is a product, Adams, of Paris, where *everyone* knows . . ." James's voice dropped very low on the word "knows" and his eyes became very round and comical. Caroline and Del laughed. Adams did not because it was now time to talk of Thee-oh-dore. Caroline wondered if all Americans, of this particular set anyway, were obliged to speak of Theodore Roosevelt at least six times a day, rather the way convent nuns told their beads at regular intervals. She herself had never met the Colonel, as he was currently known, thanks to what John Hay had dubbed, publicly, "a splendid little war," giving offense in many quarters, not all of them Spanish. But although Theodore and his Rough Riders had caught the popular imagination, Caroline found it odd that he should be so interesting to his social equals, not to mention elders. Adams sought to explain him: "He is *all* energy. I suppose that is his attraction . . ."

"For those who find crude mindless energy attractive." James put three teaspoons of sugar in his tea.

"Well, he is not mindless, entirely, that is." Adams was judicious. "He wrote an excellent history of our Navy in the War of 1812 . . ."

"A subject that even at this far remove, causes my pulses to slow. Was that the war where the participants were exhorted not to shoot until the whites of certain distant hostile eyes were visible?"

"Oh, you expatriate! You will not allow us what history we have."

"Of course I will. I just want a lot more of it; and written always by you. But what will become of the hero of our Cuban *Iliad?*"

"He is running for governor of New York State," said Del. "The Republican machine had to take him. You see, he isn't corrupt. And they are. So he will make them respectable."

"But surely, they will make him corrupt, too, if they elect him." Obviously, thought Caroline, Mr. James was more interested in American matters than he let on.

"I think he's far too ambitious," said Adams, "to be corrupted."

"Then, there it already is! The true corruption. I'm afraid I cannot, dear Adams, in my heart, endure your white knight, Theodore. I have just—tell no one—reviewed his latest . . . latest . . . well, *book* for want of a description other than the grim literal paginated printed nullity, called *American Ideals*, in which he tells us over and over—and then over once again—how we must live, each of us, 'purely as an American,' as if that were something concrete. He also warns us that the educated man—himself, no doubt—must not go into politics as an educated man because he is bound to be beaten by someone of no education at all—this he takes to be some sort of American Ideal, which he worships, as it is American, but which, he concedes, presents a problem for the

educated man, whom he then advises to go into the election as if
he had had no education at all, and presenting himself to the
electorate—yes, you have grasped it!—purely *as an American*, in
which case he will win, which is what matters. There is, dear
Adams, as far as I can detect, no mind at all at work in your
friend."

"Perhaps it is not mind so much as a necessary, highly energetic
cunning. After all, he was useful at Washington on the Civil
Service reform commission. He has also made a name as a reformer
of the New York Police."

"My father says that he has yet to meet a reformer who did not
have the heart of a tyrant." Del made his contribution.

"Let's hope he keeps that cruel conviction a secret from Theodore." Caroline could see that Adams wanted to defend Roosevelt
but James's contempt for his celebrated friend was plainly disturbing
to him. "At least," Adams rallied, "when he was assistant secretary
of the Navy, he got the fleet ready, something the secretary and
Congress were not about to do. He also ordered Admiral Dewey to
the China coast, just in case of war. Then, when the war came, by
resigning to go fight, he showed that he was entirely serious."

"Serious?" James frowned. The light in the garden was turning
from silver to deep gold. "Serious, as a Jingo—yes, he is that. And
also serious, I suppose you mean, *purely* as an American . . . ?"

"Oh, James, you are too suspicious of a man who after all
embodies the spirit of our race, as we now move onto the world
stage, and take our part, the leading part, which history's law
requires."

"What law, may I ask, is that?" James was mischievous.

"That the most efficient will prevail."

"Ah, your brother's law! Yes, that the world will go to the . . . uh,
cheapest economy. Of course. And why not? We should do well to
get ourselves an empire on the cheap, assuming that the British will
let theirs go, which I don't see them ever doing, not while German
kaiser and Russian tsar and Japanese mikado are all rattling their
sabres in the once peaceful stillness of the Orient . . ."

50

"A stillness we have broken. You know, Brooks is close to Theodore. Brooks is also close to Admiral Mahan. The three of them are constantly plotting our imperial destiny."

"According to Brooks's immutable laws of history?"

"Yes. Of course he likes to apply laws. I don't. I prefer to understand them."

"The Adamses . . . !" James's exclamation was both comic and fond; and on that note, tea ended; and the electrical-motor car returned them, without incident—though not without numerous warnings from James that they might yet become the martyred subjects for one of Hay's dread Transportation Ballads—to Surrenden Dering.

When Caroline came down to dinner, she found Clara Hay, swathed in pastel colors that made her large bulk seem more than ever monumental, at a desk, writing letters. "I am never caught up any more," she said, smiling at Caroline. Is she to be my mother-in-law? Caroline wondered. Am I, at last, grown-up? She asked herself this question a dozen times a day. It was as if the prison door of childhood had simply opened of its own accord and she, without thinking and, certainly, without a plan—had stepped into the outside world. She had always wanted to do as she pleased; had never dreamed that such a thing was possible. Then the Colonel vanished, which was how she thought of his death; and she had slipped through the open door.

"Did you meet Clarence King this summer in Paris?" Clara continued to write.

"No. I met a George King, who had just married a girl from Boston."

"That was Clarence's brother. They were all together. Then Clarence went off—someplace. To look for gold, or whatever. He is our *brilliant* friend. . . ."

Caroline saw that the letter-paper was the same that Elizabeth Cameron had confiscated. "The Five of Hearts," she said.

Clara put down her pen; and looked at Caroline. "How do you know about that?"

51

"I saw the letter-paper, on the desk. Mrs. Cameron was very mysterious. She said I was not to mention the subject to Mr. Adams."

"She's right. You mustn't. You see, once upon a time there were five of us, and we called ourselves the Hearts. This was in the early eighties, in Washington. There was Mr. Adams, Mr. King, Mr. Hay. There was also Mrs. Adams—now dead—and me. So there are only four Hearts left, of which three, I am happy to say, are here in this house, as I write to the fourth, in British Columbia."

"But did you have—do you have a secret society? With passwords, and curious handshakes, like the Masons?" Colonel Sanford had been devoted to Masonry.

Clara laughed. "No, nothing like that. We were just five friends. Three brilliant men, and two wives, of whom one was brilliant and the other's me."

"How—nice that must have been." Caroline was aware of the inadequacy of the word "nice" but then she was equally aware of the inadequacy of Clara's explanation. "Mr. Adams never speaks of Mrs. Adams?"

"Never. But he does like it when people speak of the memorial to her, Saint-Gaudens's statue in Rock Creek Cemetery. Have you seen it?"

"I've never been to Washington."

"Well, we shall alter that soon, I hope."

Brooks Adams entered the drawing room, talking. "A nation that faces two oceans must have colonies everywhere in order to protect itself."

"Oh, dear," murmured Clara Hay, folding the letter to King and placing it in an envelope. "Dear Brooks," she added; and fled the room slowly.

"That is not just my view," said Brooks, staring hard at Caroline. "It is Admiral Mahan's. When was the last time you reread his *The Influence of Sea Power upon History?*"

"I've never actually read it once," said Caroline, trying not to lose her balance and fall into those mad flinty eyes. "Or," she added, finally detaching her gaze from his, "heard of it till now."

"You must reread it at least once a year." Brooks listened to no one but himself and Henry. "The logic is overpowering. Maintain a fleet in order to acquire colonies. Then, in turn, the colonies will provide you with new wealth in order to maintain an even larger fleet in order to acquire even more colonies. Theodore has finally learned this lesson. It took me years to bring him around. Now he understands that if the Anglo-Saxon race is to survive—and prevail—we must go to war."

"With whom?"

"With anyone who tries to stop us from the acquisition of China. We shall need a different president, of course. McKinley has been superb. But now we need a military man, a dictator of sorts. I'm instructing the Democratic Party to support General Miles. He's a war hero, after all. He's commanded all our forces. He's deeply conservative."

"Will the Democratic Party do as you tell them?" Caroline was now convinced that Brooks Adams was more than a little mad.

"If they want to win, of course. Wouldn't you vote for General Miles?"

"Women do not vote, Mr. Adams."

"Thank God. But if you could?"

"I don't know him."

"You don't know who?" Mrs. Cameron was brilliant in watered blue silk.

"Mr. Adams's candidate for president, General Miles."

"Nelson?" Mrs. Cameron's eyebrows contracted.

"That's right. He's willing. We're willing."

"Then that's that, I suppose." Don Cameron and Henry Adams entered the room together, and Brooks abandoned the ladies for the real quarry. "Poor Brooks," said Mrs. Cameron. "But then poor Nelson, too, if he's got the bug."

"Is Nelson, General Miles?"

"Yes. He's also my brother-in-law. I can't imagine him as

53

president. But then I can't really imagine anyone until, of course, they are. Del says you are leaving tomorrow."

Caroline nodded. "I must talk to lawyers. In New York."

"Our summer's ending far too soon. You to New York, Mr. Hay to New Hampshire. Mr. Adams to Paris . . ."

"Mrs. Hay just told me who the Five of Hearts are."

Mrs. Cameron smiled. "So now you know who they are. But did she tell you *what* they are?"

"What they are?" Caroline was puzzled. "But weren't they just five friends, to begin with?"

"No. They were not just friends," Mrs. Cameron was suddenly, annoyingly, mysterious. "It is *what* they are that most matters." Then Mrs. Cameron turned to greet two strange ladies, who had just arrived. Could it be, wondered Caroline, much intrigued, that these five—now four—elderly people are the gods of Olympus in disguise?

2

Blaise Delacroix Sanford had little appetite for food and less for drink, and so he had got into the habit of turning the lunch hour into a long walk up Fifth Avenue, starting at the *Journal* office and ending with a visit to the Hoffman House bar in Madison Square. Here he would drink a mug of beer and dine off the vast buffet, the only tariff, as it were, the expected twenty-five-cent tip to the waiter, which insured the solid clientele of New York's most sumptuous bar against the hordes of hungry dangerous men who lived beneath the elevated railroad along Sixth Avenue a block away. Although there was an unwritten treaty that there be no traffic between wealthy Fifth and depraved Sixth Avenues, the idle stranger had been known to appear in the bar-rooms of the Fifth Avenue Hotel, that acropolis among hotels, and wolf down a complete meal from the celebrated "free lunch," some sixty silver platters and chafing dishes containing everything from terrapin stew to a boiled egg.

Blaise, in his sturdy youth, preferred the boiled egg to any other food. He had been so spoiled by great cooking all his life in France that simplicity at table was a bleak joy he could now indulge in. As he stood at the bar, beer mug in hand, he looked about the glittering high-ceilinged rooms that ran the hotel's length. Slender, fluted Corinthian columns supported an elaborately coffered ceiling. Every square inch of wall was vividly decorated: half-pilasters in elaborate stucco, painted Arcadian scenes in gilt frames, cut-crystal gas lamps now electrified, and in the place of honor over the mahogany bar the famed nude woman, the notorious master-piece of a Parisian unknown to the Parisian Blaise, one Adolphe William Bouguereau. The painting was still regarded by New York men as "hot stuff." For Blaise it was simply quaint.

As Blaise studied the stout burghers who came and went, talking business, he was relieved to see none of his fellow journalists. Although he enjoyed their company, to a point, that point was often too swiftly reached whenever a bottle was produced. He had known a few heavy drinkers at Yale; had even been drunk himself; but he had never encountered anything quite like the newspaper-men, as they called themselves. It seemed that the more talented they were, the more hopeless and helpless they were in the presence of a bottle.

There was a mild stir in the bar as the former Democratic president Grover Cleveland, a near-perfect cube of flesh, as broad as he was tall, made a stately entrance, shook a number of hands absently, and then took the arm of the smooth Republican Chauncey Depew and together they vanished into an alcove.

"Who'd think they were once mortal enemies?" Blaise turned and found himself looking into the handsome, if somewhat slant-eyed, face of his Yale classmate Payne Whitney. The young men shook hands. Blaise knew that although his classmates considered him somewhat scandalous for not bothering to graduate, he was thought to be highly enterprising—in a criminal sort of way—for having gone to work for William Randolph Hearst and the *Morning Journal*, a newspaper whose specialty, according to the newspaper-

56

men, was "crime and underwear," an irresistible combination that had managed to bring, in two years, Pulitzer's *New York World* to its knees. At thirty-five, Hearst was the most exciting figure in journalism, and Blaise, who craved excitement—American excitement—had got himself introduced to the Chief. When Blaise had said that he had left Yale, just as Hearst had left Harvard, in order to learn the newspaper business, the Chief had been non-committal; but then, at best, he found it difficult to express himself in spoken words. Hearst preferred printed words and pictures; he was addicted to head-lines, exclamation points, and nude female corpses found, preferably in exciting chunks all round the town. But when the Chief had learned that young Mr. Sanford was heir to a considerable fortune, he had smiled, boyishly, and welcomed him into the bosom of the *Journal*.

Blaise sold advertising; rewrote stories; did a bit of everything, including expeditions into darkest Sixth Avenue, and Stygian Hell's Kitchen. He had been bitterly disappointed when the Chief had not taken him to Cuba to enjoy Hearst's victory over Spain. Theodore Roosevelt may have won a small battle but everyone conceded that Hearst had himself started and won a small war. Without Hearst's relentlessly specious attacks on Spain, the American government would never have gone to war. Of course, the sinking of the *Maine* in Havana harbor had been decisive. The plot had been as crude as it was lurid: a ship of a friendly nation on a friendly visit to a restive Spanish colony sinks as the result of a mysterious explosion, with the loss of many American lives. Who—or what—was responsible? Hearst had managed to convince most Americans that the Spanish had deliberately done the deed. But those who knew something of the matter were reasonably certain that the Spanish had had nothing to do with the explosion. Why should they antagonize the United States? Either the ship had exploded from a spontaneous combustion in the coal-bins, or a floating mine had accidentally hit a bulkhead, or—and this was currently being whispered up and down Printing House Square—Hearst himself had caused the *Maine* to be blown up so that he could increase the *Journal*'s circulation with his exciting, on-the-spot coverage of the war. Although Blaise rather doubted that the Chief would go so far as to blow up an American warship, he did think him perfectly capable of creating the sort of emotional climate in which an accident could trigger a war. Currently, Hearst was involved in an even more fascinating plot. At one-thirty, Blaise, a principal in the plot, was to report to the Chief at the Worth House, where Hearst lived in unlonely bachelor splendor.

Payne Whitney wanted to know what Hearst's next move might be. Blaise said that he was not at liberty to say, which caused a degree of satisfying annoyance. But then Blaise was now in the world while Whitney and his Yale roommate, Del Hay, were still boys, on the outside.

"I heard from Del, in England. He said your sister . . ."

"Half-sister," Blaise always said, and did not himself know why. It was not as if anyone cared.

". . . was visiting the same house. I think Del likes her." Whitney looked like a ruddy-faced Chinese boy; a very wealthy Chinese boy between his father, William Whitney, who had been involved in numerous streetcar and railroad ventures, many of them honest, and his doting uncle, Oliver Payne, known to Blaise's father as one of the truly "filthy rich," which always put Blaise, as a boy, in mind of a dark dirty man wearing a large diamond stickpin. Whitney ordered the Hoffman House special cocktail, the razzle-dazzle.

"I think Caroline likes him, too. But she does not exactly share her heart with me." At the thought of Caroline, Blaise had started to think in French, a bad habit, because he found himself translating automatically in his head from French to often-stilted English. He wanted to be entirely, perfectly, indistinguishably American.

"I suppose they are all coming back, now Mr. Hay's secretary of state. Just as I was about to go over, and start my grand tour."

"Oh, *this* is the grand tour!" Blaise, perhaps too Gallically, used both hands to embrace the Hoffman House bar, a habit he must break, he reminded himself. American men never used their hands, except to make fists in order to punch one another. Once angered, Blaise's own instinct was not to punch but to draw a knife, and kill.

Payne Whitney laughed. "Well, you were born on the Grand Tour. I haven't made mine yet." He finished his cocktail; and said good-by. At exactly one-thirty Blaise left the Hoffman House by the Twenty-fifth Street entrance. The sky was an intense cloudless blue. The wind was like gusts of cool electricity, vitalizing everyone, including the old hack-horses. A solitary motor car cruised noiselessly along the street; then the reason for the absence of noise became evident—the engine had stopped. The hack-drivers were delighted and, as always, someone shouted, "Get a horse!" Meanwhile, on every side, men—women, too—could be seen, puffing hard as they succumbed to the latest fad, bicycling.

Just opposite the huge marble Hoffman House was the small Worth House. Blaise was respectfully greeted by a chasseur in a splendid, for no reason, Magyar officer's uniform. An ornate fretwork lift slowly lifted him to the third floor—the whole of it rented by Hearst; here he was greeted by George Thompson, a plump blond man in frock-coat and striped trousers. George had been the Chief's favorite waiter at the Hoffman House. When the Chief had decided to set up housekeeping, he had asked George to keep house for him, which George was happy to do, regulating the traffic so that the Chief's mother on one of her impromptu visits from Washington never actually met any of the ladies who were apt to be visiting her son at unconventional hours.

"Mr. Hearst is in the dining room, sir. He says you're to join them, for coffee."

"Who's them?"

"He's with Senator Platt, sir. Just the two of them."

"Not much talk?"

"Conversation flagged, sir, after the fish. There has been mostly silence since, I fear."

Blaise knew that he would be needed as a conversational buffer. Although Hearst was not particularly shy, he gave that appearance because no one had ever explained to him just how conversation worked. He had a good deal to say in his office; and even more to say in the composing room. But that was that. For Hearst the ideal evening would be a show, preferably one starring Weber and Fields, who would tell jokes that made Hearst laugh until he wept with delight. He also liked minstrel shows, chorus girls, late nights. Yet he neither drank nor smoked.

The dining room was panelled with dark walnut. Italian paintings hung over the sideboard and the mantelpiece; several leaned against the walls, as they waited their turn to be hung. Hearst bought objects with the same boyish greed that he bought writers and artists for his two newspapers.

Hearst was six feet two inches tall, heavily built and not very well put together, to Blaise's critical eye; but then Blaise was a natural athlete, and though only five feet nine inches tall, he carried himself like a circus acrobat, according to Caroline. The muscular body balanced, often as not, on his toes, as if he were about to make a double somersault in the air. Blaise also knew that with his blue eyes and dark blond hair he was definitely, perhaps even permanently, handsome, unlike Hearst, whose pale face with its long thin straight nose and wide thin straight mouth was seriously uninteresting except for the close-set eyes, which were very difficult to look into, more like an eagle's than a man's— the palest blue irises rimmed black pupils that seemed to be forever acquiring whatever he looked at, the brain within a *camera obscura* in which, given time, he would have the whole world's image fixed and filed. Hearst's clothes were definitely "Broadway." Today he wore a plaid suit in which there was a bit too much green and yellow; while the necktie was, simply, a sunset.

On Hearst's right sat the white-haired benign Senator Platt, the Republican boss of New York State. Although Hearst himself was nominally a Democrat, he dealt even-handedly with politicians of every sort. They needed him, he needed them. But the Chief was not to be taken for granted. To everyone's amazement, in the election of '96, he had not supported his father's friend, the Major. Instead, Hearst attacked the Major as a puppet of the archetype

Ohio boss Mark Hanna; he also tried to get Payne Whitney's father to be the Democratic candidate. But when it was plain that William Whitney could not be nominated, the young William Jennings Bryan took the convention by storm. Bryan was a formidable populist orator who had but one speech, "the cross of gold," on which the wealthy had crucified the American people, and the only way to get them down from the cross would be to increase the money supply by coining silver at a rate of sixteen silver units to one of gold.

Although every businessman in the country regarded Bryan as not only mad but potentially revolutionary, Hearst's *Journal* had been the only major paper in New York to support the Democrats. Personally, Hearst thought that Bryan's silver policy was absurd. But Hearst was a Democrat, with populist tendencies. He enjoyed supporting the party of the people against the rich. He also enjoyed Bryan's marvelous oratory. But then who did not? Despite McKinley's election, Bryan was still a great force in the country, and Hearst was his high priest in Babylon, as New York was known to the South and the West where Bryan's strength lay. As George pulled out a chair for Blaise to sit at Hearst's left, Senator Platt said, "I knew your father."

"I heard him speak of you many times, Senator," said Blaise, whose father had never mentioned Platt, or any senator for that matter, except one named Sprague who had married Kate Chase, to his father's fury.

After Senator Platt's confession and Blaise's lie, the room was silent except for the sound of George, filling coffee cups. Plainly, the Chief and the Republican boss had exhausted their small talk while their big talk could never be shared with someone as junior as Blaise. The Senator took a cigar from a box that George offered him; then he asked, "Are you a Methodist, Mr. Sanford?"

Blaise felt his cheeks grow warm, and knew that they were now bright red. "No, sir. We are—my half-sister and I—Catholic."

"Ah." There was a world of regret and contempt in that single

61

exhalation. "France, I suppose. All those years. Explains why you're a Democrat, like Mr. Hearst."

"Oh, Blaise and I aren't what you'd call good party men." Hearst's voice was high and slightly quavery. "If we were, we wouldn't be breaking bread with the Republican czar of New York."

"There are times when serious men must unite. You know what Scripture says." They did not know. He told them. Blaise was much amused to learn that New York's great lord of corruption was also a deeply committed Christian, active in the Methodist church, and an enemy of all vice that was not directly profitable.

"That's why I thought you'd cotton on to Theodore." Platt blew not smoke rings but cloudy globes of impressive diameter.

"Well, we invented him." Hearst was sour. But then Theodore Roosevelt was the only man that the Chief ever showed signs of envying. Theodore was only six years older than Hearst; yet he was now being given credit for Admiral Dewey's conquest of the Philippines, while his own victory in the field at Kettle Hill— renamed San Juan in the interest of euphony and dignity—had been played up by Hearst himself as a battle equal to Yorktown or Gettysburg, and all for the sake of increasing the *Journal*'s circulation in the real war, which was against not Spain but the *World*.

"Yes, you invented him, all right, and I had to take him."

"Didn't you want him to run for governor?" Blaise did his best to appear innocent. Everyone knew that Platt had only taken the "reformer" because thanks to a series of scandals involving the Erie Canal, the Republican Party was in danger of a serious defeat. "We're always open to the better element." Platt was serene. "We welcome reformers."

"Better to have them inside the tent than out," Hearst agreed.

"I'm just sorry you don't see your way to helping out."

"We're committed to the Democrats this time. We're for Judge Van Wyck all the way." The Chief made an effort to sound enthusiastic. "I hate those pink shirts."

"What pink shirts?" Blaise was intrigued.

"Roosevelt's. I also saw him once with this silk . . . thing," the Chief's vocabulary was not rich, "around his waist instead of a waistcoat."

"He wears statesman's black now," said Platt, moodily eyeing Hearst's sunset cravat and riotous plaid.

"I don't like the way he talks either." The Chief's voice quavered; his own accent was Western, modified by Harvard, while Roosevelt's accent was all Harvard. Worse, Roosevelt's voice became falsetto when he orated. Over the years, sensitive to charges of effeminacy, Roosevelt had learned to box and to shoot; had written popular books about his heroic exploits as a rancher in the Badlands, equalled now by his hour of immortal glory in Cuba, charging, ever charging amongst the flying bullets—and the writing journalists—up Kettle Hill.

After another long silence—Platt's defense of his candidate stopped short of a defense of the voice—the Senator rose to go. He made a few cryptic remarks, which the Chief understood; and Blaise did not. Then the long smooth papery hand shook Blaise's somewhat sweaty youthful paw. "You can find me most afternoons at the Fifth Avenue Hotel. I like to sit there in the long corridor, and watch the world go by."

"You sit there and you tell it where to go!" The Chief laughed at his own marvelous acuity. Then the Senator departed; and Blaise followed Hearst into his study, which looked onto the marble façade of the Hoffman House. Hearst sat at an Empire table, all gold eagles and honey-bees, beneath a portrait of Napoleon, one of his heroes; the others were all equally *heroic* heroes, world conquerors. Blaise found himself vacillating between amazement at the Chief's simplicity and absence of even the sort of culture that Harvard might have given him had he bothered to notice that such a thing existed and the marvelous energy and inventiveness that he demonstrated when it came to publishing a newspaper. Hearst alone had discovered a truth so obvious that Blaise, a fascinated newcomer to the American world, was amazed that no one else had grasped it: if there is no exciting news to report, create some.

When the artist Remington had cabled Hearst that he wanted to come home from Cuba as there was nothing happening for him to draw, Hearst had replied, "You furnish the pictures, I'll furnish the war." Whether or not Hearst had literally sunk the *Maine* was irrelevant, because he, far more than Roosevelt, had made war not only inevitable but desirable. Now the Chief had a new project, and Blaise was at its center because, among other things, he knew French.

"You bring the latest dispatches from Paris?"

Blaise gave the Chief a series of cables which had arrived that morning from France; a number were written in a code of his own excited devising. Since January, the Chief had had his heart set on what Blaise thought of as "the French Caper." But the war with Spain had intervened and all other projects were suspended, as Hearst orchestrated public opinion with the magical reverberant phrase "Remember the *Maine!* And buy the *Journal!*" When Hearst's war was declared, he had offered to finance and command a regiment. McKinley had said no; he had not forgotten those cartoons of him on Hanna's knee. Ever the gracious patriot, Hearst then made the Navy a present of his yacht, aptly named the *Buccaneer*; with his own military services included. The Navy took the ship but refused the services. So Hearst commandeered another ship and went to war on his own and in style, accompanied by *Journal* writers, artists and photographers.

The Chief's dispatches from the front, including his personal capture of twenty-nine Spanish sailors, had caused great distress to Mr. Pulitzer at the *World*. The Chief was also obliged to play up Colonel Roosevelt's derring-do; and he did so conscientiously but without relish. Instinctively, the dashing politician knew almost as much about publicity as the Chief himself. Certainly, from the Chief's occasional remarks about the Colonel, it was plain to Blaise that each had seen the war as *his* war and that each had wanted to capitalize politically on the subsequent victory, not to mention imperium. But of the two, the Colonel, if elected governor, seemed to be in the better position. On the other hand, Hearst had now decreed that Judge Van Wyck be governor; and the fact that Senator Platt had come to the Chief to cut, as the politicians would say, a deal was proof that the Democrats were comfortably in the lead. But if Hearst's next coup were to succeed, the election might easily be obscured by William Randolph Hearst's daring.

The plan was nothing less than the removal from Devil's Island, in the Safety Islands off Guiana on the South American coast, of the world's most celebrated prisoner, Captain Alfred Dreyfus, a Jew, who had been accused, falsely according to Hearst and half the world (but not Blaise's half), of giving French military secrets to the Germans. Although the case had been reopened in Paris, and the actual spy supposedly identified, the French General Staff would not admit that justice, no matter how skewed by fashionable anti-Semitism, had miscarried. They acquitted the actual spy; and kept Dreyfus in solitary confinement on Devil's Island. At that moment, in January, the Chief had said to Blaise, "You work this one out. You're French. Make the case for what's his name. We'll pour it on. Every day. Then if the French don't let him go, I'll outfit the *Buccaneer*, and we'll go down there and shoot our way in and bring that Jew back to civilization, and if the French want to take us on in a war, we'll knock those frogs to bits."

Before January, it had never occurred to Blaise that Captain Dreyfus might be innocent. But the more that he investigated the case, the more certain he was that Dreyfus had indeed been falsely accused. When "that French dirty writer," as Hearst always called him, "you know, the one whose name begins with Z, like Zebra," Emile Zola, accused the French government of covering up the truth, he was obliged to flee to England. That was when the Chief gave orders for the *Buccaneer* to stand by. He himself would lead the attack on Devil's Island, with Blaise as his eager second-in-command. But then Spain not France became the enemy of Truth and Civilization; and the spring and summer were devoted to the expansion of the *Journal*'s circulation and, incidentally, the American empire. Now, as Colonel Roosevelt ran up yet another hill, as a politician, Hearst was prepared, at the least, to offer himself to the world as a hero; at the most, to change world history by precipitating a war with France.

The Chief put his feet upon the desk, and daydreamed, eyes half-shut. "We'll need, maybe, a thousand men. We might hire some of Roosevelt's Rough Riders, that'd embarrass him." The Chief giggled. Blaise, his eyes on Bonaparte, wondered if that world hero was prone to daydreaming and giggling. "Check out the Rough Riders. Don't tell them what we've got in mind. Just say a filibuster. You know, an adventure. In Latin America. Go after the tough ones, the real Westerners. We don't want any New York swells."

Blaise felt that he should interpret the latest news from Paris. "The government's just promised a new trial for Dreyfus."

"Court-martial is the phrase, I heard." Just when Blaise had decided that Hearst was totally ineducable, not to mention in thrall to his own daydreams, he would suddenly demonstrate that in his crude but highly intuitive way he had got the point, usually before anyone else. "They'll drag it out another year at least. We need a good story for the fall. *Before* November. Before election. This should do in Roosevelt."

"How can you and Captain Dreyfus lose him an election in New York State?" Usually Blaise could follow Hearst's peculiar logic: the key to it was entertainment. What would most excite the average uneducated man?—who would then part with a penny to read the *Journal?*

Hearst opened very wide his pale blue eyes and the usually straight brows arched with what looked to be wonder: *he* was ready to part with that penny. "Don't you see? It's all the same. Teddy winning a battle that was already won but getting the credit because he is who he is and all the newspaper boys were right there with him because I'm selling the war to the world. He couldn't lose because I couldn't lose. Well, if I break into Devil's Island and free that poor innocent Jew, why, no one will pay any more attention to Teddy, who'll be last summer's news while I'm this fall's news, and so Van Wyck gets elected."

In a lunatic way, Blaise saw the point. Hearst's meddling in French internal affairs, successful or not, would certainly be a sensation; and a diversion from the election. Blaise was also beguiled by the fact that Hearst could never remember Dreyfus's— or any Frenchman's—name.

"You've got the plans of the fort, haven't you?" Hearst gazed out the window at the Hoffman House, where a line of carriages were depositing the guests for some sort of Democratic meeting. As the Fifth Avenue Hotel was sacred to the Republicans, so the Hoffman House was to the Democrats.

"Yes, Chief. They're in your safe at the office. Also, the size— estimated—of the garrison, and the number of guards that look after Dreyfus."

"I don't suppose we could free *all* the frog prisoners." Hearst's imagination seemed now to be positively Mosaic, as he led all of those who had been slaves into the promised land of Manhattan.

"I think you'll have quite enough to do just freeing Dreyfus."

'I suppose you're right. Well, I'll go over all this with Karl Decker. He'll be your side-kick. He's got a real gift for these . . . uh, things."

Karl Decker was a knowledgeable journalist who had managed to free from a Cuban prison an attractive young woman, who had been a passionate—what else?—enemy of Spain and its beast-like governor. Hearst had got a lot of play out of that adventure; now he wanted more. "I expect you to be right there with us, in the lead, after me." The Chief looked very much like a small boy about to play pirate.

"I'd like nothing better."

"Because you're the only one who can talk to what's-his-name. You know? In French. I never could pick up the lingo. You think you like publishing?" The small boy pirate had suddenly turned into a bland full-grown businessman, the worst of pirates.

"Oh, yes!" Blaise was as enthusiastic as he sounded. "I think it's more exciting than anything else, especially the *Journal*."

"Well, I have my critics." The blandness was now absolute.

Although Hearst was daily denounced by all right-thinking men and women, he seemed perfectly indifferent to the opinions of others. He liked stories, adventures, fun. He liked being number one in circulation if not yet in advertising. "I've also pretty much used up my mother's . . . present. These wars can cost you a lot of money."

Blaise was surprised not that Hearst had spent the seven and a half million dollars that Phoebe Hearst had given him three years earlier but that Hearst would admit it; however, that was part of the Chief's enigmatic charm, to know who was what and how he should be treated. Employees were always treated with grave politeness; and Hearst's voice was seldom raised. He was generous, in every sense; all he wanted in return was the absolute best of its kind. But he did not make friends with those he hired, even the editors. He was not to be seen in the bars around Printing House Square. He was also not to be seen in the men's clubs of his class for the excellent reason that a cannonade of black balls would have shot down any proposal that he might be made a member of any one of them. "I've also been on the outside here," he would say, more to himself than to Blaise; and Blaise decided that the Chief was quite happy to remain where he was, outside, yes, but terrorizing those inside.

When Blaise had left Yale in his junior year, Colonel Sanford had been furious. "What will you do? What are you equipped to do in life?" Blaise was too tactful to point out that the Colonel himself had not been equipped to do anything at all in life except spend the money that he had inherited from *his* family; although to be fair—something Blaise found difficult to be with a father who had always embarrassed him—the Colonel had, rather absently, made a second fortune after the war in railroading, using Delacroix money, a source of irritation to the family of Blaise's mother, since none of it ever came their way.

"My son's a Delacroix," Sanford would say expansively, "you'll get it back through him." But when that same son left Yale, and moved to New York, and said that he wanted to go into the newspaper business, the Colonel was appalled; he was even more distressed when Blaise, who had always been fascinated by newspapers, declared that it was his ambition to be exactly like William Randolph Hearst, whose very name was a synonym for cad in the Sanford world. But the Colonel had yielded to the extent of instructing his lawyer, Dennis Houghteling, to arrange a meeting between Blaise and the dark—or rather bright yellow—prince of journalism.

Hearst had been gravely interested in the young man. "The business part's easy to learn," he said. "You just hang around the people who sell the advertising, and the people who do the accounting, and then you try to figure out how the more papers I sell, the more money I lose, and the more red ink they write their numbers with." Hearst's smile was not exactly winning. "The other end, the paper . . ."

"That's what I like!" They were seated in the Chief's office, overlooking Park Row. Hearst had rented the second and third floors of the Tribune Building, that monument to the honest founder of all that was best—if hectoring—in modern journalism, Horace Greeley. From Hearst's window the domed City Hall was visible while the magnificent new Pulitzer Building was not visible, unless you put your head as far as you could out the window and looked up the block and so saw the skyscraper headquarters of "the enemy" *World*.

"Well, the other end of putting out a paper depends partly on how much money you've got to spend and partly on how good you are at keeping the folks interested in . . . in . . ."

"In Crime and Underwear?" Blaise was brash.

The Chief frowned uncomfortably. "I don't use words like that," he said, somewhat primly. "But the folks like scandal. That's true. They also need to be looked out for because there's no one in a city like this who will take the side of the average citizen."

"Not even the politicians?"

"*They* are what you have to save the folks from, if you can. I suppose you'll want to invest in a paper." Hearst looked at a number of random tear-sheets on the floor; they would, once he'd arranged them in order, become the *Sunday Journal*.

"As soon as I know what I'm doing, if I'll ever know, of course. You don't learn much at Yale, I'm afraid."

"I was kicked out of Harvard, and glad to go. Well, you can start in here anytime; and we'll see what happens." Not long after this exchange, Hearst had declared war on Spain and won it. Now he would free Captain Dreyfus. Defeat Colonel Roosevelt. Start a dozen new papers. Everything seemed possible except, and the Chief looked Blaise in the eye, the face as tense as that of Bonaparte behind him, "I've used up all the money Mother gave me, and we're still in the red."

"Ask her for more." Blaise was brisk; he saw what was coming.

"I don't like to. Because . . ." The high voice gave out. The Chief scratched his chin; then his ear. "I saw Houghteling yesterday. At the Fifth Avenue Hotel."

"He's a good Republican." Blaise braced himself for the assault.

"I suppose so. But he don't like pink shirts any more than I do. He tells me your father's will is coming up for probate."

"Well, it's a slow process." The Colonel had been killed in February; now it was September. The process of the law had stopped during the summer. "It might not be before the first of the year."

"Houghteling says next week." The Chief's voice was flat. "There's a lot of money there."

"Oh, I don't know." Blaise was beginning to feel clammy. "Anyway there are two of us, my sister—half-sister—and me."

"Now is the time to get in on the ground floor," said Hearst. "Now's your chance. I've got my eye on Chicago, Washington, Boston. I want a paper in every big city. You . . ." The voice trailed off.

"Aren't I sort of young to be . . . a partner?" Blaise suddenly went on the offensive. Why, after all, should he be nervous with Hearst when he had—or would soon have—the money that Hearst needed?

"Well, no one said anything about you being a partner." Hearst might have laughed if he had thought of it. But he did not; he continued to frown. "I guess you could certainly buy an interest."

"Well, yes. I guess I could." But Blaise had spent enough time with the *Journal*'s dispensers of red ink to know that everything belonged to Hearst, personally; and there was, thus far, no sort of "interest" that could be sold. Blaise chose not to press the matter. He had his own plan, which might, or might not, include the Chief. More to the point, "I really don't know how much I'm going to end up with, or for how long," he added cryptically.

"Well, that's your affair."

George was at the door. "Miss Anita Willson and Miss Millicent Willson to see you, sir." George kept the straightest of faces.

"Tell them to wait in the parlor." Hearst rose.

"Get on to Decker."

"Yes, sir."

As Blaise walked down the hall, he saw the Willson sisters, staring at themselves in a mirrored screen in the parlor. They were plump, pretty, blond. At the paper there were those who thought that the Chief favored Millicent, who was only sixteen; others thought that he preferred the older Anita; a few thought that he enjoyed each of them, either separately or together, according to what degree the imagination of the speculating journalist had been depraved. All agreed that the two girls were very effective as part of a dancing group called the Merry Maidens, currently appearing at the Herald Square Theater in *The Girl from Paris*. As George opened the front door for Blaise, the Chief must have entered the parlor, because there were delighted cries. "Oh, Mr. Hearst! Mr. Hearst! We never dreamed there was that much chocolate in the world!" The voices were tough Hell's Kitchen Irish. Hearst's response was not audible. George's eyes became slightly more round. Blaise stepped into the elevator.

Park Row was crowded with end-of-day traffic. Streetcars rattled down the center of the street while smart and less smart carriages stopped at City Hall. Blaise made his way, tentatively, from street

71

corner to curb, careful to avoid as best he could the mounds of horse manure that the Mayor had promised would be removed at least twice a day. Blaise tried to envisage a city without horses; in fact, he had already tried his hand at fantasy. In the *Sunday Journal*, he had described a future world of horseless carriages. As it was, the Chief himself drove a flashy French automobile, fuelled by gasoline. Unfortunately, the only vivid difference between a horseless future and the present would be the necessary and unmourned absence of something that Blaise and the Sunday editor, the young indecorous Merrill Goddard, spent a whole morning trying to find euphemisms for. At the end, Goddard had shrieked, "Sanford, call it shit!"

Blaise smiled at the memory, and started unconsciously to mouth the word as he crossed the coupolaed hall at whose center a number of Tammany types had gathered about His Honor the Mayor, Robert Van Wyck, brother to the gubernatorial candidate.

But Blaise was doomed never to know what wisdom the Mayor was dispensing in the rotunda, because a tall old man with silver hair and rose-tinted side-whiskers, Dennis Houghteling, the Sanford family lawyer, signalled him from the marble staircase. "I have been with the Clerk of Wills," he said in a low conspiratorial voice, the only voice that he had. Because the Colonel refused even to visit, much less live, in the United States, Mr. Houghteling had been, in effect, the Sanford viceroy at New York, and once a month he reported in careful detail the state of the Sanford holdings to its absent lord. Since Blaise had known Mr. Houghteling all his life, it was only natural that when it came time to probate the last of his father's many wills, the matter would be entrusted to the senior partner of Redpath, Houghteling and Parker, attorneys-at-law.

"All is well," whispered Houghteling, putting his arm through Blaise's, and steering him to an empty marble bench beneath a statue of De Witt Clinton. "All is well as far as the *law* is concerned." Houghteling began to modify; and Blaise waited, with assumed patience, for the lawyer to tell him what the problem was. Meanwhile, the Mayor was making a speech beneath the cupola.

The vowels echoed like thunder while the consonants were like rifle shot. Blaise understood not a word.

"As we know, the problem is one of interpretation. Of cyphers; or of a single cypher to be precise—and its ambiguity."

Blaise was alert. "Who will ever contest our interpretation of an ambiguous cypher?"

"Your sister will certainly contest our interpretation . . ."

"But she's in England, and if the will's been probated, as you say . . ."

"There has been a slight delay." Houghteling's whisper was more than ever insinuating. "Your cousin has spoken up, on behalf of Caroline . . ."

"Which cousin?" There were, that Blaise knew of, close to thirty cousins, in or near the city.

"John Apgar Sanford. He is a specialist in patent law, actually . . ."

Blaise had met Cousin John, a hearty dull man of thirty, with an ailing wife, and many debts.

"Why has he got himself involved?"

"He is representing your sister in this."

Blaise felt a sudden chill of anger. "*Representing* Caroline? Why? We're not in court. There's no contest."

"There will be, he says, over the precise age at which she comes into her share of the estate . . ."

"The will says that when she's twenty-seven, she'll inherit her share of the capital. Until then I have control of the entire estate. After all, Father wrote that will himself, with his own hand."

"Unfortunately, he—who usually refused to speak French—wrote his will in rather faulty French, and since the French number one looks just like an English seven, though unlike a French seven, your cousin is taking the position that the Colonel intended for this will to conform with the earlier ones; and that your father meant for Caroline to inherit at twenty-one, not twenty-seven, half the estate."

"Well, it looks like twenty-seven to me. How did it look to the clerk?"

"I translated the text for him. *Of course*, the English version says twenty-seven . . ."

"So what's the problem?"

"Twofold. Your cousin says that we have deliberately misinterpreted your father, and he will now contest our . . . interpretation of the figure."

"*He* will? How can he? Only Caroline can and she's three thousand miles away."

"Your first supposition is correct. He obviously cannot contest a will with which he has nothing to do. Your second supposition—the geographical one—is mistaken. I have just spoken to your sister. She arrived this morning from Liverpool. She is stopping at the Waldorf-Astoria."

Blaise stared at the old lawyer. In the background, someone proposed three cheers to Mayor Van Wyck, and the rotunda reverberated with cheering; like artillery being fired. Martial images filled Blaise's head. War. "If they contest what my father wrote, I shall take them through every court in the country. Do you understand, Mr. Houghteling?"

"Of course, of course." The old man tugged at his rose-pink whiskers. "But perhaps, it would be more seemly to come to an agreement. You know? A compromise, say. A settlement . . ."

"She must wait for her share." Blaise got to his feet. "That's what my father wanted. That's what I want. That's what it is going to be."

"Yes, sir." Thus, the crown passed from Colonel Sanford to Blaise, who was now sole steward, for the next six years, of fifteen million dollars.

John Hay stood at the window of his office in the State War and Navy Building, a splendid sort of wedding cake designed, baked and frosted by one Mullett, an architectural artificer who had been commissioned a dozen years earlier to provide mock-Roman shelter for the three great departments of state, all in a single building within spitting distance of that gracious if somewhat dilapidated Southern planter's home, the White House, to the east. From the window of the Secretary of State's office the unlovely greenhouses and conservatories of the White House—like so many dirt-streaked crystal palaces—were visible through the trees, while in the distance Hay could make out, across the Potomac, the familiar green hills of Virginia, enemy country during the four years that he had been President Lincoln's secretary.

Now here I am, he thought, trying hard to summon up a sense of drama or, failing that, comedy; he got neither. He was old; frail; solitary. Clara and the children had stayed on at the Lake Sunapee house in New Hampshire. Accompanied only by Mr. Eddy, Hay had marched into the State Department that morning at nine o'clock, and taken control of the intricate and confusing department, where more than sixty persons were employed in order to . . . what?

"I am curious, Mr. Adee. What does the Secretary of State actually *do?*" Hay shouted at his old friend, *dear* friend, Alvey A. Adee, the second assistant secretary of state. They had first met when both had been posted in Madrid during the time that the self-styled hero of Gettysburg, the one-legged General Dan Sickles, American minister to Spain, was scandalously ministering to Spain's queen as her democratic lover. Seven years Hay's junior, Adee had even collaborated with Hay on a short story that had been published in *Putnam's*; and, joyously, they had divvied up the cash. Madrid had been a quiet post in the late sixties.

Now Adee carefully groomed his gray Napoleonic beard and moustaches; he used a tortoise-shell comb but, happily, no pocket mirror as in the old days. Adee was the most exquisite of bachelors, with a high voice which, in moments of stress, broke into a mallard's cackle. Although deaf, he was very good at guessing what it was that people said to him. All in all, he was the ablest man in the American foreign service as well as a superb literary mimic. At a moment's notice, Adee could write a poem in the manner of Tennyson or of Browning; a speech in the style of Lincoln or of Cleveland; a letter in the style of any and every sort of office-holder. "Each of the secretaries comes here with his own notion of work." Adee put away the comb. "Your immediate predecessor, Judge Day, spent his five months here fretting about his next judgeship. Of course, he only took the job as a favor to the President when poor Mr. Sherman . . ." Adee sighed.

Hay nodded. "Poor Uncle John, as we call him, was too old by the time he got here. If this were a just world . . ."

"What a conceit, Mr. Hay!" Adee produced an amused quack.

"I am prone to the sententious. Anyway, he should have been president years ago."

"Well, the world's all wrong, Mr. Hay. Anyway, you tried hard enough to get the old thing elected." Adee took a small vial of cologne from his pocket and shook a drop or two on his beard.

Hay rather wished that Adee were able to present a somewhat more virile face to the world. As it was, the Second Assistant was not unlike Queen Victoria, with a glued-on beard. "Obviously, I don't work hard enough. But my question's quite serious. What do *I* do?"

"What you *should* do is let me do most of it . . ."

"Well, we are old collaborators, of course . . ."

"I'm serious, Mr. Hay. Why wear yourself out for nothing? There are dispatches from all around the world to be read—and replied to. I do most of that, anyway. I also write a really masterful letter of sympathetic rejection to would-be office-seekers, many of them nephews to senators."

Hay had a sudden, vivid vision of the tall fragile figure of President Lincoln, looking very much like "the Ancient" that his two young secretaries had nicknamed him, besieged in the upstairs corridor of the White House by men and women, shoving petitions, letters, newspaper-cuttings at him. "Whitelaw Reid now wants the embassy at London," Hay began.

But Adee was studying his glistening nails, and did not hear him. He must read lips, Hay thought. When Adee's eyes are not upon your mouth, he does not hear. "You'll be relieved to know that you now have nothing to offer anyone. The President has given away just about all the posts to keep his senators happy."

"I can still pick the first assistant secretary . . ."

"There is a rumor . . ." Adee began; but a soft knock at the door interrupted him. "Come," said Adee, and a smiling Negro messenger entered to present Hay with a silver-framed photograph. "This just arrived, Mr. Secretary. From the British embassy."

Hay placed the extravagantly signed photograph on his desk, so that Adee could also enjoy the figure depicted, a somewhat larger, stouter, bemedalled version of Adee's own. "The Prince of Wales!" Adee's accent now became, unconsciously, British. He mimicked compulsively, as the chameleon shifts its color to suit the landscape. "We've all heard what a success you were with the royal family. In fact, Her Majesty was quoted in the *Herald*, indirectly, of course, as saying that you were the most interesting ambassador that she had ever known."

"Poor woman," said Hay, who had read the same story with quiet pleasure. "I told her Lincoln stories. And dialect stories. It was like being out on the Lyceum circuit. No matter how old the joke—or the Queen—the audience laughs."

Adee's accent recrossed the Atlantic and hovered somewhere near Hay's native Warsaw, Illinois. "I reckon your main job will be to help our good President, who knows nothing of foreign affairs and has no time to learn. He is mortally tired now of having been his own secretary of state for two years while running and winning a war and instructing our delegation to the peace conference in Paris, except he's not sure what he wants them to do." Adee stared at Hay's lips. "As far as I can tell, that is," he added.

Hay had heard the same rumor: indecision in the White House; hence, confusion in Paris. "Do get me all the Paris dispatches. I'd better find out just what's been said so far."

Adee frowned. "I'm afraid we don't get to see them here. Judge Day always reported directly to the President."

"Oh." Hay nodded, as if he approved. But the first warning bell had now sounded. Unless he acted quickly, he was to be excluded from the peace treaty by his predecessor's indifference.

Mr. Eddy was at the door. "The White House just telephoned, sir. The President can see you anytime now."

"Have we a *telephone?*" asked Hay, who disliked the invention, not only for its dreadful self but for its potential threat to his beloved Western Union.

"Oh, yes," said Adee. "We are very modern over here. We have one in our telegraph office. Personally, I hear nothing at all when I put it to my ear. But others *claim* to hear voices, like Joan of Arc. There's also one in the White House, in what was the President's war-room."

"Surely, the President doesn't, personally, use that . . . that menacing contraption?"

"He says that it is addictive." Adee was judicious. "He says that he enjoys the knowledge that he can always hang up when he is being told something that he doesn't want to hear, and then he can pretend that the connection was broken by accident."

"The Major has become guileful."

"He's a successful war-leader. It is inevitable," said Mr. Adee. "Shall I walk you over to the mansion?"

Hay shook his head. "No, I'll go alone. I need to arrange my thoughts, such as they are."

"What to do with the Philippines?"

"Above all." Hay sighed. "We must decide, and soon."

Hay stepped out into the dim high-ceilinged corridor, where a single policeman stood guard. Usually, the State Department was one of the most tranquil, even somnolent, of the government's ministries, on the order of Interior, where, barring the rare excitement of the odd Indian war, a man could sleep his way through the life of an administration, or get a book written. But since the events of the summer, new translators had been added to the State Department, and the slow stream of paper into and out of Mr. Mullett's masterpiece was now engorged.

Hay was greeted respectfully by numerous functionaries whose functions were as unknown to him as their persons. But he pretended to recognize everyone, the politician's trick, with a raise of an eyebrow if the face looked remotely familiar, a bob of the head if not; geniality was the politician's common tender.

Outside, in Pennsylvania Avenue, Hay was pleased at the absence of journalists. He was not expected until the next day, when he would take the oath of office. For now, no one paid the slightest attention to him except an old black man who was pushing a cart that contained everything needed for the sharpening of knives, the repair of scissors. They had seen each other for years in the street. After a solemn greeting, the old man said, "I didn't know you was living on this side of the road."

Hay laughed. "No. I'm still living there." He pointed to the dark red brick fortress, all turrets and arches, where he and Adams, like two medieval abbots, lived. "But I'm working here now."

"What sort of work they do in there?" The old man was genuinely curious. "I watched them building the thing. They say it's, oh, just government, when I asked."

"Well, that's what it still is. Remember the old State Department Building there?" Hay pointed roughly to what was now a section of the huge gray-stone Treasury Building which nicely obstructed any view of the Capitol from the White House.

The old man nodded. "I can still see Governor Seward, with that big nose of his and those baggy pants, going back and forth across the road here, with this big cigar all the time."

"Well, I've taken his place, and now we do in here what he used to do in that little shack."

"Everything keeps getting bigger," said the old man, without much pleasure. "This was a real small town back then."

"Well, now it's a real small city," said Hay, and continued on his way. He was pleased to note that the brilliant pains in his lower back had migrated to his left shoulder, where they gave him less dazzling discomfort. For an instant, a particle of an instant, John Hay remembered what it was like to be young, as he walked up the familiar semi-circular driveway to the north portico of the White House where thirty-three years earlier, he had been Lincoln's "boy" secretary. Somehow or other in the blurred interval between then and now, a generation had come and gone, and quick-stepped boy had changed to slow-moving man.

In front of the portico Hay paused; and looked up at what had been the window to the office that he had shared with the first secretary, John G. Nicolay; and half-hoped to see his own young self, with dashing new moustaches, look out the window at his future self, with . . . disgust, Hay decided, accurately. He had not, like so many old men, forgotten the boy that he had once been. The boy was still alive but locked up for good—or life, anyway— in an aging carcass.

The head doorkeeper, one Carl Loeffler, was waiting for Hay; plainly, the telephone wire between White House and Mullett's masterpiece was in good working order. "Mr. Secretary, sir." The stocky German—in Hay's day, only Hibernians were entrusted with the door—showed Hay into the entrance hall where the enormous, even astonishing, Tiffany screen, a fantasy of stained glass and intricate leading, rose from tessellated floor to ornately stuccoed ceiling, the gift of that most elegant of all presidents, Chester Alan Arthur, who had dared to do what other presidents had wanted to do but dared not. He had put up a screen in order to hide the state apartments, the Red, Blue and Green rooms, from the eyes of the multitudes who came to do business with the President, whose office and living quarters were still, as in

Lincoln's day, on the second floor, and reached by a shabby old staircase to the left of the entrance. Hay noted that the heavy dark wood railing was more than ever shiny with sweat, from the nervous hands of office-seekers. At present, a mere dozen political types were ascending, descending.

As the head doorkeeper showed Hay up the staircase, he said, "Mr. McKinley's in his office," as if the President might have been in the boiler room. Suddenly, with wonder, Hay realized that he had not walked up this particular staircase since Lincoln's time. Although he had been assistant secretary of state under President Hayes, he had never been summoned to the President. So, accompanied by a lifetime of ghosts, not least among them his youthful self, Hay stepped out into the long corridor that bisected the second floor from the offices at the east end, where he now was, and the living quarters at the west. The oval library, a no-man's-land in the middle, followed the oval shape of the Blue Room directly beneath. The Lincolns had used the upstairs oval as a sitting room; other presidents had used it as an office.

The corridor was much the same; but the world was different. Where once there had been new gas-lamps, there were now electric lights, with dangling wires criss-crossing the shabby walls in every direction. Fortunately, the unlovely greenhouses did produce quantities of flowers and plants that were placed on every table and in every corner; as a result, the inevitable tobacco and whiskey smell of politicians was hardly detectable in that rose-crowded place, where efficient-looking, highly modern young men strode decisively, at least whenever they got near the reception room where the petitioners daily gathered. The effect of a swift-moving modern office was somewhat undone by the floor, which not only shook with every step but vibrated whenever a streetcar passed. Termites, Hay thought; and knew that he had come home.

Hay entered his old office, with its view—now of Hay's own house across Pennsylvania Avenue. But instead of his own young self, he was greeted, somewhat to his disappointment, by George B. Cortelyou, the President's second secretary. "Mr. Hay!" Cortelyou was in his forties; a short-haired, short-moustached, straight-featured, short man. McKinley, in an uncharacteristic move, had hired a Connecticut swell named Porter as secretary. But Porter had proved disastrously inept, and so McKinley had, with characteristic tact, turned over Porter's duties to Cortelyou, managing to offend no one. "Can't tell you, sir, how happy—how relieved—I am that you're here and that it's—well, it's *you*."

"Your predecessor?" Hay indicated the office. "I always sat back to the window. The stove was there. I see you've got a steam radiator. This place gets cold in winter."

"I often think of you in this room, sir. And Mr. Nicolay across the way."

"Do you, really?" Hay could not believe that those two young men of long ago were remembered by anyone, except their aging, ailing selves. Nicolay was often ill these days. Fortunately, he had a small pension from his days as marshal of the Supreme Court; and there was still income from the various Lincoln books that, together with Hay and separately, he was involved in.

"I particularly thought of you during the war this summer. The scale was different from your war, naturally, but . . ."

Hay nodded. "The anxieties are always the same. You never know when you start where and how you'll end."

"You were lucky, sir. So were we. So far." Courtelyou led Hay out into the corridor. "We've changed a lot of things around since your day. In fact, since Mr. Cleveland was here. The secretary—Mr. Porter, that is—has the corner office at the end there, and the President has the middle office. Then there's the Cabinet room, which connects with the oval library. Only the President can't put up with the crowds, so he's moved out of his office, which we now use for the visitors, and into the Cabinet room, where he camps out, he says, quite comfortably, at one end of the Cabinet table."

"How *is* Mr. McKinley?"

"He's weary, sir. The pressures are very great from the Hill . . ."

"The Senate . . . ?"

"The Senate. On top of that he's developed eye-strain; can't read small print, has headaches. He also doesn't get enough exercise, but I tell him that that's *his* fault. He used to ride. But now he doesn't." Cortelyou stopped at the dark mahogany door to the Cabinet room. A doorkeeper stood guard. Cortelyou signaled the man to open the door.

Cortelyou stood in the doorway and said, "Mr. President, Colonel Hay is here." Then Cortelyou shut the door behind Hay, who crossed what had been, in his day, the Reception Room to the long table at whose end, beneath an elaborate bronze lighting fixture, stood William McKinley, a man of medium height with a large full smooth-shaven face and an equally large high firm paunch contained by an elegant white piqué waistcoat. The frock-coat was open, as if to frame the splendidly clothed, curved belly; in the presidential lapel a dark red carnation glowed like some exotic foreign order. The entire effect was impressive; and highly agreeable. McKinley's smile was always directed at the person to whom he was speaking and not set in permanent place by grim necessity. As Hay shook hands, he stared for a moment into the large, marvelously expressive—but of what other than generalized good will?—eyes, and, suddenly, for no reason at all, Hay recalled that as Lincoln had been the first bearded president, McKinley was now the first clean-shaven one in a generation. Why, Hay wondered, had he thought of that? In his place, Adams would be drawing some vast historical Plutarchian distinction between two paragons while all Hay could think of was beards; and hair coloring. The President, he noted, did not dye his thin graying hair, unlike Hay, who had recently taken to using some of Clara's Special Gentlelady's Henna, with a reasonably authentic result. Clara claimed that he still wanted to be the youth he had been rather longer than most men; and Clara was right.

"Come, Colonel. Pull up a chair next to me. Take that one there, on the right. That will be the one you will sit in when the Cabinet meets." The Major's voice was deep and mellifluous. Although he had no discernible style in *what* he said, the way that he spoke was, simultaneously, inspiring and soothing. Hay tended to agree with

Adams that McKinley, whether by accident or by design, was the first great president since Lincoln. Hay looked, inadvertently, at McKinley's hand. The President smiled, and raised his right hand; he wore a thin gold ring on the third finger. "I almost always wear your ring. For luck, which I've been in need of almost constantly."

"Which you've deserved." Hay was sincere. He also sincerely hoped that McKinley had honored his request never to reveal who it was who gave him, just before the inauguration, a gold ring containing a lock of George Washington's hair. Hay had had engraved on one side of the ring the initials "G. W. " and on the other "W. M." He had also written the Major, whom he had never known particularly well, a somewhat too effusive letter, expressing the hope that he would indeed be the new Washington. The cynically minded—the Five of Hearts, say—might have thought that ring, letter and financial contribution had got Hay first his embassy and now the greatest appointed office of state. And the cynically minded, Hay knew, would not have been entirely wrong, for he had indeed made one last effort, at age fifty-nine, to obtain an office so that he might exert power in a field where he knew that he was more competent than any other possible contender, foreign affairs. The Major had nicely taken the bait, and the world generally applauded. After all, as an editor of the *Tribune*, John Hay was the cultured voice of the Republican Party; as a man-of-letters, its poet laureate; as a man, its living link to the martyred Lincoln. The President produced a box of cigars. Then, with practiced hand, McKinley snipped the ends of two of them. "From Havana," he said, contentedly.

"The spoils of victory?"

"You might say. I cannot thank you enough." The Major took a long draw on his cigar; and Hay was aware that he was now an intimate of a president who was never *seen* to smoke, or drink anything but iced water. "For the way you handled Whitelaw Reid in London. He is the most . . . well, touchy man."

"Not to mention ambitious. He lusts for office." Hay wondered at the spontaneity of his own hypocrisy; he sounded, he thought with some amusement, like Cincinnatus, torn from his plow to do reluctant service to the state. But, to be fair, his own ambition was a small thing compared to that of his old friend and colleague Whitelaw Reid, who had inherited the editorship of the *New York Tribune* from Horace Greeley, and then passed it on, in '89, to Hay, when President Harrison appointed Reid minister to France; later, Reid was Republican candidate for vice-president, on a losing ticket. Now Reid wanted to be ambassador to England. "But Senator Platt has said no." McKinley shook his head sadly. "And I can't appoint a New Yorker without Mr. Platt's consent—and advice, which I get quite a lot of as it is."

"I told Reid to make up with Senator Platt, but he won't."

"Or can't. Mr. Platt's a very hard sort of man," said the soft-looking President, contentedly puffing smoke at Hay, who congenially puffed smoke back at his chief. "I am so relieved to have you here, Colonel. I don't think I have ever, in my life, been so tired and so . . . torn, as the last few months, and so without any help of any kind when it comes to foreign relations."

"You may be tired, sir, but you've accomplished a great deal more than any president since Mr. Lincoln, and even he didn't acquire an empire for us, which you have done." Hay laid it on, with sincerity.

McKinley liked having it laid on—who does not? thought Hay. But the Major was too shrewd not to anticipate fortune's capriciousness. "We are going to have to decide, in the next weeks, whether we are really going to set up shop in the empire business or not."

"There is a question?" Hay sat up very straight; and was rewarded with what felt like a meat-cleaver falling hard on his lower spine.

"Oh, Mr. Hay, there is the biggest question of all in my mind." McKinley looked oddly bleak for someone whose whole physiognomy was, essentially, cheerfully convex. "I came here to help the backbone of this country, business. That's what our party's all about. We are for the tariff. We are for American industry first, last and always, and we have a very big country right here to look after. Now we've got to decide if we really want to govern several million small brown heathens, who live half the world away from us."

"I think, sir," Hay was diffident, "that the Spanish converted most of the Filipinos. I think they're just about all of them Roman Catholics."

"Yes." McKinley nodded; he had not been listening. "All of them heathen and completely alien to us, and speaking—what?"

"Spanish, most of them. Of course, there are local dialects . . ."

"I've tried everything, Mr. Hay, including prayer, and I still can't decide whether or not it's in our interest to annex the Philippines."

"But we must keep Manila, sir. We must have fuelling stations all across the Pacific, and up and down the China coast, too." Hay began to sound, a bit anxiously, like a state paper. "The European powers are getting ready to divide up China. We'll lose valuable markets if they do, but if we are entrenched nearby, in the Philippines, we could keep the sea lanes open to China, keep the Germans and the Russians and the Japanese from upsetting the world's balance of power. Because," Hay realized glumly that he was parroting Brooks Adams, "whoever controls the land-mass of Asia controls the world."

"Do you honestly think we're quite ready for that?" McKinley suddenly resembled nothing so much as a seventeenth-century Italian cardinal: bland, clever, watchful.

"I don't dare speculate, sir. But when history starts to move underneath you, you'd better figure how you're going to ride it, or you'll fall off. Well, sir, history's started to move right now, and it's taking us west, and we can't stop what's started even if we wanted to."

The Italian cardinal produced a faint self-deprecating smile. "Mr. Hay, *I* can still get off the horse, if I need to. I can let the Philippines go."

"Would you leave them in Spanish hands?"

86

"Between us, I'm tempted to keep Manila. As for the other islands, if they seem incapable of self-government, like most of those natives out there, I'd let Spain stay on. Why not? Oh, Mr. Hay," the cardinal was now a harassed Republican politician from Ohio, "I never wanted any of this war! Naturally, I wanted Spain out of the Caribbean, and that we've done. Cuba is now a free country, and if the Puerto Ricans were capable of self-government, I'd free them, too, because I honestly believe it's a mistake for us to try to govern so many colored heathens whose ways are so different from ours."

Hay now presented his own foreign policy, already rehearsed in the course of several well-received speeches in England. "Mr. President, I have always thought that it was the task of the Anglo-Saxon races, specifically England, now shrinking, and ourselves expanding, to civilize and to," Hay took a deep breath, and played his best if most specious card, "*Christianize* the less developed races of the world. I know that England is counting on us to continue their historic role, and they believe, as I believe, that the two of us together can manage the world until Asia wakes up, long after we're gone, I pray, but with our help now, a different sort of Asia, a Christian Asia, civilized by us, and so a reflection of what was best in our race once history has seen fit to replace us."

McKinley stared a long moment at Hay. Then he said, "Colonel Bryan was in here last week."

Hay felt deflated; his eloquence for naught. But then he had forgotten the first rule of politics: never be eloquent with the eloquent. "Who is Colonel Bryan, sir?"

McKinley's smile was both warm and malicious. "He is a very new untested Army colonel, stationed in Florida. You perhaps know him better as William Jennings Bryan."

"The cross of gold?"

"The same. My opponent. He came here to try to get me to release him from the Army, but as we still have military problems in the Philippines, I took the position that I just can't let every politician go home when he pleases." McKinley was enjoying

87

himself. "Particularly when there's an election starting up."

"On the other hand, you let Theodore go home and run for governor."

"How could I say no to a genuine war hero? Colonel Roosevelt is a special case."

"As well as a Republican."

"Exactly, Mr. Hay." Suddenly, McKinley frowned. "Mr. Platt's worried. He tells me it's going to be a pretty close race for us in New York. Of course, the mid-term election's always bad for the incumbent party."

"Not when the party leader's fought and won a war in a hundred days." All in all, Hay rather wished that he had not used the now much quoted phrase "a splendid little war," as if he were a jingo, which he was not. The phrase had come to him as he somberly compared the war with Spain to the Civil War, and found the war with Spain both splendid and blessedly unlike the bloody ordeal of Lincoln's war to preserve the union. Hay had long known that it was good politics never to try to have the last word in a dispute; now he had begun to see the wisdom of not trying to have the first word either.

"I have the impression," said the Major, stumping out his cigar in a cheap ceramic souvenir mug, depicting his own head with a detachable Napoleonic hat for lid, "that Bryan is going to give us a difficult time on annexation. His people—the South, the West, the farmers, the miners—seem to have lost interest in free silver, which, thank Heaven, he has not."

"But the speech is so good he'll never give it up."

"Luckily for us. Even so, there is a feeling out there that we ought not to be like the European powers, with colonies full of heathens and so on, and I understand that feeling because I share it, to a point. But Cleveland—usually very sound—is being very difficult while Andrew Carnegie . . ."

"Has he written you, too?" The wealthy irascible Scots-born Carnegie had been bombarding Hay with letters and messages, denouncing the annexation of the Philippines, or anything else, as sins against the Holy Ghost of the Republic.

"Yes, yes, he has." McKinley held up the Napoleonic mug, as if searching for some secret message hidden in what, after all, was his own smooth painted face. "I shall go to Omaha," said the President; he had obviously received a secret message from his ceramic self.

"Omaha? And what will you do in Omaha?"

"I shall make a speech. What else?" The small cardinal's smile was visible again; the large eyes glowed. "Omaha is Mr. Bryan's city. Well, I shall begin my tour of the West—which I haven't visited since '96—with Omaha. I'll beard him in his own town, and I'll persuade the folks to . . ." The President paused.

"To welcome the annexation of the Philippines?"

"I'll see what I find there first."

Hay nodded. There were those who liked to think that McKinley was Mark Hanna's puppet, but anyone who had known either man back in Ohio, as had Hay, knew that the President was the perfect political animal, endlessly cunning and resourceful with a genius for anticipating shifts in public opinion, and then striking the right note. Hanna—now a senator from Ohio—was simply McKinley's crude moneyman. Currently, he was "milking," as he put it, every wealthy Republican in the country to ensure Republican majorities in the Senate and the House of Representatives.

"How are the negotiations in Paris?" Hay realized that McKinley was not going to volunteer anything.

"There are problems. The first is, simply, what do we want? I'll know that better at the end of October. I'm going to St. Louis, too. When in doubt, go to St. Louis." The Major looked cryptic; a cardinal again. "The Spaniards will cede whatever we want. But there is bad feeling."

"I would suggest a payment for the islands."

McKinley looked surprised. "I thought the cost of the war was the cost of the islands."

Hay had given the matter some thought. He had also got the

idea from his old friend John Bigelow. "If we pay, as we did for Louisiana and Alaska, then there is no doubt of the legitimacy of the ownership. The bill of sale is the proof. Otherwise, we can be accused of theft, or brutal imperialism, which is not our way, or ought not to seem to be our way."

"That is a very good idea, Mr. Hay." McKinley got to his feet. He touched a button on his desk. "Explain it here tomorrow morning, when the Cabinet meets. But I warn you. Foreign relations are now *your* department. I am free of such entanglements."

"Except for the peace conference in Paris." Hay was dogged. Should he be left out of that, he might as well have stayed on in London; or retired to 1603 H Street.

"Judge Day likes to deal with me. But while I'm gone, Cortelyou will keep you informed. When does Mrs. Hay join you?"

"In a couple of weeks." Cortelyou was now in the doorway. "She has to stop off in New York to do the Christmas shopping."

"Christmas shopping? In September?" The Major was astonished.

"Actually September's a bit late for my wife. She usually does all her Christmas shopping in August."

"We could certainly have used her at the War Department." McKinley put his arm through Hay's and they crossed together to the door.

"How is Mrs. McKinley?' The delicate subject.

"She is—comfortable, I think. You will come to dinner, I hope. We don't really go out. What is your son Adelbert doing now?"

"I didn't know you knew him." Was this the politician's trick of boning up in advance whenever someone important called? or had Del, unknown to him, got to know the President?

"He was down here in June, before he graduated. Senator Lodge brought him by. I was most impressed. I envy you, having a son." The McKinleys' daughter had died young. It was said that their bedroom was a shrine to the dead child. "Perhaps we can find some work for your boy here."

"You are kind, sir." Actually, Hay had considered taking on Del at the State Department, but then decided against it. They did not, for reasons obscure to him, get on. There was never unpleasantness; there was simply no sympathy. Hay was happier with daughters; as Adams was happiest with nieces, real or honorary.

As the President and Hay stepped into the corridor, a tall, gaunt figure stared intently at Hay, who stared, bewildered, back. McKinley said, "You remember Tom Pendel, don't you? He's been a doorkeeper here ever since your day."

Hay smiled, not recognizing the old man. "Why yes," he began.

"Johnny Hay!" The old man had no teeth. But his handclasp was like a vise. "I was new here, remember? One of the guards back then when you and Mr. Robert were in the parlor there, when I came in to tell you the President had been shot." Hay had a sense of vertigo. Was he about to faint? or, perhaps, poetically, die? Then the world righted itself.

"Yes," he said, inadequately. "I remember."

"Oh, it was terrible! I was the last one here to see Mr. Lincoln into his carriage, and he said to me, 'Good-night, Tom,' just like that."

"Well, the sentiment, under the circumstances, was not unnatural." Hay tried to make light of the matter. He had been warned that McKinley did not enjoy hearing about his predecessors.

"I was also the last man here to see off General Garfield that summer morning when he left for the depot, and said, 'Good-bye, Tom.' Just like that, and then he was shot, in the depot, and lingered on and—"

McKinley was growing restive. "Our Tom has seen so many of us come and go." Cortelyou signalled the President. "I must go to work. I'll see you tomorrow morning. Cabinet meets at ten." McKinley and Cortelyou vanished into the Cabinet room. A dozen ladies, making a tour of the White House, stared with awe at the President's back.

As Hay extricated himself from the highly historic Tom Pendel, he was told that Colonel Crook, who had been Lincoln's body-guard, was also still on duty. "But the rest are all gone, sir, like snowflakes upon the river. You were so young back then."

"I am not," said Hay, "young now."

3

Caroline had not realized the extent of her own courage as she walked, all alone, in Peacock Alley, a corridor as long as that block of Thirty-fourth Street between Fifth and Sixth Avenues, which was encased—exquisitely entombed, she had begun to feel—by the magnificence of New York's newest and most celebrated hotel, the Waldorf-Astoria. Even in Paris, the new hotel had been written about with, for the French, wry respect: one thousand modern bedrooms, untold restaurants, palm courts, a men's café and, most intriguing, the Peacock Alley, which ran straight through the double building, a splendid promenade with walls of honey-colored marble that reflected rows of relentlessly glittering electrified chandeliers. Between potted palms and the mirrored entrances to alluring courts and restaurants, sofas and armchairs lined the alley; here sat what looked to be all New York, watching all New York go by. Like the city itself, the Waldorf-Astoria never slept.

There were late-night supper rooms as well as early-morning cafés where men in white tie and tails could be seen drinking coffee with men in business suits, drones and worker-bees all in the same buzzing honey-filled hive.

Caroline had been warned that no proper young lady could ever be seen alone in Peacock Alley. But as she was there to meet a gentleman, she would not be alone for very long; and so she took pleasure in the interest that she—and her Paris Worth gown—aroused, as she proceeded from lobby to Palm Court, all eyes upon her progress. So, she decided, animals in the zoo watch their human visitors. Certainly, the notion that it might be she who was on display in the monkey house, and the fleshy ladies on their divans and the stout gentlemen in their armchairs were the human audience, she found perversely amusing; also, she noted, in their general grossness, the New York burghers were more like bears than monkeys: upright and curious, dangerous when disturbed.

Just ahead of Caroline, two by no means fleshy girls were walking, arm in arm, like sisters. Were they, she wondered, prostitutes? Worldly ladies had told her that even in the most splendid—or particularly in the most splendid—of New York's extraordinary hotel lobbies, businesswomen patrolled. But now with the invention of the Waldorf-Astoria, it had become fashionable not only for respectable women but for grand ladies to be seen, properly escorted, in hotel lobbies and even, though this was very new, to dine in a hotel restaurant, something unknown to the previous generation. In a fit of charity, Caroline decided that her dark suspicions about the "sisters" in front of her were simply that, and that they were indeed, like herself, young ladies curious to see and be seen.

Two-thirds of the way down the Alley, John Apgar Sanford sprang to his feet; promptly, his head vanished in the fronds of the palm tree that shaded his chair. "Are you hiding from me?" asked Caroline, delighted.

"No, no." Sanford emerged from the fronds, his thin curly hair in disarray. He shook her hand gravely; he had her father's small mouth—were they second or third cousins?—but the rest of him was all his own, or an inheritance from ancestors not shared with Caroline. At thirty-three he lived with a chronically ill wife in Murray Hill. "I've made a reservation in the Palm Garden. How was your trip?"

"When not terrifying, very dull. There is no middle way on a ship. How wonderful!" The Palm Garden *was* a wonderful jungle of palm trees set in green Chinese cachepots. From the high ceiling crystal chandeliers were all ablaze though it was daytime. Noon on a tropical island, thought Caroline, half expecting to hear a parrot shriek; then heard what sounded like a parrot shrieking but was merely the laughter of Harry Lehr, young, fair, fat and damp; he was leaving the Palm Garden in the company of a thin elderly lady. "You're expected," he said, clasping Caroline's hand. "At five sharp." He looked at Sanford appraisingly. "Alone," he added; and was gone.

"That . . . cad!" Sanford had turned the color of Murray Hill brick. Caroline took his arm protectively; and together they followed the headwaiter to a table set in front of a gold-velvet banquette for two, on which they could sit side by side, close enough to be able to speak in low voices, far enough apart to emphasize the innocent decency of their relationship in the eyes of that considerable portion of the great world having tea in the Palm Garden. Much more opulent than Paris, Caroline noted; but also more coarse. "Why is Mr. Lehr a cad?"

"Well . . . I mean, *look* at him."

"I have looked at him. I have listened to him. He is a bit on the fantastic side. But very amusing. He's always been kind to me. I can't think why. I'm not yet fifty. Or rich."

"What—*where* are you expected at five? Of course, it's none of my business." Sanford suddenly stammered. "I'm sorry. But I thought you were just off the boat. I mean, he seemed to be expecting you."

"I am just off the boat; and I haven't seen Mr. Lehr since spring; and, yes, he always seems to be expecting you, and so I shall have tea with him. That's all."

"At Mrs. Fish's?"

"No. At Mrs. Astor's. When he mentions no name like that it is always Mrs. Astor. The Mystic Rose, as they call her. But why a rose? Why mystic?"

"Ward McAllister called her that. I don't know why. He was court chamberlain before this—this little brother of the rich, as they call his sort." Tea was brought them, followed by liveried waiters, bearing cakes.

"Well, he makes me laugh, which is probably his function in life. I suppose he makes Mrs. Astor laugh, too. Hard to imagine."

"I shouldn't think she'd feel like laughing in here." Sanford placed a thick envelope on the table between them. "This used to be Mrs. Astor's ballroom, the one that McAllister said could only hold four hundred people, the only people who mattered socially, he said. Another little brother."

"I thought the hotel was all new?"

"The hotel's new. But half of it's built on the site of Mrs. Astor's old house, and half on the site of her nephew's house."

"Ah, of course! I remember. They hate each other. Oh, the raging passions of the Astors! I can't get enough of them. They are like the Plantagenets. Everything on such a monstrous scale, like this hotel."

Caroline knew all about the rivalry between nephew and aunt. The nephew, William Waldorf Astor, was oldest son of oldest son; this meant that he was *the* Astor and his wife was *the* Mrs. Astor. But upon his father's death, his aunt had declared herself *the* Mrs. Astor, causing her niece much pain, not to mention confusion, as invitations were constantly being sent to wrong addresses. William Waldorf then declared war on the Mystic Rose. He tore down his house, which was next to hers, and put up a hotel. Unable to bear the presence of a hotel's shadow on her garden, the Mystic Rose persuaded her husband to tear down their house and put up a second hotel. Though uncle and nephew were also at war, they were sufficiently practical to see the advantage of joining the two hotels into a single unique monument to the fierce passions of their turbulent family, and so they styled the result, somewhat uneasily, the Waldorf-Astoria.

"Now everyone can sit in Mrs. Astor's ballroom."

"Everyone certainly does." Sanford was sour; but then his mother was an Apgar, a self-regarding old family whose brownstone rectitude and gentility were forever grimly opposed to the white marble vulgarity of the buccaneer rich whose palaces now extended not only up Fifth Avenue to Central Park but also to the west, where, not long ago, one enterprising millionaire had discovered, to everyone's astonishment, the Hudson River; and so the Riverside Drive was now a place where the new rich could build their palaces, and live in a rural, riparian splendor, like so many upstate Livingstons with the marvelous amenity of the nearby Columbus Avenue elevated train, which could get them to any part of Manhattan in a matter of minutes. "The world is very much changed," said Sanford, now all Apgar.

"I wouldn't know." Caroline was enjoying everything about the Waldorf-Astoria. "The only world I know is now."

"You are young."

"That is the problem, isn't it?" Caroline indicated the envelope, flanked by a chocolate torte and a blond, pale, damp cake, reminiscent of Harry Lehr's face.

Sanford nodded; opened the envelope; withdrew some documents. "I have gone on appeal. There are the documents in question. They are . . . well, I'll leave them with you. Read them carefully. I've also obliged Mr. Houghteling to produce the Colonel's earlier wills, for comparison. In every will that I know of, each of you was to inherit his half of the estate at the age of twenty-one. But in the last will . . ."

"Father appears to have written a seven instead of a one." At first Caroline had thought it some sort of joke; then she realized that the Colonel must have, by mistake, written a French one. Now, for the first time, she was able to examine a copy of the will. "Surely if I'm not to inherit until I am twenty-seven, then the same condition—that is, the same confused cypher—must apply to Blaise, who is only twenty-two."

"Look." Sanford tapped the document. She read: ". . . my son,

Blaise, who is of age, to inherit his portion; my daughter, Caroline, when she is of age, at 27, to inherit her portion, as described above . . ." Caroline put down the will. "This makes no sense. I was twenty when he made the will. Blaise was twenty-one, and Father says he is of age. So why am I *not* of age when I am twenty-one, as the previous wills stated?"

"You know, I know, Blaise knows, Mr. Houghteling knows, that Colonel Sanford meant twenty-one. But the law does not know this. The law only knows what is written down and witnessed and notarized."

"But the law must, sometimes, make sense."

"That is not the law's function, I'm afraid."

"But you're a lawyer. Surely lawyers make the law . . ."

"We *interpret* the law. So far the interpretation in this case has all been done by Mr. Houghteling, who says that the Colonel decided that you, as a young inexperienced woman, must wait until you are twenty-seven, before you inherit. Blaise, at twenty-one, he regarded as being competent, and of age."

Caroline stared at the will, which now seemed to her even more of a jungle than the Palm Garden, where a string trio was playing softly, *La Belle Hélène*. "What can I do?" she finally asked.

"What do you want?"

"My half of the estate *now*."

Sanford crumbled bits of chocolate cake with his fork. "That will mean going to court, an expensive process. It will also mean overthrowing this will, since your father's peculiar number one is now accepted by everyone hereabouts as a seven."

"Why," Caroline was thinking hard, "did he draw up this will? I mean, is it any different from all the others?"

"Yes. Apparently, he changed his will every time there was a new . . . uh, housekeeper." Sanford was ill-at-ease. Caroline was not. "He would make a bequest to the new one. There are seven such bequests in all. But the bulk of the estate has always been evenly divided between his two children."

"If I should lose," Caroline had yet to speculate on such a catastrophe but the palms were suddenly filled with menace and the waltz from *La Belle Hélène* sounded like a funeral march, "what happens?"

"You will be paid, from the estate, thirty thousand dollars a year until you are twenty-seven. Then you will inherit your half."

"Suppose Blaise loses it all. What then?"

"You will have half of nothing."

"So I must get my share now."

"What makes you think Blaise will lose instead of make money?" Sanford eyed her curiously. For Caroline, a banquette's advantage was that with a slight turn of the head one's features—half-visible at best—were no longer on display. She looked toward the next table, where an actress whom she had often seen on stage was trying to look obscure in order that everyone might see how young she looked offstage, when, of course, for an actress, the Palm Garden was the ultimate stage.

"Blaise is ambitious, and ambitious people almost always fail, don't they?"

"That's a curious notion, Miss Caroline. I mean, there was Caesar and Lincoln and . . . and . . ."

"Two excellent examples. Both murdered. But I wasn't thinking of that sort of huge ambition. I was thinking of people who are in a hurry, very young, to make others take notice of them. Well, Blaise is rushing into the world like . . . like . . ."

"Like Mr. Hearst?"

"Exactly. He tells me, proudly, that Mr. Hearst has lost millions of dollars on his two newspapers."

"But Mr. Hearst—a true rotter—will make other fortunes. He is made for this degraded time."

"Perhaps he will. Perhaps he won't. But his mother is richer than our father was, and I don't want to end up with half of nothing."

Sanford looked at her curiously. "If what you call ambitious men lose fortunes, what sort of a man do you think makes one?"

"My father." The answer was prompt. "He was indolent. He

paid no attention to business, and he more than doubled his inheritance." Caroline turned, full face, to Sanford. "We must find a way to force Blaise to give up what's not his."

"But Mr. Houghteling has already taken the first steps. I think a court case might be risky."

Caroline involuntarily shuddered: anger and fear commingled. "Surrender is riskier. Isn't this the city where everyone can be bought? Well, let us buy a judge, or is it the jury one pays for?"

Sanford smiled to show that he was not shocked; and looked very shocked indeed. Caroline felt a certain compassion for her upright relative. "Our city officials are *generally* corrupt," he said. "But I wouldn't know how to deal with that sort of thing. You see, I am with the reform movement. I helped Colonel Roosevelt when he was police commissioner. Of course, reform is dead for the moment and Tammany's back in power again with Van Wyck, who's Boss Croker's man. Croker's back, too." The string trio, as if cued, began to play the song of the year, the sickening, to Caroline's Parisian ear, "The Rosary." Sentimental religiosity and public stealing, that was the new world. Well, she decided, she had better master it; or be mastered herself. There was, all in all, a certain advantage to having been brought up by a lazy father who could not speak the language of the country where he lived. As a result, Caroline had been in charge not only of her own life but of Saint-Cloud-le-Duc, never really yielding her authority to any one of the resident ladies. In the long run, the managing of the ladies had taught her patience and diplomacy. Unfortunately, the world of men had been closed to her. Blaise, who might have been a link, was always away at school either in England or in the United States; and since the Colonel was like no other man, what she had learned in the managing of him was obviously not going to be of much use to her with the brutes of the Palm Garden. The celebrated actress—who was she?—was listening, head to one side, eyes half-closed, to "The Rosary"; she appeared to be having a religious experience, to the awe of her companions, rude bewhiskered New Yorkers, with red faces, and a reverence for the finer things, of which the actress was, so expensively, one.

"Will you see your brother?" Sanford was tentative; but then he had never known what her relations were with the half-brother who had, so suddenly, turned pirate. Caroline herself was not certain just what she felt, other than fury. She had always appreciated Blaise's energy, both athletic and moral, if moral was the word for a highly immoral or amoral will to rise. She had even found Blaise's beauty attractive in the sense that they complemented one another; he was blond and she was dark. He should have been a bit taller with long, less-bowed legs; but then she might have been more usual had she been shorter and fuller—much fuller, since fashion had now decreed magnificent poitrines for the ladies while nature had decreed, in her case, otherwise. Although Worth had made up the difference artfully, the disappointment of her future husband was a source of not exactly pleasant daydreams.

Caroline rose. "Blaise is taking me to the theater. Then we shall go to supper, the two of us, at Rector's, which I can now enter, as I am a woman of twenty-one though not yet an heiress of twenty-seven." Caroline saw that she had made her point. Sanford nodded; looked grim; he would do battle for her. As they swept into the Peacock Alley, Sanford said, "You must be very careful of what you say to your brother."

"I always am. But he does know that we mean to fight, doesn't he?"

"Yes. I've made that clear to Mr. Houghteling. Perhaps you shouldn't mention the matter to Blaise."

"Perhaps," she said.

They entered the high-ceilinged, resonant lobby, suggestive of a Bernini nightmare, thought Caroline, darkly approving the excess of gold and crystal and red damask, through which moved the hotel staff, evenly divided between those dressed to look like officers of the Habsburg court and those got up as members of some very superior parliament where Prince Albert frock-coats were cut to perfection and trousers were subtly, grayly striped. Caroline walked Sanford to the door. He seemed disturbed; then blurted out: "You must have someone with you, you know."

"A governess?" Caroline smiled. "But surely I've been governed all my life."

"I meant a suitable lady, a relative . . ."

"Those who are suitable are not available, those who are available . . . Don't worry. I have Marguerite. She's been with us all my life. She sleeps in a small room next to my bedroom. The hotel was relieved to see her honest, ugly face."

"Well, then, I suppose . . . But when you go out, she goes with you?"

"When we take the air, yes. But I'm not going to take her to Mrs. Astor's. She's far too intelligent for those people. She has read Pascal."

Sanford looked puzzled; then said, "Good-by. I'll see you tomorrow, if I may. After I've talked to Mr. Houghteling and you . . ."

". . . have not talked to Blaise." Caroline smiled, as he left; and kept on smiling all the way to the elevator; then caught a glimpse in the mirrored door of her own face, made perfectly stupid by the insipid smile. She frowned; beauty regained.

Caroline's beauty—such as it was—was again lost at Mrs. Astor's. Although she had made up her mind not to smile, habit undid her; and she looked, she knew, exactly the way she was expected to look: stupid, innocent, young. But then, she thought dourly, she was all three and the absolute proof of her stupidity was the fact that she knew it and could do nothing about it. She had had a superior education with Mlle. Souvestre. She had read the classics; she knew art. But no one had ever explained to her how *not* to be cheated out of a fortune.

Harry Lehr pranced toward her as she crossed the first drawing room, empty except for the two of them. "Oh, Miss Sanford! You are a sight for sore eyes!"

"In that case, I shall go live in Lourdes and make my fortune."

"You won't need to go anywhere for that." Lehr had not heard of Lourdes; and Caroline was not in an instructive mood. "*She's* pouring tea herself, in the library. Just a few people, the chosen ones, you might say."

"And then again might not." Caroline enjoyed Lehr's deep silliness. Paris was filled with similar lapdogs. There seemed to be a universal law that the greater the lady the more urgent it was for her to have a Lehr to make her laugh, to collect gossip and new people, to be always at her side and yet never give her cause to fear compromise. Lehr was in his late twenties; from Baltimore. He lived by his wits. He sold champagne to friends. On occasion, he liked to dress up as a smart lady; and make people laugh.

Caroline followed, happily, the conventionally dressed Lehr through a second drawing room to a library, newly paneled with ancient wood. Here a dozen "old" New Yorkers sat in a semi-circle around the tea service, where Mrs. Astor presided; she was very much herself, as always, beneath a jet-black wig. The old woman gave Caroline a finger to touch; a thin smile to respond to; a cup of tea to drink. "Dear Miss Sanford," said the Mystic Rose, "sit beside me."

Caroline sat next to the old lady, a mark of honor that did not go unnoticed by the other guests, most of whom she recognized but none of whom she could identify. New York had always been like that for her, a series of strange drawing rooms filled with familiar-looking strangers, and familiar-sounding names. She assumed that once she could put the right name to the right face she would be, at last, home, for she had decided that she was going to be what her father pretended, uselessly, *not* to be, an American. Nevertheless, New York was still a foreign city to her, unlike Paris, where she was at home, or even London, where she had often stayed with family friends or with girls she had known at Allenswood; over the years, she had graduated from children's parties to the grown-up world, marked, officially, four years earlier, when she had put three feathers in her hair and in the company of the Dowager Countess Glenellen, mother-in-law of a schoolfriend, she curtseyed low to Queen Victoria. Now she sat next to the Queen's

American equivalent, who put her uneasily at ease as is royalty's way. "You will not have cake?"

Caroline had refused the cake offered her by a maid. "This is my second tea, Mrs. Astor. I had my first in your old ballroom."

"The Palm Garden." Mrs. Astor pronounced each syllable with the same emphasis. "I have seen the Palm Garden. But only from the corridor. You are stopping at the hotel?"

"Yes. It is most comfortable." Caroline was finding this sort of exchange oddly more tiring in English than in French, where the ritual exchange of polite phrases could be, occasionally, charged with meaning. "I think the hotel is unique." And now, why not, she wondered, get the reputation for being much too clever for a girl? She launched herself, "The Waldorf-Astoria has brought exclusivity to the masses."

Mrs. Astor's range of expressions did not include astonishment, as, like her British counterpart, she could not, by definition, ever be observed in so fallen a state; but polite disapproval was very much in her repertoire. The eyes, which slightly drooped at the corners, opened wide. The short-lipped mouth was now pursed, as if she might be inclined to whistle. "Surely," she said in her usual clear uninflected voice, "that is not possible. I also wonder how one so young, though brought up in France," Caroline did not wince at the low thrust, "could know of these things."

"Oh, Mrs. Astor, we are nothing if not exclusive . . ."

"I meant," said Mrs. Astor, "the . . . masses." She blinked her eyes, as if a tumbril had come into view. But it was only the maid with bread and butter. Mrs. Astor helped herself, as if falling back on a basic necessity in order to fortify herself against the mob. "Your grandfather," Caroline was pleased that Mrs. Astor had made a connection, "wrote a book which I have still in this library," her dark eyes stared vaguely at a row of magnificent tooled morocco volumes, emblazoned with the name Voltaire, "that told of what happened in Paris when the Communists overthrew the regime. It is a work which gave me many a sleepless night. Those fierce common people, after killing poor Marie

Antoinette, then proceeded to eat the entire contents of the Paris
Zoo, too dreadful, from antelope to . . . to emu."

Caroline smiled politely in order not to laugh out loud. Mrs.
Astor had managed to confuse 1870 with 1789. "Let us hope that
the mob will be kept happy here by the Waldorf-Astoria with its
one thousand bedrooms."

Mrs. Astor frowned slightly at the raffish word "bedroom": but
then, as if recalling her young guest's unfortunate upbringing, she
said, "Your grandfather always said he was the wrong Schermerhorn and the wrong Schuyler. I was born Schermerhorn," she
added quietly, as if she had pronounced the ultimate royal name
Saxe-Coburg-Gotha.

"I know, Mrs. Astor, and I hope you don't mind but I have taken
to pretending that my grandfather was the right Schermerhorn."

Mrs. Astor's genuine smile had considerable charm. "I suspect,
my child, that the distance between the right and the wrong
Schermerhorn has never been much wider than a ledger." Thus,
Mrs. Astor unfurled the Jolly Roger of trade, under whose cross-
and-bones all America sailed, more or less prosperously. Before
Caroline could think of something memorable—stupid or otherwise—to say, Lehr neatly replaced her on the sofa with an elderly
man and Caroline, on her feet, was now face to face with a woman
not much older than she. "I'm Mrs. Jack," said the woman in a
husky voice. "You're the French Sanford girl, aren't you?"

"French, no. Sanford yes; living in France . . ."

"That's what I meant. Jack and I visited your father at Saint-
Cloud. *That's* the way to live, I said, not like the way we do in the
Hudson Valley, in wooden crates." Then Caroline realized that
Mrs. Jack was Mrs. John Jacob Astor, the daughter-in-law of the
Mystic Rose. The war between the two ladies was a source of
delight to New York. Although friendly when together in public,
each tended to disparage the other when apart. Mrs. Jack found
her mother-in-law's social life boring, while Mrs. Astor thought
Mrs. Jack's circle fast. Worse, in the eyes of the Mystic Rose, her
son had political interests if not ambitions. Like so many of New

York's young grandees, Jack Astor had been inspired to clean up the Augean stables if not of the republic, an impossible undertaking, of the city. He had been a colonel in the recent war; he was said to be an inventor; he had published a novel about the future. None of this gave pleasure to his mother. On the other hand, she herself had recently won the only family war that mattered: not only had William Waldorf Astor exchanged New York for London, he had also renounced his American citizenship. Caroline Schermerhorn Astor reigned alone. "I can't think where my mother-in-law finds these people." Mrs. Jack looked about the room. She was very handsome, Caroline decided; and very fashionable in the English rather than the American way. "I think they must be kept in cedar chests when they're not here. Harry amuses, of course. Did you know Ward McAllister?"

"I think," said Caroline, "he was under a cloud when I first stepped onto the stage."

Mrs. Jack looked at her with some interest. "Yes," she said, "it is very much a stage, our world. But the clouds are real, if one's not careful."

"The problem must be," Caroline wished to sound tentative, and succeeded, she thought, "at least *my* problem is, what is the play that we are supposed to be acting in."

"The play, Miss Sanford, is always the same. It is called 'Marriage.'"

"How boring!"

"How would *you* know?" Mrs. Jack gave a sudden great hearty deep laugh. "One has to be married to know just how deeply boring the play is."

"But if that's the play, I'm well into the first act. *Getting* married is at least a third of the drama, isn't it?"

"To Del Hay, I hear. Well, you could probably do worse."

"Who knows? Perhaps I shall, Mrs. Astor."

"Call me Ava. I shall call you Caroline. Do you play bridge?"

"Not yet."

"I shall teach you. I used to play tennis until Jack took it up.

Now I play bridge. It is exactly like being alive. You'll love it. The danger. The excitement. We shall see each other from time to time. We shall lunch at restaurants together, something that drives my mother-in-law mad. We shall compare notes on the play, between terrible yawns. I do hate my life, you know." On that intimate if somewhat somber—not to mention theatrical—note, Mrs. Jack bade her new close friend farewell; kissed ritually the cheek of the Mystic Rose; and departed.

"Ava is always bored," said Mrs. Astor to Caroline, as if she had overheard their conversation. "I am never bored. I recommend that you never be bored either. There is nothing so boring as people who are always bored."

"I shall remember that," said Caroline, fearing that she would.

"I am told that your brother, Blaise Sanford, is in the city. He has not come to see me, though your d'Agrigente brothers have. *They* are French," she mysteriously emphasized; then regained her subject, Blaise. "He works with that Mr. Hearst."

"Yes. Blaise also plans never to be bored. He finds Mr. Hearst very exciting."

"It is possible to be too exciting."

"I've not been so lucky."

"I see Mrs. Delacroix each summer in Newport, Rhode Island. She does not think Mr. Hearst a good influence on her grandson. She tells me that journalism is bound to draw Blaise into the company of politicians and Jews. She is deeply distressed."

"I've not met her, you know."

Mrs. Astor's dark stare was curiously disconcerting. She looked at Caroline as if, indeed, Caroline were an actress on stage and she the critical audience when, Caroline was certain—or was she?—that it ought to be the other way around. "That is right. You had different mothers. I knew both. Your mother I knew very slightly. She was dark—like you. She was the Princess d'Agrigente. Then Denise Delacroix Sanford died, and your mother married your father."

"Yes, I know the sequence intimately."

"Yes," said Mrs. Astor. "I suppose you must."

Harry Lehr then amused everyone; and the tea was over.

At midnight Broadway resembled itself at noon, except that the millions of white electrical lights used to spell out the names of theaters and plays, lacking all color, drained Broadway of color, too. There was something arctic about the scene, thought Caroline, as the carriage entered Longacre Square, a lozenge-shaped area whose south end was dominated by an odd triangle of a building. At midnight the square was almost as crowded as at noon. Streetcars rattled by; carriages stopped and started, as the night people got in, got out.

Blaise was entirely at home, thought Caroline, with a twinge of envy. She was still a foreigner; he was already a New Yorker. At the theater, he pointed out all sorts of New York figures in the audience, including a man who invariably bet a million dollars on almost anything, and another man, very fat and covered with diamonds, who ate a dozen dinners a day but drank only orange juice, a gallon at each meal.

"Here's Rector's." Blaise was at his most attractive when he was excited, and New York excited him—electrified him, she thought, feeling a dozen years his senior. But despite her own new *gravitas*, she had enjoyed the play almost as much as the intermissions. Neither had mentioned the will; presumably, over supper, they would begin their business, and she would ignore her cousin's warning.

Rector's occupied a low yellow-brick building between Forty-third and Forty-fourth Streets on the east side of Longacre Square. Over the doorway hung an electrical griffin. "There's no other sign," Blaise explained happily. "Everyone knows this is Rector's."

As Caroline entered Rector's the orchestra was playing what she had come to think of as the city's anthem: "There'll be a Hot Time in the Old Town Tonight." She was not certain whether the war had made the song popular, or the other way around. In either case, she preferred this jaunty tune to the lachrymose "The Rosary." A thick, heavy man—but then all New York men were thick, heavy—Mr. Rector himself, greeted Blaise; and was pleased, if somewhat surprised, to learn that Caroline was his sister. "We'll put you in the back, Mr. Sanford. A quiet table."

"Has Mr. Hearst been in?"

"No, sir. But the evening's young."

They sat facing one another across a corner table. The room was overheated, and smelled of roast beef and cigar smoke.

"You'll like the Chief. At least I think you will."

"Mrs. Astor—"

"Oh, those people hate him. You see, he does everything his own way. They really hate that, you know. They also can't believe it. Like Brooklyn Bridge . . ." The maître d'hôtel took their order for supper. Although Caroline could not get enough of Long Island's oysters, she disliked France's allegedly more delicate and distinctive oysters. The Atlantic was colder here than there; or so someone had said, trying to explain to her the crucial difference. Meanwhile, she ate as many oysters as she dared.

"What about Brooklyn Bridge?" Meekly Caroline accepted every delay that Blaise saw fit to contrive; and he was in a delaying mood. She had begun, almost idly, to wonder what he was really like. She had, of course, analyzed him to their Sanford cousin, but even as she had held so sententiously forth on Blaise's form of ambition, she now realized that she hardly knew this sharp-faced, high-colored blond youth sitting opposite her. They had been apart too often. Was he, for instance, in love with anyone? Or was he what Mrs. Astor's circle called a libertine? Or was he simply interested in himself, in thrall to his own energy as she was to hers?

Blaise told her about the Brooklyn Bridge. "The Chief decided that after all the fuss about the bridge—you know, the biggest and the best and so on—that the bridge was about to fall down. So we ran a series on how it's about to collapse. Lovely stuff. Except there was nothing wrong with the bridge. Then when people found out that the bridge was safe, everyone was so mad at the Chief that he goes and publishes a big front-page story, saying that Brooklyn

Bridge is safe at last, thanks to the *Journal*. It was a wonderful series!"

"Doesn't it bother . . ." Caroline shifted tactfully from "you" to, "him that these things aren't true?"

Blaise shrugged; and looked, momentarily, French. "It's just for circulation. No one cares. There's always another story tomorrow. Anyway, he makes things happen."

"You mean, they *seem* to happen."

"It's all the same here. It's not like other places. Where's Del?"

"In New Hampshire, I think."

"You like him?" Again the bright blue eager stare.

"Do you like him?" Caroline was curious.

"Yes. He's very—old-fashioned, I guess. Is he going to work, or is he just going to be a clubman?"

"Oh, he'll work, I suppose. He talks about the law. He talks about the diplomatic service."

"Well, he's set up there. Old Hay's back on top."

"Old Hay is not so well, I think. I liked them, the old people, this summer."

"I can't stand old people." Blaise scowled. "They always act like they are judging us."

"I don't think they notice us at all."

"Oh, they do! They notice the Chief anyway. The only old person he knows is his mother, and she's jolly enough, for an old lady."

"I hadn't realized that you had developed this phobia for—old folks."

"It's New York!" Blaise grinned. "It's the only place to be young in."

"Well, I intend to do my best," said Caroline, ready now to broach the delicate subject. But the one person in all New York who ought never to know their business approached the table. It was the infamous Colonel William D'Alton Mann. Florid, white-bearded, definitely elderly and thus entirely unacceptable to Blaise, the gentle-seeming Colonel, whose style of address was antebellum courtly—he had actually been a colonel in the war—was known to all New York as the city's preeminent blackmailer. He published the irresistible weekly *Town Topics*, where, as "the Saunterer," he confided to his readers a man-about-town's inside knowledge of society's dark side. The Saunterer gave the impression that he was more than eager to print not only devastating truths but ingenious libels about the rich and powerful. But this vivid impression was, largely, for effect. In actual fact, a truth too devastating or a libel too ingenious would first be submitted to the victim, who then had the opportunity to buy off the Colonel, usually with a loan of money, at a nominal interest rate, that became, in due course, a thoroughly bad debt. Smaller truths and minor libels were kept out of print by the payment of fifteen hundred dollars a year for a subscription to the Colonel's luxurious annual volume, called, rather pointedly, *Fads and Fancies of Representative Americans*. Caroline was delighted to meet a villain of such stature. Blaise was less than pleased.

"Dear boy," said the Colonel, seating himself uninvited in an empty chair beside Caroline. "How I revel in what the Chief is doing to the Secretary of War. Mr. Alger is indeed a murderer, just as the Chief says, killing American soldiers with poisoned beef, the same old trick that was played on us who fought in the War Between the States. You must give him my compliments. He is the best thing to happen to journalism since—"

"Since *Town Topics* was revived by you," said Caroline, eager to show that she was up-to-date. To her pleasure the Colonel's dull red face began to take on a purple coloring at the edge of the snow-white whiskers.

Colonel Mann was all honey. "How rare it is to find a young lady who appreciates—well, courage, I suppose is the word."

"That's one word," said Blaise.

"*The* word," said Caroline. "I can't get enough of your newspaper, and I don't know why so many people I know are made uneasy by your . . . saunterings." Caroline flattered.

"I am, at times," the Colonel's confession gave every appearance

of shyness, "unkind, even—yes, a fault admitted is a fault miti-
gated—unfair. For instance, there is something about Mrs. Astor
that annoys me, possibly because we're all good Democrats, aren't
we? Well, the jewels that she wears in just one evening could
rebuild the thousand and one Astor tenements that paid for them."

"The Colonel's turned socialist." Blaise had not yet learned how
to turn social disgust to fascinated rapture. Caroline had been well
taught by Mlle. Souvestre.

"No, my boy. I simply voted the way the *Journal* told me to vote,
for Bryan." He took a pinch of snuff from a silver box. "Have I
your permission, Miss Sanford."

"Of course! How nice to know one another without being
introduced. Versailles must have been just like . . . Rector's."

"God," said Blaise to the oysters that had just arrived.

"You will live here, I hope?"

Caroline nodded. "It is the city of the future, and so perfect for
someone like me who has no past, as you know best of all."

"Oh, the Saunterer is not that much of an ogre. Believe me. You
must get on with supper." He rose, as champagne arrived, a
present from Mr. Rector. "Mr. Houghteling tells me that everything is going nicely now, which is plain," he spread his hands as
if to embrace the young couple, "to even my Saunterer's eyes!"
Colonel Mann moved on to the next room, and the men's bar.

"He's a monster. How can you talk to him like that?"

"I'm fascinated by monsters. How does he find out things? You
know, dark secrets?"

Blaise toasted the air; and drank. Caroline satisfied herself with
a single sip: this was not a time to be unalert. "He bribes servants
mostly, and he pays people like Harry Lehr to give him gossip.
They say he has a safe which is full-up with the dirt on everyone
famous in the town."

"Break into it!"

"What?" Blaise stared at her, as dumbly as his sharp features
could allow.

"Well, wouldn't that be a coup for the Chief? To publish the contents of Colonel Mann's safe."

"They might really run him out of town, if he did that." Thus announced, the Chief himself appeared, with two young girls; all three in evening dress. Blaise introduced Caroline to Mr. Hearst, and the two Misses Willson. Hearst's presence at Rector's caused considerable excitement. Admirers shook his hand; detractors turned away. The Chief stared intently at Caroline and then, as the orchestra, this time in Hearst's honor, began to play "There'll be a Hot Time in the Old Town Tonight," he said, in an odd thin voice, "Would you like to see me put the *Journal* to bed?"

"I thought the *Journal* never slept . . ."

"It goes to bed when they make it up, the front page, for the last time before they print." Blaise was helpful.

Hearst was forceful. "Come on," said the Chief. The Misses Willson continued to smile in unison. Hearst took Caroline's arm, most politely. "Miss Sanford," he said. She looked up at him; he was well over six feet tall. Caroline smiled; and understood why her brother found Hearst so exciting: he was one of those rare creatures who make, as Mlle. Souvestre would say, the weather.

A perilous old elevator, operated by an ancient Negro, took them to the second floor of the Tribune Building, where several men were still at work in a long ink-smelling room, rather like a livery stable except that instead of bridles and saddles attached to walls or mounted on sawhorses, there were long sheets of galley paper, drawings, photographs. The overhead electric light bulbs on their cords swayed whenever a heavy wagon made its way along Park Lane. The editor, Willis Abbott, both dapper and deeply weary, presided over a mock-up of the front page, whose principal headline advised the reader that President McKinley was to make a major address on the Philippines, in St. Louis.

"Oh, no," said Hearst mildly. 'Unless we can tell them something they don't know—like he's going to annex the whole place, or burn down Manila . . ."

"A Hot Time in the Old Town Tonight" sounded, unbidden, in

Caroline's head. With both amusement and awe, she watched as Hearst put a number of strips of text and squares of illustration on the floor and then got down on his knees and, like a child happy with a puzzle, began to create—no other word—the next day's news. But news was not the right word. This was not news but entertainment for the masses. A murder at the bottom of the page began, inexorably, to move higher and higher up the page. A drawing of the murdered woman, idealized to a Madonna-esque purity, found its way to the page's center while the President sank to the page's bottom, and a statement by Secretary of State Hay moved to the third page. During this, the Willson girls practiced a new dance step at the far end of the room beneath a large drawing of the Yellow Kid, a cartoonist's invention for the *World* which Hearst had appropriated for the *Journal* (along with the cartoonist), causing the aggrieved Mr. Pulitzer to engage a new creator of Yellow Kids and, in the process, giving the generic word "yellow" to popular journalism.

"The Chief's amazing," Blaise murmured in Caroline's ear. "He's like a painter."

"But is it *always* murder first?" Caroline's voice was low, but Hearst, now on all fours, heard her. "Rape's better," he said, "if you'll forgive the word."

The Willson girls shrieked with delight. Hearst received an enlarged headline from a copy-boy: "Murdered Woman Found!" He placed it above the Madonna face. "We also like a good fire."

"And a good war," said Mr. Abbott dutifully.

"Look," said Blaise. On the wall opposite, beneath an American flag, the huge headline "*Journal*'s War Won!"

"*Your* war, Mr. Hearst?"

"Pretty much, Miss Sanford. McKinley and Hanna weren't ever going to fight. So we got the war going so they'd have to . . ." Hearst sat on his heels, a strand of blond dull hair in one eye. "Mr. Abbott, wasn't the murdered woman found nude?"

"Actually, no, Chief. She was wearing a sort of gingham dress . . ."

"Well, make that a slip . . . a *torn* slip." Hearst smiled up at Caroline. "I hope this doesn't shock you."

"No. Blaise has prepared me."

"Blaise has got a real knack for this." The great man then started in on page two, with running commentary to Abbott, mostly asking for more pictures and large headlines; also, "We're giving too much space to that dude Roosevelt. Remember. We're for Van Wyck. And sound government, and all that."

"You mean Tammany, Chief?" Abbott smiled.

"Platt's better than Tammany any day. But Van Wyck's our crook. Roosevelt's theirs. But we'll clean up this city one of these days."

"Reform?" asked Caroline, who knew in theory what the word meant; knew, in practice, what it meant when applied to New York City's politics; knew nothing of what the word meant to Hearst.

"Yes, Miss Sanford. The whole country, too. Bryan's hopeless. McKinley's just a front for old money-bags Hanna." Hearst stood up. On the floor, his masterpiece: the front page for the next morning's edition of the *New York Journal*. "So we need somebody new, clean."

"That's what they *say* Roosevelt is." Blaise was cautious.

"He's Platt's candidate. How can Platt be reformed? Anyway, he's going to lose. Mr. Abbott." Hearst turned to the editor just as that more than ever weary figure was presenting the intricate mosaic of the front page to the printer.

"Yes, Chief."

"I've decided on our next president." Even the Willson girls stopped dancing when they heard this. Everyone looked very solemn; even Caroline was impressed.

"Yes, Chief?" The editor was imperturbable. "Who?"

"Admiral Dewey. Hero of Manila. 'You may fire when you are ready, Gridley.' That's as good as 'Don't shoot till you see the whites of their eyes.'"

"But did Admiral Dewey really say those—those inspiring

words?" Caroline was now caught up in the excitement of inventing history, not to mention of creating presidents.

"Well, we said he said it, and I suppose he probably did say something like it. Anyway, he hasn't denied it, and that's what matters. Besides, he beat the Spaniards and got us Manila. Do you know him?" Although Hearst was looking at Caroline, the question was to Abbott.

"No, Chief. But I suppose we could write or cable him and inquire . . ."

"Nothing in writing!" Hearst was firm. "Send someone to Manila, to sound him out. If he's willing, we'll nominate him to run against McKinley."

"Is the Admiral a Democrat?" asked Blaise.

"Who cares? I'm sure he doesn't."

"But," asked Caroline, "does he want to be president?"

"Oh, everyone does over here. That's why we call ourselves a democracy. Fact, just about anyone can be president, particularly if the *Journal* promotes him right."

"You, too?" Caroline was bold; despite Blaise's evident dismay.

But Hearst was bland. "Do you like Weber and Fields?"

"The shoemakers?" Caroline had heard the names before. "In Bond Street."

The Willson girls giggled in harmonic unison. "No. Comedians. In vaudeville. I can't get enough of them. We must take her with us sometime," Hearst said to Blaise; then to Caroline, "Now get this. Weber and Fields are in this fancy French restaurant, and the waiter comes up after dinner and the waiter asks Weber if he wants a demitasse, and Weber says yes. Then the waiter asks Fields if he'd like a demitasse, too, and Fields says, 'Yes,'" at this point Hearst began to laugh, "'Yes, I'd like a demitasse, too, and,'" Hearst was now shaking with laughter while the Willson sisters clung to one another, giggling, "'and I'd also like a cup of coffee.'" The office echoed with laughter; and Caroline assumed that her question had been dramatically answered.

Blaise drove her back to the Waldorf-Astoria; escorted her to the suite where old Marguerite, in her night-dress, greeted him with a cascade of pent-up French. "She will not learn English," said Caroline, presenting Blaise with a new bottle of brandy, which he opened. As he filled a glass for each, Marguerite delivered herself of a tirade celebrating the beauties and comforts of Saint-Cloud-le-Duc as contrasted with the horrors of New York; then she went to bed.

Every vase in the Louis XVI sitting room was filled with chrysanthemums despite Marguerite's piteous pleas that they be taken away, for, as the civilized world knows, chrysanthemums are flowers suited only to memorialize the dead. Although Caroline told her not to be superstitious, she herself was somewhat troubled by those *memento mori*. But she kept them where they were, all bronze and yellow, as a proof of her new unsuperstitious Americanism.

"Do you like the Chief?" Blaise sipped at his cognac. Caroline poured herself Vichy water.

"I don't think I'd ever find him very easy to like. But he's certainly fascinating to watch—to listen to. Is he so powerful?"

Blaise nodded. "He can really make someone president . . ."

"But he didn't say *some*one. He said *any*one."

"Well, he exaggerates at times."

Caroline laughed. "At times? I should think that *that's* his power. He exaggerates all the time."

"It sells newspapers."

"That's all that he cares about?"

Blaise refused to be led into deeper waters. "As a publisher, yes. That's what I want to be."

"With Mr. Hearst?"

"No. I want to be my own Mr. Hearst."

"He doesn't know that yet, does he?"

"How can you tell?" Blaise gave her his best boyish smile; and it was still most boyish even though she knew the amount of adult calculation that went into it. Charm was Blaise's most formidable weapon. Charm was Caroline's most fragile defense.

"The way he treats you. With everyone else, he is very *grand seigneur*. He is polite, the way we are to servants. But he treats you as an equal, which means that he expects you to invest money—perhaps all your money—in his papers." Caroline had not intended to get so directly to the will but she trusted her instinct about Hearst's attitude to Blaise.

Blaise frowned, not at all boyishly. In fact, he looked like his father at the card table, trying to recall the bidding. "I'm not about," he said finally, "to make this kind of investment."

"But you've allowed him to think that you will." Caroline understood Blaise. Did he, she wondered, hardly for the first time, understand her? "That could be dangerous, with a man so—unusual."

"Father meant twenty-seven." Blaise struck hard. "Mr. Houghteling ought to know. He was his lawyer. He says there is no doubt of intention."

Caroline sat very straight in her chair. Back of Blaise's head a mass of bronze chrysanthemums were arrayed as for a funeral. An omen? If so, his funeral or hers? "It was a lucky accident for you that Father's pen slipped. We both know what he meant. But what I want to know is what *you* mean. Why do you want my share of the estate? Surely, there's enough for both?"

"There isn't. For what I want to do." Blaise looked at her bleakly.

"To start a newspaper?"

Blaise nodded. "I'm learning how it's done now. When I'm ready, I'll start my own, or buy one. Maybe here . . ."

For once, Caroline could not stop herself from smiling. "In competition with Mr. Hearst?"

"Why not? He'd understand."

"There's no doubt he'd understand! He'd understand that you had betrayed him. He'd also understand that if you tried to compete with him, he'd be obliged to crush you, as he seems to have crushed Mr. Pulitzer."

"The *World*'s doing all right. Mr. Pulitzer just isn't number one any more."

"So there might yet be Hearst, Pulitzer and Sanford?"

"Yes," Blaise said; and said no more.

Caroline was impressed; and appalled. "You will lose the entire inheritance."

"No," Blaise said; and said no more.

"Lose or gain, for six years you will have the use of my capital. Then—what happens?"

"According to Mr. Houghteling," Blaise was deliberate, "you'll inherit the amount which represents half the estate at the time the will was probated."

Caroline began to see her way through the labyrinth; and not as a victim but as the Minotaur. "Should you double my share of the estate, you will keep half?"

"That seems only fair. *I* will have doubled it, not you."

"If you lose . . ."

"I won't lose . . ."

"If you lose, what do I get?"

Blaise's smile was radiant: "Half of nothing."

"So I lose everything if you are unfortunate and gain nothing if you are lucky."

"You'll be paid thirty thousand dollars a year for the next six years. You can live nicely on that here. Even better, back at Saint Cloud."

Caroline began to see a way through to—the treasure. She was not yet sufficiently New York predator to demand living flesh for her dinner. She had begun by wanting what was hers. Now she was eager to take what was his, as well. Although family history had always bored her, she had been sufficiently intrigued by her father's cryptic references to the fact that Charles Schermerhorn Schuyler, her grandfather, had been an illegitimate son of Aaron Burr. At Mlle. Souvestre's school she had had the good luck to have a history teacher who did not, like all the others, disdain American history. Together they had read all that they could—

which was not much—about her great-grandfather, who seemed more artist than rogue, more Lord Chesterfield than Machiavelli—and, of course, Burr was *her* maternal ancestor, not Blaise's which gave her an advantage if there should be anything to the laws or, rather, whims of heredity. Burr had been narrowly cheated of the presidency; had been rather less narrowly, to say the most, cheated of the crown of Mexico; had lived long enough to see another illegitimate son, if the gossip was true, become president. Burr had been called a traitor but, in actual fact, he had been something far worse and more dangerous to his world, a dreamer. Because of this sublime subversive trait, he had enchanted Caroline. Finally, as Aaron Burr had treated his only legitimate child as if she were a son, so Caroline had vowed when she left Europe for America that she would now become Burr's great-grand*son*, and live out, on the grandest scale possible, that subtle creature's dream of a true civilization with himself as its center, whether in the provincial capital Washington or the even more unlikely Mexico. But where the man Burr had wanted high office—even a crown—his great-grand self-styled son was, after all, unmistakably and completely a woman, and so for Caroline there would be no high office in a nation where only males were allowed to occupy such visible places; yet there was something far better than mere office, and she had got a glimpse of it that evening on the second floor of the Tribune Building in Park Lane; there was, simply, true power. Although money was the source of power in this rude place, now even less of a civilization than it had been in Burr's day, what she had seen and heard of Hearst that night had convinced her that the ultimate power is not to preside in a white house or open a parliament while seated on a throne but to reinvent the world for everyone by giving them the dreams that you wanted them to dream. She doubted if Blaise—heir to prosaic Delacroix but not to the arch-dreamer Burr—grasped this. He saw simply an exciting game to play, with money and the illusion of power as its reward. While she saw herself creating a world that would be all hers, since she, like Hearst, would have reinvented all the players, giving them their dialogue, moving them in and out of wars: "Remember the *Maine*," "Cuba Libre," "Rough Riders," "Yellow Kids" . . . Oh, she could do better than any of that! She too could use a newspaper to change the world. She felt giddy with potentiality. But, first, she must see to her inheritance. She got to her feet. Blaise did the same.

"I suppose," she said, "we'll next meet in court."

Blaise blinked. "You have no case."

"I shall accuse you of altering the will."

"I didn't."

"I know you didn't. But the accusation will always be there, all your life. Mr. Hearst can afford not to be respectable. You can't."

"You can't prove a thing. And I'll still win."

"I wouldn't be so certain. Anyway, remember this."—*Remember the Maine!* Had Aaron Burr ever so rapturous a vision?—"I shall do anything to get what's mine."

"All right." Blaise turned to go. "I'll see you in court." He opened the door to the suite. "Do you know how much litigation costs here?"

"I took the liberty of removing the four Poussins from Saint-Cloud. They are in London, with a dealer. He says they should fetch a marvelous price."

"You *stole* my pictures?" Blaise was white with fury.

"I *took* my pictures. When we divide the estate, evenly, I'll give you your half of what I get from the sale. Meanwhile, I shall be able to buy quite a lot of wonderful American law."

"*Comme tu est affreuse!*"

"*Comme toi-même!*"

Blaise slammed the door hard behind him. Caroline remained standing in the center of the room, politely smiling, and singing, rather loudly, and to her own surprise, verse after verse of "There'll be a Hot Time in the Old Town Tonight."

2

The bronze busts of Henry James and William Dean Howells stared off into space, as did the earthly head of Henry Adams beside the fire. It was John Hay's turn to be host to his friend and neighbor, and from his armchair he surveyed the three heads with a pleasure he was quick to identify to himself as elderly. Each belonged to a friend. If nothing else, he had done very well when it came to friends. Although he was not the man-of-letters that James or Howells was, or the historian that Adams was, he felt extended through them beyond his natural talents. Had he wanted to turn round in his chair, he could have stared into Lincoln's bronze face, surprisingly life-like for a life-mask. But Hay seldom looked at the face that he had once known far better than his own. During the years that he and Nicolay were writing their enormous history of the President, Hay was amazed to find that he had lost all firsthand memory of Lincoln. The million words that they had written had had the effect of erasing Hay's own memory. Nowadays, when asked about the President, he could only remember what they had written, so dully he knew, of that odd astounding man. Hay and Adams often discussed whether or not a memoir might not have the same effect—a gradual erasing of oneself, bit by bit, with words. Adams thought that this would be ideal; Hay did not. He liked his own past, as symbolized by the two busts, one life-mask. He had always suspected, even in moods melancholy and hypochondriacal, that he would end his days in comfort, with abundant memories, seated at his fireside on a February night in the last year of the nineteenth century, in the company of a friend not yet bust-ed. Of course, he had not counted on being secretary of state at the end of the road, but he did not any longer object to the dull grind, which he had turned over to Adee, or to the battles with the Senate, which he allowed Senator Lodge to conduct for him, with considerable help from Lodge's old Harvard professor Henry Adams.

Now the old friends waited for Mrs. Hay, and the dinner guests and "the shrimps," as Hay addressed his children: two out of four were in the house. Alice and Helen were deeply involved in the capital's social life. Clarence was away at school. Del was in New York, perhaps studying law. Hay had always found it easy to talk to his own father; yet found it impossible to talk to his oldest son. Some bond of sympathy had, simply, not developed between them. But then Hay had been a country boy like Lincoln, with nothing but his wits—and a connection or two; while Del, like Lincoln's son Robert, was born to wealth. Lincoln father and Lincoln son had not got on well, either.

"Will Del marry the Sanford girl?" Adams often strayed into Hay's mind.

"I was just thinking of Del, as you must have known, with those other-worldly Adams psychic powers. I don't know. He doesn't confide in me. I know he sees her in New York, where she's set up for the winter."

"She's uncommonly clever," said Adams. "Of all the young girls I know . . ."

"The brigade of girls . . ."

"You make me sound like Tiberius. But of the lot, she is the only one I can't work out."

"Well, she's not like an American girl. That's one reason." Hay had found Caroline disturbingly direct on small matters and unfathomable when it came to those things that must be taken seriously, like marriage. There was also the problem, even mystery, of her father's will. "I think she's made a mistake, contesting the will. After all, when she's twenty-five, or whatever, she'll inherit. So why fuss?"

"Because at her age five years seems forever. I hope Del brings her into the family. I should like her for a niece."

"He threatens to bring her here, for a visit. But he hasn't."

The butler announced, "Senator Lodge, sir." Both Hay and

Adams rose as the handsome, were it not for a pair of cavernous nostrils that always made Hay think, idly, of a bumblebee, patrician-politician glided into the room. "Mrs. Hay has got off with Nannie. Neither one can bear to hear me say another word about the treaty."

"Well, we want to hear nothing else." Hay did his best to be genial; and, as always, succeeded. The problem with Henry Cabot Lodge—aside from the disagreeable fact that he looked young enough to be Hay's son—was his serene conviction that he alone knew what the United States ought to do in foreign affairs, and from his high Republican Senate seat he drove the Administration like some reluctant ox, toward the annexation of, if possible, the entire world.

Worse, at a bureaucratic level, Lodge meddled so much with the State Department that even the patient Adee now found unbearable the Senator's constant demands for consulates, to reward right-thinking imperialist friends and allies. But the President wanted peace at any price with the Senate, and the price in Lodge's case was patronage. In exchange, however, Lodge had taken charge of getting the Administration's treaty with Spain through the Senate, a surprisingly difficult task because of the Constitution's unwise stipulation that no treaty could be enacted without the concurrence of two-thirds of the Senate, an august body filled with men of the most boundless conceit, as Adams had so neatly portrayed in an anonymous, highly satiric novel which even now no one, except the remaining Hearts, knew for certain that he had written.

Apparently, the Senators were, once again, running true to form, according to Lodge, whose British accent offended Hay's ears. But then Hay still spoke near-Indiana, and deeply loved England, while Lodge spoke like an Englishman, and hated England. La-di-da Lodge was one of the less unkind epithets for Massachusetts's junior senator, who was now denouncing his state's senior senator, the noble if misguided anti-imperialist George F. Hoar, who had told the nation that "no nation was ever created good enough to own another," a sly paraphrase of Lincoln. "Theodore writes me almost every day." Lodge stood, back to the fire, rocking from side to side on short legs. "He says that Hoar and the rest are little better than traitors."

Adams sighed. "I would think that Theodore would have quite enough to do up in Albany without worrying about the Senate."

"Well, he does think of the war as his war." Lodge smiled at Hay. "His *splendid* little war, as you put it. Now he wants to make sure we keep the Philippines."

"So do we all," said Hay. But this was not strictly true. Hay and Adams had thought, from the beginning, that a coaling station for the American fleet would be sufficient recompense for the splendors and miseries of the small war. This was also the view of several of the American commissioners at the Paris Peace Conference. In fact, one commissioner—a Delaware senator—had written Hay a curiously eloquent telegram to say that as the United States had fought Spain in order to free Spain's colonies from tyranny, the United States had no right to take Spain's place as tyrant, no matter how benign. We must, he said, stick to our word.

Hay had put the case to the President, but St. Louis, as it were, had inspired McKinley with a sense of mission. After ten days in the West, McKinley returned to Washington, convinced that it was the will of the American people, and probably God, too, that the United States annex the entire Philippine archipelago. He instructed the commissioners to that effect; he also offered Spain twenty million dollars; and the Spanish agreed. Meanwhile, something called the Anti-Imperialist League was breathing fire, and an odd mixture they were, ranging from the last Democratic president, Grover Cleveland, to the millionaire Republican Andrew Carnegie, from Henry Adams's own brother, Charles Francis, a one-time president of the Union Pacific Railroad, to Mark Twain.

"I wish, Cabot, I could be as certain as you are . . ." said Adams.

"About everything?" Lodge was amused and slightly, thought

Hay, patronizing. Hay had observed the phenomenon before: when the pupil has surpassed—or thinks he has—his teacher.

"No. I have *never* wished for senatorial certitude." Adams was dry. "That is beyond me. I'm always uncertain."

"You were certainly certain that the Spanish must be driven out of Cuba," began Lodge; to be stopped by Adams, who suddenly raised a pale small poodle-like paw.

"That was different. The only important contribution that my family ever made to the United States was the invention of the doctrine that is known by President Monroe's name. The western hemisphere must be free of European influence, and the Cuba Libre movement was the last act—the completion—of my grandfather's doctrine. Now, in the large sense, Spain is gone from our hemisphere, along with the French and for all intents and purposes, the British. The Caribbean is ours forever. But for us to end up with vast holdings in the Pacific, that strikes me as potentially dangerous, as more trouble than it's worth. I've sailed the South Seas . . ."

"Old gold," murmured Hay, the phrase Adams had used to describe the entrancing native women of Polynesia.

Adams affected not to hear. "Now you want us to take over a hostile population, made up of worthless Malay types, and Roman Catholics, as well. I thought you had enough of those in Boston without taking on another ten million or so."

Lodge was airy. "Well, unlike the ones in Boston, we won't let your worthless Malays vote, at least not in Massachusetts elections. And they're not hostile, at least not the ones who matter, the people of property, who want us to stay."

"Those are the tame cats, the ones who liked the Spanish. But all the rest follow this young man Aguinaldo, and they want independence." Adams tugged at his beard, which was a white version of Lodge's beard as Hay's beard was a grizzled compromise. Hay was touched that a relatively young politician should want to emulate his elders when modern politics now required clean-shaven men like McKinley and Hanna, or the moustachioed

Roosevelt. What did beards imply? he wondered. The early Roman emperors, like the early presidents, were clean-shaven; then decadence—and beards; then Christianity and the clean-shaven Constantine. Was McKinley to be a religious leader, as well as imperial consolidator?

Hay gave the latest news of Emilio Aguinaldo, whose troops had fought with Admiral Dewey on condition that once the Spaniards were gone there would be an independent Philippine—or Vishayan—republic. But McKinley's change of heart had put an end to that dream. Now Aguinaldo's troops—mostly from the Tagal tribe—had occupied the Spanish forts. Aguinaldo had also occupied Iloilo, the capital of Panay province. Thus far, neither side had been eager to begin hostilities. "But this can't last much longer," said Hay, completing his tour of the archipelago's horizon as viewed from the State Department. Elsewhere in Mullett's wedding cake of a building, Hay knew that the War Department was contemplating games that he knew nothing of; and did not want to know about.

"Obviously some sort of incident now would get us our two-thirds vote." Lodge sat in the armchair opposite Adams and adopted the same meditative pose as his old professor—and editor. After Lodge had graduated from Harvard, Adams had hired his former student to be an assistant editor of the *North American Review*, with one standing instruction: when editing historians, strike out all superfluous words, particularly adjectives. Hay had always envied Adams's continence in the matter of English prose. Adams wrote like a Roman, with an urgent war to report; Hay's prose simply idled, waiting for a joke to turn up.

"We had—you had—the two-thirds vote two weeks ago." Adams scowled. "Then the whole thing was frittered away. How I wish Don Cameron was still in the Senate . . ."

"And La Dona across the square," Hay added. Without Lizzie Cameron, Adams was incomplete. But the Camerons were wintering in Paris; and Adams was more than usually irritable and restless in Washington.

For once, Lodge did not make an excuse or, rather, more characteristically, blame someone else for the erosion of support in a Senate where the Republicans not only had a majority but he himself was the guiding spirit of the Foreign Affairs Committee. "I've never seen so much pressure brought to bear, never heard senators give so many positively crazed reasons for not doing the obvious. Anyway, we now have help from Mr. Bryan. Or Colonel Bryan, as he calls himself . . ."

"And who does not, who can?" said Hay, himself a major in the Civil War, who had never fought because he was Lincoln's secretary. Then, the war won without his participation, he was brevetted lieutenant colonel; hence, always and forever, he was Colonel Hay just as the President was always Major McKinley. But the President had actually seen action under his mentor, Ohio's politician-general Rutherford B. Hayes, whose own mentor had been yet another politician-general, James Garfield, and Hay's dear friend, as well. When General Garfield, the golden, had been elected president, he had offered Colonel Hay the position of private secretary; but Hay had gently declined. He could not be in middle age what he had been in youth. Now, of course, all the political generals from Grant to Garfield were dead; the colonels were on the shelf; and the majors had come into their own. After them, no more military-titled politicians. Yet every American war had bred at least one president. Who, Hay wondered, would the splendid little war—oh, fatuous phrase!—bring forth? Adams favored General Miles, the brother-in-law of his beloved Lizzie Cameron. Lodge had already declared that Admiral Dewey's victory at Manila was equal to Nelson's at Aboukir. But of course Lodge would support McKinley, who would be reelected; and so there would be no splendid little war-hero president in the foreseeable future.

Hay caught himself daydreaming; and not listening. In his youth, he could do both. What *was* Lodge talking about? "He holds court in the Marble Room back of the Senate. They come in, one by one, to get their instructions. He's like the pope." Bryan.

Colonel Bryan was in town to persuade the Democratic senators to support the treaty on patriotic grounds; then, the treaty passed, they would support a separate resolution to the effect that, in due course, the Philippines would be given their independence. Hay decided that Bryan was probably clever. If imperialism proved to be as popular as McKinley sensed it was in St. Louis, Bryan could enter the next presidential race as one who had joined the army and then favored the treaty and temporary annexation; but if imperialism, for some reason, should not be popular, he was on record as favoring the independence of the Philippines while the Major was now firmly for annexation. "He's also like the pope in that he is not a gentleman." Lodge could not resist the double thrust. Hay, who had not begun life as a gentleman by Lodge's standards, had become one; so much so, in fact, that he, unlike Lodge, never saw any need to use the dangerous word in any context. Politicians, no matter how patrician their birth, were a vulgar infantile lot. "We should be grateful to him, of course, wild man that he is. Because if the treaty passes . . ."

"No 'if,' please." Hay refused to envisage the treaty's failure.

"It's going to be close, Mr. Hay, very close. But Bryan's changing votes. I'm changing votes, I think, and . . ."

"And Mark Hanna's buying one or two," said Adams. "Such is the way of our world."

"A very good thing, too. Corruption in a good cause is a good thing. So who cares that a senator's been bought in the process?" Hay got to his feet, with some difficulty. Although the mortal ailment was, temporarily, in recession, he had lately developed an exciting new set of pains, both arthritic and sciatic; as a result, what felt like jolts of electric energy kept assaulting his nerve ends while odd tendons twitched quite on their own and joints, for no reason, would suddenly lock. "I've come around, Cabot. At first I thought it not only wrong but inconvenient to try to govern so many Catholic Malays. But time's running out on us. The Europeans are partitioning China. The Russians are in Port Arthur. The Germans are in Shantung . . ."

"I want us in Shanghai." Lodge's eyes gleamed at the prospect of yet more Asiatic victories.

"Well, I want us in Siberia," said Adams. "We have no future in the Pacific, but when Russia breaks up, as it must, there's our opportunity. Who controls the Siberian land-mass is the master of Europe and Asia."

Happily, Hay was spared an Adams meditation on the world's ever-shifting balance of power by the arrival of ladies. Hay greeted Mrs. Lodge, known as Sister Anne or Nannie, at the door, aware that her suspicious eye was on her husband. She did not entirely approve of Lodge when he was too much the senator; husband gave wife an innocent look. "Henry and I talk and talk about the treaty, while Cabot, who knows everything, just sits and listens, quiet as pussy," said Hay, maintaining peace in the Lodge family. "In fact, cat's got his tongue tonight."

"There is no cat," said Nannie Lodge, "large enough to get Cabot's silver tongue."

Meanwhile, Clara Hay and their two daughters quite filled the study, and Adams began to shine, as he always did when young women were present, while Lodge grew ever more courtly, and Sister Anne witty. Three of five Hearts in the same room: Hay was content. But contentment ceased in the midst of the bombe-glacée, Clara Hay's ongoing masterpiece. Although cooks came and went over the years, Clara, who could not, as they say, boil water, nevertheless was able to pass on the secret receipts to a number of all-important dishes of which the bombe-glacée was the quivering, delicate, mocha-flavored, creamy, filigree-sugared piece, as Hay called it, of least resistance.

Hay's fork was posed for a stab at this perfection when the butler appeared in the doorway to announce, "The President, sir. He would like you to go over to the mansion."

The dining room was silent. Lodge's dark eyes shone; and the bumblebee nose looked as if it scented pollen. Adams gave his old friend a mournful look. Clara was firm. "He can wait until we've finished dinner."

Hay had discovered a new and almost painless way of getting out of a chair; he used his relatively strong right arm rather than his relatively bad knees to get to his feet. Now he pushed hard against the arm of his chair; and was, almost painlessly, upright. "Henry, you be host. I'll be back—when I'm back."

"I can't think," said Clara, "what the Major is doing up at this hour. Over there, they go to bed with the chickens."

"A fox," said Lodge, "is loose in the chicken house."

At the foot of Hay's majestic staircase stood Mr. Eddy and a White House messenger. Hay's descent was cautious; the scarlet runner a magnificent peril. "What is it, Mr. Eddy?"

"I don't know, Mr. Secretary."

"I don't know either, sir," said the messenger.

"All I know, sir, is he wants you straight away, sir."

"In mid-bomb," Hay murmured sadly, as the butler got him into his fur-lined coat.

Although February had been lethally cold, no snow had yet fallen, and the three men were able to walk across the avenue to the White House, where the offices in the east end were ominously lit up while the downstairs was dark.

The German doorkeeper greeted Hay in the near-darkness of the entrance hall; he said, somewhat surprisingly, "The President's waiting in the conservatories." An usher stepped out of the shadow, to lead the way. In the dim light of a single lamp, the Tiffany screen looked incongruously Byzantine.

During Lincoln's time the conservatories had been modest; now they covered acres. One greenhouse was devoted exclusively to orchids, another to roses, another to exotic tropical fruits. At evening receptions, the Marine band would play in the rose house, and the young couples would wander from glass-house to glass-house, invariably getting lost. But there had been no such evenings since the sinking of the *Maine*.

The President was in the carnation greenhouse, seated in an armchair, smoking a cigar, a stack of papers in his lap. Hay was quite overwhelmed by the scent of flowers, not to mention the moist warmth in such marked contrast to the icy night beyond the panes of glass, which were now so many black mirrors reflecting the artificial-looking colors of the carnations on their green straw-like stalks. Electric lights made summer noon of winter night.

"I come here when I want to get away." The Major started to get up but Hay's hand on his shoulder kept him in place. Hay got into a chair opposite him; they were at the center of a perspective of carnations, arrayed in tables according to color. Those at hand were pale pink, a color Hay disliked and the Major doted on. "Tonight I've been working on my speech to the Home Market Club in Boston. It's for the sixteenth. I want to make the case, once and for all, for annexation. Please go over the text. Add anything, subtract anything. Just make it right. You're the best I know for this sort of speech."

Hay wondered if the President might not be a little mad: to summon him away from a dinner party, admittedly a late one, to sit in a stifling greenhouse in order to discuss a speech two weeks away. "Is that the text?"

"This?" McKinley held up the top paper on his lap; the huge waistcoated belly had crumpled an edge of the paper where belly rested upon vast presidential thighs. "No, Mr. Hay. This is what we have to talk about. It is from the Manila correspondent of the *New York Sun*. It will be in all the papers tomorrow."

As Hay read the cabled story, the agitated President spun his eye-glasses on their silken cord; first clockwise, then counterclockwise. On the island of Luzon, Aguinaldo's gun-men had opened fire on American troops. Hay returned the cable to the President. "I am not surprised," he said. "It was only a matter of time—and timing."

"We have a second war on our hands, so close to the other." The Major sighed. "It is always the unexpected that happens, at least in my case. I thought my administration would be a quiet affair, dedicated to sound business, sound money. Instead I am thrust by events into war after war . . ."

"Mr. Lincoln said I do not act. I am acted upon. My policy is to have no policy."

"In this, we are as one." McKinley suddenly shook the cabled report as if it were a child in need of discipline. "How foolish these people are! Don't they realize that this will get us our treaty? The people will insist on it now."

Hay nodded; he was also growing suspicious. "Do we know who fired the first shot?"

"All we know is what you've just read. It sounds as if they fired the first or provoked us to fire first. I've cabled General Otis for a report. Just the other day he said he thought he'd need as many as thirty thousand troops, to run things properly. I disagreed. As it is, our army of occupation is twenty thousand men, all—"

". . . wanting to go home."

The massive ivory head—a perfect egg save for the cleft chin—nodded and the round luminous eyes were suddenly hooded. "Now that Spain's surrendered, we are committed to getting the troops home as soon as possible. They did not sign up to fight Filipinos, Colonel Bryan has reminded me."

"So they—Aguinaldo, that is—have really done us a great favor. We can't bring the troops home if there is an insurrection." But as Hay began to make the Administration's case, he was by no means certain to what specific end they were about to commit themselves and the country. After all, the word "insurrection" assumed that the United States government was the legitimate government of the Philippines; but they were not a legitimate government; they were, allegedly, liberators, and the so-called insurrection was actually a war for independence from foreign liberators turned conquerors, with Aguinaldo in the role of Washington and McKinley in that of George III. Hay now began to weave new language: the word "trustee" emerged; "temporary," also. Suddenly, he stopped, aware that the President was not listening. McKinley's eyes were shut; and he was breathing deeply. Was he asleep? or in a trance? Could the President, like his wife, be epileptic? Hay wondered, somewhat wildly. But then McKinley cleared his throat; and opened his eyes. "I was praying," he said, simply. "Do you pray often, Mr. Hay?"

"Not, perhaps, often enough." Hay recalled the Jesuit injunction that the wise man never lies, as he has already seen to it that he need not tell the whole truth. Hay was truth-full and god-less.

"I think God answered me the other night." McKinley picked a carnation and held it up to his nose. "I actually got down on my knees—not an easy thing," he smiled, indicating the broad stomach that had overwhelmed his chest, "and asked for guidance. I was in the oval library. Ida had gone to bed. I was alone. I told God that I had never wanted any of this war, and that I certainly had never wanted those islands. But the war had come, and the Philippines are ours. What am I to do? Well, number one, I said to God, I could give the islands back to Spain. But that would be cruel to the natives, who hate Spain. Number two, I could let France or Germany take them over. But that would be a very bad business for us commercially . . ."

"I'm sure God saw the wisdom of that." Hay could not resist the interjection. Fortunately, McKinley was too preoccupied with his divine audience to note Hay's impiety.

". . . and discreditable, too. Number three, we could simply go home and let them govern themselves, which they could never do, as everyone knows. But at least we'd be out of it. That's the easy way, of course. It was then that I felt—something." McKinley's eyes seemed to glow in the light which had transformed the glass panes of the greenhouse into so many onyx mirrors. "There was a presence in that room, and I found myself summing up in a way that I had not planned to. I had simply wanted to put the case to God and hope. But God answered me. I heard myself saying, aloud: Number four, in the light of numbers one through three, as I have just demonstrated, Your Honor—God, that is—we have no choice but to take all of the islands and govern the people to the best of our ability, to educate and civilize them and to Christianize them—and in my sudden certitude, I knew that God was speaking to and through me, and that we would all of us do our best by them, or our fellow men for whom Christ also died. Well, Mr. Hay, I have never been so relieved. I had the first good night's sleep in a year. Then, the next morning, without telling you or any of the Cabinet I sent for the chief engineer of the War Department, and I gave him an order." McKinley opened up on his legs a world map. "Here is what I told him to do."

Hay took the map and held it up. At first he noticed nothing unusual; then his eye strayed to the Pacific Ocean and there, in the same yellow color as the United States, an ocean away, were the Philippines with the legend "U.S. Protectorate."

"*You* annexed them?"

McKinley nodded. "With God's assurance that I must. And, of course," he smiled, and took the map from Hay, "some assistance from Admiral Dewey and Colonel Roosevelt. I *know* I have done the right thing."

"But if the treaty fails to pass the Senate, there is no protectorate . . ."

"The treaty will pass. That's why I took you into my confidence, to show you why I am so certain and so—fatalistic. Because," McKinley stood up, "I never wanted any of this. But it is God's plan now, and we are His humble instruments."

"I hope God will give us some hints on how best to handle Aguinaldo."

But McKinley was now moving, in his stately way, down the long aisle of carnations to the door. At the President's request, Hay joined him in the shaky coffin-like elevator to the living quarters, where, upon arrival, McKinley led him into the oval library to show him the exact spot where the interview with God had taken place. But Mrs. McKinley, not God, was now in possession of the hallowed place. She sat in her invalid's chair, knitting bedroom slippers. She was slender, pale, surprisingly pretty; she spoke, however, with a nasal sing-song whine that Hay found as disagreeable as Lodge's British accent. Was there to be no happy American mean? "When they told me the Major was with you, I felt better. You never keep him up to all hours like some of them do."

Hay bowed, as if to Victoria. "I returned him from the carnation room as quickly as I could and as good as new, I hope."

Cortelyou appeared in the doorway. "There's no more news, Mr. President. Secretary Alger says that General Otis's report will be ready first thing tomorrow."

"Thank you, Mr. Cortelyou. You go to bed now."

Cortelyou withdrew. Hay was about to do the same when Mrs. McKinley delivered herself of an *ex cathedra* judgement on Washington's worldly ladies. "Why, they even brag about how they tuck their poor tired husbands into bed and then they go out gallivanting to parties on their own. Imagine! Well, I tell them that when I tuck Mr. McKinley into bed, I get right in with him, which is what we're going to do now."

"I, too," said Hay, adding indecorously, "in my own bed, of course."

But Mrs. McKinley was staring narrowly at his shoes. "Draw me an outline of your shoe-sole, and I'll make you slippers next."

"With pleasure, Mrs. McKinley."

Then, to Hay's astonishment, Mrs. McKinley stuck her tongue out at him; gave him a lascivious wink; and became rigid, only the whites of her eyes visible. The President, with an unhurried, practiced gesture, took a huge silk handkerchief from his pocket; and covered her head. "I am troubled by the Teller Amendment in the Senate." McKinley stared absently at the veiled Ida. "How to interpret it? The amendment is clear that we cannot retain Cuba. But will the Senate try to extend the amendment to cover the Philippines?"

"No, sir. Your Benevolent Assimilation Proclamation has been accepted by all except a few die-hards—and blow-hards like Bryan. If the treaty passes, the archipelago is ours. Paid for in cash to Spain. Twenty million dollars for ten million Filipinos." Hay found this talk of empire curiously exciting; and even humorous. "That's two dollars a head," he added.

"Colonel Hay." The President was gently reproving. Then he

bade Hay good-night. "We'll discuss the insurrection tomorrow. Before the Senate vote."

"Yes, Mr. President." But as Hay walked down the east wing stairs, having just vowed never to use the west wing elevator—too like a coffin—ever again, he was beginning to have his doubts about the Major's new "protectorate."

- 3 -

But all doubts were dispelled on Monday when at Lodge's insistence and against Hay's better judgement, he entered the Marble Room of the Capitol, as a somewhat casual guest of the Senate, which was now, in its chamber next door, busy biting the proverbial bullet. The voting would begin on the treaty in one hour, at three o'clock. From the windows of the gilded, mirrored, marbled chamber, White House and Washington monument were visible against a sky as dark as steel. Only Mr. Eddy accompanied Hay; on principle, Adams refused to set foot in the Capitol—or, for that matter, his family's one-time home, the White House.

Fresh from the Senate cloakroom and its intrigues, Lodge joined Hay: more than ever a bumblebee today. "I think we've got all the Republicans, except Hoar. We're getting several Democrats. I may bring them in here to you."

"I'll do what I can, dear Cabot. But what can I do?"

Lodge was not listening. But then Hay knew that senators, particularly when they were at home on their side of the Capitol, lost their never overwhelming auditory powers. Lodge produced a press-cutting from his frock-coat. "Did you see this? In yesterday's *Sun?*"

Hay had indeed read their friend Rudyard Kipling's contribution to the American political process. Although English, the prodigious Mr. Kipling had lived for some time in the United States; during 1895, he was a good deal in Washington, where Hay

and his circle had come to know and admire him. Theodore
Roosevelt, in particular, had taken him up, and their muscular
minds, Hay's happy phrase, lifted, as it were, dumb-bells together.
Now Kipling had launched a thunderbolt, in the form of a poem,
carefully timed to affect, if possible, the treaty vote. "Theodore
sent me an advance copy last month. He thought it poor poetry
but good for the expansionist cause. I happen to think it's quite
good as a kind of hymn, pretending to be a poem."

"A hymn to the god of war," said Hay, who had indeed been
struck by the poem, not least by its alarming title, "The White
Man's Burden."

"I'm using some of it in a speech." Lodge quoted,

> " 'Take up the White Man's burden—
> Send them forth the best ye breed—
> God bind your sons to exile
> To serve your captives' need.'

I also like the warning to us, that we must take over from England,
the torch is passing and we must—where is it? Oh, yes." Again
Lodge read,

> " 'To wait in heavy harness
> On fluttered folk and wild—
> Your new-caught sullen peoples
> Half devil and half child.'

That describes those Malays to a T, don't you think?"

"Well, they are certainly sullen at the moment. And even the
excellent Rudyard admits that we're in for trouble." Hay took the
cutting and read the quatrain that had most struck him:

> " 'Take up the White Man's burden—
> And reap his old reward:
> The blame of those ye better,
> The hate of those ye guard. . . .' "

"What's that?" asked a deep voice from behind them.

Hay turned toward the door, where stood a tall, noble-looking young man in a frock-coat that had been made famous—like the wide mouth, square jaw—by a thousand cartoonists. Lodge greeted William Jennings Bryan with a cry of joy. Hay never ceased to delight in the spontaneous hypocrisy of the true politician, always at his most appealing when faced in the flesh by a bitter enemy. But the enemies were, this day, allies. As titular head of the Democratic Party, Bryan had been rallying his troops in the Senate to the treaty. But senators are seldom anyone's troops, particularly those of a defeated presidential candidate. Bryan's task was made more difficult by the ambition of one Senator Gorman, who saw anti-imperialism as the means to get for himself the Democratic nomination in 1900. Although the weekend had been hectic, Bryan looked calm and at ease. No, he had not seen Kipling's poem. As he read it, lips moving, sounding the phrases, Hay wondered if Bryan had indeed ever heard of Kipling before. Then Bryan returned the cutting to Lodge. "Well, it can be read two ways," he said. The smile was wide, perhaps a trifle cretinous; but the eyes were shrewd and watchful. "And, all in all, I'd rather not have either way read today. We're having a hard enough time as it is. There is no one more anti-imperialist than I . . ."

"Colonel Bryan, we're all agreed that there will be no long-term annexation. We're all anti-imperialists." Lodge lied with perfect sincerity.

"We'd better be," said Bryan; and left the room in order to avoid his nemesis, fat, white Mark Hanna.

"I can't stand seeing that anarchist in this place," growled Hanna. "Where's Hobart?"

No one had seen the vice-president, an obscure New Jersey corporation lawyer who had been chosen to be vice-president by Hanna for no reason that Hay could see other than his wealth. Would wealthy men one day buy the great offices of state as they had during Rome's decadence? Adams thought that the practice was already common. After all, state legislatures elected United

States senators. Many legislators were for sale. Hadn't New York's sardonic Roscoe Conkling boasted that he had paid only two hundred thousand dollars for his seat? A bargain price back in the seventies? Hay argued that the presidency was still different. A party leader, like McKinley, slowly and openly evolved; or, thanks to a sudden shift in popular opinion, he emerged like Bryan. In neither case could the leadership have been bought, assuming that the would-be leader had had the money, or access to it. But it was on the word "access" that Adams looked dour. Hanna had financed McKinley on a scale unknown until now. What would prevent a Carnegie or a Jay Gould from selecting some nonentity and then, through adroit expenditure, securing for himself the presidency's power, all in the nonentity's name? Hay felt that Adams, once again, took too dark a view.

They were joined by another of McKinley's intimates, Charles G. Dawes, a personable, red-haired young politician from Nebraska, who had played a significant role in the election of McKinley. When Bryan began to take the country by storm and the multitude thought him the greatest orator in American history, Hanna panicked. Although the money interest was solidly behind McKinley, the South and the West were for Bryan. Since the farmers were penniless, Bryan promised to increase the money supply. Silver coins would be minted, sixteen to one in relation to gold. America, intoned Bryan, in speech after speech to the largest crowds anyone could remember, would not be crucified upon a cross of gold. Meanwhile, McKinley seldom strayed from his hometown of Canton, Ohio, where he conducted his own low-key campaign from his own comfortable front porch, a gift of admirers. After twelve years in the House of Representatives and four as Ohio's governor, he was a poor man; hence, honest. Hanna thought McKinley should take to the stump. McKinley was tempted; but, as Hay had heard it, young Mr. Dawes persuaded the Major to stay right where he was. When it came to demagoguery, he could not compete with Bryan; so why try? As McKinley recounted it later to Hay, "If I hired a train to campaign in, he'd hire a single car. If I bought a Pullman car berth, he'd buy a cheap seat. If I bought a cheap seat, he'd ride the freight. So I decided to stay put." In response to Bryan's cross of gold, McKinley was vigorous and vague. He was, he declared, in favor of *both* gold and silver money, an admirable sentiment as acceptable as it was unintelligible, to get the largest popular vote. Finally, crucially, a majority preferred the Major's placid solidity to Bryan's fieriness. For a moment, class war was in the air. Then the border states, which had made Lincoln president, shifted from Bryan to McKinley; and he was elected with the largest popular vote of any president since Grant.

Young Mr. Dawes had been astonished not to be included in the Cabinet; but the Major had soothed him with the office of comptroller of the currency, where he could amuse himself with the chimera of bimetallism while his wife, Caro, amused Ida McKinley.

Dawes greeted-Hay warmly; introducing him to a tall young man named Day, the assistant comptroller and a Democrat. "On his way home to run for Congress, something I should be doing. You, too, Mr. Hay."

"Oh, not me. Not now. I'm not even an Ohioan any longer." Neither Adams nor Hay, as full-time residents of the District of Columbia, ever voted in those presidential elections which so entirely absorbed them. If the irony had been, by some accident, lost on them, Lodge and a host of others were quite willing to torment the self-disenfranchised statesmen. Hay had been offered a seat in Congress in 1880; but the price quoted by the local Republican boss was too high, or so his father-in-law decreed. Then came the move to Washington; and a limbo that was now quite filled with power's unexpected rainbow.

"I think we'll win, with three votes to spare." Dawes had taken a notebook out of his pocket. Hay could see that it contained a list of senators with pluses and minuses and question marks next to each name.

"I think we'll win it," said Mr. Day. "Colonel Bryan's changed a half-dozen votes for you folks."

'You anarchists ain't winning nothing today," said Hanna; and, Hay noted, there was no twinkle in those dull red eyes. A buzzer sounded: a Senate roll-call. "I got to go join the animals. If anybody sees Hobart, tell him I'm looking for him." Hanna waddled toward the Senate chamber.

Day looked after Hanna, with some distaste. "Personally, I wish Colonel Bryan had let the thing go hang."

"And let Senator Gorman take over the party? No," said Dawes, "that's not in the cards. Bryan's riding two horses just fine."

Hay turned to Eddy. "I don't seem to be needed, after all."

Dawes took Hay's arm, companionably. "Let's go up in the gallery and watch the vote." He turned to Day. "Come on, anarchist," he said. "Now's your chance to throw a bomb."

Hay took his seat in the front row of the distinguished visitors' gallery. Nearby, the press had filled up their section; while Washington's ladies were out in force. As always, on such senatorial occasions, Hay was reminded of the bull-fights in Madrid. Admittedly, Washington's ladies, all in winter furs, were not so vivid as Spanish women in summer, but there was the same excited focus on the arena—in this case, the Senate chamber beneath them.

A senior senator presided in the vice-president's chair, high on its dais. The roll-call was about to begin. Senators were now taking their seats opposite the dais. Hay's presence had been noted. Graciously, he bowed to this one and to that, as this one and that waved or bowed to him; happily, he had no idea who anyone was. He was getting like the nearly blind Chief Justice Chase, who, toward the end of his life, had taken to greeting everyone with the same, solemn, studied joy on the ground that he did not want to offend anyone who might still see in him a potential president.

As the roll-call was being taken, Dawes chattered: "There's a story going to break that we provoked those natives to attack us, but it won't hit the papers till tomorrow, and by then it won't make any difference."

"No difference?" Mr. Day was not shy, Hay decided, mildly curious as to how a Bryan Democrat could be holding office in an administration which took very seriously the notion that to the victors belong the spoils. Naturally, Civil Service reform was dear to every progressive Republican heart; but office for the worthy was dearer. "Do you realize what a difference it will make if people find out that it was us who started the trouble over there?"

"It meant no difference to the vote today, which is what matters. I'm also not saying we started it. I don't know. It's just a rumor." Dawes turned to Day. "You folks have been getting nowhere with silver since they found all that gold in the Klondike, so now you've got to hit us with something new, like going into the empire business."

"Are you related to my predecessor, Judge Day?" Hay found the young man personable, for an anarchist. From his accent he could have been from Indiana, too; in fact, he was not unlike, Hay thought, his own young self, only taller, stronger.

"No, sir. But I do know your son, Del."

Hay was not surprised. As he himself saw Del so little nowadays, he had no idea whom his son saw. "Then tell me, what has become of him?"

"I think he's in New York. I haven't seen him since last month when he took me over to the White House, to play billiards, down in the cellar."

Hay was truly startled. "In the cellar of the White House?"

"Yes, sir. It's a terrible place, too. Slimy—like a dungeon. But there's a billiard room where some of the staff meet . . ."

"And the President?"

"He looked in, while we were playing."

Before Hay could unravel the secret life of his son and the President, Vice-President Hobart, now in his chair, entertained a motion from the floor that the peace treaty be, herewith, voted upon. As the senators answered with an aye or a nay when their names were called, Dawes would scribble in his notebook and mutter "Hell" or "Maria," presumably "bad" and "good." When the name Elkins was called, Dawes said, "Now we'll see if your man Bryan's done his work." The whole chamber was still. Elkins was a Democrat; and an anti-imperialist. Elkins allowed the silence after his name to last as long as possible; then he shouted, "Aye!" Applause exploded in the gallery. Hobart, resembling an aged walrus, struck his gavel hard on his desk. While a familiar lah-di-da voice intoned, "Bravo!"

Day turned to Dawes. "Well, Colonel Bryan's gone and got you your empire."

"*You* don't follow your leader?" asked Hay.

"I think he's made a mistake. We have enough to do here at home without . . ."

But cheering had again filled the chamber: the necessary two-thirds vote had been achieved, with one vote to spare. The Senate had voted fifty-seven to twenty-seven to uphold the Administration's peace treaty, and annex the Philippine Islands, now in rebellion against their newly legitimate, by act of Congress, masters.

"Hell and Maria!" shouted the delighted Dawes. "I must go tell the Major."

Eddy helped Hay to his feet. Various dignitaries shook his hand, as if this had been his treaty rather than the President's. At the foot of the gallery stairs, Lodge met Hay with the words: "We have done it." Hay noted that Lodge looked distinctly unwell. "I have never in my life gone through such an ordeal."

Hay gave him the praise that he wanted; and deserved. In the end, only two Republicans had voted against the treaty: Lodge's colleague Hoar, who had somewhat startlingly offered to be beheaded in the Senate if that would stop the annexation, and Hale, the hereditary senator from Maine, who had kept his hard head, and said no. Otherwise, Hanna's money and patronage, Bryan's eloquence and smile, and Lodge's perseverance had carried, just barely, the day. "The ship of state is in the open sea at last," said Hay, bowing to left and right, as he and Lodge crossed the rotunda where Washington's ladies now mingled with the weary proud legislators.

"Ship is the right image," said Lodge, somewhat grimly. "And I've just spent a month in the engine room . . ."

"The cloakrooms of the Senate."

"Exactly. I'm caked with grime."

At that moment, as if to emphasize the nature of the grime, a tall burly youthful man, surrounded by admirers, all simple Western folk, passed them without a glance, or a pause in his tirade: "I never thought I'd live to see the day when any man dare try to give, openly and in broad daylight, a bribe to a United States senator so as to get him to change his vote."

"Who," asked Hay, "was that?"

"The honorable senator from Idaho, Mr. Heitfeld, who in a well-run world would be, at this moment, planting wheat back home."

"Not, dear Cabot, in Idaho, in February. *Was* he offered a bribe?"

Lodge shrugged. "Not by me. But Hanna's been from one end of the cloakroom to the other, whispering. Bryan, too. So who knows? Anyway, all that matters is that the ship is now full speed ahead. We are on the high seas at last, Mr. Hay. What England was, we are now, as of today. Asia is ours."

"Well, not yet." They were outside the Capitol. The sky was black; a cold wind blew. Fortunately, the secretary of state took precedence over everyone but vice-president and speaker; and in no time at all, the State Department carriage creaked and rattled to a halt, at the head of a long line of carriages, their waiting horses blanketed against the cold. Hay completed the nautical image. "Let's hope the barometer's not falling, now that we're on the high seas."

"Oh," said the driver, thinking that he had been addressed, "there's a blizzard on its way, sir. Worst of the season, they say."

"That," said Hay to Lodge, "is not a good omen."

"So I'll keep killing Capitoline geese until I find one whose liver predicts good sailing weather." Lodge and Eddy helped Hay into the carriage. "Seriously," said Lodge, seriously, "this was the closest, hardest fight I have ever known. I doubt if we'll see another in our time, when so much was at stake."

"I make no predictions when it comes to earthly matters." An elaborate burst of pain at the bottom of Hay's spine brought earth into its true material perspective, the inexorable refuge for the lot of them and, for him, more soon than late. "As opposed to heavenly ones. Let us say the ships are afloat, and the legions are fighting on the Asian marches."

"Ave Caesar!" Lodge laughed.

"Hail McKinley." Hay smiled in the icy darkness. "Pacific lord of the Pacific Ocean."

4

At the end of the long broad corridor that divided the ground floor
of the Fifth Avenue Hotel, Blaise waited in what was known from
one end of the political city to the other as the Amen Corner. He
had yet to discover why the corner was so named. Presumably it
was here that "amen" was put to fervent prayers by the current
master of the Corner, Senator Thomas Platt. Seated at the center
of a gilded horsehair sofa, the so-called Easy Boss presided over
the fortunes and misfortunes of all members of the so-called
organization, the machinery that controlled the Republican Party
in the state of New York and, presumably, the new Republican
governor, Theodore Roosevelt, who had promised to give Blaise an
interview after his weekly breakfast meeting with Platt. When
Congress was in session, the Senator came up from Washington on
Friday evening and returned to the capital on Monday morning.
The fact that each Saturday the Government came down the river
from Albany to breakfast with the Easy Boss indicated the nature

147

of their relationship, or so the Chief darkly maintained.

Blaise was nervous. He had never met the Governor; he was, of course, used to him ("habituated," he said to himself, reverting to French). By now he had watched the energetic figure on a dozen stages, the incarnation of, if nothing else, energy. Now the Chief wanted the Governor interviewed; thought the time was right for Blaise to try his hand at the deceitful art; wanted certain things asked, which Blaise had written down on a pad of paper, already smudged from sweaty fingers. He was nervous; and wondered why. Was he not *habituated* to the great? He was a Sanford; a Delacroix, too. He reminded himself of his father's deep contempt for all politicians, which had been deeply and permanently satisfied at Newport, Rhode Island, when President Chester A. Arthur had made the mistake of visiting the Casino, where everyone had blithely ignored him. Worse, when it came time for Mr. Arthur to leave, he was obliged to stand, quite alone, while the carriages of Astors, Belmonts, Delacroixs, Vanderbilts swept past him, as he himself shouted, "The President's carriage!" Colonel Sanford had revelled in the situation. But Blaise lacked his father's patrician disinterestedness.

At eight-thirty of a Saturday morning, the Fifth Avenue Hotel was uncommonly tranquil. A few guests were to be seen in the distant lobby, while several potential justices of the peace from upstate tentatively occupied the Amen Corner. They reminded Blaise of the sort of furtive men one saw in the Mulberry Street police station, standing in the criminal line-up.

Two members of New York's police force guarded the door to the private dining room where their one-time commissioner was breakfasting, heartily—the usual adverb—on chicken pan-fried steak, with a pair of fried eggs, like magnified eyes on the steak, and a quantity of fried potatoes. Blaise had questioned the maître d'hôtel earlier. Apparently, the Governor was a big eater, in the Western frontiersman style; he liked his "grub" plain and plentiful and always fried.

Suddenly, a large, round, dark-waistcoated belly, packed with fried meat, appeared in the dining room's doorway; the belly's attachment, Governor-Colonel Theodore Roosevelt, said something to the two policemen which made them frown, and which made their old commissioner hoot with laughter, like a screech-owl, thought Blaise, swooping down upon a nocturnal rodent. The Governor was accompanied by the pale and more than ever weary-looking Platt. To Blaise's surprise they had breakfasted without aides or—witnesses, he immediately thought. The Chief's dark conspiratorial view of the world was contagious; and probably correct.

The policemen then saluted the Governor, who crossed to Blaise, ignoring the would-be supplicants. "Mr. Sanford? From the *Journal*. Our favorite paper, isn't it, Mr. Platt?"

"There are worse, I suppose," moaned Platt softly, moving toward his familiar settee; he was like the now proverbial man with a hoe come home to rest. "Mr. Sanford," he murmured, touching Blaise's hand with his own delicate one. Then Senator Platt sank on to his throne in the Amen Corner, ready to rule as well as reign, while the nominal ruler of the state was left free to charm and delight a young journalist. As supplicants surrounded Platt, the boss waved Governor and Blaise a mournful farewell.

"Well, now, Mr. Sanford, why don't you drive uptown with me to my sister's house. We can talk on the way." During this Roosevelt had taken Blaise's left elbow into his right hand, a curious gesture which might seem a demonstration of intimacy or at least good feeling to an observer, but to the victim, so Blaise felt himself, it was more like a gesture of physical control, as the Governor forced him to walk rapidly alongside him, and in perfect step; again he was reminded of the Mulberry Street police station. But although the Governor was like a policeman, he was hardly the robust physical specimen that legend proclaimed. Roosevelt was as short as Blaise, who had spent a half-dozen years praying for half as many inches more; but he had stopped growing at sixteen. Yet where Blaise was muscular, Roosevelt was simply rubbery, with an enormous head and neck, the first emerging from the second like a tree's section. The belly was definitely fat; the limbs were definitely thick but not muscular. Nevertheless, Roosevelt walked swiftly, purposefully, like an athlete with an appointment on some as yet undetermined playing field. Meanwhile, Blaise was bemused to discover that the Governor's conversation was exactly as recorded by the press. In the lobby, when strangers asked to shake his hand and wish him well, he would flash those huge rock-like teeth and exclaim, in three distinct syllables, "Dee-light-ed!" When told something that he approved of, he would actually say "Bully!" like a stage Englishman. He even responded, in the street, to cries of "Teddy," a name that Blaise knew no one ever dared call him in or out of the family.

A light April rain was dampening Fifth Avenue, if not Governor Roosevelt, who leapt inside his carriage, using Blaise's elbow, still held in his right hand, as fulcrum. Blaise was happy to note that the brougham was closed. Otherwise, he had an image of the exponent of "the strenuous life," the title of a lecture recently given in the Midwest, riding up Fifth Avenue in a rainstorm, shouting "Bully!" at the elements.

"You should go west," said the Governor, predictably. "A boy like you should develop his body, and morals."

Blaise found himself blushing, not at the word "morals," a subject that he, the French-reared young man, could have lectured the Governor on, but the word "body"; he prided himself on a musculature unequalled by any Yale classmate, the work of nature, admittedly, but still all his own, unlike the thick suet-pudding beside him. Close to, Roosevelt did not look young; but then, for Blaise, forty was not exactly a man's optimum age. Deep lines radiated from behind the gold-framed pince-nez. The short-cropped hair was grizzled. Like a parenthesis of hair, the Chinese-style moustache framed—and disguised?—red, full, curiously voluptuous lips. The eyes were bright and quick and of no distinctive color, other than bright. The body was unhealthily fat. "I can beat you," said Blaise, to his own amazement, "at Indian arm-wrestling."

The Governor, who had been staring out the window, hoping to be recognized by a passing umbrella, turned an astonished gaze on Blaise. The spectacles were allowed to drop from his nose onto his chest—where they swung on their chain like a pendulum. The eyes, Blaise could see at last, were blue. "You! A city dude?" There was a burst of high laughter; then: "You're on," said the Governor.

The two men then arranged themselves on the back seat so that each could rest an elbow on the middle cushion as they interlocked forearms. Blaise was perfectly confident; he was stronger, he knew, as he began to force down the older man's arm. But Roosevelt was heavier; finally, faced with defeat, he simply cheated. Aware that he was about to be beaten, he surreptitiously slid his feet under the folding seat opposite and, with this leverage, abruptly forced Blaise's arm down. "There!" shouted the Governor, delighted.

"You had your feet under the seat."

"I did not . . ."

"Look!" Blaise pointed; the feet were quickly withdrawn.

"An accident. They slipped." For an instant Roosevelt looked furious, like a small child caught out. Then he roared. "Bully for you, my boy! Come on in. You're no city dude. Whatever you are. A Sanford. Which Sanford?"

The family game was swiftly played through. The Colonel, a perfect snob like so many tribunes of the people, was quite at home with a Sanford; but somewhat intimidated by a Delacroix. As they got out of the carriage in front of 422 Madison Avenue, the brownstone house of the Governor's youngest sister, Mrs. Douglas Robinson (Blaise took meticulous notes), Roosevelt said, "Do you box?"

"Yes," said Blaise, who did.

"We'll go put on the gloves in the basement, once breakfast's settled."

Mrs. Robinson, addressed as Conie by her brother, was a dark, bright-eyed woman, who led them into a small parlor, dominated by the head of a buffalo shot by the Governor when he was a cowboy in the West. The resemblance, Blaise noted, was eerie between victim-beast and victor-man. "I used to be a taxidermist myself," said Roosevelt. "Birds, mostly. But I really wanted to be an ornithologist, a naturalist. Why Hearst?"

"Well, why not, sir?" Blaise sat in a William Morris rocking chair while Roosevelt worked off his breakfast by walking vigorously, if pointlessly, about the room. From the back parlor, a telephone rang from time to time and a low masculine voice would answer it. Apparently, the state of New York was being strenuously governed even as they spoke.

"He is against reform, of course. He is a Democrat, not that I am strict in such matters. But I think Boss Croker is, perhaps, unsavory, even by Tammany standards."

"That's true, sir. But he did stand by when you were running for governor, and you won by eighteen thousand votes because he wouldn't really go all out for Judge Van Wyck."

Roosevelt chose not to hear this. "Last week, Mr. Hearst was at the Tammany Hall dinner, in Grand Central Palace, presided over by our friend Croker, home from Ireland, or *away* from home, in Ireland. *I* would not want to be so closely allied with such a man."

"I think, sir, the Chief was there to listen to Mr. Bryan."

"I can't think why a newspaper publisher, who went to Harvard, should want to involve himself in politics when he has, as far as I can tell, no politics at all."

Although Blaise had been more amused than bemused by the Chief's sudden obsession with politics and the holding of high office, he could not tell Roosevelt that much of the Chief's interest had been created not, as many thought, by the career of his father, Senator George Hearst, but by that of the thick small restless shrill-voiced man who was marching about the room like a toy soldier that someone had wound up but forgot to point in any particular direction. Blaise had now given up on conducting an interview with the Governor. Those whom Roosevelt regarded as social equals, and Blaise was one, were not treated as a part of the solemn consistory of reforming angels at work with bucket and shovel in the stables of the republic; rather, they were treated as a fellow boy by a boy who despite—or because of—small stature and bad eyesight, was a born bully and, perhaps, leader, too, if anyone could be persuaded to follow him. Certainly, whatever crossed his plainly quick mind, he felt obliged to express.

Hearst now ceased to interest the Colonel. Instead, he was distracted by a model of a battleship, not, Blaise was reasonably certain, a treasured possession of Mrs. Robinson's. "I was given this when I was assistant secretary of the Navy. *Build more,* I said. Have you read Admiral Mahan on sea-power? Published nine years ago. An eye-opener. I reviewed it in the *Atlantic Monthly.* We are fast friends. Without sea-power, no British empire. Without sea-power, no American empire, though we don't use the word 'empire' because the tender-minded can't bear it. Like Andrew Carnegie, that old scoundrel, who says that if we don't give freedom to our little brown brothers in the Philippines, we will be cursed. By what? His money? He told Mr. Hay that if an American soldier fires—as they've had to do—on the Filipinos, we will lose our republic at home. Incredible! Thanks to Mr. Carnegie and his friends our government was obliged to fire on a great many American workers at the time of the Haymarket riots, and the old fraud was dee-lighted. Hypocrite. But Mahan's not. *He's* a patriot. The torpedo boats. I have him to thank for the theory. The Navy has me to thank for arming us, in time . . ."

". . . and you to thank for Admiral Dewey." Blaise took advantage of a pause during which Roosevelt clicked his teeth together three times, like a dog; the sound was as disconcerting as the expression of the face was alarming. "Well, I did get him the job in the Pacific. Took a bit of doing. Had to get a *senator* to sponsor him first. Imagine! What a country! If we hadn't found us a senator to sponsor him, another officer would have got the job, and we'd not be in Manila. Good man, Dewey. Good officer. They'll try to run him for president, of course. I hope he's wise. And stays out."

"Mr. Hearst thinks the Admiral would be better than Bryan . . ."

"Dear boy, *you'd* be better than Bryan. Didn't my sister Anna visit your father a few years ago?"

"Did she go to Allenswood?" Suddenly Blaise remembered a charming, excessively plain, large-toothed woman, very much at home in France.

"No. But she studied with Mlle. Souvestre when she still had her school in France. Before she moved to England . . ."

"My sister Caroline was there, too. In England . . ."

Roosevelt talked through him. ". . . did wonders for Bamie's French and general knowledge but I'm not so sure of morals. She's now a freethinker, like Mlle. Souvestre . . ."

"Who's an atheist, actually."

Roosevelt ground his teeth in a lively imitation of rage. "So much the worse for my sister. And yours . . ." Like so many politicians who never ceased to talk, he heard what others said even through the comforting cascade of his own words. "At least mine learned perfect French. What about yours?"

"She already spoke perfect French. She was obliged to learn perfect English, which she did."

"We're sending my niece to her this year. We have hopes . . ." But the Governor looked grim.

"That would be the daughter of Mr. Elliot Roosevelt, sir?"

"Yes. My brother is well known to your readers." The Governor threw himself into an armchair; and glowered at Blaise, as if he were Hearst, the devil. Four years earlier, Elliott Roosevelt had died, under an assumed name, in 102nd Street, where he had been living with his mistress and a valet. Although he had been a heavy drinker for years, Blaise's father had always said that if any Roosevelt could be said to have true charm, it was Elliott, who had spent quite a lot of time in Paris, much of it at the Chateau Suresnes, a place of refuge—or containment—for wealthy alcoholics. Some years earlier, the Governor had publicly declared his brother insane, to the delight of the press. The Chief, in particular, found it almost impossible to let the Roosevelt family skeleton rest peacefully in its closet; he also never let pass an opportunity to remind New Yorkers that in order to avoid taxes, Theodore Roosevelt used to give as his place of residence not New York State but the District of Columbia. Because of this confusion over residence he had come close to losing the nomination for governor; but then the brilliant Elihu Root, a lawyer without peer, as the *Journal* would say, had talked the nominating convention around. All in all, Blaise was pleased that he himself had no political ambitions. Between private life and public, there was, for him, no contest. What, he sometimes wondered, would they do with the Chief's private life when he decided to enter the arena?

Roosevelt wondered the same. "He'll find all the newspaper fellows will be treating him the way he's treated everybody else." Roosevelt removed his spectacles; and stared near-sightedly at the buffalo, which stared into eternity, a place just above the door to the hall. "I suppose he'll support Bryan again. That would make things easy for us. McKinley's a shoo-in."

"What about you, sir?"

"I am a good party man. McKinley's the head of the party. I've been offered the editorship of *Harper's Weekly*. You can write that. You can also say I'm tempted to take it next year, when my term's up." An aide entered from the hall; and gave the Governor what Blaise could see was a newspaper slip. He wondered from which paper; probably the *Sun*. As the aide left, Roosevelt was on his feet again, marching up and down, with no precise end in view other than the pleasure that vigorous motion of any kind appeared to give him. "The President has unleashed General MacArthur on the rebels. I've proposed unconditional surrender on our terms, not that the humble governor of New York has anything to say in such great matters."

"But they listen to you, sir." Blaise was beginning to work out a theme if not a story. "You are for expansion—everywhere?"

"Everywhere that we are needed. It is to take the manly part, after all. Besides, every expansion of civilization—and we are that, preeminently in the world, our religion, our law, our customs, our modernity, our democracy. Wherever our civilization is allowed to take hold means a victory for law and order and righteousness. Look at those poor benighted islands without us. Bloodshed, confusion, rapine . . . Aguinaldo is nothing but a Tagal bandit."

"Some people regard him as a liberator," Blaise began, aware that the Governor could thunder platitudes by the hour.

But there was no braking him now. Roosevelt was now marching rapidly in a circle at the center of the room. He had been seized by a speech. As he spoke, he used all the tricks that he would have used had Blaise been ten thousand people at Madison Square Garden. Arms rose and fell; the head was thrown back as if it were an exclamation mark; right fist struck left hand to mark the end of one perfected argument, and the beginning of the next. "The degeneracy of the Malay race is a fact. We start with that. We can do them only good. They can do themselves only harm. When the likes of Carnegie tell us that they are fighting for independence, I say any argument you make for the Filipino you could make for the Apache. Every word that can be said for Aguinaldo could be said for Sitting Bull. The Indians could not be civilized any more than the Filipinos can. They stand in the path of civilization. Now you may invoke the name of Jefferson . . ." Roosevelt glowered down at Blaise, who had no intention of invoking anyone's name. Blaise stared straight ahead at the round stomach whose gold watch-chain quivered sympathetically with its owner's mood, now militant, imperial. "Well, let me tell you that when Jefferson wrote the Declaration of Independence, he did not include the Indians among those possessing *our* rights . . ."

". . . or Negroes either," said Blaise brightly.

Roosevelt frowned. "Slavery was something else, and solved in due course in the fiery crucible of civil war."

Blaise wondered what the inside of a politician's mind looked like. Were their drawers marked "Slavery," "Free Trade," "Indians"? Or did the familiar arguments hang on hooks, like newspaper galleys? Although Roosevelt was a respectable historian, who wrote and even read books, he could never say anything that one had not already heard said a thousand times. Perhaps that was the politician's art: to bring to the obvious the appearance of novelty and passion. In any case, the Governor was enchanted by his own rhetoric. "Jefferson bought Louisiana, and never once consulted the Indian tribes that he had acquired in the process."

"Or the Delacroix family, and some ten thousand other French and Spanish inhabitants of New Orleans. We still hate Jefferson, you know."

"But, in due course, you were incorporated as free citizens of the republic. I speak now only of savages. When Mr. Seward acquired Alaska, did we ask for the consent of the Eskimos? We did not. When the Indian tribes went into rebellion in Florida, did Andrew Johnson offer them a citizenship for which they were not prepared? No, he offered them simple justice. Which is what we shall mete out to our little brown brothers in the Philippines. Justice and civilization will be theirs if they but seize the opportunity. *We shall keep the islands!*" Roosevelt suddenly began to click his teeth rapidly, alarmingly; he was like a machine, thought Blaise, wondering how on earth he could describe, in mere words, so odd a creature. Again the image of a wound-up toy soldier. "And we shall establish therein a stable and orderly government so that one more fair spot," fist struck hand a powerful blow, "of the world's surface shall have been snatched," two stubby hands seized the innocent warm air of the parlor, saving it from winter cold, "from the forces of darkness!" There was a bit of froth at the edge of the Governor's full lower lip. He brushed it away with the back of the hand which still held the one fair spot snatched from darkness.

"Are you absolutely sure that Mlle. Souvestre is an atheist?" The Governor suddenly settled into a chair. He had put away the Philippines in their drawer; and locked it.

"So I've been told. I don't really know her." Blaise was neutral. "She's been very active for Captain Dreyfus." This was not such a nonsequitur, since freethinkers tended to be Dreyfusards. In any case, the Governor was not listening.

"Bamie—my sister, that is—says that one can just ignore her on religious matters. It's worth the chance, I think, for my niece,

Eleanor." The Governor then lectured Blaise for an hour. He wanted stronger proconsuls in Cuba and the Philippines. He would discuss the matter with the President. He thought that the sooner Secretary of War Alger—the man responsible for feeding the troops tinned, tainted meat—left the Cabinet the better. Blaise managed to ask a question or two about the Governor's relations with Senator Platt. They were, apparently, "bully," even though everyone knew that the two men could not bear each other, and that Platt had only taken Roosevelt because, after the scandals of the previous Republican governor, the party would have lost the state. At the same time, Roosevelt, the zealous reformer, needed the Republican machine in order to be elected governor. It was also no secret that he would like to join his friend Lodge in the Senate; it was also no secret that Platt was not about to surrender his own seat to accommodate a governor who was currently insisting that any corporation with a public franchise must pay tax. Specifically, this struck at William Whitney, a Democrat millionaire, who owned numerous streetcar lines as well as, some said, the golden key to Tammany Hall. Whitney had served in Cleveland's cabinet; had fathered Blaise's classmate Payne.

As the Governor declaimed, he would shift his voice from effete questioner to stern Jehovah-like answerer; he played a dozen different parts, all badly but engagingly. Blaise wondered, idly, as he so often did in this still strange city, whether or not such a man would have a mistress, or go to brothels (there were more in the Tenderloin District than in all of Paris), or would he confine himself, with iron resolve, to the indulgences of his second wife?

The thought of Payne Whitney had made Blaise think of sex. Once, innocently, at Yale, Blaise had asked the high-spirited Payne if there was a decent brothel in New Haven. The boy had gone red in the face; and Blaise had realized that his twenty-year-old classmate was a virgin. Further highly covert investigations convinced Blaise not only that most of the young men of his class were virgins but that this unnatural state explained their, to him, inexplicable long and dull talk of the girls that they knew socially, combined with heavy drinking of a sort that he associated, in Paris, with workmen of the lowest class. As a result, he never let on that since his sixteenth year he had been involved in an affair with a friend of his father's, Anne de Bieville, twenty years his senior and happily married to a bank manager; her oldest son, two years Blaise's senior, had taught him how to shoot at Saint-Cloud; for a time, he was Blaise's best friend. As it was tacitly assumed that Blaise was the mother's lover, the subject was never mentioned between the boys. Consequently, prim New Haven had come as something of a shock.

"Perhaps Anglo-Saxons develop later than we do," said Anne, amused at the sight of so much virginity on the playing fields of Yale; actually, not the playing fields but at a dance for the senior class. Blaise had introduced violet-eyed Anne as his aunt; and she had caused a sensation. "Well, physically, they are all there," said Blaise; many seniors wore thick moustaches, heavy sideburns. "But something happens—or doesn't happen—to their brains over here."

"Their livers, too, I should suspect. They drink too much."

Theodore Roosevelt was again on the march around the room. Blaise tried to imagine him in a love nest in 102nd Street; and failed. Yet the brother, Elliott, had had a mistress with him when he died—a Mrs. Evans, whom the Roosevelt family had paid off because there was a *Mr.* Evans, who had threatened to shoot the Roosevelt lawyer if her income was not increased. Elliott had also loved a Mrs. Sherman, who lived in Paris but was not received in the Sanford world.

Blaise decided that Governor Roosevelt was not the sort to enjoy women as he did, say, food. On the other hand, to Blaise's youthful cynic's eye, Roosevelt seemed very much the sort of person who would, after much heart-searching and hand-wringing, seduce the wife of his best friend, and then hold his best friend entirely responsible for the tragedy. That seemed to be the Anglo-Saxon style. A secretary brought news of a telephone call from Albany. Thus, the interview was concluded.

"Good luck, my boy. I hope you can make something of my tendency to ramble. So much to talk about. So much to do. Next time I'll give you a boxing lesson. As for your Mr. Hearst . . ." The bright eyes narrowed behind the gold-edged lenses. "We disagree on many things. Bryan, free silver. Those plaid suits. He wore," Roosevelt's voice moved up half an octave, with scorn, "a *chartreuse* plaid suit with a *purple* tie at the Mayor's reception last month. And he wonders why no club will take him in." The hand-clasp was heavy; and Blaise's departure swift.

The Chief was amused by the Governor's sartorial disdain. "Well, at least we stopped him from wearing those pink shirts and fancy sashes." The Chief lay full-length on a sofa in his living room. A bust of Alexander the Great at his head; one of Julius Caesar at his feet. On the floor lay a banjo. The drama critic of the *Journal*, Ashton Stevens, had vowed that he could teach Hearst to play the banjo in six lessons. But, after fourteen lessons, the longed-for virtuosity was still longed-for. Apparently, the Chief, despite his passion for popular music, was tone-deaf. For two weeks, he had been trying to learn "Maple Leaf Rag," that essential exemplar of rag-time, with results that could only be regarded as sinister. The Chief was again in plaid; but this time of a subdued gray travertine hue, like a fashionable foyer's floor, thought Blaise, as he finished his report on Governor Roosevelt.

"Pity about what's his name, the frog," was all that Hearst had to say. He had moved on.

"It would have been a great coup." Blaise was also sorry that their hare-brained but exciting plot to rescue the prisoner of Devil's Island had been preempted by the French government. Dreyfus was home: a free man. The *Journal* must look elsewhere for dragons to slay.

"The 'Man with the Hoe' thing . . ." the Chief began; he did not need to finish. Recently, he had published, in the *San Francisco Examiner*, some verse by an obscure California teacher. Overnight, the poem had become the most popular ever published in the United States, ". . . and now they say that I'm a socialist! Well, maybe I am. Even so, *a poem!*" Hearst shook his head; and picked up the banjo. "Whoever thought a poem would increase sales?" Hearst had one more go at "Maple Leaf Rag." Blaise felt his skin crawl. "I think I've got the hang of it," said the Chief, striking a chord never before heard on earth; and holding it.

George was at the door. "There's another house-agent, sir."

"Tomorrow. Tell him nothing above Forty-second Street. I don't want to be a farmer."

"Are you moving?"

Hearst nodded. "They're tearing down the Worth House. This year. Just as I finished fixing it up." Hearst gestured to show off what looked to be an auction warehouse. Statuary in crates, dozens of paintings turned face to wall, while others that ought to have been face to wall were displayed as in a provincial French museum; chairs piled one on top of the other, reminiscent of the Louis XV Room of the Hoffman House after a dinner. "There's a possibility in Chicago," he said, swinging his long legs to the floor.

"For a house, sir?"

"No, a newspaper. To buy."

"The *News!*"

"No. They won't sell. But I could take over another one. Cheap." Hearst glanced innocently at Blaise. "That is, cheap for you. Expensive for me right now. Next year my mother's moving back to California."

"She won't . . . help?"

"She'd rather not, she says. She's already in for, maybe, ten million. Then there's Washington. The *Tribune*'s close to shutting down. Of course, there aren't any votes in the District. But you can always have fun scaring the politicians."

Blaise was puzzled. "Votes? I thought you wanted readers."

"Well, I want both. I've got New York, San Francisco, and now Chicago—with a bit of luck. The Democratic Party's up for grabs."

"You want to grab it?"

"Somebody has to. You see, the press has a power that no one understands, including me. But I know how to make it work . . ."

"To get readers. Votes are something else."

"I wonder." The Chief stretched his arms. "My mother's met your sister."

"Oh." Blaise was guarded. He wanted no one, least of all Hearst, to know about the war between brother and sister. At the moment, they communicated only through lawyers. Caroline had appealed a lower court's ruling; now they awaited a higher court's decision on the arcana of the cyphers one and seven. Meanwhile, to Blaise's surprise Caroline had settled not in New York, where the courts were, but in Washington, where, presumably, Del Hay was. Before Blaise had been able to stop her, she had sold the Poussins for two hundred thousand dollars; she now could afford to buy a vast amount of American law. But Houghteling had chuckled when he heard the news and said that, even so, she might well be twenty-seven by the time the case was settled in her favor. Irritably, Blaise had then pointed out that *he* was the one in a hurry, not she. At the moment relations with the Chief were good; but the Chief's moods were volatile, to say the least. Now was the time to help him buy the Chicago newspaper. Later, old Mrs. Hearst might again come to her son's aid; or he might even start to make more than he spent, a not likely prospect for a man who was in the habit of offering a good journalist double his usual salary, simply to get him away from the competition.

"Your sister came to look at my mother's house. But it was too big, she said. Your sister said, that is. She's intelligent, Mother says. Why does she like Washington?"

"I think it's the Hay family that she likes."

"He's practically an Englishman by now." Hearst's short attention span had snapped. Mother, sister, John Hay were as one with Captain Dreyfus and "Maple Leaf Rag." "You go to Washington. Take a look at the *Tribune*. Don't let on you have anything to do with me. I'll scout out Chicago."

Blaise was delighted with the assignment; less delighted with the thought that he might see Caroline; alarmed when the Chief said, "Pay a call on Mother. Tell her how hard I work. How I don't smoke or drink or use bad language. And tell her how much you like schools."

"But I don't."

"But she does. She's just started one for girls, up at the Cathedral. Maybe the two of us could go there and teach the girls—you know, journalism." The Chief had come as close as Blaise had ever heard him to a smutty remark. "Give my regards to your sister."

"If I see her," said Blaise. "She moves in refined circles."

– 2 –

In March Caroline had arrived at the outermost ring of the republic's circles, when she rented a small rose-red brick house in N Street, which ran through a part of dilapidated Georgetown, reminiscent of Aswan in Egypt, where she had once wintered with her father and his arthritis. There was hardly a white face to be seen; and the owner of the house, a commodore's widow of pronounced whiteness, hoped that she would not mind "the darkies." Caroline pronounced herself entranced; and hoped, she said, to hear tom-toms in the night. The widow said that as there were, happily, no Indians nearby, tom-toms would not sound; on the other hand, a good deal of voodoo was practiced between the Potomac River and the canal. She did not recommend it, in practice. The commodore's widow left behind her a large black woman, who would "help out." It was agreed that Caroline would take the house for at least one year. On the brick sidewalk in front of the house two vast shiny-leaved magnolia trees put the front rooms in deepest shadow, always desirable, Caroline had remarked, when living in the tropics. Predictably, Marguerite was stunned to find herself marooned in Africa, with an African in the kitchen.

From the outermost circle, Caroline moved to the innermost: the dining room of Henry Adams, where breakfast was served for six each mid-day and no one was ever invited; yet the table was never empty except for this particular morning, when Caroline ate Virginia smoked ham and biscuits made with buttermilk, and the host, more round than ever, discussed his departure the next day for New York; and then a tour of Sicily with Senator and Mrs. Lodge. "After that, I shall spend the summer in Paris, in the Boulevard Bois de Boulogne. The Camerons are there. *She* is there, at least. No more coffee, William," he said to the manservant, William Gray, who poured him more coffee, which he drank. "Do you know a young poet, an American, named Trumbull Stickney?"

Caroline said, accurately, that she knew very few Americans in Paris. "While we don't seem to know any French," said Adams, judiciously. "We go abroad to see one another. I gather that Mrs. Cameron is Mr. Stickney's muse this spring. If I were young, I would not be jealous. As it is, I writhe." But Adams seemed not to be writhing at all. "You must come over—or back in your case— and show us France."

"I don't know France at all." Caroline was again accurate. "But I know the French."

"Well, I can show you France. I tour the cathedrals yet again. I brood on the relics of the twelfth century."

"They are . . . energetic?"

Adams smiled, almost shyly. "You remembered? I'm flattered."

"I'd hoped for more instruction. But just as I move to Washington, you go away. I feel as if you had created me, a second Mrs. Lightfoot Lee, and then left me in mid-chapter." Caroline was now on forbidden territory. No one was ever supposed to suggest that Adams might be the author of the novel *Democracy*, whose heroine, a Mrs. Lightfoot Lee, settles in Washington in order to understand power in a democracy; and is duly appalled. Caroline had delighted in the book, almost as much as she did in its author. Of course, there were those who thought that John Hay had written the novel (he had been photographed holding a copy of the French edition and wearing a secret smile); others thought that the late

Clover Adams, a born wit, was the author. But Caroline was certain that Adams himself had written his quintessential book of Hearts. He never, with her, denied—or affirmed—it. "The lesson of that amorality tale is—stay away from senators."

"That's not difficult."

"In Washington? They are like cardinals in Renaissance Rome. You can't avoid them. That's why I flee to the twelfth century, where there were only three classes: the priest, the warrior and the artist. Then the commercial sort took over, the money-lenders, the parasites. They create nothing; and they enslave everyone. They expropriated the priest—don't you like to hear all this at breakfast?"

"Only when there is honey in the comb," said Caroline, spreading the wax and honey over a piece of hot cornbread. "I can take quite a lot of priests expropriated. And the warriors . . . ?"

"Turned into wage-earning policemen, to defend the money men, while the artists make dresses or paint bad portraits, like Sargent . . ."

"Oh, I like him. He never tried to disguise how much his sitters bore him."

"That is our last revenge against money. See? I count myself an artist; but I am only a *rentier*, a parasite. Why Washington?"

Caroline was not certain how much she should confide in this brilliant old professional uncle. "My brother and I have disagreed . . ."

"Yes, we've heard all about that. There is nothing to do with money that we don't seem to hear about. We have lost our spirituality."

"Well, I may lose something far worse, my inheritance." Where was it that she had read that there was a certain honey that made one mad? She had just eaten it, plainly; she confided: "Blaise could control everything for five years. He worships Mr. Hearst, who loses money on a scale that makes me very nervous."

"The terrible Mr. Hearst could end up losing the Sanford money, too?"

As Caroline took more honey, she noted, in the comb, a tiny grub. Perversely, she ate it. "That's my fear. Anyway, while our lawyers duel, Blaise lives in New York and I have come here to Aswan, to observe democracy in action, like Mrs. Lee."

"Then," said Adams, pushing back from the table, and lighting a cigar, with a by-your-leave gesture, "there is Del."

"There is Del."

"He is next door, even as we speak. Are you tempted?"

"My teacher—"

"The formidable Mlle. Souvestre, now established at Wimbledon. She has advised you?"

"No. She gives no advice. That is her style. I mean no *practical* advice. But she is brilliant, and she has never married, and she is happy, teaching."

"You want to teach?"

"I have nothing to teach."

"Neither have I. Yet I run a school for statesmen, from Lodge to Hay. I am also Professor Adams, late of Harvard."

"I am not so ambitious. But I am curious what it would be like to remain single."

"With your—appearance?" Adams laughed; an appreciative bark. "You will not be allowed to stay single. The forces will be too great for you. Unlike you, your Grande Mademoiselle had neither beauty nor a fortune."

"In time, I shall lose the first, and in an even shorter time could lose the second. Besides, she is very handsome. She has had suitors."

"Perhaps," said Adams, "she prefers the company of serious ladies, like an abbess of the twelfth century."

Caroline flushed, not certain why. Mademoiselle had had a partner when the school first began at Les Ruches. There had been quarrels; they parted. Mademoiselle had reigned alone ever since. No, this was not what she herself would prefer in the way of a life alone. But then she had had no experience, of any kind. "I have not the vocation," she said, "of an abbess, even a worldly one."

The honey's power released her. Adams led her into the library, her favorite American room. The overall effect was meant to be medieval, Romanesque even, with windows so sited that one could ignore the White House across the square by looking slightly upward, to Heaven. The room's focal point was the fireplace, carved from a pale jade-green Mexican onyx shot through with scarlet threads; she had never seen anything like it before, but unlike so many things never seen before, the extraordinary silk-like stone fascinated her. On either side of the fireplace Italian *cinque-cento* paintings were arranged, as well as a Turner view of the English countryside lit by hell-fire; best of all, there was a crude drawing by William Blake of Nebuchadnezzar, king of Babylon, on all fours, munching grass in his madness. "It is the portrait of my soul," Adams had said when he showed it to her for the first time. The room smelled of wood-smoke, narcissi and hyacinth. The leather chairs were low, built to suit Adams and no one else. They quite suited Caroline, who settled in one, and said, "You must tell me when I'm to go."

"I'm already packed." Adams groaned. "I hate travel. But I can never remain in one place." William announced Mr. Hay, who limped into the room. He was in pain, Caroline decided; and looked a decade older than he had in Kent.

"What are you doing here?" Adams pulled out his clock. "It's Thursday. Your day to receive the diplomatic corps."

"Not till three. Cinderella holds the fort."

"Cinderella?" asked Caroline.

Adams answered, "Mr. Hay's name for his assistant, Mr. Adee, who does all the work in the kitchen, and is never asked to the ball."

"You've settled in, Miss Sanford?" Hay took coffee from William, who knew his ways. Caroline said that she had. Hay nodded vaguely; then turned to Adams. "I think of you, Enricus Porcupinus, as a deserter. When I need you most, you and Lodge leave town."

"You have the Maj-ah." Adams was not in the least sentimental.

"We've worked hard enough for you all winter. We got your treaty. I long, now, to see La Dona—and the Don, too, of course."

"Tell her she may have her house back sooner than she thinks."

"What's wrong with the Vice-President?"

"Heart trouble. Doctor's ordered him out of town, indefinitely."

"Well, it is not as if his absence will be noted."

"Oh, Henry, you are so hard on us poor hacks! Mr. Hobart may not be much as vice-presidents go, but he is one of the best financial investors in the country. He invests money for the Majah and me, and we all do well. Though I prefer real estate. I've been negotiating for a lot on Connecticut Avenue. It is my dream to build a many-spired apartment house. They are the coming thing in this town of transients . . ."

Caroline had hoped for, perhaps, more elevated conversation at Hearts' heart. But today the old men obviously did not inspire one another to breakfast brilliance, while her presence was now sufficiently familiar not to require any special exertion. In a way, she was relieved to be taken for granted. But that was by the old; she was, to the young Del, very much a wish ungranted. "I heard you were here," he said, as he entered the room.

Adams turned to Caroline: "Our kitchens correspond closely. From cook to cook. Our Maggie to their Flora."

"And I knew you'd be here, Mr. Adams, and Mr. Adee said Father was here, too. So I . . ."

"You were at the office?" Hay looked surprised.

"Why, yes. Then I went to the White House, where I had a meeting with the President. He's asked me to surprise you."

"Is such a thing possible? Is such a thing wise?"

"We'll soon see." Del took a deep breath. "I have just been appointed American consul general in Pretoria."

To Caroline's astonishment, Hay looked as if someone had struck him. He took a deep breath, apparently uncertain whether or not tremulous lungs could absorb so much scented Adams library air. "The . . . ?" He could not utter the literally magisterial noun.

Del nodded. "The President made the appointment himself. He wanted to surprise you. He certainly surprised me. He also didn't want people to think that I got the job because I am your son."

"Surely a republic ends," said Adams, "when the rule of nepotism—like the second law of thermodynamics—ceases to apply."

"I could not," said Hay, breath regained, "be more thrilled, as Helen used to say when we'd go inside the monkey house at the zoo." Caroline watched father and son with considerable interest. What she had always taken to be Anglo-Saxon lack of intimacy between males she now decided was antipathy on the part of the famously charming and affable father toward the equally affable and, in time, no doubt, equally charming son who had not, after all, been trained in the art of storytelling by the admitted master himself, Abraham Lincoln, who could make, it was said, a mule with a broken leg laugh.

"I thought you'd be." Del was impassive; he looked not unlike photographs of President McKinley. If this were Paris, Caroline would put the odd and the even numbers together and understand precisely the nature of the appointment. But Del had his father's eyes, mouth; and there was little chance, she decided, of Ohio, known as the mother of presidents, having produced, through unlikely presidential lust, a consul to Pretoria, which was—where? Australia? She had not liked the geography teacher at Allenswood.

"South Africa could be a turbulent post," said Adams; he, too, was gauging Hay's response to his son's abrupt elevation. "What *is* our policy, between the English and those Dutch lunatics?"

"Extreme benign neutrality," said Del, looking at his father. "In public, that is."

"Yes. Yes. Yes." Hay shook his head and smiled broadly. "Neutral on England's side. The great fun will be if there's a war down there . . ."

"Splendid, perhaps?" Adams smiled. "Little?"

"Little-ish. Hardly splendid. The fun will be how our own Irish Catholic voters will respond. They are for anyone who's against

England, including these Dutchmen, these Boers, who are not only Protestant but refuse to allow the Catholics to practice their exciting rites. I predict Hibernian confusion hereabouts. I also predict that though it's only noon, and I must greet, soberly and responsibly, the Diplomatic Corps, there is champagne no farther than the flight of a porcupine's quill. We drink to Del!"

Adams and Caroline cheered; Del's forehead remained, as always, oddly pale, while his face turned to rose.

After champagne had been ceremoniously drunk to the new consul general, Caroline announced, "I can't think why *I* am celebrating. Now that I'm settled into N Street, Mr. Adams deserts me for Sicily, and Del for South Africa."

"You still have my wife and me," said Hay. "We're more than enough, I should say."

"And I don't go till fall," said Del. "The President still has some work for me to do, at the White House." Again Caroline noted the father's perplexed look.

"Then I have a few months of cousinhood if not unclehood." Caroline was pleased that Del should still be at hand. She must learn Washington at every level, and as quickly as possible. "One must be like Napoleon, Mlle. Souvestre always said, never without a plan."

"Even a woman must always have a plan?" Caroline had asked.

"Especially a woman. We don't often have much else. After all, they don't teach *us* artillery."

Caroline had indeed worked out a plan of action. John Apgar Sanford could not believe it when she told him. He begged her to think twice; to do nothing; to let the law take its course. But she was convinced that she could bring Blaise around in a more startling and satisfying fashion; assuming, of course, that she had Napoleonic luck as well as cunning. But the key to her future was here in a strange tropical city, among strangers. She needed Del. She needed all the help that she could get. John—as a cousin, she now called him by his first name—was more than willing to help her; but he was, by nature, timid. He was also, at last, a widower.

One night at Delmonico's showy new restaurant, and with the witty Mrs. Fish at the next table, straining to hear every word (for once Caroline blessed Harry Lehr's never-failing laughter), John had lost his timidity and proposed that once his term of mourning was at an end, she take his hand in marriage. Caroline's eyes had filled with genuine tears. She had done her share of flirting in Paris and London, but aside from Del no one, as far as she could determine, had ever wanted to marry her; nor had she met anyone that she wanted to marry; hence, the comfortable image of herself alone, and in command—of her own life. Yet Caroline had been touched by John's declaration; she would, she had said, have to think it over very carefully, for was not marriage the most important step in a young woman's life? As she began to unfurl all the sentences that she had learned from Marguerite, the theater, novels, she started to laugh, while the tears continued to stream down her face.

"What are you laughing at?" John had looked hurt.

"Not you, dear John!" Mrs. Fish's not unpiscine face was now costive with attention. "At myself, in the world, like this."

Adams insisted that Caroline remain behind, as father and son departed together for the State Department across the street and what would doubtless be a very serious conversation indeed. "That," said Adams, when the Hays had gone, "was a bit of a shocker."

"Mr. Hay seemed unenthusiastic."

"You felt that?" Adams was curious. "What else did you feel?"

"That the father expects the son to fail in life, and that the son . . ." She stopped.

"The son . . . what?"

"The son has tricked him."

Adams nodded. "I think you're right. Of course, I know nothing of sons. Only daughters—or nieces, I should say. I can't think what it is that goes on or does not go on between fathers and sons. Cabot Lodge's son George is a poet. I would be proud, I suppose. Cabot is not."

"It is sad that you have no heir."

Adams glared at her, with wrath. Whether real or simulated, the effect was disconcerting. Then he gave his abrupt laugh. "It has been four generations since John Adams, my great-grand-father, wrote the constitution of the state of Massachusetts, and we entered the republic's history by launching, in effect, the republic. It's quite enough that Brooks and I now bring the Adamses to a close. We were born to sum up our ancestors and predict—if not design—the future for our, I suspect, humble descendants. I refer," he smiled mischievously, "not to any illicit issue that we have but to the sons of our brother Charles Francis."

"I cannot imagine humility ever devouring the Adamses, even in the fifth generation." Caroline enjoyed the old man. It was as if Paul Bourget had been wise as well as witty.

Adams now came to his point. "I am aware of your connection with Aaron Burr, and I seem to remember you mentioning, last summer, that you had some of his papers."

"I do. Or I *think* I do. Anyway, I don't have to share them with Blaise. They came to me from my mother. They are in leather cases. I've glanced at them, but that's all. It seems that Grand-father Schuyler persuaded Burr to write some fragments of memoir. Grandfather worked in Burr's law office, when Burr was very old. There is also a journal grandfather kept during the years that he knew Burr. There is also," she frowned, "a journal, which I've never looked at, because my mother, I think it was she, wrote on the cover, 'Burn.' But it is still in its case, and no one has ever burned it—or probably read it! At least I haven't and I don't think my father ever did."

"Clearly, your bump of curiosity is less than ordinary. It is not like my family, where everyone has been writing down everything for a hundred years, and if anyone were to write 'Burn,' we would obey, with relief." Adams placed two small, highly polished shoes on the fender to the fireplace. "Some time ago I wrote a book about your ancestor Burr . . ."

"*Perhaps* my ancestor. Though I am absolutely certain that he was. He is romantic."

"I thought him, forgive me, a windbag."

Caroline was startled. "Compared to *Jefferson!*"

Adams's laugh was loud and genuine, no longer the stylized bark of approval. "Oh, you have me there! Do you read American history?"

"Only to find out about Burr."

"American history is deeply enervating. I can tell you that firsthand. I've spent my life reading and writing it. Enervating because there are no women in it."

"Perhaps we can change that." Caroline thought of Mlle. Souvestre's battles for women's suffrage.

"I hope you can. Anyway, I've done with our history. There's no pattern to it, that I can see, and that's all I ever cared about. I don't care *what* happened. I want to know *why* it happened."

"I think, in my ignorance, I am the opposite. I've always thought that the only power was to know everything that has ever happened."

Adams gave her a sidelong glance. "Power? Is that what intrigues you?"

"Well, yes. One doesn't want to be a victim—because of not knowing." Caroline thought of Blaise and Mr. Houghteling; thought of her father, whom she had known too little about; thought of the dark woman painted in the style of Winterhalter, who was completely unknown to her, and always referred to, with a kind of awe, as "dark."

"I think you must come join your uncle in Paris. I give graduate courses to girls, too; girls, mind you, not women."

Caroline smiled. "I shall enroll." She rose to go. He stood; he was smaller than she. "I shall also let you read the Burr papers."

"I was going to ask you that. I destroy a good deal of what I write. Probably nowhere near enough. I have been considering adding my Burr manuscript to the ongoing bonfire."

"Why a windbag?" Caroline was curious. "After all, he never theorized, like the others."

"He was the founder of the Tammany Hall-style politics, and that is windbagging. But I am unfair. He made one prescient remark, which I like, when he said farewell to the Senate. 'If the Constitution is to perish, its dying agonies will be seen on this floor.'"

"Will it perish?"

"All things do." At the door Adams kissed her chastely on each cheek. She felt the prickling of his beard; smelled his cologne-water. "You must marry Del."

"And leave all this for Pretoria?"

Adams laughed. "Except for my unique, avuncular presence, I suspect that Washington and Pretoria are much the same."

Del thought not. Caroline and Helen Hay dined with Del at Wormley's, a small hotel with numerous dining rooms, both small and large, and, traditionally, the best food in Washington. Whenever the young Hays wanted to escape the medieval splendor of the joint house with Adams, they would cross Lafayette Square to the hotel at Fifteenth and H Streets, where the mulatto Mr. Wormley presided. As the senior Hays were committed that evening to the British embassy, Del and Helen invited Caroline to dinner, to celebrate Pretoria. They were joined in a small upstairs dining room by a lean young Westerner named James Burden Day. "He's the assistant comptroller of the United States, for the next few hours," said Del, as they took their seats in the low-ceilinged room with its view of the vast granite Treasury Building down the street.

"What do you assist at controlling?" asked Caroline.

"The currency, ma'am." The voice was softly Western. "Such as it is."

"He's a Democrat," said Del, "and so he's devoted to silver, sixteen to one."

"I," said Helen Hay, large and comfortable-looking, like her mother, with dimples like Del, "am devoted to shad-roe, which is coming in now, isn't it? Isn't it?" Helen had a habit of repeating phrases. The courtly black waiter, more family butler than mere restaurant worker, said that it was, *it was*, and proposed diamond terrapin, a house specialty, and, of course, canvasback duck, which would be served, Caroline knew, bloody and terrible. But she agreed to the menu. Del continued with the champagne, begun at Mr. Adams's breakfast.

"I should be giving the dinner," said Caroline. "In the consul general's honour."

"You must start to do things jointly." Helen Hay even sounded like her mother, the amiable voice, which always spoke a command. In a well-run world, what splendid generals Clara and Helen Hay would have made. During the shad course, Caroline decided that she could do a lot worse than marry Del; on the other hand, she could imagine nothing worse than a season (unless it be a year) in Pretoria. Plainly, her interest in him was less than romantic. She had often wondered what it was that other girls meant when they said that they were "in love," or deeply attracted or whatever adhesive verb a lady might politely use. Caroline found certain masculine types attractive, as types, quite apart from personality—the young man on her right, addressed by Del as Jim, was such a one. Del himself was too much, physically, created in his mother's baroque mould. But had she not always been taught that fineness of character is the best that any woman could hope for in a mate? And Del's was incomparably fine.

Thinking of Del's fineness, Caroline turned to the figure on her right; he was definitely not baroque, she decided. Gothic, in fact— slender, aspiring, lean; she tried to recall Henry Adams's other adjectives in praise of Gothic; and failed. Besides, the young man's hair was curly and its color was not gray stone but pale sand; yet the eyes were Chartres blue. Was—what *was* his name? there were three, of course, to indicate noble birth at the South: James Burden Day—was his character incomparably fine? She was tempted to ask him; but asked instead how a Democrat enjoyed working for a Republican administration. "I like it better than they do." He

175

smiled; the incisors were oddly canine; would he bite? she hoped. "But it's just another job to them, and that's all government is— in this country, anyway. Jobs. Mine should belong to a Republican, and it will in September when I go home."

"To do what?"

"To come back here," Del answered for his friend. "He's running for Congress."

"Don't tempt the gods." Day looked worried; and Caroline found this appealing.

"Then you'll have an elected job. The best kind," she said.

"Oh, the worst! The worst!" Helen was adding yet more shad-roe to a Berninian figure that threatened to erupt into extravagant rococo. The arms in their puffed sleeves already looked like huge caterpillars, ready to burst and spread huge iridescent wings. "Every two years Mr. Day will have to go home and persuade the voters that he is still one of them, that he'll get the government to give them things. It's a tiring business. Father's job is best."

"But the secretary of state must please the president, mustn't he? And if he doesn't, he goes." Caroline addressed the question not to Helen but to Del.

Predictably, Helen answered. "Oh, it's more complicated than that. The Major must also please the secretary of state. If Father should leave—let's say before an election—that would hurt the Major. Truly hurt the Major. So they must please each other."

"Both," said Del, "must please the Senate. Father hates the Senate and everyone in it, including his friend Mr. Lodge."

"Even so," Helen had miraculously consumed, in a minute, ten thousand shad's eggs, "secretary of state is the best of all the jobs in this funny place."

"I'm sure," said Caroline. She turned to Del. "I keep forgetting to ask your father. What does a secretary of state *do?*"

Del laughed. Helen did not; she said, "He conducts all foreign relations . . ."

Del said, through her, "Father says he has three jobs. One is to fight off foreign governments when they make claims against us.

Two, to help American citizens in their claims against foreign governments, usually fraudulent; and three, to provide jobs that don't exist for the friends of senators who do."

"What senator got you Pretoria?" asked Day.

Del looked contented. "That was the President. Every now and then he gets a job he can give away himself, and so Pretoria is mine."

"We hate the Boers." Helen helped herself to a roast, whose weight on the serving-dish was such a strain on the liveried butler that his forearms trembled; but without compassion she hacked and shoved at the lamb. "We are for the British everywhere."

"Maybe you are, but we're not back where I come from," said Day.

"Actually, we're neutral." Del frowned at Helen. "That's my job in South Africa, to be neutral."

"I won't give you away." Day grinned. "But Colonel Bryan's positive your father and the Major have made all sorts of secret arrangements with the British."

"Never!" Del seemed truly alarmed. "If we have any policy it's to get the British out of the Caribbean, out of the Pacific . . ."

"Out of Canada?" asked Caroline.

"Well, why not? The Major ran as a believer in the eventual, mutual, more perfect, union between Canada and the United States, because we're all of us English-speaking, you see . . ."

"Except," said Caroline, "for the millions who speak French."

"That's right," said Del, not listening. It was a characteristic of Washington, Caroline had noticed—or was it politics?—that no one ever listened to anyone who did not have at least access to power. But Day had heard her; and he murmured in her ear, "Back home we figure these fancy folks here are no better than foreigners."

"I should love to go back home with you. Where is it?"

Day listed, very briefly, the pleasures of his Southwestern state. Then the latest rumors about Admiral Dewey were discussed. Would he be the Democratic choice for president? Day thought that Dewey could defeat Bryan at the convention. But could Dewey then defeat McKinley? He thought not. The country was, suddenly, marvelously prosperous. The war had given a great impetus to business. Expansion was a tonic; even the farmers—Day's future constituency—were less desperate than usual. Finally, Helen shifted the subject to Newport, Rhode Island, and Day fell silent; and Caroline held her own, as the uses to which the summer should be put were analyzed. Apparently, Helen and her sister, Alice, planned to divide the Newport season between them. They would not go together: too many Hays, as it were, on the market. Would Caroline join one or the other of them? Caroline said that she might, if she were invited, but no one, she lied, had invited her. Actually, Mrs. Jack Astor, after making Caroline promise never to play tennis with her husband, had invited her for July, and Caroline had said that everything would depend on the state of some unfinished business. Mrs. Jack hoped that her bridge was good. Colonel Jack no longer played bridge: "It's wonderful to be inside when he's outside. Almost as satisfying as divorce." Mrs. Jack was definitely racy. She had always played tennis when her husband played bridge. Now that he had taken to the courts she had taken to the card-table. "We cannot be together," she would say, as if quoting some biblical text.

Halfway across Lafayette Park, Del put his arm through Caroline's. Helen and Day, not touching, were up ahead, long shadows cast in front of them by dull street lamps which emphasized the sylvan nature of the square's confusion of ill-tended trees and bushes, criss-crossed by paths, all converging on General Jackson's monument. "I suppose I must ask sometime." Del was nervous.

"Ask what?" Caroline felt, again, tears come to her eyes. Just who, she suddenly wondered, was she? Plainly, some part of her had never been introduced to the other.

"Well, would you marry me! I mean—*will* you marry me?"

The second invitation to a lifelong relationship had arrived, so to speak, in the mail. "Oh, no!" she exclaimed, astonishing both of them. "I mean, oh, no, not *now*." She lowered her voice to a more lady-like level. "No, not now," she improvised, feebly.

"You don't want to go to Pretoria, I can understand that." Del sounded glum. To their right, St. John's Church more than ever looked like a mad Hellenist's dream of ancient Greece (the columned portico) and Byzantium (the gold-domed tower).

"No, I don't want *not* to go to Pretoria." Caroline paused; the tears had dried on her face. "I think I have put too many negatives in that sentence."

"Well, just one is too many for me."

"It's not Pretoria. It's not you. It's me. And Blaise. And business."

"We have all summer," said Del, "to do your business in. Then . . ."

"Well, then—anything. I want," she said, to her own surprise, "to be married. To, that is," she added, surprising herself for what she hoped would be the last time, "you."

So the unofficial engagement was unofficially arrived at in the dark shadow of the Romanesque monument of the Hay-Adams house, glaring like some medieval monk across the square at the rather sporty, slightly louche, White House.

Unfinished business began the next day when Cousin John arrived at her house in a "herdic cab," a local invention, consisting mostly of glass, like a royal coach. "You can see everything," he said, as they drove along Fourteenth Street, between Pennsylvania Avenue and F Street. "This was what they used to call Newspaper Row."

Caroline saw a line of irregular red brick houses, very much in the style of the rest of the old part of the city. At the end of the line was Willard Hotel, covered with scaffolding: it was to be enlarged, redone. Willard's also faced on Pennsylvania Avenue and the recently completed—after a third of a century, everyone said with some awe—Treasury Building. At the other end of Newspaper Row was the Ebbitt House, a large hotel that stayed open even in the summer months, a true novelty. On the front of one of the red brick buildings was a faded sign, *The New York Herald.*

"All the newspapers have offices here?"

Sanford nodded. "During the war Washington *was* the news, for the first time, ever. So the journalists set up shop along here." Then he pointed across F Street. "Your friend Mr. Hay's Western Union is right across the street, and, of course, there's Willard's, where *all* the politicians used to gather—and still gather—in the bars and barber shops and dining rooms. Then when they felt particularly inspired, they'd wander across the street here, and talk to the newspaper boys."

"But the row has moved . . ."

"Regrouped." The carriage paused in front of the *Evening Star*'s building, which occupied the block between Eleventh and Twelfth Streets on Pennsylvania Avenue, a four-storey brick building painted yellow. "The color," Caroline noted, "must be a recent tribute to Mr. Hearst."

"No doubt." Sanford frowned. "Your plan . . ." he began.

"Nothing ventured," she concluded. Caroline quite liked the look of what she now took to be her future city.

The carriage turned into Pennsylvania Avenue. Down the avenue's center, there were two streetcar tracks, parallel to one another. Electrical cars glided, more or less smoothly, from northwest, the Treasury, to southeast, the Capitol, and back again. Unlike New York City, Washington had few automobiles: "devil wagons," according to the large black woman who presided over the N Street kitchen. As always, Caroline was struck by the number of black people; they seemed to *be* the city while everyone else was, like herself, a transient member of an alien race. "A city of hotels," she said, as they passed a huge Romanesque building, with a turreted tower.

"And medieval cathedrals." Sanford did not appreciate the great new post office, behind which had once flourished Marble Alley, with its thousand brothels, once known locally as "Hooker's division" since the girls had been so busily employed by that general's troops.

"The influence of Mr. Adams?"

"His architect's, yes. Washington, thanks to Mr. Richardson, has leapt from first-century Rome to twelfth-century Avignon, with almost nothing in between."

"That means there's still a renaissance to look forward to." The carriage turned into E Street, and stopped before yet another Adams-influenced building, all low arches and high-peaked roofs. Across the building's pale rough stone front, a sign proclaimed: *The Washington Post.* Out-of-town newspapers also maintained offices in the *Post*'s building, their names inscribed on upper windows. Caroline duly noted that the *New York Journal* and *San Francisco Examiner* shared an office. Mr. Hearst had already dropped his anchor at the capital in the form of a scandalously brilliant California newspaperman called Ambrose Bierce. The *Pittsburgh Dispatch* and the *Cleveland Plain Dealer* also advertised from fourth-story windows. The names of these newspapers, unknown to her a few months ago, now caused pleasurable reverberations in her head.

In front of the *Post* building, there was a large newsstand where out-of-town—and even out-of-hemisphere—newspapers were on sale. Beneath an awning, next to the busy newsstand, a high blackboard stood, covered with mysterious white and yellow lines.

"What is that for? A lottery?"

"Baseball scores. From all over the country."

"Is that the game," asked Caroline, "they play with a wooden stick?"

"Yes." Sanford smiled. "As someone who is about to become deeply involved in American life, I suggest you know all about baseball." Sanford now led her into Gerstenberg's Restaurant, next door to the *Post*. The interior was smoky, and smelled of vinegar—of sauerkraut, to be exact, she decided sadly; she had never been inclined to German cuisine. A German waiter in shirt-sleeves and red galluses led them past the crowded bar. "Newspapermen," whispered Sanford, as if warning her of lepers in a lazaret.

They were established at a table in the back, close to the swing-door to the kitchen. Huge schooners of beer sailed past them, and any moment Caroline expected to be drowned by one; but the waiters were as dextrous as they were loud. Then the man they had come to meet joined them.

Josiah J. Vardeman was a mulatto. Quite unprepared for anyone so exotic, Caroline gazed in fascination at the red kinky hair, café au lait skin and unmistakably Negroid features in which were set pale gray eyes. Mr. Vardeman was not yet forty; dapper in appearance; elaborate in manners. "I am late, Miss Sanford. Forgive me. I have been with advertisers. You can imagine. Good to see you again, Mr. Sanford."

Caroline stared at Sanford, who looked at her innocently. He had intended to surprise her; and he had succeeded. "I see you are tolerant of the opposition," she said. Vardeman looked bewildered; she explained, "I mean you come *here* . . ."

"Oh, yes. A German place. But then my father's family were German. From the Rhineland."

"I meant *here*, next to your opposition, the *Washington Post*."

"Oh, that." He laughed. "Well, we are so much older. We can afford to be nice to the new folks. I'm not saying I wouldn't mind having some of their advertisers. They're good at business, those people. We're not, sad to say. But we Vardemans are an old family, and I guess old families lose some of their vigor, don't they? Europe's full of that, I reckon."

Caroline then knew delight. "*Old* family? Oh, Mr. Vardeman, we're all of us—everyone there is—as old as Adam and Eve and no older."

"I am second to none in my belief in Scripture, Miss Sanford, but families that have had great men in them sort of dry up at the roots, you might say, and the next crop or two don't amount to all that much."

"I wouldn't know. My own family is nondescript except for one ancestor, perhaps." How on earth, she wondered, could she get this extraordinary creature deeper into genealogy?

"Who is that?" he asked.

"Oh, no one very highly regarded nowadays, or even known—Aaron Burr," she said, hoping that the name would mean absolutely nothing.

She was disappointed. Vardeman clapped his hands. "We are practically related!" Caroline was pleased to see that a number of surprised, not to mention suspicious, looks were turned in their direction. Cousin John looked very pale indeed; to compensate, no doubt, for this new relation. "My mother was a Jefferson. One of the Abilene, Maryland, Jeffersons. So your ancestor was my ancestor's vice-president."

Caroline expressed delight and wonder. She had always heard that Jefferson had had a number of children by a mulatto slave girl; no doubt, this was the descendant of one of them, passing, as perhaps they all did by now, for white. In any case, Caroline knew that she had at least one thing in common with Mr. Josiah J. (for Jefferson?) Vardeman: each was descended, literally, from a bastard. Now it was her task to have something else in common.

"I am interested, as my cousin has told you, in acquiring the *Washington Tribune*. I have developed a passion for newspapers . . ."

"Devilish expensive passion," murmured Sanford, lighting a cigar. Caroline felt like a man; like a *business* man. This was life. She wished that she knew how to smoke! A cigarette smoked openly in a German restaurant would quite overshadow Mrs. Fish's girlish capers at lofty Sherry's. Mr. Vardeman, lineage forgotten, was watching her attentively. "There are," she said, "five thousand shares in all, and all owned by you or your family."

"Yes. It's always been a family newspaper. First, Mr. Wallach owned it. Then he started up the *Evening Star*. I'm third generation of his family. A cadet branch," he added, not knowing, Caroline decided, what the phrase meant.

Caroline took a deep breath; and inhaled her cousin's cigar smoke. No, she would not take up cigarettes, she decided; she coughed once, and said: "I accept your offer of twenty-two dollars and fifty cents for each of the five thousand shares." Next to her, Sanford coughed. She had taken him by surprise. But she had not taken herself by surprise. She had spent a lot of time in N Street, thinking. She was betting almost everything that she had on a single throw of the dice.

Mr. Vardeman stared at her, as if not certain whether he was being included in a particularly high-toned verbal game. Then, as she gave no signal that she was anything other than serious, he said, "What will you do with a newspaper, if I may ask? They're not easy or cheap to run, as I can tell you firsthand. The *Tribune* loses money every issue. We'd have to close down if it weren't for our printing shop, and all those visiting cards they make for everybody. Mr. Sanford's told you about our books, I guess." Mr. Vardeman had finished his stein of beer. At the bottom of the now-empty mug, Caroline noted the ominous legend "Stolen from Gerstenberg's."

"Indeed I have," said Cousin John. "And there's no doubt that the *Tribune*'s name is a great one in the city. But the *Post* and the *Star* have sewed up the town. What can anyone do to change that?" He looked at Vardeman, who looked at Caroline, who said, "I'm sure there are new things to be done. Who would have thought Mr. Hearst could have revived the *New York Journal?*" This was a daring move, because for all that Caroline knew, Blaise and Hearst might already have been in correspondence with Vardeman. On the other hand, she had had tea with Phoebe Apperson Hearst, the sweetly stern mother of the most ambitious man in publishing, if not the United States, and Mrs. Hearst had said, "I have spent all that I intend on my son's newspapers. I now want to spend money on educating young Americans."

"So that they will be too clever to read your son's newspapers?"

The old lady had looked, first, severe; then she had laughed. "I had not thought of that." Then she had proceeded to speak longingly of California, and of a university at an exotic place called Palo Alto. What her son was doing for journalism, she would do for education. Plainly, mother and son would be forever at cross-purposes.

"Mr. Hearst's people were down here a few months ago. They

looked over the plant, the books, everything. They're still very interested." Vardeman's attempt at selling was perfunctory. He did not expect anyone to pay the price he was asking for what was, essentially, a run-down printer's shop.

"Do we have," asked Caroline tentatively, "an agreement?"

Solemnly, Vardeman extended his hand across the table. Solemnly, Caroline shook it. "The *Tribune*," said the now former publisher, "is no longer a Wallach-Jefferson-Vardeman newspaper—after forty-two long, long years," he added somewhat anticlimactically.

"It is now a Sanford newspaper." Caroline felt a ringing in her ears which could be either victory, or nausea from too much cigar smoke.

Vardeman himself took her through the *Tribune* offices, in a three-story brick building with arched windows that looked out on the north side of Market Square, a curiously ill-defined, and hardly square, open area between Seventh and Ninth Streets on Pennsylvania Avenue. "A wonderful location," said Vardeman, sincerely. "This is the heart of the commercial district, where all our advertisers are."

"Or will be," said Cousin John.

Caroline stood on the dirty stoop beneath the faded sign *Washington Tribune* and looked across the square, a riot of electrical and telephone wires, of turreted red brick modern buildings in the medieval style which she realized that Henry Adams, in his serenely ruthless way, was imposing on the capital city. To Caroline's left the Center Market loomed, a combination of windowed exposition hall and Provencal cathedral, whose brick walls were the color of dried blood—Washington's emblematic color, in which were set not stained-glass windows but dusty panes of conservatory glass. Here farmers from Virginia and Maryland brought their produce; and here in the vast interior, democracy reigned, with everyone buying and selling. Vardeman identified two banks in nearby C Street. "The one on the left held our mortgage," he said. "But not any more."

They entered a small waiting room, where no one waited. Dusty creaking stairs led to the offices and the newsroom, while a corridor, the length of the small building, led to the presses which were located in a converted stables at the back. Caroline could never get enough of the actual business of printing. Rolls of paper affected her rather the way bolts of silk affected Mrs. Jack Astor, while the smell of printer's ink gave her not only an instant headache but, equally, swift delight. In a pleasurable haze, she met her new employees. The chief printer was the money-maker; and appropriately grave. He was German; spoke with an accent; came from the Palatinate. Caroline spoke German to him; and was certain that she had won his heart. Cousin John asked to see invoices; and lost the newly gained heart.

The editorial offices overlooked Market Place. The editor was a tall Southerner, with red hair and side-whiskers. "This is Mr. Trimble, the best editor in Washington, and a Washingtonian, too. Almost as much a native as the darkies," Vardeman added; he was prone, Caroline had noticed, to mentioning darkies rather more often than was entirely necessary. "What," asked Caroline, "*is* a true native?"

"Oh, you've just got to be born here. I mean, you don't have to be like Mr. Sanford's Apgar relatives, who go back to the first day." The voice was high but not unpleasant.

"Are there Washington Apgars?"

Cousin John nodded. "Apgars are everywhere. They outnumber everyone else because they marry everyone. Some of them came here in 1800, I think. They were in dry," said Cousin John sadly, "goods."

"My family came with General Jackson," said Mr. Trimble. "You can always tell when us natives got here by our names. The Trimbles, like the Blairs, came with Jackson, and after we settled in, we never went home, any more than the Blairs did. Nobody goes back to Nashville if he can help it."

"But the President—Jackson, that is—does, or did," said Caroline, charmed by her new editor.

"Well, he couldn't help it," said Mr. Trimble. "What do you intend to do with the old *Trib?*"

"Why—be successful!" Caroline's ears were now ringing again; she wondered if she was about to faint. Where once there had been four Poussins there was now a newspaper and a printer's shop in an African city half a world away from home. Was she mad? she wondered. More important, could she win? She was certain that in the war with Blaise she had just won a significant battle if not the war itself, but Blaise was now, oddly, secondary to the newspaper, which was hers—became hers, as she sat at a rolltop desk to write out the second and final payment on her account at the Morgan Bank; and gave it to Vardeman, who then signed the various documents that Cousin John had brought with him. The transfer was complete.

"You will see a lot of me, Mr. Trimble." Caroline was now at the door. "I'm here for at least a year. Maybe forever."

"Are we to continue as before?"

"Oh, yes. Nothing is to be changed, except the circulation."

"How will you change that?" asked Vardeman, with something less than his habitual ceremony: the check in hand gave him gravity.

"Have you no murders to report?" asked Caroline.

"Well, sure. I mean, we put the police news on the last page, like always. But it's just the usual. A body found floating in the river . . ."

"Surely, from time to time, a beautiful woman is pulled out of the muddy cold dark Potomac river. A beautiful young woman perhaps divided into sections, and wearing only a negligee."

"Caroline," murmured Cousin John, so shocked that he used, in public, her first name.

"I'm sorry. I'm sorry, you're right. No negligee could survive being quartered."

"The *Tribune* is a serious paper," said Vardeman, thick lips suddenly compressed like punctured bicycle tires. "Devoted to the Republican Party, to the tariff . . ."

"Well, Mr. Trimble, let us never forget our seriousnes. But let us also remember that a beautiful young woman, murdered in a crime of passion, is also a serious figure if only to herself, while the crime—murder—is the most serious of all, in peacetime, that is."

"You want . . . uh, *yellow* journalism, Miss Sanford?" Trimble was staring at her, a look of amusement in his pale blue eyes.

"Yellow, ochre, café au lait," tactlessly, she looked at yellow-brown Vardeman, "I don't care what color. No, that's not true. I am partial to gold."

"What about the gold standard?" asked Cousin John, eager to make light of everything that she had said.

"As a friend of Mr. Hay, I favor that, too. Whatever," Caroline added as graciously as she could, "it is. You see, Mr. Trimble, I am a serious woman."

"Yes, Miss, I see that all right, and I'll send someone over to police headquarters right now to see what they got in the morgue."

Caroline recalled Hearst on the floor, making up the front page of the *Journal*, the murdered woman slowly coming, as it were, alive under the embellishments. "Do that," she said. "But remember that the illustration on the front page . . ."

"Front page," groaned Vardeman, looking out at Market Square.

". . . need not resemble too closely what is actually in the morgue."

"But we . . . you . . . the *Tribune* is a *news*paper," said Vardeman.

"No," said Caroline. "It is not a newspaper. Because there is no such thing as a newspaper. News is what we decide it is. Oh, how I love saying 'we.' It is a sign of perfect ignorance, isn't it?" The ringing in her ears had stopped; she had never felt so entirely in command of herself. "Obviously earthquakes and election results and the scores of . . . *baseball* teams," she was proud to have remembered the name of the national sport, "are news, and must be duly noted. But the rest of what we print is literature, of a kind that is meant to entertain and divert and excite our readers so that they will buy the things our advertisers will want to sell them. So we must be—imaginative, Mr. Trimble."

"I shall do my best, Miss Sanford."

In the street Cousin John turned on her, with unfeigned anger. "You can't be serious . . ."

"I have never been more serious. No." She stopped herself. "That's not true. What I mean to say is that I have never been serious about anything until now."

"Caroline, this is . . . this is . . ." He launched like an anathema the word. "Corruption."

"Corruption? Of what? The newspaper readers of Washington? Hardly. They know it all. Of the *Tribune*, a dull, dying paper? The word doesn't apply. I see no corruption in what I mean to do. Perhaps," she was judicious, "we shall offer a true *reflection* of the world about us. But you cannot blame a mirror for what it shows."

"But your mirror willfully distorts . . ."

"A newspaper has no choice. It must be partisan in one way or another. But where is the corruption in this case?"

"An appeal to base appetites . . ."

"Will increase circulation. I did not make those appetites base."

"But *that* is corrupt, to pander to them."

"To gain readers? Surely, a small price to pay for . . ." Caroline stopped; a herdic cab had seen them, and now drew up to the front step.

"To pay for what?"

"To pay, Cousin John, for power. The only thing worth having in this democracy of yours." More than a generation separated Caroline from Henry Adams's Mrs. Lightfoot Lee; now, Caroline decided, it was possible for a woman to achieve what she wanted on her own and not through marriage, or some similar surrogate. She had not realized to what an extent Mlle. Souvestre had given her confidence. She not only did not fear failure, she did not expect it. "Which is probably proof that I am mad," she said to Cousin John, as he helped her down from the cab, in the dense lemon-scented shade of the twin magnolia trees.

"I don't need any proof of that," he said, quite ignoring the nonsequitur nature of her remark: they had been talking of Blaise and Mr. Houghteling and the ever more intricate games that were now being played at law.

Caroline led her cousin into the house, to be greeted by Marguerite with complaints about the cook, who appeared, rumbling what sounded like powerful voodoo curses against Marguerite. As usual, the crisis was based upon misunderstanding. Parisian French and Afro-American seemed always at cross-purposes. Caroline was placating the confusion of two languages, as she led Cousin John into the narrow, dim, cool drawing room that ran the length of the small house, where they sat in front of a fireplace of white marble, filled now with ceramic pots containing early roses, an innovation that had caused deep laughter in the kitchen: "Flowers is for the yard. Wood's for the fire."

"I wish you were more enthusiastic." Caroline wished there was a stronger word that she could use. But their relationship was insufficiently comfortable. He seemed to think that they might yet be engaged; and she allowed him to think this on the sensible ground that as anything is possible most things are improbable. Their cousinage was also a complication. He was, above all, a Sanford; and took himself seriously, *in loco parentis*.

"You must," said Cousin John, surprisingly, "meet *my* cousins, the Apgars. They live in Logan Circle. It's not the West End, of course; but old Washington still prefers that neighborhood. You should have some solid friends here."

"Unlike the Hays?" She was mischievous.

"The Hays are too grand to be of use, if you should need them, while the Apgars are always here and ready to . . ."

"In dry goods still?"

"One branch, yes. Apgar's Department Store is the second largest after Woodward and Lothrop. Most are lawyers. I have told the ladies to call."

"I'll ask the department store Apgars to advertise in the *Tribune*." Caroline was serious. "The spring sales—is that what they call them?—have started." She had become a devoted reader of advertisements.

"Well, you could *ask*, I suppose."

"Is Mr. Vardeman common?" Caroline suddenly recalled the reddish tight curls, sand-colored face.

"I should think very."

"No, I meant is it common for mulattoes to mix with the white people?"

Cousin John was amused. "No. But he has been allowed, in many circles, to pass, and that does happen here, in certain circles. I'd be much happier if you'd settle in New York, where you belong."

Caroline surveyed the naval mementoes on the wall opposite. A crude painting of a ship in flames, from the War of 1812, about which she knew nothing, beneath crossed sabres topped by a commodore's hat. Under glass, a torn British ensign. "I feel as if I've been transported to the Roman empire," she said. "You know, the interesting part, toward the end."

Cousin John laughed. "We think it's hardly begun, the United States."

"I'm sure you're right." But Caroline was sure of nothing about this peculiar country except that its excessiveness appealed to her: there was far too much of everything except history. But that would come, inexorably, and she meant to be, somehow, in the main stream of it. Suddenly, she saw history as nothing more than the Potomac River, swift yellow and swirling about dun-colored rocks that seemed to have been hurled down from the severe wooded heights of Virginia, where grew vines whose laurel-like leaves could cause human skin to erupt in itching sores. The likeness between victor's laurel and victim's poison ivy had not been lost upon Caroline when she had first been warned by Helen Hay as they drove out to the bronze memorial that Henry Adams had commissioned Saint-Gaudens to create, a memorial to that dead Heart, Clover Adams. Almost as symbolic of the city as the poisoned laurel was the seated, sorrowing veiled figure, with no inscription and, oddly, no agreed-upon sex: it could be a young man, or a young woman. Characteristically, Henry Adams would not say which.

"I shall see Apgars." Caroline was reassuring. "Besides, I shall have no choice, this summer, with everyone gone."

"You won't stay either." Cousin John was firm. "The heat is intolerable."

"I can tolerate quite a lot. But I shall occasionally long for the cool of . . ." She stopped.

"Newport, Rhode Island?"

"No. Saint-Cloud. Is the house mine or not?"

"Divided, until a decision's made. What next—with Blaise?"

"I don't know. I shall see what he has to offer me now."

During the next week Caroline spent most of each day at the office of the *Tribune*. She got to know Mr. Trimble as well as she thought she should know an employee who was also a man and not a servant, a new sort of relationship for her. She spoke to the printer in German; tried to inspire him to an even greater output of visiting cards, wedding and funeral announcements, invitations of every sort, but the season was drawing to a close and not even her exhortations could inspire the government ladies to pay more calls on one another, or to excite even more young couples to the altars of Protestant St. John's or of Catholic St. Mary's. Most of her evenings were spent behind the magnolia sentinels, teaching Marguerite—and the African woman—English. Del was put off for the moment while she considered the awesome fact of matrimony and Pretoria, in reverse order, actually; but Del did not know that Cousin John had retreated to New York and his other life, the law. Mr. Hay was trying to avoid a war with England over Canada or with Canada over England. Caroline was amused to note that Hay never referred to Canada by name; only as "Our Lady of the Snows." Thus far, no Apgar lady had called at N Street. Thus far, no new advertisers had called at the *Tribune* offices. But Caroline was well pleased by Trimble's efforts to emulate Hearst. A corpse or two had found its way to the front page for the first time, ever. Each corpse had resulted in a dozen cancellations; each corpse had sold a thousand more newspapers on the stands. Caroline now knew what it was to be Hearst; but without his resources.

On a Wednesday afternoon, Caroline was in the compositor's room, studying the next day's front page with her printer. A cat slept on the window-sill, oblivious to the noises of Market Square. In the next room she could hear Trimble's voice, coaxing an advertiser. Disloyally, Caroline moved from the first to the third page a story concerning the Virgin Islands, which Hay thought that the United States might be obliged to buy from Denmark for the five million dollars made available by the Senate, courtesy of Senator Lodge. A robbery in the West End, specifically Connecticut Avenue, took the place of the Virgin Islands, and one Mrs. Benedict Tracy Bingham was now world-famous—or capitally famous—for having been robbed during the night of her diamonds. Caroline had inserted the adjective "fabulous" before the word "diamonds," despite the objection of the elderly reporter, who had said, "They were just run-of-the-mill stuff, Miss Sanford. A pin. A ring. Earrings."

"But aren't the Binghams rich?" Caroline toyed with the notion of a crime ring: "Connecticut Avenue's Reign of Terror" she saw a headline (as usual, with her, too long); then a sub-headline: "Where will the thieves strike next?"

"The Binghams own the Silversmith Dairies. They advertise with us, or used to. Yes, ma'am, they're rich enough. But the jewels—"

"Priceless heirlooms of one of Washington's oldest and most aristocratic families," Caroline had added to the story. "If that does not delight the Binghams, nothing will," she said to Trimble, who was amused but dubious, as always, of her inspirations. "We shall be awash with milk advertising," she promised now that Mrs. Benedict Tracy Bingham's jewels were about to be first-page news, and her place in the city's highly fluid patriciate inscribed boldly if not in a book of gold in meaningful type-set.

The black doorkeeper stood in the doorway. "There's a gentleman, Miss, who wants to talk to the publishers, to Mr. Vardeman."

"What about?" Caroline picked up an engraving of the Bingham mansion; and indicated that it was to be at the center of the column.

"He says he's from Mr. Hearst. His name's the same as yours, Miss."

Caroline stood up straight; seized the nearest of many rags and rubbed, as best she could, the ink smudges from her fingers. "Did you tell him who the publisher is?"

"No, ma'am. He was pretty clear he wanted to see Mr. Vardeman."

"I'll see him in the office." Caroline had taken for herself a small dim room overlooking the printing shed in the brick yard. A framed copy of her first front page was behind the modest desk ("Body of unknown beauty found nude at Navy Yard"). Two incongruous Louis XVI chairs were the only furniture in the room. The spring's first flies made mid-air carousels.

Blaise was satisfyingly astonished. "What are you doing here? Where's Vardeman?"

"Mr. Vardeman is devoting his time to genealogy. He is descended from Thomas Jefferson, he believes, which gives the two of us a lot to talk about . . ."

"You bought the *Trib?*"

"I bought the *Trib.*"

They faced one another: implacable enemies as only the identical can be. "You did this to spite me."

"Or delight me. Sit down, Blaise."

Sulkily, he turned the gilded chair backwards and straddled it as if he were riding a horse. Demurely, she sat at her desk, strewn with unpaid bills. She wished now that she had paid more attention to Mlle. Souvestre's excellent but dull teacher of mathematics.

"How much," asked Blaise, "did it cost you?"

"Two or three Poussins."

"*My* pictures!"

"*Our* pictures. I shall pay you your share, of course, when you give me my share of—"

"That's for the lawyers." Blaise was looking about the dismal office. Caroline was pleased at the amount of squalor she could endure. She regretted that she had not followed her first impulse to hang on the wall a lurid four-color portrait of Admiral Dewey, with the legend "Our Hero."

"You can't be serious," said Blaise.

"I've never understood why whenever someone is truly serious, someone always says that. Of course I'm serious. I am," Caroline lowered her lashes shyly, the way Helen Hay did when the waiter brought around dessert, "working here, as publisher and editor, just like Mr. Hearst."

Blaise laughed, without joy. He had seen the framed front page; and guessed that it was her work. "There's more to this than murders," he said.

"Yes. There's Mrs. Hearst's money to pay his debts. Or was. She goes back to California. She will not help him any longer."

"Who'll pay *your* debts? The old *Trib* loses money like a sieve."

"I suppose that I will. From the estate."

Blaise swept the gold chair to one side; and walked over to the window and stared through the fly-specked glass at the print shop beneath. "*That* makes money. The paper loses it." He turned around. "How much do you want?"

"I'm not selling."

"Everything has its price."

Caroline laughed. "You've been in New York too long! That's the sort of thing very fat men say at Rector's. But not everything is for sale. The *Tribune*'s mine."

"Mr. Hearst will pay you double what you paid, which must have been around fifty thousand dollars."

"He hasn't got the money, I know. I have met his mother."

"One hundred fifty thousand dollars." Blaise sat on the window-sill. He wore a light gray coat which was now, visibly, beginning to darken from the room's dust. "For everything. That's three times what this wreck of a paper's worth."

Caroline thought Blaise uncommonly attractive at this moment. Anger was his invigorating emotion. What was her own? Time would answer that, she decided; and then she made Blaise gloriously beautiful, by turning mere anger to plain fury with the words: "You don't want to buy this for Mr. Hearst. You want to buy it for yourself. You are double, as the fat men say at Rector's, crossing him."

"Damn you!" Blaise sprang from the window-sill, the back of his gray frock coat veined with spider-webs and the mummies of a dozen flies who had found in the *Tribune*'s window frame their final Egypt.

"I might—if you stop damning me—let you have half the paper if you let me have my half of the . . ."

"Blackmail! You come here behind my back, knowing that I . . . knowing that the Chief must have a Washington paper, and tricked that nigger into selling—"

"I didn't trick him. And is he really a nigger? The subject is very delicate here. It is like the Knights of Malta. You know, how many family quarterings can you produce? Anyway, if you're interested, there is a very engaging Negro newspaper here called the *Washington Bee*. Since niggers and—by association?—blackmail so much concern you, you should talk to the proprietor, a Mr. Chase. I can introduce you. He is, perhaps, too moral for Mr. Hearst, but he might sell, and then you—or Hearst—will have a true Washington paper, entirely black, like the town."

Blaise looked less attractive as fury was replaced by anger, and a revival of his native cunning. "How can you pay all those bills on your desk . . . ?"

"I didn't know you could read upside down."

"Red ink, yes."

"I have my income, such as it is. I have," she improvised, "helpful friends."

"Cousin John? Well, he can't help you, and John Hay doesn't dare unless he wants the *Journal* down on him."

"I don't think he's afraid of Mr. Hearst, or much of anyone. You see, he has," she explained demurely, "a bad back." Caroline rose. They faced one another at the room's center. As they were the same height, blue eyes glared straight into hazel ones.

"I won't give up any part of the estate," said Blaise.

"I won't give up the *Tribune*."

"Unless you go broke."

"Or sell it to Mr. Hearst, and not to you."

Blaise was pale now; he looked exhausted. Caroline recalled a precocious girl at Allenswood who had actually been seduced. The girl's highly secret report to Caroline, her best friend, was the only firsthand account that Caroline had ever received from that strange country where men and women committed the ultimate act. Although Caroline had pressed for specific details (the statuary in the Louvre had created a number of confusions, *those leaves*), the girl had been, maddeningly, spiritual in her report. She spoke of Love, a subject that always mystified, when it did not annoy, Caroline; and could not be persuaded to tear the leaf from the mystery. But the girl had described the transformation in the young man's face from the archangel that she saw him to satyr or, a kindly second thought, wild animal, and how the face, all scarlet one moment, went gray-white, with exhaustion, or whatever, the next. So Blaise now resembled a lover at transport's end. But what, Caroline wondered, was the transport itself like? Mlle. Souvestre had suggested that if her students were really curious about what she always referred to with not-so-delicate irony as "married life," they study Bernini's *Saint Teresa* at Rome. "Allegedly, the saint is in the throes of religious ecstasy, the eyes are closed, the mouth is disagreeably ajar. The expression is cretinous. It is said that Bernini was inspired not by God but by the *grandest* of human passions." When asked if "married life" at its peak was similar to a confrontation with the Holy Ghost, Mademoiselle had said firmly, "I am a freethinker and a virgin. You must apply elsewhere for instruction in ecstasy, and *after* you have left Wimbledon."

"Come," said Caroline graciously, "let me show you the paper."

Together they entered the long compositors' rooms. Trimble, in shirt-sleeves, was correcting a galley at the long table. The cat was still asleep in the window. The city reporter was writing on a new typewriter-machine, bought by Caroline during the second day of her proprietorship. "I find the noise of typing soothing," she said to the silent Blaise. "I am responsible for the Remington. It's what Henry James uses." Caroline looked at her pale brother expectantly; but his silence, if possible, deepened. "I've asked the reporters *not* to achieve the same results. Fortunately, they only admire Stephen Crane and Richard Harding Davis. This is the managing editor, Mr. Trimble."

The two men shook hands, and Caroline said, as an afterthought, "My half-brother Blaise Sanford. He works with Mr. Hearst, at the *Journal*."

"Now there is a paper." Trimble was flattering. "You know, last winter we heard a rumor that you people were going to buy us."

"Since then Mr. Hearst has drawn in his horns," said Caroline. "He's not acquiring for the moment."

"What's your paid circulation?" asked Blaise.

"Around seven thousand," said Trimble.

"I was told ten last winter."

"Mr. Vardeman liked to exaggerate, I guess. Our advertising's increased in the last month," he added.

"Cousin John got us Apgar's Department Store. They are having their sales now."

The political reporter, thin of neck, red of cheek and eye, already partly drunk, approached. "Mr. Trimble, here's an item. I don't suppose it's worth bothering with. From the White House."

"Oh, dear," said Caroline. Although she was personally fascinated by politicians if not politics, she found the subject, as dealt with by the press, sinister in its dullness. Only those who were themselves political could find exciting or even fascinating the *Tribune*'s political news. Happily, most of newspaper-reading

Washington was involved in government and they would read any political news. But Caroline, as always in imitation of Hearst, wanted to extend the readership to those who found politics as dull as she did, the majority. Graphic details of murders, robberies, rapes were what people wanted to read, a lurid golden thread running through the gray pages. But she wanted even more diversions for her readers—or readers-to-be. The political reporter, as if sent by Heaven, now gave her exactly what she wanted.

"I was over talking to Mr. Cortelyou . . ."

"The President's secretary," said Caroline, helpfully, to Blaise, who was again turning a healthy pre-transport red.

"He said there's no news from the Philippines. Then when asked what the President was doing at the moment, he said, 'He's out driving,' and I said, 'Well, that's not much of a story,' and he said, 'Well, he's driving in a *motor car* for the first time.' So there's an item, I guess. A smallish item, I guess."

Trimble sighed. "A very smallish item. For the social page."

"No," said Caroline. "For the front page." She had never felt so entirely heroic as she did now, showing off to Blaise.

"What's the lead?" asked Trimble.

"First president ever to drive in an automobile." Caroline was prompt.

"But is that true?" asked Trimble.

"Mr. Hearst wouldn't care, and, I'm afraid, I don't either."

"I think it's true," said the political reporter. "Grover Cleveland tried to get into a motor car several years ago. But because he's so fat, he wouldn't fit. Fact, nothing fits him except this one orange summer suit that his young wife hates, and finally got him to give away when she threatened to denounce him to the Irish as an Ulsterman."

"Wonderful!" Caroline was indeed pleased. "That's what we want in your story. Do write it all. Now."

As the reporter was shuffling toward the Remington, Caroline stopped him. "What sort of motor car was it?"

"A Stanley Steamer, Miss Sanford."

Caroline turned to Trimble. "Put that in the sub-head. Then we shall ask the Stanley Steamer people to advertise."

"Well . . ." Trimble was grinning now; he had got her range. Then both started as the door to the room was slammed shut. Blaise had fled.

"Your brother's kind of . . . moody?"

"Well, his mood is certainly black today. He and Mr. Hearst did want this paper. In fact, he just asked me to sell it to him, and I said no."

Trimble frowned. "Would you make a profit?"

"Yes."

"You should sell. We haven't a chance. The *Star* and the *Post* have us beat."

Caroline's pleasure in the Stanley Steamer story was now replaced by that sense of doom which often visited her when she awakened in the early hours of the morning, and wondered what on earth she was doing in a small house in Georgetown, publishing a newspaper that might, eventually, ruin her. "If it's so hopeless, why does Hearst want to buy?"

"He'll pour in money. He don't care what he loses. And he'll have a Washington power-base. He's running for president."

Caroline was momentarily distracted. "How do you know that?"

"Friend at the *Journal* told me. Hearst thinks Bryan can't win, and he can."

"How curious! The first time I spoke to him, he said he wanted Admiral Dewey." But Caroline had grasped a point interesting to her in a way that politics was not. "You haven't been talking to the *Journal* about a job, have you?"

Trimble's pale blue eyes now avoided her own, she hoped, steady gaze. "We're losing circulation every month," he said.

"Not on the newsstands."

"That's no money really. Advertising rates are fixed by your paid subscriptions."

"Then we'll hold a—what is it?—you know, money for nothing? A lottery."

"With what money?"

"If you stay, I'll go in deeper."

Trimble looked at her, most curiously. "Why are you doing this?"

"I want to."

"Is that all?"

"I should think that that was everything."

"But no woman . . . no lady has ever run a newspaper that I know of, and there aren't many men who have the knack either."

"You will," said Caroline, no question in her voice and no appeal, "stay."

Trimble smiled. They shook hands gravely.

5

– I –

From one end to the other of the Brooklyn Bridge, electric lights spelled out "Welcome, Dewey," so many points of arctic light against the night sky; while downriver, the Admiral's flagship, the *Olympic*, was equally illuminated. Sirens blared. Occasional fireworks exploded along the Palisades. The hero of Manila had come home.

Blaise sat beside the Chief in the back of his motor car, the top put down the better to enjoy the display, and the cool autumn night. Madame de Bieville sat in the seat opposite, next to Millicent and Anita Willson. To Blaise's surprise, Anne was amused by the girls and, like all women, bemused by the Chief. For a week, Anne had taken the girls shopping in order to dress them up—or rather down—for Europe. Hearst had decided to go to Europe in November; winter would be spent aboard a yacht, on the Nile. Although Blaise had been cheated of his return to

202

Europe, Anne's arrival was consolation. Together they had gone to Newport, Rhode Island, and the fierce Delacroix grandmother had been openly scandalized and privately thrilled by the liaison between her youthful grandson and this French woman of the world. But like all good Newporters, Mrs. Delacroix dearly loved a French lady and a moneyed one was even more lovable. She had installed Madame in the east wing of her Grand Trianon and Blaise in the west wing, and when Mrs. Fish had suggested that there might be wedding bells between June and October, Mrs. Delacroix had said, in a voice, reputedly, of thunder, "Mamie, mind your own business." Mrs. Fish had done so: a business that included a picnic on the rocks by the sea, with Harry Lehr in charge of an artificial waterfall; but instead of water, champagne, sold by Lehr on commission, cascaded over the rocks.

Anne had said to Blaise that she now understood the French Revolution. Blaise had said that he now understood why there could never be an American revolution. The sumptuous extravagance of the rich suited everyone, particularly the readers of the *Journal*. It was still believed, he was magisterial, that in the United States anyone could strike it rich, like the Chief's father, and, once rich, "anyone" was obliged to live out every dream that everyone had ever had. There was still wealth to be had for the lucky; as for the rest, they could daydream, their imaginations fed by the *Journal*. Anne could not believe that it was possible to keep the unlucky forever content with stories of the fortunate and their extravagances, but Blaise thought it possible to string them, as the Chief would say, along forever, or as long as there were still mountains of gold and silver to be broken into and new inventions to be thought of. The native-born American still believed that hard work would earn him all the beef his family required; believed, also, that blind luck might translate him overnight to a palace on Fifth Avenue. The immigrants were somewhat different.

Blaise recalled a conversation with a manufacturer at Mrs. Fish's dinner table: "The Germans are the best workers, if they haven't been told about socialism and labor unions. The Irish are the worst, and always drunk. Dagos and niggers are lazy. All in all, the best worker is still your average Buckwheat." A "Buckwheat," it turned out, was the name employers gave to any sturdy young native-born Protestant from the countryside. The Buckwheat obeyed orders, worked hard and stayed sober. If he dreamed, he dreamed only the right sort of dreams, which might even come true. Anne found all of this mystifying. In France everyone knew his place; and wanted to change it or, more exciting, change someone else's for the worst. Of course, France was filled up, while the United States was still relatively empty. Although the frontier had ended with the invention of California, the newly acquired Caribbean Sea and Pacific Ocean were now American lakes, filled with rich islands and opportunities, and the far-away look could once again be detected in the noble Buckwheat's eyes. Blaise had composed a panegyric to the Buckwheat, and gave it to the managing editor, Arthur Brisbane, who took out everything original, including the word "Buckwheat," and published it in the *Sunday Journal*: "No derogatory nicknames for the native-born American," said Brisbane.

The Chief told the chauffeur to drive them downtown. "I want to see the arch lit up," he said. "I want to see Dewey," he added, looking at Blaise, as if Blaise were the Admiral's keeper. "I want to talk to him."

Blaise did his best to give an impression that he would deliver the Admiral to the *Journal* offices for the next day's editorial meeting. "The messenger to Manila," as the Chief's courier was known at the paper, had got nothing at all out of the old hero, who seemed interested only in his new admiral-ate. Mention of the presidency bored him, the courier had reported.

As the motor car glided through the cool autumnal darkness of Central Park, the Willson girls broke beautifully into song: "I Met Her by the Fountain in the Park," a particular favorite of the Chief, as well as of the girls, whose father, a buck-and-wing dancer-singer, had made the song famous in vaudeville. Hearst's high toneless voice joined in. Anne beat time with a gloved hand, and smiled at Blaise, who felt embarrassed. It was always hard to present the Chief to the world as a serious man; yet he was.

Just north of Madison Square on Fifth Avenue, the crowds began. Everyone was moving toward the arch which had been built over the avenue at Twenty-third Street. Special lights had been craftily arranged to illuminate the white magnificence of what the *Journal* had called the most splendid triumphal arch ever shaped by the hand of man. Mr. Brisbane, not Blaise, was the author of this hyperbole. But the huge version of Rome's arch of Septimius Severus was indeed impressive, despite the streetcars that passed, diagonally, in front of it, toward Broadway as it converged with Fifth Avenue. Three sets of columns on either side of the avenue made an approach to the arch. On top of the arch, a statue of Victory held a laurel wreath. Life-size military figures, entwined with banners, sabres, guns, adorned column-bases; upon the arch itself, the Admiral was depicted, a latter-day Nelson come home to glory in a confusion of floodlights, hansom cabs, motor cars and red-and-white bunting, courtesy of Knox's Hats on the Avenue's east side. The Hearst car stopped in front of Knox's, and even the Chief was impressed by the masses of people who, although it was after midnight, wanted to pay homage to the hero—or his monument.

As the horse of a hansom cab predictably reared in passing the alien motor car, the Chief observed with predictable pleasure, "Roosevelt must be chewing up the carpet with those big teeth of his." But Anne said, shrewdly, Blaise thought, "Why should he chew? The Admiral's old. He's young."

"Dewey's sixty-two. That's not too old to be president." The Chief looked uncharacteristically sullen. "He's in love."

"*At sixty-two?*" The Willson girls spoke as one; and everyone laughed. A newsboy, selling the *Journal*, waved a paper in Hearst's face. "Evening, Chief!"

"Hello, son." The Chief was again smiling; he gave the boy ten cents, to the ragged accompaniment of a group of Sixth Avenue types who were now singing "There'll Be a Hot Time in the Old

Town Tonight." Opposite them, beneath a column, a well-dressed woman wept. "He's all set to marry John McLean's sister. She's a general's widow. He's a widower. She's *Catholic*," the Chief added, brightening somewhat.

"There is still such a feeling against Catholics?" Madame de Bieville looked almost her age by the harsh light of a street lamp directly overhead. Blaise wished she would turn her head to the left an inch, and allow flattering shadows to mask her. Talk of age always disturbed him when she was present. The Willson girls had already worked out his relationship to what, in their eyes, despite her foreign glamor, was an old woman. If the Chief suspected, he made no allusion. But then, in sexual matters, he had a maiden's tact.

"Well, it's the Irish mostly that keep on giving Catholics such a bad name," said Hearst vaguely. "Germans, too, I guess. He's a powerhouse, her brother." The Chief looked at Blaise, without reproach, which was the worst reproach of all.

John R. McLean was the owner of the *Cincinnati Enquirer*. He lived in Washington where his mother and wife jointly reigned much as Mrs. Astor did, alone, in New York. McLean was fierce, partisan, powerful. He would do anything to keep Hearst out of Washington. Blaise's failure to buy the *Tribune* was a blow to Hearst, who was not about to begin, from nothing, a newspaper in the capital. The *Tribune* had been an ideal acquisition, and Blaise could never adequately explain to his partner—employer no longer: Blaise merely lent the Chief money at the going rate—that he had lost the paper to his own sister, who, to his surprise, eight months later, was still, if only barely, in business. They now communicated through lawyers. Anne thought that he should come to terms with Caroline, but Blaise refused. He would fight her to the end, which would come, rather anti-climactically, one way or another, in five years.

"Who built the arch?" Anne changed the dangerous subject.

"A committee," said Blaise. "The National Sculpture Society."

"The American style." She smiled into the light; and the

resulting lines made Blaise both nervous and sad. "And what is
the arch made of? Marble? or stone?"

"Plaster and cheap wood," said the Chief with obscure pleasure.
"And lots of white paint."

"But then when the winter comes . . ."

"It will fall apart." The Chief's tone was dreamy.

"But there's a subscription to rebuild it in marble. This is just
the model." As a young, new New Yorker of means, Blaise had
already made his contribution to the fund.

"It doesn't look at all temporary." Anne was admiring.

"That's the American *way*," said the Chief. America personified,
Hearst thought of himself; and, perhaps, thought Blaise, he was.
Everything here was equally new, self-invented, temporary.

– 2 –

The secretary of state and the new secretary of war, Elihu Root,
stared at one another across Hay's desk. Root had replaced Alger
in August. A New York lawyer of uncommon brilliance and sly
wit, Root gave Hay more pleasure than the rest of the admittedly
dim Cabinet combined. Root's hair was cut short like Julius
Caesar's, with a dark fringe over the brow, and a modest moustache. The black eyes were as quick as the wit; and the swift smile
was both frank and agreeably murderous. "If you really want the
Philippines," said Hay, "you can have them. I've got too much on
my hands as it is."

"I don't *want* them, dear fellow. I've got quite enough with
Cuba." Root lit a cigar. "In fact, I've told the President that State
should have all our island possessions. War just isn't suited to run
a peacetime colonial government. Of course, Cuba isn't really a
colony." Root frowned. "I wish we could think of a better word
than 'possession' for our . . ."

"Possessions?" Hay smiled; the pains in his back were in

remission. A summer in New Hampshire had restored if not his weary soul his spinal column. "We must face what they are."

"I've just divided Cuba into four military districts, rather the way we did the South in 1865. In due course, we'll come home, but then what happens to Cuba?"

"Germany?" Lately the "German menace" was much discussed at Cabinet, where it was generally thought that the German fleet was making itself too much at home in both the Caribbean and the Pacific; and all—or almost all—agreed that if Germany were to obtain a single port anywhere in the Caribbean, there would be war.

The Major's recent discovery of the Monroe Doctrine had been galvanizing. But then, as Henry Adams always said, his family's masterpiece only came to irritable life once every other generation or so. Plans were now afoot to buy the Virgin Islands from Denmark; unfortunately, the Danes had assumed that the government of the United States was so corrupt that it would be necessary to pay off the relevant officials. Hay himself had been crudely approached; severely, he had told the eager Dane, "You must pay off Senator Lodge first. He is the key, and a very expensive one, too, because he is from Massachusetts, and their senators still idolize—and emulate—Daniel Webster, who was 'retained' by everyone." Cabot had not been amused by the subsequent advances. Adams had not stopped laughing for a day.

"I don't think Germany is going to amount to much on this side of the Atlantic." With a forefinger, Root dusted the silver-framed portrait of the Prince of Wales. "Poor man. He'll never be king, will he?"

"Queen Victoria cannot live forever, as far as we know. She has been queen all my life; yours, too. She adds whiskey to her claret at table."

"That explains her longevity. It's going to be Leonard Wood in Cuba."

"As governor-general?"

Root nodded. "Or whatever we'll call him. He wants to clean

up, literally, Cuba. You know, collect the garbage. Educate the children. Give them a constitution where only men of property can vote."

Hay inhaled the smoke from Root's cigar: Cuban, he noted, of the best quality. "No one can ever accuse us of exporting democracy. Poor Jefferson thought that he had won, and now we are all Hamiltonians."

"Thanks to the Civil War."

Adee opened the door, and put his elegant head into the room. "They are coming, Mr. Hay," he softly quacked.

"Who," asked Hay, "are they?"

A high screeching falsetto shouting "Bully!" promptly identified one of *them*.

"I should have warned you," said Root, baring his teeth in an anticipatory smile.

"Theodore approaches . . ." Hay held on to the edge of his desk, as if battening down, whatever that nautical verb meant, a hatch.

"With his invention . . ."

The door was flung open and in the doorway stood the portly young Governor of New York, and the portly old Admiral Dewey. "There you two are! We've been with Secretary Long. Nice to have the three of you all in the same building. You look bully, Hay."

"I feel . . . bully, Theodore." Hatch battened down, Hay had risen to his feet with some pain. Root's murderous smile was now in place. He started to shake the Admiral's right hand; and was given the left. "My arm's still paralyzed from shaking hands in New York," he said. Dewey was small and sunburned, with snow-white hair and moustache.

"The hero of the hour," said Root, reverently.

"Hour? The century!" shouted Roosevelt.

"Which ends in less than two months." Hay was pleased to deflate Theodore. "Then we shall be, all of us, adrift in the frightening unknown of the twentieth century."

"Which begins not in two months but in a year and two months from now." Root was pedantic. "On January one, 1901."

"Surely," Hay began; but Roosevelt broke in.

"Why frightening?" The Governor removed his glasses and cleaned them with a silk handkerchief. "The twentieth century—whenever it starts—will see us at our absolute high noon. Isn't that right, Admiral?"

Dewey was staring out the window at the White House. "I don't," he said, "suppose it's very difficult, being president."

The three men were too startled to react either in or out of character. "I mean, it's just like the Navy. They give you your orders and you carry them out."

"Who," said Root, the first to recover, "do you think will give you your orders, President Dewey?"

"Oh, Congress." The Admiral chuckled. "I'm a sailor, of course, and I have no politics. But I know a thing or two about the trade. My wife, as of tomorrow my wife, that is, likes the idea. So does her brother, John R. McLean. He's very political, you know. In Ohio."

Hay was watching Roosevelt during this astonishing declaration—or, more precisely, meditation. Theodore's teeth were, for once, entirely covered by lips and moustache. The blue eyes were astonished; the pince-nez fallen.

"The house is certainly an enticement." Dewey indicated the White House, with a martial wave. "But, of course, I have a house now, at 1747 Rhode Island Avenue. The people's gift, which I've just deeded over to my wife-to-be."

Hay was speechless. For the first time in American history, a subscription had been raised to reward an American hero with a house. When General Grant had died in poverty, editorials were written about Blenheim Palace and Apsley House, national gifts to Britain's victorious commanders. Did not the United States owe her heroes something? Shortly after Admiral Dewey's return, a house in the capital was presented to him, according to his reasonably modest specification: the dining room must seat no fewer than fourteen people, the Admiral's idea of the optimum number. Now the Admiral had blithely given away the nation's gift. "Is this wise?" asked Hay. "The people gave *you* the house."

"Exactly. Which means that it's mine to do with as I please, and I want Mrs. Hazen to have it now that she's to be Mrs. Dewey. All in all," he continued, without a pause, "I think one must wait till the people tell you just when they want you to be president before you yourself say or do anything. Don't you agree, Governor?"

Roosevelt's screech sounded to Hay's ear like a barnyard chicken's first glimpse of the cook's kitchen knife.

As always, Root rallied first; and said smoothly, "I'm sure that the thought of being president has never occurred to Colonel Roosevelt, who is interested not in mere office or its trappings or, indeed, the *housing* that goes with office. No. For the Governor, *service* is all. Am I not right, Colonel?"

Roosevelt's huge teeth were again in view, but not in a smile; rather, he was clicking them like castanets, and Hay shuddered at the sound of bony enamel striking bony enamel. "You certainly are, Mr. Root. I set myself certain practical goals, Admiral. At the moment, as governor, I wish to tax the public franchise companies so that—"

"But doesn't your legislature tell you what you should do?" The Admiral's homely dull face was turned now toward the Governor.

"No, it doesn't." The teeth snapped now like rifle shots. "*I* tell *them* what to do. They're mostly for sale, as it is."

"May I quote you, Governor?" Root's killer's smile gave Hay great joy.

"No, you may not, Mr. Root. I have enough troubles . . ."

"The Albany mansion is comfortable," said the Admiral thoughtfully: plainly, housing was much on his mind.

"Perhaps you might want to be governor of New York," Hay proposed, "when Colonel Roosevelt's term ends, next year."

"No. You see, I don't like New York. I'm from Vermont."

Hay changed the delicious subject. After all, the Admiral was a McKinley-made hero, and to tarnish him would, in the end, tarnish the Administration. "How long do you think it will take us to pacify the rebels in the Philippines?"

It was hard to tell whether or not the Admiral was smiling beneath the huge moustaches, like a snowdrift on his monumental face. "Forever, I suppose. You see, they hate us. And why not? We promised to free them, and then we didn't. Now they are fighting us so that they can be free. It's really quite simple."

Roosevelt was very still in his self-control. "You do not regard Aguinaldo and his assassins as outlaws?"

Dewey looked at Roosevelt with something dangerously like contempt. "Aguinaldo was our ally against Spain. *My* ally. He's a pretty smart fellow, and the Filipinos are a lot more capable of self-government than, say, the Cubans."

"That," said Root, "will be the position the Democrats take next year."

"Damnable traitors!" Roosevelt exploded.

"Oh, I don't think that's quite right." Dewey was mild. "There's a lot to be said for good sense, Governor."

Adee was again at the door. "Admiral Dewey, the reporters are waiting for you in the Secretary's office."

"Thank you." Dewey turned to Roosevelt. "So you agree with me that when it comes to the presidency we just bide our time until the nation calls?"

A strangled cry was Roosevelt's only response. Smiling graciously, Admiral Dewey bade the three men of state a grave farewell. When the door shut behind him, Hay and Root broke into undecorous laughter; and Roosevelt slammed Hay's desk three times with the palm of his right hand. "The greatest booby that ever sailed the seven seas," he pronounced at last.

"I'm told that Nelson was also a fool." Hay was judicious; and highly pleased that he had witnessed Theodore's embarrassment, for he had, from the beginning, taken full credit for Dewey's career and famous victory.

"Let's hope," said Root, mildly disturbed, "he'll keep quiet about the Philippines in front of the press. Let's also," he smiled sweetly, "hope that he remembers to tell them about that house."

"The man's mad." Roosevelt was emphatic. "I hadn't realized it. Of course, he's old."

"He's my age," said Hay gently.

"Exactly!" boomed Roosevelt, not listening.

"At the moment," said Root, "Dewey could probably have the Democratic nomination."

"And McKinley would win again," said Roosevelt. "I am not, by the way, gentlemen, at all interested in the vice-presidential nomination next year. If nominated, I warn you, I won't accept."

"Dear Theodore," Root's smile glittered like sun on Arctic ice, "no one has even considered you as a candidate because—isn't it plain?—you are not qualified."

That does it, thought Hay, Theodore will bolt the party and we shall lose New York.

But Roosevelt took this solid blow stolidly. "I'm aware," he said, quietly, for him, "that I am considered to be too young, not to mention too much a reformer for the likes of Mark Hanna—"

"Governor, no one fears you as a reformer." Root was inexorable. "'Reform' is a word for journalists to use, and the editor of *The Nation* to believe in. But it's not a word that practical politicians need take seriously."

"Mr. Root," the voice had attained now its highest register, "you cannot deny that I have the bosses on the run in New York State, that I have—"

"You don't have breakfast any more with Senator Platt. That's true. But if you run again, you and Platt will work together again, as you always have, because you're highly practical. Because you're full of energy. Because you are admirable." Root's fame as a lawyer rested on an ability to pile up evidence—or rhetoric— and then to his opponent's consternation, turn all of it against the point that he appeared to be making. "I take it for granted that you *must* be president one day. But today is not the day, nor even tomorrow, because of your passion for the word 'reform.' On the other hand, the day that you cease to use that terrible word, so revolting to every good American, you will find that the glittering thing will drop—like heavenly manna—into your waiting lap. But, for now, we live in the age of McKinley. He has given us an empire. You—you," if air could bleed, Root's razor-like smile would now so have cut it that there would be only a crimson screen between him and the stunned Roosevelt, "you have given us moments of great joy, 'Alone in Cuba,' as Mr. Dooley expressed it, referring to your book on the late war. You also gave us Admiral Dewey, a gift to the nation we shall never cease to honor you for— or let the nation forget. You say unpleasant things about arrogant corporations, whose legal counsel I happen to be. And I thrill at your fierce words. You have been inspiring in your commentaries on the iniquities of the insurance companies. Oh, Theodore, you are a cornucopia of lovely things! But McKinley has given us half the islands of the Pacific and nearly all the islands of the Caribbean. No governor of New York can compete with that. McKinley, working closely with his God, has made us great. Your time will come, but not as vice-president to so great a man. It is also too soon to remove yourself from the active life of strenuous reformation, not to mention the vivacious private slaughter of animals. You must allow yourself to grow, to see points of view other than the simple, deeply held ones that you have evolved so sincerely and so publicly. Work upon understanding our great corporations, whose energy and ingenuity have brought us so much wealth . . ."

With a cry, Roosevelt turned to Hay. "I said it was a mistake to put a lawyer in the War Department, and a *corporation* lawyer at that . . ."

"What," asked Root, innocently, "is wrong with a corporation lawyer? What, after all, was President Lincoln?"

"What indeed?" Hay was enjoying himself hugely. "Of course, Lincoln was just beginning to make money as a railroad lawyer when he was elected president, while you, Mr. Root, are the master lawyer of the age."

"Do not," whispered Root, with a delicate gesture of humility, "exaggerate."

"Oh, you are both vile!" Roosevelt suddenly began to laugh. Although he had no humor at all, he had a certain gusto that eased relationships which might have proven otherwise to be too, his favorite word, strenuous. "Anyway, I don't want the vice-presidency, which others, Mr. Root, want for me, starting with Senator Platt . . ."

Root nodded. "He will do anything to get you out of New York State."

"Bully!" The small blue eyes, half-hidden by the plump cheeks, shone. "If Platt wants me out I must be a pretty good reformer."

"Or simply tiresome."

Roosevelt was now on his feet, marching, as to war, thought Hay. He never ceased to play-act. "I'm too young to spend four years listening to senators make fools of themselves. I also don't have the money. I have children to pay for. On eight thousand dollars a year, I could never afford to entertain the way Morton and Hobart did." At the mantel, he stopped; he turned to Hay. "How is Hobart?"

"He is home. In Patterson, New Jersey. He is dying." The President had already warned Hay that in accordance with the Constitution, the Secretary of State would soon become, in the absence of an elected vice-president, heir to the presidency should the President himself die. Hay was agreeably excited at the thought. As for poor Hobart himself, Hay had only a secular prayer; and the practical hope that were the Vice-President to die, Lizzie Cameron could return to the Tayler house in Lafayette Square a year before she had planned, thus keeping happy the Porcupinus, who was still in Paris, porcu-pining for Lizzie, who, in turn, was in love with an American poet, twenty years her junior. As she had made Adams suffer, so the poet made her suffer; thus, love's eternal balance was maintained: he loves her, and she loves another who loves—himself. Hay was quite happy to have forgotten all about love. He had not Adams's endless capacity; or health.

"I've proposed you, Mr. Root, for governor, if I don't run again." Roosevelt gave a small meaningless leap into the air.

"I have never said that you were not kindness itself." Root was demure. "But Senator Platt has already told you that I'm not acceptable to the organization."

"How did you know?" There were times when Hay found the essentially wily Roosevelt remarkably innocent.

"I have an idle interest in my own affairs." Root was equally demure. "I hear things. Happily, I don't want to be governor of New York. I don't want to know Platt any better than I do; and then, like Admiral Dewey, I dislike Albany."

"But the Admiral does like the governor's mansion," Hay contributed.

"He is a simple warrior, with simple tastes. I am sybaritic. In any case, Governor, you'll be happy to know that I have surrendered to you. Next month your friend Leonard Wood will become military governor of Cuba."

"Bully!" Two stubby hands applauded. "You won't regret it! He's the best. Who's for first governor-general of the Philippines?"

"You?" asked Root.

"I would find the task highly tempting. But will the President tempt me?"

"I think he will," said Root, who knew perfectly well, as did Hay, that the farther away McKinley could send Roosevelt, the happier the good placid President would be. The Philippines were Roosevelt's anytime he wanted them, once the bloody task of pacification was completed. Tens—some said hundreds—of thousands of natives had been killed, and though General Otis continued to promise a complete submission on the part of Aguinaldo and the rebels, they were still at large, dividing the United States in what would soon be an election year, while Mark Twain's answer to Rudyard Kipling would, Hay had been told by their common friend Howells, soon be launched. Meanwhile, the old Mississippi boatman, now of Hartford, Connecticut, had told the press that the American flag's stars and stripes should be replaced with a skull and crossbones, acknowledging officially the United States' new role as international pirate and scavenger.

"The Major," Hay was cautious, "has said you'd be an ideal governor once the fighting stopped."

"I might be helpful there," said Roosevelt, wistfully: he truly liked war, as so many romantics who knew nothing of it tended to. One day's outing with bullets in Cuba was not Antietam, Hay thought grimly, where five thousand men died in less than an hour. It was generally assumed that because Roosevelt's father had so notoriously stayed out of the war, the son, filled with shame, must forever make up for his father's sin of omission. Hay could never decide whether he very much liked or deeply disliked Roosevelt. Adams was much the same: "Roosevelts are born," he had observed, "and never can be taught," unlike Cabot Lodge, a creature of Adams's own admittedly imperfect instruction.

"Save yourself, Governor." Root rose; and stretched. "We have so much to do right now. There is an ugly mood out there." An airy wave of an arm took in the mud-streaked glass of the White House conservatories. "And an election next year."

"Ugly mood?" Roosevelt sprang to his feet. For a man so plump, he did exert himself tremendously, thought Hay, whose every rise from a chair was a problem in logistics, and a source of pain.

"Yes," said Hay. "While you have been enjoying the company of Platt and Quay and the refinements of the Albany mansion, we—the Cabinet and the Major—have been ricocheting about the country for the last six weeks. As there were elections in—"

"Ohio and South Dakota. I'm a Dakotan myself. When I—" Roosevelt got everything back to "I."

Root raised a hand. "We shall all read *The Winning of the West*. To think! You are not only our Daniel Boone but our Gibbon, too!"

Roosevelt blew out his upper lip so that lip and moustache fluttered against the tombstone teeth. "I hate irony," he said with, for once, perfect sincerity.

"It will do you no harm," said Root. "The fact is the labor unions are giving us more and more trouble, particularly in Chicago. We barely squeaked through in Ohio, where the Presi-

217

dent made a special effort, and though Mark Hanna spent more money than ever before, John McLean engineered a big victory in Cleveland for the Democrats."

"Out of the twelve states voting, we carried eight." Roosevelt was brisk. "Only cranks opposed us . . ."

"But in our own party," Hay began.

"*Every* party has its lunatic fringe." Roosevelt's recent coinage of this phrase had given him great pleasure, which he shared with the world. "Luckily for us, the Democrats have Bryan. He's just carried *his* Nebraska with a fusion ticket, which means he'll be nominated, which means we will win."

"Unless the Admiral hears the unmistakable cry of a grateful people," said Hay, working himself out of his chair, "and puts himself forward as a candidate opposed to the very same empire that he—guided by you, Theodore—brought us. Now that would be a splendid *big* election."

"That would be a nightmare," said Root.

"That won't happen," said Roosevelt.

Adee appeared yet again in the doorway. "Colonel Roosevelt, Admiral Dewey wants to know if you would be willing to submit yourself," for some reason, today, of all days, Adee was more than ever quacking like a duck, thought Hay, as he shoved himself to his feet, "to something of a photographical nature, which sounds like—our telephone has developed a strange sea-like sound, like the inside of a sea-shell when you hold it to your ear . . ."

"Mr. Adee is stone-deaf," said Hay to the others, his face averted from Adee, who could then neither hear his voice nor read his lips.

"Sounds like *what?*" Roosevelt's eyes gleamed. He loved all forms of publicity.

"Biograph, Governor."

"Biograph?" Hay was puzzled.

"It is a *moving-picture*," said Roosevelt, bounding toward the door. "Gentlemen, good day."

"Do nothing, Governor," Root was beaming, "until you hear the unmistakable call of the people."

"You," said Roosevelt, waving a fist at Hay, "and Henry Adams have a great deal to answer for, with your deprecatory ironic style, which is like ... like yellow fever, this *unremitting* cynicism." Roosevelt was gone.

Hay looked at Root and said, "If nothing else, Teddy's more fun than a goat."

"Unremitting cynicism." Root laughed. "He comes to Washington as a candidate for vice-president with the backing of Platt and Quay, the two most corrupt political bosses in the union."

"Doubtless, he means to betray them, virtuously, in the interest of good government and, of course, reform . . ."

Root nodded thoughtfully. "I confess that to betray without cynicism is the sign of a master politician."

"Certainly, the sign of an original." Hay started to the door. "I must visit the Major."

"I must go to work." Root opened the door, and stood to one side so that the senior Cabinet member could go first. Hay paused in the doorway. Adee was at his desk, back to them; thus, wrapped in impenetrable silence. Hay looked at Root and said, "You know who the Major wants for vice-president?"

"Don't tell me Teddy . . ."

"Never Teddy. He wants," Hay studied Root's face, "you."

Root was impassive. "The Republican National Committee wants me," he said precisely. "I don't know that the President was ever influenced by them."

"He isn't."

"It is," said Root, "a long time until next summer and your— not my—twentieth century."

Behind Adee's back, Hay bet Root ten dollars, even money, that the new century began the coming first of January, 1900, and not a year from that day.

3

For Caroline, marriage to Del was postponed until he had returned from Pretoria, in a year's time. Yes, she would come to South Africa to see him. No, she did not want a formal engagement. "A woman does that sort of thing for a mother, and I am not so burdened." They came to these terms in the large victoria which was used by the Secretary of State for weddings, and funerals.

They drove through a light rain across Farragut Square to the K Street house of Mrs. Washington McLean, who, with her daughter-in-law Mrs. John R. McLean, as vice-reine, presided jointly over Washington society in a way that no President's wife could, even were she not epileptic. The senior Hay had decided not to attend the afternoon reception for Mrs. Washington McLean's daughter, Millie, now wife to Admiral Dewey. As head of Ohio's Democratic Party and proprietor of the *Cincinnati Enquirer*, John McLean, now the Admiral's brother-in-law, was particularly unpopular with the Administration. But Del saw no reason why he shouldn't go, and Caroline was eager to meet her fellow publisher, Mr. McLean. Thus far, their paths had not crossed in Washington's jungle. But then Caroline had kept pretty much to her own bailiwick throughout the summer, which had proved to be as equatorial as Cousin John had promised. Fortunately, to Caroline's surprise, she had proved as strong as she had boasted. There was no gasping retreat to Newport, Rhode Island, or Bar Harbor, Maine. She had divided the furnace-season between Georgetown and Market Square; and duly noted that by mid-July the city was entirely African. The President had retreated to Lake Champlain. Congress had gone home and the gentry had fled to cool northern spas. As a result, she had never so much enjoyed Washington. For one thing, there was the newspaper to be fathomed. For another, there were the legal maneuverings of

Houghteling and Cousin John. To make no progress was Houghteling's masterly aim; and no progress had been made. Meanwhile,
Trimble taught Caroline the newspaper business, which seemed to
have very little to do with news, and even less with business, in a
profitable sense. Yet circulation had begun, slowly, to increase,
thanks to Caroline's bold imitation of Hearst. Both the *Post* and
the *Star* had sent reporters to interview her, but she had refused to
see them.

In a city where all power was based on notoriety, she was
thought eccentric—a rich young woman perversely playing at
being a newspaper proprietor. She was not distressed by what they
wrote. She now knew, at first hand, that nothing written in a
newspaper should ever be taken seriously. She might herself not
know how to produce a successful newspaper but she certainly had
learned how to read one. Simultaneously, Trimble had shown an
unexpected, even original, interest in the corruption of city officials,
and though she doubted that the subject was of much general
interest, she encouraged him to reveal what crimes he could.
Meanwhile, she exulted in the river's catch of beautiful bodies,
often torn, literally, to bits by raging passions. She was now
experimenting with abandoned live babies in trash-cans, having
failed to ignite the city's compassion with abandoned dogs and
cats.

"How long will you keep it up?" asked Del. In front of them,
Admiral Farragut, all in metal, rested a spy-glass on his raised left
knee. Farther on, off the square in K Street stood the McLean
mansion.

"Oh, forever, I suppose." Their carriage now joined a long, slow
line in front of the K Street mansion.

"But doesn't the paper lose a good deal of money?"

"Actually, there is a small profit." She did not add that the
profit still came from calling-cards, and now that Congress was
due to assemble in December, orders were coming in at rather
more than the seasonal rate. "Anyway, I do it to amuse myself,
and others."

Del tried not to frown; squinted his eyes instead. Caroline had come to know all his expressions; there were not many but they were, for the most part, agreeable to her. He had grown more confident since his diplomatic appointment; and somewhat stouter. He was his mother's child. "You do find quite a lot of crime here." Del tried to sound neutral. "I suppose people like to read about that."

"Yes, there is a lot of crime to be found here. But the real point is," and Caroline frowned, not for the first time, at the thought, "does it make any difference if you tell people what is actually happening all around them? or do you ignore the real life of the city and simply describe the government in the way that it would like you to?"

"You are a realist. Like Balzac. Like Flaubert . . ."

"Like Hearst, I'm afraid. Except that Hearst's realism is to invent everything because he wants to own everything, and if you've invented the details of a murder or a war, why, then it's *your* murder, *your* war, not to mention your readers, your country."

"Do you invent?"

"We—*I* do nothing, really. Like Queen Victoria I encourage, advise and warn—we sometimes put in what others leave out . . ."

"As a matter of good taste . . ."

Caroline laughed. "Good taste is the enemy of truth!"

"Who is truth's friend?"

"No one in Washington—that I've met, anyway. I hope my peculiar *métier* doesn't embarrass you." To say that Del was conventional was to say everything.

"No, no. You are like no one else, after all."

"You will do well in . . ."

"Diplomacy?"

"Pretoria." They both laughed; and entered the "sumptuous mansion," as the *Tribune* always described any home with a ballroom, at whose center stood the splendid Mrs. Washington McLean, flanked by her daughter Millie, a handsome little woman, aglitter with diamonds, and the happy white-haired, teak-faced, gold-braided bridegroom. Although Caroline had not been to many of

Washington's hard-pan affairs (so named because these new rich had, often as not, made their millions with a hard pan in some Western creek, prospecting for gold), she recognized from her own newspaper's reports numerous city celebrities, permanent residents, often from the West, builders of new palaces along Connecticut and Massachusetts Avenues, those two great thoroughfares of the fashionable West End. She herself always caused something of a stir, as a grand Northern or European, or whatever she was, personage who had taken on the proprietorship of a dull small-town newspaper and made it incontrovertibly and shockingly yellow. No one could guess her motive. After all, she was a Sanford; engaged, more or less, to the equally rich Del Hay; yet she spent her days in Market Square, dealing in murders and, lately, civic corruption; and her evenings at home, where few of Washington's cliff-dwellers or hard-panners were ever invited, assuming that they would come to the house of so equivocal a maiden.

For company, Caroline had taken up with the Europeans, particularly with Cambon, the French minister; and with the recently ennobled British ambassador, Lord Pauncefote. Although she found the twice-divorced Russian ambassador, Count Arthur (surely, Arturo? she had said) Cassini, amusing and predictably gallant, she had followed Mrs. Hay's advice and steered clear of him and his beautiful sixteen-year-old "niece," who was, actually, his daughter by a one-time "actress," now installed at the Russian embassy as the girl's governess. The Washington newspapers had been almost as savage as the Washington gossips. Out of deference to Clara Hay, Caroline had avoided the Cassinis and the McLeans. Now she felt exhilarated as she stepped into the gilded room. Where the Hays and the Adamses and the Lodges were discreetly wealthy, and lived lives of muted splendor, prisoners to good taste and devotees of civilization at its most refined, the McLeans flaunted the inexhaustible contents of their hard pan. Guiltily, Caroline was more delighted by the vulgar kingdom than by the known one.

Caroline and Del made their way down the receiving line. The

Admiral was gracious. "Tell Mr. Hay how much I appreciated his letter."

"I will, sir."

"Is Mr. Hay coming?" asked Millie, a pretty woman, Caroline decided, for forty-nine.

"I believe he is with the President tonight," Del lied smoothly, and Caroline was pleased that he had taken so well to the world that he would be obliged to make his way in.

"We *expected* the President." The new Mrs. Dewey smiled hugely; the teeth were discolored. But the huge doll's eyes were a marvelous blue.

"There is a crisis," murmured Del. "In the Philippines."

The small, imperial Mrs. Washington McLean regarded the young couple with mild curiosity. "We don't see much of you, Mr. Hay," she said. "We don't see you at all, Miss Sanford." This was neutral. The style was very much that of *the* Mrs. Astor.

"I hope," said Caroline, "that that will change."

"I do, too." A thin smile hardly lit a face entirely shadowed by a diamond-studded bandeau lodged half an inch above small eyes. "I shan't be here forever."

"You go back to Cleveland, to be renewed?"

"No. To Heaven, to be redeemed."

Then Caroline found herself face to face with John R. McLean himself. He was tall, with the limpid blue eyes of his sister, and a neatly trimmed moustache. "Well, it's you," he said, staring down into Caroline's face. "Come on. Let's talk. Unless you want money from me. I don't give money, outside the family."

"How wise." Then, exquisitely pretentious, Caroline began to quote Goethe in the original German: apropos a father's duties.

Startled, McLean completed the quotation, in German. "How did you know I speak German?"

"You were at school at Heidelberg. You see? I study my fellow publishers."

McLean began to hiccup, eyes misty with pleasure, or so Caroline hoped. "My stomach," he said, "has been eroded by its own acids. Come into the library. Away from these people."

They sat before a huge fireplace, where great logs burned. The firelight was reflected in the dark blue leather bindings of the books, arranged like so many Union soldiers on parade in their mahogany shelves. "You can never make that paper a success." He gave her a glass of champagne; he poured himself soda water. The library door was firmly shut to the other guests. When McLean noticed that her eyes were on the door, he laughed. "Two publishers can't compromise each other."

"Let us hope Mr. Hay sees our relations so practically."

"I am told that he's an agreeable young man. We're all of us from Ohio, you know. At least Clara Stone is. John Hay's from nowhere. A sort of gypsy who's taken to stealing power instead of babies."

"How else," asked Caroline, displeased, "is power obtained if it is not taken from someone else? I realize, of course, some power is inherited, the way you inherited the *Enquirer* . . ."

McLean was amused. "Me, an idle heir! Well, that's a new one. I built on an inheritance, you might say—like your friend Hearst." From a log, bright blue Luciferian flowers suddenly bloomed.

McLean stared at Caroline a moment. "I won't ask you why you're doing this," he said finally. "I get pretty tired of people asking me that. If they can't see why you—why we—do it," he was suddenly attractive to her, now that he was collegial, "there's no way of telling them. But since you're a handsome young woman with a fortune, and Del Hay to marry, how long can you be so . . . original?"

"As long as you, I suppose."

"I'm a man. We're allowed to marry and we're allowed— delighted to do business. No lady that I know of has ever set out, so young, while single, to do anything like this."

Caroline studied the white smoke which had replaced the blue flame-flowers. "Why," she asked, "are you so eager to be president?"

"How do you know I am?"

"That's coy, Mr. McLean. That is maidenly. You give me the sort of answers that I'm supposed to give you. Why do you want it so badly that you took on the President in his own home state, and lost, as you knew you were going to?"

McLean's hiccups returned, louder than the fire's hissing and sputtering. "I didn't expect to lose. It was close. The President's on spongy ground back home. This empire business isn't popular with the folks."

"But prosperity is, and the President's clever. That war of his ended the bad times, and even the farmers are complaining less than usual, which means that McKinley will defeat Bryan again." How proud, Caroline thought, Mlle. Souvestre would be: one of her girls dealing with a man on equal terms.

McLean stared at Caroline with true wonder. "Somehow or other, I got the impression that you were only interested in the more revolting contents of our city's morgue."

Caroline laughed. "I'm not entirely ghoulish. In fact, I don't like the contents of the morgue at all. But I am curious as to how living people manage to end up on marble slabs, and I share my curiosity with our readers, few as they are."

"Mr. Hay—the father—must talk freely with you."

"I listen—freely—to everyone." Caroline stood up. "We've been here too long. I am compromised. Shall I scream?"

"I would be deeply flattered, and Mrs. McLean would be deeply proud—of me." McLean got to his feet. They stood in front of the fire. Over the mantel hung a splendid fraudulent Rubens. Caroline had seen two exact copies of the same painting in New York. In dealing with innocent Americans, Old Europe's forgers had grown careless. "You are interested in our political life, and I am surprised. Most young ... most women are not. How did this happen?"

"I went to a good school. We were taught to question everything. I do. Now then, Mr. McLean, which of us—the *Enquirer* or the *Tribune*—shall question the war?"

"The war?" McLean blinked. "What war?"

"The Filipino war of independence, what else? We seem to be losing it."

"Losing it? I guess you didn't see this morning's Associated Press wire. General Otis has captured the president of the so-called Philippines Congress, and has made secure all of central Luzon. The war, as you call it, is just about over."

"Aguinaldo is still free. But you know far more than I about all this." Half-heartedly, Caroline turned herself into polite *jeune fille*. "I had only hoped that someone might explain just how the . . . the morgues in those islands got so filled up, and why."

McLean took her arm; he was suddenly paternal, and almost, for him, affectionate. "You know more than any young woman I've ever met. But you haven't quite got the clue to all of this . . ."

"Clue?"

McLean nodded. They were at the door. "I'm not going to tell you, either. You're too smart as it is."

The door was flung open, and there stood Mrs. John R. McLean, small of chin, blue of eyes, dark of skin. "You two are a scandal," she observed mildly.

"We are at that." McLean was wry. "But then that's our business. Now, young lady, a question."

"Before my very eyes," said Mrs. McLean, plainly not disturbed.

"And ears," her husband added. He turned to Caroline. "Do you mean to sell out to Hearst?"

"No. I also don't mean, if I can help it, to sell out to my brother—half-brother—Blaise."

"If you can help it?" McLean watched her face closely, as though studying a clock which may or may not be keeping correct time.

"Blaise has tied up my share of our inheritance. I may not get what is mine until 1905. It is possible that I shall run out of money before then. . . ." Caroline could see that Mrs. McLean was far more shocked by this talk of money than she would ever have been by the thought of a romantic interlude between husband and young woman. But McLean had seized the point.

"If you ever need money for the *Tribune*," he said, "come to me."

"Pop!" Mrs. McLean's dark complexion seemed smeared with ash by firelight. The pale eyes protruded.

"Mummie!" McLean responded in kind, their princely eminence abandoned for the homely lowland of the common hard pan. McLean turned to his wife and took her arm. "Don't you see that the best thing in the world is for me to have this lovely child running the *Tribune*, with my money, than have her go sell it to that bastard . . ."

"Pop!" The voice resounded like thunder.

"I have heard the word," said Caroline. "In Market Square," she added, demurely.

" . . . William Randolph Hearst." McLean concluded; and led the two ladies back into the ballroom.

Caroline was greeted by her new friends of the diplomatic corps. Jules Cambon was a lively cricket of a man, always pleased to see what he regarded as a countrywoman. He was also, he liked to say, an *American* bachelor: Madame Cambon had refused to join him in the Washington wilderness. Lord Pauncefote was a lawyer turned diplomat; he had been posted to Washington for ten years, and knew the intricacies of the capital even better, Hay liked to say, than the Secretary of State. Pauncefote's face was wide, made even wider by fleecy side-whiskers, whose white was emphasized by the rich red claret color of the huge face. Pauncefote was also an expert on the legal intricacies governing international canals. He had been involved in the creation of the Suez Canal; now he was again at work, with Hay, drawing up the protocols which would govern the canal that the United States was planning to build across the Central American isthmus. Once Atlantic and Pacific oceans were connected, America's military power would be doubled, while, it was whispered in the Senate cloakroom, England's would be halved.

"We are hopeful," said the old man to the group of government officials surrounding him. As Congress was not yet in session, there were few tribunes of the people present to celebrate the hero of

Manila Bay. Pauncefote bowed to Caroline. "Miss Sanford. I am speaking shop, and will now desist."

"Don't! Go on. It is my shop, too. The *Tribune* has already thundered its approval of the Hay-Pauncefote Treaty."

"Would that the Senate will do the same next month." Actually, the *Tribune* editorial, the work of Trimble, had suggested that since the United States was building—and paying for—the canal, the United States must have the right to fortify the canal, which the treaty, out of deference to an 1850 convention between England and the United States, would deny. But just as Pauncefote began to express his government's views of canals, Mrs. Admiral Dewey joined them, a sumptuous doll, Caroline decided, who had at last found herself a proper doll's house. She explained to Caroline, "We couldn't live in that tacky house in Rhode Island Avenue. So I've bought Beauvoir, a pretty place in Woodley Lane. Do you know it?"

Caroline did not.

"It's like being in the country, but still in the town. I can't wait to start fixing it up. For years I've owned quantities of the most lovely blue-and-white Delft tiles, and now I'm going to be able to use them."

"In the kitchen?"

Mrs. Dewey's huge doll's eyes blinked like—a doll's. "No. In the drawing room. Of course, the house is rather small, but then we don't need anything large. There are no children now. Only my husband's trophies. And what trophies! You saw the gold sword the President gave him at the Capitol?"

"From a great distance." The ceremony had been impressive, if somewhat bizarre. Never before had a reigning president sat in front of the portico while the center of attention was not himself, the sovereign, but a military man. McKinley had carried off his difficult assignment with his usual papal charm, and Caroline had accepted, gratefully, Hay's characterization of the President as a medieval Italian prelate. While the Admiral was being celebrated by the vast crowd, the President had smiled beautifully at no one.

Only once was he utilized. He was obliged to present a gold sword to the Admiral, with a few murmured words, no doubt in Church Latin.

"The sword's only gold plate, by the way. Too shocking! Congress said that it was to be *solid* gold, of the highest quality . . ."

"And from the hardest pan?" Caroline could not resist.

But Millie Dewey seemed not to know the phrase. "I would have thought solid gold would be the only thing suitable for the first admiral we've had in thirty years. The Admiral now outranks every military man in the country," she added proudly. "Which is causing all sorts of problems, I can tell you. You see, General Miles," and, indeed, Caroline could, literally, see that warrior, formidable in appearance with his equally formidable wife, Mary Sherman, the older sister of Lizzie Cameron, "well, General Miles may be chief of staff of the Army but he is only a lieutenant general, while my husband is admiral of the Navy, the first to hold that rank since Farragut, who only won a little victory in Mobile Bay during the War of Secession while *my* admiral gave us all Asia . . ."

"Surely, not *all*. There is still China."

"We shall have that, too, he says, if the Russians and Japanese don't get there first. Speaking of Russians, this is my Aunt Mamie." They were joined by a small, fat woman with dyed red hair; quantities of huge jewels, set in massive gold, were attached to her ears, bosom, waist. She looked Byzantine; and she was. "Madame Bakhmetoff lives in St. Petersburg, far, far from home."

"About as far as one can get," Caroline agreed. The ramifications of the hard-pan families never ceased to amaze her. One sister might be a farmer's wife in Iowa; another Duchess of Devonshire.

"The Russians aren't civilized," said Madame; then added, unexpectedly, "That's why I feel at home there. We're so much alike, Americans and Russians. Here's mine."

Mamie's Russian was as ugly as she. He wore a monocle; and presented to the world a gargoyle's face, scarred deeply from smallpox. He kissed Caroline's hand; and without thinking—or did he calculate?—slipped into French, presumably excluding Mamie and Millie. "You are an unexpectedly splendid apparition for this bleakest of capitals." Bakhmetoff's tone was agreeably flattering; and sharp.

"How could you tell I am not a native?"

"First, I know who you are . . ."

"You have been to Saint-Cloud-le-Duc . . ."

"No. But I admired your mother a century ago. You must come see us one day, at the edge of the Arctic Circle."

"I prefer the equator, for now."

Mrs. Dewey, in perfect if heavily accented French, said, "I understand every word. After all, my late husband and I were at the Austrian court for ages . . ."

Del saved Caroline from further displays of international glamor. "They are Beales, and can never forget it."

"What's a Beale? And why can such a thing never be forgotten?"

"Their father. He was a general in the war, and then he struck it rich in California . . ."

"To strike . . ." Caroline paused. "What a funny expression, 'to strike it rich,' like a blow of some kind against someone else."

"Well, many people never recover from those strikes."

"I think," said Caroline, "my father might have been one."

"But he was very rich to start with."

"He made more, like Mr. McLean."

Lord Pauncefote stopped Del at the door to the ballroom. "We have had good news from South Africa," he said. Caroline turned her back on them, so that the old man could tell whatever it was that he wanted Del, in turn, to repeat to his father. As Caroline surveyed the room, she saw the exquisite figure of the Cassini child, as elegantly dressed as a Paris lady of fashion, with a round chubby face, small features, and the bright eyes of a young fox. "They say," said Mrs. Benedict Tracy Bingham, "that she is neither daughter nor niece but," the low excited voice dropped even lower and became more excited, "mistress."

"Oh, surely not!" Caroline was mildly shocked. She might have been even more shocked had she not known Mrs. Bingham altogether too well. Mrs. Bingham was Galatea to Caroline's Pygmalion, monster to Caroline's Baron Frankenstein. Ever since she had so off-handedly thrust Mrs. Bingham and her fabulous jewels, aristocratic lineage, magisterial presence onto the front page of the *Tribune*, she had received not only a number of advertisements for the Silversmith Dairies but a large number of invitations to Mrs. Bingham's "sumptuous mansion," where, at last, Caroline met all of her Apgar connections as well as much of pre-hard-pan Washington. The cave-dwellers, or cliff-dwellers as they were alternately known, seldom mingled in the new palaces of the West End and never in the world of official Washington. But Mrs. Bingham, and one of the Apgar ladies, were twin poles of Washington's high if dowdy social world, to which Cousin John had assigned Caroline her place, a place she filled as little as possible and then only on condition that in return for the pleasures of her company she be given advertising for the *Tribune*. As a result of her relentlessness, she had increased the paper's revenues by twelve percent, much to Trimble's amazement. "It is a charge," Caroline had explained, "for my appearance at their functions. They think I am rich, so they are willing to give me money. If they knew how poor I really am, I'd be cut dead."

As it was, every mother of a marriageable son wanted to entertain Caroline, with due pomp and gravity; the present mootness of Caroline's heiressdom was either not known or not understood. The fact that her brother Blaise was never to be seen had been noted by all, and the Apgars, rehearsed by Cousin John, spoke sadly of an estrangement. Meanwhile, Caroline's proprietorship of what was, after all, the cave-dweller's favorite unread newspaper was considered a charming folly due to her European upbringing.

Certainly, Mrs. Bingham revelled in the fact. Until Caroline's highly creative account of the Connecticut Avenue robbery, Mrs. Bingham had led a decorous life, a monarch of much of what she surveyed, including the ancient dairyman, her husband. But once identified as a sort of Mrs. Astor disguised as a Washington milkmaid, there was now no stopping her. She courted the press. Every visiting celebrity was summoned to her mansion; and those few who obeyed her summons were then written up at length in the *Star*, *Post* and *Tribune*. All in all, Caroline quite enjoyed her monster. For one thing, Mrs. Bingham was a treasury of scandal. There was no one that she did not know something discreditable about; best of all, there was no one whom she would not slander, joyously, to her inventrix, Caroline, who now stared at the lean, yellow-faced woman of sixty, whose moustache was like fluff of the sort that Marguerite constantly found under Caroline's bed, and could not persuade the African either to acknowledge or identify, much less remove.

"How can you tell? I mean that she's his mistress?"

The deep voice sounded like a cello when a bass chord is, mournfully, struck. "My butler's sister is upstairs maid at the Russian embassy. She says, late at night, there are *footsteps* from *his* room to *hers*."

"A heavy Cossack tread?"

"Booted and spurred!" roared Mrs. Bingham, delighted at her own wit. Caroline suspected her of constant improvisation. Mention Queen Victoria, and she would promptly give lurid details of the Queen's secret marriage to a Scots servant, in a cottage at Balmoral; and mourn the fact that the Queen, once a symbol of fertility for all the world, was now so many decades past the ability to conceive: "Otherwise, there would be Morganatic Claimants to the Throne!" This said in a hushed voice, awed by the grandeur of her subject.

"You must 'do' society for me, Mrs. Bingham. You know everything."

"But I *say* nothing," said Mrs. Bingham, who said everything but not to everyone. "Another proof that she is his mistress," she began, true artist, to ornament her invention, "is the fact that he insists she act as his official hostess, and attend state dinners. One doesn't do that with a daughter . . ."

"In Russia, always," Caroline smoothly invented. "The wives are left home in their, ah, dachas, and the oldest daughter always escorts her father to court."

"Curious, I have never heard that before." Mrs. Bingham gave Caroline a suspicious look. Unlike most liars she was seldom taken in by the lies of others. "I'll ask Mamie Bakhmetoff," she said, ominously.

"Oh, she will lie. To save face. They all do." With that, Del took Caroline's arm, but before they could escape, Mrs. Bingham struck hard.

"Mr. Hay can tell you all about Mlle. Cassini. He sends her flowers."

Del coughed nervously. In Washington, when a man sent flowers to an unmarried girl, it meant that he was courting her. "I didn't know," said Caroline.

"I'm sorry for her, that's all. Poor girl." As they crossed the room, he bowed to the Cassini girl, and whispered to Caroline, "Father wants me to keep an eye on the Russians."

In the carriage, en route to Caroline's house, Del told her that, contrary to what Pauncefote had told him, things were not going well for the British in Africa. "The Boers are on the warpath, which is good for us."

"Aren't we—your father, anyway—pro-British?"

"Of course. But we've got the treaties to think about. When England's riding high, they oppose us everywhere from habit. When things go badly for the English, they are very agreeable. This means they'll accept Father's treaty, without fuss."

"But will the Senate?"

"Why not? Lodge is there, and the President's popular."

"But next year's election . . ."

Del was staring out the window at the Treasury, like a granite mountain in the rain. "There's talk in New York, of Blaise and an older woman, a Frenchwoman."

234

"Madame de Bieville? Yes. I know her. She has great charm. They are old friends."

"But isn't she married?"

"Not seriously," said Caroline. "Anyway, she is now a widow." Caroline was obliged, always, to conduct herself with rather more caution than was natural to her whenever this sort of subject came up. Did Americans really believe what they said or were they simply fearful of that ominous majority whose ignorance and energy set the national tone? They certainly never ceased to pretend in public that marriage was not only sacred but the stately terminus to romance. Although she constantly heard, and not just from Mrs. Bingham, of this or that bad marriage, adultery was seldom alluded to within the pale of respectability.

Del confirmed her not so native caution. "Blaise ought to remember that New York's not Paris. We have different standards here."

"What about Mr. Hearst?"

Del flushed. "First, he is outside society. Second, he is never without a chaperon, as far as one knows. He is afraid of his mother, after all, and she has the money."

Caroline nodded, as gloomy now as the November day. "She's struck it rich again, with a silver mine somewhere."

"Copper. In Colorado."

"She's giving him money again."

"To buy the *Tribune*?" Del looked at Caroline, most curiously. She knew that he was mystified by her life as a publisher; scandalized, too, she feared. Ladies did not do such things. Ladies did not, in fact, do anything at all but keep house and wear the jewels that the gentlemen they were married to gave them, as outward symbols not of love or of fidelity but of the man's triumphant solvency in the land of gold.

"Oh, I won't sell, ever. Besides, he now has his eye on Chicago. He needs the Midwest. He wants everything, of course."

"Like you?" Del smiled.

But Caroline took the question seriously. "I want," she said, "to be interested. That is not easy for a woman. In this place."

6

The twentieth century began, according to Hay, but did not begin, according to Root, on January 1, 1900. Although in idle moments John Hay had been practicing writing "19" he could not get used to the change from the familiar, even consoling "18" into which he had been born and during which he had now lived more than sixty years to the somewhat ominous "19" which, if nothing else, would mark his end. At best, he might have ten years more; at worst, when the pains began, he prayed for prompt extinction.

Hay and Clara breakfasted alone in a window recess of the great dining room, with a view of Lafayette Park and the White House beyond. The park was full of snow that had fallen during the night. In the White House driveway black men were covering white snow with sawdust. Comforted by the labor of others, Clara ate heartily. Hay ate sparingly. With time's passage, she had grown larger and larger; he smaller. Another century and she would quite fill the room at her present rate, while he would have shrunk to nothing.

Between them, on the breakfast table, was a telegram from Henry Adams in Paris. "Sail from Cherbourg January 5."

"I can't wait to see the Porcupine in action again, keeping Cabot in line, and all the senators." Actually, Hay dreaded the presentation to the Senate of what was now known as the Hay-Pauncefote Treaty, a document carefully designed to place in a new perspective relations between England, busily at war in South Africa, and the United States, busily at war in the Philippines. For once, the United States was, if not in the lead, in the higher ascendant. White reported to Hay regularly on the purest honey that dropped from the British ministry whenever relations with the now imperial republic were mentioned. Boundary problems with Canada were no longer of any urgency. Let the Canadians work out their own dimensions, the prime minister had been heard to say, the partnership of London and Washington was the hope of the world, not to mention of the busy, efficient, right-minded Anglo-Saxon race.

"It will be a nightmare." Clara put down the *Washington Post.* The pale gentle moon face shone upon Hay. "The *trains,*" she added; and moaned.

"You seem to have travel on your mind. But we are going nowhere. There are no trains in our immediate future, nightmarish or not."

"The reception today. There." She indicated the White House. "The ladies. They have. All of them. *Trains.* This year." The pauses were accompanied by a thoughtful chewing of cornbread, from a special coarse meal water-ground at Pierce's Mill beside the Rock Creek.

"Trains to their dresses." Hay understood. "But what's so bad about that?"

"In the crush? A thousand ladies, each with a three-foot train?"

Hay understood. "We shall be there for the entire twentieth century."

"Mrs. McKinley has said that she will come down." Clara sighed. "I've noticed that she is at her best when others are uncomfortable. The Green Room was seriously overheated last week. Two ladies fainted. But Mrs. McKinley looked in her element, and stayed on and on."

"A hot-house blossom. What a wretched life those two must have." Hay was surprised at his own observation. He made it a point never to speculate on the private lives of others, particularly with Clara, who sat in constant judgment, studying every shred of evidence, and weighing all hearsay in the scales of her own perfect justice.

"I don't think they *know* they are wretched." Clara held up a napkin as if to blindfold herself, like Justice, and pronounce verdict. "They do go on and on about the child they lost. But I think that gives them something to talk about. She worships him, you know. While he . . ." Clara stopped to give Hay his moment in the stand to speak as witness for the male.

"He *seems* devoted. There is no one else, either."

Clara began to frown: irregularity in marriage disturbed her almost as much as an ill-run house. Hay quietly added, "I speak, my dear, of friends, men or women. The Major is quite alone, it seems to me, which makes him very like the President."

"He is the President."

Hay smiled; pushed a crumb out of his beard. "When I say the President like that, seriously, I mean only one."

"Mr. Lincoln. I wish I'd known him."

"I wish I had, too." Hay tried to visualize the Ancient, but could only summon up the dead life-mask in his study. Lincoln had been erased from his mind by too much—or too little?—thought upon the subject. "But no one knew him, except Mrs. Lincoln, who was often mad, while no one at all really knows the Major . . ."

"Not even the dreadful Mr. Hanna?"

"Particularly not the dreadful Marcus Aurelius Hanna. No, Mr. McKinley has done it all alone." Hay laughed.

Clara looked at him sharply. She hated to be excluded from anything. Whenever she caught him smiling at remembered dialogue or rehearsing phrases to be used, she would say, "Tell me!

Tell me what you're smiling about. It must be very funny." Now she added, "What are you thinking of?"

"I was thinking of something the Major said the other evening. We were in the upstairs oval room, the two of us, and he said, 'From the Mexican war in 1848 until 1898, we were sound asleep as a nation. Internationally, that is. Happy in our isolation. Now all that has changed. We are everywhere. We are treated now with a respect which we were not when I was inaugurated.'"

Clara blinked. "True enough, I suppose. But why did you laugh?"

"I laughed because when I reminded him that, originally, he had been inclined to give the Filipinos their freedom, he said that that had *never* been his intention. From the beginning, he said, he had meant to hold on to everything. When I reminded him of his conversation with God, he gave me his secret kindly Borgia smile."

"Is he greater than Lincoln?"

"He is as . . . crucial, which puts them on a par, in a way." Hay picked up the *Washington Tribune*. A headline celebrated the burning of a livery stable in Arlington. "Our putative daughter-in-law has a fixation about fire."

"If she would only confine herself to that sort of flame." Clara was severe.

"I quite like what she does," said Hay, who quite liked Caroline. "Del is lucky."

"I think I like her, too. But she is not like us. She is French, really."

"The French are not, all of them, so very wicked. Look at M. Cambon."

Throughout their marriage Clara had been torn between a desire, on the one hand, to know everything about Hay's many years in Europe and a conviction, on the other, that she must keep all knowledge of sin from her. She vacillated between frivolous desire and stern conviction. She vacillated now. "I suppose it's her independence that I can't get used to. She is like a young man . . ."

"Rather better to look at than any young man I've ever met."

"Del seems so young beside her." Clara shifted ground. She had never been able to accommodate the unusual, which Hay not only accommodated easily, but often courted.

"There is always," Hay noted that the snow was now starting to fall again, as it always did once the White House carriage ways had been laboriously cleared, "the Cassini girl."

"Do you think he likes her?"

"I told him to woo her, for his country's sake."

"Patriotism!" Clara sighed. Hay was never certain that his wife understood his jokes. She registered them politely; but seldom laughed, once the registration had been made.

"She's uncommonly pretty . . ."

"But not legitimate, they say." Clara was remorseless in such matters. In July, she had refused to attend Kate Chase's funeral in Glenwood Cemetery. Husband and wife had quarrelled; and Hay had gone alone to say good-by—to himself. Kate herself had been said good-by to when he last saw her, with bloated face, dyed hair, trying to sell him eggs from her Maryland farm.

"No. She is legitimate. I had our ambassador in Petersburg find out. But after Cassini's other wives, and all his losses at gambling, he never dared ask the Tsar for permission to marry her mother, an actress, someone so far beneath him, hard as *that* is to visualize." Across the square the sky was like a gray iron plate, and the shovellers at the White House were now striking attitudes of despair, as the snow began, once more, to pile up. The reception was going to be chaos. Snow and trains. He shuddered.

"What matters," said Clara, "is Del. The young people seem to think that he is in love with Mlle. Cassini. Ever since he took her to the Bachelors' German at the Armory."

"Where you presided."

"Of course *I* have no objections to . . ." Clara's unfinished sentences were often her judgments.

"To foreign girls like Marguerite Cassini or Caroline Sanford, who is as good as foreign. But you prefer the native stock for Del."

"Am I wrong?"

"You are never wrong, Clara."

"There are so many girls right here, like the Warder girls, and Bessie Davis and Julia Foraker . . ."

"Don't! You make me think of votes in the Senate. As for Del and the Cassini girl, I've learned a lot. The Russians and the French plot against us and the British in China." Hay relayed to Clara what Del had learned about Holy Russia's intentions in Asia; and Clara smiled approvingly, and listened not at all. Marriage mattered. China did not. Meanwhile, the White House had disappeared behind a screen of falling snow. Fortunately, the Hays would not be obliged to join the long procession of carriages. Since Vice-President Hobart's death, John Hay was now the President's constitutional heir, a matter of midnight panic, when he saw himself suddenly elevated by death to the presidency, an office which he had always pined—rather than fought—for, and now no longer had the strength to fill. Fortunately, McKinley's health was excellent.

On the other hand, Hay suddenly found that he did have the unexpected strength to join Clarence and some of his friends in a pillow fight in the rough-room; and only Clara's warning, "We'll be late if you don't get dressed," stopped the delightful game. Clarence was both thoughtful and playful; unlike the ever-mysterious Del, who had said that, yes, he would be at the White House reception but, no, he would get there on his own.

The snow had stopped falling as Hay and Clara got into their carriage. Driveways that had been cleaned of snow that morning now resembled the steppes of Siberia. An endless line of carriages moved slowly beneath the portico of what Count Cassini had referred to as "a pleasant country home." Groundmen scattered sawdust beside the driveway as, in pairs, pedestrians moved slowly along Pennsylvania Avenue and into the White House grounds.

By earlier agreement with Mr. Cortelyou, Hay's carriage went round the White House to the south entrance, which was used only for special visitors. As the city vanished beneath feathery fronds of snow, he tried to recall what winters had been like in Lincoln's day; but as he had been young then, all that he could recall of that far-off time was a constant, languorous high summer, broken by fits of malarial fever.

One of the German door-keepers helped the Hays from their carriage. "Mr. Cortelyou would be pleased, sir, if you were to go directly to the Blue Room."

In the relative gloom of the lower White House corridor, Hay and Clara, arm in arm (she supporting him more than he her), made their way up the stairs just back of the Tiffany screen which hid the state apartments from the sort of curious crowd that was now gathering in the entrance hall. Green, Red and Blue Rooms were already filled with distinguished guests. As Clara had predicted, the trains were a nightmare, not improved by the slush and mud from shoes. The carpets were like wet burlap sacking, reminding Hay of Congress in his youth when tobacco-chewing was universally popular and, at session's end, the deep red carpet of the Senate would be river-mud brown.

The Blue Room contained the members of the Cabinet and the chiefs of diplomatic missions. As always, Hay was charmed and amused by the costumes of the—he always thought of them as *his*—diplomats. Pauncefote wore what looked to be an admiral's uniform laced with enough gold to please a Byzantine emperor. Lady Pauncefote, plain and mild in everyday life, had suddenly grown from her mouse-gray hair, like antlers, a tiara so splendid that it seemed to aspire to be a crown. In her silver dress, she reminded Hay of an icon; even her constitutionally sallow face looked as if it might have been darkened by the smoke of votive candles. She was in marked contrast to her usual untidy self, invariably wearing a highly unbecoming shawl, "the gift," she would murmur, "of our dear Queen." Cambon was red and gold; Cassini more gold than anything else, while his daughter, Marguerite, glowed at his side, the only youthful, beautiful object in the room. If Hay had been Del, he would have carried her off and married her.

The ambassadors greeted Hay with the punctiliousness that his rank required. Clara flattered the wives. In the entrance hall, the Marine band played.

Mr. Cortelyou drew Hay to one side. "We have a problem, sir."

"Never say 'we' to me. *You* have a problem, and I won't take it on."

"Well, sir. It's protocol . . ."

"Ask Mr. Adee. He loves protocol."

"It's the Navy, sir."

Hay was now interested. "They want to take precedence over the Army?"

"Yes, sir. It's been a terrible week. It's due to the war, and what the Navy did . . ."

Hay knew the problem; all Washington did. "Admiral Dewey outranks General Miles," said Hay promptly, "so he wants the Navy to go in to see the President ahead of the Army."

"Then you do know, sir?"

"No, I didn't know. But I'm pretty good at figuring out this sort of thing. Stupidity has always been kind of a specialty of mine. Now I suggest the person you deal with . . ."

" . . . is me." Elihu Root now stood between them. "I gave a very hard ruling. Since the beginning of the country, the Army has taken precedence over the Navy. And that's that, I told Dewey."

"What did he say to you, sir?"

"He said I should talk to Mrs. Dewey." The Root smile glittered like a knife. "I told him I was much too busy. I also have no small talk."

"I never realized that before," said Hay comfortably. "Is *all* your talk big?"

"Gargantuan."

"Well, mine's all small. So I guess I don't ever really understand a word you say."

Cortelyou hurried away; unamused by senior-statesman facetiousness. Root then came to the point. "Ten dollars, Hay. Fork it over. I win."

"About the start of the century?"

243

Root nodded; he withdrew a press cutting from his frock-coat. "This is authority," said Root. "*The Review of Reviews.*"

"Hardly . . ." Hay began.

But Root was inexorable; he read: "'With December 31' . . . Dr. Shaw is referring to yesterday . . . 'we completed the year 1899—that is to say, we round out ninety-nine of the hundred years that are necessary to complete a full century.' Now, dear Hay, attend closely to his reasoning . . ."

"You know I'm hopeless when it comes to figures, dear Root."

"As your vast real estate holdings testify. Anyway, you are sufficiently numerate to get *this* point. 'We must give the nineteenth century the three hundred sixty-five days that belong to its hundredth and final year, before we begin the year one of the twentieth century.' You will like this part." Root beamed contentedly. Just back of him, Hay noted that Mrs. Dewey, all sapphire blue, had somehow got herself to the Blue Room's center, where Cortelyou stared at her, deeply alarmed.

Root continued, unaware of the drama in the making. "'The mathematical faculty works more keenly in monetary affairs than elsewhere. . . .' One would think that Dr. Shaw knew you personally, Hay."

"I am Everyman, Root. You know that. An on-going exemplar of the ordinary and the modest. Something to be found on any grandmother's sampler."

"Be that as it may, none of the people who have prepared to allow ninety-nine years to go for a century would suppose that a nineteen-hundred-dollar debt had been fully met by a tender of eighteen hundred and ninety-nine dollars. Well?"

"You are brutal." Hay gave Root ten dollars. "You win. And now it is possible—probable even—that I shall have my wish and die in the nineteenth century."

"What a curious ambition. My God, there's Mrs. Dewey."

"She has captured Mr. Long. He is her Cavite Bay."

The great china-doll eyes of Mrs. Dewey were turned on the

Secretary of the Navy, while a tiny doll's hand rested gently, imploringly, on his forearm.

"Mischief is afoot," Hay began; but then the Marine band broke into "Hail to the Chief," and the guests who had been waiting in Green, Red, and Blue Rooms now stationed themselves at the foot of the stairs as the President and—to general amazement—Mrs. McKinley made their slow, stately descent. She clung to him; he held her upright. There was something poignant, Hay felt, in their perfect ordinariness. The other guests were already crowded into the East Room.

McKinley nodded, first, to Hay, who bowed; and then fell in behind the last of the diplomatic corps, the Cabinet behind him.

Suddenly, Hay was aware that Mrs. Dewey had moved into position at his left elbow, while clinging to the right arm of the Secretary of the Navy. "Happy New Year, Mr. Hay!" She was brightly innocent; even the eyelashes were like those of a doll, in odd clusters, giving a starry artificial look to the china-blue eyes.

"What a joy," murmured Hay, never so happy as when he was able to indulge in a minor insincerity, "to find you here with us, in the Cabinet."

"It was dear Mr. Long who took me in. I told him that the Admiral and I must leave early, and if we were to wait until Cabinet, Court, diplomats, Congress *and* Army went through the line, why, we'd be here longer than my Admiral's whole war, and Mr. Long said he'd take me through. So kind . . ."

Hay felt Clara's disapproval on his right; and saw Root's amused anger or angered amusement at Mrs. Dewey's bold victory over the Army, and himself.

At the door to the East Room, the President paused; and looked anxiously down at Mrs. McKinley, who looked up, wanly, at him. Then the President made his entrance, going straight to the throne-like blue chair at the room's opposite end; here he deposited Mrs. McKinley, who sank into the chair, clutching a bouquet of orchids to her bosom.

As Hay and Clara entered the crowded room, he was careful to avoid, as always, his single superstition, the cleared space at the center, where Lincoln had lain in his coffin. Otherwise, the East Room had no particular significance for Hay. It had always been a sort of theater, whose star was the president of the moment, whose audience were the dignitaries who came and went, usually without trace; yet, simultaneously, Washington was a city that although it never missed anyone never forgot anyone, either. Again, Hay thought of the house—the city, too, and the republic beyond—as a theater, with a somewhat limited repertory of plays; and types. The only time the East Room had ever come alive was during the weeks that a Kentucky regiment of volunteers, eager to protect President Lincoln, had bivouacked in the room, where they had used the fireplaces for cooking. Later, Mrs. Lincoln would make the East Room splendid, at a stunning cost to the government and to her husband, who insisted on paying for some of her madder luxuries. Now the East Room was, again, shabby, and depressing; rather like a resort hotel out of season. Where Mrs. Lincoln's glorious sea-green carpet had unfurled its expansive expensive length there was now a bright yellow mustard-colored carpet, presently a bright perfect foil for muddy footprints. Between windows and fireplaces rows of shabby, pumpkin-shaped seats were placed, each with a stricken palm tree rising from its center. The effect was peculiarly dismal in the glare of the huge electrified chandeliers.

Mrs. McKinley endured her high estate for an hour; then the President himself took her upstairs; and the guests were now free to roam outside their hierarchical orders. Mrs. Dewey's preemptory strike had been noticed by all; and General Miles looked very grim indeed. The Admiral seemed not to have noticed anything as he and triumphant wife departed, while Hay was taken to one side by Lord Pauncefote. Across the room the Russian Ambassador glared at the two conspirators. Hay knew that Cassini regarded him as not only an Anglophile but a dupe of England. Actually, in most matters of any consequence to the United States, England followed America's lead; in exchange, the Administration reciprocated by tacit encouragement in South Africa. Hay was prepared to discuss the Hay-Pauncefote Treaty, soon to go to the Senate, but to his surprise, Pauncefote had not canals but China on his mind. "You know, Mr. Hay," the old man's seductive barrister's voice buzzed agreeably in Hay's ear, "that the dismemberment of China continues, with the Russians busiest of us all . . ."

"'Us'? *We* are not busy."

"I speak of wicked Europe, of course, not innocent America."

"Thank you."

"They are consolidating Manchuria. They will soon be Russifying Peking and North China, an essential market for your textile industries, which the Russians mean to close."

Cassini, a few yards away, clamped his monocle into his left eyesocket; and glared at them over the head of Cambon. Cassini seemed to be listening to every word.

"The New England delegation to Congress is very sensitive to all this." Hay was soothing. "And so am I. Did you know that Mr. Henry Adams thinks that Russia will disintegrate in the next twenty-five years, and that we shall then be obliged to Americanize Siberia, the only territory worth having in Asia?"

Lord Pauncefote gave Hay a sharp look to see if this might be some sort of Yankee joke to which he had not got the point. When Hay said no more, Pauncefote smiled. "Mr. Adams does not hold office, does he?"

"No. Alas. For us."

"Yes," said Pauncefote, Adams forever dismissed from his mind. He then steered Hay to one of the depressing pumpkin seats, where, beneath a palm whose fronds were brown from overheating, he came to his point. "Unlike Russia, China is already disintegrating. The question is, who shall pick up the pieces? Russia and Japan have got the most already. The Kaiser fishes wherever he can. The French . . ."

"As you know, we are the only non-fishers." Hay wondered to what extent he should take Pauncefote into his confidence. Hay had already worked out a formula which, he was certain, would place the United States at the center of the entire China equation; yet cost nothing. Hay proceeded, by instinct. "We sit on our extremely uncomfortable Philippines and stare with dismay at the Gold Rush for China. Of course we're nervous about the Shansi province. Will Russia shut the north of China to us? If they do, will our textile industry collapse? I have," Hay decided to take a shallow, experimental plunge, "gone round Cassini, who is impossible to deal with, as we all know. He is vain and somewhat silly. Worse, he's also been ambassador in China, and he knows, perhaps, too much for . . . *our* good. So I've been dealing directly with Count Mouravieff in Petersburg. Last week he wrote me a straightforward letter—straightforward, that is, for a Russian. I had asked for only one thing. An open door to China for all nations. He wrote me that outside of the territories currently leased by China to Russia—"

"Leased!" Pauncefote shook his head; shut his eyes, to blot out the extent of human perfidy.

"Isn't Kowloon leased to England by China?"

"A straightforward business, involving a single port." Pauncefote was quick. "Nothing like taking over all Manchuria, and Port Arthur, a whole kingdom."

"Anyway, he guarantees Russia will honor the old Chinese treaties with each of us."

"Do you believe him?"

"Of course not. But I have forced him to make a move, something Russians hate. They want nothing spelled out, ever. Well, now he's given me an opening to put as large a construction as I can on his words. So, in a few months, I shall make my move. I think that I—that *we*, dear Pauncefote—can box them all in."

"You seem to be getting the hang of this." Pauncefote was dry.

"I appeal only to the decent instincts of all mankind."

"Wait till you deal with the Japanese. They are not decent. They are not even mankind."

"Extra-terrestrial?"

"Lunatics, yes! Moon-men."

The President was again in the East Room. But this time he was accompanied not by Mrs. McKinley but by Del and Caroline. "They look like son and daughter," said Pauncefote, without much tact.

"Surely son and daughter-*in-law*," Hay rallied. He had yet to comprehend what attraction Del had for the President. Certainly, Del told him nothing. Only by accident did he ever learn that Del had had a family dinner with the McKinleys or that he had accompanied the President on a drive. Plainly, the boy was a born courtier.

Caroline had thought the same but now she was not so certain. For the first time, she had been invited to "supper" with the McKinleys. The other guests were Del and Mr. and Mrs. Charles G. Dawes. She now inclined to the son-that-he-never-had view. It was the President who played courtier to Del, advising him on everything, including what to eat. As it was, the food in the family dining room was plentiful. The conversation was not. Mrs. McKinley drank consommé; and ate a chicken wing. The Daweses talked and laughed enough for four, their function, Caroline decided. The President ate for two; and Del was demure.

Now they stood in front of a marble fireplace at one end of the truly, to Caroline's eye, hideous East Room, and the President shook hands and made stately conversation with those who came up to him. In the brief intervals between what Caroline had come to think of as the laying on of hands, the President talked to her of Del. "As long as I am here," he said, in his mellifluous, even to Caroline's critical ear, voice, "he will go very far indeed. He is the sort of person we need in this place where . . ." Somehow or other, McKinley never allowed any potentially interesting sentence to arrive at a conclusion; thus, he avoided, masterfully, ever being quotable. Caroline had first been bored by the President; then she was fascinated by the perfect caution with which he spoke, allowing fortune not a single hostage. If not intelligent, he was highly subtle in the practice of his political art. But then Caroline had already realized that her own criterion for intelligence was both conventional and European. For her, intelligence was, simply, to what degree a mind had been civilized. As a result, she had been in no way prepared for a mind that, innocent of civilization, was still capable of swift analysis and shrewd action. McKinley barely knew of Caesar and Alexander; yet he had conquered almost as much of the earth as either, without once stirring from the ugly national house with its all-important telegraph-machine and no less potent telephone.

"He's very much," said McKinley, "the way his father must have been when he was here." Del had told Caroline that the President seldom mentioned any of his predecessors by name, a perhaps unique trait that he shared with Lincoln. "I think Pretoria will season him and then . . ." The appearance of Senator Lodge caused the President to smile with what looked to be genuine warmth. There was, thought Caroline, a lot to be learned about acting from Mr. McKinley. Meanwhile, Del, out of earshot, was screening would-be celebrators of the new year—new century— with the President. At the far end of the room, Marguerite Cassini looked very lovely; indeed, like a ballet girl, dressed up, thought Caroline with swift unkindness, as a lady. She was enchanting a number of elderly congressmen, her eyes on Del; apparently, he had flirted more seriously with Marguerite than he had ever admitted to Caroline, who was disturbed to find herself jealous; and was not jealousy a sign of love? she asked her own Marguerite, who had replied sourly, "More likely a sign of a very selfish disposition."

The President had finished congratulating Senator Lodge on his awesome brilliance; and Lodge turned to Caroline, with a foxy smile. "You are still enjoying this barbaric country?"

" 'Barbaric' is your word, Mr. Lodge. I am enamored of your— *our* civilization. A light to all the world, I should say."

"You *do* say in the *Washington Tribune*."

"Oh, I never read the leaders. I only like . . ."

"Murders?"

"Lost children is our current passion. But I didn't think that you read our paper."

"Oh, I keep careful track of you."

"Our murders?"

"Lost children, too."

"Treaties?" Caroline struck, sweetly she hoped. She had the pleasure of producing a frown on the stern senatorial face. Lodge was suspected of working against his friend Hay's canal treaty.

"My dear Miss Sanford. A treaty is only a Platonic essence before it comes to the Senate. Then we—two-thirds of us—make it corporeal."

"May I quote you?"

"Let me quote myself first in the Senate. Then it is all yours. You will go on?"

Caroline was now quite used to the question. "Why not? Besides, Mr. McLean is willing to finance me."

"McLean? Why?"

"So that I won't be obliged to sell out to Mr. Hearst."

"Oh!" Lodge was delighted. "You'll find a lot of us will pay you anything you like to keep him out of Washington." Lodge looked at Del. "When does he go to Pretoria?"

"Next month."

"Alone?"

"Alone."

– 2 –

Henry Adams gave the farewell dinner for Del; and Adams was, Hay thought, every bit as grim as February itself, Washington's least favored month. Hay arrived first; and found Adams looking more like a diabolic hedgehog than the legendary angelic porcupine of Lafayette Square.

"I have lost all interest in tobacco and champagne." Adams

stood beneath Blake's celebration of Nebuchadnezzar's madness. William brought more wood for the fire.

"You still have La Dona." Hay lit his forbidden-by-Clara before-dinner cigar.

"She is the muse of a poet, Heaven help us. A ridiculously young poet." Adams was very round indeed; and almost as irritable as he claimed to be. "I've had a letter from Don Cameron. He's down in St. Helens and wants me to visit. I remind him of his wife, I suppose. If it were not for the thirteenth century, I would kill myself."

"Then we have more to thank Madame Poulard for than her omelettes."

"They, too, are as Gothic as Mont-St.-Michel." Hay was not as enamored of the idea of the Virgin as Adams had become. He was beginning to fear that his old friend might yet turn Catholic on him.

"Perhaps too agreeable an image. Cabot is not coming tonight."

Hay felt a sciatic thrill in his left leg. "Does this mean he'll oppose the treaty?"

"I don't know what he means any more. He is as bad as Brooks."

Hay had just read Brooks Adams's most recent novelty, *Natural Selection in Literature*. With all the positiveness of a Karl Marx, Brooks traced England's decline through its literature, from vigorous rural warrior Walter Scott to effete, urban, cowardly and fearful Charles Dickens. Apparently, the rise of Mr. Micawber heralded England's eclipse. "Brooks writes me regularly," said Hay, somewhat cautiously, aware how much younger brother irritated older brother. "He has decided that Russia must either undergo a social revolution internally or expand externally."

"Why not both?" Adams was more than ever bristling porcupine.

"He prefers either-or to simultaneity. He has confided to me that if the Russians and the Germans were to obtain China's Shansi province, we would be at their mercy . . ."

"So we must arm to the teeth. That means more ships, more Admiral Mahan, more noise from Teddy! Oh, I am sick of the whole lot." The fire, sympathetically, exploded behind Adams. Both men started. Then Adams sat in his favorite small leather chair opposite Hay's favorite small leather chair. The children's study, the large Clara had called the room, designed as it was entirely for the comfort of great small men, and charming nieces. "I admire Brooks's theory as far as I can understand it—nations as organisms. Nations as stores of energy, slowly depleting unless refuelled. I grasp all that. But I want only to understand the theory, which I don't, really, and neither does he, while Brooks wants to *apply* the bloody thing. He's mad. He's got all sorts of people who should know better excited, including you."

"Nothing excites me, Henry, except your excitement."

"Well, I am excited when I think of him. Brooks thinks England will collapse soon. So do I. He thinks we'll inherit their empire. I don't, at least not for long. I want us to build a sort of Great Wall of China, and hide behind it as long as possible. In the next quarter century the world's going to go smash. Well, I'm for staying out of the smash as long as possible. You see, I'm anti-imperialist. Don't tell Teddy or Lodge or Mahan. I'm for letting the whole thing smash up, and then, later, we might find some pieces worth picking up. Meanwhile, forget the Philippines. Forget China. Let England sink. Let Russia and Germany try to run the machine, while we live on our internal resources, which are so much greater than theirs. They'll end by going bust, and why should we go bust with them?"

"Perhaps," said Hay, startled by so much unexpected vehemence, not to mention so vast a sea-change in the Adams cosmogony, "we shall not be allowed to stay out, in order to pursue your—scavenger policy, of picking up the pieces."

"Scavengers thrive on the battles of others. Anyway, we are getting in much too deep in Asia."

"I thought you always wanted us to have Siberia . . ."

"But only as a scavenger, as loot, after the Tsar and his idiot

253

court—those thirty-five grand dukes—have managed to destroy their ramshackle empire. I certainly wouldn't send Admiral Dewey and General Miles to Port Arthur."

"What about Teddy? We could always send him, alone, with a gun over Petersburg. In a balloon, of course."

"Filled with air from his own strenuous lungs. I saw him when he was here last week. He swore, yet again, that he did not want to be vice-president."

Hay sighed. "The Major doesn't want him. Mark Hanna has already had one heart attack, attributable to Teddy. He was at his desk in the Senate, reading a newspaper account of Teddy's fierce determination *not* to be vice-president, when, with a terrifying cry, he slumped to the floor, near dead of a Teddy-inspired heart attack."

"Well, he is now completely recovered." Adams stared gloomily into the fire. "He was brought here to breakfast."

"Mark Hanna!" Hay was horrified; no one so low had ever come to an Adams breakfast. "Who *dared* bring him?"

"Cabot. Who else? It was, he said, for my—education."

Clara and Helen made a joint entrance. Adams and Hay rose to greet them as if they had not all just met at tea beneath their joint roof. In order to maintain perspective, as Hay put it, meaning sanity, he walked every afternoon, no matter how cold, with Adams; then they would join Clara at her tea-urn. During these long walks, Hay was able to relate exactly what was on his mind while Adams was able to tell him, with great charm, what was not on the Secretary of State's mind but ought to be.

Helen was now thinner; and altogether lovely to her father's prejudiced eye. It was taken for granted that, in a year's time, she would marry Payne Whitney, a handsome son of a handsome father, who was also deeply corrupt politically, and a master of Tammany. William C. Whitney was also a maker of money and, like Hay himself, a marrier of money, in the form of the large— why were heiresses always so large?—Flora Payne, who had died, leaving not so much a bereaved husband as a bereaved bachelor brother, Oliver Payne, the wealthiest of the lot. Then when Whitney remarried, Oliver Payne declared war on his one-time brother-in-law and with extraordinary and elaborate monetary bribes detached two of Whitney's four children from their father: a daughter, Pauline, and a son, Harry Payne Whitney. Happily, the stormy brothers-in-law that once had been both approved of Helen, who behaved like a minister plenipotentiary as she made her way between the warring houses. William Whitney, once spoken of for president, was now being investigated by Governor Roosevelt because he owned streetcar lines in New York City. Whitney had been in Cleveland's Cabinet; was an ally of Bryan; was, thought Hay, more than a match for Teddy, whose reforming tendencies, thus far, were more rhetorical than real.

"Colonel Payne is coming, isn't he?" asked Helen, with more anxiety than her father felt warranted.

"He is doing me the honor, dearest infant. But then I hold open house for all Ohio, always. It is the Adams destiny in the fourth generation."

Clara laughed. "One Stone and one Payne are hardly all Ohio."

"But one Mark Hanna and one McKinley are one nation," said Hay.

"One Republican Party, anyway. It seems," said Adams, brightening, "that all presidents now come from Ohio. Garfield, Hayes, the Major. And they have quite obliterated the founders with their Western Reserve glory."

"Dear Henry," murmured Hay, "you do lay it on."

The room filled up. Adams had invited twenty guests, the optimum number, he felt, for a dinner party. There was a possibility of general conversation, if someone other than the host proved to be brilliant. If no such paladin emerged, guests could speak across the table if they chose, an impossibility at a vast formal dinner where conversation, in Noah's Ark twos, shifted to left and right with each course.

Hay noted several senators of the sort that Adams would never have invited were it not for Hay's treaty: he appreciated the

255

Porcupine's sacrifice. Dowdily, Lord and Lady Pauncefote arrived, an equally dowdy daughter in tow.

Adams—the worst of guests; in fact, guest no longer of anyone except the Hays—was the best of hosts. Expertly, he moved his menagerie around the study like a sheepdog. But Del got past him to speak to his father. As they talked, Hay studied his own nose at the center of Del's face; thus, nature would continue him through Del and, after Del, their plainly unlosable nose would be carried on into future generations, a reminder of one Johnny Hay from Warsaw, Illinois, master of all trades, as he once vaingloriously proclaimed to Adams, and a jack of none.

"The President says you're to instruct me, Mr. Secretary."

"You have no instructions, Consul-General, except the general one that I always give. What you have never said cannot be used against you."

"I shall be silent to the Boers and silent to the English . . ."

"But write long reports to me and—to the President?" Hay was curious to know just what the Major expected of Del.

"I am to keep him informed, he said. Nothing more. You know how he is."

"Not as well as you." Del blushed at this. "You have his confidence." Hay was aware of the sententious note in his voice. "Do not abuse it." Why, Hay wondered, was he so expert at always striking the wrong note with Del when, with everyone else, he had always had—owed his career to, in fact—perfect pitch?

"Why should I?" The gentle Del was now angry; and Hay could not think how to placate him. He looked for a diversion, and one stood in the doorway, the last of the guests, wearing a splendid dark gold gown. Caroline was greeted by Adams, who kissed her hand, something he rarely did with nieces, but then she was more fine Paris lady than humble American niece. Hay had always thought her a splendid catch, unlike Clara, who was less than enthusiastic but could give no reason why Del ought not to marry someone so extraordinarily rare. Yet Clara still went on and on about foreignness as if she had never left Amasa Stone's house in

Cincinnati. It was Hay's fear that Caroline would take the year of Del's absence and find someone more grand. Hay did not have the usual American *nouveau riche* conviction that to be new and rich was a sign of God's anointment and so to be preferred to quarterings and coronets and money that had been aged in land. He had come from nowhere, like his father-in-law, and he could, he always feared, revisit nowhere at a moment's notice. Fortunes lost were less of a novelty at century's end than fortunes won.

Caroline joined them. "You're late," said Del.

"I have been," suddenly Caroline stammered, "at the office. Isn't that a terrible thing for a woman to say?"

"Say or do?" asked Hay, charmed.

"Both. At first, the fact that I have an office was a novelty here. Now it is a source of—*chagrin.*" She used the French word.

"The other girls are just jealous," said Del.

"Oh, the 'other girls' rather like the idea. It means that I am completely out of the way, and no competition. It's the men who grow distressed."

"We are the superfluous sex." Del looked at her more than fondly. If he was as much in love as Hay suspected, he was to be envied; at least, by his father, whose fondness for Clara had never once resembled love. Of course, he and Clara had been older when they met; and the world much younger; and marriage a matter, mostly, of sets of silver and linen, and relatives to be shared and propitiated, and money.

"What kept you at this sinister office of yours?" Hay quite liked the idea of a young woman publishing a newspaper in sordid Market Place.

"You," said Caroline; the hazel eyes looked directly into his own. Wildly, he imagined that he, not his son, was engaged to this splendid creature, who had, on her cheek, like a beauty mark, a small delicate charming smudge of printer's ink. Hay had spent much of his own youth among printing presses.

"What about Father?" Del seemed anxious. Hay could only

delight in the pale rose-pink cheek with its coquettish dot of blue-black ink.

"Wouldn't you rather wait until after dinner?" Caroline started to back away, and stepped into Root, who was approaching them.

"I won't be able to eat unless I know what horrors the press plans to rain down upon my head." Hay could not make up his mind which he despised more, the loud ignorant venal Senate or the equally loud ignorant venal press. On balance, as he had been both a journalist and an editor, he despised the press more. He understood the journalist in a way that he could never understand the egomaniacal senator, who saw himself as the nation incarnate and mindless, and loud, loud, loud.

"Miss Sanford, don't keep us in suspense. What has come over the wire?" Root looked at Hay. "The War Department has been cut off from the world ever since the last freeze. We could be invaded, and never know it."

"The *New York Sun* would probably keep you informed," said Caroline, producing from her handbag a press cutting. "This is tomorrow's *Sun*. Governor Roosevelt has attacked your treaty."

Hay took the cutting, and pretended to read, though he could see nothing without the pince-nez which rested on his chest. "I suppose," he observed mildly, "that this is why Cabot did not come tonight."

"I grow bored with Teddy," said Root, baring his teeth. He took the cutting from Hay. "He wants the canal to be armed, by us."

"If the Senate does not accept the treaty," Hay's words sounded to himself as if from a great distance, "I shall have no choice but to resign."

"If you do," said Root thoughtfully, "you will take Teddy down with you. The President will never forgive him."

"Then I shall have done *two* excellent things." Hay remembered to smile. "Let us not," he said, "discuss this with the others. Let them read of my shame tomorrow."

He turned to Caroline. "You are publishing Teddy's statement?"

"On page three . . ."

"Where it belongs," said Root.

"I have an entire family murdered by a single ax, on page one," said Caroline.

"Good girl!" Hay was amused at last. "First things first, always. Is Del's nose like mine?"

"Yes. A perfect copy. I'm fascinated at the way physical features continue in families from generation to generation." She echoed, nicely, his own perception.

"Your mother . . ."

"I know."

But Hay was certain that Caroline did not know the rumors about the famous Princesse d'Agrigente.

After dinner, Caroline and Del and Helen Hay were bundled into the back of a sleigh for a long moonlight ride to the hamlet of Chevy Chase.

"Russia must be like this. Just like this!" Helen exclaimed, as they passed from town into open snowy country: a world without color, only black, white and shades of gray, and sudden flashes of diamond-glitter as moonlight struck ice. Clara had insisted, without subtlety, that Helen join them on their last ride, and Caroline had been as pleased as Del was displeased. Caroline got no joy from having her hand pressed beneath a sable rug, while a stolen kiss, anywhere, simply depressed her. She was not like other girls; she had accepted her uniqueness without distress; she was prepared, or so she thought, for everything, including the whole business of two anatomies entwined, and the prickling of fig-leaves or whatever, but she could not bear the step-by-careful-step American courtship. At least in Paris, marriages were business affairs, like the mergers of railroads.

Helen chattered incessantly of Payne. How he and his sister Pauline had chosen their bachelor uncle, Oliver, over their hand-some—*handsome*, she repeated—father. She would make no judgment, while the other brother, Harry, and sister, Dorothy, chose to remain with their father. "You cannot know, Caroline, what it is like to live in a family with such, such Shakespearean emotions, emotions!"

"But I can *imagine*, Helen." Actually, Caroline suspected that there had been something Jacobean about her own parents. Why did her father never mention the, always, "dark" Emma? Why had Blaise told her that Mrs. Delacroix's eyes entirely vanished at the mention of Emma? Then, back of all, there was Aaron Burr, worth a dozen Whitneys, a gross of Paynes. Nevertheless, old Oliver Payne, who seemed to Caroline to be all malignancy, coming between father and children and buying two of them outright from their father because the father had remarried three years after the death of Oliver's sister, Flora, deified by brother, it was said, as once he had deified or at least revelled in his handsome, handsome, as Helen would say, brother-in-law. "But then we always think our own families more original than anyone else's." Caroline thought that she had scored a point as their driver hurtled over a smooth untracked ivory field, close by a farmhouse where a single window filled space and time with a square of yellow light, the only color in their night world.

"Oh, *we're* not original," said Helen. "We are very dull, aren't we, Del?"

"Some of us more than others." Del was judicious. Under the robe his hand, a trifle damp, held Caroline's.

"But your father's life has been so interesting." Caroline was now working herself up to the eventual embrace that their last evening together required. At times, she felt that she was involved in an elaborate peasant dance, which had not been entirely explained to her. Now the hand is held; now the heel is stamped; now the head turns; and then the kiss.

"I don't think Father really believes he lived it," said Helen, unexpectedly.

"Who does he think did?" Caroline stared at Helen's profile, back-lit by snow-glare.

"I don't think he thinks about that. He's always in the present, you see; and there's something always wrong, so he's disturbed. I showed him a copy of that famous picture of him with Nicolay and President Lincoln. You know, sitting in front of the fireplace in the President's office, and he said he had no memory when it was taken, but he was certain that he'd never once laid eyes on the skinny young man, who called himself John Hay."

"He remembered enough about the picture to say it was made in a studio and that the background was painted in later." Del clutched hard Caroline's hand. Should she clutch back?

"I hope I'll never be so old." Helen sounded as if she meant what she said. "I think he will resign, if the Senate rejects his treaty."

"I don't," said Del; and Caroline withdrew her hand, and made a fist. "The President needs him. And what would he do if he went? Hatred of the Senate keeps him alive."

In Chevy Chase, they stopped at an eighteenth-century tavern; and drank hot buttered rum in front of a great fire. At the next table what looked to be four local farmers played cards in silence. Helen, tactfully, excused herself.

"I wish you were coming to Pretoria."

"So do I." Caroline was almost sincere. After all, was there anyone nicer than Del? "But I've got the paper, and I've got Blaise to deal with."

"Why does he take so hard a line with you? After all, you'll inherit anyway in a few years."

"Because my plan misfired. He's more like me than I suspected. I thought he'd give way once I had something that he wanted. Now, of course, he'll never give way."

"Are *you* like that?"

"If tested, yes, I think so. Anyway, that is the way I am with him. Mr. Hearst is also very angry with me," she added happily.

"When we're married . . ."

The dance had started up again; a moment of panic; what was her next step? "Yes, Del?"

"You won't go on, will you?"

"You'd rather I didn't?"

"Do you think it's the sort of thing a wife should do?"

"There are," said Caroline, sagely, "wives and wives. Wouldn't I be more useful to your father and the President with a paper than without?"

"Would you be more useful to me?"

"I don't know." Caroline had given the matter no thought. She realized that she was now several steps behind in the mating dance. "If you're to be a diplomat and live abroad—well, no. But you say you'd rather be here after Pretoria—in politics!"

"Or business. I don't know. Pretoria's for the President. He wants someone there he can trust to tell him what's really going on between the English and the Boers. He thinks Father is too . . ."

"Pro-British?"

Del laughed. "I can't say that to a newspaper publisher, can I?"

"Fortunately, you don't have to. The *Tribune* is already on record. Remember?"

"When some senators complained to the President that the Secretary of State was a product of the English school . . . ?"

"The President said, 'I thought he was a product of the school of Abraham Lincoln.' Yes, we got that story first. And everyone's copied us."

"Was it true?"

Caroline laughed. "The gist of it, yes. I am in too deep at the *Tribune*, for now."

"But if *I* were to buy it . . . ?"

"Oh, I'd warn you against buying! I owe you that much."

"You lose a great deal?"

"We make a small amount." Actually, between the increase in the newsstand sales and the additional advertising revenue relentlessly extorted by Caroline from Mrs. Bingham's friends, not to mention all of Apgardom, the paper was for the first time, if barely, in the black. Mr. Trimble was suitably awed; and Caroline suitably conceited. "I have something for you." Caroline now chose to adapt the dance to her own measure. She removed a small package from her handbag; and noted that Del was astonished at this change in the dance's familiar pattern: a german had become a waltz. He opened the package: and took out a heavy gold ring in which was set a dark fire opal. "This was my father's," said Caroline, suddenly uneasy. Had she gone too far? "Opals bring bad luck but it brought him good luck and if it's your birthstone . . ."

"As it's mine," he said, and slipped on the ring, and kissed her, as indifferent to the card players as those solemn men were to the young, now engaged, couple. Caroline had been openly wearing her sapphire, without explanation, for a month. Marguerite had complained, as had the ancient Miss Faith Apgar, who now lived under the eaves of N Street, an official duenna, put in place by the Apgars. Without a formal engagement, no man's ring could be worn. Now a woman's ring was in place on a man's finger; and the scandal, if anyone were to know, would echo from flashy Lafayette Square to stolid Scott Circle. Apparently, no girl had ever given a man a ring before.

But Del did not mind; quite the contrary. "Look!" He showed Helen the ring, as she sat down.

"Good Heavens! How beautiful! How daring! How unlucky!"

"Not for me, the opal," said Del.

"My father wore it, and lived a long time; happily, I suppose."

"He died in an accident," Helen began.

"Rather a better end than most of his contemporaries made," said Caroline. "He was old," she added.

"As a poet, I am thrilled. Thrilled!" Helen had published one volume of verse quite as good, if not as popular, as her father's youthful work. "As a sister, I think we should take a mutual vow of silence until you two are safely married."

The three drank to that, and Caroline felt herself, suddenly, part of a most agreeable family, something she had never known at home and only caught glimpses of on visits to the houses of school friends. Was it possible, she wondered, as they took the sleigh back to the city, that she would not always be alone?

7

— I —

Blaise stood in front of the four-story brownstone on Twenty-
eighth Street, off Lexington Avenue. New-planted trees were in
somewhat mangy leaf on either side of the chocolate-colored steps.
The old Worth House was now a muddy hole in the ground. But
Hearst, with his usual flair—or was it good luck?—had managed
to buy the townhouse of that most fastidious and fashionable—if
not the only fastidious and fashionable—of presidents, Chester
Arthur.

George opened the door. "Well, it's home now, Mr. Blaise," he
said. "Practically a palace, I'd say, from the number of rooms I
have to look after."

Blaise followed George up a flight of mahogany steps to a
baronial panelled sitting room filled with crates of unopened art or
"art," while the walls were covered with paintings and tapestries
and, sometimes, paintings supported by nails impatiently driven
through ancient Aubusson and Gobelin tapestries. Egyptian

mummy cases and statues were scattered about the room, like a newly opened pharaonic tomb, loot from the Chief's winter on the Nile.

The Chief himself stood in front of a large map of the United States, with numerous red pins in it. Like George, he was in shirt-sleeves. Also, like George, he was somewhat larger than he had been at the Worth House. Otherwise, he was unchanged. He was still loyal to the Willson girls, but not ready to marry. For company, he currently allowed his editor, the courtly Arthur Brisbane, to live in the house. Brisbane reminded Blaise of a somewhat obsequious tutor to a somewhat dim rich boy.

"National Association of Democrat Clubs. Where they are. Each red pin is one club." The Chief explained either too much or too little.

"And you're the chairman."

"I'm the chairman. I don't know." Hearst fell onto a sofa and kicked off his shoes: the socks were striped mauve and yellow. "It looks like Chicago," he said at last.

"For the Democratic Convention?"

"Newspapers, too. I agreed. The *Chicago Evening American*. I like the word 'American.' For a paper."

"What about 'Evening'?" Blaise sat in an armchair next to a life-size sphinx, assuming that in life sphinxes were the same size as chorus girls.

"You may have to start with 'evening.' Then you sneak up on 'morning.' Takes time. I think I've made a joke. By accident. How's your French lady?" Hearst could never remember any French names.

"In France. Where French ladies live."

"She's very well-dressed," said the Chief thoughtfully. "The girls like her clothes a lot. And her, too," he added, staring at the mummy case, which, Blaise hoped, did not remind the Chief too much of his mistress.

"Who did you agree with?"

"About what? Brisbane says that mummy case is a fake, but how would he know?"

Blaise let Brisbane slip by. "About starting a paper in Chicago."

"The Democratic National Committee. They said they won't have a chance this year without a Chicago paper, so after they made me chairman of all those clubs—all across the country, see? Three million members." He waved his hand at the map. This was to be his powerbase within the party. "So I said I'd start up a paper. First issue is July second, two days before the Democratic Convention. Bryan is going to start up the presses."

"Bryan's the nominee?"

The Chief grunted. "*I'm* not,' he said, neutrally. "This is going to cost a lot." From under the sofa he pulled out the dusty banjo. He ran his thumb across the strings; in defiance of the law of averages, each was out of tune. Happily, Hearst did not try to play.

Blaise prepared himself for what he knew was the Chief's next move. But Hearst did not make the expected move. "Mother's luck is better than Father's ever was," he said. "She's in on the Homestead Mine. South Dakota Gold. They're making six million dollars a year now and she's chief shareholder."

"That takes care of money." Blaise was, momentarily, relieved.

"That could. Croker's on his way here. He's got Tammany lined up for Bryan. That's the city. I'll get him the rest of the state."

"Do you want Bryan?"

"Can't stop him. But he's promised to go easy on silver. He owes me a lot. You'll come in on Chicago?" That was the way that Hearst got Blaise to invest. Although Hearst maintained full ownership of all his papers, he was obliged to take out personal loans, involving pieces of paper which were, in effect, IOUs. The idea of sharing a newspaper—or power—with anyone was unthinkable. The detail about the Homestead Mine was to remind Blaise that Mrs. Hearst would always bail out her son. According to Hearst's man of business, Solomon Carvalho, Mrs. Hearst's fortune was now larger than

266

the one that her husband had left her. Luck was a Hearst family friend.

"I suppose so. I'll talk to Carvalho." Blaise preferred to do business with businessmen and not with—but what was the Chief? A visionary? Hardly. More an innovator, entrepreneur, fact of nature.

"You do that. How's the Washington paper?"

"My sister hangs on."

"She can't forever."

"John McLean has said he'll stake her if she ever needs money, to keep you out of town."

Hearst's thin mouth ceased to be a mouth; a thin fissure now split the white face. "I'll buy the *Post* one day. To keep McLean out of town. He wants it. But old Wilkins won't sell to him. He will to me."

Blaise both admired and deplored the Chief's certainty that, in time, he would have everything that he had ever wanted. "I'm looking at the *Baltimore Examiner*."

"Not bad," said Hearst. "Cheap. Potential for growth." He echoed, unconsciously, Carvalho's businessman's talk. "They need it—or they could need it—in Washington."

George announced Mr. Richard Croker, lord of Tammany and the Democratic equivalent of Senator Platt, with whom he was never too proud to do business. In fact, the Irish-born Croker regarded himself as nothing more than a simple businessman who, for a fee, would work with any other businessman. He controlled the politics of the city. He enjoyed the company and even the friendship of the magnates of the Democratic Party, particularly William C. Whitney. But then each kept stables, and raced horses. Croker had stud farms not only in New York State but in England. He was an impressive figure, all gray from hair and beard to expensive English tweeds.

Croker shook Hearst's hand as languidly as Hearst shook his; then he shook Blaise's hand vigorously. Blaise was somewhat awed by this street youth who had risen so high. He had begun as a henchman of the infamous Boss Tweed, in whose behalf he might or might not have murdered a man on a long-ago election day. The jury—twelve bad men and false—had been unable to make up its mind; and so he was allowed to go free; and rise. "I seen my opportunities," he would say of his long career, "and I took 'em." He took "clean graft," money for city contracts. Dirty graft was the sort of thing that the police went in for, extorting protection money from saloon-keepers and prostitutes. Although Croker highly disapproved of dirty graft and never touched it himself, he had once said, almost plaintively, to Blaise, "We've got to put up with a certain amount. It's only common justice. After all, the police see us doing all this good business, and then they see the Astors making all that money out of all those tenements, and breaking every law, which, Heaven forgive us, we let them do because we do business with the Four Hundred like everyone else who's respectable, so how can I be too hard on an overworked police sergeant with ten children who asks for ten dollars a week from some saloon-keeper for a bit of protection?" Blaise had had several fascinating talks with Croker; and tended to admire him more than not. Croker was particularly fierce on the subject of the reformers. He now displayed his ferocity to Hearst and Blaise.

"I have never known such a bunch of hypocrites in my life." He lit his cigar; puffed smoke at the Chief, who coughed, unnoticed by his guest. "The worst is Roosevelt, because he knows the game. He *plays* the game . . ."

"He takes money?" Blaise regretted his question, as two sets of pitying eyes were turned, briefly, on him.

Neither man bothered to answer so naïve a question. "He acts, every day, as if he's just discovered sin when his family and every other grand family in this city is supported by us, by the city, by the way we get around the laws he and his sort make, so a man can do business here, and do well here. Who is Platt?" The deep voice rumbled stagily. The gray eyes turned on Blaise, who was wise enough to attempt no answer. "Platt's Croker and Croker's

Platt, with a brogue and no education. But we do business the same way. We get out the vote of the quick and the dead and the immigrants, including the ones who think they're living in Australia. Heaven help us! Well, I've no heart to tear the scales from their eyes, you can be sure." Croker continued, comfortably, in this vein until the Chief signalled for him to stop.

"You know, Mr. Croker, whenever I want to know what the Republicans are up to, I ask you, and when I want to know about the Democrats, I ask Platt."

Croker nodded; and nearly smiled. "You'll get something close to the truth, going round the back way, you might say."

The Chief nodded; and put his feet up on the back of the sphinx, a creature plainly puzzling to Croker. "What's Platt doing about Roosevelt?"

"He wants him out of the state fast. We all do. It's not that he *does* anything. Don't get me wrong. But he talks so much. He gets the rich folks all riled up on account of us, not that they don't know better."

"He's a demagogue." Blaise made his vital contribution.

Croker nodded. "You could call him that. Poor old Platt's gone and broken a lot of ribs. He's in plaster of paris up to here." Croker indicated the place where his own neck was, assuming that he had such a feature, hidden back of gray beard, gray tweed. "He's poorly, today. With a fever. But he's made up his mind he won't let Teddy run again for governor."

"How does he stop him?" asked Blaise.

"Throw us the election is one way. Teddy didn't do all that well first time around. It's not like Platt and me haven't arranged an election together before. But Platt's got other plans this year. He wants McKinley to take Teddy on as vice-president."

Hearst scratched his stomach, idly; gazed into the middle distance at a cow-headed Egyptian goddess, who stared back. "Dewey's done for," he told the goddess.

Croker laughed, an unpleasant sound. "That interview in the *World* did the trick."

"I could have managed him." Hearst shut his eyes. "I could've elected him president."

"But you couldn't have managed Mrs. Dewey, and that's the truth."

Like everyone else, Blaise had read, with wonder, the Admiral's interview. After a bit of thought, the Admiral had declared his readiness to be president, an easy sort of job, he declared, where you simply did what Congress told you to do. Mrs. Dewey was given full credit for the resulting farce.

"No one," said the Chief, opening one eye and keeping it firmly on Croker, "wants Teddy."

"Since when does that matter? Platt wants him out of New York. The only way is to make him vice-president. Boss Quay in Pennsylvania—"

"Got thrown out of the Senate."

"A bag-," said Croker, enjoying each syllable, "a-telle. Who needs the Senate? But everyone needs Pennsylvania, and Matt Quay's got that. New York and Pennsylvania will make Teddy vice-president."

"Bosses." Hearst's tone was neutral; he had now widened both eyes in imitation of the cow-goddess.

"So what's Mark Hanna? He's boss of the whole Republican Party."

"No." Hearst was unexpected. "McKinley runs the show, and lets Hanna collect the loot, and take the blame. Teddy was in Washington last week, begging for the job, and Hanna said, no, never, and McKinley said, may the best man win. McKinley wants Allison."

Blaise had yet to learn the entire roster of American statesmen. Vaguely, he was aware of an elderly Iowa senator named Allison, who, with serene fidelity, represented not Iowans but corporations in the Senate. "McKinley won't get Allison," said Croker. "Which means he don't really want him."

"Maybe that's why he *says* he wants him." The Chief, each day, sounded more like a politician than an editor. Blaise doubted the wisdom of this metamorphosis. Bright butterflies ought not to change into drab caterpillars. "Dolliver's the man the White House boys like. Dawes wants him."

"Dolliver." Croker allowed the name to remain in that perpetual limbo from which those who might have been figures of the highest degree in the great republic fail to rise even to the surface, like iridescent scum, wrote Blaise in his head. He was beginning to get the knack of newspaper writing. Whatever phrase came first and most shamefully to the mind of someone who read only newspapers was the one to be deployed in all its imprecise familiarity.

"Lodge supports Long. New England supports Long." Hearst plucked at a single string of his banjo, and even the hardened Croker winced at the sound.

"Lodge works day and night—for Teddy." Croker stared at the banjo as if it were a city judge whose price had doubled. "He has to be for Long. That's the cover. The New England candidate, like Dolliver—not Allison—is the real Midwesterner. Now Root . . ."

"Yes, Root . . ." Hearst frowned. Blaise could follow only so far into the maze when politicians lapsed into their own curious vernacular, so similar to that of Paris thieves. Plainly, Root impressed each man. Plainly, Root was a non-starter.

"Who do *we* want, Mr. Hearst?" Croker was, finally, direct.

"Anyone but Teddy." Hearst was as direct.

"That's you, of course. Me, I'm like Platt. I want him out of New York. He's tiresome to do business with."

Hearst turned to Blaise. "I've fixed it. He says you're the only gentleman we've got around here. So you can go down with him, in his car. Make all the notes you can every day and telephone them in and we'll write it up."

"By 'he' you mean Colonel Roosevelt?"

Hearst stared at a splendid school-of-Tintoretto painting, the work, to Blaise's eyes, of a student destined not to matriculate. Anyone could sell the Chief anything if it was Art. "You're booked into the Walton Hotel, same floor as Teddy. You leave Friday. Pennsylvania Station. Noon. All your badges and so on are at the office. The convention don't start till Tuesday, so Teddy's getting a headstart. He's going to be rushing around telling everyone how he's *not* a candidate, too young to be put on the shelf, too poor for the job. You don't have to take any of that nonsense down. Mr. Brisbane can write the usual Teddy interview in his sleep—in *their* sleep." The Chief had finally made something close to a joke. The thin voice was asthmatic with uncontrollable laughter.

"As good as Weber and Fields," beamed Croker, suddenly turning before their eyes into a dear wee leprechaun, straight from the Emerald Isle.

Blaise was less indulgent. "Where's Hanna in all this?"

"He's staying with rich friends in Haverford. He'll be at the Walton by Saturday. But Charlie Dawes is the man to keep your eye on. He's the one who'll be talking on the telephone to McKinley in the White House. If Teddy starts to bore you, head for Dawes." Blaise had a vague memory of a reddish-haired young man, said to be one of the President's few intimates. "He'll be with the Illinois delegation." Hearst gave a few more instructions; then Blaise said farewell to Chief and Boss.

As Blaise left the room, he heard, once again, the sly sing-song voice of the leprechaun, "And then we'll be needing a governor all our own, once Teddy's gone to Washington, a fine famous sort of man, Mr. Hearst, with whom we can do business."

"I'm for reform, Croker."

"Who isn't? As autumn leaves fall and the first Tuesday in November, that precious gift of our brave forebears who fell at Bunker Hill, comes round, and we elect a new governor of this state—a reforming governor—why not William Randolph Hearst?"

Unfortunately, George shut the door before Blaise could hear the Chief's reply to the siren's song.

2

Theodore Roosevelt welcomed Blaise heartily into his railroad car, a somewhat shabby affair for the governor of so great a state, with dirty antimacassars on dirty green armchairs; and filled, for the most part, with aides, journalist friends, and the upright remains of Senator Platt, who seemed to have been dead for some time. The face was pale blue, in nice contrast with the white whiskers, while the upper torso beneath the frock-coat was encased in plaster, giving the effect not only of death but of advanced rigor mortis as well.

"Delighted you could come!" For once Roosevelt did not make three or even two words of "delighted." He seemed uncharacteristically subdued, even nervous. With a sudden shake, the train started. Blaise and Roosevelt fell together against Senator Platt's chair. From the chair came a soft cry. Blaise looked down and saw two accusing eyes set in a livid face, glaring up at them.

"Senator. Forgive me—us. The train . . ." Roosevelt stuttered apologies.

"My pills." The voice was of a man dying. The pills were brought by a porter. The Senator took them, and sleep—opium, not death—claimed the Republican boss.

"He's in great pain," said Roosevelt, with some satisfaction. Then he frowned. "But so am I." He tapped one of his huge teeth on which Blaise always expected to see engraved "RIP." "Agony. No time to have it pulled either, with so many speeches to give. Wouldn't do. Must suffer. I am simply a delegate-at-large, you know. I am not a candidate for vice-president. Why won't people believe me?"

Blaise restrained himself from saying, "Because you're lying."

Roosevelt read his silence correctly. "No, I'm not being coy," he said. "It's a complicated business. There's one thing being a true choice of all the people, and quite another being forced over a convention by," from force of habit, he struck left hand with right fist, "the bosses."

The boss of New York heard this; opened his drugged eyes; sneered slightly beneath his white moustache; and resumed his drugged sleep.

"Well, you've got Platt and Quay behind you," Blaise began.

"What is a boss, finally, but someone led by the people?" This was a new variation. "They make judges and mayors and justices of the peace and—deals, yes. I know all that. But he," Roosevelt lowered his voice and pointed to Platt, whose back was now to them, "didn't want me for governor, and doesn't want me for vice-president either, but the people push and push and so the bosses get out in front like . . . like?"

"Mirabeau."

"Yes! The very man! When the mob was loose in the street, he said, I don't know where they're going but as their leader I must lead them, wherever it is, he said."

"Or something like that," Blaise murmured. But Roosevelt never heard what he did not want to hear. Blaise, however, forced him to explain why, if he was not a candidate, he should want to be in Philadelphia three days before the convention started; and Mark Hanna was out of town.

"Senator Lodge says I'm making a great mistake. He always says that, of course. No matter what anyone does." Roosevelt swung a fat thigh over the arm of his chair. A waiter brought him tea. Blaise ordered coffee. Covertly, the other journalists watched Blaise, waiting for him to vacate the chair beside the Governor. But Roosevelt seemed to need the company of a gentleman at so delicate a moment in his history. Blaise got the impression that the Governor was not only nervous but undecided what to do. In effect, he was arriving at a convention controlled, in McKinley's name, by his enemy Hanna. The Colonel was a national hero, but conventions were no respecters of popularity of the sort bestowed by a press so easily manipulated and its gullible readers.

Roosevelt acknowledged this. "I got the governorship on a hurrah, after Cuba. But how long can a hurrah last in politics?"

"With Admiral Dewey only a few months."

"To have thrown all that away." Roosevelt shook his head with wonder. "I captured one hill. He captured the world. Now they laugh at him, and that *permanent* victory arch of his is falling to pieces in Fifth Avenue. I just told the Mayor to tear it down. But he doesn't—the Mayor—listen to me. Because I'm not a war hero any more. I'm just a hard-working governor, who's taken on the trusts, the Whitneys, the insurance companies . . ." The Governor's voice was now a high and, to Blaise, familiar drone. When there was a pause in the litany of brave achievement, Blaise surrendered his chair to the *New York Sun*, the Roosevelt paper.

Toward journey's end, Platt opened his drug-dimmed eyes; saw Blaise; motioned for him to draw near. "Mr. Sanford, of the Roman Catholic Sanfords." A smile's shadow made hideous the corpse-like face. "How is Mr. Hearst?"

"Expanding, Senator."

"In circulation? Weight? Politically? As chairman of all those clubs?"

"Into other cities. More newspapers."

"Well, he *knows* papers." Platt sat up even straighter and grimaced with pain.

"I wonder, sir, what you think of Senator Hanna's support for Cornelius Bliss, as vice-president."

"I think it shows what a damn fool Hanna is, and always has been." Two marks of red, like thumb-imprints, appeared at the center of each ashen cheek. "What is Hanna but a stupid tradesman—a grocer? No, don't quote me. Let me say it in the Senate first—or last. All Hanna knows how to do is raise money for McKinley. But he don't know nothing about politics. Bliss, damn his eyes, is mine!" Twice, the religious Platt had sworn in Blaise's presence. The opiates had had an effect; he was also feverish.

"Yours, sir?"

"Bliss is from New York. *I* am New York. Hanna is Ohio. How can he work for someone from *my* state?" Platt shut his eyes; and appeared to have fainted. The scarlet thumbprints faded to ash.

Roosevelt insisted that Blaise ride with him and his secretary in a carriage to the Walton. "You'll be able to tell Mr. Hearst, firsthand, how I have not sought the nomination." As Roosevelt spoke, he kept poking his head out the carriage window, smiling aimlessly at the crowds in Broad Street. But as no one expected a non-candidate to arrive so early, he was not, to his chagrin, noticed. The secretary sat between Blaise and the Governor, a round black box on his knees.

Blaise had never been in Philadelphia before. For him, the city was simply a stop on the railroad between Washington and New York. Curiously, he stared out the window, and thought that he was in some sort of Dutch or Rhineland city, all brick and neatness; but the people were unmistakably American. There were numerous Negroes, mostly poor; numerous whites, mostly well-to-do, in light summer clothes. Blaise, who was hatless, noted that almost every man wore a hard round straw hat to shield its owner from the near-tropical heat.

As the carriage stopped in front of the Walton, a considerable crowd had gathered, to watch the great men appear, as it were, onstage. There were all sorts of colored placards, among them eulogies to "Rough Rider Roosevelt." But over all brooded the round smiling face of McKinley, like a kindly American Buddha.

"Quick!' Roosevelt tapped the box on his secretary's lap. The man opened the box just as the doorman opened the carriage door and the crowd moved forward to see who was inside. Roosevelt took off his bowler; gave it to the secretary; then he took from the black box his famous Rough Rider's sombrero, which he jammed on his head at an angle. Then with an airy gesture, he pushed up part of the brim and, aching tooth forgotten, he turned on the famous smile, like an electrical light; and leapt from carriage to sidewalk.

The cheering was instant, and highly satisfying to the Governor, who shook every hand in sight, as he made his way into the hotel.

"It's my impression," said Blaise to the secretary, "that the Governor is available for the nomination."

"Whatever the people want, he wants." The secretary was smooth. "But he does not seek the office, and he will certainly not accept anything from the bosses."

Although the boss of Pennsylvania, Senator Quay, was not in Roosevelt's suite to greet him, his deputy, Pennsylvania's other senator, Boies Penrose, was on hand; and the two men communed in the bedroom while the sitting room filled up with Roosevelt supporters.

Blaise went to his own room, farther along the musty hall, already heavily scented with cigar smoke and whiskey. He prepared his notes; then he went to the telephone room off the lobby and rang Brisbane in New York. "The story is the hat," said Blaise, highly pleased with himself. For once, he had got the lead into a story right. Brisbane was delighted. "Would you say that it was an acceptance hat?"

"If I don't say it, you will, Mr. Brisbane."

"Good work, Mr. Sanford. Keep us posted. Tomorrow's the day."

"But—tomorrow's Sunday."

"Politicians—and Moslems—do not observe the Sabbath. Keep your eyes open. Roosevelt wants to stampede the convention before it starts."

Sunday the Governor of New York did indeed neglect the Sabbath. As far as Blaise could tell, no church pew held him that day, nor did he, as the Lord enjoined, observe a day of rest. He resembled, in his hotel suite, a Dutch windmill, arms constantly flailing high and low as he made his points; arms descending at regular intervals to shake, vigorously, proffered hands.

Blaise sat, unobserved, in a corner with an elderly political reporter from the *Baltimore Sun*, who advised Blaise to warn Hearst against buying the *Baltimore Examiner*. "The paper's a regular jinx," said the old man, removing a dented silver flask from his pocket and taking a swig of what smelled like corn whiskey.

"Philadelphia's dry on Sunday," he said, as if in explanation. Opposite them, back to the window with its view of the surprisingly narrow Broad Street, Roosevelt was spluttering to the delight of delegates whose eyes reflected not only excitement—even lust— but anxiety: the drama was not yet written, and until it was, this entirely self-conscious chorus had no idea whom to laud. If Dolliver, the current favorite, were to be nominated on Wednesday, there would be no chorus in the Roosevelt suite, and the now exuberant windmill in front of the window would no longer revolve once the warm winds of choric frenzy had ceased.

"What is happening?" asked Blaise. When in doubt, ask someone knowledgeable, was Brisbane's obvious but too often ignored advice to journalists.

"Everything. Nothing. The dude," he pointed to Roosevelt, "can't make up his mind. He thinks if he gets to be vice-president he's done for. They sort of disappear, by and large. He'd like to be reelected governor, but Platt won't let him. So should he take on Platt? Fight it out? He don't dare. This is about all he's got left."

"He's still young." Blaise was now used to referring to the fat little governor, almost twenty years his senior, as "young."

"He's aiming to be president next time around. But he knows that every vice-president's been passed over since Van Buren. But governors of New York are always in line. Now Platt's kicking him out—or upstairs. That's why he's going around in circles."

Indeed this seemed a proper description of the Governor, who was now, literally, marching about the room in circles, talking, talking, talking. Senator Penrose had withdrawn, having declared that Pennsylvania's delegation was for Roosevelt. "Machine," said the old man from Baltimore. "Funny thing for a reformer, to be the number-one choice of the bosses."

But the next delegation was un-bossed California. There was cheering from Roosevelt's supporters, and a brilliant smile from the Governor, as he greeted, by name, a number of the Californians. "We're with Roosevelt all the way!" shouted the chairman of the delegation.

"The West for Roosevelt!" someone else shouted.

"The 'rest'?" asked the old man, beginning to make notes on his large dirty cuff.

"The West," Blaise said.

"I'm a bit deaf," the old man smiled. Huge dentures moved about his mouth. "There's your key. That's what Teddy's looking for. He doesn't want people to think of him as Platt and Quay's invention. But to be the candidate of the West . . ."

"A cowboy . . . ?"

"A cowboy. A Rough Rider. Now he's getting it together."

"Can Hanna stop him?"

"Will McKinley stop him? That's the question."

"McKinley can keep him from being nominated?"

"McKinley can put him out to pasture for good—in the bad-lands. But will he?"

Monday morning Blaise was in the crowded hotel lobby when Mark Hanna made his not-so-triumphant entrance. The once thick-set, rather doughy political manager, made famous by a thousand cartoons of which the wickedest were Hearst's, was now a stooped haggard figure who walked with a noticeable limp. Behind him, to Blaise's surprise, was Senator Lodge, Roosevelt's closest friend, whose support of Secretary of the Navy Long was considered to be no more than a holding operation for an eleventh-hour strike by the Governor. The eleventh hour was now striking. Blaise tried—but failed—to get near Hanna. He caught Lodge's eye; and received a courtly nod, no more. But then Lodge had always taken the firm line that if a gentleman were to work for Hearst either he was not a gentleman or the word was in need of redefining.

Blaise then retreated to the marble stairs to the mezzanine, where he knew Hanna would be quartered. The day was oppress-ingly hot; and the smell of the delegates overwhelming. Blaise felt like Coriolanus as, trying not to inhale, he climbed the stairs to the mezzanine, which was filled with huge portraits of McKinley trimmed with red, white and blue bunting. A large placard, over an exit door to a fire escape, announced, humorously, "Republican National Committee."

James Thorne, a *San Francisco Examiner* reporter, took Blaise in hand. He was a young, thin, hard man, who did the actual work of the Washington bureau which Ambrose Bierce adorned, weaving his verbal wreaths, in prose and verse, of marvelous poison ivy. "Hanna's using this room," said Thorne. "Does he know you by sight?"

"I doubt it."

"He knows me, so I'm keeping my hat down over my eyes. If I do get kicked out, you'll take notes, won't you, Mr. Sanford?"

"I think I probably can," said Blaise. He was used by now to being treated as a feeble-minded rich boy.

Thorne and Blaise occupied two straight-backed chairs in front of a window. "That's so the light will be in his eyes," said Thorne. "He won't be able to see us. I hope. One thing about a national convention. Nobody's ever seen anybody before. So you can get away with a lot by just pretending you belong wherever you happen to be."

Blaise did his best to look as if he belonged in front of an open window in a large room filled with gilt sofas and chairs. In the corner of the room there was—most important of all—a telephone booth. "It's rigged up to the White House," said Thorne.

Suddenly the room was filled with politicians, and Hanna was carefully placed in an armchair. He was, Blaise decided, not long for this world. Lodge was nowhere in sight.

One by one the state leaders were admitted to the presence. Hanna questioned each carefully; each questioned Hanna. Was it true that McKinley was taking no position?

Hanna's response was always the same. He was in close touch with the President. The convention was open. Everyone hoped that the best man would win. Wherever Roosevelt was alluded to as a potential "best man," Hanna would glower. Then he would speak of Dolliver, Allison, Long, Bliss: seasoned men, good Republicans, reliable. But after each delegation had come and gone,

Hanna was more and more drained. He sweated; and the dull red eyes were glazed.

One of Hanna's aides came out of the telephone booth. "No word, Senator."

"In that case," said a Roosevelt supporter from the West, whose name neither Thorne nor Blaise had heard, "the convention's under your control, Senator."

Hanna glared at the Westerner. "My control? No, it is not. Everyone's doing what he damn well pleases."

One of Hanna's aides tried to stop him; but the fit was upon him. "I am not in control. I should be. But I'm not. McKinley won't let me use the power of the presidency to defeat Roosevelt. He's blind or afraid, or something. I'm finished. I'm out. I'm not running this campaign. I'm quitting as national chairman." The tirade went on. Thorne and Blaise both made rapid notes.

A California delegate entered the room, unaware that he was interrupting Hanna's definitive performance as King Lear. "Well, Senator, the whole West is now for Roosevelt . . ."

"Idiot!" Hanna bawled. The Californian reeled back as though struck. With the help of three men, Hanna staggered to his feet. "Don't you fools realize that there would be only one man's life between that madman and the presidency?"

At this propitious moment, the madman entered the room, clicking his teeth with what could have been joy or, Blaise thought more likely, a carnivore's hunger. "Senator Hanna, dee-lighted."

Roosevelt seized the hand of the swaying Hanna. The room was now filled with Roosevelt supporters. "I'm sorry to cause so much commotion." Roosevelt adjusted the Rough Rider's hat. "I thought I'd just slip into town, as a humble delegate-at-large . . ."

Softly, Hanna screamed. But no one paid the slightest attention to him. At the eleventh hour the madman held center stage. "I had not realized how undecided everyone is . . ."

Hanna found his voice. "Undecided? We're all decided. You're not going to be the nominee. You come in here, dressed up like a cowboy, and try to stampede the convention, when Long and Dolliver are the true candidates."

"Senator Lodge tells me that Mr. Long is not all that serious, and . . ."

"If I say he's serious, Governor, he's serious."

"What does the President say?" Blaise admired this instinctive leap for the jugular.

"May the best man win. That's what we all say. That's what's going to happen, too. All you've got, Governor, is Platt and Quay. Well, we can't go into an election with Bryan with a candidate who's the invention of the big-city machines. McKinley speaks for the heartland, not Boss Platt, not Boss Quay . . ."

"Not Boss Hanna?" asked a voice in the doorway.

"Boss? Me, a boss! I do like I'm told. Don't go believing what you read in those Hearst papers. I follow orders, and I've got one from the President which I'm going to follow to the end. No deal with the big-city bosses. *They* may want you, Governor. But *we* don't want nothing to do with them. Is that clear?"

Roosevelt was now very red in the face and breathing hard. "My support is from reform; from the West . . ."

"Platt and Quay. Platt and Quay!" Hanna drowned him out, and Blaise could tell that Roosevelt had been, momentarily, beaten back.

"Naturally, I stand where I've always stood." Roosevelt's hand touched the tooth which Blaise knew to be aching. "I would like renomination as governor of New York . . ."

"Make a statement to that effect. By four this afternoon, we'll want it for the wire services." Hanna had pulled himself together. "I'll get the word to Platt, and the New York delegation. You may think you have the West, but we have the South, and Ohio." Hanna was now in the doorway, surrounded by his revivified troops. "May the best man win!" he shouted at Roosevelt, who was staring at Blaise, and not seeing him, or anyone else. The teeth that had been clicking so ominously were now set close together. Behind the gold pince-nez the small dull blue eyes were unfocussed. What next? Blaise wondered.

The next day was Hanna's. He was given an ovation when he

appeared on the stage of the convention hall, a vast hot building set in West Philadelphia. Blaise was seated in the press section, with a good view of the state delegations below him. New York's banner was close to the stage; but there was no black-hatted Rough Rider to be seen. The Governor had indeed done as he was told by Hanna; he had given a statement to the press that he would prefer to continue as governor. When asked to comment, Senator Platt had said that he was in such exquisite pain that he no longer cared who was elected what. According to Roosevelt's secretary the Governor had made no move to woo the Southern delegates away from Hanna; instead, he was searching desperately for a dentist who could stop the pain in his tooth without removing it. The thought of a huge gape in those tombstone teeth was terrifying to all Roosevelt supporters.

As the speeches began, Blaise sat next to Thorne. During the night Thorne had spent some time with Dawes, who was now the President's eyes and ears at the convention. "Something's happened between McKinley and Hanna." Thorne was mystified. But Blaise, who knew nothing of politics but a good deal about human vanity, had the answer. "He's tired of those cartoons of ours, showing him being led around by Boss Hanna."

But Thorne suspected all sorts of dark intrigue. Meanwhile, the New York State delegation was trying to make up its mind whom to endorse. For some mysterious reason, Theodore Roosevelt was not even considered; then, on the second day of the convention, word swept the hall that the New York delegation had selected as a favorite-son non-candidate Lieutenant Governor Timothy L. Woodruff, one of Platt's less gorgeous inventions. Simultaneously came the news that Roosevelt had defied Platt. "This makes no sense," said Blaise to Thorne, as each tried to cool himself with a palmetto fan in the airless hall.

But for once the political reporter could instruct the man of the world. "Teddy's pulled it off, and so has Platt. Teddy can't ever appear to be Platt's candidate, so they cooked this up to make the

West and the South and the country think that Roosevelt's fallen
out with the boss of his own state."

"This is all Platt's doing?"

Thorne nodded; and smiled. "It's smooth work, Mr. Sanford.
Seamless, you might say."

By afternoon, the West and Wisconsin had come out for
Roosevelt. Then the permanent committee chairman, Senator
Lodge, was escorted to the platform by his old friend the Rough
Rider himself. As Roosevelt and Lodge appeared onstage, the
convention hall exploded with sound. "It's all over!" Thorne
shouted into Blaise's ear.

Roosevelt stood to one side of the lectern where Lodge had been
installed. Roosevelt appeared to be genuinely surprised by the
ovation. First, he looked at Lodge; then he gestured for Lodge to
take a bow; but the elegant Lodge merely smiled a small smile,
and folded his arms, and bowed to Roosevelt.

At that moment the band struck up "There'll Be a Hot Time in
the Old Town Tonight." Roosevelt removed his hat and waved it
like a plume. Under the Ohio banner, Senator Hanna fell back in
his chair, and shut his eyes.

On Thursday, the matter was settled. Blaise had talked to
Dawes, whom he found to be intelligent as well as charming, a
rare combination in a professional courtier. "It's no secret the
President started out not wanting Roosevelt. Now he thinks it's all
for the best."

From the press section, the convention floor was, suddenly,
colorful as plumes of red, white and blue pampas grass were
waved, worn, held. The Kansas delegation, wearing yellow silk
sunflowers, demonstrated for Roosevelt. Then Lodge banged his
gavel for order; and introduced Senator Foraker of Ohio, who
proceeded with due pomp and collegial zeal to renominate for
president William McKinley. A demonstration resulted. The band
played "Rally 'Round the Flag" in memory of the Civil War, of
the origins of the party itself and of Major McKinley. Afterward,
there was silence, as Lodge took his place at the lectern, and the

elegant voice sounded throughout the hall, "To second the nomination of President McKinley, the Governor of New York . . ."

With that, the hall was in eruption. Even Blaise found himself
excited. Whoever had stage-managed Roosevelt was a master.
Again the band played "There'll be a Hot Time," by now the
anthem of the Spanish-American War. Rough Rider hat held high,
the stout small near-sighted man raced down the corridor from his
post beneath New York State's banner and up the steps to the
stage. Again, the ovation was fortissimo, and Roosevelt seemed to
grow ever larger as the cheering filled him up, as hot air does a
balloon. The teeth shone (the pain must somehow have been
killed); the hat was held above his head like a victor's laurel.

Lodge, much moved, shook his hand and led him to the lectern.
Roosevelt's shrill voice resounded throughout the hall. He said
nothing memorable; but he himself was memorable as . . . Blaise
could not think what. Taken detail by detail, he was as absurd a
creature as Blaise had ever met, but taken as the whole that was
now being presented to the nation, he seemed all high-minded
probity, fuelled by the purest energy; he was, literally, phenomenal.
As Roosevelt seconded the nomination of McKinley, he himself
seized the crown. At last he was at the center of the republic's
stage, and he would never again leave it, Blaise thought, suddenly
conscious of history's peculiar inexorableness. The speech was
mercifully short. History does not enjoy too close an examination
of its processes.

The roll-call of the states began. But there were so many cries to
make unanimous the renomination of McKinley that Lodge, in a
general storm of confused parliamentarianism, did precisely that,
and Iowa jumped the gun and nominated Roosevelt for vice-
president. There was more confusion. Finally, Lodge declared that
Governor Roosevelt was indeed the unanimous choice of the
convention for vice-presidential candidate, having received every
vote save one. The Governor, in a paroxysm of modesty, had
declined to cast a vote for himself. At that glorious moment, a huge
stuffed elephant appeared in the hall, attended by waving red,

white and blue pampas grass. History had been made.

As Blaise entered the Walton Hotel, Senator Platt was leaving, surrounded by members of the press. The Easy Boss was more than ever easy; and the ashen color of the weekend had been replaced by his normal pallor; but he moved stiffly, carefully, as though afraid he might break. "Are you pleased at Governor Roosevelt's nomination?"

"Oh, yes. Yes," murmured Platt.

"But, Senator, weren't you for Woodruff?"

'We are all of us for the Republican Party," said Platt gently. "And the full dinner pail."

"The full what?"

"Dinner pail," another reporter answered.

This must be, Blaise thought, a campaign phrase, to emphasize the new prosperity in the land, thanks to McKinley's policy of expansion and, of course, high tariffs.

"Any other thoughts, Senator?"

"Naturally, I am glad," said Platt, now at the door, "that we had our way."

"What?" asked a journalist, affecting surprise. "I mean, who's 'we'?"

Platt covered himself smoothly. "The people have had their way." The Senator disappeared through the door.

Blaise found Thorne in the bar, not yet crowded with delegates. The convention was still in session. The two men sat at a small round marble-topped table, more suitable for an ice-cream parlor than a serious hotel bar-room. Blaise joined Thorne in whiskey, not his favorite drink. "I've already filed," said Thorne, contentedly. "In fact, I filed this morning before the convention. The whole story."

"You knew what would happen?"

Thorne nodded. "Easy to see it all coming. Now I've sent on the details. The *Examiner*'s going to have everything first. In the West, that is."

"I just telephoned Mr. Brisbane. Then he makes it all up."

"Same thing. Now Bryan will be renominated in July, and we'll have the election of '96 all over again. I can write that one in my sleep. Sixteen to one silver versus solid money . . ."

"What about imperialism?"

"The party of Lincoln," said Thorne quickly, "has freed from the yoke of Spanish bondage ten million Filipinos."

- 3 -

John Hay sat with the President in the Cabinet room. Dawes had finished his report of the convention. McKinley was seated at his usual odd angle to the end of the Cabinet table, left elbow resting on the table, his legs, as always, off to the right and never under the table. He even wrote with his weight on his left elbow, his right arm crossing the considerable waistcoated paunch. He seemed to regard the entire seating arrangement as being, in some way, temporary. Hay occupied his usual Cabinet chair. Dawes sat across from them. Overhead, an electrical fan slowly stirred the humid air. To Dawes's left the large globe of the world needed dusting. In fact, thought Hay glumly, the entire White House needed a thorough cleaning. It was curious how quickly in the absence of an energetic presidential wife the place took on the appearance of a politicians' somewhat sleazy clubhouse.

"I suppose, all in all," said McKinley at last, "it was the hat that did it."

Hay laughed inadvertently. The President could be mildly droll, but seldom humorous. "The acceptance hat, it was called." Hay quoted a newspaper story.

"What's the proper name for those Rough Rider hats?" McKinley seemed genuinely curious.

"I think they're called sombreros," said Dawes "Teddy never took it off, the whole time. Except to wave it, of course."

"A curious creature," said McKinley, stretching his legs so that the great paunch, as large and round as the globe of the world itself, rested comfortably on his huge thighs. "I suppose we can live with him. Of course, we're going to hear a lot about the bosses from Bryan." McKinley frowned; removed his eyeglasses; rubbed his eyes.

"Mark Hanna's taken the whole thing very well," said Dawes, picking up rather too rapidly, thought Hay, on the President's reference to Platt and Quay.

"He's poorly, I think. He's a bad color. I worry about him. What did he say?" McKinley looked over his left shoulder at Dawes, who was nicely reflected in the glass of a mahogany credenza, containing documents that no one, as far as Hay could tell, had ever examined.

Dawes chuckled. "He said he was going along with the party, as always. But with Roosevelt as vice-president, it was your constitutional duty to survive the next four years, to save us from the wild man."

McKinley smiled. "Well, that's the constitutional minimum, I suppose. Who was the last vice-president to be elected president when the president's term was up?"

"Martin Van Buren," said Hay. "More than sixty years ago. Poor Teddy's on the shelf, I'm afraid."

Dawes laughed. "You know what Platt said when they asked him if he was coming to the inauguration? He said, 'Yes. I feel it my duty to be present when Teddy takes the veil.'"

Hay's own feeling toward Roosevelt, never entirely sympathetic, was now more hostile than not. In March, Lodge had risen in the Senate to denounce the Hay-Pauncefote Treaty, using language similar to Roosevelt's but adding the insufferable thesis that the treaty-making power was, essentially, the Senate's preserve. Hay had then written out his resignation, and given it to the President at the end of the Cabinet meeting. McKinley had responded with charm and firmness. Hay was to remain until the end. They would fight side by side for virtue. Hay remained, as he knew all along that he would. Without good health, without office, there would be, simply, no life left. Also, he had enjoyed a considerable success with his marvellously imaginative approach to collapsing China. Hay had serenely announced, as the world's policy, an "open-door" approach to China. He had informed the relevant predatory nations that this was the only sensible course for them to pursue, and though the Russians and the Germans had been privately outraged, they were obliged to subscribe, if only by silence, to the cause of international virtue and restraint. Overnight, Hay had become a much applauded world statesman. Even Henry Adams praised his friend's guile. The formula is meaningless, of course, the Porcupine had noted, but no less powerful for its lack of content. Hay regarded the "open door" as buying time until the United States was in a stronger position to exert its will on the Asian mainland. For the American press, the popular author of "Jim Bludso" had acted in a straightforward, decent, American way; he would, one editorial maintained, "Hole her nozzle agin the bank, 'til the last galoot's ashore." McKinley had read this editorial to the Cabinet, sonorously quoting "Jim Bludso." Hay had felt his usual hatred for the poem that had made him famous.

Dawes asked for news of the disturbances in China. McKinley sighed; and turned to Hay, who said, "'The righteous, harmonious fists'—better known as the Boxers—are pounding away. We've had no word out of Peking. Most of the foreign diplomats are in the grounds of the British legation."

"Are they dead?" asked Dawes.

"I assume not." It was Hay's view that the Chinese zealots who had risen up to drive the foreigners out of China would be the first to tell the world if they had, indeed, been able to kill the various ambassadors who had taken refuge in Peking's Tartar City. After all, that was the object of their desperate enterprise.

"This is very delicate." McKinley pushed his chair farther away from the table so that now his back was to Dawes, the papal left profile to Hay, the eyes on the lighting fixtures, a new tangle of wires from the ceiling now able to incapacitate several Laocoöns and their sons. "Bryan will talk imperialism for the rest of the year, as he's been talking all along . . ."

"Anything to get away from silver." Dawes was the Administration's authority on Bryan.

"Whatever." McKinley had no personal interest in any of his opponents, which made him unlike any other politician that Hay had known. Even Lincoln enjoyed analyzing McClellan's character. But McKinley *was* papal. He was, to himself, so securely right and in the place where he ought to be that he seemed hardly to notice those who tried to unseat him. In any case, he allowed the devoted, the impassioned, the—why not the word?—besotted Mark Hanna to lay about him, bloodily, in order to secure the McKinley throne.

"I think we are—home free on the Philippines issue." McKinley gazed, without visible pleasure, at the tangle of electrical cords. "I speak only for the purposes of the election," he added. He looked at Hay. The dark circles beneath the large eyes gave him the look of an owl in daytime, deceptively brilliant of eye, intensely staring, blind. "Judge Taft is a popular choice, I think."

McKinley had gone to the Federal bench and appointed a circuit judge from Cincinnati—always Ohio, thought Hay, himself a beneficiary of that state's political mastery of the Union. Although Judge William Howard Taft had not been, as Taft himself had somewhat nervously put it, an imperialist, McKinley had persuaded him to take charge of the commission whose task would be to restore a degree of civilian rule to the archipelago, where the fighting continued to be fierce and Aguinaldo continued to assert his legitimacy as the first president of the Philippine republic, now supported, he had recently maintained from his jungle retreat, by the Democratic Party and its anti-imperialist leader Bryan. Bryan's Marble Chamber work for the treaty in February of 1899 was apparently unknown to Aguinaldo.

"How do we keep from the press Judge Taft's problems with General MacArthur?" Dawes was not supposed to know of Judge Taft's reception in Manila on June 3 when the General—filled with proconsular self-satisfaction—refused to greet in person the commission. But the next day he had deigned to tell the commission that he regarded their existence as a reflection upon his regime and that, further, he disapproved of bringing any sort of civilian rule to the islands while a war was being fought.

Hay had been in favor of the immediate removal of MacArthur, an unsatisfactory if not entirely unsuccessful military commander. McKinley had murmured a few words, half to himself, in which the only word that Hay had heard clearly was "election," while Root had said that *he* would be more than happy to explain to his insolent subordinate the meaning of civilian rule. Hay was reminded of Lincoln's complaints about generals in the field who spoke with the authority of Caesar while performing with the incompetence of Crassus.

"We shall have to do something in China." The Major looked more than ever like a Buddha.

"Surely, an 'open door' is more than enough."

"Unfortunately, the Boxers have shut the door. We must open it again, Colonel Hay, or seem to. First, the Boxers." The Buddha smiled, for no reason other than delight in the perfection of his enlightenment. "Then the Boers—"

"Yes, the Boers," said Dawes, frowning. He was directly involved in the reelection of the candidate. China was far away; and the Boxers were exciting but exotic. As long as they did not kill any Americans, they would not affect the election one way or another. Even their evil genius, the sinister Dowager Empress, had her admirers in the popular press. But the Boers were a matter of immediate concern. German and Irish voters hated England. For them, the Boers were honest Dutch folk, fighting a war of independence against England. Therefore, all right-thinking Americans must be against England, except the intelligent ones, like Hay himself, who saw the Boers as primitive Christian fundamentalists at war with civilization in all its forms.

McKinley inclined to Hay's view. But he needed the votes of the Irish and the Germans. Meanwhile, earlier in the spring, a delegation of Boers had appeared in Washington. Hay had received them with all the charm that he could simulate. Del had written him alarming reports from Pretoria. Apparently, England could lose the war. Hay's earlier offer to mediate between the two sides was no longer possible. England would lose any mediation. McKinley had been willing to play the honest broker, but Hay persuaded him that between the Boers and the English, the United States needed England. He reminded the President of England's support during the war with Spain, when Germany threatened to move against American forces in the Far East.

"I believe, Mr. Dawes," Hay looked straight at the little man across the table, "that *I* must be given full credit for being a dupe of England, while the President is above the battle, working hard for American interests." The Buddha's smile was more than ever sublime during this. "As well as German and Irish interests," Hay added; and the smile did not lessen.

"We must be wary," said McKinley. "Did you know that Judge Taft weighs three hundred pounds?" He looked thoughtful. "While, according to the *Sun*, his fellow commissioners each weigh over two hundred pounds."

"Does this create a good impression, Major?" Dawes—small and lean—frowned.

Absently, McKinley patted his own fawn waistcoated belly. "In Asia, it seems that, inadvertently, I am regarded as a political genius. Fat men are held in the highest esteem, and the Filipinos have never before seen so many truly *large* white Americans as I have sent them. I am sure that it is now only a matter of weeks before Aguinaldo surrenders to . . . to . . ."

"American weight?" Hay provided the image.

"I must," said McKinley, sadly, "exercise more."

Dawes reported on Bryan's mood. He would attack the Republican management of the new empire but not the empire itself. Silver would be soft-peddled, as a result of Congress's acceptance, in March, of the gold standard for American currency.

Mr. Cortelyou announced General Sternberg, the surgeon general of the Army. Hay and Dawes rose to leave. McKinley sighed. "Imperialism may cease to be an issue," he said, "if we don't stop the yellow fever in Cuba."

"It's just the result of all that filth, isn't it?" asked Dawes.

General Sternberg overheard Dawes, as he entered the Cabinet room. "We think it's something else."

"But what?" asked the President, giving the small general his largest warmest handclasp.

'I'm sending out a commission of four medical men to investigate, sir. With your permission, of course."

"Of course. There is nothing, in my experience, quite so efficacious as a commission." Thus, McKinley made one of his rare excursions into the on-going humor of government's essential inertia, in itself the law of energy in reverse, thought Hay. If nothing could possibly be done, nothing would most certainly be, vigorously, done.

Hay returned, alone, to the State Department. Already there were signs that the government was shutting down for the hot months. Except for important-seeming naval officers, the steps to the colonnaded masterwork were empty.

Adee hissed a warm welcome. "I am writing some more open doors for you, Mr. Hay. I do love writing open doors."

"Don't let me stop you. Any word from Peking?"

"The diplomats have vanished, as far as we can tell. They are, probably," Adee giggled, inadvertently, Hay hoped, "all dead."

As Hay entered his office, he glanced at a stack of newspapers to see which ones contained stories about him—marked in red by Adee, with an occasional marginal epithet. Except for the *Journal*, which maintained that he was England's secret agent in the Cabinet and a sworn enemy to the freedom-loving Boers, the press was not concerned with the Secretary of State. The vice-presidential candidate governed the headlines.

Wearily, Hay took up his "tactful" silver pen, the gift of Helen. For some reason this particular pen, once set to work upon the page, could, in a most silvery way, celebrate whomever he was writing to, in a tone of perfect panegyric, with no wrong notes struck. This letter was, of course, to "Dear Theodore."

Without thought or pause, Hay's hand guided the pen across his official stationery: 'June 21, 1900. As it is all over but the shouting, I take a moment of this cool morning of the longest day in the year to offer you my cordial congratulations." With any other pen Hay might have been tempted to add, "and my congratulations to Platt and Quay who have given us *you*, a precious gift," but the silver pen lacked iron as well as irony. "You have received the greatest compliment the country could pay you . . ." This brought a tear to Hay's own eye: he must have his blood pressure taken; such tears were often a sign of elevated pressure. ". . . and although it was not precisely what you and your friends desire," Hay had a glimpse of the sweating Roosevelt slapping mosquitoes as governor-general of the Philippines while sly Malays shot at him from behind jungle trees, 'I have no doubt it is all for the best." Here, Hay and his silver pen were as one. There was no mischief that a vice-president could make under a president as powerful as McKinley. More gracious phrases filled up the page. What small liking that Hay had ever had for Roosevelt was currently in abeyance, thanks to his sabre-rattling over the canal treaty, abetted by the treacherous Lodge. Henry had promised to bring Lodge around; and Henry had failed. Hay's pen signed the letter, warmly. Hay himself sealed it. As he did, Adee entered. "I sent around the copy of Del's letter to Miss Sanford. But she is gone."

"Where to?"

But Adee was looking out the window; and heard nothing. Hay shouted, "Where has she gone?"

"No answer to your letter to the Mikado." Adee liked to pretend that his hearing was acute at all times. "You know how long Tokyo takes to answer anything."

"Miss Sanford's gone where?"

"There is no news from Port Arthur either. We should be thankful that Cassini is abroad. The Tsar is supposed to be ready to recognize his daughter."

"As the Tsar's?" Hay was momentarily diverted by the usual Adee confusion.

Adee opened a box of Havana cigars; and offered one to Hay, who took it, in defeat. As Adee lit the Havana cigar he said, as if he'd heard all along, "Miss Sanford's gone to Newport, Rhode Island. She left us her address. She stays with Mrs. Delacroix. Her half-brother's grandmother."

"How do you know such details?" Hay was curious; and impressed.

"In the absence of a court and a Saint-Simon, someone must keep track."

"We have so many courts in this country."

"There is only one Newport, Rhode Island." Adee, without a by-your-leave, helped himself to a cigar. Then the two old friends methodically filled the office with fragrant smoke, successfully eliminating the cloying odor of summer roses, arranged in every vase. "She left me a note, saying that anything that she hears from Del she will let you know, and hopes that you will do the same."

"Yes." The pains in the lower back had, ominously, ceased. For some reason, Hay had always felt that a degree of pain was not only reasonable but a sign that the body was correcting itself, as new things went awry in the furnace, the plumbing and the electrical arrangements. But now there was only a general weakness in every limb; and a sensitivity to heat, which made him constantly sleepy, a condition that sleep itself did not improve. He must soon withdraw to New Hampshire or die; or both, he thought, without fear, glad that he could at least enjoy, in the present instant, Adee's inspired misunderstanding of the word "Tsar."

The appearance in the doorway, unannounced, of the Secretary of War caused Adee, graciously, like Saint-Simon indeed, to withdraw, never turning his back on the great ones while never ceasing to puff at his cigar.

Root sat on the edge of Hay's desk. "The Major wants all Americans out of China."

"How are we to do that, with the Boxers surrounding them in Peking?"

"I told him I thought it was a bad idea, unless the Russians were to go, too, which they won't. He's worried about the effect on the election."

Hay sighed. "I now leave Asia in your hands. I leave the State Department in your hands. I leave . . ."

"You leave too much."

"Well, I don't leave you Teddy." Hay looked at the now sealed letter to the Governor of New York. "He will speak in every state, he says."

"It will be interesting to see if he mentions the President." Root's contempt for Roosevelt was entirely impersonal and spontaneous. At the same time, they got on well politically: two practical men who needed each other. Teddy had already written Root his version of the convention, which Root had shown Hay; "It was a hard four days in Philadelphia." Teddy made his own nomination sound like a war won. "What will the Major do?"

"He is going home to Canton," said Hay. "He will sit on his front porch until election day, chatting to the folks . . ."

". . . and waiting for the telephone to ring."

"We're weak on the Philippines." Root was abrupt. "Taft's too easy-going. MacArthur's too much of the military proconsul."

"You can handle the General."

Root chuckled. "Oh, I'll break him to sergeant if he disobeys me. But I can't give Taft a backbone. If there's trouble between now and November . . ."

"Bryan won't know what to do about it. We shall be reelected, and I shall no longer be the heir-presumptive to the republic. Are you certain you wouldn't like my place?"

Hay, genuinely, for the moment at least, wished to relinquish office. But Root would have none of it. "We make a good team, the way we are." He picked up a copy of the *Washington Tribune* from a side-table where the national press was each day arranged, much as Hay himself used to prepare it for President Lincoln. But unlike

Lincoln, who had never been a journalist, Hay should have known better than to take seriously the press. But fabulists, Hay knew, tend to believe tall tales.

"Del's fiancée seems to be making a go of this."

"She says that she does not lose money," said Hay, "and she is amused."

– 4 –

But Caroline had lost money since spring; and she was not amused. She had spent far too much money covering the national conventions. Since Hearst had given every journalist in the country an exaggerated idea of his worth, she had been obliged to pay a former *New York Herald* journalist more than she could afford to write what proved to be, surprisingly, an excellent account of the Philadelphia convention. Could it be that Hearst was right? that one did get what one paid for? Now she sat on the lawn of the Delacroix "cottage" and read the *Tribune*'s account of the nomination of William Jennings Bryan at Kansas City on July 5. As a running mate, Bryan had selected Grover Cleveland's ancient vice-president, Adlai Stevenson of Illinois. Caroline carefully compared the account in her paper to that of the rival press. Although Hearst was hearty in his endorsement of Bryan, nothing much was said about silver, while Bryan's anti-imperialist views were barely acknowledged by imperialist Hearst. Happily, Hearst and Bryan were as one on the "Criminal Trusts," whatever *they* were, thought Caroline, turning to Hearst's new paper, the *Chicago American*, officially launched on July 4, with all of the Chief's characteristic energy and rich inaccuracy.

"It is curious indeed," said a deep feminine voice, "to see a young lady reading the vulgar press, and getting ink on her gloves in the process."

"Then I shall take off the gloves." Caroline dropped the stack of newspapers onto the grass, and removed her white gloves. "But I must keep on reading my competition; and perfect my own vulgar art."

Curiosity had, finally, brought them together. When Caroline, vanquished at last by Washington's heat, had agreed to spend July with Mrs. Jack Astor, Mrs. Delacroix had written her that she must stay with what was, after all, the nearest thing that she had to a grandmother. And so Caroline had transferred herself from Mrs. Jack's to the splendors of the Grand Trianon, set high on Ochre Avenue above the bright cool Atlantic; and from this sea-fragrant height the steaming heat of Washington was soon forgotten.

Mrs. Delacroix was small and thin, with a face whose lines resembled an intricate spider's web, framed by silver-gray hair so elaborately curled and arranged—not to mention thick—that half Newport was convinced she wore a wig like her contemporary Mrs. Astor. But hair—and spider's web—were all her own. When the old lady spoke, her speech was swift with oddly clipped syllables, a reminder of her New Orleans origin. As Mrs. Delacroix approached Caroline, she held a parasol between pale skin and bright sun; she seemed, to Caroline, like some highly purposeful ghost; with truly bad news from the other side.

"Mr. Lispinard Stewart, our neighbor, has come to call. I said that I thought that you were indisposed. But of course if you are disposed . . ."

"I am entirely at *your* disposition."

"They do teach you girls how to talk over there in Europe." A footman in livery appeared from behind a hedge of lilac, and placed a chair behind Mrs. Delacroix, who sat in it without once looking to see if the chair was in place. "Mr. Lispinard Stewart owns the White Lodge down the road. He is very snobbish."

"Like everyone else here. Or so I've been told," Caroline added; she had vowed not to be critical, in conversation.

"Some of us have more occasion to be snobbish than others. Mr. Stewart is a bachelor whom everyone would like to marry. But I suspect he will remain in his current state of immaculate chastity, as the nuns used to say in my youth, until he is one day called to a higher station, as a bridegroom of Christ."

Caroline could never tell when the old lady was being deliberately droll. In either case, she laughed. "It was my impression that Jesus contents himself only with brides."

"We must not," said Mrs. Delacroix serenely, "question the mysterious ways of the Almighty." With the point of her parasol she was turning over the pile of newspapers on the lawn. "You're the first young lady that I have ever known who reads the front part of the newspapers."

"I am the first young lady you have ever known to *publish* a newspaper."

"I would not," said Mrs. Delacroix, "boast."

"Boast? I had hoped to arouse your sympathy."

"I have none." Mrs. Delacroix looked quite pleased with herself.

"None at all—for anyone?"

"Not even for myself. We get what we deserve, Caroline." From the first day, the old woman had addressed the young woman as both child and relative. "But what I most particularly deserve, you don't have." She abandoned turning over the newspapers; and frowned with disappointment. "It's not here."

"What were you looking for?"

"*Town Topics*. I read nothing else. It's always wise to know what the servants think of us. The things that that paper prints!"

"It's what they *don't* print—the omissions—that I study it for."

Mrs. Delacroix carefully readjusted her huge pastel yellow hat with its swept-back veil of lace. Gold ornaments clung haphazardly to her bust. "Surely those *not* mentioned are virtuous, and so of no concern to our servants."

"Or they pay Colonel Mann large sums of money to keep their names out of his 'Saunterings.'"

"Cynical!" Mrs. Delacroix's voice tolled like the sea-bell on the sharp rocks beneath the house. "That's what comes of reading newspapers! They soil one's soul as surely as they soil white gloves."

Caroline held up her gloves. They were indeed smudged with ink. "I must change again," she said.

"Wait until we dress for lunch." Caroline had been relieved to discover that Newport required no more than five changes of dress a day, assuming that one did not play tennis or go yachting or riding. In Paris, seven changes of costume was thought the fashionable minimum. As a result of this new dispensation, the asthmatic Marguerite was in Paradise: enraptured by the sea-air's coolness, as well as by the thousand or so French maids employed along the ridge where Newport's "cottages" were set apart from the old town whose year-round inhabitants had been dubbed by Harry Lehr, in a literal translation of Louis XIV, "our Footstools." Although the Footstools loathed the fashionable Feet, they served them grimly during the eight-week season of July and August; after the last fête, Mrs. Fish's Harvest Festival Ball, the huge palaces were then shut for the remaining ten months of the year and Newport was again the property of the Stools.

"Why must you quarrel with Blaise?" Suddenly, disconcertingly, Mrs. Delacroix resembled a withered version of her grandson.

"We only quarrel over money. Surely, that's usual—and permissible."

"One *disagrees* over money but one does not quarrel. You could be such a good influence on him."

"Does he need a good influence? I thought," Caroline was mischievous, "that Madame de Bieville now stood *in loco parentis*."

With some effort, Mrs. Delacroix managed not to smile. "*I* am *in loco parentis*. The poor boy's last blood relation—except for you, of course."

"And I am so young, inexperienced, still a *jeune fille*, while Blaise is a man of the world, with Madame to guide him—when you are not there, of course."

"Now you make fun of me." The dowager looked almost girlish.

"But you seem more at ease in these parts than Blaise. You select your friends with care . . ."

"Girls never select. We are selected."

"Well, you have, somehow, acquired the Hay family. Helen dotes on you. She's arriving today, with Payne Whitney. Naturally, they go to different houses. We are not French, yet. But Blaise comes and goes and except for the delightful Madame de Bieville, he has no friends in Newport . . ."

"No friends? Why, there is Payne, and Del Hay, when he's here, and all those Yale classmates . . ."

"He thinks only of Mr. Hearst and newspapers . . ."

"Like me. I sometimes think our wet-nurse must have fed us ink instead of milk."

Mrs. Delacroix put her hands over her ears. "I did not hear that!" A footman arrived with a silver tray on which two near-transparent cups of bouillon were placed. "Drink up," said the old woman. "You'll need your strength. We have a formidable season prepared."

"You are good to invite me." Caroline looked at her hostess; and began to be fond of her. Although she had not expected to find anything but a dragon, breathing fire, the invitation (summons?) had proved to be a sign of belated—not quite affection but deep curiosity: of the two emotions always the more interesting one in Caroline's view. But then she, too, was curious about Mrs. Delacroix for many reasons.

Thus far, there had been no talk of the past. A portrait of Denise Sanford hung in the drawing room; she looked very young, and rather startled; except for her expression, she looked like Blaise. There was no portrait of their father, William Sanford. "I must have put it away," said Mrs. Delacroix. "Would you like to have it?"

"Yes, I would."

"He is in uniform. In the war, he fought on the Yankee side."

"Hardly fought," Caroline could not resist.

"That is the best thing I have heard said of him. We continued to know one another only because of Blaise, who is my last living grandchild, my last relative, in fact, outside New Orleans, that is, where I am related to everyone."

"What a burden!"

Mrs. Delacroix took Caroline's arm and they walked, carefully, up the lawn to the pink marble terrace. "Mamie Fish is giving us lunch. She's very curious about you."

"I am not," Caroline said, "curious about her."

"Do tell her! She will be shattered. She thinks herself the most interesting woman on earth, and now that old Mrs. Astor's started to fade, Mamie means to take her place, or, rather, Harry Lehr means to install Mamie as our uncrowned queen."

"Such excitement," murmured Caroline, wondering if there might not be a story to be passed on, most anonymously, to the *Tribune*.

They entered the cool boiserie-lined study, where a marble bust of Marie Antoinette gazed, like a regal sheep, out the window at a lawn ready for munching. "When Mrs. Leiter was here, she asked me if Rodin had made that head."

On principle, Caroline laughed at any mention of the wealthy Chicago lady who had launched, successfully, three splendid girls into the great world's marriage market, of whom the most attractive married Lord Curzon, now viceroy of India, where the vicereine was known as Leiter of India. "Naturally I told Mrs. Leiter that Rodin had sculpted the entire French royal family, starting with Charlemagne. She said that she was not surprised as he did only the best people. In fact," Mrs. Delacroix suddenly inhaled, making a sound that could only have been described as a snort, "Mrs. Leiter said that I must see the *bust* that he has just done of her daughter's hand."

Then Mrs. Delacroix proposed that they drive to the Casino, a rustic shingle-and-wood building which provided marble Newport with a sort of village center, a Petit Trianon for would-be simple folk. Here tennis was played on grass courts, while in the Horse Shoe Piazza, Mullalay's orchestra could be heard throughout the day as unenergetic ladies took the air, often together, while the energetic men were all at sea in sailboats and the unenergetic ones had withdrawn to the Casino's Reading Room, where they were safe from ladies, cads and books.

But Caroline said that she had—she almost said the unsayable word "work" but quickly remembered the common phrase—"letters to write," and clothes to be changed. Mrs. Delacroix let her go; and took to her carriage alone except for a poor relation called Miss Aspinall, who acted as companion during the high season. The rest of the year, Miss Aspinall rusticated at Monroe, Louisiana, where she could enjoy the quiet pleasures of a pastoral spinsterhood.

Marguerite had laid out an elaborate costume from Worth; perfection, except that it was three years old, a fact that the sharp eyes of Newport's ladies would be quick to notice. But Caroline's reputation for eccentricity had its social uses. Also, was she not a Sanford? and had she not been taken in by Mrs. Delacroix, supposedly a mortal enemy of her mother, Emma?

Supposedly? Caroline sat in an armchair covered with worn Aubusson and looked out at the sea where sailboats tacked this way and that, and white spinnakers filled with wind; blasphemously, she found herself thinking of pregnant nuns; the influence, no doubt, of her hostess. What indeed did the old woman feel about her mother? What indeed did she feel about her mother's daughter? and why the sudden peremptory invitation that had taken precedence over the annoyed Mrs. Jack? Yet they had come to enjoy each other's company; also, there were, despite the high season, no other houseguests, something of an oddity. Vague references to Louisiana relatives who were too ill to travel suggested to Caroline that she might be a stopgap, a last-minute improvisation. If anything, the emptiness of the huge marble house was more to be revelled in than not. The servants were well-trained; that is, invisible when not needed; and a number were French, to Marguerite's uninhibited joy. The great cool, sunlit rooms smelled of roses, lemon furniture-wax and, always, the iodine-scented sea-air.

There was a good deal to be said for idle luxury, thought Caroline, carefully placing side by side on the parquet floor the front pages of the nine newspapers that were her daily reading. By now, each newspaper was like an old acquaintance. She knew why one newspaper relentlessly played up—when the editors did not invent—every Boer victory in South Africa: the publisher's wife and daughter had *not* been received at the Court of St. James's; while another newspaper spoke only of British victories, a tribute to the managing editor's long affair with a British lady whose husband owned an auction house in New York City. Caroline was now able to predict how any American newspaper would respond to almost any important event. Only Hearst occasionally baffled her, because he was, in his way, an artist; mercurial, unpredictable and devoted to invention.

Newport itself was featured inside two New York City papers; and not much elsewhere. Currently, Newport was in the news because William K. Vanderbilt, Jr., had driven a French motor car from Newport to Boston and back, some one hundred sixty miles, in three hours and fifty-seven minutes. She memorized the item. This would get her nicely through Mrs. Fish's lunch, where Harry Lehr was now fulltime major-domo. Old Mrs. Astor no longer entertained as much as she had; she preferred to remain in her cottage, receiving only the faithful. Power was shifting—everyone said—to Mrs. Fish, though Mrs. Ogden Mills, born Livingston, was the ranking American archduchess at Newport, and when Mrs. Astor let the sceptre fall she should, by the very number of her democratic quarterings, succeed. When asked her views of the Four Hundred, Mrs. Mills had said coldly, "There are really only twenty families in New York." Mrs. Mills did have one marvelous, even unique, gift: she could make absolutely anyone feel ill at ease in her presence. "A priceless gift," Mrs. Delacroix had observed, mournfully, unaware of the permanently terrified expression of the spinster Aspinall, always at her side.

Other, lesser, candidates for the throne included the lively, clever Mrs. Oliver Belmont, "the first *lady* ever to marry a

Vanderbilt," she would say with some satisfaction, particularly if there was a descendant of the old tugboat commodore in the room, "and the first lady ever to get a divorce, on her own terms. I was also the first American lady to marry her daughter to a duke of Marlborough, for which I shall, doubtless, suffer in the afterlife. But I meant well. And, of course, I am the first lady ever to marry a Jew, my darling Oliver Belmont. Now," she would say, with a formidable glare in the dark intelligent eyes that fascinated Caroline, "I shall be the first woman—*not* lady—to see to it that every American woman will one day have the vote. For women are the hope of this country. If you doubt this, then pray to God," she had said when she first met Caroline, and tried to recruit her for women's suffrage, "and *She* will help you." Caroline revelled in Alva Vanderbilt Belmont, but no one else in the great world did. She was too shocking and too advanced to be popular; she was also too rich and too powerful to be ignored. But she was definitely not in the line of succession to Mrs. Astor; nor wanted to be, any longer. There had been a time when Alva had threatened to replace the Astor-Plantagenets with the Vanderbilt-Tudors. But divorce had intervened; and, more dismally, good works.

Mrs. Stuyvesant Fish, heiress-presumptive, greeted her guests in the great hall at Crossways, a Colonial-style mansion, with a dining room that could seat two hundred, said Harry Lehr, greeting Caroline warmly.

"That means you must eliminate half the Four Hundred," said Caroline. "So which will it be? The gentlemen or the ladies?"

"We shall never experiment, because Morton won't let us. Sixteen is now his limit for lunch."

Morton was the English butler, who had served rather too many dukes, thought Caroline, who also wondered why Mrs. Fish was so impressed by the number of his grand employers while ignoring the briefness of his service with each. Morton was a tall florid man, who treated Mrs. Fish and her guests with a disdain that they may have deserved but ought not to have allowed. Caroline was not charmed.

The ladies proved to be the season's best; the men were not. The young and vigorous were sailing off Hazard's Beach; or driving motor cars. Lispinard Stewart was present, however; he seemed to have stepped from the pages of a "silver fork" novel of the early nineteenth century; he was elegant, effeminate and wondrously boring. He fluttered about Caroline; who fluttered, as best she could, in the general direction of Mrs. Fish, who stood, one eye on the door to the dining room, to make sure that the magnificent Morton would not be kept waiting once he had announced that dinner was served.

Mrs. Fish received Caroline with an interest that might have passed for warmth had Caroline been less experienced in the social wars. Mamie Fish was a plain but interesting—and interested-looking—woman with deep-set wide eyes beneath arched brows; but the rest of the face had not been worked out with the same care: the jaw was large but characterless and the mouth had been crudely sketched in, rather as if the Divine Artist—plainly, a woman, as Mrs. Belmont maintained—had decided not to undermine with incongruous beauty the easy wit of Mamie Fish, who had, in any case, captured early in life a descendant of not only the Puritan but the Dutch founders of the nation, one Stuyvesant Fish, known fondly to Mamie in Puritan parlance as "the Good Man." As it was, the good man preferred his old house at Garrison on the Hudson to Newport or New York, an arrangement that perfectly suited Mrs. Fish and the sparkling Harry Lehr, now grown plump and somewhat less sparkling of eye.

"I feared we should never capture you." Mrs. Fish stared interestedly at Caroline. "We are used to Blaise in New York. But you are the enigma of Washington, a city no one ever visits. Old Mrs. Astor—not well, you know, not well at all—thinks you a great addition. But to what? I asked."

"Washington, perhaps." Caroline was tentative. "Where, if you're right, no one will ever visit me."

"Washington does not matter, dear child. If you like that sort of a place, try Charleston, during the azalea season, or New Orleans, where Mrs. Delacroix still keeps slaves. Oh, she'll deny it! But the war has never been accepted in that part of the world. Just as we don't accept Washington. Are you quite sure you don't want to marry one of us?" The question was delivered with the famous Mamie Fish drawl.

Caroline was surprised to find herself blushing. "There is so much to choose from." Caroline indicated the nearest man, James Van Alen, a moneyed widower, who had modelled himself on the sort of English gentleman seen not so much in London society as on the Broadway stage. When Van Alen had first met Caroline at Mrs. Belmont's, he had said, loudly, "Zounds!"—a word Caroline had never before heard *spoken* in real life—then, as he withdrew, still staring at her, he announced, "A most delectable wench, forsooth"; and placed a monocle over one eye.

"I think," said Mrs. Fish, "nothing could be simpler than for you to become the bride of Mr. Van Alen."

"I am rather near-sighted." Caroline blinked her eyes. "I didn't see who it was."

"But then you are going to marry Del Hay. You see? We do keep up. But when will he come back from South America?"

"South Africa."

"It's all the same, sweet pet. Anyway, here's Helen. And Payne."

Caroline and Helen embraced. Payne's wrist was in a sling, from tennis. "Otherwise, I'd be in the race today." He looked with youthful displeasure at the room filled with elderly beaux, each armed, as it were, with his hereditary silver spoon as well as fork.

"Father's in New Hampshire. New Hampshire!" Helen seemed more than usually exuberant. "He's been told to spend at least two months there, even if all his open doors slam shut."

"Has he heard from Del?"

"Nothing since you heard last week. Everything's diplomatic pouch. So he can't say what he means. But the English are losing. Losing! It's horrible!"

At that moment Morton, ominously, announced lunch, and, dutifully, even hurriedly, Mrs. Fish took the ranking gentleman's arm and hurried to her place at the Sheraton mahogany table, which, although set for Morton's optimum sixteen, had all its leaves in place, giving each guest a considerable amount of room to accommodate the season's enormous skirts. Down the center of the table an elaborate solid gold series of pagodas and bridges complemented the somewhat chinoiserie appearance of the hostess.

Caroline was placed—as she knew that she would be—between Lispinard Stewart and James Van Alen. Longingly, she thought of her small office in Market Square, and of the flies, both living and dead, her familiars.

"The test of a good cook," announced James Van Alen, "is codfish cakes."

"Is Mrs. Fish's cook going to give us some?"

"Egad, Miss! This is *not* breakfast."

Lispinard Stewart explained to her, in elaborate detail, his relationship to the Stuarts, and why his family had modestly replaced the "u" with "ew" in order not to embarrass the current ruling house of England, who feared, more than anything else, a claimant from his family to their throne, "which, by rights, is ours, as they know."

"And of what kingdom," asked Caroline, remembering at last how to make conversation, "is Lispinard the royal house?"

There was a dance that night at The Elms, given by the Burke-Roches. When Mrs. Delacroix announced that she was going home early, Caroline went with her. "Tomorrow," she said, "I must spend the morning on the telephone, talking to Washington."

"When I was young, I danced all night. I was always in love."

"I am not in love, Mrs. Delacroix. So I sleep . . . and talk on the telephone."

"We enjoyed ourselves more. There were no telephones, of course." They were seated in the small study off the drawing room. Although it was late July, the night was cool and a fire was burning. Mrs. Delacroix poured herself brandy, while Caroline took Apollinaris water. The old woman laughed. "Mamie's completely under that butler's thumb. He's convinced her that in all great English houses, Apollinaris water must first be boiled."

"I would boil him if I were her."

Mrs. Delacroix held up a small painting on ivory. "This is your father, and my daughter."

"I thought you had no painting of him except in uniform?"

"I suppose that's because I never look at him when I look at this. I see only Denise. She was so happy. Can you tell?"

But Caroline, like the old woman, only saw what she wanted to see—not the pretty rather banal girl but the round-faced, small-lipped young man whom she had never known, and could not associate with the red-faced loud figure of her own youth. "They were both happy," said Caroline, neutrally; and gave the picture back.

"Your mother came here once in the summer of '76. She was beautiful."

"She was happy, too. Wasn't she?"

"My daughter died, giving birth to Blaise." The spider's web across the old woman's face tautened suddenly: had a fly been trapped? was the spider, ever watchful, close by? "Your mother was her best friend, at that time."

"This is all before I was born." Caroline did not like the direction that the conversation was taking. "My father never spoke—to me, at least—of his first wife. He seldom spoke of my mother, either. So Blaise and I are each motherless."

"Yes." Mrs. Delacroix crossed her tiny ankles, just visible beneath the watered pale blue silk of her evening gown. "It is curious how Emma died in much the same way as Denise, as a result of giving birth."

"Emma. At last. You have said her name. Now tell me, was she really so dark? And *why?*" Caroline hurled the question at the old lady, who visibly winced; then rallied. "Your mother," she said, most evenly, "killed my daughter, and *that* is the precise nature—and quality—of her darkness."

Caroline had often observed women swoon either from too-tight corseting or as an act of desperate policy. She wondered whether or not this was a proper moment for her to experiment, entirely as a matter of policy, with a sudden dead-faint. But she recalled herself. She would give blow for blow. "How was this . . . murder, as you do not quite call it, achieved?"

"Denise had been warned that she could never have a child. Your mother encouraged her to have one, by the man your mother wanted to marry, even then, your father-to-be, Colonel Sanford."

Caroline bared her teeth in what she hoped might be mistaken by firelight for a young girl's sweet smile. "I find no darkness here. Only your surmise. How does one woman encourage another to have a child, when each knows the consequences?"

"There was a lady—I use the word ironically—who specialized in such matters. Emma sent for her. Emma got her to say—paid her to say—that Denise would survive. Since my daughter wanted a child very much, she had one. Then she died, and her husband went on to marry . . ."

"Darkness?"

"Yes. Then you were born, and in due course *she* died, a proper vengeance I always thought."

"I do not believe your story, Mrs. Delacroix, nor can I understand why you choose to tell me so terrible a thing, assuming you *believe* what you've told me, when I am a guest—briefly, may I say—in your house."

"I hope not briefly." The old woman poured herself more brandy. "I have told you because I cannot tell my grandson."

"Are you afraid—of Blaise?"

The head, silver hair aglitter with diamonds, nodded. "I am afraid. I don't know what Blaise might do, if I were to tell him."

"As he seems to have been born entirely without conscience, he will do nothing at all. He will not be interested."

"Now you are unkind to him. You see, he is so like her." Quite unexpectedly, tears began to leak from the bright black eyes. "I look at him, and it's Denise come back to me. You see, I'd given her up. The way we must always give up the dead until such time . . . So, having forgot my child, let her go, kept only a picture or

two, poor likenesses all, she suddenly comes back to me, alive and
young, and I look at her—him—and can't believe what I see.
Think I am dreaming. I see the same eyes, hair, skin, voice . . ."

"Blaise is very much a male."

"A beloved child is without gender to its creatrix, as you may
have the good—or bad—fortune to discover." Mrs. Delacroix
withdrew a lace glove from her left hand; dried her eyes with the
wadded glove. "He is my heir, not that I am as wealthy as people
suppose."

"Good. Perhaps you can then persuade him to give me my share
of our father's estate."

But the old woman was now removing, one by one, her huge
old-fashioned diamond rings, a slow and complicated process, for
the fingers were bent with arthritis. "I shall also remember you in
my will."

"I trust that when you come to write it you will not mistake a
one for a seven like my father." But Caroline knew that there is no
egotism to compare with that of someone old, embarked upon a
crucial venture, involving money.

"Blaise has treated you badly. I don't know why. But I suspect
why. I think, somehow, he knows what happened."

Caroline shook her head. "If he knew, he would have told me
long ago. Also, if he knew, he would not, I'm afraid, care at all. He
lives only for himself."

"Your father knew." Mrs. Delacroix now only heard what she
chose to hear. "He never dared to see me, not that I would have
spoken to him. He settled in France to avoid me, and what he'd
done, what *she* had done."

Caroline rose. "I am tired, Mrs. Delacroix. I am also ill-
pleased." In anger, Caroline's English began to take on a somewhat archaic sound. She longed to burst into a proper French
tirade.

"Surely not with me, my dear." The old lady was now her
gracious, formidable self again. She swept her rings into her
reticule; and rose. "I have taken you into my confidence because,

when I am dead, I want you to tell Blaise the true story."

"I suggest," said Caroline, "that you put it all in writing, as part of your will. Let him find out at the same time he gets the money. If you like, I'll help you put it into French Alexandrines. They are particularly useful for this sort of—theater."

"It's not theater, my child. I only want you to—"

"Why want *me* for anything, since I am the daughter, in your eyes, of so much darkness?"

To Caroline's astonishment, Mrs. Delacroix crossed herself, and whispered something in Latin. Then: "I believe in atonement."

"I am to atone for my mother?" Without thinking, Caroline crossed herself, too.

"I think you must. Besides, you and Blaise are all that's left of the Sanfords, the real ones, that is. So you must make up. This is one of the ways."

"I can think of less hazardous ways."

"I am sure you could." In the falling firelight the small room had taken on a rosy color, and Mrs. Delacroix looked almost girlish, spider's web erased. "Blaise is in Newport," said the suddenly young-faced old woman, taking Caroline's arm. "He's at Jamie Bennett's Stone Villa. Poor Jamie's still an exile in Paris. But, of course, you know all that. Anyway, each year he leases his cottage. Blaise has taken it for August."

"I'm sorry that I've kept him from staying here, with you."

"No, no. I want *you* here. He's close enough."

"Too close, perhaps, for me." But Mrs. Delacroix had preceded Caroline from the room.

The next morning Caroline arrived alone at Bailey's Beach, where she was greeted with a smart salute by the gold-braided field marshal whose task it was to know not only members but their friends by sight. How he was able to discern a member from an intruder was a source of wonder to all Newport. But he was infallible, and the small beach, awash with slimy dark green and dull red seaweed, was the most exclusive patch of sand in the world, as well as, Caroline noted, one of the most malodorous. In the night, an armada of Portuguese men-of-war had attacked Bailey's, and today their iridescent, bloated, gelatinous shapes were strewn upon the pale sands. Although the field marshal's helpers—boyish Footstools, as Harry Lehr would say—raked as hard as they could, corpses of the men-of-war still outnumbered Bailey's members beneath the brilliant sky.

Caroline made her way to the tented pavilion maintained by Mrs. Delacroix; nearby, the Fish house-party was already on the beach, the ladies in morning frocks. There would be no bathing for them this day, but, like a sea-god, Harry Lehr was costumed for his native element. The upper vest of his emerald-green bathing suit had been cut in daring décolleté to show off an alabaster-white chest and neck, while the ruddy face was barely visible beneath a curious sort of burgundy-red sunbonnet which kept the sun from his face as surely as Caroline's parasol protected hers. The legs, however, gave great joy to the beach. The suit stopped just above two large dimpled knees which were, in turn, covered by sheer peach-colored silken stockings that set off shapely calves that he like to compare, complacently, with those of Louis XIV. To Caroline, they were more reminiscent of the legs of certain Paris lady circus-riders. In any case, he was a marvel of androgynous charm; and as indifferent to the sniggers of the boyish Footstools as they raked up the gummy jellyfish as he was proud of the true admiration with which *his* circle regarded him. Harry Lehr was an original, which he proceeded to demonstrate to Caroline, to the chagrin of the Fish party farther along the beach. "Such beauty!" he exclaimed. "All alone at Bailey's!"

"Yours, Mr. Lehr? or mine?"

"You make fun of me. I love that, you know." The laugh was rippling, and sincere. Then he sat beside her, cross-legged on the sand. The legs *were* beautiful, Caroline decided; but then nature always had a habit of mixing things up. Blaise, who dearly wanted a moustache, could not grow one, while Mrs. Bingham, who did not want a moustache, was obliged, each day, with wax, to rip hers off. Caroline would not in the least have minded exchanging

Harry's legs for her own, which were too slender for contemporary taste. At school, numerous references to the taut beauty of Diana of the Hunt had not appeased her. "You could be such a success here. You know that, don't you?"

"But aren't I? A success, that is. Within my limits, naturally."

"Well, you are you, of course, and so you're a success by birth, and the way you look. Though I'd dress you better. More Doucet, less Worth."

"Less Worth, more money?"

"What's money for? I'm like Ludwig of Bavaria. I hate the bareness of everyday life. It withers my soul. But I don't have money, like you. Like everyone here." Beneath the sun-visor, the blue eyes narrowed. "So I make my way by amusing others. It's certainly better than sweating in an office."

"But harder work, I should think." To Caroline's surprise she found herself growing interested in Harry Lehr, as a human case. Was she now falling victim to his famous—or infamous—charm?

"Oh, easier than you might think. Most people are fools, you know, and the best way to live harmoniously with them and make them like you is to pander to their stupidity. They want to be entertained. They want to laugh. They'll forgive you anything as long as you amuse them."

"But when you grow old . . ."

"I shall marry soon. That will take care of that."

"Have you picked the . . . girl to be honored?"

Lehr nodded. "You know her, in fact. But you'll probably think . . ." Lehr's concentration was broken by the approach of two young men. One very slender, even gaunt, and the other smaller, more compact, muscular. It was the second youth that caused Lehr to frown. "Would you say his legs are better than mine?"

"Oh no!" Caroline was all tact. "He has too many muscles, like a jockey. And, like a jockey, see? his legs are slightly bowed, while yours are exquisitely straight."

"You must be very far-sighted to see him in such detail." Lehr gave her a mischievous womanly smile.

"Oh, I know nearly all his details. You see, he's my brother."

"Blaise Sanford! Of course." Lehr was excited. "I should have recognized him. So attractive, so elegant."

"If you like stable-boys from Brittany, he is attractive; I would not call him elegant."

"Well, the other one is. He's like a stork but the face is interesting."

"I'm afraid, dear Mr. Lehr, he is yet another of my brothers. The beach is littered with them today, like Portuguese men-of-war."

Now the two young men had joined them, and Lehr greeted the bemused Blaise with coquettish charm; and bowed low as he took the hand of Caroline's oldest half-brother, the Prince d'Agrigente, known as Plon, who looked twenty-five but was thirty-seven; and separated from his wife, by whom he had had five children, each, it was rumored at the Jockey Club, where everything interesting is known, miraculously his own.

"Plon wanted to escape from Paris. I wanted to escape from New York. So we took old Jamie's villa. It's full of mildew," Blaise added, staring at Lehr as if he were, somehow, responsible.

"The servants don't air the Stone Villa properly. Because the owner never comes. I must introduce you two splendid creatures to Mrs. Fish—"

"I know her." Blaise was flat.

"'Fish' as in *poisson*?" murmured Plon in his deep voice.

"We have splendid names in America—" Caroline began.

"But not Lehr as in *menteur*," said Lehr, taking the lead; and the match. Suddenly, the two young men laughed; and Lehr was able to withdraw in triumph to Fishland.

"We have one of those at Paris." Plon was thoughtful. "I didn't know you had one here, too."

"You must travel more, *chéri*." Caroline gave him the sisterly kiss she withheld from Blaise. "We have everything here. Including the most exclusive beach in the world."

"Is it always covered with garbage?" Plon rubbed his nose, as if the smell might be pushed away.

"Only human," said Blaise.

At that moment, Mrs. Jack appeared on the boardwalk that ran the length of the clubhouse. She was in what she called "tennis costume": white tennis shoes, black stockings, white silk blouse and skirt beneath which could be seen—daringly—bloomers; on her head a sailor hat held in place two veils like mosquito netting. When Mrs. Jack saw them, she swept aside her veils so that they could see her. "Caroline," she called. "Do come here, and bring your young men." Caroline did as she was ordered. The young men pleased Mrs. Jack, who delighted them when they heard her name, and listened to her imperious nonsense, all delivered in a husky Comédie Française tone. "You are exactly what I want. You both play tennis?"

"Yes, but—" Blaise began.

"Perfect," said Mrs. Jack. "I gave up tennis for bridge when my husband took up tennis. Now he has taken up bridge again, and is giving a bridge party. So I shall take to the court with you two splendid young men. You are clever, Caroline, to have so many brothers."

"Half-brothers . . ."

"Better and better. One needs only to be half-fond of them." Mrs. Jack was gone.

"We have one of those in Paris, too," said Plon, "but she's very old."

"That's *the* Mrs. Astor. This is her daughter-in-law. La Dauphine. She'll make you laugh. She hates everything."

"She's quite good-looking," said Plon. "Is she . . . vivacious?"

"This is America. The ladies are all pure." Caroline was warning.

"I know," said Plon, glumly. "I shouldn't have come."

Half the Astor house-party played tennis, and the other half played bridge. Mrs. Jack took over Blaise as a partner, leaving Caroline with Plon, who was as vague and kindly and impecunious as ever. "When Blaise heard my purse was *vide* . . . how you say?"

"Broke."

"Broke. He offered to pay to bring me over for the summer. So here I am."

"Looking for a new wife?"

"We are still Catholic. Aren't we, Caroline?"

"Yes. But there are always arrangements."

Plon shook his head, his eyes on Mrs. Jack's elegant figure, and haphazard game of tennis. "Maybe I could give tennis lessons," he said. "They play very badly here."

Idly, they gossiped beneath the huge copper beech tree. Occasionally, Colonel Astor would come out on the verandah and gaze, rather bewilderedly, at his wife. He was an eccentric man, with a full moustache and a bald forehead that receded in agreeable sympathy with his chin. He was happiest, it was said, on his yacht, the *Nourmahal*, away from Mrs. Jack. Since Mrs. Belmont had so fiercely blazed an exciting new path through the wilderness of society, the sword not Excalibur but divorce in her hand, it was now, for the first time, conceivable that even an Astor might get a divorce. Admittedly, the Vanderbilts were still a number of rungs beneath the Astors on the gilded ladder, but what Alva Vanderbilt Belmont had done Ava Willard Astor might also do. "Divorce will become a commonplace." Caroline was sententious, a habit that was growing upon her now that she was being taken seriously as a newspaper publisher, and general authority.

"Not in France. Not with us," said Plon. "I like your Mrs. Astor."

"But only to seduce. You are so French, Plon."

"*You* are so American," said her half-brother bleakly. "I am told that that curious creature with you on the beach . . ."

"The pretty man?"

"The lovely man . . . that he sells champagne to these rich Americans. Perhaps I could do that. I know a good deal about wine." He blinked his dark seemingly depthless eyes, and Caroline realized that she was looking into her dead mother's eyes. Mrs.

Delacroix had inspired her to search for likenesses, clues.

"You have our mother's eyes," she said.

"So they say." Plon was watching for the occasional glimpse of Mrs. Jack's ankles as she careened wildly about the grassy court.

"What was she like?"

"What was who like?" Plon's mind was on the court.

"Emma. Your mother. My mother."

"Oh, it was so long ago. She was American like you."

"Plon, are you really so stupid or is this your idea of how to charm American ladies?"

The handsome aquiline face was turned toward her; he smiled, and showed good teeth. "Surely, I don't have to charm a *half*-sister. Or is there something a trifle Egyptian about this Newport of yours?"

Caroline allowed this tasteless gallantry to go unnoticed. "Do you think Emma might have—"

"Killed the first Mrs. Sanford?" Plon was still staring at the court, where Mrs. Jack had just, for the first time, perhaps ever, scored a match point. "Bravo!" Plon shouted. Mrs. Jack turned, her usual look of annoyance in place, but when she saw the lean admiring Frenchman, she gave a small curtsey.

"You should get at least a cigarette case," said Caroline sourly, "for attendance."

"I'm afraid I shall need more than a cigarette case."

"You've heard the rumors?"

"Only what everyone hears. The dull Colonel Astor prefers his boat to his wife. They have a son, so she has done her duty . . ."

"I speak of Emma!"

"You do have a thing about the past, don't you? All right. She was, for me, adorable. When I went driving with her, I always hoped that people would mistake her for my mistress. Yes, yes, I know. I am very French. I was also fourteen when she died, and full-grown for my age."

Caroline tried to imagine the boy Plon and the dark lady of the portraits together in an open carriage, driving through the Bois de

Boulogne; and failed. "I was prejudiced, of course, against your father. I thought him very . . . very . . ."

"American?"

"The exact epithet I was searching for. He was very American except that he had no energy at all, an impossible combination, we thought. But Maman always did her best to bring us together. She was very weak those last months, particularly after . . ."

"I was born."

"Yes. She just faded away. We were sorry, my brother and I, to see her go like that."

"No more than sorry?"

"Boys are like that. One develops a heart much later."

"If at all."

"Maman would never have killed anyone."

"Then why the rumor, which I've just heard, yet again, right here."

Plon gave a stage Frenchman's shrug, and crossed his long legs. "Rumors are eternal in our world. No, *chérie*, if anyone killed the first Mrs. Sanford—which I highly doubt—it was your abominable father, who was capable of anything to get his way."

Caroline felt as if she had been given a sudden electric shock. "I don't believe you," was the best that she could do.

"I couldn't care less what you believe." The dark eyes stared at her, with an expression that she had never seen before. Could this be Emma, she wondered, looking, so directly, into her daughter's eyes?

"Now you credit him with energy." Caroline turned away. Plon's eyes were suddenly neither human nor animal; they were of another order of nature altogether, a mineral that reflected nothing at all.

"He would have had the energy for that." Plon yawned. "Anyway, it's all done. It's very American," he suddenly grinned, "to think always of the past."

Caroline was horrified to find herself suddenly unmistakably attracted to the Prince d'Agrigente in a way quite different from

319

the perverse attraction of the golden enemy, Blaise. "I must," she said, "go in."

Mrs. Jack had already preceded Caroline into the house. She was removing her tennis veil; the pale face was agreeably flushed; a young plain boy, clutching a nurse's hand, stared up at her.

"Caroline! This is my son. He's nine. Say how-de-do to Miss Sanford."

The boy bowed politely from the waist. "How do you do?" Caroline was as polite as she would have been to the father, whose back could be seen in the drawing room, at one of the dozen bridge-tables, all occupied.

"Is he to be John Jacob the Fifth or the Sixth?" asked Caroline. "Your family is getting like the Hanovers with all their Georges."

"I've broken the line. He's William Vincent. Frightfully plain, isn't he?" said Mrs. Jack, as the boy was led away. "It is one of those rare cases when the paternity is absolutely certain. He has Jack's depressing features, and hangdog eyes. But the maternity's very much in doubt. He doesn't look a bit like me. Tell me about that handsome creature, your half-brother."

As Caroline told her about Plon, Mrs. Jack looked very interested. "We must have him to dinner, with Blaise, too," she added. "I'll ask all the Stone Villa, and you, of course, and Mrs. Delacroix, if she doesn't disapprove of me this year."

"Just don't smoke in her face."

"How petty the old are! He looks very young for thirty-seven," she added. Poor Plon; Caroline was compassionate. He already had more cigarette cases than he knew what to do with. Presently, he could have yet another one. In the long run, he would have to go back to his wife, who at least paid for the cigarettes that filled the cases.

If Caroline imagined that she could see in Plon their dead mother, she saw nothing at all of her father in Blaise. Doubtless, Mrs. Delacroix was not exaggerating when she had alluded to his remarkable resemblance to Denise. As Caroline dressed for dinner, she imagined Emma's eyes staring out of Plon's face, and watching

Denise's face as worn by Blaise. What would the two young men make of that? she wondered, and if Mrs. Delacroix's mad story proved true, was Blaise in danger? Rather the opposite, she decided, as Marguerite laced her into a ball gown, from unfashionable Worth. "We should come here more often," said Marguerite, putting the last touches to Caroline's ivory-colored gown. "It's almost like civilization."

"You don't have to speak English all day is what you mean."

"And your two brothers are here. That is very right, you know. To have a family." As a spinster entirely devoted to herself, Marguerite liked delivering homilies on the pleasures, duties and rewards of family life. She could not wait for Caroline to marry; and be truly unhappy like all the other ladies of her class. Happiness in others tended to have a chilling effect on Marguerite, who liked nothing better than offering desperate ladies sympathy, and a spotless cambric handkerchief scented with lemon verbena in which they might harvest bitter tears.

Plon was waiting for Caroline in the marble hall. Mrs. Delacroix had taken herself to bed, and Plon would escort Caroline to the Casino, where a dance in celebration of something was to be held. Neither Plon nor Caroline could remember what the something was. Plon thought that it might have to do with Mr. Vanderbilt's motor car. He himself had hired an open carriage, and they drove through the warm moonlit night to the Casino, which was lit with Japanese lanterns and filled with Mullalay's music. Plon brought her up to date. Mrs. Jack had proved incredibly cold, even for an Anglo-Saxon; no cigarette case would arrive from that quarter; worse, despite the fact that he had made a considerable point of his total marriedness, hostesses kept putting him next to single girls at table or, even more ominously, vivacious widows, eager for a second chance. "I can't tell them that I only like married women."

"No," said Caroline, "you can't."

They made a stately entrance into the Casino. Plon soon vanished, taken over by Lady Pauncefote and one of her numerous unmarried daughters. Lord Pauncefote looked curiously unimpressive in plain evening clothes. Caroline much preferred him in gold braid, with decorations pinned to his stomach. He had quickly found Helen Hay, and Caroline joined them, to help out Helen, who was being given a thorough and entirely misleading account of the British war against the Boers. Helen embraced Caroline. "But you will have heard the latest, from Del. From Del."

"I mailed the last letter he wrote me straight to your father in New Hampshire."

"The young man has made an excellent impression in Pretoria." Lord Pauncefote pronounced judgment.

"Don't you wish you'd gone?" Helen was mischievous.

"Oh, I would be so useful in the . . . veldts? Is that the word?"

"So close to the German word for wealth," said Blaise, at Caroline's back. "Payne's looking for you," he said to Helen, liberating her from Pauncefote, who was now, in turn, taken captive by James Van Alen.

"Zounds, my lord!" he boomed; and led the Ambassador off to the bar. "Methinks you have a dry look to you."

"There are," said Caroline, "many very serious bores here at Newport."

"Do you include half-brothers?"

"Only as half-bores, I suppose. I thought we were not speaking this year."

Blaise took her arm; and led her, somewhat against her will, to a flowery alcove at the edge of the dance floor, as far as it was possible to get from Mullalay's orchestra. Here they sat, side by side, primly, as if at school, on wooden chairs. "I saw my grandmother at lunch. At Mrs. Astor's. You have charmed her."

"Mrs. Astor?"

"Mrs. Delacroix, a much more difficult lady to . . . charm."

"You make me sound as if I had designs upon your grandmother."

"Don't you?"

Caroline looked at him; and thought of his mother, Denise. "I have no designs on anything except my own property."

"The courts—"

"No, Blaise. The clock. The calendar. Each breath I breathe brings me closer to what is mine."

"Don't tempt fate." Blaise made the sign to ward off the evil eye. "My mother was dead before she was twenty-seven."

"I shall not have children. That's one safeguard."

"You'll never marry?"

"I didn't say that. But I don't want children."

"Such things are not so easily arranged."

"How is Madame de Bieville?"

Blaise responded serenely. "At Deauville. What news of Del?"

"At Pretoria."

"The Chief's giving Mr. Hay a hard time."

"But that's the Chief's specialty, isn't it?"

"This summer, anyway. He's going all-out for Bryan."

"All-out?" Caroline smiled. "He doesn't take seriously Bryan's nonsense about silver, and he loves the empire that Bryan keeps attacking."

Blaise laughed in spite of himself. "Well, they don't like the trusts, and they don't like Mark Hanna."

"Very statesmanlike. The *Chicago American* is losing money, I hear."

"Quantities."

"*My* money?" asked Caroline.

"Some of it is my money, yes. But most of it is old Mrs. Hearst's. They keep finding gold in South Dakota." Harry Lehr swept by, a plain young woman on his arm. "Elizabeth Drexel." He said the name as if half-brother and half-sister were wholly interested. "I," he added, with a lizard's swift blink at Blaise, "am the Funmaker."

"You must make some fun for my numerous half-brothers." As Caroline sensed Blaise's furious disapproval, she found herself quite liking Lehr.

"First, you must let Wetzel make your suits, and Kaskel your pajamas and underwear . . ."

Lehr's public association of Blaise with pajamas, much less the pruriency of any reference to underwear, brought a coughing fit as Blaise's phlegm, mistakenly inhaled, choked him—with wrath, of course, thought Caroline with satisfaction. Lehr was delighted to have caused so much distress, while the Drexel girl—the future Mrs. Lehr?—looked as embarrassed as Blaise. They were saved by the majestic approach of Mrs. Astor, with her daughter-in-law, Mrs. Jack. Caroline felt as if she ought to curtsey, while even Blaise—no longer choking—bowed low at the great ladies' approach. Lehr pranced about the old sovereign like some huge blond dog. The two Mrs. Astors regarded him with stares worthy of the two bronze owls that decorated the gateposts to the Casino. Plainly, Lehr was going to pay for his defection to Mamie Fish.

"You must come see me, Miss Sanford." The huge dark wig was aglitter with rubies. "You, too, Mr. Sanford, though I have heard that you have no time for old ladies."

Blaise blushed becomingly. "We've only arrived, Mrs. Astor, my step-brother and me . . ."

"The Prince has a great deal of time for ladies," said Mrs. Jack in her low drawl, "of any and every age."

"How you comfort me." Mother-in-law smiled with dislike at daughter-in-law, who was now examining Blaise speculatively.

"Don't," said Mrs. Jack, "get married."

"I have no intention of marrying." Blaise recovered his poise. He was a match for Mrs. Jack if not her mother-in-law.

"Like dear Harry?" asked Mrs. Astor, finally acknowledging the fawning creature at her side.

"I don't know about that." Blaise was staring boldly at Mrs. Jack, who suddenly looked away. Was she cold? Caroline wondered; and what, after all, was coldness but a strategy in the dangerous American world where a lady's fall from grace could cause her extrusion—no matter how resonant her name or heavy her wealth—from the only world that mattered? Paris was filled with extruded American ladies, paying dearly for adulteries of the sort for which a French lady would have been applauded.

324

"I won't be a bachelor forever," Lehr trilled. The Drexel girl pursed her lips, as if to kiss the air. She was the one, poor creature, thought Caroline. But, then, perhaps, they were well-matched. She might be another Mlle. Souvestre.

"We are told," said Mrs. Astor, "that you and Mamie—so original, isn't she?—" Mrs. Astor's malice was royal in its self-assurance—"plan to give a dinner for dogs."

"Dogs?" Mrs. Jack's deep voice dropped to an even lower, almost canine register.

"Dogs, yes." Lehr yelped. "Each with its owner, of course."

"How amusing." Mrs. Astor made of "amusing" three full evenly emphasized syllables.

"At the same table?" asked Caroline.

"There will be different tables, of course."

"So that you can tell the dogs from their masters?" As Caroline spoke, she knew that she had, once again, gone too far. Wit had always been disliked and feared at Newport, while wit in a woman was sufficient cause to be burned as a witch anywhere in the republic.

The Astor ladies chose to ignore Caroline's slip. But she knew that each would give damning evidence should she, indeed, be tried for witchcraft.

Lehr took charge of the Astor ladies and swept them into the party. "He's awful," said Blaise.

"But think how much duller this place would be without him."

"Plon needs a rich widow." Blaise changed the subject.

"Don't look at me. I'm no help. I'm outside this world. In Washington . . ."

"Why don't you take him there, in the fall?"

"I'll take Plon anywhere, of course. I adore him, as you know . . ."

"As I know." They stared at each other. The orchestra was now playing *Tales of Hoffmann*. "I hear that Cousin John's wife is dead."

Caroline merely nodded; and said, "How is Mr. Houghteling?"

"Lawyers!" Blaise let the subject go. Neither had much emotion left to bear on the subject of the money that divided them. "I've told Plon that Mrs. Astor—the young one—only flirts."

"I think he's worked that out. But he thinks that he understands American women better than he does because he has seduced so many of them in Paris."

"Does he tell *you* such things?"

"Doesn't he tell you?"

"Yes, but I'm a man."

"Well, I'm not an *American* woman. Anyway, what those creatures do in Paris is one thing." Caroline thought of the beautiful Mrs. Cameron with her beautiful boy poet, of the majestic antlers once again sprouting from Don Cameron's head, not to mention a delicate unicorn's horn from the pink marble baldness of Henry Adams's brow.

Lord Pauncefote joined them, having no doubt exhausted Helen Hay with his notorious and habitual long answers to questions not put to him. "Your friend Mr. Hearst is in splendid form." He acknowledged Blaise's identity. "He accuses poor Mr. Hay of being England's creature."

"Oh, that's just to fill space," said Blaise.

"Between murders," Caroline added.

"Actually, he's going to have some more fun with Roosevelt!"

Pauncefote shut his eyes for a long instant, always a sign that he was interested; that a message to the Foreign Office would soon be encoded. "Yes?" Pauncefote's eyes were again open.

"The Chief's been in touch with some of the leading goo-goos . . ."

"The leading what?"

"Goo-goo," said Caroline, "is what reformers of the American system are called by those who delight in the system. Goo-goo is an—abbreviation?—of the phrase 'good government,' something Governor Roosevelt, like all good Americans, holds in contempt. Isn't that right, Blaise?"

"Not bad." Her brother's praise was grudging.

"Goo-goo," murmured Pauncefote without relish.

"The goo-goos are attacking Roosevelt because he's a creature of the bosses but likes to talk about reform, which he's really as much against as Senator Platt. The Chief's going to have some fun with all this when the campaign starts."

"I suppose," said Pauncefote, "Governor Roosevelt is too much the soldier for this—heady political life."

"Soldier!" Blaise laughed delightedly. "He's just a politician who got lucky in Cuba."

"But that was a famous victory over Spain, and he was part of it."

"As architect, yes," said Blaise, and Caroline was surprised that her brother seemed to know of the plotting that had gone on amongst Roosevelt and Lodge and the Adamses and Captain Mahan. "But not as a soldier. The real story in Cuba—which the Chief will never print—is not how we bravely defeated the Spanish but how seven hundred brave Spaniards nearly beat six thousand incompetent Yanks."

Pauncefote stared, wide-eyed, at Blaise. "I have never read this in any newspaper."

"You never will, either," said Blaise. "In this country, anyway."

"Until I publish it." Caroline was indeed tempted to puncture the vast endlessly expanding balloon of American pomposity and jingoism.

"You won't." Blaise was flat. "Because you'd lose the few readers you've got. We create news, Lord Pauncefote."

"Empires, too?" The Ambassador had recovered his professional ministerial poise.

"One follows on the other, if the timing's right." Blaise was indifferent; and most Hearstian, thought Caroline.

"I shall reexamine the careers of Clive and Rhodes, with close attention to the *Times* of their day."

"Lord North's career would be more to the point." Blaise was hard. Caroline wondered who had been educating him; certainly not Hearst. Plon joined them; and Pauncefote withdrew.

"Have you found a rich lady?" asked Caroline.

"Oh, they are—what do the English say?—thick upon the ground. But they cannot talk."

"Bring him to Washington." Caroline turned to Plon. "We are rich in ladies whose husbands are *under* the ground. And *they* talk—the ladies, that is."

"Perhaps we'll both come, after the election." Blaise stared, idly, at a pale blond girl who was approaching them, on the arm of a swarthy youth. What color, wondered Caroline, would the children of so contrasted a couple be? "But New York is more Plon's sort of oyster."

"Oyster?" Plon's grasp of idiom was weak. "*Huitre?*" He translated, tentatively.

To Caroline's amazement the blond girl greeted her warmly. "Frederika, Miss Sanford." The voice was Southern; the manner shy; the profile, turned to Caroline, noble. "I'm Mrs. Bingham's daughter. From Washington. Remember?"

"You've grown up." Caroline had hardly noticed the child in Washington; a child, literally, until this summer.

"It's the dress, really. Mother won't let me dress up at home."

"Mrs. Bingham *is* Washington," Caroline declared.

"Is she a widow?" asked Plon, in French.

"Not yet," murmured Caroline. The swarthy young man proved to be from the Argentine embassy, a representative of what John Hay wearily termed "the dago contingent" until Caroline had allied herself sternly with the entire Latin race and "dago" was no longer a word used in her volatile presence.

Frederika was thrilled by the half-brothers; they were characteristically indifferent to her. She was too young and pure for Plon; and Blaise's mind—Caroline never thought to associate the word "heart" with so blond and fierce a beast—was elsewhere.

"Is your mother here?" Caroline knew that there was no earthly way, as yet, for Mrs. Benedict Tracy Bingham, wife to Washington's milk king, to break into Newport's Casino on such a night.

"Oh, no. I visit friends. You see, Mother likes Washington in the summer." There was a sudden mischievous, even collusive, look in Frederika's eyes. As Caroline was deciding that the girl had possibilities, the Argentine swept her away.

"Her father," said Caroline, to Plon, "makes all of Washington's milk."

"How funny!" Plon laughed delightedly.

"Why funny?"

"It's my English, I suppose, but for a moment I thought you said he made 'milk.'" Caroline let the subject go. Plon was better in Paris. Blaise—and she—were better suited to this new world of energetic and mindless splendor, of waste—of absolute waste of everything and, she wondered, suddenly feeling disagreeably faint, of everyone?

8

Four of the original Five Hearts were gathered in Henry Adams's study, to John Hay's delight. Although the pale April sun filled the study, Adams as always had a fire blazing and the smell of woodsmoke mingled agreeably with that of the masses of daffodils and lilies-of-the-valley the incomparable servant, Maggie, had placed everywhere. The fourth Heart—Clarence King—stood with his back to the fire, Adams to his right, all admiration like a schoolgirl, and Clara to his left, all fondness like a sister while King talked rapidly and brilliantly and coughed and laughed at his own coughing, and coughed again. "I have a spot on my lung now, the size of a dollar—why always a dollar, I wonder? But better the coin than the greenback. I thought the sun would cure me, as it always has before, but Florida has failed me, as Florida has failed so many before me, including you, John. Didn't you want to be a congressman from there in 1864?"

"*From* there, oh, yes," said Hay. "I like to pretend it was President Lincoln's idea, to get friends into Congress. But the carpetbag I took to Florida was all my own . . ." And then, Hay completed to himself, just as I was about to quit as the President's secretary, he was shot. Hay wondered, yet again, how strange it was that he, who dreamed now so much at night, no longer encountered the Ancient in his dreams.

Although Clarence King was dying, he was determined to go in a great display of mind and wit and energy. He was bearded like Hay and Adams: the three had more or less synchronized their beards, each allowing the rakish moustaches of youth to act as foundation for the stately beards of middle age.

Hay had been shocked at the change in King, who had arrived some days before, haggard and ill-kempt. But William and Maggie had taken him in hand; put him to bed; fed him magnificently. "Tuberculosis does wonders for the appetite," King had announced at the first meal—High Communion, Adams had called it—of the Hearts, and Hay noticed that a fifth place had been left at table for the fifth never-to-be-mentioned Heart, Clover Adams. Except that King, quite naturally, would repeat something that Clover had said, and Adams seemed not at all perturbed; but then King could do no wrong for Henry Adams, who had declared his friend the greatest man of their generation, causing Hay a pang of ignoble envy; but then Henry Adams had always been in love— there was no other word—with the geologist, naturalist, philosopher, world-traveler, creator of mining enterprises, Renaissance man who, now that his life was near its end, had managed to fail on the grandest scale. He had been wiped out in the depression of '93, and though he still went exploring in the Yukon and other parts of the world, he was now merely a brilliant geologist, employed by others. There would be no King mine, no King fortune, no King widow and children; only the memory that the Hearts all had of a glorious companion who could sit up till dawn speaking on the origins of life, and, presumably, they could go look at a mountain called Clarence King, a superb peak in the Sierra Nevada.

A mountain and a memory were not much, thought Hay; but then what a life King had had. While Adams and Hay had sat at desks, reading and writing, or hovering on the periphery of power, King had explored and mapped the West, and written marvellously of the new world he had discovered, not to mention the geological wealth that other men would exploit. So taken with the idea of King was Adams that he had fled from Harvard to the Far West to travel with King, to rough it. In later years they had often travelled together, most recently to Cuba. Each had developed a passion for Polynesian women, "old-gold girls," as they would cryptically refer to these palpable visions, unknown to Hay. Then, in 1879, King become director of the United States Geological Survey, a bureau created largely for him, with considerable assistance from Senator James G. Blaine, who was less than amused when the novel *Democracy*, suspected to be a work by one of the Hearts, lampooned him as the venal Senator Ratcliff. Hay had often wondered if Henry Adams had, somehow, instinctively, harmed the man he loved and envied above all others. By 1880, King had departed the only office that he had ever wanted; he had also entered the lives of John and Clara Hay; and, thus, due to highly elective affinities, Five Hearts beat as one until Clover Adams swallowed potassium cyanide; and then there were Four. Soon, Hay thought bleakly, as April light made glitter King's feverish eyes, there would be Three; then Two, One, None. Why?

King answered, as if he had looked into Hay's mind. "When I went mad that day in the lions' house in Central Park, I was positive that I had seen God, and He was, simply, a huge mouth, maw, with teeth, sharp, sharp—and hungry, oh, so hungry to dine on us. That's why we exist, I thought, to feed Him. Then a Negro—someone's butler from a house in Madison Avenue—enraged me, and I struck him. One tends to violence in the lion house, particularly in the presence of one's Maker who is also one's devourer, and I was taken away by the police in a state of purest ecstasy, and committed to the Bloomingdale Asylum . . ."

"On Halloween," said Adams, happy to contemplate, yet again, the sacred story. "Then we went off to Cuba in February. There were no lions there."

"Ah, but there was that maw, always in attendance. Always

hungry. Is Theodore as dreadful as ever, now he's vice-president?"

"I had hoped that name would not be spoken on this day of days," said Adams. "Theodore's luck is relentless and inexorable, like the Chicago Express."

"He was," said Clara, justly, "less noisy than usual. You must give him credit for that, Henry."

"But there weren't many occasions for noise." Hay had been surprised by the dignity of Teddy's inaugural speech to the Senate, given during a lull in a particularly squalid filibuster. In that cigar-smelling chamber where weary senators dozed, Teddy had taken the oath of office as vice-president; and then, cryptically, he had spoken of the great things in store for this particular generation of Americans. "As we do well or ill, so shall mankind in the future be raised or cast down." At that moment, a storm broke over the Capitol and the sound of rain on the skylights of the Senate chamber put Hay, suitably, in mind of war. Given the chance, Teddy would try to expand the American empire; but vice-presidents are not given such opportunities, as Teddy knew. "This office is the ultimate grave of my political career," he had said to Lodge accusingly; but then he liked to blame Lodge for driving him to accept a nomination never offered him by President or party leaders. Teddy had simply seized the prize—or, as Hay always thought of the vice-presidency, "persimmon." During the autumn, he had spoken in twenty-four states to audiences that so thrilled him that he was inspired to refer to William Jennings Bryan as "my opponent." The Major *said* that he had been amused by these slips; but Hay suspected that the Major's tolerance for the Colonel was not great. Certainly, the overwhelming Republican victory in November was spoiled for McKinley by those who suggested that it was not he but his glamorous running-mate who had ensured the million votes by which the Republicans had won.

"Teddy was not in town very long," said Adams. "He presided over the Senate on March fourth. Then Congress adjourned until next December, and he went home to that ugly house of his on Long Island."

"I wonder," said the practical Clara, "where they will live. And

333

how. Edith says there's no money, and all those children. Bamie—his sister—has found a house here, but only for herself."

"Our Madame Maintenon?" asked King, moving from fireplace to an armchair too low and narrow for the second-largest of the Hearts. Clara, the largest, had her own special non-Adams-proportioned chair. "Otherwise, I shall simply stand when I'm in your study."

"We could do worse." Adams extended alabaster hands toward jonquil-yellow flames. "She's sounder than Teddy. But he'll vanish from public life. He was astonished to find that between March fourth and next December, the vice-president has no duties at all. He will probably write another half-dozen books."

"No," said Hay, delighted that he could delight his fellow Hearts with the higher gossip. "Teddy has suddenly succumbed to ambition. He means to . . . what word shall I use? He means to do something that only Clarence among us has ever done."

"Lechery in the South Seas?" Adams's eyes were bright.

"No. Something more unusual, more . . . alarming."

"What?" cried Clara.

"Work!" shouted Hay.

"Oh, Lord save us! Save *him!*" Clarence sank from chair to floor, on his knees—no great distance—hands clasped in prayer. "Theodore Roosevelt will actually work for a living?"

"Something Henry and I would never dream of doing . . ."

"No, no. You are not pure, John." Adams was stern. "You have worked as an editor and a journalist and a businessman. *I* have never worked . . ."

"Professor at Harvard? Editor of the *North American Review?*"

"Neither was proper work. Certainly, I did not make my living from all that showing off . . ."

"What, please tell me," King was still on his knees, "is the vice-president going to work at?"

"The law! He is going to go to law school." Hay was pleased by the general excitement.

"An American vice-president, in office, at *law* school?" Adams's horror was not affected.

"I can't imagine your great-grandfather taking courses at Columbia while waiting for General Washington to die, but Teddy . . ."

". . . is out of sight," said King, an addict of Bowery slang. Then he pulled himself, with some difficulty, Hay noticed, back into the tiny armchair. "How do you know this?"

"At the White House, he cornered the Chief Justice, and told him that as he was still quite young with a lot of time on his hands, he wanted to qualify for the bar. The Chief Justice was alarmed, of course. But when he saw how serious Teddy was, he said that he'd give him a reading list for the summer, and once Congress convenes, he'll tutor Teddy, 'quiz him' was the phrase he used to me, every Saturday night."

"Theodore is not like other people," said Clara, as neutrally as she could say anything.

"If Clarence is our Renaissance man . . ." Adams began.

". . . Teddy is our Baroque boy," completed King. "We live in wondrous times. What does the Major think of all this?"

"If I didn't know, I'd tell you," Hay repeated Seward's favorite line. "Actually, the President is more than ever the Buddha these days. He's leaving at the end of the month for a six-week trip around the country, accompanied by, among others, me. At last," said Hay, turning to King, "I shall see your California. The President launches a battleship at San Francisco, and I'll be there, chatting of open doors and peace, while General MacArthur continues his slaughter of Filipinos." Hay wondered what errant electrical circuit in his brain had made him advert to the one subject that he—and the Administration—never acknowledged. Particularly now, when the war—no other word for it, privately—was over. Aguinaldo had been captured in March, shortly after the inauguration. Presently, before they started across the country, the President would issue a decree declaring the "insurrection" at an end.

Hay did not allow the others to pick up on his unexpected use of the word "slaughter." "By the end of the month, of course, the business is over." He spoke rapidly, and was aware of a shortening of breath. Heart? To die, suddenly, at the heart of the Hearts would be poetic. "I shall get them, by the way."

"Get what?" asked King, through a series of dry coughs. Perhaps all the Hearts might stop at once, like four clocks someone had forgotten to wind.

"The Philippines. The Major thinks that the State Department, not the War Department, should administer them. Root agrees, I am happy to say. In October I shall be lord of all the isles."

"What about the canal?" King coughed. "Will you be lord of the isthmus, too?"

"We must get the treaty through the Senate first." Hay was again short of breath: must not panic. "They've rejected two versions so far, despite England's surprising complaisance. Pauncefote and I are now ready with a third version, which we will submit to our masters in the Senate come December." Hay took a deep breath; felt better; noticed that Clara was watching him with some alarm, which, in turn, alarmed him. Did he look—did he sound?—so ill? He glanced at Adams to see if the Porcupine had noticed anything wrong, but the Porcupine was looking at Clarence King, whose lower face was covered with a handkerchief, even though the fit of coughing had stopped. How fragile we have become, thought Hay; then he rallied. "Of all our friends I hate Cabot Lodge the most."

"John." Clara was reproving.

"Oh, Cabot's hateful." Adams turned his gaze from the dying King to the blazing fire. "I've always detested him, while delighting in his friendship. I think that Cabot's problem is shyness."

"No senator was ever shy." King chiselled out the sentence as if on marble.

"Shyness?" Hay had not thought the ever-grinding Cabot shy. But perhaps he was, and disguised the fact with endless commentaries broken by sudden acts of treachery toward friends.

"Yes, shyness," Adams repeated. "He is one of nature's Iagos, always in the shadows, preferring to do evil to nothing . . ."

"And nothing to good." Hay made his addition to the indictment. "So if Cabot's Iago, McKinley must be his Othello."

"No, no." Adams was firm. "After all, Othello trusted Iago. I think it most unlikely that our Ohioan Augustus trusts—or even notices—Cabot. No. I see Theodore in the part of Othello. They complement each other. Theodore all action and bluster, Cabot all devious calculation. Cabot is the rock on which Theodore will sink."

"I like Cabot." Clara put a stop to the conversation. "He is also Brooks's brother-in-law. He is practically your relative, Henry."

"That is no recommendation, Clara, to a member of the house of Atreus . . ."

"From Quincy, Mass." King liked to deflate the Adamses. Their peculiar self-esteem was matched only by their sense of general unworthiness. All in all, Hay was happy not to be the member of a great family's fourth generation. Better to be one's own ancestor; one's own founding father. What would Del become, he wondered, in the twentieth century that had begun, as Root had maintained, January 1, 1901? Hay had already spent four months in the new century (Queen Victoria had wisely died after three weeks of the new epoch) and was more than ever convinced that it was just as well that he would miss nearly all of it. Del, on the other hand, might experience more than half the century. Father wished son luck.

– 2 –

Caroline greeted Del at the door to her office, abuzz with the first—and always precious to her—flies of spring. Del was larger than when he had left; there was more chest, more stomach; he also seemed taller. They shook hands awkwardly. Mr. Trimble watched them, all benignity. He had given his unsought blessing to the match. "A woman must not be alone too long," he had said, "particularly in a Southern town like Washington."

Caroline had just returned from New York, where she had said good-by to Plon, who had sailed for home, enriched by two cigarette cases.

Now Del had come to take her to lunch. They faced each other across the rolltop desk. "Were you really pro-Boer?" asked Del.

"Were you, really, secretly pro-British?" Much of Bryan's attack on McKinley had been the President's pro-British policy, the result of that conniving Anglophile the Secretary of State, John Hay, and his equally sinister son, who was American consul general—nepotism, too!—at Pretoria.

"Yes," said Del, to Caroline's surprise. "But only secretly. No word ever passed my diplomatically sealed lips. I was the soul of caution, like Father."

"Well, we were pro-Boer because our readers—and advertisers—are, or were. Anyway, now it's over. Your team has won. Ours has lost."

"And the Irish and the German riff-raff have all joined the Democratic Party where they belong. What next?"

John Hay had told her that he doubted Del would want to stay on in the diplomatic service; but then Hay usually said what others wanted to hear. He knew that Caroline could not bear the thought of being a diplomat's wife, moving from post to post around the world.

But Del chose not to answer her directly. "You'll see what's next."

"When?"

"Today. At lunch."

Mystified, Caroline took her place in the Hays' family carriage, which proceeded from Market Square into Pennsylvania Avenue, then headed north. "There are more electrical cars," Del observed. "And telephone wires." Like spaghetti, wires were strung every which way on posts in the bright noon-light, which made their shadows on the avenue resemble an elaborate spider's web. The trees along the sidewalk were in new bloom. Washington's April was so like Paris's June that Caroline was, suddenly, homesick: by no means the proper mood for a young lady who had not seen her fiancé for a year. She noted her opal ring on his finger; tried to imagine a wedding ring on her own; thought instead of Saint-Cloud-le-Duc. She and Blaise had agreed that neither would go there until the will had been finally settled. Marguerite was suicidal. Caroline was stoic.

"I am stoic," she said to Del, apropos nothing at all. But he was speaking to the driver. "We'll go in from the south side." They were now opposite the immaculately restored and redecorated façade of Willard's. Black children stood on the sidewalk, holding out clusters of daffodils and blossoming dogwood switches, pale pink, white. White.

"The White House?" asked Caroline.

"Yes. We're having lunch with the President." Del's small eyes gleamed; he would be, one day, as large as his mother, she thought, and she wondered if she could be happy with so huge a masculine entity.

Although the south door of the White House had been originally designed as the mansion's great entrance, nothing in Washington ever turned out as planned. For instance, the Capitol on its hill faced, magnificently, a shanty town, while its marble backside loomed over Pennsylvania Avenue and the unanticipated city's center. The city had been expected to grow west and south; instead it had grown east and north. The Executive Mansion had been designed to be approached from the river through the park, with a fine view of Virginia's hills across the river; but the unexpected primacy of Pennsylvania Avenue had obliged the tenants to make the northern portico the main entrance, and only secret or private visitors were encouraged to drive through the now muddy park to the somewhat forlorn grand entrance, where curved stairs looked as if they had been designed for an al fresco republican coronation of the sort that the Venetian doge endured atop stairs of equal pomp.

The downstairs corridor was empty. As always, Caroline was fascinated by the casualness of the White House. Except for a single policeman, who sat reading a newspaper inside the door, they had the shadowy corridor to themselves. "How easy it would be," whispered Caroline, though if ever walls had no ears, it was these, "to stage a coup d"état."

"Who would bother?" Del seemed genuinely surprised by the idea. "The place is too big."

"This house is very small."

"The house is nothing," said Del, as they started up the creaky steps to the main floor. "It's the country that's too big for that sort of thing."

In the main entrance hall, crowded as usual with visitors, Mr. Cortelyou greeted them in front of the Tiffany screen. "The President will join you in the family dining room. *She's* joining you."

"She's better?" asked Del.

But Cortelyou was now stowing them in the small presidential elevator; then he shut the door, and remained behind. Rattling alarmingly, the elevator rose. Caroline clutched Del's arm: would the machine be stuck? Would they die of suffocation before help came? But after what seemed like a purgatorial if not presidential term, they came to a halt, and Del led the way into the living quarters. One of the Germans opened the door to the dining room, where the table was set for four. To Caroline's surprise, Mrs. McKinley was already in her place. Had she been carried in, and set upright, like a doll? The face was unreal in its prettiness. Like so many women whose career is illness, she looked younger than her years. "Miss Sanford," the voice was nasal, like a crow's crawing, "I'm glad to see you again. Sit down here, next to me. The Major sits on my other side. I don't know why Mr. Hay's department fusses so when a husband and wife want to sit together at supper. After all, that's why you get married, isn't it?"

"I'm not sure, Mrs. McKinley. But, then I'm not married . . ."

"Yes," said the First Lady, and smiled. The smile was indeed lovely; and like a young girl's. "Well, you'll make a fine couple, and with money, too. Did you know that the Major's the only honest man we've ever had as president? Mr. Cleveland came here poor as can be, but when he left he was able to buy that mansion of his in Princeton. Well, the Major and I have finally, after all these years of scrimping, been able to buy our old house in Canton, Ohio, and guess how much we paid?"

"I don't know," said Caroline, who did know. The *Tribune* had already carried the story.

"Fourteen thousand, five hundred dollars, and the Major's going to spend three thousand more—which is all we have left—on fixing it up so that when I'm feeling poorly, like last summer, we can just hole up there, and he can still be president, with the telephone and all. Do you play cribbage, dear?"

"No. But I can always learn."

"You ought to. Euchre is a good card game, too. I always win, you know. It's important when you're a wife, to have something to do."

"Miss Sanford has her newspaper." Del meant to be helpful; and failed.

Mrs. McKinley buried her sudden frown in the bouquet of hot-house roses beside her plate. "I never read those . . . things."

"Neither do I," said Caroline quickly. "I only publish, which is very much like . . . like cribbage, I think," she added nonsensically. Why, she wondered, was she here? Obviously to be approved of by the Major and his lady as Del's wife; but why was that so important?

The Major stood in the doorway, large and serene, eyes glowing with—was it opium he was supposed to take? In his left silk lapel he wore a pink carnation, to set off Ida's pink roses. Caroline got up from her chair and curtseyed. The President crossed to her; he took her hand and, gently, seated her again. The low and beautiful voice was as rustic as Ida's but without the canting nasality. "I'm glad you could come, Miss Sanford. Sit down, Mr. Hay. Ida . . ." Fondly, he touched his wife's face; fondly, she kissed his hand. Caroline noted how pale each was. But then he had nearly died of pneumonia after the New Year's reception, and she had had a nervous collapse the previous summer. Caroline tried to imagine what it was like to be at the head of such a vigorous, loud nation; and failed.

Lunch was as simple and as enormous as the President's dove-gray waistcoated paunch, which began very high indeed on his frame and curved outward, keeping him from ever sitting close to table, which accounted, no doubt, for the single shamrock-shaped gravy stain on the black frock-coat that hung in perpendicular folds to left and right of the huge autonomous belly, like theater curtains drawn to reveal the spectacle. Quail was followed by porterhouse steak which preceded broiled chicken, each course accompanied by a variety of hot bread—wheat muffins, corn sticks, toast, and butter. Butter flowed over everything, and the Major ate everything while Ida picked at this and that. Del, Caroline noted with alarm, kept pace with the President: two of a kind, obviously. Would Del be as fat? Across Caroline's future fell a shadow, every bit as large and fateful as President McKinley's stomach.

The President spoke of the coming trip across the country. "Mrs. McKinley will make the effort." He gazed at her fondly. She munched a quail's leg. "Her doctor comes, too. And your father, of course. In fact, I want the whole Cabinet with me. Not everyone can get to see us here in Washington . . ."

"*Seems* like everyone does." Mrs. McKinley frowned.

"But they don't. So we'll go to them. It's very frustrating for me, these front-porch campaigns, having to stay home in Canton. Because I like . . . I really like going to see the folks . . ."

"*I* don't." Ida spread butter over a length of cornbread. "Never have. Always wanting something, the folks, from my dearest."

The President ignored her obbligato. "You get a sense of what they're thinking about, which you don't in this place. You also get a chance to talk straight to them, without the papers coming in between."

"You know, Miss Sanford has one of those newspapers, dearest. I told her she should learn to play euchre. Much better way to pass the time. You can win money, too, if you gamble, which is a sin." Ida looked suddenly sly.

"I like your paper, Miss Sanford. Much of the time," the Major added with a droll blink of the huge eyes.

"We like your Administration, Mr. President. Much of the time."

McKinley laughed. "You may like us even more of the time after this trip."

"The President," Del made his contribution, "is going to speak out, against the trusts . . ."

"Like Colonel Bryan?" Caroline could not resist.

"Perhaps more like Colonel Roosevelt." The Major was bland.

"But *most* like President McKinley." Del was enthralled by the Major, Caroline decided.

"The President's going to meet the problem head on. He's also going to discuss the tariff. He wants commercial reciprocity."

Ida hissed at Del. The President's face did not change expression. Del did not stop talking. "He's going to challenge the Senate at last . . ."

Ida hissed Del even more loudly. As Caroline turned to look at her hostess, McKinley with a practiced gesture flipped a buttery napkin over his wife's head; but not before Caroline had got a glimpse of the mouth as it set in a ghastly rictus, while the wide-open eyes showed only the whites. Beneath the napkin the hissing continued.

"I hope you won't write this in your newspaper." McKinley helped himself to a Spanish omelette which had appeared just when Caroline had prayed for deliverance from food.

"No, Mr. President. I understand that all this is," Ida was now making a gurgling sound, "in confidence."

"Caroline is discreet, sir." But Del was nervous.

"I'm sure. Unlike Mr. Hearst." McKinley shook his head; spoke with his mouth full. "Have you been reading the *New York Journal?* Not only am I the most hated creature on the American continent, their exact words, in spite of my reelection . . ."

"You even beat Bryan in his home state . . ."

"But I lost New York City by thirty thousand votes. Anyway, they've now written that if bad men can be got rid of only by killing, then the killing must be done."

"That is—atrocious!" Caroline was shocked; she was even more shocked that she had not seen the story. Del explained why. "After the first run, Mr. Hearst killed the story. So it wasn't in the later editions. For once, the Yellow Kid figured he'd gone too far, even for him. And Blaise," Del added. Mrs. McKinley was now silent beneath her napkin.

"All the more curious," said the President equably, "because Mr. Hearst had just sent me one of his editors to apologize for the things they wrote about me during the election."

When a Kentucky governor had been killed, Hearst's irrepressibly savage employee Ambrose Bierce had written a quatrain that had shocked the nation:

> The bullet that pierced Goebel's breast
> Cannot be found in all the west;
> Good reason, it is speeding here
> To stretch McKinley on his bier.

"Hearst wants to be the Democratic candidate in '04," said Del. "He figures Bryan's had his last chance, now he's getting into place."

"I wish him luck." McKinley was mild. Caroline wondered if he was as serene as he appeared; or was he, simply, a consummate actor? "Anyway, I shall be out of it. I shall never run again."

"That will upset Father," said Del. "He's already talking you up for a third term."

"We'd better put a stop to that." McKinley turned to his wife. As neck and shoulders were no longer rigid, he removed the napkin.

"There's nothing more boring—I say—than talking about the tariff." Ida picked up where she had left off.

"Then let's not talk any more about it." The Major smiled at her; and indicated for the waiter to bring them the first of several pies. "I want my second term to be truly disinterested. I want to do the sort of things that ought to be done but which you can't do if you're fretting about being reelected."

"Poor Mark Hanna," murmured Caroline.

McKinley gave her an amused, appreciative look. "He'll have his problems, I suppose. But I've made up my mind."

"He's sick." Ida sounded pleased. She helped herself to apple pie; if nothing else, the fit had given her a good appetite. Did she know? Caroline wondered. Or did she not notice that the game course had abruptly given way to dessert?

"Do you think," asked Caroline, "that there's *any* chance of Mr. Hearst being nominated?"

McKinley shook his head. "He is much too unscrupulous—too immoral—too rich. But if, let's say, he managed, somehow, to *buy* the nomination, he could never be elected. Curious that he should call me the most hated creature in America, when I am— reasonably popular, while he is the one who is hated."

"Reasonably hated," added Caroline.

"Reasonably hated," McKinley repeated; then he turned to Del. "Have you told her?"

"No, sir."

"Have you told your father?"

"I've told no one at all."

"It was," said Ida, staring intently at Caroline, "my idea."

"What is—*it*, Mr. President?"

"I'm appointing Del assistant private secretary to the president, with the understanding that when Mr. Cortelyou moves out and— and up, Del will be secretary."

Del turned pink with pleasure.

Caroline saw immediately the eerie symmetry. "It is the same position that John Hay had, when he came to Washington with President Lincoln."

"I think it fitting." The President smiled; dried his lips with a napkin, just missing a shiny buttery spot on the Napoleonic chin.

"Oh, that was so long ago." Ida was entirely in the present when she was not out of time altogether.

"But to look a long way ahead," said Caroline, "thirty-eight years from now, if you are like your father, you will be secretary of state."

"In the year," McKinley paused; not so much to count as to

345

marvel, "1939. What on earth will we be like then?"

"Gone, dearest. In Heaven, with little Katie. And good riddance to everybody else." Mrs. McKinley put down her napkin. "We'll have coffee in the oval parlor." The President helped her up, while Caroline and Del flanked the sovereign couple. "I'm glad Del's marrying you." Thus Ida gave her blessing to the appointment and the marriage. Caroline was relieved, for Del's sake. Whether or not she married him, she wished him well; realized that this was the greatest day of his life so far. As Lincoln had lifted the young John Hay out of the irrelevant mass and placed him squarely in history, so McKinley now lifted the son.

They proceeded into the oval sitting room, where the coffee service had been set up.

"When do you start work?" Caroline helped the President arrange the drooping First Lady in a green velvet chair.

"In the fall," said Del.

"After the tour." In his antimacassared rocking chair, McKinley rocked slowly back and forth, gently settling the contents of that huge stomach. "Shall I tell your father? or do you want to?"

"You should, sir."

"No." Caroline was firm. "Del must confide in his father, this one time, anyway."

"Your young lady is a born politician." The Major bestowed the highest accolade within his gift. Then smiled at Caroline, and she was struck, yet again, by the beauty of his plain face. Over the years, goodness of character had transformed what might otherwise have been a dull, somewhat bovine appearance into an almost god-like radiance—almost because, unlike most gods, there was no fury, no malice, no envy of mortal happiness in William McKinley, only a steady radiant kindness, like a comforting nimbus about that great head, whose rounded chin reflected the afternoon sunlight, thanks to the butter with which it was, like some sacred balm, anointed.

3

Nicolay was propped up in an armchair beside a coal fire. A faded tartan-patterned blanket covered the lower part of a body preparing soon to be in fact what it looked even now to be, a skeleton. The beard was wild, long, white. The eyes—nearly blind and oversensitive to light—were covered by a green shade. Hay recognized nothing in this old man of the young secretary who had persuaded President Lincoln to bring Johnny Hay to Washington as assistant secretary. "We can't bring *all* Illinois," Lincoln had complained. But Hay had joined the White House staff; shared a bed and an office with Nicolay, five years his senior. Later, in the aftermath of that heroic era—the American *Iliad*, Hay always thought—the two men had together spent a decade writing the story of Lincoln. Then Nicolay had been given a sinecure as a marshal at the Supreme Court; then he became ill and retired. Now he lived in a small house on Capitol Hill with his daughter, on the margin of the American present but at the center of its past.

Although Nicolay no longer resembled the man that he had been, Hay was conscious that despite his own numerous debilities he himself was still very much Johnny Hay, who had simply glued on a beard and lined his face with a pencil in order to impersonate an old man—an old man of state; and so had managed to fool everyone but himself. He knew that he was doomed to be forever what he had been, young and appealing and—the word that he had come to hate, charming, even as he charmed, and charmed. Those whom the gods wish to disappoint they first make charming.

"You're making headway, I hope." Hay indicated the desk where papers and open books were piled. Nicolay was at work on yet another Lincoln book, recently interrupted by a trip up the Nile.

"Oh, I try to work. But my head is not what it was." Hay

marvelled that the Bavarian-born Nicolay still spoke with a German accent.

"Whose is?"

"Yours, Johnny." Back of the wild white King Learish beard, the young Nicolay was smiling. "You grow more fox-like with time . . ."

"The fox is weakening, Nico. The dogs have got the scent. I hear the huntsman's bugle." Hay was a master of the elegiac note.

"You'll go to ground." Nicolay's hand shook as he pulled the tartan tighter about himself. The hand was white, bloodless, dead. "It is good news about your boy."

Hay nodded, wondering why he himself had not been pleased. In recent years, since Pretoria, in fact, he had come to admire and like his son; yet he did not want him to be so vividly and precisely his own replacement. Now that the son had started up glory's ladder, the father must prepare to surrender his own place higher up; ladder, too. "Del will go far," he said. "I never thought he'd have what it would take, but the President did—does. Del's like a son to the President."

"And not to you?" Nico stared at Hay, who looked at a copy of the now faded lithograph of Lincoln with his two secretaries, Nicolay and Hay. Had he ever been so young?

"Well, yes, to me, too. But he's more like his mother . . . . Anyway, he's at the start and we're at the end."

"You're not." Nico was flat. "I am. I'll die this year."

"Nico . . ." Hay began.

Nico finished, "I think there's nothing next. What do you think?"

"I don't—think. There's not much now. I'll say that."

"Religion," Nicolay began, but stopped. Both stared at the neutral fire.

"I go, at last, to California." Hay's mood lightened at the thought. "We start tomorrow. The President and the Postmaster General and I and forty others. We shall, yet again, bind up the wounds of the South, and then on to Los Angeles, and a fiesta, and San Francisco, where the rest of the Cabinet joins us, except clever Root, who says he must stay close to the War Department, where he directs our far-flung empire. Do you think it wise?"

"What wise?" Nico was drifting off.

"The empire we're assembling. Do you think," Hay was curious to know what Nico would answer, "that the Ancient would approve?"

Nico's response was quick. "The Ancient, no. The Tycoon, yes. He was of two minds, always."

"But he *acted* with a single view."

"Yes, but he thought for such a long time *before* he acted. The cautious Ancient and the fierce Tycoon held long debates, and Mr. Lincoln, in the end, arbitrated, and handed down his decision."

"The Major took a long time making up *his* mind."

"The Major is not Mr. Lincoln."

"No. But he is as essential to us in his way. I think we have done the right thing. I was persuaded of it when I was in England, and saw what prosperity—and civilization—empire had given them. Now they begin to falter. So we must take up the burden."

Nico looked at Hay directly. "Mr. Lincoln would never have wanted us to be anyone's master."

"Perhaps not." Hay had long since given up trying to imagine how Lincoln would have responded to the modern world. "Anyway, it's done. We are committed."

"When does Del move into the White House?"

"In the fall. For now, he'll be working with Mr. Adee at the State Department while I'm gone . . . . He plans to marry the Sanford girl."

"The Hays have a dowsing rod for money."

"Del is also a Stone . . ."

"A golden Stone. Well, are you pleased?"

Hay said that he was; and he was. "They will marry in the fall. Helen, too, I think, to the Whitney boy . . ."

"We've come a long way from Illinois."

"I wonder." With age, Hay was more than ever conscious of what might have been; yet could not conceive of any ladder that might have been better than the one that he had climbed, almost without effort, almost to the top. "I don't think I ever wanted to be president." Hay addressed the coal in the grate.

"Of course you did. Have you forgotten you?" Nico addressed Hay.

"I must have."

"I haven't. You were ambitious. You tried, twice, to go to Congress. Surely it was not for the company you'd find there."

"Perhaps you're right." Hay answered Nico's not-so-rhetorical question. "Anyway, I have pretty much forgotten me. Even so, it is odd that for one year I was next in succession to the President. So I did get pretty high up that particular ladder, which I may—or may not—have wanted to climb."

"McKinley's health is excellent." Nico laughed; and coughed.

"Unlike mine. After this trip, I go to New Hampshire for the rest of the summer. We'll all be there. Del and Caroline, too." Hay indicated the lithograph on the wall. "Do you ever dream of him?"

Nico nodded. "All the time. I dream of you, too. As you were then."

"What sort of dreams?"

"The usual, for those of us at the end." Nico's fragile fingers pulled at his wiry beard. "Things have gone wrong. I can't find important papers. I go through the pigeon-holes in his desk. I can't read any of the handwriting, and the President is anxious, and the trouble—"

"'This big trouble.'" Hay nodded. "He never said 'Civil War.' Fact he never said war at all. Only this big trouble. This rebellion. How does he seem to you in the dreams?"

"Sad. I want to help him, but can't. It's very frustrating."

"I don't dream of him at all any more."

"You're not so close to the end as I."

"Don't say that! But what's the end got to do with dreams? I dream most of the night, and nearly everyone I meet in my dreams is dead. But I never dream of *him*. I don't know what that means."

Nico shrugged. "If he wants to pay you a call he will, I suppose."

Hay laughed. "Next time you see him tell him I'd like a visit."

"I'll tell him," said Nico with Germanic gallows humor, "face to face. In Heaven, or wherever it is we politicians end up."

4

Blaise and Payne Whitney crossed the quadrangle, festooned with banners celebrating various class reunions. This was their third reunion, and Blaise had agreed to attend only because Caroline had said that Del Hay would be there, the first member of their class to have made his mark in the world. "You will be envious," she had said, well pleased. They would all meet in New Haven, and then Del and she and Payne would take a trip on Oliver Payne's enormous yacht; then Del and she would go on together to Sunapee in New Hampshire, where Mr. Hay was enjoying his ill-health in the bosom of the family. When Blaise had told the Chief about the reunion, the Chief had said, "Cultivate young Mr. Hay."

Connecticut's high summer was tropical in its heat, and the air was fragrant with the scent of roses and peonies and the whiskey that the graduates were drinking from flasks as they hurried from party to party. Blaise wondered why he had not enjoyed Yale more than he had. "You were in too much of a hurry to get started," said Payne, breaking into his thoughts. "You should've stayed long enough to graduate instead . . ." Payne broke off not so much out of tact as for lack of sufficient polite vocabulary to describe Hearst, devil incarnate to his class.

"Graduate or not, it's made no difference at all." Blaise was accurate. They were now at the edge of the pseudo-Gothic campus. Beyond a row of trees was Chapel Street and their hotel, the New Haven House. A streetcar gasped to a halt. Men in straw hats and women in wide-brimmed hats and flowery dresses got off, and made their way onto the campus. Del and a group of classmates were still at the hotel, where there would be, he had assured Blaise, champagne, "to celebrate my victory over the Boers and the English."

"Are you Mr. Hearst's partner?" asked Payne, as they crossed the street, filled with carriages and electrical cars, all converging upon the college.

"I don't know. I don't think so." Blaise was never entirely sure just what his relationship to the Chief was. Principally, he was a moneylender. He would have preferred to be an investor, but Hearst allowed no one to buy any part of a Hearst newspaper. Also, casual as Hearst was about money, he always paid back his debts to Blaise, with interest. Meanwhile, Blaise learned the business; learned it better, in a sense, than Hearst himself, for Blaise saw the business as just that, while Hearst, more and more, regarded his newspapers as mere means to an all-important end: his own presidency in 1904, followed, no doubt, by a Napoleonic dictatorship and self-coronation.

Although Blaise had no political ambition, he quite liked the power that went with the ownership of a newspaper. A publisher could make and break local, if not national, figures. Blaise had also watched, with a degree of fury, Caroline achieving what he ought to have done by now. She was taken very seriously in Washington because her newspaper was read and she no longer lost money. Inadvertently, he had driven her to be what he wanted to be. The irony of the situation was peculiarly unbearable. More than once, he had considered handing over her inheritance in exchange for the *Tribune*; yet such an exchange would have been an admission that she had, totally, won. Also, he was by no means certain that she would agree to the arrangement. In a few years, she would not only have her inheritance but the newspaper, too—not to mention the President's secretary for a husband, while Blaise would still be in Hearst's shadow, holding a purse that was less and less needed, as gold flowed from the Dakotas into Phoebe Hearst's account. At the corner of the hotel, Blaise vowed that he would buy the Baltimore newspaper, jinx though it was supposed to be. He must start his life.

"I suppose the best time of my life was here at Yale." Payne at twenty-four was nostalgic. "I don't suppose there'll be anything to top having rowed for Yale at Henley, even if I was a substitute oar."

"Oh, I'm sure something else will happen to you, during the next fifty years."

"I'm sure it will, too. But don't you see? I'll be old by then. I was young here." This threnody was cut short by a sudden eruption of young men and women from the hotel lobby into the street. Blaise and Payne were shoved against a wall. To Blaise's amazement, one of the young people was Caroline; in her right hand she held high an empty champagne glass, as if she were about to propose a toast.

"Caroline!" Blaise shouted. But if she heard him, she paid no attention, as she hurried to join the others, now gathered in a circle on the sidewalk opposite an ice-cream vendor. To an idle observer, it looked as if a dozen young people had been possessed, like so many medieval zealots, by an overpowering passion if not for God for ice cream. But then, as Blaise and Payne hurried to join the party, the ice-cream vendor abandoned his livelihood and joined the circle, from whose center a loud cry sounded, chilling Blaise's blood. He had never before heard Caroline so much as weep, much less cry out like a wounded animal.

Blaise pushed to the crowd's center, where he found Caroline on her knees, still holding the empty champagne glass carefully balanced, as if she were fearful of spilling its long-since-spilled contents. In front of her, on his back, was Del Hay, arms and legs flung wide, akimbo, like a comic doll.

Caroline touched Del's face with her unencumbered hand; Del's mouth was ajar, and blood streamed down his chin, while the gray eyes stared, intelligently, upward at his recent friends.

"Stand back! Stand back!" A voice of authority was heard. But no one heeded it. "Caroline," Blaise murmured in her ear; she did not look at him but she did give him her glass to hold. "He fell, from the third floor," she said. "He was sitting in the open window, talking to us, and leaned back, and fell. Like that." Blaise helped her up. The others had now made a passage for two policemen, who stared, dumbly, at the figure on the sidewalk. Then one of them squatted down and felt for the pulse in the right wrist; as he did, the hand flopped over, revealing a gold ring, without its jewel.

"My ring," said Caroline. Blaise had never seen her so marvellously collected; or so entirely mad, from shock. "The opal's gone." While the policeman examined Del for signs of life, Caroline got down on her hands and knees on the red-brick sidewalk and searched for the missing jewel. Amazed—and embarrassed—bystanders stood back, as she, politely, said, over and over again, "I'm sorry. Do you mind moving? His ring is broken, you see. The stone fell out."

"He's dead," said the policeman, who was now checking the neck for a pulse; then he shut the staring eyes.

"Oh, good," Caroline exclaimed, "I've found it!" She got to her feet, triumphantly. "Look," she said to Blaise, as the policemen carried away Del's body, and the crowd dispersed. "Here's the fire opal—for luck, for some, they say. But," she frowned at the stone in the palm of her hand, "it's cracked in two." Sunlight struck the stone in such a way that for a moment Blaise's eyes were dazzled by what seemed to be firelight. "I wonder if it can be fixed." Caroline's hand shut over the stone. Blaise took one arm. Payne took the other.

"I'm sure it can," said Blaise. "Let's go inside."

The lobby was dim and cool after the bright heat of the street. Just inside the door, Caroline became herself again. She turned to Payne. "How do we tell Mr. Hay?"

"I don't know." Payne was now in shock. "Thank God Helen isn't here."

"Let Mr. Hay find out on his own." Blaise was practical. "There's nothing we can do . . ."

"That we've not done." Caroline put the broken stone in her handbag. "I should have taken the warning seriously, that opals are bad luck." Happily, they were joined by Marguerite, loudly wailing; and as Caroline comforted her maid, Blaise knew that she would be all right. On the other hand, he wondered, briefly, about the universe. Was *it* all right? or was the whole thing meaningless and random, and insensately cruel?

9

―――――

"Why," asked Lizzie, "are autumn flowers darker than summer flowers which are darker than spring flowers?"

"Is that a question?" Caroline sat on the lawn, a shawl between her and the damp grass. "If it is, you've asked the wrong person. I was brought up to believe that what is out-of-doors should stay there, and not be encouraged in any way."

"The French love flowers." Lizzie was assembling bouquets of zinnias and early chrysanthemums; she, too, sat on the lawn, a blanket beneath her, a wide-brimmed straw hat pushed to the back of her head: she looked like a handsome country boy.

"But we like to discover them indoors, in vases. You're not afraid of chrysanthemums?"

"No. But then I'm not afraid of anything," said the niece of General Sherman; and Caroline believed her.

"I'm glad Marguerite's not here. She would make a scene. Chrysanthemums are only for the dead, we believe. *She* believes, that is."

355

"She will come back?"

Caroline nodded. "The end of this month, when I go back to Washington. Thank you for my holiday."

"Thank *you*. Without you, I would have gone mad in this house, with only my loved ones to keep me company."

"The Senator's less restless than he was." Caroline was neutral. Don Cameron was ageing visibly; and drinking invisibly. Although never exactly drunk in their presence, he was never entirely sober. Daughter Martha was at what promised to be the sort of awkward age that might well last a lifetime. She was large, ungainly, unhappy; an exact opposite to her beautiful and gallant mother. Lizzie, wanting to do her best for the girl, did her worst. They had nothing in common but blood, that least of bonds. It was Henry Adams who had arranged that they take this house at Beverly, on Massachusetts's north shore, not far from Nahant, where the Cabot Lodges summered. Only this summer, the Lodges and Adamses had gone to Europe, leaving the Camerons to their own devices, with only the Brooks Adamses for company, at not-so-nearby Quincy.

Earlier in the year, Don had cut back Lizzie's allowance. She had barely been able to live in Paris on eight hundred dollars a month. When she had asked for a thousand, Don reduced the eight hundred; and then decided, capriciously, that they should all economize together, in the United States, where Martha must soon take her place in society, not to mention at school. Father, mother and daughter were now situated on the aptly named Pride's Hill, surrounded by rented rural beauty, with only Caroline for company.

After Del's death, Caroline had, with some misgivings, joined the Hay family in New Hampshire. She would have preferred to spend the summer in Washington's heat, working at the *Tribune*, or even return to Newport, Rhode Island, and Mrs. Delacroix, but Clara Hay had been insistent; and so Caroline had gone, to Sunapee, to act the part of the widow that she might have been.

Hay had taken the death hard. "I see his face all the time now, always before me and always smiling." Then he had read aloud to

Caroline a curiously intimate and uncharacteristic letter from Henry Adams to Clara. For the first time, according to Clara, Adams alluded to the suicide of his wife: "I never did get up again, and never to this moment recovered the energy or interest to return into active life." He had cautioned Clara not to allow Hay to break down as he had done, with the result, he had duly noted with devastating self-knowledge, that "I have got the habit of thinking that nothing is worthwhile! That sort of habit is catching, and I should not like to risk too close contact at a critical moment with a mind to be affected by it." Hay had been both touched and amused by the Porcupine's sharp clarity, charity.

When the Camerons had invited Caroline to Beverly, Clara had insisted that she go. "They are so deeply interested in themselves that you won't have any time to think of yourself." Caroline accepted the invitation; then sent Marguerite back to France to see the inevitable ailing mother that every lady's maid possessed, even to her hundredth year, as a constant *memento non mori*.

The Camerons were indeed full of themselves, but as Caroline could never get enough of Lizzie, she was content to drift with them to summer's end. Now the sea-wind was sharp with an autumnal chill. Soon the house, always sea-damp, would be shut up, and the Camerons would go—where? They were like so many flying Dutchmen, each on a separate track, and only briefly, as now, did their courses coincide.

They were joined by Kiki, Lizzie's small overweight poodle, who leapt onto Lizzie's lap and began, methodically, to lick Lizzie's firm chin.

"Martha's problem is that she is both lazy and vain. Which is worse?" Lizzie appeared to be addressing Kiki.

"I find both qualities endearing, at least in friends. Lazy people never bother you, and vain ones don't involve themselves in your life. I wish I had such a daughter," Caroline added, surprising herself; Lizzie, too.

"You really *want* children?"

"I just said that I did, so I suppose I must." But, curiously, Caroline could never imagine having given birth to a child by Del.

Worse, she had never been able even to fantasize what it might be like to make love to him.

"She wears my last year's clothes." Lizzie was neutral. "Don delights in her. She is more Cameron than Sherman. We are not so large. I think that she would like to marry that Jew. But I got her away in time."

Earlier in the year, at Palermo, Lionel Rothschild, a nineteen-year-old Cambridge undergraduate, had affixed himself to Martha. "The odd thing," said Lizzie, "is that he is absolutely enchanting but . . ."

"A Jew." Caroline had lived through the Dreyfus case in a way that no one who was not French could understand; and Caroline was, for all practical purposes, a Frenchwoman, impersonating an American lady. Caroline had favored Dreyfus in the civil war that had broken out in the drawing rooms of Paris. She had skirmished on many an Aubusson, heard the ominous hiss of enemy epigrams, the thudding sound of falling tirades; yet she herself knew no Jews. "At least the Rothschilds are very rich."

"Worse!" Lizzie pushed her straw hat even farther back on her head. "The boy's charming. But the race is accursed . . ."

"You sound like Uncle Henry."

"Well, that is the way of our world, isn't it? Anyway, she's too young to marry . . ."

"And I'm too old." Caroline got the subject back to herself. Since Del's death, she had become more than ever interested in herself; and more than ever puzzled what to do about this peculiar person. She was apt to live a long time. But she had no idea how she was to occupy her time. The thought of half a century to be lived through was more chilling to her than the thought of an eternity to be dead in.

"No, you're not too old." Lizzie was direct. "But you'd better make your move soon. You don't want to be the first—and last—woman publisher in the world or Washington or whatever, do you?"

"I don't—I really don't know. I miss Del."

"That's natural. You've had a shock. But some shocks are good—after the pain, of course. Have you ever noticed a tree after

358

lightning's struck it? The part that's still alive is twice as alive as before and puts out more branches, leaves . . ."

"Unlike a woman struck by lightning, who is decently buried."

"You *are* morbid. You're also lucky. You are—will be—rich. You're not like me, dependent on a man who is—happiest alone."

The man, happiest when alone, seemed delighted to be walking arm in arm with Martha, dark-browed, tall, heavy. They came from the house, whose old-fashioned frame porch—piazza they called it locally—was ablaze with potted hydrangeas, neatly regimented by Lizzie. Kiki abandoned Lizzie; and leapt into Martha's arms, while the red-faced patriarch smiled upon this homely scene.

Don Cameron was now nearly seventy; nearly fat; nearly very rich, though a sudden fall in the stock market the previous month had obliged him, for some days, to drink for two. Now news from the outside world had shaken them all. History was at work, "overtime," in Lizzie's phrase.

"There are still no newspapers," said Don, slowly, carefully, arranging his bulk on Lizzie's blanket. Martha stood, holding Kiki in her arms—Virgin with canine god, thought Caroline.

"Anyway, we think we can pronounce the name," said Martha, and she pronounced, "Leon Czolgosz," with two shushing sounds. "He is Polish, it seems."

"An anarchist!" Don growled. "They're everywhere. They're out to kill every ruler in the world, like the king of Italy last summer, and before him, what's her name?"

"Elizabeth," said Caroline, "empress of Austria. They also— whoever they are—killed the prime minister of Spain and the president of France . . . . She was so beautiful." Caroline had always been told that her mother had been very like the Kaiserin, whose death from a knife through the heart, as she was getting aboard a ship, had appalled the world. It was, somehow, unnatural that a woman as beautiful as the Empress should be so gratuitously murdered.

"Funny thing," said Cameron. "Hanna's been worrying for more than a year now. 'I want more guards,' he kept telling the

359

Secret Service. Then they find that list of those wops over in New Jersey, with the names of all the rulers they meant to kill, and Hanna was fit to be tied, because there was the Major's name but the Major wasn't interested; very fatalistic, the Major."

"Very lucky, the Major," added Lizzie, reclaiming the faithless Kiki from Martha's arms. Martha now sat, cross-legged, on Caroline's shawl. The four of them then proceeded to contemplate history.

A few minutes after four o'clock in the afternoon of September 6, 1901, in the Temple of Music of the Pan-American Exposition at Buffalo, New York, President McKinley stood before a large American flag, with potted plants to his left and right. An organ played Bach. The day was hot. The presidential collar had twice been changed. Mrs. McKinley was, as usual, ill; and bedded down in the International Hotel. The President was attended only by Cortelyou, and three agents of the Secret Service. Exposition police were also on hand, but when the President gave the order to throw open the doors, so that the people could come shake his hand, there was more than the usual confusion. For one thing, the line was not orderly and rapid, the way the President preferred: one citizen's hand succeeded rapidly by another, one pair of eyes deeply, if briefly, transfixed by the President's luminous stare. Instead, the citizens of the republic advanced slowly, hesitantly, singly, in couples, even in groups. There was no sorting them out.

A young, slight man approached the President with a bandaged right hand. Face to face, there was a moment of confusion. As McKinley's right arm outstretched automatically, he was presented with a problem. Did one shake a bandaged hand? or would its owner offer him his left hand? The young man solved the problem. He darted forward, pushing to one side the President's arm while, simultaneously, firing twice a pistol that he had been holding in the bandaged hand. The stunned President remained standing while guards threw the man to the floor; then, as they dragged him from the hall, a chair was brought for the President, who sat down and, dazedly, felt his waistcoat, where blood was oozing. But he seemed more interested in the assailant than in his wound, and he said to Cortelyou, most calmly, "Don't let them hurt him." Then, when he saw the blood on his fingers, he said, "Be careful, Cortelyou, how you tell my wife."

Eleven minutes later, the President was on the operating table of the Exposition's emergency hospital. One bullet had grazed his chest; the other had entered the vast paunch, and gone through the stomach. The surgeons were able to repair the points of entry and of exit; the bullet, however, was not found. Then the President was sewed up. No vital organs had been harmed; on the other hand, the wound was not drained, and there remained the possibility of infection, not to mention shock to a system that might not prove to be as strong as it appeared.

During the next few days, Vice-President, Cabinet, and Mark Hanna, as well as McKinley's sisters and brother, came to Buffalo. But after a feverish weekend, the President's temperature returned to normal; and he was pronounced out of danger. The Vice-President vanished into the Adirondacks, while the Cabinet dispersed. Meanwhile, Leon Czolgosz was closely questioned. When he confessed to an admiration for a leading anarchist named Emma Goldman, she was immediately arrested in Chicago; and declared the originator of the plot to kill the President.

But at Beverly Farms, news was slow in coming. Don Cameron relied on visitors to bring him day-old newspapers. As there was neither telephone nor telegraph office nearby, Caroline wondered if she should go back to Washington, to her command post at the *Tribune*. But Lizzie said, "There's no one in the government left in town. What news there is is at Buffalo, and who wants to go there?"

Kiki began to bark; visitors had appeared on the piazza of the house. Brooks Adams and his wife, Daisy, waved to the group on the lawn. Then Brooks shouted, "Teddy!"

"Teddy what?" responded Cameron, getting first to his knees; then, laboriously, onto his feet.

"Teddy Roosevelt," roared Brooks, as his wife, frowning, put her hands over her ears, "is president of the United States."

"Oh, God," murmured Cameron.

Caroline crossed herself. The poor good McKinley was now as vanished from the story as Del. Then to Kiki's delight, everyone ran toward the house.

"When—how?" asked Lizzie.

"Yesterday evening. Friday the thirteenth. Gangrene set in. At two-fifteen this morning, he died. Teddy was off in the woods, somewhere. But he should be in Buffalo by now, being sworn in. The Cabinet's all there except for Hay, who's in Washington, holding together the government. No one knows the extent of the conspiracy. The Spanish-Cubans are thought to be behind it, out of revenge, for what McKinley did—and did not do—in Cuba." Brooks spoke rapidly, without a pause for breath. Then, like a child, he began to jump up and down on the porch; and Kiki jumped alongside him. "Teddy's got it all now! Do you realize that he occupies a place greater than Trajan's at the high noon of the Roman empire?" Brooks, like his brother, never spoke when he could lecture. "There has never been so much power given a man at so propitious a time in history! He will have the opportunity— and the means—to subjugate all Asia, and so give America the hegemony of the earth, which is our destiny, written in stars! Also," Brooks came to earth with a crash, "today is a day of great importance to Daisy and me. It is our wedding anniversary."

"History does seem to have us by the throat," said Lizzie mildly. "Come inside."

"Champagne," said Cameron, brightening. "For your anniversary . . ."

"And for Theodore the Great, whose reign has, at last, begun."

"No period of mourning for Mr. McKinley?" asked Caroline, who felt, suddenly, an intense grief for Del, the Major and, not least, herself, bereft.

"The King is dead," Brooks was cold. "Long live the King."

2

In the brightly illuminated reception room of the Pennsylvania Station, John Hay sat in a gilded armchair. Adee stood beside him, while a half-dozen Secret Service men prowled about the small, ornate, musty room reserved for dignitaries. The train from Buffalo was due to arrive at eight-thirty; aboard was the new president, and the body of his predecessor. Hay had arranged for the White House ushers to escort Mrs. McKinley and Cortelyou to the mansion, where McKinley would lie in state, while his family helped Mrs. McKinley to pack her belongings, a melancholy task that Hay had twice before witnessed when the widows of Lincoln and Garfield had each been obliged to deal with a life's end in the most humiliating and public way.

Once again, to Hay's amazement, as there would be no vice-president for another four years, he was constitutional heir to the President. If only for this reason, he was confident that Roosevelt would replace him as secretary of state. The President—the youngest in history at forty-two—must not have as his potential successor a sixty-two-year-old wreck, which is how Hay thought of himself, literally a wreck in body—mind, too. The death of Del had shaken him; the death of McKinley had sunk him into a melancholy of a sort that he had never before experienced. "I am a harbinger of death," he would say aloud, dramatically, when alone: he had yet to find the person with whom he could share his desolate vision of himself. In the nation's history, only three presidents had been murdered in office, and each had been a close friend of John Hay. It was curious, too, how essentially benign the three murdered men had been; it was not as if they had been tyrants, tempting the gods. Although, and Hay began to redefine "tyrant," many Filipinos and Spanish-Cubans did view McKinley as a tyrant. But, thus far, the Secret Service had been unable to link Czolgosz's anarchists to those Spanish-Cubans who were supposedly eager to avenge wrongs done them by McKinley.

Although Roosevelt had announced in Buffalo that, as he was simply a continuation of McKinley, he would keep the Cabinet intact, Hay expected, after a decent interval, to be let go. On Sunday morning Hay had written Roosevelt a letter of commiseration and congratulation, all couched in a valetudinarian style: "My official life is at an end—my natural life will not be long extended, and so in the dawn of what I am sure will be a great and splendid future, I venture to give you the heartfelt benediction of the past." Hay had wept when he wrote that line; now, recalling it, his eyes again filled with tears, for all the selves that he had been; and would be no more.

Suddenly, Hay heard the noise of a crowd outside the reception room. As he got to his feet, and started across the room, the station master flung open the door and said, "The President"; and disappeared.

Theodore Roosevelt, thick, sturdy, small, bounded across the room, and shook Hay's hand. Teeth bared but not smiling, he spoke rapidly. "I've seen your letter. Of course you will stay on with me, to the end, or as long as you like. As for your talk of age, that's affectation. You're not old. It's not your true nature to be old, any more than it's mine."

"Mr. President—" Hay began.

"Theodore, please. As I have always, disrespectfully, called you John, you must call me Theodore, as you've always done, except, of course, when people are about and we must both acknowledge the majesty of our estate . . ."

"You are too kind . . . Theodore." Hay was amused at the Rooseveltian vehemence. Obviously, on the long train ride, he had been busy working out how protocol would affect his various personal relationships.

"I don't want to cut myself off from old friends socially, the way the other presidents have tended to do. I want to be able to dine like any guest at your house, or Cabot's, but, of course," he became very grave, somber even with majesty, "I must preserve the prerogative of the initiative." Before Hay could think of a response,

Roosevelt was off on another tangent. "Root swore me in. It was very moving, all of us in that parlor. Root couldn't say the oath of office for some ten minutes. Odd. I never think of him as being an emotional man. For the time, I want to keep the Philippines in his department. You don't mind?"

"No, no. I have quite enough to do. Your wife and young Ted are here. They arrived this afternoon."

"Good! Let's join them."

Theodore grabbed Hay's arm, and marched him, rather too fast for Hay's perfect comfort, into the main waiting room of the station, where a small crowd cheered the new president, who solemnly raised his hat, but did not, Hay was relieved to note, mar the occasion with the huge, toothy Roosevelt smile. A dozen policemen then made a ring about them, and escorted them outside.

In the distance, the dome of the Capitol was illuminated like a confectionery skull, thought Hay. Since Hay had ordered the White House to make no announcement, there was no crowd outside the station; the public did not expect the new president to arrive until the next day. Neither Roosevelt nor Hay chose to notice the huge ebony hearse, with its six black horses, ready to bear McKinley's body to the White House. For a moment, Roosevelt paused on the sidewalk; started to speak; said nothing.

"You needn't wait," said Hay.

Roosevelt looked relieved; and sprang into the presidential carriage, followed by Hay. "Seventeen thirty-three N Street," said Roosevelt, as if he were in a taxi-cab.

"They know," said Hay, amused. "It's their job."

"Quite right. I must get used to that. I must get used to a lot of things now, like the White House. I want the stationery changed. I can't stand 'The Executive Mansion.' From now on, we'll just call it 'The White House.' Less pompous. How many bedrooms are there?"

"Five in the living quarters; and three of them are pretty small."

"What's on the third floor?"

"I haven't been up there since Tad Lincoln mixed up all the

bells in the mansion—house, that is—and I had to unmix them."

"I suppose we can make extra rooms up there. Alice must have her own room now that she's about to be eighteen." Roosevelt stared at the post office, where an illuminated flag was at half-mast.

"All flags should be taken down at sunset. It's depressing," he added, uncharacteristically. "To come here as president, and everyone is mourning."

"Murder is always depressing—and alarming."

"Do we know who's behind that anarchist?"

"The Secret Service wants to arrest everyone in sight. They remind me of Stanton after Lincoln was shot."

"Let's hope with better result. I wouldn't mind being shot—like Lincoln, that is, not poor McKinley. Lincoln never knew what happened."

Hay shuddered, involuntarily. "I'm not so sure. When we were writing his life, I read the autopsy report. Apparently the bullet entered not the back of his head but the left temple, which meant that he had heard Booth at the door to the box, and that he had turned around to see who it was . . ."

"And saw?"

"And saw, for an instant, the gun."

"How grisly!" Roosevelt was plainly delighted by this macabre detail.

In front of the N Street house of Anna Roosevelt Cowles, two policemen stood guard. From a second-story window a huge American flag drooped at half-mast. "Why *don't* they take down these flags?" Roosevelt was querulous; and Hay suspected, some-how discomfited by the tribute to his predecessor.

In the downstairs parlor, Roosevelt greeted his wife, Edith; sister, Anna, whom he called Bamie; and son, Ted. The ladies wore mourning; they were in excellent spirits. The ladies made much of Hay, who was pleased to be treated like a piece of rare porcelain from an earlier time. He was helped into an armchair, and encouraged to smoke a cigar, which he refused. Meanwhile, the new president was prancing about the room, asking everyone questions to which he alone had the answers. During this display, the admirable Edith maintained her stately calm. Hay had always preferred her to the noisy—no other word—Theodore.

Edith Kermit Carow was descended from Huguenots who had inter-married with the family of Jonathan Edwards. She had known Theodore all her life. The Carow family had lived in New York's Union Square next door to the house of Theodore's grandfather. Edith had been a bookish girl, no great recommendation in their world, but a link to the high-strung asthmatic Theodore, who was not only bookish but, to compensate for physical weakness, doggedly athletic as well.

Hay had always thought that Theodore took too much for granted his perfect wife. Certainly, he had taken her so much for granted that, perhaps to her surprise—who would ever know, as she was all tact and reserve?—Theodore, on his twenty-second birthday, had married a beautiful girl named Alice Lee, and Edith Carow had, serenely it was reported, been a guest at the wedding. In due course, Alice Lee gave birth to a daughter, Alice; not long after, Alice Lee died within a day of Theodore's mother. The two sudden deaths drove Theodore out of politics—he had been a member of New York's State Assembly; out of New York City, too. He bought a ranch in the Badlands of the Dakotas; lost money on cattle; and wrote with marvellously contagious self-love of his own bravery. Four Eyes, as the bespectacled Theodore was known to the Western toughs, was very much a hero in his own eyes, while giving much pleasure to his friends the Hearts, if not in the way that he might have liked. After all, he was a mere dude compared to Clarence King.

As Hay listened to this most unlikely of American presidents, he was reminded of the chilling prescience of Henry Adams's letter from Stockholm, which had arrived on the day that the President was shot. "Teddy's luck" was the letter's theme; fate's too, as it proved. Theodore was, Adams had proclaimed, "pure act," like God: endless energy without design.

Finally, Roosevelt had returned from the West, poorer than when he had left but better-known to magazine readers. After losing an election for mayor of New York in the autumn of 1886, he and Edith Kermit Carow were married, most fashionably, at St. George's in Hanover Square, London; the groomsman was Cecil Spring-Rice, the Hearts' favorite British diplomat. Then the Roosevelts returned to the ugly comfortable house that he had built on Sagamore Hill at Oyster Bay, Long Island. Here he wrote the six-volume history *Winning the West*; filled the house with children; and plotted, with Henry Cabot Lodge, a political career that had been interrupted not only by personal tragedies but by a mistrust of the Republican Party's leader James G. Blaine; fortunately, this dislike had not led to apostasy of the sort that had caused the truly virtuous to bolt the party and raise high the banner of Independence and Mugwumpery. Roosevelt and Lodge were too practical for this sort of idealistic gesture. They stayed with Blaine, who lost to Cleveland in 1884.

While Theodore was turning out biographies of Thomas Hart Benton and Gouverneur Morris and essays in celebration of Americanism of the sort that had given Henry James such exquisite pain, he was also busy president-making. One president thus made was Benjamin Harrison; and Theodore's political carpentry was rewarded with a place on the Civil Service Commission.

Both President and Theodore had been eager for him to be under-secretary of state, but the secretary, James G. Blaine himself, had the usual politician's long memory, and Theodore was forced to content himself with Civil Service reform, an Augean stable where not even Hercules would have dreamed of putting hand to shovel. Although Theodore was no Hercules, he was, by nature, busy. In 1889, at the age of thirty, he made himself the commission's head. He railed against the spoils system, and the press enjoyed him. When Republican President Harrison was replaced by Democratic President Cleveland, Roosevelt was kept on. During the six years he served on the commission, he entered the lives of the Hearts. In 1895, a reform mayor of New York City appointed Roosevelt president of the board of police commissioners. Roosevelt proved to be a fierce unrelenting prosecutor of vice; and the press revelled in his escapades. Since the law that forbade saloons to dispense their poisons on the Sabbath was often flouted, Roosevelt closed down the saloons, which meant that the saloon-keepers need no longer pay protection to Mr. Croker of Tammany Hall. But Mr. Croker was more resourceful than Roosevelt; he got a judge to rule that as it was not against the law to serve alcohol with a meal, a single pretzel ingested while drinking a bottle of whiskey made lawful the unlawful.

Roosevelt was also introduced to a world from which he had always been sheltered, the poor. He took for his guide a Danish-born journalist named Jacob Riis, who had written a polemical book called *How the Other Half Lives*. Roosevelt was shown not only the extent of poverty in the great city but the complaisance of the ruling class, which included his own family.

Hay had never been much impressed by Theodore's occasional impassioned denunciations of the "malefactors of great wealth"; after all, as Henry Adams liked to say, they were all of them consenting parties to the status quo. Though the Police Commissioner got himself a reputation for the disciplining of dishonest policemen, when the journalist Stephen Crane—previously admired by Roosevelt—testified in court against two policemen who had falsely arrested a woman for soliciting, Roosevelt had sprung to the defense of the policemen, and denounced Crane, an eye-witness to the arrest. Since Crane was much admired by the Hearts, Roosevelt had been taken to task. But he stood by his men, like a good commander in a war.

In March, 1897, the thirty-eight-year-old Roosevelt met, as it were, his luck. The new president, McKinley, appointed him assistant secretary of the Navy, ordinarily a humble post, but with a weak and amiable secretary, Roosevelt, in thrall to the imperial visions of Captain Mahan and Brooks Adams, was now in a position to build up the fleet without which there could be no future wars, no glory, no empire. The next four years were to wreathe with laurel the stout little man who now stood, if not like a colossus athwart the world, like some tightly wound-up child's toy, dominating all the other toys in power's playroom, shrill voice constantly raised. "Germany, John. There's the coming problem.

Coming? No, it's here. The Kaiser's on the move everywhere. He's built a fleet to counter us—or the British, one or the other, but not—*not* both together—yet. Also, if he makes the bid, he will have to look to his rear, for there is savage Russia, huge and glacial, waiting for the world to fall like a ripe fruit into its paws." Theodore smote together his own paws. Hay tried to imagine the world smashed in those pudgy hands. "Russia is the giant of the future," Theodore proclaimed.

Hay felt obliged to intervene. "I don't know about the future— but at the moment the only kind of giant that Russia is is a giant dwarf."

Theodore laughed; and clicked his teeth. Bamie was now pouring coffee, with Edith's assistance. Neither paid much attention to Theodore; but their absent-mindedness was benign. "I'll use that, John, with your permission."

"Don't you dare. *I* can say such things in private. But you can't, ever. We have enough trouble here with Cassini, with Russia. You may *think* such things," Hay conceded, "but the president must always avoid wit . . ."

"And truth?"

"Truth, above all, the statesman must avoid. Elevated sentiment and cloudy tautologies must now be your style . . ."

"Oh, you depress me! I had hoped to make a brilliant State of the Union address. Full of epigrams, and giant dwarfs. Well, all right. No dwarfs."

"We must extend the hand of friendship," Hay intoned, "through every open door that we can find."

Roosevelt laughed; or, rather, barked; and started to march about the room. "The thing to remember about the Germans is this. They simply haven't got the territory to support their population. They've got France and England to the west—and us back of them. They've got your giant dwarf to the east, and back of it China. There's really no place, anywhere, for a German empire . . ."

"Africa," Hay broke in.

"Africa, yes. But Africa *what?* A lot of territory, and no Germans

willing to go there. In the last ten years, one million Germans—
the best and the pluckiest of them all—moved out of Germany.
And who got them? We did—or most of them. No wonder the
Kaiser's eager to set up his own empire in China. But he'll have to
deal with us if he moves into Asia . . ."

"Suppose he moves into Europe?" Hay's back pains had
returned; and Bamie Cowles's coffee had created turbulence in a
digestive system more than usually fragile.

"Spring-Rice thinks he might, one day. I like Germans. I like
the Kaiser, in a way. I mean, if I were in his situation, I'd try for
something, too."

"Well, we did not like them in '98, when they tried to get
England to join them to help Spain against us."

"No. No. No. But you can see how tempting it must have been
for the Kaiser. He wanted the Philippines. Who didn't? Anyway,
the British were with us." Roosevelt suddenly frowned.

"Canada claims," Hay began.

"Not now! Not now, dear John. The subject bores me."

"Bores you? Think of me, hour after hour, day after day, in close
communion with Our Lady of the Snows . . ."

"Boring Lady, in my experience."

"Now, Thee." Edith's warning voice was a bit lower than her
normal voice; but no less effective.

"But, Edie. I was just commiserating with John . . ."

"I suppose," said young Ted, "that I will be able to endure
Groton another term."

"Is this a cry for attention?" asked the father, balefully clicking
his teeth.

"No, no. It was just an observation . . ."

"Where is Alice?" asked the President, turning to his wife.

"Farmington, isn't she?" Edith turned to her sister-in-law.

"In my house, yes. Or she was. She's very social, you know."

"I don't know where she gets that from." Theodore appealed to
Hay. "We are not—never have been—fashionable."

"Perhaps this is an advance, a new hazard for an old
fortune—"

"No fortune either!" sighed Edith. "I don't know how we'll live now. This black dress," she slowly turned so that her husband could appreciate her sacrifice, "cost me one hundred and thirty-five dollars at Hollander's this morning. That's ready-made, of course, and then I had to buy a truly hideous hat with black crepe veil."

"One can only hope that there will be numerous similar funerals for you to attend," said Hay, "of elderly diplomats, of course, and senators of any age."

Theodore was staring at himself in a round mirror; he seemed as fascinated by himself as others were. Then he confided, "I have to go to Canton after the services here." Then he spun around, and sat in a chair, and was suddenly still. It was as if the toy had finally run down. He even sat like a doll, thought Hay; legs outstretched, arms loose at his side.

"Shall I go?" asked Hay.

"No. No. We can never travel together again, you and I. If something should happen to me, you're the only president we've got."

"Poor country," said Hay, getting to his feet. "Poor me."

"Stop sounding old." The doll, rewound, was on its feet. "I'll meet with the Cabinet Friday, after Canton; the usual time."

"We shall be ready for you. As for Alice, if she does decide to visit Washington, Helen says that she can stay with us."

"Alice worships your girls," said Edith, without noticeable pleasure. "They dress so beautifully, she keeps reminding me."

"Alice doesn't like having poor parents," said the President, as he led Hay to the door.

"Give her to us. There's plenty of room."

"We might. Pray for me, John."

"I have done that, Theodore. And will again."

3

Blaise found the Chief in, of all places, his office at the *Journal*. As a rule, he preferred to work at home when he was in New York, which was seldom these days. In Hearst's capacity as presiding genius of the Democratic clubs, he travelled the nation, rallying the faithful, preparing for his own election four years hence. He had been in Chicago when McKinley was shot.

Brisbane was seated on a sofa while the Chief sat feet on his desk, and eyes on the window, through which nothing could be seen except falling, melting snow. Neither man greeted Blaise; he was a member of the family. But when Blaise asked, "How bad is it?" Hearst answered, "Bad and getting worse." Hearst gave him a copy of the *World*. Ambrose Bierce's quatrain was printed in bold type. Hearst's deliberate incitement to murder was the theme of the accompanying story. As Blaise read, he could hear the steady drumming of Hearst's fingers on his desk, always a sign of nervousness in that generally phlegmatic man. "They're trying to make out that the murderer had a copy of the *Journal* in his pocket at Buffalo. He didn't of course."

"They will invent anything," said Brisbane sadly. The two founding fathers of invented news were not pleased to find themselves being reinvented by others no less scrupulous. The irony was not lost on Blaise.

"The *Chicago American*'s got close to three hundred thousand circulation." Hearst's mind worked rather like a newspaper's front page, a number of disparate items crowded together, some in larger type than others. "I'm going to add the word 'American' to the *Journal* here. Particularly now. Croker's leaving Tammany Hall. Murphy's taking his place. The saloon-keeper, who was also dock commissioner. The one we caught owning stock in that ice company."

"Even so," Brisbane sounded confident, "I'm willing to bet he'll nominate you for governor next fall."

"I'm not so sure." The right foot now began to waggle, and the drumming fingers were still as the energy moved to the body's opposite end. "Maybe you should try him out. See if he'll nominate you for Congress in the Eleventh Ward. All you have to pay is your first year's congressional salary. After that, they leave you alone in Washington, except on votes that concern the city, which nobody else cares about." The Chief stared at Blaise.

"But I don't want to go to Congress," began Blaise.

"I was talking to Brisbane." The Chief was equable.

"We've discussed it before." Brisbane's urbane whiskerless face looked, suddenly, statesmanlike. He had, it was rumored, socialist tendencies. "A sort of trial balloon. The Chief needs to win one high office before 1904, and governor of New York is the one that will put him in the White House."

"What about Colonel Roosevelt? He's bound to run again." Blaise could not imagine the Chief, for all his journalistic skills, as a match for the dynamic, evangelical Roosevelt. More to the point, the Chief hated public speaking; hated crowds; hated shaking hands—his limp damp grip was much imitated along Newspaper Row.

A sub-editor entered with a newspaper proof. "The President's message to Congress. We just got it on the wire." Hearst took the long sheets of paper, and read rapidly; found what he was looking for; read aloud, imitating Roosevelt's falsetto, not so different from his own: "Leon, however his name's pronounced, was, according to our new president, 'inflamed by the teachings of professed anarchists . . .'"

"Poor Emma Goldman," said Brisbane.

"'. . . and probably also by the reckless utterances of those who, on the stump and in the public press,' that's me, I hope Mother doesn't read this, 'appeal to the dark and evil spirits of malice and greed, envy and sullen hatred. The wind is sowed by the men who preach such doctrines, and they cannot escape their share of responsibility for the whirlwind that is reaped.'"

Hearst made a ball of the sheets of paper, and aimed it, successfully, at the waste basket beside Brisbane. Then he swung his feet off the desk, opened a drawer and withdrew a revolver, which he slipped into his coat pocket. "I've been getting death threats," he said to Blaise. "And Mr. Roosevelt's speech won't help. Well, we'll get him, too, one of these days."

"With another bullet, to put him on his bier?" Blaise found dark comedy in the Chief's melodramatic view of the world.

"Heaven forbid." Hearst turned pale. "I hate violence. I was sick to my stomach when I heard about McKinley. Frightful. Frightful." Blaise realized that, in some curious way, Hearst lived in a kind of dream where real people were turned, by his yellow art, into fictional characters that he could manipulate as he pleased. On those rare occasions when his fictions and the real world coincided, he was genuinely shocked. It was all very well for him to report that one Jack had taken a ride into Heaven aboard a bean stalk and quite another thing for an actual bean stalk to lift *him* up above the world.

Brisbane left them. The President's message must be printed and commented on. Then Hearst asked for news of the Baltimore newspaper, and Blaise told him the truth. "It's just a stepping-stone."

"To where?"

"I want Washington. After all, you have everything else worth having."

"You could run one of my papers." Hearst stared at the snow, which was now sticking to the glass of the window. The room was filled with an odd refracted blue light.

"*You* run them. I want my own."

"In Baltimore?"

"The *Examiner*'s a beginning until . . ." But Blaise did not know where or what the "until" would be.

"She'd probably have sold, if the Hay boy hadn't been killed." Hearst liked to analyze Caroline. By and large, women did not interest him as people. But Caroline was now beyond mere womanhood, she was a publisher.

"I'm not so sure. She likes owning a newspaper."

"I know the feeling." Hearst made one of his rare mild jokes about himself. "Well, I'll miss you around here." With that, Blaise was dismissed. He was no longer of financial use to the Chief, whose mother's fortune was even larger than when her son first set out to spend it all. Now that Blaise was himself a publisher, there was no need to continue the master-apprentice relationship. "Are you going to live in Baltimore?" The Chief seemed genuinely curious.

"No. The management's good enough as it is, without me." This was untrue, but Blaise was not going to tell Hearst that he was already planning a raid on the *Chicago American*'s editorial staff. He had an excellent managing editor in view, who would have to be paid more than Hearst paid him, which was far too much, but if anyone could salvage the *Baltimore Examiner* it would be one Charles Hapgood, a native of Maryland's eastern shore and eager to abandon Chicago's arctic winters and tropical summers for equable Baltimore.

"You should do well." Hearst did not sound passionately convinced. "I mean, you've got the money, that's what counts. Buy the best people and—that's the ticket." The pale gray eyes glanced for a brief instant in Blaise's direction; and Blaise decided that the Chief knew about Hapgood. "You been giving any thought to the magazines?" This was the Chief's new interest. He had been impressed by the amount of advertising that certain ladies' magazines could command. But when he had tried to buy one of them, he had been put off by the cost. He would now have to start one— or two, or a thousand.

"I don't know enough about how they work." Blaise was direct. "Neither do you. Why bother?"

"Well, we could learn the business, I reckon. I've been thinking about, maybe, a magazine called *Electrical Machine* or something . . ."

"For ladies?"

"Well, they drive, too. But I'd aim that at men. Just a thought. I'm marrying Miss Willson one of these days."

Blaise was surprised. "*Before* the election?"

"Well, that part's up in the air. Maybe I'll . . ." The thin voice trailed off. Obviously, Hearst was afraid that scandal might be made of his long liaison with a showgirl; although marriage would silence the sterner moralists, might it not draw attention to the earlier liaison?

Blaise rose to go. The Chief gave him several limp soft fingers to squeeze.

"Which one?" asked Blaise, as he walked toward the door.

"Which one what?"

"Which Miss Willson are you marrying?"

"Which . . . ?" For an instant, Hearst seemed entirely to have lost his train of thought. Marriage often had that effect on men, Blaise had noticed. "Anita," said Hearst. Then corrected himself. "I mean Millicent, of course. You know that," he added, with a hint of accusation. Hearst was that rare thing, the humorless man who could recognize humor in others, and even at his own expense. "Your French lady," Hearst began a counter-attack.

"She has retired to the country. I am to see her no more."

"So that's how they do it in France."

Blaise left Pennsylvania Station aboard the parlor-car with every intention of stopping in Baltimore, but the sight, from the train window, of those interminable brick row-houses, all alike, with scoured white stone steps, depressed him, and he continued on to Washington.

During the train journey, Blaise thought, rather more insistently than usual, about himself. He was twenty-six; he was rich; he was attractive to women, even though he was not seriously attracted to them. Anne de Bieville had called him *gâté*—spoiled. But there was more to it than that, he knew, as the town of Havre de Grace, bleak under snow, moved slowly past his window. He had become too used to being the one wooed; and seduced. Except for occasional visits to the Tenderloin's more exclusive bordellos, Blaise had made no efforts to find himself a mistress, much less a wife. Plon had been amazed, and wondered, solicitously, if Blaise might not be in ill-health, suffering perhaps from some debilitating malady of the sort that begins, as all things French must, with the liver and then moves, inexorably, devastatingly southward. But as Blaise was as sturdy as a young pony, Plon had, finally, come to the sad conclusion that the illness was not of the flesh but the spirit: Anglo-Saxonism, a state of mind notoriously debilitating to the whole man. Plon had suggested more exercise, like tennis.

Blaise was duly impressed by the renovated lobby of Willard's, which still extended from street to street. Just behind the monumental cigar stand, the city's political center, there was a new telephone room. Here he gave the telephone operator the number of the *Washington Tribune*. She plugged various wires into sockets.

"Your number is ready." She indicated a booth.

When Blaise lifted the receiver and asked for Caroline, a deep Negro voice said, "There is no Miss Sanford here. This is the Bell residence."

"But isn't this number—"

"No, sir, it isn't. We have been getting wrong numbers here all week." The man hung up. After two more attempts, Blaise got through to the *Tribune*.

Caroline was delighted with Blaise's misadventure. "Now we can write the story. Everyone in Washington knows that the only telephone that never works properly is Alexander Graham Bell's. 'Inventor without honor.' How's that for a head? But, of course, he's got plenty of honor for inventing the telephone. Perhaps 'Inventor without a repairman.'" Caroline agreed to meet Blaise at Mrs. Benedict Tracy Bingham's "'palatial home.' The occasion is humble. She is pouring tea for the new members of Congress. I have to be there. You don't, of course. Oh, but you do. You're a publisher, too—at last!" she added, with bright, impersonal malice.

Mrs. Bingham stood before a palatial fireplace, taken from a Welsh castle, she said, belonging to Beowulf, an ancestor of Mr. Bingham on the maternal side. As usual the milk lord of the District of Columbia was nowhere to be seen. "We are surrounded by Apgars," said Caroline, who had met Blaise at the door. But Blaise could not tell an Apgar from anyone else in the crowded room, where the new congressmen and their ladies looked supremely ill at ease despite Mrs. Bingham's deep-throated welcomes. Although she was not learned in matters of history, much less myth, she had the politician's ability to remember not only names but congressional districts. After many consultations with Caroline, it had been decided that Mrs. Bingham's destiny was to fill the void at the center of Washington's social life and become a political hostess. There had been no proper salon in years. The Hay-Adams drawing room was far too rarefied for mere mortals, much less itinerant politicians; embassies were out of bounds, while the White House was essentially a family—even tribal— affair now that the Roosevelts were all arrived. So Caroline had encouraged Mrs. Bingham to move to the high—relatively high— ground; and there set her standard.

"Blaise Sanford!" she exclaimed, as Caroline approached, half-brother on her arm. Blaise found himself transfixed by dull onyx eyes, and a powerful handclasp. "Baltimore is closer than New York, *and blood*," she added, significantly, "*thicker than water.*"

"Yes." Blaise had never found talking to American ladies, as opposed to girls, easy. But then ladies like Mrs. Bingham had conversation enough for two. An occasional "yes" or "no" could see a young man safely through this sort of encounter. "You'll live here, naturally. Baltimore is out of the question. Washington's more convenient, in every way. Caroline, have you heard? Alice Roosevelt has lost all her teeth, and only eighteen years old. I think that's so romantic, don't you? Such a great calamity, at so tender an age."

"How," asked Caroline, "did she lose the teeth?"

"A horse kicked her." Mrs. Bingham looked almost youthful as she bore, yet again, ill tidings. "Now she's developed an abscess in her lower jaw, and all the teeth fell *crashing* out . . ."

"Poor girl," said Blaise. He had never met Miss Roosevelt, but she was known to be clever and eager to have a social life of great intensity anywhere on earth except in dowdy Washington. He could not blame her. Idly, he wondered if he should marry her. She was said to be good-looking. But then the thought of the dentures that she soon must wear erased any fantasy of a White House wedding.

Caroline helped Mrs. Bingham greet the arriving guests, and Blaise was taken off by an Apgar lady, "your fifth cousin," she said. They kept track, the Apgars, of their vast cousinage. As Blaise tried to make conversation, he looked about the room, all gilt and crystal and old-fashioned shiny black horsehair, and tried to recognize who was who among the politicians, and failed. But he was able to tell which man present *was* a politician—the uniform black Prince Albert frock-coat was the give-away, not to mention the inevitably large mouth and huge chest, suitable for speech-making to enormous crowds. So many opera tenors, he decided, disguised as preachers. Caroline, he noted, seemed in her element; she was supremely poised, as Mrs. Bingham introduced her to the new men of state; and once each had realized that this young lady was proprietor of the *Tribune*, her hand would be taken not in one hand but two glad-hands, and her arm pumped, as if from the depths of her being printer's ink might be summoned up, to spell out, again and again, the politician's name in stories that would give pleasure to his constituents and profits to his sponsors.

Bleakly, Blaise realized that the *Baltimore Examiner* could never have the same effect on these overexcited men, excepting, always, the Maryland delegation, to a man to be avoided. Fortunately, Hapgood had promised to act as buffer; and Hapgood knew them all.

A wiry young man with a full head of coppery hair—for some reason, a full head of hair was a rarity in the republic's political life—turned to Blaise, and said, "You're Mr. Sanford. Caroline's brother." The young man's handshake was highly professional. By gripping hard the other man's fingers, the politician got the first grip, thus saving himself from the malicious working-man, whose superior strength could, with a grinding squeeze, reduce even the sturdiest man of state to his knees. McKinley's famous trick of simultaneously shaking the honest yeoman's hand while appearing gently to caress its owner's elbow was simply a precaution. Should the other begin to crush the presidential fingers, the affectionate grip on the elbow would be transformed to a sudden sharp blow, calculated to cause such unexpected pain that the grip would be loosened. Blaise had learned all the tricks, in the Chief's service.

"You're one of the new—congressmen?" Despite the political handclasp, the young man seemed far too athletic and handsome to be a tribune of the people; but that, indeed, was what he was. "James Burden Day," he said; and named his state and district; also cousinage. "We're all of us Apgars," he said.

"Yes." Blaise was vague. He had no memory of James Burden Day, but he was not displeased to have a distant cousin in the Congress, particularly one who looked like a gentleman even if he did represent a barbarous state, whose barbarous accent he also affected, if it was not, grim thought, his own.

"I was here before, in the comptroller's office. That's when I got to know Del Hay and, of course, Miss Sanford." They exchanged condolences on Del's death. "After he went off to Pretoria, I never saw him again. He was going to marry Miss Sanford . . . ?" Day inserted a question in his voice.

"Yes. This month, I think. He was also going to join the President's staff."

"Poor . . . Mr. Hay," said the young man, unexpectedly; and his pale blue eyes looked suddenly, directly, embarrassingly, into Blaise's. With one hand, Blaise touched his own forehead, as if to deflect by this meaningless gesture that sharp disquieting gaze; and wondered why he should find Mr. Day disturbing. After all, the inference that Caroline did not care for Del was none of Blaise's business. But Day had made him uneasy, which he did not like. He was also reminded, yet again, that although he was *the* Sanford, Washington was very much Caroline's city. She had made herself a high place; and he had none yet.

Day said the expected things. Del dead so young; President dead so tragically; Mr. Hay devastated. "Even more so now," said Blaise, wishing that he was as tall as Day, who was able to speak to him with such intimacy and warmth, and yet could look, whenever he chose, over Blaise's head to see what new magnate had entered the room. But Blaise continued: "Mr. Hay's oldest friend just died, Clarence King. You know, the geologist."

"I didn't know . . ."

"My sister tells me he died in Arizona a few weeks ago. So in six months poor Mr. Hay has lost his son, friend and president."

"Well," said Day, with sudden cold-bloodedness, "he hasn't lost his job, has he? Funny that Roosevelt hasn't replaced him. But then," and the smile was boyish and engaging, "I'm a Democrat, and I carry a spear for Bryan, in the people's name."

"We're crucifying them," said Blaise, matching the other's boyish coldness, "upon a cross of silver this time around." Both men laughed.

"I'm Frederika Bingham." A pale blond girl, with a languid manner, introduced herself. "I know who you are, of course, but Mamma thinks that you should know who I am." She smiled at Blaise, a somewhat crooked smile that revealed curiously sharp incisors. She smelled of lilac-water. Day smelled of not quite clean broadcloth. Of all Blaise's faculties, the sense of smell was the strongest and, in sexual matters, the most decisive. "I saw you at the Casino, at Newport," he said.

"You will go far in politics," said the young woman, her voice on a dying fall, her eyes not on Blaise but on James Burden Day.

"Except Mr. Sanford doesn't go into politics at all," said Day. "He doesn't have to, lucky man."

"I get everyone mixed up," said Frederika contentedly. Blaise could see that Day attracted her; and that he didn't. Masculine competitiveness began, like a tide, to rise, for no reason other than the moon's disposition, or was it lilac, or the other? The other . . .

Caroline joined them. She, too, was attracted, Blaise could see. A storm of male resolve broke—behind his eyes or wherever such storms break. One male—admittedly taller than he—had attracted two women. He must, somehow, establish his own primacy. "You have come back, as you said you would," Caroline greeted Day warmly. "In Congress, at last."

"Father wants you to do something about milk," said Frederika, gazing thoughtfully at Blaise. At least, he had willed her attention from the other.

"But I don't come from a dairy state," said Day, answering for Blaise.

"You are naive!" Caroline seemed to be bestowing a high compliment; but Day blushed, as she meant him to do. "The fact that there is not a single cow in your state means that when you finally do something for all the cows in the nation—I don't know just what you'll have to do, but Mr. Bingham will tell you— you will be thought disinterested and altruistic and a true friend of . . ."

". . . of the dairy interests," finished Day, habitual healthy bronze heightened.

"No. No. Of the cows." Caroline was emphatic.

"Father really likes them." Thoughtfully, Frederika smiled her crooked smile at Blaise. "Cows, that is. He can moon around that dairy of his—the one in Chevy Chase—all day."

"I know how he feels." Blaise could tell that Caroline was about to improvise an aria. She could, with no effort, say what others would like to hear, with astonishing spontaneity. "I was like that at Saint-Cloud-le-Duc. Remember, Blaise? The cows, the milking rooms, the churns where they still make butter the way they did when Louis XV stayed there? It was Paradise, and at its center not God but the Cow . . ." Before Caroline could complete her panegyric, Day pulled a small, plump, pretty woman to his side, and said, "This is my wife, Kitty."

"The cow . . ." Caroline repeated absently; then her voice trailed off as, politely, she gave the woman her hand. "But this is thrilling," she began.

Blaise understood her disappointment. Since James Burden Day was uncommonly fetching, Blaise suspected that Caroline's phantom list of possibilities might once have included him. The speed with which Caroline now set out to charm Kitty convinced Blaise that he was right. "Mr. Day never hinted that he might . . . And to *you!*" she exclaimed, eyes radiant, as if with admiration for Kitty. "Oh, he is lucky! *We* are lucky to have you in Washington. Aren't we, Blaise? Except you live in Baltimore . . ."

"Oh, no, I don't," Blaise growled.

But Caroline was not to be stopped. "Was it so sudden? We heard nothing here, and between Frederika's mother and the *Tribune*'s 'Society Lady,' we're supposed to know everything."

"Well, it was sudden," said Kitty. She had a low nasal voice of the sort that Blaise liked least in a country where nearly everyone's voice got on his nerves.

"We got married," said Day, "on election day. We'd always planned that," he added.

"Only if you were elected." Kitty was flat in her humor. "I wasn't about to marry somebody who was going to stay on in American City, and practice law like everybody else. No, sir," she said to Caroline, who took the "sir" in easy stride. "I wanted to get out of the state almost as bad as Jim, Representative Day, I guess I have to call him now."

"Surely not at breakfast." Caroline was gracious.

Mrs. Bingham, sensing discord or at the least drama, approached and Frederika fled. "Isn't this a surprise?" The voice was accusing. "Mr. Day never lets on that he was going home to get both elected and married, to Judge Halliday's daughter. Judge Halliday," Mrs. Bingham explained, "is to that state what Mark Hanna is to Ohio, and then some."

Blaise noticed that Day was smiling, with embarrassment. On the other hand, Kitty looked as if she had indeed, like the fabulous feline, swallowed the canary. As Caroline now prepared to rise to new heights of insincerity, Blaise was suddenly conscious of the degree and intensity of his sister's sexuality, no less powerful for her innocence or, rather, ignorance. He wondered, perversely, what it would be like to switch roles with her; then, looking at Day and Kitty, thought better of it. The sort of wall that a man might breach no woman could, at least not in their world. Here the cards were entirely stacked against women; only men could play a relatively free hand.

Kitty spoke of houses and servants, and Caroline offered to help with both. Day turned to Blaise. "I hope we'll see you, now that you're nearby."

"I hope so, too." Then Blaise added recklessly, "But I won't be nearby. I'll be right here."

"In Washington?" The sandy eyebrows arched.

"Yes, in Washington. New York's too far away and Baltimore is nowhere at all. I'm looking for a house," he improvised, inspired by Caroline. She was not the only one who could spin a bright web in company.

"Then we'll see more of you." Day was easy; charming. "It won't be the same, though, without Del."

"I think I shall build a house," said Blaise, allowing for no sentiment. "In Connecticut Avenue. The best of country life, the best of village life. She would never," Blaise lowered his voice, not that Caroline and Kitty could have heard either of them in the noisy room, "never have married Del."

"What makes you so sure?"

"I know her," Blaise lied. "Better than myself," Blaise told the truth.

– 4 –

John Hay was at the window to Henry Adams's study, looking down on the passersby. The Porcupine was always amazed at how many people Hay could recognize, particularly now that everyone they knew had been so dramatically transformed by age. "General Dan Sickles, with crutches," Hay announced, as the aged, bleareyed warrior, murderer, and queen's lover hobbled beneath the window in icy H Street.

"Surely, he's dead." This season, Adams affected to believe that everyone of their acquaintance was dead unless proven otherwise.

"He may well be dead." Hay was judicious. "But he has taken to moving about, like Lazarus. Where is his leg, by the way?"

"Shot off at the battle of Gettysburg, which he nearly lost for us, the four-flusher."

"No. No." Hay turned round in the window seat, and settled his back as comfortably as he could against cushions. "When the leg was detached, by cannonball, Sickles sent someone to find it. Then he had a charming box made for it so that he could carry it around with him. I think he said he was going to give it to one of his clubs in New York."

"Another point against New York. I would not allow Sickles in *any* club, much less his leg." Adams sat beside the fire; he wore a mulberry velvet smoking jacket. As always on Sunday, the breakfast table was set more elaborately than usual. At noon, the guests would arrive. Hay was never entirely sure how many were directly invited and how many simply showed up. When queried, Adams looked mysterious. "All is random," he would murmur. "Like the universe."

But this morning, all was not random in their lives. Adams had come back from Europe at the end of December, in time to attend, on New Year's Day, Clarence King's funeral in New York City. He had stayed on in the city longer than usual. He had been, he wrote Hay, astonished by King's will; but said no more.

The previous night, at dinner with the Hays, Adams had whispered in Hay's ear that he would like to see him, alone, before breakfast the next day. When Hay arrived, Adams had been maddeningly mysterious, as he went slowly through the drawers of his escritoire, collecting bits of paper, while Hay, finally, retreated to the window and the view of the passersby, many of them slipping and falling most agreeably upon the frozen pavement. Only the one-legged Sickles was entirely sure-footed.

"The will," Adams said, at last.

"The estate . . . ?" Hay was more to the point.

"Well, there will be money. Our friend's collection of pictures and bric-a-brac is stored in Tenth Street, in New York City, and once sold off at auction should provide enough money for any reasonable contingency."

"What, dear Henry, is 'reasonable' and what is the 'contingency'?"

But Adams was staring at the fire as if it were the sun and he a worshipper. "You know, John, that for King, in his robust way, and for me, in my crabbed way, woman is all things in Heaven and earth . . ."

"Your twelfth-century virgin . . ."

"*Our* Virgin; as revered in that last cohesive century, and memorialized at Mont-St.-Michel and Chartres."

Although Hay never wearied of Adams's enthusiasms, currently focussed on the idea of woman as virgin, and mother of God, he failed to make any connection between the Porcupine's ongoing literary work of celebration and Clarence King, who had died a bachelor. But Adams was not to be hurried, and Hay settled back in the window seat, and stared at Blake's mad Babylonian monarch, on all fours, munching grass. "King always saw the male as being rather like the crab's shell, to be discarded when no longer needed, by the crab—by woman, that is. *She* is the essential energy that uses the shell, and then lets it go. Obviously, King was a more primitive, basic man than I. Although each of us celebrated the idea of woman, I see her as the virgin queen of an ordered, perfect world while he celebrated an earthier, more primitive great-mother goddess, rich in the inheritance of every animated energy back to the polyps and the crystals."

Even for Adams, this was highfalutin, thought Hay. Admittedly the two men had obviously run amok in the islands of the South Pacific, paying court to old-gold women, but to make a universal system out of two inhibited nineteenth-century American gentlemen's good luck was, perhaps, too much.

"In any case, our friend was to find his ideal, his inspiration, and in 1883, he married her."

Hay nearly fell from the window seat. "Clarence King was married?"

Adams gave a maddeningly diffident bob of his pink-bald head. "In Twenty-fourth Street, in New York, he married one Ada Todd, by whom he was to have five children."

"*In secret!*" Hay had the sense of going mad.

"In such secrecy that he never actually told Ada his true name until the very end. He called himself James Todd, and he settled her, and their children, in a lovely rural New York retreat called Flushing."

"Henry, if you have turned to novel-writing again . . ."

"No, no. Truth is bizarre enough for the mere historian. King was still able to produce sufficient money to keep his family in comfort in their Horatian rusticity, where the ginkgo trees run riot, and loyal servitors were able to maintain them in Arcadian if anonymous comfort."

As Hay grew more and more impatient, Adams grew more lyric. "As you might suspect—I saw your face subtly change when I used the word 'anonymous.' There were excellent reasons why King did not want the world—or even the Hearts, sad to tell—to know of his secret life. Ada was his ideal, of course, an earth goddess, essential, a custodian of cosmic energy . . ."

"Henry, in God's name—"

"John." Adams raised a hand in gentle remonstrance. "I've not finished with the secret life. Just before King went west again, he decided that it would be best for his family—still called Todd—to move to that part of the world which currently gives you so much trouble, over the infamous Alaskan boundary . . ."

"Canada?"

"Our Lady of the Snows, yes. He moved the lot of them to Toronto, where the sons have been enrolled in," Adams glanced at the paper on his lap, "something called the Logan School . . ."

"Why Canada?"

"Because there is a tolerance there quite unlike our own—oh, *fierceness* on the subject of identity, one might say. Our national disapproval of any and every misalliance."

Hay nodded. "I can understand that, particularly now that he has given her his name. He has, hasn't he?"

Adams nodded. "If she wants to use it, of course. He also made it clear in his will, which you'll get a copy of, in due course. You are a trustee . . ."

"Why do you have a copy, and I don't?"

"A friend—*our* friend, Gardiner—gave me this early draft. Once the will is probated, and King's bric-a-brac is sold, the widow will be able to live in moderate comfort as Mrs. Todd or Mrs. King, in Toronto or Flushing or . . ."

388

"This sounds like one of poor Stephen Crane's stories. The gentleman and the fallen lady, the illegitimate family, the false names . . ."

"Oh, it's a much bolder story than anything Mr. Crane put his hand to. You see, dear John, King's perfect woman, mother of his five children, emblem of the original universal goddess for whom the male has no use once his biological function is complete, this glorious creature from pre-history, this Ada Todd, is a Negress."

Hay exhaled suddenly; and all the blood went from his head. For an instant, he thought he might faint. Then he rallied. "Clarence King married a Negress! But—that's impossible."

"You did not go to Tahiti." Smugly, Adams gazed into the fire, framed by luminous Mexican jade.

"But you did, and I fail to see a dusky Mrs. Henry Adams on these premises . . ."

"Only because I moved on—and up. To the Virgin of Chartres, to another more perfect avatar of the primal goddess, who . . ."

"I'll be damned," said John Hay, as William slowly opened the door to the study and said, "The young ladies would like to pay their respects . . ."

Adams rose; and assumed his avuncular mask, though a certain unfamiliar gleam in his eye suggested that there was still something demonic latent in his nature.

The room was filled by three girls. Hay had never been able to figure just how it was that his two daughters and their friend Alice Roosevelt could take up so much space, breathe so much air, create so much atmosphere—for want of a better word—but they did.

The three swarmed over Uncle Henry; receiving chaste touches of his hands, now raised in papal blessing. Helen was more and more like Clara, while Alice was like himself. The President's Alice was, happily, not like her father, except for a thin mouth full of large snaggled teeth. Alice Roosevelt was more handsome than pretty, with a slender figure, and gray marbly eyes; she stood very straight, and comported herself like the regal princess she saw herself as. She was also given to demonstrations of manic energy,

and there were already signs of a dextrous, most undemocratic—
yet hardly royal—wit. Henry Adams affected to find her intimidating. Eager to please, she proceeded to intimidate Uncle Henry.
"You must come to the party. It's not every day I have a debut in
the White House . . ."

"I am too old, dear child . . ."

"Of course you are. So we'll prop you up like who was it at the
feast?"

"Themistocles . . ."

"Mr. Hay, make him come!" Alice Roosevelt turned to Hay, one
arm raised high like the goddess of victory.

"I'll do what I can."

Helen threw herself, with rather too much of a crash, into the
chair opposite Adams, the large chair consecrated to her mother,
who was still larger, Hay was relieved to note, than their daughter.
He was also relieved that Helen would marry Payne Whitney the
following month. Were she to become even larger . . . He dared
not think of what it would be like to live in a house between that
massive Scylla, his wife, and a prospective spinster of equal
grandeur, Helen, as Charybdis.

"Everyone *else* is coming." Alice Roosevelt perched on a stool.
"Of course, it will be boring. Father and Mother refuse to spend
money. Other girls get a cotillion. Do I? Of course not! Simple
republican Alice gets only a dance, and punch. Not even champagne. Punch!" she exclaimed, as her father might have shouted
"Bully!"

"Surely punch is suitable for young people." Hay, making kindly
grandfatherly sounds, could think only of voluptuous black women,
heavy-breasted and sinuous, crabs to his relevant shell, to appropriate Henry's ugly image. How lucky King had been. Even as he
was dying, he had had "a woman," and, apparently, such a woman
as the unadventurous Hay had not known since he was a very
young man, living a bachelor life in Europe. Was it now too late?
Of course, he was dying, but then King had been dying, too.
Where there was a will, there was Eros. There was, also, Thanatos,

390

he grimly completed his reverie. He would never again touch warm silken skin.

"We're to have a hardwood floor in the East Room instead of that awful mustard carpet, and those round seats with the palms sprouting out of them. It's a horrible house, isn't it, Uncle Henry?"

"Well, it has never been a *fashionable* house," Adams began.

"Father is going to redo everything, as soon as he makes Congress cough up the money. It's intolerable, all of us upstairs, and Father's office, too, in such a small place. We're going to do over the entire floor, from west to east . . ."

"And where will the President have his office?" In Hay's memory, every administration had tried to change the White House; and except for the odd Tiffany screen, nothing much had been altered since Lincoln's time.

"Father's going to tear down the conservatories, and put his office where they were. So he'll be practically next door to you at the State Department."

"Is this wise?" Even the iconoclast Adams—and what mustier icon than the White House was better suited for his smashing?—was dismayed.

"Either our family grows smaller or the house grows larger." Thus the Republican princess decreed.

"Alice knows her mind, her mind!" Helen applauded.

William was again at the door; this time he stood very straight, as he announced, "The President."

All rose, including the Republican princess, as Roosevelt, dressed in morning suit, skipped into the room, as if he were still racing upstairs, two at a time, his usual practice, which would, sooner or later, Hay thought, with true pleasure, cause that thick little body to break down. "I've been to church!" The President shared the great news with all of them. Lately, he had taken to dropping in on Hay after church, which gave sovereign and minister a few often crucial moments alone together, away from secretaries and callers. The President, Hay had duly noted, could not be alone. Even when he was reading, a family passion, he liked to have fellow-readers all about him. "I heard you were over here, for breakfast . . ."

"Join us, Mr. President." Adams was silky.

"Oh, no! Your food's much too good for the likes of me."

"Chipped beef will do for the President." Alice grimaced. "And a nice hash with an egg on it. And ketchup."

"Perfect breakfast! If Alice ever exercised, she'd eat hash, too. Prince Henry of Prussia." Roosevelt flung the name at Hay; then took up an imperial position before the fire; and clicked his teeth three times.

"Father!" Alice shuddered. "Don't do that. You know, the slightest breeze makes my bottom teeth sway . . ."

"I'm not making a breeze."

"But you're clicking your teeth, which reminds me . . . Look," Alice opened wide her mouth, "the horror!"

But all Hay could see was a lower tier of teeth somewhat smaller than the tombstones above. "*They are all loose*," she said triumphantly, mouth still open, diction suffering.

"Do shut, please!" Roosevelt, in turn, as if by paternal example, pursed his own lips tight-shut.

"I should have had them all pulled out. Every debutante in America would have imitated me, of course. A nation of toothless girls—like the Chinese women, with their bound feet . . ."

"Alice, your teeth have exhausted us as a subject . . ."

"I," said Adams, "was just beginning to enjoy this dental— permutation on Henry James's American girl . . ."

"Effete snob!" Roosevelt glared.

"Prince Henry of Prussia." Hay retrieved the lost subject.

"Oh, yes. He's to come in February, to pick up the yacht we're building for the Kaiser, or so I was informed at church by old Holleben, who had converted to Presbyterianism, at least for the day. What do we do?"

"Give him a state dinner. But try to keep him from getting around the country . . ."

"Since I am a debutante," said Alice, "I shall be asked to charm him. Is he married?" Alice was now moving about the room in imitation of her father, only as she walked, she swept her long dress this way and that, as if it were a royal train. "If I married him, I'd be Princess Alice of Prussia, wouldn't I? So much nicer than Oyster Bay . . ."

"Princess Henry, I should think." Adams was in his avuncular glory. "You will civilize the Teuton. If that's possible."

"Barbarize them even more." Roosevelt was brisk. "Anyway, he's married, and no Roosevelt's going to marry a Prussian."

"Unless the next election looks very close," added Hay.

"Extraordinary!" Roosevelt added at least one too many syllables to the word. "The loyalty common Americans have to Germany. Imagine if we felt the same way about Holland."

"We've been away longer," said Alice. "Come on, girls." She swept from the room with Hay's daughters in tow.

"You are good to take Alice in." Roosevelt sat in the chair vacated by Helen. "She is so—strenuous."

"Like her father." Hay thought of black women; and spoke of Prince Henry. "He's here for one purpose. To stir up the German-Americans."

"We won't allow that. He's supposed to be a gentleman. Not like his brother. The Kaiser's a cad, all in all. Well, one day he'll go too far. He'll put out his neck and place it on the block." Roosevelt clapped right hand with left; the sound was like a pistol shot. "No head. No Kaiser."

"Then we shall be king of the castle?" Adams's voice was mild, always, Hay knew, a dangerous sign. Adams was growing more and more restive not only with the bellicose President but with his own brother, Brooks, who never ceased to make the American eagle scream.

"That may be." Roosevelt was equally mild; and guarded.

"Brooks believes that we are now at the fateful moment." Adams smiled at Nebuchadnezzar. "The domination of the world is between us and Europe. So—which will it be?"

"Oh, you must come on Thursdays, and enlighten us." Roosevelt was not to be drawn out. He was wily, Hay had discovered, rather to his surprise. Under all the noise, there was a calculating machine that never ceased to function. "We meet at nine o'clock and listen—"

"To my brother. I could not bear that, Mr. President. I'm obliged to hear him whenever I—*he* likes."

"We'll pick a Thursday when he's not there." Roosevelt was on his feet. "Your breakfast guests will be coming soon. Gentlemen." Adams and Hay rose; their sovereign beamed upon them; and departed.

"He will have us at war." Adams was bleak.

"I'm not so sure." Hay approached the fire, suddenly cold. "But he wants the dominion of this earth, for us . . ."

"For himself. Curious little man," said Adams, himself as small as Theodore, as small as Hay; *three* curious little men, thought Hay. "Now there are three of us." Adams looked at Hay, forlornly.

"Three curious little men?"

"No. Three Hearts where once there were five."

Hay felt a sudden excitement of a sort that had not troubled him for years; certainly, not since he had begun to die. "Is there a photograph?" he asked, voice trembling in his own ears. "Of her?"

"Of who?" Adams was bemused by firelight.

"The black woman." The phrase itself reverberated in Hay's head, and his mind was, suddenly, like a boy's, filled with images of feminine flesh.

"As the trustee of his will, I suppose you could ask her for one. *Droit de l'avocat*, one might say. King outdid us all. We died long ago, and went on living. He kept on living long after he should've been dead."

Two Hearts gone, thought Hay; three left. Who would be next to go? he asked himself, as if he did not know the answer.

10

As usual, the apostle of punctuality was late. John Hay stood in the doorway of the Presbyterian Church of the Covenant, watch in hand held high to dramatize the lateness of the presidential party. Inside the church, the nave was crowded with dignitaries. To the dismay of the church elders, admission to God's house—unlike Paradise—was only by card. The Senate, the Cabinet, the Supreme Court and the diplomatic corps were all represented, with sufficient omissions to cause social anxiety for the rest of the season. It had been Clara's inspiration to place Henry Adams between the Chinese ambassador, Wu, and the Japanese ambassador, Takahira. As a result, the angelic Porcupine now resembled an ancient not-so-benign mandarin, engulfed in the Orient.

The Whitney family had given Hay rather more trouble than the canal treaty. The rupture was not about to be healed between William C. Whitney, with two of his children loyal to him, and his former brother-in-law, the bachelor Oliver Payne, with two of Whitney's children loyal to him, including today's groom, Payne.

395

Hay had placed the Payne faction on one side of the aisle and the Whitney faction on the other. There had been even more confusion when William Whitney arrived at the church without his card, and the police had tried to stop him from entering, to the bleak joy of Oliver Payne, secure and righteous in his pew. As Hay got Whitney past the police, he was struck, as always, by the speed with which oblivion surrounded even the most celebrated of men when he no longer held office. Whitney, king-maker and king-that-might-have-been, was just another guest at his son's wedding to Helen Hay.

Like a stagecoach pursued by rustlers, the presidential carriage came hurtling down Massachusetts Avenue, horses steaming in the cold. Before the guards in front of the church could open the carriage doors, the President sprang out, wearing a silk top hat. Then Edith Roosevelt, more majestically, descended, followed by Alice, got up like a Gainsborough painting in dark blue velvet, with a dashing black hat. Hay stood, watch held before him like the host.

"We are *exactly* on time," the President lied.

"Of course. Of course."

Church ushers appeared in the doorway. Quickly, their republican majesties drew themselves up, and then, with hieratic—that is, to Hay's eyes, waddling—gait, they proceeded down the aisle to their pew in the front row.

The moment that the Roosevelts were seated, the wedding march began, and Hay, curiously weak of limb yet free of pain, went to collect the terrified Helen, magnificent in white satin and tulle but no—she wanted to be original—lace; then, in due course, under official Washington's eyes, Hay delivered his daughter over to the tall, handsome Payne Whitney, while Clara wept softly in the background, and Henry Adams, surrounded by Asia, looked incredibly old and small.

The wedding breakfast greatly appealed to Hay's sense of drama, never entirely dormant. He had invited seventy-five guests, which meant overflow from dining room into his study, where, in the bay window, he had set a table at which, side by side, he had placed William C. Whitney and Oliver Payne. As the President

and Mrs. Roosevelt were also at the round table, good behavior
was assured. Hay had also added the Whitelaw Reids, whose never
allayed ambition for social distinction would be temporarily sated.
The President was at Clara's right; and Mrs. Roosevelt at Hay's
right.

There was no need to fear awkward silences. Theodore, very
much aware of the two men's enmity, delivered himself of a lecture
on the trusts; an occasional glance at the two money princes acted
as a reminder that today, at least, and in more ways than one, they
were in the same boat. The handsome Whitney was, as always,
calm, but Payne, a choleric man, could barely speak for rage.

The situation was too curious for words, thought Hay, happy
that Theodore's flow of talk could not be deterred by mere curiosity
of situation. For once, Edith did not give her husband a warning
look, followed by a small cough, followed—if that did not staunch
the flow—by "Oh, Thee!" in a stern voice. She, too, was awed by
the hatred of the two men, who spoke, politely but briefly, to each
other whenever the President paused for breath. The Whitelaw
Reids, for once at rest in the still circle of perfect social preemin-
ence, glowed benignly, as course after course was served, and the
round table in the bay window became luminous with bright
winter sunlight, an Arthurian table at the Arctic, thought Hay.

"Helen loved your gifts, Mr. Whitney." Clara made motherly
sounds. "They are so very grand, the rings, the brooch."

"I'm glad." Whitney was Chesterfieldian in his politeness. He
had had a great deal to contend with lately. He had given up his
political career. He was under fire for his various business connections. He had not been invited to his son's bachelor dinner, held at
the Arlington Hotel by Colonel Payne, the usurper. Yet he acted
as if nothing in his world was amiss. On the other hand, Payne
was incoherent with mysterious rage. Hay wondered why. The fact
that after the death of Oliver Payne's sister Whitney had remarried
could not have been sufficient reason for so long-lasting a ven-
detta—long-lasting and infinitely resourceful. There was something positively Luciferian in the relentless way that Payne had
gone about buying two of Whitney's children, one of whom was

now Hay's son-in-law. Perhaps childlessness was at the root of it all. Envying Whitney's charm and fecundity, Payne robbed him of two children; and tried to ruin him financially as well. But though Oliver Payne was the richer of the two, Whitney was the cleverer; and not made for failure.

Edith Roosevelt made the error of asking Oliver Payne what *he* had given the young couple. "Not much," he said, eyes on his plate, where a quail in aspic seemed, somehow, obscene. "Diamonds, the usual," he mumbled. Whitney drank champagne, and smiled at Mrs. Whitelaw Reid. "The house in Thomasville, Georgia," said Payne. "They'll honeymoon there. Good hunting, Georgia."

The President, mouth full, could not let the subject of hunting pass unannotated. "*Wild* turkey!" he choked.

"Thee!"

But guns and wild turkeys were now the subject of that powerful energetic boy's mind. "I'm also lending them my yacht," said Oliver Payne to those of the table who were not entirely attentive to the presidential hymn to the slaughter of wildlife. "The *Amphitrite*. They'll go to Europe on it, this summer . . ."

"An *ocean*-going yacht?" Mrs. Whitelaw Reid's happiness was complete.

"Yes," said Oliver Payne, looking not at Whitney's face but his far shoulder. Thus he emphasized his own greater wealth.

"It's the size of an ocean-liner," said Hay, allowing Reid his moment with the President, who, sensing that he had lost the table in general, was now concentrating all the more on Reid, whose sycophantish smiles and bobs of the head caused the President to give a detailed history, from prehistoric times to the present, of the beagle.

"I'm also building them a place in New York." Oliver Payne turned to Clara, as an interested party. "Your daughter said she preferred New York to Washington . . ."

"And *you* to us!" Clara's sudden laugh cut the beagles just short of François Premier, and a hunting party at Poitiers.

"She never said that," murmured the very rich man. "But New

York's right for Payne, and her. I've found them a lot on Fifth Avenue near Seventy-ninth Street, where I'll build a house . . ."

"And we can be," said William Whitney, "all together, on Fifth Avenue."

That stopped both Oliver Payne and Theodore Roosevelt. Hay wished that Henry Adams could have shared this comic interlude.

"How is young Ted?" asked Clara in the pause.

"Weak but recovered. Groton's looking after him well enough."

Young Ted had nearly died of pneumonia, and both Roosevelts had gone to Groton to be with him, leaving Hay as the acting president. Occasionally, he still day-dreamed of what it would be like should Theodore himself fall victim to pneumonia or an assassin's bullet, or simply a trolley car, like the one that had smashed into the President's carriage the previous autumn, killing a Secret Service man. Had Theodore and not the Secret Service man died, John Hay would have been the president. Old and ill as he was, the thought was not entirely without its appeal. Of course, he was too fragile to do much. On the other hand, he would have a free hand to guide the United States onto the world stage, as an equal party with England. Between the two fleets—nations, he corrected his reverie—the entire world would be theirs for the foreseeable future. Although Theodore was on the same course, he was fitful and easily diverted; he was also concerned with being elected president in his own right in 1904. Disturbingly, despite the closeness of his friendship with Cecil Spring-Rice, he resented, as only a Dutch-American could, England's long ascendancy in the United States, achieved at the expense of his ancestors. He had even said to Hay, apropos Pauncefote, that the Englishman is "not a being I find congenial or with whom I care to associate. I wish him well but I wish him well at a distance." This was most unlike McKinley, whose benign neutrality in the Boer War had been of such importance to England.

Whitelaw Reid spoke of Russia, and the President gave Hay a quick glance. They were *not* to discuss the current problems with that, to Hay, mindless grasping barbarous nation. "We can say nothing, dear Whitelaw." Hay made of his old colleague's first name a sort of formal title, White Law, White Rod, Black Law, Black Rod, like those ancient ceremonial servitors of the British crown. "Because Cassini is lurking on the premises, and he will tell the Tsar everything."

"Did you see him avoid Takahira?" The President was about to be tactless.

Hay intervened. "Cassini doesn't see too clearly. It's the monocle, I think . . ."

"What will Japan do about Russia, and Manchuria?" Whitelaw had refused to take Hay's hint. Thus a man lost a foreign mission.

"We must ask the Japanese." Hay was bland. "Certainly, none of us wants the Russians to occupy the industrial parts of Manchuria . . ."

"Shansi province!" Roosevelt erupted; and Hay shuddered, as he heard Brooks Adams's suave low voice turned into Rooseveltian falsetto. "The principal goal of every empire on earth today. Who holds Shansi province holds the key to the balance of power . . ."

"Theodore, they are going to cut the cake." Edith rose in tandem with Clara, and Hay was relieved. Although Hay did not in the least disapprove of the coming American hegemony, as outlined by Brooks in his soon to be published polemic *The New Empire*, he felt that the Administration ought never to associate itself with such un-American concepts as empire. Let the empire come in the name of—the pursuit of happiness, of liberty, of freedom. If the United States was not always high-minded, the world might take less seriously the great new-world charter that set off this extension of the British empire not only from the motherland but from all other restless, expanding nations.

Once the bay-window table had been abandoned, Whitney and Payne separated, as if by prior arrangement. The Hays escorted the Roosevelts into the dining room, where all the guests were standing, champagne glasses at the ready. Back of the huge white cake Helen and Payne stood, ready for the toasts; and the cutting of the cake.

As a bridesmaid, Caroline wore a light gray silk crepe gown, a not entirely satisfactory color or non-color, but Helen had insisted that she be a bridesmaid, "since you were supposed to be my matron-of-honor." To this appeal, Caroline had surrendered.

Now Caroline stood between Henry Adams and Cabot Lodge, and the three responded to the various toasts, particularly an exhilarating one from the President, who had moved in between the bride and groom as if, somehow, their wedding if not their marriage might have been incomplete without his nearness, even centrality.

"Theodore," murmured Adams, "is quite drunk with himself."

Lodge's laugh was not the prettiest of sounds; but, under the circumstances, Caroline found it irresistible. "He can't bear for anyone else to be the center of attention. He wants to be groom . . ."

"And bride," Caroline contributed.

"*Everything*," said Adams. "What, I wonder," he added with a macabre smile, "will he be like at a funeral?"

"In the coffin," said Lodge.

"If it's a state funeral," Adams agreed. "So much energy for everything, including death."

"We're lucky." Lodge was now grave. "To have him where he is, at such a time."

"Handing round cake?" Caroline was deflationary but Lodge was a true believer, and Theodore's star was his star.

To Caroline's surprise, Frederika Bingham was in the room, uncommonly pretty in pale green. Although Mrs. Bingham had yet to enter the gilded gates of the highest society, the crooked smile of her daughter seemed, somehow, to open every door. Caroline was admiring. After all, the pursuit of a high social career was, perhaps, the only challenge that a wealthy American girl might ever meet and, with luck, overcome. "Alice invited me," Frederika read Caroline's mind.

"Roosevelt?"

"Hay. I never knew there were so many people in Washington I did not know and so few," the smile was implicit rather than visible, "so wonderfully few, congressmen."

"Your mother has *them*."

"She can keep them. I suppose these are New York people."
Frederika looked about the room as if she were in New York's
legendary lion house, where Clarence King had seen fit to go mad.

"I'm a foreigner." Caroline still fell back on this identity; but, of
course, she was now, like it or not, old Washington. "There are
many people here from Ohio. Like Colonel Payne. And the Stones.
And Senator Hanna." They were bowed to by the fat, pale Mark
Hanna, who resembled, for an instant, all Ohio. "Is your brother
here?" asked Frederika, as the two young women followed the
newlyweds and the adhesive President into the drawing room.

"No. He's vanished. But he's supposed to be building a house
here."

"He's not in Baltimore?"

"Not if he can help it." Caroline had just received, unofficially,
an accountant's report of the *Examiner* losses for the year just
ended. The paper was going to be expensive to maintain. The
Tribune, thanks to Mr. Trimble and her own inspired negligence,
was profitable. Mr. McLean had even made a New Year's offer to
buy; and Caroline had declined, joyfully, to sell and, sorrowfully,
he had said that he might now be obliged to buy the *Post*.

"I think Mr. Hearst must be fascinating." Frederika was unexpected. As a rule, nice young ladies deplored the national villain.

"Well, if you think that, you and Blaise think alike. He's drawn
to him like . . . like . . ."

"A moth to a flame?"

"I'd hoped to avoid that phrase but then, as a publisher, I ought
not, ever, to avoid the too familiar. Exactly. A moth to a flame. I
hope he isn't burned." Caroline said exactly what she meant; but
then she no longer regarded Blaise as an enemy. After all, had he
not behaved as he had, she might have been simply another
transatlantic young heiress of the sort that Mr. James wrote more
and more elaborately about. Instead, she had made a place for
herself like no other; and though Marguerite might mourn the
irregularity of their situation, Caroline was delighted to be free,
and—why deny it?—powerful in the world of Washington, which
was becoming very much the world that mattered. She glanced at

the ring that she wore on her left little finger. As Del's fire opal had split in equal halves, she had had them set on either side of an irregular yellow sapphire. The effect was more evocative than beautiful; emblematic of a life that had broken in half, had not been lived . . .

At the door to the drawing room, Caroline was astonished to see Mrs. Jack Astor, like some celestial peacock—or was it hen?—in the Washington back yard. "It is like one of those Brueghel paintings," the deep voice sounded in the crowded room. "The wedding of village swain to milkmaid."

"Attended by a fairy godmother, all in gossamer and jewels . . ." Caroline began.

". . . *witch,* dear Caroline. What am I doing in so bucolic a place?"

"It reminds you of Newport, Rhode Island, I suppose."

"No. Rhinebeck-on-Hudson when we give our annual harvest feast to the yokels, and I see to it that their trestle tables are wreathed in poison ivy." Mrs. Jack's laughter was enjoyable if not precisely contagious. All round them, awed Washington ladies were staring at the fashionable Mrs. Astor, never before seen in the capital city. Caroline was agreeably aware that her own stock was rising rapidly.

"Are you a friend of the Hays?" asked Caroline.

"No, not really. But I am enamored of this creature, so young, so potentially appalling . . ."

Mrs. Jack had put out an arm and swept the imperious Alice Roosevelt toward her. "You see? I came. Your rustic revels are now complete."

"So proud the Astors!" exclaimed Alice, in no way, ever, to be outdone, even by the superb Mrs. Jack. "When they were nothing but German Jews, kosher butchers, when we Roosevelts . . ."

". . . were running away from the Indians, in your clumsy wooden shoes, which I see you're wearing today," she added, glancing down at Alice's rather large squared-off slippers. "How suitable . . ."

"Isn't she foul!" Alice turned, delighted, to Caroline.

"No, no. She is fair. But her bite is lethal."

"Rabid!" Alice gazed with delight on Mrs. Jack. It was no secret that the President's oldest child was also, in his own words, "the only one of us with any money," inherited from her dead mother. She was also bent on being a Fashionable, something unknown in Roosevelt circles, a family not unlike the Apgars when it came to dowdy self-satisfaction.

There was a sudden murmur all about them, as the President and Mrs. Roosevelt approached, led by John Hay, like an ancient chamberlain. "Alice, we're leaving," the President announced.

"You're leaving. I'm staying."

"Alice," murmured her stepmother.

"Mrs. Jack Astor." Alice presented the swan to the barnyard geese.

Mrs. Jack made an elaborate curtsey.

"Do stop that!" The President was unamused.

"She does it very well." Edith smiled a queenly smile.

"Thank you." Mrs. Jack rose now to her full height. "Why do you call us 'the idle rich'?" She gave the President a mocking smile. "We are never idle."

"Some are less idle than others," began the President, plainly not comfortable.

"While some are less rich than others," acknowledged Mrs. Jack. "Even so, you must not generalize about your loyal subjects, or we shall all vote for Bryan next year."

"Then *everyone* will be less rich." The President was now retreating from the room. Alice remained. If nothing else, Caroline found her refreshing. But then the entire Roosevelt family was a surprise to a world that had come to look upon the White House as a seedy boardinghouse for dim politicians *emeriti*. Caroline's "Society Lady," as the woman in question signed herself in the pages of the *Tribune*, was thrilled with the change in Washington's *ton*, as she liked to call it, rhyming the French word, to Caroline's immeasurable joy, with the English word that denotes a measurement of weight.

"This place has possibilities." Mrs. Jack was looking about the room. The diplomatic corps was its usual colorful self; and the few men of state were, if not actually gentlemen, got up as if they were. Only the wives—the poor wives, as Caroline thought of them— gave away the game. They were redolent of the back yards of small towns; and always frowning with anxiety, fearful of letting down the *ton*.

Caroline had been disagreeably surprised to meet the wife of James Burden Day. For one thing, she had not expected him to marry so unexpectedly, and, for another, to marry someone from "back home" when he had already entered the relatively great world of Washington, where he was, relatively, related to those ubiquitous gentlefolk the Apgars. Caroline assumed that Day's wife was the price of his congressional seat. None of this was her business.

"If the wives were subtracted," Mrs. Jack said aloud what Caroline was thinking, "the result would be a lot more amusing than anything we've got in New York."

"Only," said Caroline sadly, "they refuse to be subtracted."

"Try division." Mrs. Jack gave her a sudden sharp, knowing look; and Caroline, for no reason that she could ascertain, gasped.

Clara Hay gathered them up. "Come on, you two. Amuse Colonel Payne."

"Surely, he dislikes ladies," began Mrs. Jack.

"Who doesn't?" whispered Caroline, taking advantage of Clara Hay's deafness.

"All the more reason for him to make a fuss over *you*, Mrs. Astor." Clara was firm, always firm; she was also generally right. Colonel Oliver Payne was thrilled to be surrounded by Mrs. Astor and Miss Sanford.

"We must," said Mrs. Jack, voice more throaty and menacing than ever, "find *you* a husband—I mean, a wife, Colonel."

Blaise had accompanied his editor Hapgood to New York City to observe the election of the Chief to Congress, a foregone election, as Hearst had left nothing to chance. The original Democratic nominee, Brisbane, had stepped aside, to make way for his employer; and Hearst was duly confirmed as Tammany's Democratic nominee in the Eleventh District. For this safe Democratic seat, the new head of Tammany, the cheerful Charles Francis Murphy, asked only that the *Journal* whole-heartedly support Tammany's candidate for governor. Hearst had agreed.

Now Blaise and Hapgood stood in windy Madison Square, where some forty thousand people were gathered to hear the election results, and view the fireworks laid on by the *Journal*. "He sure knows how to spend the money," observed Hapgood, with awe.

"Sometimes I think that that's all he knows." Blaise was sour. He, too, had spent money in Baltimore; in fact, the money spent was now at his side, a stout Teutonic man with a huge moustache, the paradigm of Hearst journalists in the copious flesh. But even Hapgood had so far failed to increase circulation figures. Currently, their hopes were based on a series about miscegenation, the one subject certain to thrill their readers, or so Hapgood, the Marylander, maintained. Blaise envied Caroline *her* city. When the capital was dull, there was Embassy Row; when the embassies were short of news, there was the White House, a never-ending source of "warm human interest," to use the current phrase. Stories about the Roosevelt children and their ponies in the elevator, their appearances at state sessions on stilts, their snakes and frogs at table, and, above all, the Jovian sovereign Theodore, conducting himself like a king, destined by birth to his high estate. Caroline need do nothing to fill the columns of her paper; they filled themselves. All he had was miscegenation; and then what?

Blaise had wanted to join Hearst at the Lexington Avenue house, but Hapgood suggested that they get a sense of the crowd first. "After all, if the Chief"—although he worked for Blaise now, the Chief was still the Chief—"is going to be the candidate in '04, we'll get some sense of it now, from the crowd."

"A lot of Bowery." Blaise knew his Manhattan crowds. "Also Tammany." Everyone was in a gala mood. Huge transparencies celebrated Hearst's victory of fifteen thousand eight hundred votes over his dim Republican adversary; and his lead over the entire ticket by thirty-five hundred votes, which made him the largest Democratic vote-getter in the state. Tammany's governor-to-be was not-to-be: in a close race, he had lost to the Republicans. This then was the night that Hearst had dreamed of. He had won his first election in the biggest possible way.

Blaise and Hapgood found themselves not far from a band which kept playing, rather tactlessly, "California, Here I Come," a tribute to Hearst's origin rather than to his adopted domicile, which was now dispatching him to Washington. Overhead a manned balloon was lit up with colored lanterns. The crowd was festive, as well they should be; free schooners of beer were being served at one end of the square beneath the legend "William Randolph Hearst Labor's Friend," while nearby an electrical sign proclaimed, "Congress Must Control the Trusts," a not-so-subtle reminder that the current president was less than arduous in his efforts to master the country's owners.

Hearst's socialism—if that was what it was—always bemused Blaise, who never ceased, for a moment, to be loyal to his own class and could not conceive any other loyalty. Although Hearst would have to pose as a friend of the working-man and the enemy of the rich if he wanted to replace William Jennings Bryan as the plain people's tribune, he was not entirely the demagogue others thought him. The rich Mr. Hearst, who had inherited his money, disliked those other rich men, who had inherited theirs. He was genuinely attuned not so much to the hard-working worthy poor as he was to those excluded from society itself. Himself a sort of outlaw, he not only lived outside the law but used law to flout law.

Hearst might yet strike that nerve in a still-savage land which would make him its natural leader. Blaise was, suddenly, aware that he was present at an historic moment, the genesis of what might be an astonishing, even Napoleonic career.

As if to emphasize and punctuate the Napoleonic image, Madison Square exploded—literally exploded. Blaise fell to his knees on the pavement, while Hapgood sat down beside him with a crash. Soundwaves buffeted them like Montauk surf. The band stopped playing. Then the screaming began; and the sound of ambulances. Overhead the balloon hovered; then began its descent. The electrical sign still threatened the trusts, but the various transparencies had been abandoned, as people ran, in panic, from the square, where something, Blaise could not tell what, had blown up.

"Anarchists!" Hapgood was now on his feet, ever the reporter, the Hearst reporter.

In the cool autumn air there was the acrid scent of—what?—gunpowder, Blaise decided, as he and Hapgood, like brave soldiers in a battle, hurried against the fleeing crowd. Let others run from battle; *they* would go to war.

The fire department arrived just as Blaise and Hapgood found the source of the explosion, a small cast-iron mortar inside of which a fireworks bomb had gone off, igniting dozens of other bombs. The principal damage had been to the windows of a building nearby. The glass had been pulverized, and like so many icy lethal bullets had laid low dozens of men, women and children. Some stood, screaming, faces bleeding; others lay ominously still on the pavement. Blaise stared down at a man, spread-eagled face down; in the back of his neck there was a diamond-shaped piece of glass which must have severed the spine. To Blaise's amazement there was no blood, only the glass, shining in the lamplight, and the dark slit, rather like a letterbox into which someone had tried to insert a glass message.

"How many dead, wounded?" Blaise was delighted by his own coolness; and realized what a truly easy time of it Roosevelt must have had at San Juan Hill. Everything so fast, so shocking, so pointless.

"At least a hundred, I'd say." Hapgood's notebook was out; and he was writing and looking simultaneously; then police and firemen made them move on.

Hearst was seated at his Napoleonic desk; he had foregone, no doubt forever, the bright plaids and festive ties of his Prince Hal days. Now he was in a statesman's black frock-coat, with a black bow tie and a white shirt. The legs once so haphazardly arranged upon the desk were set, side by side, beneath it, as he talked into the telephone to Brisbane at the *Journal* office. George Thompson, now elephantine in appearance, had warned Blaise that the Chief was "handling the misadventure in Madison Square."

Blaise sat on the sofa opposite, as he had so often before in his days as apprentice. The Willson girls, each in a glittering ball gown, were at the opposite end of the museum-like room, playing Parcheesi. Somewhere, a supper party was being laid on to celebrate the victory of the rising political star. But for now, Hearst listened, murmured questions, shut his eyes as if better to visualize not the explosion in the square but the headlines that would describe it. Finally, he put down the receiver.

"I was there," said Blaise.

With professional skill, Hearst questioned Blaise; took notes; ignored the chatter of the Willson girls. "There will be lawsuits," he said finally, "even though the district attorney's prepared to exonerate us. Well, it's done. The important thing is to keep Roosevelt on the run. He's been an ass over the coal-miners. You see, he's the worker's enemy."

"Yes," said Blaise. It was odd to hear the Chief express political opinions. As a rule, he was indifferent to the rights and wrongs of any issue. All that mattered was how to play the news. Now he himself meant to be the news. Blaise wondered if Hearst understood the risk that he was running. He who had devoted a lifetime to making lurid fictions of others was now himself a candidate for re-creation. Blaise was not certain what a petard was but he understood about self-hoisting. Meanwhile, he congratulated the newest star in the political firmament.

Hearst was matter-of-fact. "I should've gone for the governorship. But there wasn't the time, and 1904's almost here, and we've got nobody to put up against Roosevelt. I've got Los Angeles."

"Los Angeles?"

"A paper there. The *Examiner*, I'm calling it. Then Boston's next."

"What about Baltimore?"

"I'll need some organizing there, Blaise. Maybe you could see to it." Hearst swung back and forth between newspapers and politics as if the two were the same, which perhaps they were to him at the moment, and if they were, Blaise saw trouble ahead. One could not be both inventor of the American world and the thing invented.

George Thompson was at the door, round face more than usually flushed with late-night celebrating. "The gentleman you are expecting, sir," was the cryptic announcement.

Hearst leapt to his feet; as did Blaise. The Willson girls continued to play Parcheesi. The doorway now framed the unmistakable statesmanlike figure, in black alpaca frock-coat and string tie, of William Jennings Bryan.

"Colonel Bryan!" Hearst presented five fingers to the Great Commoner, as Bryan was nown to the inventive press; and the Great Commoner squeezed the fingers in his experienced grasp, and smiled his thin wide smile. Blaise had never seen the idol of the masses at such close quarters; was surprised to find him as impressive close up as he was in the illuminated distance of an auditorium, the voice surging from that barrel chest like a force of nature uncontrolled by mere man, much less by Bryan himself.

"You have won the first of many victories." Bryan's speaking voice was agreeably low, not at all like the thunder of the hustings. "I, too, started with an election to the House of Representatives," he added, as if, thought Blaise, this was necessarily a recommendation. After all, he had been beaten for every office since.

Hearst introduced Colonel Bryan to the Misses Willson as "my fiancée and her sister." The Great Commoner maintained his Old Testament poise. As for Blaise, he complimented him on a recent editorial in the *Baltimore Examiner*, convincing Blaise that Bryan intended to be a third-time candidate for president in 1904, unless the Chief could bring him up short. "We are all three publishers,"

410

observed Bryan, sitting in a golden throne, covered with Napoleonic bees, an original, Hearst always said, "the property of the Emperor himself," unaware that every railroad hotel in France had a similar set of chairs. Bryan removed from his pocket several copies of his newspaper, the *Commoner*, published from his home town of Lincoln, Nebraska. "For your amusement, gentlemen."

Hearst riffled the pages professionally; shook his head sadly. "I see, Colonel, you don't follow my advice."

"Well, Mr. Hearst, I aim at a quieter public than yours." Bryan was benign. He even smiled, vaguely, at the Willson girls, who ignored him. Blaise found it hard to believe that this simple farmer-like man could have so seized the nation's imagination. Was it all art—or artifice? Could oratory alone create such passionate fervor, and such enduring antipathy? For at least a third of the nation, Bryan could do no wrong, ever; and if the inventors of the American world, through the press, had not so successfully cast him as a villain, a socialist, anarchist, leveller, he would now be the country's president, and even more popular than the sly Roosevelt, for Bryan's popularity was just that—populist, based on the plain people at large, whose voice he was.

Bryan spoke knowledgeably—and not optimistically—of the election. "Usually, the party that's out picks up congressional seats. But Roosevelt's life is singularly charmed. We hold our own, and no more, which is why your election is deeply meaningful."

Hearst nodded his agreement. Blaise wondered if the Chief would make the mistake of thinking himself not only cleverer but more popular than Bryan. The Chief was sufficiently unused to the ways of the world to be overwhelmed by an election that had been entirely arranged for by Tammany. Blaise feared that the Chief, who could be surprisingly innocent, might mistake his large vote for personal popularity of the sort which Bryan generated in such quantities that only great money, shrewdly spent by Hanna, had kept him from the presidency. "I am honored, naturally," said Hearst, slowly, as if speaking to a slow-witted journalist, "by the confidence that the people—the poor people—of the Eleventh District have shown in me, and I will do my best to fight labor's battle against labor's sworn enemy Theodore Roosevelt."

During this, Blaise watched Bryan's face. Politicians, like priests, do not enjoy the exalted visions of laymen. Bryan's square jaw and thin mouth were a study in parallel and vertical lines at precise right-angles. No wonder he was so easy to caricature. "I'm sure you'll do very well in Washington." Bryan's eyes shifted for an instant to the dazzling Willson girls; then, guiltily, he blinked his eyes. "If I may advise," he began humbly, "we have yet another rich line of attack against our would-be emperor, and that is the empire itself."

As Hearst generally supported America's imperial presence in the Philippines, he did not quite rise to Bryan's bait. "I think Mr. Taft has the Philippines under control . . ."

"No, Mr. Hearst. I'm not referring to crimes that we have already committed. I mean the one that Theodore is dreaming of. He glories in war, which I hate. Hate!" There was a rumble, like approaching thunder, in the room. The Willson girls abandoned their Parcheesi, to stare at the great—what else?—star, who seemed ready to perform. They might not care for politics, but there was nothing that they did not know about show-business, to which, all in all, Bryan, the spell-binder of the Chautauqua circuit, belonged, too. "I hate the love of war he demonstrates every time he speaks." Bryan, aware that he had got the attention of the two girls, the equivalent now to at least two states of the union, grasped his lapels in a familiar gesture. "At West Point, he told the cadets, 'A good soldier must not only be willing to fight, he must be anxious to fight.' So much for Scripture, and the words of our Lord, Jesus Christ." The voice's famous lute-song filled the room, as did Arthur Brisbane, and a half-dozen Hearst employees, who entered, unannounced by George. "They estimate more than a hundred are dead!" Brisbane was excited; he became even more excited when he recognized the Great Commoner in the Napoleonic throne. "I'm sorry, W.R. I didn't know . . ."

"That's all right. Colonel Bryan and I are, as always, as one. We complement each other." Blaise knew that the Chief had never worked out the differences between "compliment" and "complement"; fortunately, he did not have to.

"Would you join us, Mr. Brisbane?" This was the Chief's polite way of telling everyone else to go, including the Willson sisters, who continued to stare at the great actor, who smiled gravely at them, as they passed him in a glitter of gold thread, a cloud of heavy perfume.

Brisbane sat opposite Bryan; he was no enthusiast of Bryan for the simple reason that no man in history had ever been great without blue eyes. When Blaise had mentioned Julius Caesar, Brisbane had replied that the written evidence was not clear; also, what evidence there was about Caesar's life indicated sexual irregularity of the sort that would preclude greatness. Blaise thought that the conquest of the world might weigh something in the balance, but Brisbane was an American moralist, and there was no arguing with him.

"Colonel Bryan is here," said Hearst, grasping his own lapels in imitation of Bryan, "to discuss his European tour."

Brisbane nodded. "I've made all the travel arrangements, sir. You will leave in two weeks' time; the terms are—as agreed."

"They were, when last we corresponded, agreeable. I am, after all, just a country newspaper editor." Blaise was both surprised and impressed. Somehow, Hearst had managed to put the Great Commoner on his payroll. Obviously, the Chief would do anything to secure the nomination in 1904, and why not? If the party's leadership could be bought, he would pay the price. He had made, as it were, a first down-payment by signing up William Jennings Bryan to tour Europe and write a series of articles for the Hearst press, now six newspapers, soon to be eight. There *was* something Napoleonic in the way the Chief went about his conquest of the Democratic Party; and the republic for which it hardly stood.

Brisbane spoke of details. Hearst gazed at the ceiling. Bryan seemed more than ever a monument to the common man. "I'm sending one of our best writers with you. His name is Michelson, and he'll do the actual writing. Naturally, you'll decide what you want to cover, of course."

413

"Of course. I want to meet Tolstoi, the Russian count." Bryan was unexpected. "From what I read of him, we have a lot in common. Fact, I am said to have had a great influence on his own speeches—books, I mean. Also, Russia is important for us, very important, and it seems that he speaks for their common man as I speak for ours."

"I hadn't realized," said Brisbane, plainly startled, "that you were a reader of Count Tolstoi's books."

"No, I can't say I've ever *read* one of them. But I've read a whole lot about him, in the magazines mostly, as he has read about me. We'll get on like two houses afire." Bryan rose, as a monument must rise, thought Blaise. The other three men did, too; and bowed low to the embodiment of the people. There was something formidable about the man's gravity and serene confidence. "I look forward to the food," he said, as he and Hearst parted at the door. "You know, I have spent most of my life at railroad counters, eating on the run, between speaking engagements. I think it was one of your reporters who wrote that Colonel Bryan has probably eaten more hamburgers than any other American."

At this, even Hearst remembered to laugh. Then Bryan was gone.

"He's washed up," said Brisbane.

"But will he support me, like I supported him both times?" Hearst was fidgety; could not sit down.

"Why not? There's no one else on the scene."

"He'll want it for himself, again," said Blaise, who now understood as well as anyone the nature of the American political animal.

Hearst nodded gloomily, and said, "Which means if he can't get it, he'll make it impossible for me—or anyone else—to win."

"We're going to be sued by a lot of people." Brisbane's mind was on Madison Square.

"Let them try." Hearst was indifferent. "Act of God, the law calls it."

"Act of Hearst, Mr. Pulitzer will call it," said Blaise.

"Same thing," Brisbane chortled.

Hearst simply stared at both of them, hands gripping his lapels as if he could, thus, summon forth Bryan's eloquence. This time, Blaise noted, he forgot to laugh. "Bryan's only forty-two," said Hearst. "Roosevelt's forty-three. I'll be forty in April. I'm pretty far behind. I'm taking Elihu Root's house in Lafayette Park, right down from the White House."

"Then you'll only have to move across the street two years from now." Brisbane seemed, truly, to believe in the inevitability of Hearst. Blaise did not. He saw the Chief as someone rather greater than a mere president, who did things that were news only if Hearst himself were to decide whether or not those acts were to be recorded, or reinvented, or ignored. Hearst was something new and strange and potent; and Blaise gave Caroline full credit for having perceived this novelty before anyone else that he knew. Now Hearst, the creator, was trying to create himself. It was as if a mirror, instead of reflecting an image, were to project one out of itself. Hearst could alter, in any fashion, what was there, but what was there must first be there before he could perform his curious magic. Could a distorting glass reflect itself when nothing at all was placed before it? Was Hearst real? That was the question. Blaise was glad that he would be living in Washington during Hearst's term as congressman.

– 3 –

Mrs. James Burden Day ("You may call me Kitty, Miss Sanford") was at home on Easter day, and Caroline, accompanied by Mr. and Mrs. Trimble, helped fill her home in Mintwood Place, on a bluff just off Connecticut Avenue, with a wild, even primordial, view of Rock Creek Park, abloom with white and pink dogwood and flowering Judas.

"We should get to know the Democrats," said Caroline to Mr. Trimble, who was himself a Bryan man, and found it difficult to follow Caroline's circumspect line in regard to Roosevelt. The

Tribune was intended to be read by everyone, and this meant that true political controversy, of the sort that Mr. Trimble affected to like, was not possible in a city dominated by the Roosevelt family with its ever-increasing royal style of entertaining. The novelty of a patrician in the White House had quite undone not only Washington's old guard, so used to looking down on White House occupants, but the diplomatic corps, traditionally condescending when it came to the social arrangements of what was still thought to be a rustic republican capital, set in the Maryland woods. Since Caroline was popular with the Roosevelts, she was careful not to do anything that might jeopardize her useful, for the *Tribune*, entrée. Of all the Roosevelts, she was most charmed by the serene Edith, who managed the Roosevelt circus with what looked to be no effort at all.

The plump, noisy, small President, in his passion to be thought sinewy, eloquent and tall, had taken to vigorous exercise in the White House, where wrestlers and acrobats were always welcome, and he would join in their gymnastics, with such gusto that a medicine ball, stopped by his red perspiring face, had nearly knocked out one of his eyes. Although this had been kept secret from the press, Caroline had discovered from Alice what had happened; from other sources, she had later discovered that the President was blind in one eye. But the public knew nothing of this; and he continued his strenuous life, riding horses at full speed along Rock Creek's dangerously steep trails and bridle-paths, shouting at those in his path, "Stand aside! I am the President!"

Between court life and the rarefied world of the Hay-Adams house, Caroline was far removed, as Trimble accused, from those readers who were plain folk, and followers of Bryan. "But the *Post* is the Democratic paper. Why shouldn't we be the Republican?" Caroline had thought Mr. Trimble unreasonable; but, of course, he was right in the sense that a newspaper that existed largely to entertain need not ally itself so exclusively with one faction. To please him, she had taken advantage of Mrs. Day's invitation.

The Days lived in one of a row of similar houses, with steep porches, Gothic windows, and a roof that sprouted unexpected crenellations. The overall effect was of a fortress built to dominate Rock Creek.

Kitty sat behind her silver teapot, her silver coffee pot, and her regiment of cups. With the help of what looked to be an elder sister, she poured and greeted, and spoke of the weather. Caroline recognized a number of Democratic legislators, by face if not by name. Only the minority leader of the House, John Sharp Williams of Tennessee, was known to her from dinner parties. A sardonic, dishevelled man, never entirely sober, he was feared for his wit. He collected her by, simply, putting his arm through hers, most indecorously, and guiding her toward the dining room, where a lonely decanter of whiskey had been placed, for his use. "I'm Jim Day's boss, you know. He's got to look after me." While Williams poured himself whiskey, Caroline noted the nice pattern that a number of dark tea leaves made at the bottom of her cup, escapees from Kitty's coarse strainer. "I didn't know you knew Kitty, Miss Sanford."

"I don't. I know her husband." Caroline paused; then added, "Slightly, when he was at the comptroller's office."

"He'll go far, with Kitty's father behind him."

"The Judge?"

"The Judge. Oh, he's a powerhouse, that man. He's only got the one leg, you know. He got Jim the election."

"Is that why Mr. Day married the Judge's daughter?" Caroline softened the bluntness of the question with what she hoped was a deprecatory laugh. "I *am* a working journalist, Congressman."

"Didn't know the *Tribune* went in for that kind of story." Williams's round red face became solemn, a look that Caroline had come to know: the politician who has said to the press more than he intended to say, and fears the result.

"We don't. My 'Society Lady' might hint around *if* I let her. But I won't. Marriage is sacred to us."

"Spoken like a true guardian of the morals of this republic, which you are, Miss. I make no bones about that." Williams looked about the room. "Why, there's the Speaker."

"Mr. Cannon?" Caroline looked about her, eager to see this

august personage. But Williams was mistaken. Someone who bore a slight resemblance to the Speaker had entered the parlor. Caroline recognized the man, a Washington realtor whose specialty was getting members of Congress "settled." "It's not Mr. Cannon." Williams seemed relieved. "But then, most everybody's headed back home by now. I'm surprised so many of us are still lingering on . . ."

"Potomac fever?"

"That's for when you're defeated. Then you can't leave the town, ever. But *we* still come and go, and the more we go—home, that is—the longer we can stay around here."

"I can't wait until you all come back in November."

"That's kind of you, Miss Sanford." Williams beamed at her, and for an instant, Caroline felt a hand lightly brush against her hip. At least, she had been spared a pinch of the sort certain notorious senators were known to bestow on ladies whose contours pleased them, often leaving blue-black badges on delicate flesh.

"I was not thinking of Congress in general," said Caroline, deftly sliding a dining-room chair between them, "but the arrival of William Randolph Hearst."

Williams scowled. "He's already sent me his first orders. He wants to be on the Ways and Means Committee *and* on Labor."

"You have obliged him?"

"In hell, yes. That's where he'll get those committees, not from me. You know, that fool is getting himself up to run for president. He takes the cake, that one."

"Surely, he's not the first fool to do that, or," Caroline added, aware that Day was approaching her, "the first fool to be elected, if he is, of course."

Williams laughed a loud whiskey laugh. "That's pretty funny, Miss Sanford. Yes. There have been fools galore in the White House, and there are times when I think we have a precious one there right now, with all that 'Bully!' nonsense, and double-dealing. . . . Jim, I never knew you aspired to the higher social circles."

Day smiled, at Caroline; shook her hand. "We're old friends, or so I like to think. I knew young Mr. Hay," he said to Williams, who looked appropriately grave.

"Struck down, as if by lightning, in his prime," intoned John Sharp Williams; then, whiskey in hand, he left host with guest.

"We've not done so well," observed Day, neutrally, an angel food cake between them from which one large slice had been taken. Ladies hovered at the table's other end, eating small pink shiny cakes, balancing teacups, gossiping.

"You mean the election?"

"That's all we ever mean here." He looked at her; the eyes were what the Society Lady had lately taken to referring to as "candid blue." Lately, Caroline had rather hoped to encounter a pair of duplicitous blue eyes, which she could confound the Society Lady with. Meanwhile, the Society Lady herself, hugely incarnate, was working her way, methodically, through a plate of ladyfingers: it was her method to begin with the "fingernail," a glossy blanched almond, and then, in two bites, to finish off the finger, and mourn the unbaked hand that she could not bite though it fed her, thought Caroline, rather wildly, head aswim with metaphors involving food, and all because the young man, towering beside her, was attractive, and made her think of—food. Was there a connection? Would she turn praying mantis, and devour him, as if he were angel food cake, or would she surrender to him, as all the romances—and the insistent Marguerite—required, her flesh mere cake to his sweet tooth? Perhaps, she decided, tiring of food metaphors, neither would devour the other; instead, they would resemble naked statuary in the gardens of Saint-Cloud-le-Duc, where, marble arms entwined, they would strike poses, in the rain—yes, she saw them both shining and wet in a heavy summer rain, a male and a female statue, side by side—no, stomach to stomach, Venus and Mars, dripping rainwater, face to face. On the back of the hand that held the teacup, she saw a pattern of sand-colored hairs and tried to picture the statue Mars entirely covered with interesting patterns of hair; but then the rain slicked down the hairs like a wet dog's; yes, the hairy male most resembled a dog when he was not cake or marble but warm alien flesh, wet.

Caroline was not certain that she would entirely enjoy the man's real body, even if it were placed on offer, which he showed, newly married as he was, no sign of wanting to do.

"Every day on my way to the Capitol, I watch your brother Blaise's house going up. It's going to be about the same size as the Capitol, I'd say."

"I can't think what he wants a house here for." Caroline's victory in Washington was by means so total that she could bear fraternal competition. After all, Blaise still controlled the Sanford fortune; and Washington was for sale even to the lowest, or only, bidder. Once Blaise had taken a wife, she would be *the* Mrs. Sanford, and Miss Sanford, the spinster sister, publisher though she was, would fade. Who then would come to the small house in Georgetown when there was a marble palace in Connecticut Avenue, with a court always in session? She must marry. She must build a house. She must take to bed James Burden Day. "Of course, he wants to buy the *Post*, but Mr. Wilkins will never sell."

"A good thing. We need one Democratic paper here." Caroline noticed that the pattern of light hairs on the hand vanished at the wrist and then spread out on that part of the forearm that was just visible beneath his loose cuff. Marguerite had already warned her that if her virginity were to be kept for one more season, she would, simply, dry up. Significantly, Kitty entered the room, bearing a plate of small cakes each adorned, most ominously, with a glazed bit of preserved fruit. "No, no." She moved the plate away from her, mildly sickened. "No, *thank* you," she added graciously, aware that she had been too vehement. "So delicious, your—angel food cake."

Kitty looked suspiciously at the great gap in the cake, and Caroline realized that Kitty now thought that she had eaten it all herself, a devouring woman, no doubt of that. "Banked fires give off the most heat" was one of Marguerite's folkloric observations, as she observed, with disapproving eyes, her virginal and, at twenty-five, aged mistress.

"Mr. Williams says that President Cleveland will run again, for a third time." Unlike most Washington wives, Kitty was herself a politician, trained by her father.

"I should think that he'll think twice, and stay home in Princeton." Day was staring at Caroline's chin. Was it dusted, lightly, with sugar from one of Kitty's confections? "I'm sure Bryan can have it again. I'm for him. We're all for him where I come from."

"I've never seen a man eat so much," said Kitty; and she left them. How, Caroline wondered, had food become the prosaic leitmotif for the—with relief, she shifted to music as compelling metaphor—*Liebestod* so soon to sound between them? She stared not at cake but at the lean face bent down toward hers; the lips curved upwards at the corners like a Praxiteles faun. But marble fauns were not patterned with coppery hairs, and she was not quite certain how she would respond to love's unveiling. The theory of a man's body and the fact of it must be as unlike as the theory of American government with all its airy platitudes and the sleazy, disagreeable, democratic practice. But whatever the surprises in store for her, he was not fat, like Del.

Faun-lips shaped for love now spoke, softly, of the recent coal strike. "You know, the country was close to shutting down before the election. There was real panic back home, let me tell you! There was winter coming and no coal. We should have taken the lead, but Roosevelt got to the owners and the miners first. He's on the owners' side, of course. But he made them give up a few pennies, which was easy for them to do if the miners would agree to a ten-hour day, which they had to. Oh, we'll have our showdown one of these days . . ."

"The Democrats and the Republicans?"

"No. The owners of the country and the people who actually do the work."

"Surely, the owners work, too. Overtime, in fact."

Day grinned; the teeth were white, but one of the front teeth had a curious crack in it like—again, marble; no, alabaster. But since the effect was more Mars than faun, Caroline now willed herself to be the mate of Mars, Venus. Perhaps, miraculously, her breasts would double in size between now and the union of war and love. Marguerite had proposed exercises; and plenty of cream—to be drunk. But the exercises were boring, and the cream sickening; and the breasts remained more Diana, chaste goddess of the hunt, than Venus. Caroline began to chatter nervously. "How close it was last fall, to our having Mr. Hay for president . . ."

"Poor old man . . ."

"Oh, not too old, though much frailer since Del died." Mistake to mention Del; must not pause for condolent phrases. "Anyway, he was most excited when word came from Pittsfield that a trolley-car had run into the President's carriage, and the Secret Service man was killed, and Mr. Roosevelt was sent sailing through the air like . . . like a huge doughnut," food yet again, and inappropriate at that, "and of course no one knew just how seriously hurt he was . . ."

". . . is. They say his brain's addled."

"No more than usual. I saw a good deal of him at Jackson Place, where he had to move after they started tearing up the White House. He had—has—an abscess of the leg, the bone. But that's all. He's still full of energy, and Mr. Hay did not become president."

"Worse luck. I ride on Sundays." The faun lips at last shaped expected phrases. "Along the canal. To Chain Bridge. After Sunday dinner . . ."

Caroline stopped any further reference to food, forever, between them. "I'll join you," she said.

As it turned out, he—not she—said, "I've never done this before." They lay side by side, entirely nude, not the modest way to couple in the United States, if the *Tribune*'s Ladies Page was to be trusted, or interpreted correctly, for all was euphemism when it came to matters so intimate.

"Surely, you and Kitty have at least *tried* to do what we've managed to do." Caroline's virginal fear of the male body had, at first, been confirmed by so much overpowering muscle, hair, size. The scale was much too heroic for a mere woman. She felt not like a doll, which might have had its enchanting helpless side, but like a midget, which was definitely unattractive. The yards of male sinew beside her seemed the god-like norm and her own white slender body so like—like a rib torn out of him. Perhaps the biblical story did contain a kind of truth. Happily, he was as fascinated by her as she was by him, and he kept caressing her, as if not certain that she was indeed real. She, on the other hand, was more chary of touching him; fearful of explosions that might be set off if she were to explore too closely the brown-rose surfaces of that huge, mysteriously animated body.

"No. I meant that I haven't been with anyone since we . . ." The voice trailed off.

"Well, I have been with no one at all." She broke the news, as his hand strayed toward her groin. The hand froze where it was; she thought of the petrified citizenry of Pompeii, each last act caught and preserved in lava. Drusilla, virgin, with Marius, gladiator: in her end was her beginning.

"*I'm* the first?" He stared at her with unattractive amazement.

"Surely, it's no martyrdom for you. One has to begin sometime, with someone . . ."

"But if I'm the first," he repeated, eyes most unattractively fixed upon the source of all life, which Henry Adams never ceased, euphemistically, to celebrate.

"Why is there no blood?" Marguerite had explained all this to her; and she explained to him, with growing irritability, her years as a youthful equestrienne with its eventual reward not of trophies won but of hymen ruptured.

"I've never heard of that," he said.

Although Caroline had not expected romance, neither had she expected so clinical a discussion after what had been, nearly, ecstasy. Firmly, she placed one hand over the faun-like mouth; with the other, she began experiments of her own, of an hydraulic nature; plainly, ecstasy was going to take a good deal of patience, not to mention hard manual work.

The second time was better than the first, and Caroline saw definite possibilities in the famous act. She was critical, however, of the Great Artificer who had designed both men and women with too little attention to detail, and too much left to chance. Nothing was quite angled right. Junctions, though possible, involved acrobatics of an undignified nature. Only childbirth, which she had witnessed, was less dignified, and, of course, exquisitely painful. Fortunately, there was no pain in all their maneuverings upon the bed; while pleasure, when it arrived, was sharp and unexpected and quite obliterated the sense of self, an unanticipated gift of Eros. Obviously, the Great Artificer intended that each be a conduit for the other, as well as for the race itself, which He had so haphazardly designed to go on and on, doing what they were doing in order to achieve pleasure, the small reward that the Artificer had thrown in, as they, doggedly, fulfilled what was the only perceivable purpose of the exercise: more, ever more, of the same until earth chilled or caught fire, and no one was left to couple.

Later, Jim, as she now called him, lolled contentedly in the tub, while Caroline followed Marguerite's instructions with an elaborate douching in a Lowestoft china basin, involving a cold tisane guaranteed to discourage any little stranger from assembling itself in her no longer virginal loins.

Aware that Jim was watching her perhaps too expert handling of herself, she said, "Marguerite has given me full instructions. She's also a midwife, though I pray we won't ever need her for that."

"Frenchwomen know an awful lot, don't they?"

"Some know more awful things than others. But when it comes to the basic things, yes, they know a lot, and they tell one another, mother to daughter, for generations."

"Americans never talk about—those things."

"That is why newspapers are so necessary. We give people something to talk about. Politics, too," she added, remembering her manners. Now, as she put on a silk peignoir, she wondered if she was going to be in love. She rather doubted it. After all, she lacked the first requisite: she was without jealousy, she had noted, watching him get into the tub. Kitty got to see this homely but also exciting spectacle every day while she could only attend the miracle play on Sundays; yet she did not envy Kitty. To have a man always with you, even one as well-proportioned and charming as Jim, was not a dream that she had ever wanted to come true. She had been a bachelor too long. Of course, she had ceased to be a virgin only an hour earlier, and who knew what fires hitherto banked—why did sex require so many similes, metaphors?—might flare up out of control, and devour her with lust, for that particular body, and no other? *Je suis la fille de Minos, et de Pasiphaë*, she murmured, and thought it curious that the great celebrators of women's lust had been men like Racine and Corneille. Nothing much was left of burning Sappho's celebrations, while the other ladies who had written on the subject were careful not to give away the game, if indeed there was a game to be given away. Perhaps the whole thing was an invention of idle poets—of men with nothing better to do, unlike women, who had to bear and raise children and keep house, and rapidly lose their charms, leaving idle men free to invent love. But then Caroline thought of the various women that she had known who had been in love, and as she recalled their sufferings, she decided that they could not all have been acting. There had been pain or at least *chagrin d'amour*, which was probably worse. She wondered if she would ever suffer so much for any man, or woman—she must be honest with herself, as a pupil of Mlle. Souvestre. She doubted it; she was too used to being just herself, watchful, engrossed by others, amused by vanity, and was not jealousy simply vanity writ large? Yet when she saw Jim, fully clothed, the beautiful body that she was beginning to learn how to work for her own pleasure now covered up, she did feel a mild pang that she could not start all over again, and unveil the godhead, as she had come to think of that absurd-looking but entirely necessary organ. She would have to wait—impatiently?— until next Sunday.

The faun-lips were surprisingly soft, while the surrounding skin was scratchy, a nice contrast. He smelled of cedar, and the horse that he had been riding. "You and Kitty must come here to dinner," said Caroline, leading him to her bedroom door.

Jim looked amazed. "*Both* of us?"

"Well, it is usual to invite married couples together, or so my Society Lady instructs us."

"You'd *like* Kitty here?"

"Very much. We have," Caroline smiled, "so much in common."

"I guess you do at that." He could be as cool as she, and that would make their relationship all the easier, she decided; and smiled, when she heard the front door slam. As it did, Marguerite, arthritis forgotten, hurtled into the room like a witch on the devil's breath; and embraced Caroline, weeping loudly, shouting her congratulations, mixed with cautionary do's and don't's and did she remember? and how was it, it, it?

"I have come through, Marguerite." Caroline spoke to her in French; and felt a bit like Joan of Arc at the crowning of the Dauphin. "I am a saint—I mean a woman, at last."

"Praise God!" Marguerite positively howled.

11

John Hay looked out over the Atlantic, and thought of Theodore Roosevelt; but then practically everything reminded Hay of the President, who had summoned him to the strenuous confusions of Oyster Bay to concert a policy toward Russia, which had refused to accept a protest, forwarded by the President, deploring the Easter massacre of the Jews of Kishineff. American Jewry, headed by one Jakob Schiff, was up in arms; and, on the opposite side, so was Cassini in Washington. The President, like the Atlantic, obeyed his own tides, mindless tides, Hay had decided, entirely directed by the moon of his destiny. In the confusion of children, ponies, neighbors, it was decided to make no official remonstrance to the Tsar, but to play up, in the American press, the refusal of the Tsar's government to accept a message on the subject.

"I believe the country would follow me if I were to go to the extreme." Roosevelt was standing before his house, jaw held high; but since jaw and neck were all of a piece, Hay thought, queasily, of a chunk of roast beef.

427

"You mean war with Russia?" Hay leaned his back against the bole of a sycamore tree; and the pressure relieved, somewhat, the pain.

"*I* could lead the people in such a war . . ."

"Well, if you couldn't, there wouldn't be much of a war, would there?" In a year the Republicans would hold their convention, and Roosevelt dearly wanted to be the nominee. As a war leader, at the head of his legions in Manchuria, he would be, he thought, another Lincoln and so, overwhelmingly, elected. Hay lived now in dread of Theodore's activism, like the Atlantic when the moon was at the full and the wind north-northwest.

"I favor only splendid little wars, as you know . . ." Hay began.

But Theodore Rex was now in full repetitive flow. "Who holds Shansi province dominates the world." Hay wished that Brooks Adams had been born mute or, better, not at all. As Theodore trumpeted the Brooks Adams line, Hay made the usual demurs; then, inspired, he said, "Now if you want a useful small war, there's Colombia."

"I'd hoped you would say Canada." Roosevelt suddenly laughed; and stopped playing emperor. "Yes. We've got good cause to send the troops to Bogotá. They are endless cheats. I know you'd just as soon place the canal in Nicaragua, but Panama's the more likely spot, and if the Colombians *don't* come to terms . . ." More Atlantic menace flowed up and down the lawns of Sagamore Hill; then the President went off to play tennis, and Hay fled to Edith for comfort.

Now Hay was again at Newport, Rhode Island, in the house that Helen and Payne had rented for the season. "The sea-air will do you good," even Henry Adams had said that, as *he* fled to France; and the sea-air had indeed done him so much good that he had, that very morning, written out his resignation as secretary of state. The strain of keeping Theodore in line was too much for a sick man. Root was far better suited than he; also, Root rather frightened Theodore, which Hay certainly did not. Finally, Root was planning to give up his post as secretary of war; therefore, the graceful thing for Hay to do would be to stand aside, allowing Root to take his place, as Theodore's keeper.

"I shall be free." Hay addressed the Atlantic, which indifferently glittered in the bright July light. "I shall be able to enjoy life." Then he laughed aloud when he recalled what Henry Adams had said when he had heard Hay fretting that by the time he left office he might have lost all zest for life.

"Don't worry, sonny," said his old friend, with exuberant malice, "you've already lost it."

Slowly, Hay descended the curved marble staircase to the round marble entrance hall—inspired by Palladio's Villa Rotunda. Colonel Payne rented only the best for his stolen Whitney son. Hay did not like Colonel Payne; but, to the Colonel's credit, he did not thrust himself upon the family of Helen Hay Whitney. Thus far, he had not been seen in Newport; nor had William C. Whitney. Each maintained the symmetry of their feud through absence.

In a panelled study that resembled the interior of a cigar box, Clara was writing letters beneath the portrait of the house's owner, a railroad magnate, gone abroad. "You have resigned," she said, without looking up.

"How did you know?" Hay was no longer astonished by Clara's astonishing knowledge of him.

"The way you walk on your heels when you think you've—put your foot down. I'm writing Edith. Shall I say anything about your resignation?"

"No. No. Theodore must hear it only from me." Hay produced the letter. "My freedom."

"Yes, dear." Clara continued to write; and Hay felt robbed of all drama.

"It's not every day the secretary of state resigns," he began.

"Well, it *seems* like every day in your case. I wish," Clara signed her letter with a flourish, and turned the entire huge bulk of her body toward him, "that you really would go through with it. I want to get you back to Bad Nauheim, to the treatments, to . . ."

"Clara, I've done it! We can leave for Europe next month. Adee keeps the department running smoothly whether I'm living or dead, and the President . . ."

". . . will stop you, as always. He wants you for next year, for the election. You'll have to stay on, worse luck. Of course, the sea-air . . ."

". . . agrees with me. But, how can I take another year of the Senate and Cabot . . . ?" Hay shuddered at the thought of that narrow pompous man whom he had once thought of as a friend.

"We must put up with him because of Sister Ann. She's worth a dozen of him . . ."

"And he is a dozen truly dreadful senators rolled into one . . ."

Helen swept, very like her mother, into the room. Marriage had enlarged everything about her. "Mrs. Fish gives a reception for the Secretary of State Saturday. So Mr. Lehr has decreed, decreed . . ."

"What dogs are to be asked?" Hay had been rather more pleased than shocked by the Lehr-Fish dinner party for the dogs of the Four Hundred. Roman decadence had always appealed to his frontiersman soul. The fact that decadence so enraged Theodore was also a point in its favor, particularly now that Theodore was himself showing late-imperial signs.

"Alice is arriving." It was no longer necessary to ask which Alice. *The* Alice always arriving was Roosevelt. The press revelled in her; and called her Princess Alice. She delighted; she shocked; she powdered her nose in public, something no lady was supposed to do even in private, and it was even whispered that she, secretly, smoked cigarettes. Plainly, late, very late, Roman decadence now luridly lit up the White House, and the President had even joked to Hay that he himself had been taken to task by a lady in Canada who had read that he had actually drunk a glass of champagne at Helen Hay's wedding, thereby placing in jeopardy his immortal soul.

"Your father has resigned."

"I suppose she'll stay at the Stone House. But we could always have her here . . ."

"Is that all that you have to say at the close of my long career?"

Hay realized that his affectation of melancholy was too close to the real thing to be convincing.

"Oh, you won't resign. You won't *really*. Don't be silly, Father. You'd have nothing at all to do. Anyway, the President won't let you. So that's that, isn't it?" Helen appealed to Clara, who nodded, with sibylline dignity.

Hay was ill pleased, for he had, indeed, meant to resign once and for all, and now every omen was wrong. Only death could free him of office; and that would come soon enough. "You two are merciless," he observed.

"You must also see to it that we get that canal from Colombia," said Helen, adjusting her hair in a mirror. She was now nearly as large as her mother; and dressed in the same dramatic style. "Why are they being so difficult?"

"They are dawdling because next year the old French Concession for a canal, which we took on, runs out, and then they'll want us to pay all over again."

"Thieves," said Helen, curling a lock of hair with a finger.

"To put it mildly. We may have to—intervene. The people who actually live in the isthmus, the Panamanians, hate the Colombian government."

"We must give them their freedom." Helen was emphatic. "That is the least we can do, the very least."

"You and the President think alike," said Hay. "Four times in the last two years the Panamanians have revolted against Colombia . . ."

"The next time we'll help them, and then they can enter the Union like . . . like Texas."

"Oh, surely, *not* like Texas," said Clara, obscurely.

"One Texas may be too much." Helen was reasonable. "But if Panama wants to belong to us, we should let them."

"Or," said Hay, "we should say that we'll build the canal in Nicaragua. Just the threat will bring Colombia round." This had been Hay's policy; and Roosevelt had concurred, for the time being. "I shall resign," he repeated, as he left the room. Neither lady responded. Helen's hair had fallen, disastrously, down her back, while Clara's letter-writing totally absorbed her.

In the marble hall, Hay gave the butler his letter to be mailed to the President at Oyster Bay; and the butler presented Hay with a newly arrived dispatch-case, full of business from Cinderella at Washington.

As Payne came down the stairs, Hay gave the dispatch-case to the butler. "I'm playing hooky today," he said. "Put this in my room."

"I'll take you driving, sir." Payne gazed down at his tiny father-in-law. "The Pope Toledo's just arrived."

"The what?"

"The Pope Toledo, my new motor car . . ."

"It sounds like a picture you might see hanging in the Prado."

"Shall we ask the ladies?" Payne looked toward the study.

"No," said Hay. "I'm no longer speaking to them. I've resigned as secretary of state, and they simply won't accept it—my resignation, that is."

"Let's drive by old Mrs. Delacroix's. Caroline and Blaise are there."

Had Payne heard him? Hay wondered, as he followed the young man through the front door to the porte-cochère, where stood a marvellously intricate, shining piece of machinery.

The butler helped Hay into the front seat beside Payne, who showed as little interest in Hay's resignation as the ladies of the family. Perhaps I am already dead, thought Hay, and everyone's too polite to tell me. Perhaps I am dreaming all this. Lately, Hay's dreams had been getting more and more life-like—and unpleasant—while his waking life was more than ever dream-like, and almost as unpleasant. Surely, it was all a dream that young Teddy was president and that he had just been to see him at Sagamore Hill and Teddy had discussed the possibility, even desirability, of a war with Russia. This sort of thing happened in dreams. In real life, there were real presidents, like Lincoln and McKinley; and real secretaries of state like Seward, not himself in masquerade, little Johnny Hay from Warsaw, Illinois, barely grown, with a new moustache, in a horse and buggy, driving down the rutted mud main street of Springfield, not being sped along inside an elegant contraption on rubber wheels that gave the sense they were floating on air, as Bellevue Avenue slipped past them, its palaces more suitable for Paradise—or Venice—than mere earth.

The Secretary of State was recognized as he was borne by Pope Toledo to the Delacroix cottage, and hats were raised, and he nodded graciously at the strangers who held him—or rather, his office—in such awe. When one was dead did one actually know it? as in the sort of dreams when the dreamer knows he dreams? That seemed an urgent question to put to Henry Adams, who knew everything.

In the Delacroix drawing room they were greeted by Caroline, who held in one hand a dozen newspapers. "You catch me with my knitting," she said.

"Mine too," said Hay, "only I've sworn off reading the stuff until September."

"If only I could." Caroline greeted Payne rather as if she were the sister-in-law that he might have had, and Hay wondered what sort of marriage she and Del would have had. He was fairly certain that Del would not have wanted her to go on publishing a newspaper, and he was equally certain that she would not have given it up. She had a good deal of will, Hay had long ago decided; and if there was one quality that he himself would not have wanted in a wife it was will, of Caroline's sort, which was like a man's, unlike Clara's, which was formidable, in its way, but entirely womanly, wifely, motherly.

"Mrs. Delacroix is surrounded by Louisiana ladies, and Blaise is playing tennis with Mr. Day."

"Which rhymes with Hay," said Hay, "and who is Mr. Day?"

"James Burden Day. He's an Apgar, too. He's in Congress."

"Why isn't he home, looking after the folks, like all the other tribunes of the people?" Hay looked with longing at an armchair, but the sound of ladies' voices kept him on his feet; he could no longer bear too many standing ups and sitting downs.

"He wanted to see Mr. Hearst in New York. Mr. Hearst wants to be elected president next year. He is very ambitious."

"He married the chorus girl," said Payne, who had moved, before his marriage, in glamorous Broadway circles.

"She will make a stunning first lady." Caroline was solemn.

"What a lucky country!" Hay was amused; until the room filled up with ladies from Louisiana.

Mrs. Delacroix had aged, she told everyone, but she looked no different to Hay from the way that she had always looked during the thirty years that he had casually known her. "I am now aged beyond recognition," she said, giving Hay her hand, while she removed a large hat with the other.

"You are unchanged," said Hay. "But the hat shows its age."

"How rude! It's only ten years old." A chorus of approval from the ladies, who were now taking cups of tea from the Irish housemaid, circulating among them. "Sit down, Mr. Hay. Please. You look peaked."

"It was the Pope Toledo," said Hay, sinking into an armchair.

"Pope who?" Mrs. Delacroix looked anxiously at the Irish maid. Catholicism, Hay knew, was always a delicate subject in the presence of servants.

"My new car," said Payne.

"Blaise is here, too. Isn't it wonderful?" Mrs. Delacroix addressed this sentiment to Payne, as Blaise's one-time classmate.

"But doesn't he always come to see you?" Payne's own strong familial life was so rich in furious drama that he had little appetite for the family dramas of others.

"Not when Caroline's with me. Now they have made up." Mrs. Delacroix turned to Caroline, and smiled.

"No, we haven't. We simply ignore any differences when we're under your roof. It is our affection for you, not one another. It is also my—atonement."

"Yes. Yes." Mrs. Delacroix smiled at Caroline; then sat opposite Hay, while the Louisiana ladies hovered around the grand piano, as if they expected to break into song.

"Is it still the inheritance?" asked Hay, who had once known, from Del, all the intricacies of the Sanford testament, which had

434

proved to be every bit as stupid as Sanford himself, Hay's exact contemporary.

"Yes. But in less than two years I shall inherit under the mysterious terms of the will . . ."

"The one that looks like a seven?" Hay recalled the portentous detail.

"Exactly. Well, when I *am* twenty-seven, the one will at last be a seven; and what is mine will be mine . . ."

"You must marry." Mrs. Delacroix frowned. "You're much too old to be a single girl."

"I am a spinster, I am afraid."

"Don't!" Mrs. Delacroix made the sign to ward off the evil eye. "Payne, why don't you marry her?"

"But I am married, Mrs. Delacroix. To Mr. Hay's daughter."

"I quite forgot."

"We haven't," said Hay, agreeably. "It's still very much on our minds."

"Such a splendid wedding," Caroline contributed.

"You must come to New Orleans, Caroline. We have a great many young men there, all ready to marry and settle down."

"Not too young," said Caroline. "Not at my age." Hay wondered why so handsome a young woman should so much enjoy depicting herself as old and, essentially, unattractive. Perhaps she was, as she had said, one of nature's most curious creatures, a spinster. He had always somehow doubted that Del would ever succeed in marrying her. She was too self-contained; too—cold? But that seemed the wrong word to describe a character of such charm and amiability. She was, simply, independent in a way that their world was unused to.

"Don't wait too long," was Mrs. Delacroix's conventional wisdom.

Blaise and the young congressman stood in the doorway. They wore white cotton shirts, flannel trousers; they were sweating. It was a sign of great old age, thought Hay, when congressmen looked like schoolboys.

"Don't come in!" ordered Mrs. Delacroix. "Go change, both of you."

The young men vanished, to the apparent sorrow of the Louisiana ladies. "I want," said Payne, to Mrs. Delacroix, "to ask all of you to come out on Uncle Oliver's yacht, for lunch."

"I hate boats." Mrs. Delacroix was firm. "But I'm sure the young people will want to go. Caroline?"

"Oh, yes. I love boats." Suddenly she stood up. Hay noted that she had ripped in two the lace handkerchief that she had been playing with. Was she ill, too? Or was so much talk of spinsterhood disturbing to her?

"I'll be right back," she said; and slipped out of the room.

"Their reconciliation has been the joy of my life," said Mrs. Delacroix, with somber joy.

"Funny, isn't it? how family quarrels are *always* about money," said Hay, who had had his problems with his own wealthy father-in-law.

"What else is there to quarrel about?" asked Payne, unexpectedly, himself the victim of a family quarrel, whose origin, whatever it was, was not money.

"Unrequited love," said Hay, and observed with pleasure that his son-in-law had blushed. Hay had always suspected that Colonel Payne had been in love with brother-in-law Whitney, and as a love so sulphurous in its possibilities could never manifest itself, Oliver Payne had allowed it to turn so violently to hate that at least the same quantity of violent emotion might be used up in the process.

Caroline stood over the commode in her bathroom; and vomited. She felt as if she might turn herself inside out, so powerful were the spasms and of such long duration. She would not, she decided, ever commit suicide by poisoning. Then the spasms ceased, and she washed her face in cologne, noting how red and swollen her eyes had become.

Suddenly, Marguerite was at her side. "What's wrong? What's wrong?"

"Dear Marguerite, you, of all people, how can you ask me that?" Caroline put down the linen towel. "I'm pregnant," she said. "In my fifth month." Then, before Marguerite could cry out, Caroline placed her hand firmly over the old woman's mouth. "*Maintenant le silence*," Caroline whispered.

Blaise, in a bathrobe, entered Jim's room, which adjoined his own. The bathroom door was open and his tennis partner stood, eyes shut, beneath the shower. When it came to plumbing, Mrs. Delacroix did not share the prejudice of so many old Newporters, who believed that hot water was not really luxurious unless humanly transported in metal cans up many steps from cellar kitchen. Every bedroom of her Grand Trianon had its own bath with huge copper fixtures kept perfectly polished. Blaise stared, thoughtfully, at his tennis partner; and wished that he himself were as tall and well-proportioned. Where his own legs were short and muscular, Jim's were long and slender, like the rest of him; he had a classical body in every sense, heroic even, suitable for showing off in a museum, once a suitably large leaf had been found.

Jim opened his eyes, and saw Blaise, and smiled, without self-consciousness. "We can't buy a shower anything like this in Washington," he said. "Kitty's looked and looked."

"I think you have to have them specially made." Blaise turned away, as Jim shut off the shower, and picked up a towel. "How did you like Brisbane?"

While Hearst was abroad with his new wife, Arthur Brisbane was in charge not only of the newspapers but of Hearst's political career. Hearst had wanted to know James Burden Day, who had wanted to know Hearst. As Democratic members of Congress, each could be useful to the other. Unfortunately, Day could only be in New York when Hearst was abroad. But Blaise had arranged a meeting with Brisbane, followed by an invitation to join Blaise at

Newport, which Day had accepted without his wife. Caroline seemed glad to have the young congressman as a guest, and Blaise was now able to observe his half-sister in a new light as she and Day talked politics like two professionals. Certainly, she made more sense than Hearst, her model, she liked to claim, knowing how much it annoyed Blaise.

Jim dressed himself quickly, from long habit, he said. "I rush from boardinghouse to picnic ground to depot, no time to dress, think, do anything except politics."

"I couldn't imagine that sort of a life."

"I couldn't—*can't* imagine being rich, like this." Jim looked around the bedroom, all, more or less, in the style of the original Grand Trianon.

"It's sort of like being born with six fingers instead of five. You don't pay attention to it, but others do. So, what was your impression of Brisbane?"

Jim was now combing out his wet curls, and wincing with pain as the comb's teeth struck snarl after snarl. "He doesn't know as much about politics as he thinks he does. At least not our kind, in the West and the South. He thinks Bryan's some sort of fool . . ."

"*Isn't* he?"

Jim laughed. "I reckon you think all of us Westerners are yokels, which we are when you coop us up in a place like this, but we know a thing or two about the country that people with six fingers to the hand don't know."

Then Blaise laughed; and could not resist saying, "If you know so much, why do we keep beating you in these elections?"

"Money. Give me what Mark Hanna gave McKinley and gives Roosevelt, and I'll be president, too."

"You'd like that?"

The boyish head was turned toward a gilded mirror but the mirror reflected both their heads. Jim looked at Blaise through the glass. "Oh, yes, why not? It's there, after all."

"But you need six fingers?"

"I need *friends* with six fingers." Jim sat on the foot of the bed and tied his shoelaces. "Except when there's trouble, the money power isn't really everything. There's a lot of labor out there, and the farmers, and all the new people coming in from Europe. We'll get most of them. That's why Hearst interests me. He's set up all these Democratic clubs, which is the best way of enrolling them, but I'm afraid he's so busy trying to use the clubs to get the nomination for himself that they aren't much use to us, to the party, that is . . . so far."

"Do you think he has a chance?"

Jim shook his head. "He's too rich for us Democrats. He'd be better off with you people. But those papers of his have done him in with all the respectables. You know, I'd like to let Bryan try again, but . . ."

"He'd lose."

Jim nodded, somewhat forlornly. "They've turned him into a sort of national fool, the papers. They always do that when somebody comes along who wants to help the working-man."

Blaise could never tell with any politician where truth ends and expedient cant begins. Did this handsome, god-like youth, admittedly a rustic god, more Pan than Apollo, really give a damn about the working-man or the price of cotton or the tariff? Or were these the noises that he was obliged to make, like a bird's mating call, to gain himself what he wanted in the world? Blaise did not pursue the question. Instead, he reminded Jim that Hearst had helped to invent the populist if not popular Bryan. "So they, the six-fingered owners of the country, haven't totally distorted him. He has his rich admirers, too."

"Yes, that's been lucky for us. Hearst has done us some good, no doubt of that—and no matter why." Jim stood up; and Blaise realized that he himself was not dressed. Blaise walked toward the open door to his own bedroom. "We're having lunch on Payne's ocean-liner," he said. He paused at the door. "Did Brisbane say that you would go far in politics?"

Jim laughed. "Yes, he did. And he told me why."

"Because you have blue eyes."

"Exactly. Is Hearst just as crazy?"

"Crazier in a way."

"We must," said Jim, as he left the room to rejoin the house party, "keep an eye on him."

"A cold blue eye."

"On those six fingers, particularly."

Despite Marguerite's pleas, Caroline joined the yachting party. "I must seem absolutely all right," she said, "until . . ."

"Until . . . what?"

"I do what I have to do." This sentence released a torrent of mercifully silent tears. Actually, Caroline had no plan for the coming catastrophe. She must be cool, she told herself; do nothing rash; tell no one, certainly.

The father of her child-to-be looked very handsome, as he lounged on the after-deck of the yacht, the unlovely bulk of Block Island just back of him. The other guests were in the main salon, waiting for lunch to be announced. Although Caroline had been careful to avoid Jim, she had not been able to resist fresh air. She who had never in her life fainted now feared just that. The sensations inside her body were ominous, to say the least; and anything could happen.

"I probably shouldn't have come," Jim smiled. "But Blaise insisted, and I'm in his debt—for Mr. Hearst, or Mr. Brisbane, I suppose."

"I'm glad you're here." Caroline managed to animate her voice. "Of course," she added.

"I'd no idea people really lived like this."

"Does it tempt you?"

"No. What I do is more interesting. I'm never bored, while these folks . . ."

"Give dinner parties for their dogs."

"I just met Mr. Lehr." Jim grimaced.

"I will not protect you . . ."

"That poor girl he's married to . . ."

"You saw that?"

"We're not all that simple back home."

"I never thought you were." Caroline was pleased that, thanks to the shock of her situation, she felt no desire at all for Jim. He, on the other hand, was radiating sexual energy like one of Henry Adams's dynamos. She would have to discourage him, she decided, not quite certain what the etiquette of a pregnancy at this point required, or allowed. The doctor that she had visited, anonymously, in Baltimore, had been so interested in his fee for the planned abortion that she had not gone back to him. Instead, she had waited; she did not know for what.

"You'll be going back to American City now . . . ?"

Jim nodded. As the mouth still had its appeal for her, she gazed upon Block Island instead. "On Monday. Kitty's pregnant."

"Oh, no!" Caroline's astonishment was so genuine that she feared that she had given herself away.

But Jim simply grinned. "Well, that's what you get married for, you know."

"I don't—know." Caroline saw a good deal of gallows humor in the situation. "I can imagine, naturally." She was her usual self now. "Is she ill? I mean does she have—spells of sickness?"

Jim nodded, without much interest. "There's always a bit of feeling bad, I guess."

"When will it . . . the child, that is, be born?"

"October, the doctor thinks."

The same month that Caroline's would be due. He had gone from one bed to the other, perhaps even on the same day, like a rooster. For the first time, she realized just how dangerous the male was. The superior physical strength was bad enough, but the ability to start new life, with a single inadvertent thrust, was truly terrifying. Mlle. Souvestre had been right. Better the Sapphic life, the "white marriages" between ladies, than this sweaty black magic.

Blaise appeared in the doorway. "Lunch is ready." For once, Caroline was grateful for his interruption.

"I have no appetite," she said, accurately, and entered the ship's

441

salon just as a gong sounded from the dining room. Harry Lehr took her arm, as if for a cotillion.

"I had no idea our congressmen were so attractive." For a guilty instant, Caroline wondered if Harry Lehr knew. But, of course, he could not know, and her heart beat less rapidly. She wondered if she was going to become entirely furtive in character, thus giving away her game to everyone.

"You mean Mr. Day?" Caroline smiled at Mamie Fish, who nodded in a queenly way. "He's Blaise's friend."

"They're an attractive couple, aren't they?" Lehr laughed, musically. Caroline joined in; she had, suddenly, a plan.

– 2 –

At exactly noon, Caroline entered the Waldorf-Astoria's Peacock Alley, now largely deserted. Fashionable New York could not be found within a hundred miles of the city, while working New York was largely shut down. The emptiness and stillness of the great rooms was somewhat alarming. Paris must have been like this, she thought, when Bismarck was at the gates.

Beneath a potted palm sat John Apgar Sanford, somewhat balder, somewhat grayer than the year before when they had last met in Washington, and he had reported his usual failure to budge Mr. Houghteling. Since she would inherit soon, no matter what, they had given up the case. "You didn't say in your telegram what you wanted to see me about, but I assumed it would be the case, so I've brought the key documents." He held up a leather case.

"That's all right," she said, and seated herself opposite him. "It's not about the case, actually." She had rehearsed a number of openings but none was right. She would, she had decided, depend on inspiration; but now that she was with him, there was none, only a mild panic.

John asked about various Washington Apgars. Caroline began with a wrong move. "One has even been elected to Congress.

442

James Burden Day. I think his mother was an . . ."

"Grandmother, I believe," John nodded, "was an Apgar. I've met her."

"The wife is charming." Then Caroline abandoned this most dangerous of subjects. "You must find . . ." She could not finish this sentence.

But John took in stride the sentiment. "Yes, it is quite lonely for me. In spite of a plentitude of Apgars, I have no family life now, none at all."

"We Sanfords are also few."

"Very few indeed. Blaise . . ." John did not finish.

Caroline did not begin. That subject was abandoned, stillborn. "I have been thinking," she said at last, in lieu of inspiration, "about getting married."

"I suppose that is natural, of course." John seemed unsurprised; also, uninterested.

"Soon, there will be the inheritance." She played her great card at once.

"Yes. You will be very well-off indeed. From what I gather, Blaise did not—do as we feared. There are still certain loans to Mr. Hearst outstanding, but Mr. Hearst is good for them. Otherwise, the inheritance is intact. I hope," John smiled wanly, "you are not being married for your fortune . . ."

"Like one of Mr. James's poor ladies? No, I don't think that enters my . . . calculation, so far. Is patent law so difficult?"

John looked surprised. "It is not difficult, no. But it is not easy to make a living at it. I've changed firms, as you know. But my wife's long illness . . ." The voice trailed into embarrassed silence.

"Things have not been easy for you, John. I know that. I'm sorry. Truly," she added, pleased by her own display of warmth. She quite liked him; she also liked very much her liking him. "You once did me the," Caroline stared up at the palm tree, half expecting to see if not a monkey a coconut ready to fall, "honor of proposing to marry me."

"Oh, I do apologize," John stammered; turned pale. "It was after . . . after . . ."

443

"She had died. I wished that I had known her. She was a . . ."

". . . a saint," John filled in.

"Exactly the word that I was going to use. I have now thought over your proposal—somewhat slowly, I must admit. It's been—what? Four years at least. And I accept." It was done.

Caroline decided that John's look of astonishment was not the greatest tribute ever paid her. Had she, somehow, imperceptibly, aged? Or was he otherwise engaged? Certainly, she knew nothing of his life. For all she knew, he might have a full-time and exigent mistress, perhaps a Negress, living in Flushing like Clarence King's secret wife. "But . . . but, Caroline . . ."

"You cannot say that this is so sudden, John." Caroline was beginning, almost, to enjoy herself.

"No. No. Only I never dreamed . . . I mean . . . why me?"

"Because you asked me. Remember?"

"But surely others have . . ."

"Only Del Hay, and he is dead. You and I, we are both—survivors."

"I can't think what to say." John looked as if a coconut had indeed fallen from the trees, and struck him a sharp blow.

"You can say yes, dear John. Or you can say no. I can accept either. But I can't accept indecision. You must not think it over in your deliberate legalistic way. I want the answer now, one way or the other."

"Well, yes. Yes. Of course. But . . ."

"What is the but?"

"I have lost everything. We were—my family, that is—wiped out two years ago, when the Monongahela Combine failed, and then her illness . . ."

"I have," said Caroline softly, "enough for two. Or I will have soon enough."

"But it's not right that the wife support the husband . . ."

"Of course it's right. It is done all the time, even in Newport, Rhode Island," she added for dramatic emphasis.

"I don't know what to think."

She was relieved that there was no sexual aura to John. He was more like a brother to her, a conventional *American* brother, she felt obliged to note in her deposition to the high tribunal of her conscience which was now sitting in judgment on her. Blaise, though only half a brother, was possessed of the same sort of dynamo that she had responded to in Jim. But John Apgar Sanford was like Adelbert Hay; he was comfortably, undisturbingly present; and no more.

"I shall be able to help you financially," she said, abandoning any attempt at coquetry, which even if it were her style was irrelevant to the current proceeding.

"That would be mortifying." John was acutely uncomfortable.

"'A fair exchange is no robbery,' as the French say." Caroline gazed at the palm fronds overhead. "So I shall explain exactly what is to be exchanged for what. I know that you are, of all the family here, the most worldly, the most experienced." Caroline saw fit to lay it on rather heavily, as she was by no means certain what his response was going to be. "You handled Blaise superbly, and I am, of course, grateful." The fact that John had done nothing at all for her was beside the point, as she methodically set him up for man-of-the-worlddom.

"I did what I could. . . . He's difficult, yes." John was at sea.

Caroline threw out her net. "In marrying me, you will not only get the support that you need in your . . . our, endeavors but you will be able to provide me with a father for my child." Caroline gazed at him, with what she hoped were luminous, madonna-like eyes.

John had gone pale. John had misunderstood. "Naturally, in marrying, the thought of a family is all-important to me, to carry on the name . . ."

"*Our* name," Caroline murmured, wondering how to explain herself.

"Our name, yes. We are both Sanfords. So your monogram won't change, will it?" He laughed without mirth. "I always regretted not having children with my wife, my first wife, but her illness . . ." The voice again trailed off.

"I think, John, I have not expressed myself with that clarity which you, as a lawyer, so rightly pride yourself in." Caroline now felt rather like one of Henry James's older European ladies, ready to launch some terrible bit of information at a dim-witted American ingénu. "I was not speaking of a future hypothetical fatherhood for you, but of an imminent motherhood for me . . . in October to be precise, which is why I am eager to be married this week, at City Hall, where I have already made inquiries."

John gasped, but at least he had understood. "You . . ." But he exhausted all his breath in startled exhalation.

As John inhaled, Caroline said, "Yes, I am pregnant. I cannot tell you who the father is, as he is a married man. But I can tell you that he was my first—and only—lover. I feel like that chaste king of Spain who . . ." But caution stopped her from repeating Mlle. Souvestre's favorite story about how the ascetic King Philip had finally gone to bed with a woman and promptly contracted syphilis. John might not be ready for this story.

"He—the father is in Spain?" John was doing his best to grasp the situation.

"No, he is in America. He is an American. He has visited Spain," she improvised, hoping to erase King Philip from the court—courtship?—record.

"I see." John stared at his shoes.

"I realize that I am asking for a very great deal, which is why I said at the very beginning that there would be an exchange between us, useful to each." Caroline wondered what she would do in John's place. She would, probably, have laughed, and said no. But she was not in John's place, and she could not measure either his liking for her person or his need for her fortune. These two imponderables would determine the business.

"Will you continue to see him?" John came swiftly to the necessary, for him, point.

"No." Caroline lied so seldom that she found it quite easy to do. Would she now become addicted to lying, and turn into another Mrs. Bingham?

"What will you do about the newspaper?"

"I shall go on with it. Unless *you* would like to be the publisher."

This was definitely Mrs. Binghamish: Caroline had no intention of ever losing control of the *Tribune*.

"No. No. I am a lawyer, after all, not a publisher. I must say, I have never come across a . . . a case like this." He looked at her, worriedly; a lawyer mystified by a client.

"I thought that pregnant ladies were always getting married in the nick of time."

"Yes. But to the man who . . . who . . ."

"Made them pregnant. Well, that is not possible for me."

"You are in love with him." John was bleak.

"Don't worry, John. I shall be as good a wife as I can, given my disposition, which is not very wifely, in the American way, that is."

"I suppose you will want to look at my books . . ."

"You are a collector?"

"My *financial* books . . ."

"I am not an auditor. You have debts. I'll pay what I can now. When I inherit, I'll pay the rest. I assume," Caroline suddenly wondered if she ought not to bring in an auditor; she laughed uneasily, "I assume that your debts are not larger than my income."

"Oh, much less. Much less. This is embarrassing for both of us."

"In France our relatives would be holding this discussion, but we're not in France, and I can't imagine Blaise handling any of this for me." When Caroline rose from her chair, John sprang to his feet: yes, he was hers, she decided. So far so good. Now all that needed to be worked out was the marital bed. She had no intention of sleeping with John, and it was plain that he had every intention of claiming his conjugal rights. For the moment she was safe: her family history of difficult, even fatal, pregnancies could be invoked to keep him at a distance. Later, she would, she was certain, think of something.

Caroline took John's arm, as a wife takes a husband's. "Dear John," she said, as they made their way down the deserted Peacock Alley, the only sound that of the revolving overhead fans.

"It's like a dream," said John.

"*Exactly* what I was thinking," said Caroline, who had never felt more awake.

– 3 –

John Hay could still not believe the change in the White House. The entire upstairs was now home to the Roosevelts and their six children, who seemed, to Hay, more like twelve. The entrance hall which had been so long graced by President Arthur's Tiffany screen was now an impressive eighteenth-century foyer to a sort of Anglo-Irish country house whose drawing rooms, *en suite*, were now directly accessible to the hall, where the old pols' wooden staircase had been replaced by a marble affair down which the presidents could descend in glory. The west staircase had been removed in order to enlarge the state dining room, whose new fireplace had been inscribed with the pious Rooseveltian hope that only men as noble as he would ever preside in this republican palace.

Then, as ushers opened doors, Hay entered the new west wing, where the executive offices were comfortably quartered. The President's architects had nicely duplicated the oval of the Blue Room for his office, which looked south toward the Potomac. The Cabinet had its own room at last, with the office of the President's secretary separating it from the sovereign's oval.

Theodore was standing in front of his desk throwing a medicine ball at the tiny German ambassador, a particular friend, and the source of remarkable trouble for Hay because Cassini was now convinced that Theodore and the Kaiser were in secret league against the Tsar. Hay was required, at least once a week, to soothe the Russian. The new French ambassador, Jusserand, was more worldly and less excitable than his predecessor, while Sir Michael Herbert, Pauncefote's successor, was himself like a member of the President's own family, and rode each day with Theodore through

Rock Creek Park, and joined him in loud, clumsy games of tennis where the President's ferocity and near-blindness made for every sort of exciting danger.

Hay bowed to President and Ambassador. "If I am interrupting," he began.

"No. No, John." Theodore heaved the medicine ball at von Sternberg, who caught it easily. "That was splendid, Speck!" Hay was always amused at how like his numerous imitators the President could sound, except for the clicking of the teeth, which no one had ever quite duplicated.

The Ambassador said good-morning to Hay and left the room, carrying the medicine ball with him.

Roosevelt mopped his face with a handkerchief. "The Kaiser affects indifference." He was very unlike his imitators when he was at work; and there was now a great deal to be done. "You have the telegram?"

Hay gave him the draft which he and Adee had just completed. Four days earlier, a junta had declared Panama independent of Colombia. The arrival, the previous day, November 2, 1903, of the USS *Nashville*, *Boston* and *Dixie* had inhibited the Colombians, who might, otherwise, have put down the insurrection. The presence of the American Navy had been necessary, according to the President, because American citizens might have come to harm during the course of a revolution, which had not, as of November 2, taken place. Neither Roosevelt nor Hay had been particularly pleased with their somewhat hollow explanation, but the thing had turned out marvellously well. The revolution, which had started November 3, ended on the fourth, when the Republic of Panama was proclaimed, and now, on the sixth, the United States was preparing to recognize this splendid addition to the concert of nations, freed at last from Colombian bondage.

"'The people of Panama,'" read the President, in a grave voice, "'have, by an apparently unanimous movement,' I like that, John, 'dissolved their political connection with the Republic of Colombia . . .' Very like Jefferson, that."

"You flatter me."

"It's better than these jackrabbits deserve." Roosevelt read the rest of the telegram quickly; then gave it back to Hay. "Send it."

"I'm also drawing up a treaty for the canal, which we should get signed before the end of the month. Then, if Cabot allows the Senate to ratify . . ."

"Cabot will call for a voice vote, and his own voice will be the loudest." Roosevelt was plainly delighted. "There were casualties, after all," he said. "Root just sent over a message. One dog was killed, and one Chinaman." With a laugh, the President settled into his chair. Hay also sat, not with a laugh but a groan.

"The terms for Panama will not be the best, of course . . ." Hay wondered how much pain the body could take before death provided anesthesia.

"They are independent, aren't they? Well, *we* made that possible. So we deserve something, I'd say."

"I'm thinking of next year."

Roosevelt nodded; and frowned, as he always did when he contemplated his reelection or, to be precise, his first election to the presidency. "Well, the anti-imperialists can't really fault us. We must have a canal, and it has to be somewhere along the isthmus."

"But it could have been in Nicaragua, with no fuss, no fleet, no dead dog or Chinaman; no hint, shall we say, of collusion, between us and the Panamanian junta."

"Of course there was collusion." Roosevelt pounded left fist into right hand. "We are for free people everywhere, and against foolish and homicidal corruptionists of the sort that govern Colombia . . ."

". . . and now Panama."

"You have never favored the canal, have you?"

Hay often forgot that under all the noise, the President was both shrewd and watchful. "I've always thought," said Hay, "that the railroads could do the job quite as well as a canal, which will be difficult and expensive not only to build but troublesome—in the future, anyway—politically. Yes," Hay added before the President could taunt him, "I'm a large investor in the railroads, but that's not to the point."

Idly, Roosevelt spun the globe of the world beside his desk. "The point, John, is that we have done something useful for our country. Our fleets can go back and forth, quickly, between Atlantic and Pacific."

"You see a future so filled with war?" Hay wished, suddenly, that he had not allowed the President to talk him out of the July resignation.

"Yes, I do." The high harsh voice was suddenly low and almost, for its owner, mellifluous. "I also see our own mission, which is to lead where once England led, but on a world scale . . ."

"All the world?"

"It could come to that. But so much depends on the sort of people we are, and continue to be." He grimaced. "There is a weakness running through our people, a love of ease, a lack of courage . . ."

"You must continue your demonstrations, and inspire us."

"That is exactly what I try to do." Roosevelt was entirely serious. Hay thought of Henry Adams's phrase, "the Dutch-American Napoleon." Well, why not? How else is an empire to begin?

"And now, Mr. President, I shall provide the legal underpinnings to our latest acquisition."

"The Attorney General has assured me that we must not let so great an achievement suffer from any taint of legality." Roosevelt's laughter was like that of a frenzied watchdog.

As Hay rose, the room appeared to be full of dark green smoke, through which small golden stars shone. For a moment, he thought that he was about to faint. But Theodore was now suddenly at his side, holding him up.

"Are you all right?"

"Yes. Yes." The room was itself again. "I'm often faint when I get up too quickly. But the odd thing was—I thought I was in Mr. Lincoln's office. You know, with its dark green walls, and the gold stars, one for every state, we used to say, that was trying to get away."

Roosevelt walked Hay to the door, his thick arm firmly through the older man's. "I see him sometimes."

"The President?"

Roosevelt opened the door to his secretary's office. "Yes. That is, *imagine* him vividly. It's usually at night in the corridor, upstairs, at the far end . . ."

"The east end." Hay nodded. "There was a water-cooler in the hall, outside his office. He would drink cup after cup of water."

"I'll look for that next time I see him. He is always sad."

"There was a good deal to be sad about."

"My problems are so slight compared to his. Curious, to measure oneself with him. I don't think I'm immodest when I say I'm very much superior to most of the politicians of our time. But when I think of what greatness *he* had . . ." Roosevelt sighed, a most un-Rooseveltian sound. "You must get some rest, John."

Hay nodded. "Once the treaty's done. I'm going south."

"Bully!" Roosevelt was again his own best imitation.

– 4 –

The great hollow sound of metal striking the thick bole of a magnolia tree brought Caroline and Marguerite to the window of the Georgetown house. A motor car had, somehow, got from N Street onto the sidewalk and into the largest of Caroline's two magnolias. At the wheel was Alice Roosevelt, a feathered hat now jammed over her implacable blue eyes, while at her side Marguerite Cassini, looking both beautiful and terrified, waved her hands in front of her, in a gesture which Caroline took to be, literally, the wringing of hands, something that only her own histrionic Marguerite ever did.

Caroline hurried into the street, where an elderly Negro man was working hard to open the door on Alice's side of the car; it had jammed.

"The brakes!" Alice was accusing. "They don't work. It's your chauffeur's fault."

"It's *my* fault, when Father finds out." Marguerite got out of the car. Caroline helped the Negro to free the Republican Princess, who then shoved her hat back in place; leapt to the ground; thanked the Negro, and said, "Tell the police to take this bit of junk back to the Russian embassy, in Scott Circle. It is the ugliest house there. They can't miss it."

"My father—" Marguerite began.

"Your father? *My* father. That's the problem. He wouldn't let me buy a car, you know." Alice led Caroline into her own house, while Marguerite Cassini gave the Negro elaborate instructions. "I can't fathom him. There are times when he seems to be living in another century. I had picked out this splendid roadster. Too killing. And he said, no. Never. Women are not to drive, or smoke, or vote. I agree on the vote, of course. It will just double the same old vote. Even so . . . What's it like, being married?"

They were now in the back parlor, overlooking the small garden where, because of the season, only late ominous chrysanthemums grew. The trees had lost their leaves; and in the small goldfish pond, a large goldfish had bellied up, a victim to overeating.

"Serene. The same, actually. John's mostly in New York with his law firm. I'm mostly here with the paper; and the child."

The two-month-old Emma Apgar Sanford was less noisy than Caroline had anticipated, and though not yet the best of company, she was a benign presence in the house, and Caroline, against Marguerite's advice—no longer heeded, ever—breast-fed her daughter, and noted with awed wonder how large her gravid breasts had become. She was, for the first time in her life, *à la mode* in the grand fleshy world.

Marguerite Cassini now made her hardly climactic entrance. Caroline admired her beauty; but nothing more. The shadow of Del seemed, mysteriously, attached to her. Caroline had heard it said that the opal ring that had broken in half on the New Haven pavement had been a gift from Countess Cassini. Plainly, fiction's war with truth was never-ending. Marguerite went straight toward the open box of chocolates from Huyler's, the city's principal confectioner. Each Washington house ordered its own mixture, and Caroline had introduced white chocolate to Washington, a novelty still controversial in those circles where the *Tribune*'s Society Lady so hungrily moved. "You shouldn't eat chocolate. You'll get fat," Alice announced. "I never eat dessert. Just meat and potatoes, like Father."

"Perhaps you'll be as stout as he is," said Marguerite, looking suddenly Mongol—or was it Tartar?—or were they the same? The friendship between La Cassini and Alice was the talk of the town, and by no means confined to the Society Lady's circles. In the current troubles between Russia and Japan, President Roosevelt tended to take the Japanese side, to the fury of Cassini, who had roared in Caroline's presence, "The man's a pagan! We are a Christian nation like the United States, and he sides with yellow savage pagans." At the White House, Russian greed was sadly deplored. The Administration was ready to acquiesce in Japan's proposal that Russia might annex Manchuria if Japan could be allowed to take over Korea as well. The *Tribune* tried to be even-handed but tended, thanks to Mr. Trimble, to favor Russia, to the President's fury. At the center of the new Cabinet room, he had made Caroline a long speech on the tides of history while a portrait of Abraham Lincoln looked wearily away from the seated woman, the marching President. Lately, Cassini tended to kiss rather too warmly Caroline's hand at receptions, and Marguerite had thanked her for her editorial support. "It's so difficult for me," she had sighed, "now that I am *doyenne* of the diplomatic corps." With Pauncefote's death, Cassini had become the senior chief of mission at the capital. As his hostess, Marguerite sailed first into every official gathering; meanwhile, the President's daughter defied her father and made Marguerite her friend, all because, as only Caroline knew, the President had refused to allow Alice to own a red automobile, and so Alice had commandeered the Russian Ambassador's machine. The previous summer Alice and Marguerite, like Arctic explorers, had driven together to Newport, to the fearful applause of the public, to the horror of pedestrians run down, of motorists forced off the road. After today's collision, Caroline was fairly certain that the relationship between Alice and Marguerite was about to undergo a sea-change. Cassini would deny them the use of his car; and Japan would triumph over Russia. *The causal links*, as Brooks Adams liked to say.

"What am I wearing tomorrow at the British embassy?" asked Alice, opening her handbag, removing a cigarette case and, as expertly as any clubman, lighting up. Caroline still experienced mild shock whenever she saw this; and had said so. "But," Alice had assured her, "everyone will be doing it now that I do."

"But you don't do it beneath your father's roof."

"I do it *out* the window, a technicality he has come to respect. So what am I wearing?"

"The dark blue velvet, with lace at the throat . . ." Caroline began.

"I *won't* lend you my sable again." Marguerite was squashing the chocolates with her fingers; she liked only soft centers.

Both Mrs. Roosevelt and Alice liked to invent elaborate costumes, which they did not possess, and then give the White House press secretary descriptions of these fabulous creations, which would be written of, ecstatically, in every "Society Lady" page. As it was, neither lady could afford much of anything to wear, though, of the two, Alice was somewhat richer. When Caroline had caught on to the White House game, Alice had asked her to help invent costumes, which Caroline would describe in the *Tribune*, to the amazement of those who had actually seen what the Roosevelt ladies had been wearing.

The maid-of-all-work appeared with tea. Caroline had planned to move to larger quarters and hire what the Apgars would call a proper staff, but John's liabilities had used up her own income for the year; fortunately, the newspaper had begun, shyly, to flourish, and she could live, comfortably, as a Mrs. Sanford in Georgetown instead of *the* Mrs. Sanford, which she would not be until March 5, 1905, some fifteen months in the future. Worse, she suspected that John had even greater debts than he had admitted to. Even worse, she suspected that Blaise knew just how insolvent her unexpected bridegroom was, because he had only recently suggested that she sell him the *Tribune*, if she were so minded. She was not so minded, she said, and continued to watch, as did all Washington, his palace take shape on Connecticut Avenue, rivalling in its ornate marble splendor those Dupont Circle palaces where reigned the Leiters and now the Pattersons, whose daughter Eleanor, known as Cissy, a restless nineteen-year-old, entered on the arm of the most elegant member of the House of Representatives, one Nicholas Longworth of Ohio, a dapper figure in his early thirties, most glitteringly bald. One day it was rumored that he was supposed to marry Marguerite Cassini; the next, Alice Roosevelt; the day after, no one at all, for "he is," his mother had confided to the press, "a born bachelor."

Caroline poured tea; made conversation, not that much of that ever had to be made in a room containing Alice, who never stopped talking, particularly when inspired to shock, and Longworth seemed her particular butt of the moment. While Marguerite Cassini glowed, in her Tartar way, and Alice spoke rudely of the House of Representatives, Cissy Patterson told Caroline her problems. Cissy's face was that of a dull red-haired Pekinese, with a small pink nose; eyes, too, for she had been weeping. "Yes, I've been crying on Nick's shoulder," she murmured to Caroline.

"The Pole?"

"The Pole. I can't believe Mother is doing this to me."

"But he is handsome . . ."

"I don't think I care for men," said Cissy, staring at Caroline in a way that made that new mother—new woman, too—somewhat uneasy; the gaze was too like Mlle. Souvestre's.

"Oh, you'll get used to them. They are too large, of course, for most uses." Caroline thought fondly of Jim, who visited her every Sunday, after his ride along the canal. He smelled, always, of horse. In fact, she now so connected sex with horses that she had suggested that perhaps he send her the horse on a Sunday, and himself go home to Kitty. He had been shocked.

"It's not that. At least, I don't think it is. Of course, I'm a virgin."

"Of course," said Caroline. "We all were once. Such happy carefree days."

"I don't know about happy. But Joseph is deeply impressed by my virginity. Apparently, there are no virgins in Europe."

"Very few, certainly." Caroline was eager to be agreeable. Cissy's uncle was Robert McCormick, whose wife's family published the Chicago *Tribune*, and he was eager to buy Caroline's *Tribune*. Cissy's brother, Joe Patterson, was a reporter for her uncle's paper; and so, like a law of nature, Pattersons had begun to gravitate toward Sanfords, printer's ink, in its way, as binding as blood. Cissy had literary dreams; she would write novels, she said; and promptly picked up Mr. James's latest effort, *The Ambassadors*, inscribed to Henry Adams, who had recommended it to Caroline, who had given up reading fiction now that she herself, a newspaper publisher, was a principal purveyor of that evanescent product.

"He's too long-winded now." Cissy had learned to say what everyone else said, a moment or two before perfect staleness made dust of the conventional wisdom. As a result, she was thought clever. "He's getting a million," she whispered into Caroline's ear, while biting off, one by one, the points of one of Huyler's very special thin chocolate leaves.

"Count Gizycki?"

Cissy nodded, tragically; mouth full of chocolate.

"That's fair, I suppose." Caroline was judicious. "In Europe, the bride brings the money while the husband provides the title, the name and the castle. There is a castle?"

"In *Poland*." Cissy sighed. "He doesn't love me, you know."

"Then why marry him?"

"Mother wants me to be a countess. Father will pay, of course. But it's very un-American, buying a husband."

"It may be un-American but Americans do it all the time. Look at Harry Lehr and the poor Drexel girl. Or read your uncle's paper, or mine, or—if you're really innocent—any of Mr. Hearst's. It's common."

"Common!" Cissy looked as if she might burst into tears. "I

wish," she said unexpectedly, "I had your mouth."

"I'll give it to you, on your wedding day—in the form of a kiss," added Caroline, uneasily aware that she was now the recipient of a "crush."

Marguerite Cassini joined them, leaving, unwisely, thought Caroline, Nick Longworth to the predatory Alice, who had her father's need to be always the center of attention. *She* was capable of marrying anyone, if she thought that that was the only way of gaining everyone's complete attention. Of the republican dollar princesses, Alice was the most interesting, and the most doomed, Caroline decided, to unhappiness. It was all very well to be the most famous girl in the United States, but then, more soon than late, all-powerful presidents turned into obscure ex-presidents, while glamorous girls became women, wives, mothers, forgotten. She could not imagine Alice old; it would be against nature. Meanwhile, the beautiful Cassini was consoling Cissy, with countessly wisdom. "The family is a great one—for Poland, of course. And his best friend is very close to us, Ivan von Rubido Zichy, who says Joseph is over the heels head in love with you!"

"These names sound," said Caroline, "like characters in *The Prisoner of Zenda.*"

"You are so literary," said Marguerite, disapprovingly. "You must get it from having to read all those newspapers."

"*My* White House marriage will be the first since poor Julia Grant married Prince Cantacuzene." Alice hurled herself at center stage.

"Nellie Grant, Julia's mother, was married in the White House." Longworth was languidly pedantic. "That was the last White House marriage. Julia was married in Newport . . ."

"And my father, representing the Tsar, had to give permission, which he wouldn't, of course, because Julia's aunt, Mrs. Potter Palmer, wouldn't come up with a dowry on the ground that Julia was pretty enough to be married for herself alone."

"*Hardly true,*" all three girls echoed as one.

"So Father said to Mrs. Potter, 'How much do you pay *your* cook?' Then he explained that a newly wed prince and princess must also have enough money to pay *their* cook. He was overwhelming. Of course, the Prince was rich in his own right . . ."

Caroline cut short Marguerite's tsarist vainglory. "Alice, you must tell us when your White House wedding will take place; and with whom . . ."

Alice was brisk. "In 1905, probably. After Father's reelected. I haven't picked anyone yet. Blaise is very rich, isn't he?"

"Very." Caroline had often thought what a good match it would be for him, not to mention the publisher of the *Tribune*. In or out of the White House, the Roosevelts would be colorful, if nothing else. "You'd also have that new palace of his to live in."

"Oh, I'd never live *here!* Too dull. Scenes of former glory sort of thing. I don't want to be a fixture. No, I could never live here. I want New York, Paris, London . . ."

"Oyster Bay is probably what you'll get," said Longworth. "And deserve."

"Better that than Cincinnati." Alice's eyelashes were, Caroline noticed, remarkably thick; she fell just short of actual beauty. Did she care?

Then Longworth proceeded to amuse them with an impression of Theodore Roosevelt, which made even his daughter laugh: and Alice was always alert to condemn *lèse-majesté*. But Nick, like the President, was a member of Harvard's Porcellian Club and so nearly an equal.

"I was in his office Monday, talking about some business in the House, and he was in a bad mood—for him, that is. So I was getting a bit uneasy because I'd promised this young Cincinnati reporter that I'd get him into the President's office for a minute or two, and he was waiting in the next room. Anyway, after we finished our business, I said, 'You know, Colonel, there's a young journalist who'd like to say hello . . .'" With that, Longworth began a rendition of Theodore Roosevelt—snarling, grimacing, charging about the room, fists punching wildly at the air. "'Never! Never, Nick! You presume too much! You are a fellow Pork, true. We are bound together by the ties that bind all gentlemen, but, no! Of course, I am the First Magistrate, and I am accessible, *in theory,* to every citizen. But if I saw them all, there would be no time left for me to magistrate . . .' '*First* magistrate,' I ventured. 'Execute,'" the voice was now an inhuman shriek, "'my office. What's his name?' I told him. 'Never heard of him. What's the newspaper?' I told him. 'Never heard of it!' I was desperate. 'His father, so-and-so, led the movement that denied General Grant a third term.' 'I don't believe it. Send him in.' Well, the young man entered, filled with awe, and the President practically embraced him. 'I am thrilled, young man, to make your acquaintance. Do you know why? Because your grandfather was one of the greatest men I have ever had the privilege to meet. How well I remember him arguing to the party's leaders—such eloquence!—which you've inherited, I can see, in the pages of your inspiring journal. Well, sir, on that occasion your grandfather was another Demosthenes, but unlike the original, *he* stopped the tyrant, and saved the republic from corruption of a sort that it makes me shudder, even now, to contemplate. Go thou, my boy, and do likewise!' With that the President shook the ecstatic boy's hand and got him out of the room, a convert to TR for life. Then he turned to me and hissed, 'Never do that to me again!' Then he winked."

As they all laughed, Alice said, thoughtfully, "Father has depths of insincerity not even he has plumbed."

"It is the nature," said Longworth, "of our politicians' art."

The ladies asked to see the baby, who was brought down to the drawing room, a solemn wide-eyed child. Cissy promptly burst into tears at the thought of marriage and babies and money and a title, and Caroline gave her a tumbler of brandy, which she drank in a single gulp, to everyone's amazement.

As the impromptu "at-home" broke up, Marguerite Cassini took Caroline aside to announce, "Nick has asked me to marry him. Tell nobody."

Except the public, thought Caroline, who asked, "Will you?"

Marguerite nodded.

"Come on, Maggie," Alice commanded. "Nick's taking us in his carriage. I hope that father of yours fixes those brakes. *We,*" she said dramatically, "could have been killed."

"Maybe," said Cissy, darkly, to no one, "it would be for the best."

"Do be still," said Princess Alice; and they were gone.

Glumly, Caroline sat at her desk and began, yet again, to study her husband's debts. Slowly, she was coming to the realization that if his creditors refused to wait, she might have to sell the *Tribune*. She did her best not to blame John. After all, she had married him, and not the other way round. Even so, men were supposed to know about business, and she felt, obscurely, cheated. The wages of sin, she thought; and laughed aloud: she was beginning to think like a newspaper. Nevertheless, where, she wondered, could money be found?

12

Blaise stared a moment at the door to the house in Lafayette Square, exactly opposite the White House. All in all, he decided, it was a tribute to the energy and colorfulness of Theodore Roosevelt that this less than splendid house, formerly rented by Elihu Root, was now occupied by Representative William Randolph Hearst. Plainly, it was Roosevelt's powerful magnetism that drew to sleepy backward Washington Hearst and himself, not to mention the likes of Elihu Root, now gone back to New York to practice law, his place as secretary of war more than amply filled by that human mastodon William Howard Taft, the President's most trusted adviser on the Philippines, where he had reigned in viceregal splendor during the . . . whatever it was: no one had yet come up with the right word for the violent resistance of so many Filipinos to Yankee rule. As of February 1, 1904, a week ago, Taft had become secretary of war, complaining bitterly to everyone that he would not be able to live on his salary; yet while every office-holder made the same complaint, everyone accepted office and, somehow, got by, thought Blaise, cynically.

The familiar corpulent George opened the door, just as if they were still in a real city instead of this curious Southern village. "Mr. Blaise, you're a sight for sore eyes." Over the years, George had come to regard Blaise as the Chief's young brother, or even son, a role Blaise had never once had any desire to play. But play-act both men must, the omnipotent Hearst, publisher now of eight papers (Boston had surrendered), and the wealthy Blaise, who had still to make his mark at anything, particularly since yesterday's disastrous fire had destroyed his Baltimore printing press. Although Hapgood had made arrangements with a new press, the *Examiner* would not appear for several weeks.

Hearst sat, enthroned, in the wood-panelled study, listening to a small and—to Blaise—perfectly appalling Georgian named Thomas E. Watson, who had served a term in the House, as member of the Farmers' Alliance; been vice-presidential candidate of the Populist Party; might now be the Populist candidate for president in 1904. Currently, Hearst was desperately wooing him to support the Democratic Party—and Hearst, who was weak in the Godly South, thanks to the aura of scandal about his name; yet, practically speaking, Hearst was the closest thing, politically, to a socialist or Populist among the national possibilities. Certainly, he appealed to Watson; but then Watson appealed to Watson even more.

Jim Day was seated on a sofa facing Hearst; he greeted Blaise with a smile; and continued to listen to the tiny fiery Watson, who stood at the room's center, declaiming. Blaise's entrance was made little of. Hearst waved him to a chair. Watson ignored him as a preacher would a late-comer to a revival meeting.

"I dedicated my book on Thomas Jefferson to you, Mr. Hearst, because I see you as Jefferson's heir, politically, that is."

"Lucky for me." Lately, Hearst had begun, tentatively, to tell jokes. "He didn't leave a cent when he died."

"That's to his eternal credit." Watson's blue eyes flashed, unamused. "I'm writing biographies of my—and your—heroes,

Jackson and Napoleon, and I'll dedicate them all to you if you continue to fight the good fight for the people, just as they did, against the trusts, the Jew bankers, the idolatrous papists, and all the rest of the foreign element that keeps down our people, the original people of this republic." There was more in this vein. Hearst listened patiently. At the Democratic Convention in July, Watson could swing the Southern delegates to Hearst, and the nomination; at election time, Watson was worth five million votes to the nominee. But would Watson himself be a Democrat in July? or would he be the candidate of the Populists? Blaise did not envy the Chief. From what Blaise could tell of the American people— glimpsed, admittedly somewhat askew, through their tribunes— they tended to sectarian madness. Religion ran like poison through their veins, followed—or mingled with—racism of a sort undreamed of in wicked old Europe. There was always a "they" at whom a pejorative verb could be launched automatically transitiv- ing "they" to the ominous all-evil "them" who must be destroyed so that Eden could be regained. Blaise would rather be a humble worker in his father's encaustic-tile plant at Lowell, Massachusetts, than president of so strenuously mad a country as the United States. He could not fathom it; did not want to; marvelled that Caroline had got the range of the place, and all without in any way becoming one of—yes, *them.*

Watson spoke for another half-hour; then, with a peroration on the absolute necessity, if the United States were ever to know greatness, of a rural free mail delivery service, he stopped. "Mr. Watson," Hearst rose; he towered over the tiny orator, "I have admired—even simulated you . . ."

"Emulated," Blaise murmured automatically to himself. The Chief was still having his problems with English. "Now I know we can do great things together this summer, fall, forever. But where I need you—really need you—is your working for me. No, that's wrong, I'd be working for you, for your ideas, if you'd only take over as editor of the *New York American.* You're a natural."

This was exceptionally well done, thought Blaise. The Chief was learning. Watson expressed gratitude for confidence placed; but did not, quite, take the bait. After more compliments exchanged, Watson left. Hearst sighed.

"Hard work," said Blaise.

"He's a wonderful orator," said Jim. "But if you're not a crowd, he's pretty tiring."

"What do you think, Jim?" Hearst turned to Day. Blaise was, suddenly, completely jealous. They were on a first-name basis, something rare for Hearst to be with anyone. Of course, Jim was Hearst's senior in the House of Representatives; even so, it had taken a year before Hearst had called Blaise by his first name.

"I think Colonel Bryan's going to try again, and I'll be with him, as always, and he'll fail to be nominated, so I guess you'll be the candidate—or Cleveland, if he's in a Lazarus mood."

"Cleveland's really dead." Hearst turned to Blaise. "You know, I got on the Labor Committee, over Williams's dead body." To Jim: "How do you get a bill passed in the House?"

"First," said Jim, "you get somebody to write it for you. Then . . . Well, Congress isn't at all like a newspaper."

"I figured that one out. But," Hearst pointed toward the White House, "*that* place is. Roosevelt's just like me, storming around, making news . . ." Hearst turned to Blaise. "Sorry about the fire. I guess you'll start up again, won't you?"

"Next week. There's a chance that Caroline might sell me the the *Tribune*." Caroline had been, even for her, unusually intricate on the subject. He knew that she needed money to pay John Apgar Sanford's debts. On the other hand, if she could hold out for a year, she would have her share of an estate that kept growing, despite the money he was pouring into his Connecticut Avenue Italianate palazzo. Blaise had put Houghteling to work, increasing the pressure on Sanford's edgy creditors. If a crisis could be provoked . . .

"I'd love to get my hands on that paper." Hearst was wistful. "She's made a go of it. Amazing. A woman."

"Galling! My own sister."

"She even understands politics." Jim made his contribution.

"Kitty really likes her," he added. "Kitty's the politician in our family," he added to his addition.

"I want to investigate the coal-railroad monopoly," Hearst announced, more or less at Jim. "I've spent sixty thousand dollars of my own money, investigating how six railroads own eleven coal mines, secretly, and get this cheap coal, and then water their stock and sell it to the public, and the Attorney General, and that noisy fraud across the road, know all about it and they won't do a thing."

Blaise rather liked Hearst's editorial approach to politics. He rooted about for scandal; found it; publicized it. But now instead of just selling newspapers, Hearst might be able, with a scandal of this nature, to destroy the Administration. That was direct power.

"You take this one to the House Judiciary Committee. I'll show you how to go about it. But I don't think you'll be able to smoke out the Attorney General."

"Wait and see. You know, if I'm nominated, I'm going to give the Democratic National Committee one and a half million dollars for the campaign."

Jim whistled; then smiled. "Why *after* you're nominated? Spread it around before and you will be nominated." Hearst let that one go; he continued, "The idea is, the party, to raise money, won't have to go to the railroads, to the trusts, the way they do when the candidate's a conservative, with his hand out . . ."

"And only five fingers." Jim smiled at Blaise, who realized that he had never had a man-friend before, except the son of his now-retired mistress.

"What?" Hearst was baffled.

"A joke. Of ours." Blaise was delighted by Jim's "ours."

"Roosevelt," declared Hearst, somberly, "has all sorts of luck."

"Except bad," noted Jim. "There's never been anything like him."

"I hate him, I think." But Hearst's thin voice sounded more wistful than passionate. "He calls me McKinley's murderer."

"Why don't you suggest that *he* hired that anarchist to kill McKinley so that he could become president?" Blaise improvised, for Jim's amusement.

"We were never able to find a connection," said Hearst sadly, startling Blaise, who put nothing beyond the Chief, but this seemed to be, even for Hearst, a singularly grotesque caper.

"Well, when in doubt, make something up." Jim was cheerful.

Blaise recalled, word for word, the latest Henry Adams characterization of William McKinley: "a very supple and highly paid agent of the crudest capitalism." He decided not to repeat this to Hearst, who had accepted with his usual equanimity the fact that he would never be received at the other side of Lafayette Square.

But Hearst was now discussing the joys of parenthood with James Burden Day. Since Millicent would give birth in two months, she refused to leave New York City for fear that any child born in the District of Columbia would grow up to be a politician. "Or Negro," said Jim. "Law of averages."

George announced, "Miss Frederika Bingham," to Hearst's surprise. Blaise rose. "I asked her to meet me here. We're going to look at my new house. She's got ambition, as a decorator of houses. She's read Mrs. Wharton's book."

Frederika was cool. Hearst was courtly. Jim was friendly; he had met her a number of times. Blaise shook her hand.

"My mother wants to know, Mr. Hearst, why you refuse to come to her congressional-at-homes." Frederika spoke to Hearst but kept her eyes on Blaise, who admired the ease with which she could handle any social situation. In this, she resembled Caroline, no recommendation, of course. Did he hate his sister? envy her? love her? He could never make up his mind. Certainly if he were the publisher of the *Tribune*, and she a mere society lady, they would probably get on. As it was, the primal emotion was, no doubt, envy.

"I don't know any congressmen," said Hearst meekly. "Except Mr. Day and Mr. Williams . . ."

"The Speaker," said Jim, "swears he doesn't know you by sight."

"So you see, *I* wouldn't be at home, would I?"

"All the more reason for coming to our house. Mother will

introduce you to the right people. Mr. Sanford, I have only an hour . . ."

They said their farewells; and got into the Binghams' chauffeured motor car. "Did you hear about Cissy Patterson?"

Blaise confessed that he did not know who she was; he was told; then: "Last week, after the wedding, the groom didn't show up at the wedding breakfast in the Patterson house." The Patterson palace was now directly in front of them as they entered Dupont Circle. "So Cissy was in tears, and a friend of the groom, this Austrian, went looking for him, and found him at the railroad station, buying a ticket for New York. Apparently, he had gone to his bank right after the service, and they had told him that the million dollars that he had been promised hadn't been deposited."

"Did he go?"

"He stayed. The check was still being cleared. I don't think Cissy's going to be very happy, do you?"

Blaise said no.

"I'd like to be like Caroline. Independent. With something to do."

"Having children's quite enough to do." Blaise was patriarchal; French.

The Connecticut Avenue house was a vast and, to Blaise's eye, most beautiful rendering in a modern way of Saint-Cloud-le-Duc, which he more and more missed. Neither he nor Caroline had returned, according to their post-Poussin treaty, and he was more than ever homesick while she was less; yet of the two, it was she who had loved the place more, and stayed on and on, while he had turned himself eagerly into a full-time American. Now they had reversed roles.

A caretaker in a heavy overcoat let them in. The interior of the house was even colder than outside. Together they explored the double drawing room, adapted from Saint-Cloud; and the ballroom, copied from a castle of Ludwig of Bavaria. There was even a lift, which Frederika thought a mistake. "The poor Walshes thought they were so clever in putting their ballroom on the top floor. But the elevator could only hold four people at a time, so

when the guests all arrive at once, the party takes forever to begin."
She laughed; he found her easy, something that most American
girls were not. They tended to take command.

But then, as if to prove that she, too, was American and
managerial by nature, Frederika told Blaise exactly how to decorate the various rooms; and he was pleasantly surprised to discover
that he did not in the least mind so much advice. As they talked,
their mingled breaths like smoke in the icy air, Blaise thought
seriously of marriage, not to Frederika, but to someone suitable,
someone who would be able to look after the house, not to mention
Saint-Cloud-le-Duc. Both Alice Roosevelt and Marguerite Cassini
had appealed to him. But the first was far too self-important and
the second far too Slavicly sly. Alice Hay had charmed him; but
he had not charmed her, and she was now married to a New York
Wadsworth. Millicent Smith, the Countess Glenellen, was not
without a certain appeal. She had grown up in Washington; gone
to school with Caroline; married the Earl Glenellen, from whom
she was now separated after what was thought to have been the
most exciting fist-fight in the history of the American embassy at
London. Lord Glenellen had been knocked unconscious by the
fragile Millicent, who later explained to the appalled ambassador
that she had cheated, holding in her right fist, not the traditional
street-fighter's roll of coins, but a metal cigar container (cigar
inside), which had added exceptional, if unfair, force to her blow.
Millicent was also much admired for the strength of her character.
Nevertheless, the more Blaise studied the field the less any one
person appealed to him. He had considered going back to Paris;
but that would have been an acknowledgement of defeat for him,
and a victory for Caroline.

"I'm freezing. And I'm late," Frederika announced, as they
made their way to the front door, where the watchman let them
out. "Mother's at home Saturday," Frederika announced, as she
dropped Blaise off at Willard's.

"I'll be there," he said. They shook hands, formally, and he
went into the hotel. Why not, he wondered, marry Frederika? She
appealed to him in an entirely practical way; that is, there was no

passion of the sort that might end with a fist-fight in the White House's Blue Room. She could certainly manage a dozen households. On the other hand, there was Mrs. Bingham, and all those cows. No, a Sanford must marry within that gilded circle where cows could be peripheral but never central, as in the Bingham case.

– 2 –

While Blaise brooded on cows, Caroline paid court to Henry Adams, as a dutiful niece now matured by matrimony. He seemed smaller, older, and definitely sadder. "The fire that destroyed your brother's printing press also made molten my little book on the twelfth century." He sighed, stretched out his hands in a propitiatory way toward the fire, begetter of molten type-face. "I shall have to delay publication, not that I really, ever, publish. The edition is only for me, and you, and a few others . . ."

"Hearts?"

"We are only three now." He frowned. "I worry about Hay. He is being slowly worn to death by that maniac across the street, and that madhouse of a Senate. Cabot . . ." he began; and ended. "I'm in a cheery mood, as you can see." He gazed at her reflectively. "Why do we never see Mr. Sanford?"

"Because I thought it was the ageing Mrs. Sanford whose company you pretend to enjoy."

"Oh, no pretense. No pretense. I find it hard to talk to some of the new girls. But then I'm very dull. Don't you agree?"

"Yes. It's your most attractive feature. If you were older, I might have married you instead of my cousin, who is merely—not attractively—dull."

Adams laughed his muted dog's bark of a laugh. "You'll do very well."

"Surely you like Alice." Washington had taken to saying the

name "Alice" with a slight pause between syllables, to denote that *the* Alice was meant.

"I like her better than her father. But then I like everyone better than I like him. Last week, I went to my first White House dinner since 1878, during the sullen reign of Rutherford B. Hayes, where lemonade flowed like champagne. I was only asked because Brooks could not come. They needed an Adams, any Adams, while the President always needs a pair of humble ears. Mine were never so humble. He did not stop talking for two hours. The contents," Adams smiled sweetly at Nebuchadnezzar eating grass, "of that mind confound me! All history is neatly on file in that great round Dutch cheese of a head. But—so generous is he that he will share all that he knows with anyone, no matter how humble. I was awed. Speechless. Poor John, what he must go through, day after day . . ."

Caroline, aware that Adamsian gloom was about to overwhelm the bright room, said, "I just passed Alice and the Cassini girl bob-sledding on Connecticut Avenue. They start at Dupont Circle, and slide through the traffic, out of control."

"A metaphor, my child, for her father's administration."

"How," asked Caroline, "does one get money?"

For the first time in their friendship, Adams looked at her with true surprise. "In our world, you select parents who have money, and they, in turn, pass it on. If one has been careless in the selection of parents, one marries someone who was not so careless. I am very good about money, by the way. I can't think why. But I do well in financial crises. Brooks, who understands the monetary system better than anyone alive, loses money, always. It is highly gratifying. Anyway, next year—is it?—you inherit your fortune—"

"*This* year, I am desperate."

"Your husband has debts." Adams did not phrase this as a question; but then everyone knew everything in their world.

"More than I had bargained for."

"Go to your brother."

"He wants the paper."

"Go to the Jews."

"I have tried. But they don't seem eager to lend, at a bearable rate."

"I could lend—"

"I shall leave the room, and never return, if you ever hint at such—an impropriety."

Adams smiled, like a contented cat. "I knew you would reject me. Otherwise, I would not have made so rude a move. "Why not sell Blaise your newspaper?"

"Because it is all that I have, of my own. A child is never your own. It is also—the father's." Caroline enjoyed the irony. Jim had never once suspected, holding Emma on his knee, that she was his flesh and blood, blue eyes and curly hair.

"Let us be subtle. Sell Blaise half the shares of the *Tribune* minus one, which will give you control."

Caroline had thought of this. "It would mean getting to know him rather more than I'd like."

"One boy is like another." Adams disliked all males except a half-dozen aged ironists like himself. Caroline had never known a man to whom woman—if not women—was so necessary; and she wondered, as always, why had the brilliant wife killed herself, why had he never remarried, why did he maintain his peculiar, and plainly unrequited, passion for Lizzie Cameron?

"You made do with a cousin as husband. You can certainly make do with a half-brother as—junior partner."

William was at the door, announcing "Professor Langley." The accident-prone secretary of the Smithsonian Institution entered the room, without once, symbolically, slipping, Caroline noted. Although Henry Adams regarded Samuel P. Langley as the best scientific mind in the western world (Adams particularly admired Langley's invention of something called a bolometer, "which measures the heat," he would say gleefully, "of *nothing!*"). The press had, lately, taken a good deal of pleasure out of Langley's doomed attempts to fly heavier-than-air craft. He was always on the verge of freeing man from the earth; but man continued to be earth-bound, as far as heavier-than-air craft went. Lighter-than-air craft, on the order of gliders or balloons, somehow did not count. Caroline found mystifying Langley's obsessions; but she had seen to it that he was often, and favorably, interviewed in the *Tribune*. As a result, he had mistaken her for an admirer like Adams; and she had done nothing to disabuse him. Whatever pleased Adams pleased her. Besides, Langley could be interesting, when not goaded by Adams into discussing the famous dynamo that they had together glimpsed at the Paris Exhibition four years earlier. Adams wanted to find a scientific basis to history, on the order of the second law of thermodynamics. Caroline, who knew little of history and nothing of science, was convinced that there were no laws applicable to the human race, a random affair that moved neither up nor down but, simply, *on*, in fits and starts, for no reason. She had always found it odd that men required coherent reasons for things that women knew to be non-reasonable.

"There is a rumor that a pair of bicycle mechanics in North Carolina have flown in a heavier-than-air machine of their own devising." This was Langley's ponderous greeting to his old friend.

"When?" Adams was alert, as always, to the marvels of science. "And for how long did they fly?"

"Three months ago. The story's garbled. No one seems to have got it straight. Someone sent me a clipping from a Norfolk newspaper, that made no sense . . ."

"We were notified," said Caroline, recalling Mr. Trimble's amusement at the message from two brothers to the effect that they were the first, ever, to fly in such a machine. In one day they had taken off and landed several times. She recalled that they had claimed to have flown a half-mile. She reported this to Langley, who seemed more depressed than elated. Plainly this disinterested man of science wanted for himself the glory of being the first to fly like—was it Icarus? she wondered, recalling Mlle. Souvestre's injunction that one ought always to be ready with an apt classical allusion in order not to use it.

"I've heard something very like that. I don't see how it's possible. I mean who—what are they?"

"It is very odd that the press has not picked it up." Adams

473

turned to Caroline. "Why didn't you use the story?"

"Because we get so many stories like that, out of nowhere. Also, Mr. Trimble couldn't tell whether the machine wasn't just another sort of glider, like the one that took off from the Eiffel Tower."

"I shall write them, I suppose." Langley was glum. "I am so close now, so very close to the workable machine . . ."

"What use is a flying machine?" Caroline was genuinely curious, not so much about the tinkering with machinery, a male madness, but the uses to which something so impractical might be put.

"Flight will change everyone's life," said Langley. "People can be transported at great speed over long distances."

"I suppose that's a good thing." Caroline was dubious; her magnolia tree had died as a result of Alice Roosevelt's assault upon it with a highly powered swift-moving arrangement of metal.

"It will change warfare." Adams was thoughtful. "One could carry explosives over the enemy's territory and blow up—anything, I suppose."

Langley nodded. "Even in our Civil War, balloons were used, most effectively. Now, with powered air-craft . . ."

"But they will promptly discover a way of knocking them out of the sky." Caroline recalled one of the President's recent arias. He was talking of the Kaiser, whom he had come to like, thanks to Speck, the ever-charming link between the two bellicosities. Speck, according to Roosevelt, had described how the ingenious maker of munitions Krupp handled the Kaiser. "Apparently Krupp is a superb statesman." The President's pince-nez glittered with a light all its own. "He goes to the Kaiser and says, 'I've invented a steel plating that no bullet can pierce.' So the Kaiser immediately orders quantities of steel plating. Then, a year later, Krupp, looking very sad, comes back to the Kaiser and says, 'I'm afraid we've invented a bullet that will pierce the impenetrable steel plating.' So the poor Kaiser must order several tons of these magical bullets, to be followed by ever-newer impenetrable plating that will eventually be penetrated by newer bullets. The Kaiser has warned me not to be taken in, the way he's been." When Caroline repeated this to Adams and Langley, they exchanged knowing glances; and Langley said, "The Kaiser wants us to fall behind, which is why, should there be war, we must have the first flying-machine."

"But if they find a way to shoot it down . . ."

"We will invent something that cannot be shot down . . ." began Langley.

"Until it is," said Caroline. "If I may give you a matronly view, this sort of contest is endless." Caroline had been much impressed by the President's story.

"Progress, once started, is endless." Langley was sententious.

"Progress," said Caroline, "implies that one is moving from one known place to another. Isn't the problem, here, *not* knowing the proper terminus?"

"Serendipity is sovereign." Adams was not his usual candid, pessimistic self.

"We proceed because we must," said Langley. "It is like evolution."

"You have reminded me that I am Catholic, and in no way connected, genealogically, with any monkey, no matter how charming." Caroline rose to go.

"You were taken from Adam's rib, as we all know, to our delight." After Caroline had said her farewell to Langley, Adams led her out onto the landing, which smelled of out-of-season lilies-of-the-valley; in fact, the house, always overheated and filled with flowers, reminded her of the White House conservatories, now a thing of the past. "Sell Blaise a part of the paper."

"He will try to get all of it."

"Don't let him. You are a clever child." Adams patted her hand; and William showed her out.

John Hay sat alone in his moving parlor, and watched through newly washed windows the United States rush by. The Casetts of the Pennsylvania Railroad had provided the Secretary of State with their ornately furnished private car, and specially trained Negro attendants. At the President's insistence, Hay had agreed to attend the World's Fair at St. Louis, where he would make an address which, high-minded, witty and elegant, would be the opening gun in the coming battle for the presidency. There was no doubt that Theodore would be nominated by the Republican Party in June; there was little doubt that he would beat Bryan or Hearst or Parker or any Democrat in November. But Theodore saw lions everywhere in his path; and so he had sent the now always ailing Hay to the West. Clara had insisted that Henry Adams, an aficionado of world fairs, accompany them; and Adams had insisted on bringing his real-life niece, Abigail, a plain but interesting and interested girl.

Hay wrote slowly in a notebook. Speech-writing no longer came easily to him; but then nothing did. In addition to the pleasures of a diseased prostate, he had now developed angina pectoris, a new and boisterous ailment which could be counted on to stab him in the middle of a speech, leaving him breathless and faint. He had always known that life would end; he was constantly amazed that so many of his acquaintances were astonished when death at last came their way. On the other hand, he had not counted on all the games that were being played within his body, which seemed to him now rather like one of Henry's dynamos, breaking down for lack of whatever it is that keeps a dynamo serenely humming.

Theodore was one of those who could not imagine his own death, or anyone else's, which explained, perhaps, his unnatural passion for war. The one time that Theodore was forced to look death not once but twice in its bony face—when wife and mother

476

simultaneously died—he had literally fled, like that traveller to—or was it from?—Samarra. He had abandoned his just-born daughter, career, world; to hide in the Wild West, where, presumably, the distances were so great and the terrain so flat that death could be seen coming and so avoided, by further flight, if necessary. The fact that the Secretary of State was now dying did not in the least distress Theodore, who thought only of the coming election, and his own continuing glory. John Hay was now the fine figurehead of the Republican Party, which would be a half-century old in July. Therefore, Lincoln's young secretary and Roosevelt's aged minister must be borne like an icon about the country, mouthing platitudes so that Theodore might become, in his own right, president, and no longer His Accidency.

Hay's rather loose handwriting seemed to grow ever more loose with age, as he constructed his pieties and platitudes, and reined in his wit, which would never do in so crucial a year. As usual, there was the problem of the people—those famous people that the Ancient had so mysteriously exalted that hot muggy day at Gettysburg; government of, by, and for the people? Had ever a great man said anything so entirely unrealistic, not to mention, literally, demagogic? The people played no part at all in the government of the United States in Lincoln's time, and even less now in the days of Theodore Rex. Lincoln had tended to rule by decree, thanks to the all-purpose "military necessity" which gave legitimacy to his most arbitrary acts. Roosevelt pursued his own interests in his own surprisingly secretive way; he was for empire at any cost. The people, of course, were always more or less *there*; they must be flattered from time to time; exhorted to do battle, or whatever the Augustus at Washington wanted them to do. The result was a constant tension between the people at large and a ruling class that believed, as did Hay, in the necessity of concentrating wealth in the hands of the few while keeping the few as virtuous as possible, at least in appearance. Hence the periodic attacks on trusts. But labor was a more delicate matter, and though Theodore was as hostile to the working-man's demands as any Carnegie, he knew that he must appear to be their tribune, and so,

477

to Hay's amusement and annoyance, Roosevelt had given, in 1903, a Fourth of July speech at, significantly, Springfield, Illinois, where he had declared, "A man who is good enough to shed his blood for his country is good enough to be given a square deal afterward. More than that no man is entitled to, and less than that no man shall have." This breathtaking announcement had caused rage in the better clubs of the republic and less than euphoria amongst those to whom the mysterious square deal had been promised. They would vote for Bryan anyway.

Even so, Hay wrote, in large letters, "The Square Deal," with slightly embellished capitals; then he ran his pen through the phrase. He was not up to such a speech. Let Theodore do his own ranting. At the last Cabinet meeting, Root had declined the honor of serving as campaign manager; and Theodore had been plainly rattled. The post had gone to the secretary of commerce (a needless new department, created by Roosevelt), Mr. Cortelyou, a soothing presence, and reminder of McKinley's golden age, now as remote to Hay as Lincoln's time of blood. There would be no talk of a square deal at St. Louis.

Hay stared out the window, as one lonely village after another moved by the train's window, an endless cyclorama of sameness. The pale spring light made the houses seem more than ever shabby, in contrast to the bright yellow-green foliage of trees and spring wheat. Was it April 15 or 16? he wondered. Without Adee—or a newspaper nearby—he never knew the date any more. If it was April 15, then it was the thirty-ninth anniversary of the murder of Lincoln. Hardly anyone was left from that time. Mary Todd had died, mad, at Springfield in 1882; her death long since preceded by that of the beloved child Tad. Only the eldest son, Robert Lincoln, survived; a chilly railroad magnate, largely indifferent to his father's memory. Once Hay and Nicolay had finished their life of Lincoln, Hay's connection with Robert was, for all practical purposes, at an end. They were no longer comfortable with each other; yet thirty-nine years ago, they had been drinking together when the White House doorkeeper had rushed into the room with the news, "The President's been shot!" And together they had gone to the boardinghouse near Ford's Theater, to watch the Ancient die.

Hay was beginning to find concentration difficult. Usually, the familiar act of setting pen to paper caused him to think precisely. But now he wool-gathered, lulled by the regular metallic clicking of the train's wheels on the rails. Foreign affairs would be a safer subject than the evanescent square deal. The war between Russia and Japan was of great significance; but how was he to explain it to the public, when he could never explain it to the President? He found alarming the fact that Kaiser and President were growing altogether too friendly; they were not unalike in their sense of imperial charismatic mission. Each tended to regard the collapse of the Tsar's eastern empire as a good thing. On the other hand, Hay thought that a victorious Japan in the Pacific would mean nothing but trouble for the United States, and its new bright Pacific empire.

"Open Doors," Hay wrote, without his usual pride in the famous histrionic formula that had worked once; and might again. Dare he mention the mysterious enlargement of the German fleet? Was there, as some suspected, a German plot to destroy the British empire, and undermine the United States by means of all those— how many millions now?—German immigrants, with their own newspapers, communities, nostalgia? But the President put no credence in such a plot. He thought he understood the Kaiser and the Germans. Hay knew that *he* understood this barbaric tribe; and Hay feared them. With Russia crippled by Japan to Germany's east, the Kaiser could move west. "Piece," wrote Hay; was he losing his mind? He crossed out the word; wrote "peace"; then "meat." At least he spelled that right. Ever since the tainted-meat scandal during the war with Spain, government action had been called for, and, finally, Roosevelt had come up with a Meat Inspection Act, which Congress had rejected. This was definitely good government, but Hay rather doubted if he could extract much rhetorical magic from the subject.

Henry Adams coughed politely. "Do I intrude on the creative process?"

479

"I was trying to make lyrical the Meat Inspection Act. But nothing scans." Hay shut the notebook. A steward appeared with tea. "Mrs. Hay says you are to drink this, sir."

"Then I shall."

Hay and Adams stared out the window, as if expecting to see something of great interest. But all was a sameness, thought Hay.

"Theodore Rex worries about his—Rexness," said Hay, at last.

"No need, even with Mark Hanna dead." The monster of corruption had died in February, busy collecting a war-chest for the nomination not of himself but of Roosevelt. The two enemies had long since come to an understanding. As for the Democratic side, their paladin William C. Whitney had also died in February. Without Whitney, there was no one—except Hearst—who could finance a winning campaign. Everything would flow Roosevelt's way; yet Adams was puzzled. "Why didn't Root take on the job as campaign manager?"

Hay took morbid pleasure in his reply. "He was—is, perhaps, still—convinced that he has a cancer of the breast."

Adams's look of surprise was highly pleasing. "Surely, only the ladies have been chosen for this especial mark of God's favor."

"The ladies—and Elihu Root. Anyway, he had a tumor removed, and I'm sure he's all right now. What a president he might have made."

"Why do you say 'might have'?"

"He is a lawyer, too much involved with the wicked corporations and trusts. And then the miners' strike . . ." The miners' strike of 1902 had caused so much panic in the land that Roosevelt had threatened to take over the mines, as receiver; since public opinion was on the side of the miners, the threat was popular. Although public opinion was seldom heeded, Roosevelt feared that demagogues like Bryan and Hearst might try to unleash the mob, and so, to forestall revolution, he sent Root to force the ownership, J. Pierpont Morgan himself, to give the miners a wage increase while keeping them to a nine-hour day in hazardous conditions. Roosevelt took the credit for settling the strike. Root took the blame from both workers and owners for an unsatisfactory settlement; and lost forever the presidency.

"To what extent does your brother, Brooks, influence Theodore?" When in serious doubt, Hay believed in directness.

Henry Adams cocked his head, rather like a bald, bearded owl. "You are with His Majesty every day. I am not."

"You see Brooks . . ."

". . . as little as possible. To see him is to *hear* him." Adams shuddered. "He is the most bloodthirsty creature I have ever known. He wants a war, anywhere will do, as long as we end up as custodian of northern China. Domestically, 'We must have a new deal,' he wrote me, so we shall have to suppress the states in favor of a centralized dictatorship at Washington. Does he write Theodore often?"

Hay nodded. "But I am not in their confidence. I don't love war enough. What shall I say in St. Louis about our enormous achievements?"

Adams smiled, showing no teeth. "You can say that the most marvellous invention of my grandfather, the Monroe Doctrine, originally intended to protect our—note the cool proprietary 'our'—hemisphere from predatory European powers, has now been extended, quite illegally, by President Roosevelt to include China and, again by extension, any part of the world where we may want to interfere."

"This is not the Hay Doctrine," Hay began.

"This is not the Monroe Doctrine either. But my grandfather's masterpiece was already coming apart in 1848 when President Polk dared to tell Congress that our war of conquest against Mexico was justified by the Monroe Doctrine. My grandfather, by then a mere congressman, denounced the President on the floor of the House, and then dropped dead on that same floor. When Theodore recently announced that we have an obligation, somehow, inherently, through the Monroe Doctrine, to punish 'chronic wrongdoers' in South America, as well as 'to the exercise of an international police power,' *I* nearly dropped dead over my breakfast egg."

Hay himself was not entirely at ease with all the implications of a national policy in which he had, for the most part, cheerfully participated. Nevertheless, he defended, "Surely, we have a *moral*—yes, I hate the word, too—duty to help less fortunate nations in this hemisphere . . ."

"And sunny Hawaii, and poor Samoa, and the tragic Philippines? John, it is empire you all want, and it is empire that you have got, and at such a small price, when you come to think of it."

"What price is that?" Hay could tell from the glitter in Adams's eye that the answer would be highly unpleasant.

"The American republic. You've finally got rid of it. For good. As a conservative Christian anarchist, I never much liked it." Adams raised high his teacup. "The republic is dead; long live the empire."

"Oh, dear." Hay put down his cup, which chattered at him in its monogrammed saucer. "We have all the *forms* of a republic. Isn't that enough? Isn't that *everything?* Why else am I now hurtling across Ohio, or wherever we are, to make a speech to persuade the folks to vote?"

"We let them vote so that they will feel wanted. But as we extend, in theory, the democracy, the more it runs out of gas." In imitation of Clarence King, Adams now liked to use new slang expressions, often accompanied by a faintly raffish tilt to his head, like a Boston Irish laborer.

"I don't weep." Hay had made his choice long ago. A republic—or however one wanted to describe the United States—was best run by responsible men of property. Since most men of property tended, in the first generation at least, to criminality, it was necessary for the high-minded patriotic few to wait a generation or two and then select one of their number, who had the common—or was it royal?—touch and make him president. As deeply tiring as Theodore was on the human level, "drunk with himself," as Henry liked to put it, he was the best the country had to offer, and they were all in luck. For good or ill, the system excluded from power the Bryans if not the Hearsts. Hay was aware that the rogue publisher was a new Caesarian element upon the scene: the

wealthy maker of public opinion who, having made common cause
with the masses, might yet overthrow the few.

Lincoln had spoken warmly and winningly of the common man,
but he had been as remote from that simple specimen as one of
Henry's beloved dynamos from an ox-cart. One *rode* public opinion,
Hay had more than once observed. Theodore thought that public
opinion could be guided by some splendid popular leader like
himself, but, in practice, Roosevelt was mildness itself, never
appearing above the parapet of his office when hostile bullets were
aimed his way. Hearst was different; he could make people react
in ways not predictable; he could invent issues, and then solu-
tions—equally invented but no less popular for that. The contest
was now between the high-minded few, led by Roosevelt, and
Hearst, the true inventor of the modern world. What Hearst
arbitrarily decided was news was news; and the powerful few were
obliged to respond to his inventions. Could he, also, a question
much discussed amongst the few, make himself so much the news
that he might seize one of the high—if not the highest—offices of
state? Theodore sneered at the thought—had the American people
ever *not* voted for one of the respectable few? And if nothing else, it
was agreed by everyone (except, perhaps, the general indifferent
mass of the working class) that Hearst was supremely unrespecta-
ble. Even so, Hay had his doubts. He feared Hearst.

The train clattered to a stop at the depot of a small town called,
according to the paint-blistered sign, Heidegg. Clara and Abigail
appeared in the doorway to the parlor. "We're stopping," Clara
announced, in a loud authoritative voice.

"Actually, my dear, we've stopped." Hay vaulted to his feet, an
acrobatic maneuver which involved falling to the right while
embracing with his left arm the back of the chair in front of him;
gravity, the ultimate enemy, was, for once, put to good use.

Adams pointed to a small crowd at the back of the train. "We
should go amongst the people in whose name we—you and
Theodore, that is—govern."

"We'll be here fifteen minutes, Uncle Henry," said Abigail, and
led him to the back of their private car, where a smiling porter

helped them onto the good Ohio (or was it now Indiana?) earth. Hay stepped into the cool day, which had been co-existing separately from that of the railroad car, whose atmosphere was entirely different, warmer, redolent of railway smells, as well as of a galley where a Negro chef in a tall white cap performed miracles with terrapin.

For a moment, the earth itself seemed to be moving beneath Hay's feet, as if he were still on the train; slightly, he swayed. Clara took his fragile arm in her great one and then the four visitors from the capital of the imperial republic, led by John Hay, the Second Personage in the Land, mingled with the folks.

The American people, half a hundred farmers with wives, children, dogs, surrounded the Second Personage in the Land, who smiled sweetly upon them; and lapsed into his folksy "Little Breeches" manner which could outdo for sheer comic rusticity Mark Twain himself. "I reckon," he said, with a modest smile, "that well as I know all the country hereabouts—" He was positive that he was now in Indiana, but one slip . . . "—I've never had the luck to be in Heidegg before. I'm from Warsaw myself. Warsaw, Illinois, as I 'spect you know. Anyway, we're on our way now to the big exhibition in St. Louis, and when I saw that sign saying, Heidegg, I said, let's stop and meet the folks. So, hello." Hay was well pleased with his own casualness and lack of side. He did not dare look at Henry Adams, who always found amusing, in the wrong sense, Hay's Lincolnian ease with the common man.

The crowd continued to stare, amicably, at the four foreigners. Then a tall thin farmer came forward, and shook Hay's hand. "*Willkommen*," he began; and addressed the Second Personage in the Land in German.

Hay then asked, in German, if anyone in Heidegg spoke English. He was told, in German, that the schoolteacher spoke excellent English, but he was home, sick in bed. Hay ignored the strangled cries of Henry Adams, trying not to laugh. Fortunately, Hay's German was good, and he was able to satisfy the crowd's curiosity as to his identity. The word had spread that he was someone truly important, the president of the railroad, in fact. When Hay modestly identified himself, the information was received politely; but as no one had ever heard of the—or even a—secretary of state, the crowd broke up, leaving the four visitors alone on a muddy bank where new grass was interspersed with violets. As Abigail collected violets, Adams was in his glory. "The people!" he exclaimed.

"Oh, do shut up, Henry!" Hay had seldom been so annoyed with his old friend, or with himself for having handled with unusual clumsiness an occasion fraught with symbolism of a sort that Adams would never cease to remind him.

As they dined, Adams talked and talked. Clara ate and ate, course after course, marvelling, occasionally, at what remarkable dishes were emerging from the small galley. Abigail stared out the window at a great muddy river, surging through the twilight, from the Great Lakes to New Orleans. "You must—Theodore must—*someone* must," Adams declared, "cross the country, like this, by car, and stop—but I really mean stop, and stay, and look and listen. The country's full of people who are strange to us, and we to them. That river," Adams pointed dramatically at the river on whose banks were set square frame houses with square windows in which lights now began to gleam; each house was set in its own yard, strewn with scrap iron, scrap paper, cinders, "could be an estuary of the Rhine or the Danube. We are witnessing the last of the great tides of migration. We are in *Mitteleuropa*, surrounded by Germans, Slavs and—what were the people of Heidegg?"

"Swiss," said Hay, deciding that he would take his chances with broiled Potomac shad and its roe.

"You were born on this river, John, and now it's stranger to you than the Danube. When Theodore goes on and on about the true American, his grit, his sense of fairness, his institutions, he doesn't realize that the American is as rare as one of those buffalos he helped to kill off."

"We shall," said Hay, mouth filled with roe, "transform those Germans and Slavs into . . . buffalos. All in due course."

"No," said Adams, revelling as always in darkness, "they will transform us. When I was writing about Aaron Burr . . ."

485

"Whatever became of that book?" asked Clara, addressing herself to what looked like a side of buffalo.

"I have burned it, of course. Publish in total secrecy, or burn . . ."

"In secret, too?" Hay remembered that Clover had said that her husband's life of Burr was far superior to his published life of John Randolph. Hay had always thought Burr an ideal scamp to write about. But something in Burr's character or life had made Henry uneasy; he had decided that Burr was not a "safe" scoundrel to deal with, and if he were let out of the history books where he had been entombed alongside Benedict Arnold, he might cheat the world all over again. Hay rather suspected that Adams had not destroyed the book but used parts of it for his study of Jefferson.

"In his old age, Burr was walking down Fifth Avenue with a group of young lawyers, and one of them asked him how he thought some aspect of the Constitution should be interpreted. Burr stopped in front of a building site, and pointed to some newly arrived Irish laborers, and he said, 'In due course, *they* will decide what the Constitution is—and is not.' He understood, wicked creature, that the immigrants would eventually crowd us out and re-create the republic in their own image."

Abigail looked at her uncle, who had, happily, run out of breath, and said, "But the country's not all Catholic yet. That's something."

"Everyone in the Swiss Indiana village of Heidegg was Catholic . . ."

"Lutheran," said Hay, who was quick to learn essentials whenever votes were involved.

"Anyway, I incline now to Catholicism, too," said Adams perversely.

"Mariolatry." Hay's heart fluttered disagreeably. He had a vision of himself addressing twenty thousand people at the fair; and dropping dead.

"Catholic maids are always pregnant. I can't think why," said Clara.

"Luckily, steam-power, like this train, is going to make all these different races into one. The way the idea of the Virgin—hardly Mariolatry—united the Europeans of the twelfth century."

Abigail interrupted her uncle. Hay silently commended her bravery. "Why St. Louis for a World's Fair?"

Hay, as the Nation's Second Personage, answered: "It is the fourth-largest city in the country. It is centrally located. The new Union Station is the world's largest, or so they claim. Finally, the late revered William McKinley, whenever he was in doubt as to what the people of this great nation wanted him to do, would say, 'I must go to St. Louis.' The city is our heartland. Now the city fathers, to celebrate the centennial of the Louisiana Purchase— *illegal* purchase by Mr. Jefferson," Hay added for Adams's pleasure, "are holding the largest fair of its kind in the history of the world. There will be," he added ominously, "innumerable dynamos and other pieces of dull machinery."

"Oh, dear," said Abigail.

"Oh, joy," said Adams.

"Oh, waiter," said Clara, "more beef."

"Everyone," Hay sighed, "will be there."

– 4 –

Mr. and Mrs. John Apgar Sanford occupied a small suite of the Blair-Benton Hotel in Market Street, the main street of St. Louis, not far from the stone-paved Front Street, locally known as the levee, since that is exactly what it was, some four miles of riverfront which was used not only as a river-port but, also, as a promenade.

"We were lucky to get even this," said Sanford, indicating the bedroom with its single four-poster bed; he had duly noted Caroline's displeasure. They did not, except in emergencies, ever share the same bed. When Sanford had told her that a number of his inventors and their business sponsors would be at the fair, and that he, as their patent attorney, was expected to be on hand to

487

examine all the exhibitions and determine whose patent was being infringed, Caroline had told him that she thought he should go. There was a chance, after all, of additional fees for tea-kettles that were silent, for electrical sockets that did not shock, for engines that would—what was Langley's phrase?—"free man from earth." When the *Tribune*'s best reporter took ill, Mr. Trimble had convinced Caroline that she should herself describe the Exposition, at least the inaugural ceremonies. And though Clara Hay had proposed that the Sanfords join them in their private car, Caroline had spared the Hays and the Adamses the experience of John, who had grown more and more glum, no bad thing, but more and more apologetic for his life, a very bad thing indeed.

They had been shown to the suite by the manager himself. "Everyone," said the manager, "is in St. Louis this week."

"I don't mind," said Caroline, sweetly, and thanked him for his courtesy.

As John unpacked, Caroline made dutiful notes. The Louisiana Purchase Exposition, as it was properly called, covered one thousand two hundred forty acres, of which two hundred fifty were roofed over—pavilions, halls, restaurants. They had caught a glimpse of the Secretary of State and Clara riding through the brightly decorated city. As Caroline worked at an octagonal table of the shiniest black walnut, John went through a file of papers, with a worried frown. "This should be," said Caroline, by now an expert at making marital conversation, "a paradise for a patent lawyer."

"I certainly hope so. Except," John was already defeated, she could tell, "there is no longer a way of really winning a patent suit. Every inventor takes out a dozen patents for the same invention. If you threaten to sue, he'll drop three patents but keep nine others in order to confuse the courts and his rival inventors."

"What an excellent opportunity for the lawyer, endless litigation."

"They," said John, at wit's end plainly, "always settle. Is there any news?"

"Yes. I went to the Jews, as Mr. Adams would say. These

488

particular Jews are a Yankee firm by the name of Whittaker. They are devoted Presbyterians. I asked, as you requested, for half a million dollars, at the going rate."

"Why did they say no?" John had now been a husband long enough to be able to finish Caroline's sentences, if not enter, as it were, her bed. A single attempt to fulfill their conjugal duties had failed. Each had been apologetic. Caroline had given what she thought was a convincing performance of a devoted wife. She had even, against her by now better judgment, followed Marguerite's advice, which was to shut her eyes and imagine that the large body on top of her was that of James Burden Day. But the smell was wrong; the texture odd; the attack askew. She had always known that she was deficient in imagination, as their first and last attempt demonstrated; and she envied those women who could go from one new body to another, like an explorer loose in an endless archipelago of men—women, too, in Paris at least—enjoying this island for its luxuriant trees, and that for its silvery springs. She was no explorer; she was a contented land-lubber, in a familiar satisfying landscape. The attempt to leave home, as represented by James Burden Day, for John was like abandoning a perfect oasis for the surrounding Sahara. John, in no position to complain, complained. Caroline, in no position to moralize, moralized. In time, the matter was dropped. John's sexuality was soon subdued by the financial ruin which had overtaken him. He could think of nothing else, and, lately, neither could Caroline.

"Mr. Whittaker was evasive." At first, Caroline had been puzzled; then angry. "I gave the date, next March, when I am twenty-seven. I said there was no way that I could *not* get my share. He said, 'There are complications.' I said, what? He wouldn't answer."

"Of course not." John was bitter. "The Whittakers often retain, as counsel, our friend Houghteling."

Caroline experienced a sudden spasm of purest hatred for her brother. "Blaise is making it appear that the estate is in trouble . . ."

"Or nonexistent, or that there are obscure liens, or your rights

489

unclear." John the lawyer was far better company than John the husband. "I'm joining some of my clients for lunch. I may be able . . ." He did not finish the sentence. He would try to borrow money; so would she.

"I must join the Hays. He speaks this afternoon at the Exposition. Perhaps . . ." She did not finish her sentence either.

But Caroline had plans which did not include the Hays. Instead, she walked in the warm sunlight along the levee, crowded with visitors from out of town. By and large the natives ignored the river; all the houses, she noted, turned their backs on what was, after all, a phenomenal if not beautiful sight, a wide expanse of yellowish swift water, no uglier than the Tiber, say, and infinitely larger.

At a waterfront saloon called the Anchor she paused. As far as she could see along the levee, black men were loading and unloading cargo from barges, ships. Caroline thought of Marseilles, turned African.

John Burden Day, in statesman's black, approached her from the saloon. "What a surprise," he said, and looked at his watch. "You're exactly on time."

"I'm always on time." She took his arm; and they walked along the levee like a contentedly married couple, which, in effect, they were. Caroline had long since accepted as an unalloyed bit of golden good fortune the fact that they were not obliged to live together, day after day, night after night, in the same conjugal bed, listening to the midnight cries of many children, the usual marital fate in this country. Occasionally, she needed him on days other than Sunday; but that was a small price to pay for Sunday itself; and now St. Louis. "Where is Kitty?"

"She chairs the Democratic Ladies' Committee on Suffrage all morning. She will go with them to hear Mr. Hay at the Exposition. I shall go with you."

"Or not."

"Or not."

They made love in Caroline's suite at the Blair-Benton Hotel. Jim was nervous that he might be recognized. But the lobby was so crowded that no one could actually see anyone. Also, Caroline was now something of an expert on the use of hotels. Whenever she planned to meet Jim, she insisted on a first-floor suite in a hotel with at least two separate stairways from ground to first floor. Jim thought that had she been a man, she would have been a natural general. Caroline had disagreed. "But I might have succeeded at business," she answered. "I would have cornered something like wheat, and brought on a highly satisfying financial crisis."

Caroline watched Jim dress, a sight almost as pleasing as the reverse. He watched her, watching him; divined her mood. "You're thinking about money," he said.

"Its lack," she said. "John has got himself—us, that is—in the deepest water. And Blaise has seen to it that I can't borrow."

Jim frowned, as a tooth of Caroline's comb broke in his wiry coppery hair. "I broke your comb. Sorry. Why can't you borrow? Next March it's all yours, anyway. Bankers love that sort of short-term loan. How can Blaise stop them from lending?"

"By lying. Through his lawyers. Pretending the estate is compromised."

"That's easily investigated." Jim sat in a rocking chair, and rested his head on a spotless new antimacassar. All St. Louis had been cleaned up for the world's delight.

Caroline got out of bed; began to dress. "In time, I could straighten all this out. But there's no time. Blaise has been putting pressure on John's debtors. If he does not pay up now, he will be ruined." Although Caroline rather liked the sound of "he will be ruined," the reality was impossible to grasp. What was financial ruin? In her own life, there had been so many financial crises, so many friends or acquaintances "ruined," and yet they went right on eating breakfast, and seeing one another. Ruin, as such, did not mean much to her. But the thought of a forced sale of the *Tribune* was like a knife at her throat, a most disagreeable sensation.

"You will have to sell to Blaise." Jim was flat.

"I would rather die."

"What else?"

"Other than death?"

"Other than a sale. You should follow Mr. Adams's advice, and keep control . . ."

"If he will let me."

Jim stared at her in the mirror, where she was now repairing the damage that Eros does to even the simplest coiffeur. "Why not," said Jim, "let John go under? He's the one at fault, not you."

"Because, my darling, he knows who the father of my child is." Caroline looked at Jim's face, next to hers in the mirror, smaller than hers, thanks to perspective, so ably taught by the drawing mistress at Mlle. Souvestre's. Caroline enjoyed Jim's look of astonishment.

"But *he's* the father, isn't he?"

"No, he's not."

There was a long silence, broken by Jim's sudden laughter. He sprang to his feet, like a boy, and embraced Caroline from behind, kissed the nape of her neck, causing the hair, controlled at last, to come crashing down. "Oh, damn," said Caroline, for the first time in her life. "My hair."

"My child! Emma's mine, too!"

"You sound like a horse-breeder."

"Why not? I am the acknowledged stud. Why didn't you tell me?"

"I didn't want to worry you. Now if you come near my hair again, I shall . . . do something drastic." Caroline again pinned up the mountain of cleverly coiled hair, *all hers*, as Marguerite used to gloat, when she did the arranging.

Jim retreated to his chair. He seemed delighted; and Caroline wondered why. Men were very odd, certainly. Jim had two children now by Kitty; and one by her. "Are there any others?" she asked.

"Other what?"

"Children of yours that I should know about? When little Emma grows up, she will want to know all her half-brothers and -sisters."

Jim shook his head. "None that I know of." He frowned. "How does John know it's me?"

"He doesn't. I was just being dramatic. All he knows is that Emma's not his. When I discovered I was pregnant, I told him, and he married me. It was my money for his—for *my* respectability."

"Why didn't you just pretend it was his?"

"Because I've never really been to bed with him."

Jim whistled, an engaging rustic sound. "You really are French," he said at last.

Caroline was not amused. "You would be surprised just how American I am, particularly in a situation like this. I am not about to lose . . ." But this, she knew, even as she spoke, was hollow boasting. She was about to lose the *Tribune.* She had considered, seriously, allowing John to fail; but honor forbade such a course, not to mention commonsense. If she did not keep her side of their bargain, he would be free to divorce her or, worse, annul the unconsummated marriage, and tell the press why.

"Shall I work on Blaise? He seems to like me."

"More than that is my impression."

Jim's head suddenly filled with blood; the face became scarlet. The hydraulic system that produced a blush was, Caroline observed, with a certain wonder, the same as that which produced a man's sex. "I don't," he stammered, "know what you mean."

"Which means you know exactly what I mean. He is like a schoolgirl around you." Caroline rose from her dressing table, armored for the day. "Seduce him."

"That is definitely French," said Jim, himself again.

"No. It's English, actually. *Le vice anglais,* we call it, and not unknown in these parts, either."

"Would you really want me to . . . ?" Jim could not say what, after all, was unsayable in American City.

"You might like it. After all, Blaise is much better-looking than me."

"I don't think I could, even for you." Jim held her, carefully, about the waist, as they walked to the door. "But I guess I could sort of flirt with him, maybe."

"You American boys!" Caroline was now entirely amused.

"Well, it's the least I could do, for you giving me Emma."

In the lobby, they found themselves face to face with Mrs. Henry Cabot Lodge, a lady both censorious and serene.

"Caroline," said Mrs. Lodge, looking at Jim.

"Sister Anne. You know Congressman Day, don't you? And Mrs. Day," Caroline was inspired to add. Then Caroline turned to Jim, and said, "Where's Kitty? She was here just a minute ago."

"She left her purse upstairs."

Sister Anne was duly taken in. "Are you going to hear Mr. Hay?"

"Hear—and record it all, for the *Tribune*."

"Theodore is wicked, forcing him to come here like this. He should be home in bed at Sunapee." Sister Anne bade them farewell; and moved on.

"You would also make a good politician," said Jim, as they crossed over to Olive Street, where a special car would take them to the Exposition.

"Because I lie so easily?" Caroline frowned. "It's odd, though. I never used to lie, ever. But then—you."

"The apple in the Garden of Eden?"

"Yes. Since the serpent tempted me, I've not been the same. I have sinned . . ."

Caroline was not prepared for the astonishing beauty of the Exposition at night. Great airy palaces were lit by a million electrical candles whose light turned the prosaic Missouri sky into a spectacle like nothing that she had ever seen before. In the course of the evening, partners had been deftly switched. She was now with John, dining at the French restaurant with Henry Adams and his niece, Abigail. Representative and Mrs. James Burden Day were dining at the German restaurant in the company of the two senators from Jim's state, of whom one was very elderly indeed, and might do the proper thing and retire or die, leaving the place to Kitty's husband, as Caroline tended to think of Jim in his official capacity. He was entirely the creation, so people thought, of the legendary Judge, his father-in-law. Caroline suspected that the truth might prove to be otherwise, but no one was about to put the matter to the test.

"I have never seen anything so beautiful . . ." Adams was ecstatic; Abigail was bored. Caroline was sexually satisfied. John was in despair—his clients had been of no use to him.

"Surely, Mont-St.-Michel and Chartres . . ." Caroline began.

"They are different. They evolved over centuries. But this is like the Arabian nights. Someone rubbed a lantern and said, a city of light on the banks of the Mississippi. And here it is, all round us." Actually, all around them were huge contented-looking Americans of the heartland, gorging on French cuisine. Each contributing country had its own restaurant, with France, as always, in the lead.

"The question is, are we looking at the future, all this power, humming away, or is this a last celebration of the American past?" Adams was, for him, aglow.

"The future," said John, a subject that Caroline knew put him in a dark mood, ruin. "We've never achieved anything like this."

"We've imagined it, which is almost the same. But will our cities in 1950 be like this one?"

"Don't cities—like cathedrals—evolve?" Caroline nodded to Marguerite Cassini, who had just made what was intended to be— and indeed was—a dazzling entrance, on the arm of an elderly French diplomat. "And if they do, then they are bound to be hideous . . ."

"Like Chartres?" Adams was uncharacteristically cheerful. "Anyway, I have a mania for expositions. If only real life were constantly on display like this, always at its very best." Then Henry Adams spoke of dynamos, and Caroline thought of money; and despaired.

13

Beneath a revolving fan, Hay studied the file which Adee had
brought him. Adee tried, almost successfully, to look as if he were
not in the room. The heat was intolerable, and all that Hay could
think of was New Hampshire, which now seemed beyond his reach,
forever. He had been ordered to speak at Jackson, Michigan, on
July 6. Now June was nearly over, and Washington was more than
ever equatorial. But Hay was obliged to stay at his desk, because
the President was experiencing a sort of nervous breakdown.
Would he *really* be nominated? If nominated, could he, *ever*, be
elected president in his own right? To the extent that Hay found
anyone interesting any more, Theodore's sudden failure of nerve
was fascinating. He wished that he could talk to Adams about this
highly pleasurable state of affairs; but the Porcupine had fled to
France, stopping off in Washington just long enough to visit the
White House—after first making certain that Theodore was not
home—in order to urge Mrs. Roosevelt to go to St. Louis, and
experience the transcendent beauty of the World's Fair.

"Well, this is a proper mess," said Hay; but as he had not remembered to look up, Adee was not able to read his lips. Hay struck the desk with his right hand, a signal to Adee that Hay was about to speak. Adee's eyes focussed on Hay's lips. "Plainly," said Hay, "he's not an American citizen."

"Plainly. So what happens to him is none of our business."

"But the press . . ."

"And the President."

Both sighed. In May, a Moroccan bandit named Raisuli had abducted from something called the Palace of the Nightingales one Ion H. Perdicaris, son of a South Carolinian lady and a Greek, who had become an American citizen. The kidnapping was an affront to the entire American press. Hearst was particularly apoplectic: what sort of administration allowed American citizens to be held for ransom, particularly in a part of the world where once, for a moment or two, the proud fleet of Thomas Jefferson had reigned supreme? Already in a state of hysteria over the coming election, Theodore had quite lost his mind. He raged to Hay and to Taft: war, war, war! The fleet was put on alert. Hay was ordered to exert pressure on the Moroccan government. Hay had done so; he had, also, privately ordered an investigation of I. H. Perdicaris. Now the proof was in hand. Mr. Perdicaris was *not* an American citizen. In order to avoid military service in the Civil War, he had fled to his father's place of origin, Athens, where he had himself duly registered as a Greek subject; he was no longer an American citizen. The head of the Citizenship Bureau of the State Department, Gaillard Hunt, was now in Hay's outer office, with further proofs. Meanwhile, the President had, the day before, June 21, ordered Hay to demand the immediate release of Perdicaris; otherwise, war. Since June 21 was the first day of the Republican Convention in Chicago, the frantic President felt a loud trumpet note was in order.

"Send Mr. Hunt over to the White House. Have him explain . . ." But Hay knew that the mild Mr. Hunt would be no match for Theodore in his most Rexish mood. "Telephone the President's office. I am on my way."

"Yes, sir. You'll drive, I hope."

"I'd hoped to walk. But not in this heat." Lately not only had walking become painful in the always uncomfortable lumbar region but any exertion was apt to bring on an attack of angina. He doubted if he would live through this hellish summer; he rather hoped that he would not.

Theodore was ominously still as Hay entered the presidential office, unwelcome documents in hand. The vast Secretary of War started to go, but Theodore motioned for him to stay. "You have the telegram ready, John?"

"No, Mr. President." Hay was formal in address but not in action: he sat down, unbidden, suddenly weary.

"You realize that as we sit here, the convention is going on?" The famous teeth began to snap, nervously. "We're following it all on the telephone, in the Cabinet room. There's apt to be real trouble over this Moroccan business. We look weak, indecisive . . ."

"Mr. President, Perdicaris is not an American citizen. He is a Greek subject. He's no concern of ours."

Taft beamed; and chuckled, just the way fat jovial men were supposed to. Actually, whatever Taft was, jovial he was not. He was ambitious, petulant, suspicious. But his glorious fatness made him adorable in the eyes of the nation. "We're off the hook," he said. "Tell the press to go after the Greek government, and leave us alone."

As the President studied the documents that Hunt had assembled, he looked, to Hay's amazement, furious. "This ruins everything," he said at last. "*Everything!* I had counted on a powerful telegram to wake up the convention, the country, the world to the fact that no American citizen anywhere on earth can be harmed without a bloody reprisal, and now some fool clerk in your office comes up with this . . . this nonsense! No!" The high voice rose to a shriek. "He was born in America. His parents were American. Those are facts. How do we know any of this is true?" The President shoved the papers at Hay. "We don't. We'll have to verify. That means our legation in Athens will have to go through the records to see if he really gave up his nationality. That will take time. Too much time. I want a telegram sent today, to the American consul general at Tangier. Is that understood?"

"It's understood, of course." Hay got to his feet.

"Legally . . ." Taft began.

"I'm not a lawyer, Judge Taft. I'm a man of action, and this calls for action. Make it good, John—the telegram."

"I shall be classically brief, as befits a director of Western Union."

Hay was at the door when Theodore called out. "Put that whole file under lock and key, while we investigate the truth of the matter."

"But . . ." Taft began.

"Take care of yourself, John," shrieked the President from behind his desk.

"I think I've already done that, Theodore," said Hay; and left the presence. He had already thought up a message which would fit, neatly, into even a Hearst headline.

At the State Department, Hay himself dictated his instructions to the consul general at Tangier: "Perdicaris alive or Raisuli dead." The telegrapher beamed: "Good for you, sir! That's telling those niggers where to head in."

"Yes," said Hay. "It has a nice lilt to it. I can't think why I gave up poetry." Then he returned to his office, and locked the Perdicaris file in his desk. From Lincoln to Roosevelt had not been, exactly, an ever-upward spiral.

– 2 –

The Jefferson Hotel in St. Louis was the headquarters of "The William Randolph Hearst for President Committee." Hearst himself had a suite on the floor directly above the humble, single room of William Jennings Bryan, a lowly delegate-at-large from Nebraska.

499

Blaise pushed his way through the crowded anterooms to Hearst's command post, a large salesman's sample room, with a view of the river in the distance. The heat was terrible; the odor of sweat and tobacco and whiskey oppressive. Blaise tried not to breathe as he plunged through the crowd of delegates and hangers-on, all enjoying Hearst's hospitality.

Blaise knocked on the ultimate door, which was opened a crack. Brisbane's suspicious face appeared; then, appeased no doubt by the definite manly blueness of Blaise's eyes, he admitted him to the presence.

Despite the heat, Hearst was dressed in a black unwrinkled frock-coat, unlike his brow, which was very wrinkled indeed as he spoke into a telephone. "But my Illinois delegates are the legitimate ones," he said, acknowledging Blaise's arrival with a wave of his hand. A dozen political types, in shirt-sleeves, sat about the room, reading newspapers, making calculations of delegate strength. A New York City appellate court judge named Alton B. Parker was the candidate of the party's conservative wing, headed by August Belmont now that Whitney was dead.

Even Blaise had been impressed by the efficiency of Hearst's political operators. Although the eastern leadership of the party found Hearst intolerable, he had managed to collect so much support in the South and West that he had an excellent chance of winning the nomination if Parker failed to be nominated on the first ballot. At the moment, the Credentials Committee was faced with the problem of two delegations from Illinois. One had been put together by the Chicago boss, Sullivan; the other was committed to Hearst. "Then get Bryan. He hates Sullivan. He'll stop this." Hearst hung up. He looked at Blaise. "I can't get through to Bryan. He's staying right here in the hotel. But he won't support me . . ."

"He won't support Parker either," said Brisbane, soothingly.

"He's waiting for a miracle." Hearst sat on top of a long display table. "There won't be a miracle. For him, anyway."

"What are your chances, on the first ballot?" Blaise had already made his own estimate.

"With Illinois, I've got two hundred sixty-nine votes, and Parker's got two hundred forty-eight, without Illinois."

James Burden Day, in shirt-sleeves, entered the suite. "I've just been with Bryan. He's on his way to the convention hall. He's going to fight for the seating of your delegates."

The men in the room applauded; and Brisbane danced a small jig. "But," asked Hearst, unimpressed, "will he support me?"

Day shrugged. "He's not supporting anybody, so far. He wants to stop Parker, that's all."

"I'm the only one who can do that." Hearst's eyes seemed to have been electrified; they shone, balefully, at Day. "Doesn't he know that? Doesn't he know there's only me now?"

Brisbane answered for Day. "He still thinks that when he gets up in front of that audience, all will be forgiven."

Hearst turned to Day. "Make him *any* offer."

"I'll try. But he's in a bad mood." Jim left. He had not even noticed Blaise. Politics had that effect on everyone involved. Blaise had seen the same sort of total absorption only at gambling casinos, where men were so absorbed in the turn of a card or the throw of a pair of dice that not even the end of the world could distract them.

A number of delegates were then admitted, and the Chief received them with magisterial calm. Would he bolt the party if he failed to get the nomination? Of course he would not, he said: this was the party of the people, and he would never turn his back on what after all was the nation itself. Also, only the Democratic Party could keep peace in a world made more dangerous by the bellicosity of Theodore Roosevelt. But hadn't he been impressed by the swift assurance of the President when, with a single telegram, he had freed an American citizen from his Barbary Coast kidnapper? Hearst shrugged this off as "mere sensationalism." For Blaise, the Chief's new respectability was as irresistibly comic as any Weber and Fields sketch.

Brisbane drew Blaise aside. "He's got the nomination if only Bryan . . ."

"What's wrong with Bryan?" Blaise was genuinely curious; but then he had no political sense, the turn of a card meant nothing to him.

"Oh, vanity, I suppose. The peerless leader of '96 and 1900, wandering about the convention like a lost soul, his only power to help the Chief win—or lose."

"He'll want him to lose, so that Parker will be beaten by Roosevelt, and the next time—four years from now—Bryan will be back, crucifying mankind on that cross of gold of his." Blaise was rather proud to have figured out what was so obvious to Brisbane that he did no more than nod, and say, "That's about the size of it. But if he gets our Illinois delegates seated, that may do the trick." John Sharp Williams made a stately entrance. Hearst pretended delight. Brisbane said, "I hear you're buying your sister's paper."

"I'm trying to. That's really why I'm here. Not that this isn't," he stared at Hearst's alarmingly huge smile, "worth the trip. My sister's more political than me. She's here to write about the convention. She actually writes herself, you know."

"Many of us," said Brisbane, sourly, "do."

On the Fourth of July, Hearst was nominated by a San Francisco politician, a friend of the late Senator George Hearst. Blaise sat with Caroline and John Sanford in the press gallery of the huge airless hall. A six-foot portrait of Hearst dominated the stage, while a Hearst band played first *"America"* and then, as a recognition of the South's importance to the populist millionaire, "Dixie." Although Thomas E. Watson was, that very day, being nominated for president by the Populist or People's Party, he had brought a number of Democratic Southern politicians into Hearst's organization.

After the nominating speeches for Hearst, the California delegation led a parade around the floor of the convention. Blaise was surprised at how genuinely popular the Chief had become. "Of course he has no chance," said Caroline, rising from her wooden folding chair.

Blaise also stood up. "Why not?"

"His Illinois delegation wasn't seated. So that's fifty-four votes for Parker. And Bryan will never support him. Let's go get some air. I am about to faint."

For the delicate business at hand, Blaise had selected a riverboat. The owner had offered Blaise a suite when it was discovered that every hotel in the city was booked, and so he now had, all to himself, the wonders of the *Delta Queen*, a great Gothic wooden contraption with paddle-wheels of the sort celebrated in John Hay's "Jim Bludso of the Prairie Bell." The night was airless, damp, hot. The *Delta Queen* was moored to the levee near Market Street. At the gangplank, a single guard saluted Blaise casually; and bade them all welcome.

A steward received them on the first deck, and escorted them into an echoing mahogany bar, lit by a single bronze gas-lamp, beneath which sat, ominous in his cheerfulness, dreadful in his jovial smile, the pink-whiskered Mr. Houghteling. Blaise was relieved to find his ally in place. Now it was two to two. Before, he had felt outnumbered by Caroline and John—three rather than two to one, since Caroline had, in a sense, doubled herself through accomplishment while he had diminished himself by non-success. Mr. Houghteling rose, the dentured smile ghastly in the light from overhead. "Mrs. Sanford. Mr. Sanford. Mr. Sanford. At least one has no trouble with names . . ."

A figure stepped out of the shadows and said, "I'm Mr. Trimble—not Sanford."

Blaise felt, again, outnumbered. But he greeted Trimble politely; then the five of them sat at a round table, and the steward brought them champagne with the compliments of the owner. Blaise noted a spittoon had been fastened to the deck beside each chair. How, he wondered, was it emptied? and what happened if one's jet of tobacco juice changed its trajectory due to a lurch of the ship? He tried to recall the laws of physics that he had learned in school— and forgotten. Galileo on the leaning tower of Pisa. Spit on the deck. As Blaise thought, wildly, of spittoons, Sanford and Houghteling were covering the table with sheets of paper, and Caroline and Trimble were talking to each other in low collusive voices. Blaise knew that he should feel elated; instead, he was merely hot, tired, irritable. Sanford began, for the enemy. "You've had a chance to study the *Tribune*'s financial status . . . ?"

"Yes." Houghteling looked at Blaise, who looked at Caroline, who was staring now into her glass of champagne. He thought of that other champagne glass, of Del dead on a New Haven sidewalk. "Yes," Mr. Houghteling repeated, "all is in order, according to my accountant. I'm afraid I can neither add nor subtract. But he's been with me thirty years, and he does both very nicely, or so I'm told by those who know. He says all's well, so—all's well. Now," Houghteling frowned and smiled simultaneously, "we are willing to pay for fifty percent of the shares . . ."

Caroline, not her lawyer-husband, spoke. "Forty-eight percent of the shares are up for sale, not fifty percent."

Sweat rolled down Blaise's left side, tickling him mercilessly. "We agreed to fifty-fifty, you and I." He stared at Caroline, who stared back at him, in perfect innocence.

"So we did. So it is," she said. "I will sell you forty-eight percent of the shares. I will keep forty-eight percent of the shares. That's fifty-fifty. We—you and I—will own exactly the same amount, as agreed."

"Who owns," asked Mr. Houghteling, sinister smile in place but cordial scowl gone, "the remaining four percent of the shares?"

"Mr. Houghteling misled us!" Caroline was suspiciously charming. "He adds and subtracts with lightning speed . . ."

"*I* own four percent," said Trimble, turning his pale blue Brisbane-approved eyes on Blaise. "Mrs. Sanford wanted to give me a bonus when the paper was in profit. I said I'd take the bonus in the form of stock."

"It was my understanding . . ." Houghteling began.

"I thought it was all cut and dried." Sanford was now, himself, triumphantly cut, dried, thought Blaise. "Sister would sell brother half her shares for one hundred fifty-six thousand dollars. That was the meaning of fifty-fifty . . ."

"That was not my understanding." Blaise wondered if he should abandon the game right then and there.

Houghteling tapped his pile of papers. "There was no mention here, according to my accountant, of any owner other than Mrs. Sanford, the sole owner."

"You will find the Trimble shares adverted to in section five of the financial audit." Sanford sounded bored; yet it was his life that was at stake. Blaise found him almost as mysterious as Caroline, whose mystery was to be exactly what she seemed, someone intent on getting what she wanted without unduly distressing those whom she—victimized: he was now casting himself in the role of victim. Certainly, he had been subtly misled from the beginning. Caroline was nothing if not tricky.

"We," said Mr. Houghteling, "have acted in good faith from the beginning."

"I trust," said Sanford, "that you are not suggesting that we have not?"

"I suggest exactly that, yes. My client understood—as did I— that he would become half-owner of the *Tribune*. Instead, he is, to put it bluntly, a minority shareholder, who can be outvoted by Mrs. Sanford and Mr. Trimble, should they choose to act as one."

"Which they will always do." Blaise got to his feet. "I see no reason to go on with this." He looked at Caroline, who smiled and said nothing.

"I am sorry if there has been a misunderstanding." Sanford did not sound, in the least, sorry.

"There always is," said Caroline suddenly. "We specialize in misunderstandings. It is a family trait. What looks to be a one to one of us appears as a seven to the other."

Blaise experienced a moment of almost perfect rage, a highly exciting flush of blood to the head, followed by a sudden weakness. He sat down heavily. Caroline acted as if nothing untoward had been said. "If you would rather not buy, I'll go to Mr. Hearst, who will be a publisher again tomorrow, or to Mr. McLean."

This was bluff. Blaise knew that the Chief had no available money (he had spent close to two million dollars in order to secure the nomination), while John R. McLean had already said no to Caroline. "I'll buy forty-eight percent of the shares, at the agreed-on price." Blaise heard his own voice as though it were someone else's, far off, strange. But then this was the most important decision that he had ever made.

"I draw your attention, Mr. Houghteling, to the obligation of your client and my client," John was dry, correct, "in the event of a future sale of these shares, to offer one another, first, the option to buy . . ."

"Yes, yes." Houghteling presented Caroline with a sheet of paper; then he signalled to the steward. "Ask the captain or mate or whoever's on duty to witness these signatures."

In silence they waited beneath the bronze lamp, which swayed, ever so slightly, as the river's current rocked the ship. Two men in uniform joined them. Caroline signed first. Blaise signed second. The ship's officers signed. Then Houghteling signalled for more champagne; and Caroline said, "Where is my check?"

Houghteling laughed; and gave her Blaise's check. Blaise studied Sanford's face; but there was no reaction. The cause of Caroline's embarrassment appeared at ease.

Trimble raised his glass. "To the *Washington Tribune*," he said.

Solemnly they drank. Then Sanford and Houghteling put away their documents. The ship's officers excused themselves, and Trimble said, "I don't know about you publishers, but the editor has to go back to the convention hall."

"So will this publisher." Caroline rose; and turned to Blaise. "Will you join us?"

Blaise said, "Yes."

As it turned out, the only publisher to go to the convention hall was Caroline. Blaise chose to go back to the Jefferson Hotel to confer with the Chief, now in his shirt-sleeves, a telephone receiver close to one ear, as word came from the hall, where Brisbane was reporting what was—and was not—going on. What was going on was the nomination of Alton B. Parker for president. What was not going on was Willliam Jennings Bryan, who had yet to make known his choice. "I'll get one ninety-four on the first ballot," was Hearst's greeting.

Blaise responded in kind. "I bought half the *Washington Tribune*."

President-to-be Hearst put down the receiver and became Publisher Hearst. "How much?"

Blaise told him the exact amount. Word always spread; he did not say that he had bought only half of Caroline's shares. "Too much." Hearst took off his tie and collar; and looked less presidential by the moment. "I could go in with you. Maybe," he said, staring at Blaise with the same impersonal intensity with which he would glare at the mock-up of a front page.

"And then," said Blaise, lightly, "maybe not. I don't want to be involved with the *Tribune American*, and you don't either."

"I guess not. You and your sister friends?"

"I don't know."

"You'll find out soon enough."

Blaise agreed.

At four-thirty on the morning of July 8, after all the nominating speeches had been made, Blaise and Jim Day sat side by side in the press section, shelling and eating peanuts, as they tried to stay awake. Others had succumbed to fatigue or alcohol. Figures were slumped over chairs on the convention floor as well as in the galleries. The smell of stale smoke, whiskey, sweat was now so powerful that Blaise, acclimatized, wondered if he could ever again breathe fresh air. The balloting would soon begin. Hearst still had a chance. But Bryan had not come to his aid. Earlier, Bryan had nominated a nullity in the form of a Missouri senator. He did add that he would be happy to support the people's friend, William Randolph Hearst, should the convention nominate him. Then Bryan had gone back to his hotel, where, Hearst had gleefully noted, he collapsed with what seemed to be pneumonia.

"Bryan wants us to lose, I'm afraid," said Jim.

"Do you care?"

"Well, I'm safe back home. But it would be nice to have a strong head to the ticket."

Suddenly, there was a sound of applause at the back of the hall. The speaker—there was never not someone speaking from the platform—paused as, down the main isle, William Jennings Bryan made his slow, majestic way.

"This is going to be something." Jim was now wide awake. He brushed peanut shells from his trousers; and sat very straight. Even Blaise felt something of the general excitement as Bryan, plainly ill, dark of face and sweating heavily, walked up the steps to the platform. The twenty thousand delegates and visitors were now all alert. There was loud applause. There was also excitement of the sort that Blaise had only observed once before, at a bullfight in Madrid when matador (Bryan?) and bull (the convention? or was it the other way around?) began their final confrontation. For ten minutes, by Blaise's watch, the crowd cheered Bryan, who plainly drew nourishment from his people. Then he raised both arms, and the hall was silent.

The voice began, and, like everyone else, Blaise was mesmerized by its astonishing power. Illness had made Bryan hoarse; but no less eloquent for that. "Eight years ago at Chicago the Democratic National Convention placed in my hand the standard of the party and commissioned me as its candidate. Four years ago that commission was renewed . . ."

"He's going for it!" Jim's eyes were bright. "He's going to stampede the convention."

The tension was now absolute in the hall. The Parker and Hearst delegates looked grim indeed. The galleries were ecstatic, as were perhaps a third of the delegates, Bryan's men to the end.

"Tonight I came back to this Democratic National Convention to return that commission . . ."

A chorus of no's drowned him out. The eyes were glittering now, and not from fever. Again the commanding arms were raised. ". . . and to say to you that you may dispute over whether I have fought the good fight, you may dispute over whether I have finished my course, but you cannot deny," and the voice was now as clear as some huge tolling bell, "that I have kept the faith."

By the time Bryan was done, he was the convention's hero and the party's paladin forever. But, contrary to Jim's hope, he did not stampede the convention. He received his ovation and was carried off, by concerned friends, to the Jefferson Hotel, and the wild nocturnal pleasures of pneumonia.

By dawn's light, the first ballot gave Parker nine votes less than the two-thirds needed to nominate. Hearst was second with, as he had predicted, one hundred ninety-four votes. As the balloting continued, Hearst's vote became two hundred sixty-three votes, to Blaise's astonishment. How could anyone in his right mind want the Chief as president? But delegates need not be in their right mind; and money had been spent, particularly in the Iowa and Indiana delegations. If Bryan had come to Hearst's aid, the Chief would have been nominated. Actually, a race between Hearst and Roosevelt would have been, if nothing else, a splendid—what was the Greek word? *Agon.* Blaise had taken to the word in school. *Agon.* Agony. A contest for a prize; a duel; to the death, presumably.

During the balloting, Jim was with his state's delegation on the floor while Blaise sat with Brisbane in the press gallery. Caroline and husband had long since retired; only Trimble and Blaise represented the *Tribune.* Judge Alton B. Parker was duly nominated, after receiving six hundred fifty-eight votes. "We'll get Bryan," said Brisbane, furiously. "If it's the last thing we do."

"Bryan's got himself." Blaise was flat. "Forget about him. What's next?"

Brisbane looked exhausted. "I don't know. Governor of New York, I suppose."

"It's worse than gambling, politics." Blaise was aware that Jim was signalling him from the floor.

"But think of the stakes," Brisbane sighed. "The whole world."

"Oh, I don't think the White House is the whole world yet." At the main entrance to the convention hall, Blaise met Jim, who was mopping his face with a handkerchief; yet, even sweating and tired, he was masculine energy and youth incarnate.

"I'm going to bed," said Jim.

"I've got a room on the river-boat." Blaise waved for a cab. "Courtesy of the owner."

"You won't be uncomfortable?"

"No," said Blaise, as they got into the cab. "To the levee," he said to the driver; and turned to Jim. "It's closer, and why wake Kitty?"

14

In the bright winter sunlight, Henry Adams, like some ancient pink-and-white orchid, sat in the window seat and stared down at Lafayette Square, while John Hay sat opposite him, studying the latest dispatches from Moscow. Hay was delighted to have lived long enough to welcome Adams home from Europe.

The summer and fall had nearly ended him. On Theodore's orders, he had been obliged to speak at Carnegie Hall in New York City to sum up the achievements of the Republican Party in general and of Theodore Rex in particular. Hay had enjoyed perjuring himself before the bar of history. Of Roosevelt's bellicosity, Hay had proclaimed with a straight face, "He and his predecessor have done more in the interest of universal peace than any other two presidents since our government was formed." Adams had thought the adjective "universal" sublime. "He works for universal peace—whatever that is—stasis?—through terrestrial warfare. You have said it all." But Hay was well pleased with the speech, as was the President. The emphasis was on the essential conservatism of the allegedly progressive Roosevelt. The tariff needed reform, true, but that was best done by the magnates themselves. This went down very well in New York City, where the President had been obliged to go, hat in hand, to beg money from the likes of Henry Clay Frick. Thanks to the essential conservatism of Parker, the great magnates, from Belmont and Ryan to Schiff and Ochs, were financing the Democratic Party. Roosevelt, with no Mark Hanna to raise money, was obliged to make any number of reckless accommodations in order to extort money from the likes of J. P. Morgan and E. H. Harriman. Meanwhile Cortelyou was blackmailing everyone he knew to give to the campaign.

Hay had never seen anything quite like Roosevelt's panic: there was no other word to describe his behavior during the last few months of a campaign that he had no chance of losing. Bryan had stayed aloof until October; then he moved amongst his people warning them of Roosevelt's shady campaign financing practices and of his love for war. Bryan seldom had much to say about Parker, who ended by losing not only the entire West but New York State, the source of his support. It was the greatest Republican victory since 1872. Theodore was—and continued to be— ecstatic. He had also insisted that Hay stay on for the second term.

"I should get a telescope." Adams squinted in the bright sun. "Then I could see who pays calls on Theodore. I've been waiting for a glimpse of J. P. Morgan's incandescent nose ever since I got back."

"That particular incandescence is probably already out of joint. I don't think Theodore will humor him, or any of the others."

"Betrayal?" Adams's eyes shone.

"*Fidelity* to . . . earlier principles. You know, Bryan's in town, holding court at the Capitol. He's been praising Theodore . . ."

"A bad sign."

"He also says that if the Democrats were to come out for nationalizing the railroads, they would sweep the country."

"Why not?" was the response of the co-author of *Tales of Erie*, easily the most savage indictment ever made of the railroad owners, and their exuberant, never-ending corruption of courts, Congress, White House. Then, triumphantly, "Here they come!"

Hay managed to be perpendicular when Lizzie Cameron entered the room with her daughter, Martha, who was, at eighteen, larger, darker, duller than her mother, who was still, in Hearts' eyes at least, the world's most beautiful woman, the Helen of Troy of Lafayette Park, now resident, mysteriously, at the Lorraine, a New York City residential hotel in Forty-fifth Street, convenient to the theaters, and Rector's, and museums, where Martha was to be finished off at last and then, her mother prayed, grandly married. "La Dona." Adams welcomed his beloved with a deep bow; bestowed a kiss on Martha's cheek. "I never thought to see the two of you here again."

"Oh, yes, you did. John," Lizzie took Hay's hand and gave him the cold appraising Sherman look, "go to Georgia. This minute. You are mad to stay on here. I'll wire Don . . ."

"I'd be madder to go now we've got you back, if only for the Diplomatic Reception." Lizzie had asked Henry to put her and Martha on the guest list for the January 12 Diplomatic Reception at the White House. This would be, in effect, Martha's official, and inexpensive, social debut.

"I'm a pauper!" Lizzie let drop her ermine cape on the small chair by the fire, where Adams always sat. Then she sat on the cape.

"You're not a pauper. Don't be dramatic, Mother." Martha had her father's weighty manner if not actual weight. "Mother wants to reopen 21. I think she's mad."

"Everyone, it would appear, is mad today." Hay sat on a sofa's arm, from which he could stand up without effort. "Don't discourage your mother. We want her back. Next door to us. Forever."

"See?" Lizzie stared up at Martha, whose body now blocked the fire. In the bright air Hay watched as motes of dust floated and glittered like minuscule fragments of gold, a pretty sight—if of course he was not having another seizure like the one where he had imagined himself in Lincoln's office. He dared not ask the others if they, too, noted the bright dust.

Then Clara greeted mother and daughter, and their diminished circle was closed at last. "What sort of husband would you like?" asked Clara, as if she herself could provide one, according to Martha's specifications.

"Rich." Lizzie was still radiant, Hay decided; and unchanged.

Adams was still besotted with her; and unchanged. "The rich are boring, La Dona."

"I think I'd like Mr. Adams." Martha was cool. "He is never boring, except when he sees a dynamo."

Clara, a master of small talk, disliked idle talk. "Blaise Sanford. He's the right age. He's built himself a palace in Connecticut Avenue. He's half-owner of the *Tribune*, so he has something to do, always important. *And* he lives part of the year in France. I think," she turned to Hay, "we should set things in motion."

"You set them in motion. I have the Russians to deal with. They've just surrendered Port Arthur to the Japanese." Hay held up the folder containing the Moscow dispatches.

Adams was suddenly alert. "Now the pieces rearrange themselves. Brooks predicted this, you know. Now let's see if his next prediction comes true. Russia will undergo some sort of internal revolution, he says, and their empire will then fall apart or, if they survive the revolution, expand at our expense. England is at an end, civilization shudders to a halt, and . . ."

"I cannot get enough of your gloom." Hay did enjoy the Porcupine's chiliastic arias. "But we've got Japan to deal with in Asia, and a peace to be made in order to keep . . ."

"Open doors." Everyone, including Martha, repeated the magic meaningless phrase.

"I would rather be known for that than for 'Little Breeches.'"

"I'm afraid, sonny," said Adams contentedly, "your future fame will rest on an ever greater vulgarity, 'Perdicaris alive . . .'"

"'. . . or Raisuli dead!'" the others intoned.

"The fatal gift for phrase," sighed Adams, as happy as Hay had ever seen him, with Lizzie beside him, and all the remaining Hearts in the room. Then, as if to complete Adams's felicity, the door to the bright study now framed the thick rotundity of his houseguest, whose bald head shone in the winter light, like Parian marble, whose great eyes looked merrily but shrewdly on the company. "I have," intoned Henry James, "already, in the literal sense, merely, broken my fast, but as rumors of a late—ah, *collation* is being served *à la fourchette*, so much tidier than *au canif*, I have hurried home from my morning round of calls, filling the city with a veritable blizzard of pasteboard." Then, ceremoniously, James greeted Lizzie and Martha, while Adams took a calling-card from his vest pocket, and presented it to James.

"What—or, rather, who is this?" James held the card close to his eyes.

"Delivered by its owner while you were out."

"'George Dewey,'" James read in a voice resonant with awe, "'Admiral of the Navy.' My cup runneth over, with salt water. Why," he addressed the room, "would a national hero, whom I've not had the pleasure—honor—distinction of meeting, descend, as it were, from the high, glorious—ah, poop-deck of his flagship, which I can imagine moored with chains of gold in the Potomac, all flags unfurled, and submit himself to dull earth in order to pay a call on someone absolutely unknown in heroic circles, and less than a ripple, I should think, in naval ones?"

Hay found James in his old age far more genial and less alarming than in his middle age. For one thing, the appearance was milder since he had shaved off his beard; in fact, the resulting combination of bald head and rosy smooth ovoid face put one in mind of Humpty Dumpty. "You are a fellow celebrity," said Hay. "That's all. The press, which defines us all, celebrates both you and him. Now he comes to celebrate you and, in the act, celebrates himself yet again."

"He is a wondrous fool," said Adams. "Stay longer and I'll invite him here."

"No. No. No. The ladies of America are waiting for me to tell them about Balzac. So much—ah, money can be earned by lecturing, I had no idea."

James had not been in Washington since 1882; and he had not been in the United States for some years. "Contemptible, effete

snob!" Theodore Rex would roar whenever the name was mentioned. But Theodore was himself sufficiently a snob, if not effete,
to realize that since the reigning novelist of the English-speaking
world had come home to take one last long look at his native land,
the President must invite him to the Diplomatic Reception. With
each passing year in the White House, Theodore became more
royal, and his receptions and dinner parties now had a definite
Sun King style to them. Therefore, protocol required that America's great writer be received by his sovereign. James had been
delighted and, wickedly, amused by the invitation; his view of the
President was every bit as dark as the President's of him, but
where Theodore thundered, James mocked softly; Theodore Rex
was simply a noisy jingo, not to be encouraged.

"We are," observed James, as Adams led them into the dining
room, where silver and crystal sparkled, and William stood at
benign attention, "recreating the house-party at Surrenden
Dering. Mrs. Cameron. The delicious Martha—now grown.
Ourselves . . ."

Hay thought, with a sudden guilty pang, of Del, whom he almost
never thought of any more. James, aware that the party had lost a
member to death, shifted swiftly to Caroline. "What of her?" he
asked. Adams told him. James was interested, as always, in
variations from the usual. A young American woman who chose to
publish a newspaper was not quite within his grasp, but Hay had
the sense that by the time James's visit to what he called "the city
of conversation" was over, Caroline would be defined in Jamesian
terms.

Lizzie asked James, point-blank, what he thought of Washington. The Master's frown was not without charm, as he affected an
air of total concentration, like a man doing a complex sum in his
head. "The subject so—vast. The language so—inadequate," he
began, a stick of Maggie's cornbread breaking off in his hand.
"One must be subjective, no other approach will do, so—to live
here, for me, *not* John, a great minister of state or, in short, a
statesman in his proper state, the capital, or Henry, the historian,
the observer, the creator of theories of history and—ah, *energy,*

what better place to watch the world from? You, too, Mrs. Cameron, are of this world, though divided in allegiance, I suspect, with a bias for our shabby old European world, but I *see* you here, glittering at the center, with Mrs. Hay and, perhaps, Martha, too, but as for me—ah, my passion for crudely chipped beef is still remembered in this house." James filled his plate without dropping so much as a single syllable of a speaking style which hardly varied now from his novels, which were, for Hay, unlike the writer himself, too long of wind for the page while delightful when accompanied by James's beautiful measured voice, far less British in its accent than that of Henry Adams, who sounded exactly like the very Englishmen who had so resolutely snubbed him and his father during the latter's ministry to St. James's. ". . . as for me to live here would be death and madness. The politics are of no account when one is not a politician, while the constellation—not to mention promiscuous congregation—of celebrities would quite smother me . . ."

– 2 –

Caroline was surprised at how few disagreements there were between herself and Blaise. The new publisher knew his job, if not Washington. Trimble continued to put out the paper. Caroline gladly surrendered to Blaise the task of wringing advertising money from their mutual relatives, and everyone else. He had gone twice to Mrs. Bingham's; and showed no great disdain. Although Frederika was helping him furnish the palace, he seemed to have no particular interest in her, or in anyone. He had become, in some mysterious way, a creature of Hearst. It was as if their close association had made it impossible for him to find anyone else interesting; yet Blaise did not much like Hearst personally. Obviously, this was a case of inadvertent fascination. Luckily, it was a very useful one for the *Tribune*. Blaise was, by any standard, an excellent publisher.

As Marguerite helped Caroline dress for the Diplomatic Reception, she counted the number of days which would bring her to the magic, if not exactly joyous in itself, twenty-seventh birthday: fifty-two days, and she would be able to soar, on eagle-wings of gold. But soar where? What would change? other than the constant dull worry that money was in short supply. John had paid his debts; and remained, at her request, in New York. Jim seldom missed a Sunday; and she was reasonably content. But Marguerite, who was not always—as opposed to usually—wrong, was right when she said that so ridiculous a situation could not go on forever. Mrs. Belmont had made it possible, if not exactly fashionable, to divorce a husband and still remain within the world. That was progress. But divorce implied an alternative, in the form of yet another marriage, and except for Jim, there was no one who interested her; and Jim was beyond her reach, even if she had been so minded to reach out, which she was not. Still, it was now an absolute fact that Caroline had no more use for John Apgar Sanford; and he had none for her. Only Emma was satisfactory.

Blaise arrived in a motor car, with a handsome uniformed driver, who helped Caroline into the back seat, where Blaise was resplendent in white tie. "We are," Caroline observed, "a couple."

"For the purposes of Diplomatic Receptions, anyway." He was more relaxed with her now. The meeting on the river-boat had been their lowest moment. Relations could only improve, or break off entirely. They had improved. "Court will be unusually brilliant tonight." Caroline turned into the Society Lady. "Mr. Adams is not coming, but he is sending not only Henry James but Saint-Gaudens and John La Farge—literature, sculpture, painting will celebrate our sovereign and decorate his court."

"He is so full of himself."

"No more than Mr. Hearst."

"Hearst's an original. He's done something."

"Isn't the . . . the . . . the Panama Canal something?"

"Nothing compared to reporting . . ."

". . . and inventing . . ."

". . . news." This was an old debate between them, or, rather, discourse, since they were generally in agreement. To determine what people read and thought about each day was not only action but power of a kind no ruler could, with such regularity, exercise. Caroline often thought of the public as a great mass of shapeless modelling clay which she, in Washington, at least, could mould with what she chose to put in the columns of the *Tribune*. No wonder that Hearst, with eight newspapers, and a magazine or two, felt that he could—even should—be president. No wonder Theodore Roosevelt genuinely hated and feared him.

The East Room of the White House had been simplified to the point of brilliance, and the result was more royal than republican. Also, the Roosevelts had increased the number of military aides, their gold-braid loopings complementing the quantities of gold-and-silver braid worn by the diplomatic corps. The astonishing McKinley pumpkin seats, each fountaining a sickly palm, had long since vanished; the mustard rug was now only a memory of a time when the East Room was like the lobby of a Cleveland hotel. The floor was now shining parquet, the chandeliers were more elaborate than ever, while the sparse furniture was much gilded and marbled. Red silk ropes were everywhere, in order to control the public, which were allowed, at certain hours, to wander through their sovereign's palace.

The President and Mrs. Theodore Roosevelt stood at the room's center, shaking hands, as glittering aides discreetly moved the guests along. Theodore was more than ever stout, and hearty, and delighted with himself, while Edith Roosevelt was her usual calm self, ever ready to curb her volatile mate, whose self-love was curiously contagious.

"Very sound. *Very* sound on Japan, Mrs. Sanford," was his greeting to Caroline. "Things are about to happen." Then he looked very grim, as Cassini, dean of the diplomatic corps, approached, Marguerite in tow. Caroline exchanged amiable whispers with Edith Roosevelt, and moved on. President and Russian Ambassador had nothing to say to each other, and contrary to all diplomatic usage *said* nothing to each other. Marguerite looked worn. She had had a love affair that had gone wrong, and now the word was that Cassini was to be replaced. End of glory, thought Caroline, as Henry James, the embodiment of all literary glory, shook her hand warmly and said, "At last. At last."

"It has been almost seven years since Surrenden Dering," Caroline observed, with some not entirely banal wonder at the rapidity of time's passage.

"You never come to our side of the water, so I've come to yours." James lowered his voice in mock fear, as if Theodore might be listening. "Ours. *Ours!* What have I said? *Lèse-majesté des Etats-Unis.*"

"I shall be on the other side this summer," said Caroline, as they crossed the room, for the most part filled with people that she knew. Washington was indeed a village still; and so a newcomer like Henry James was a mild sensation. Once the diplomatic reception was concluded, there would be a supper for the chosen few, among them James and Caroline but not Blaise.

They paused in an empty corner, as the Hays made their entrance. "Our Henry refuses to come," James observed with quiet satisfaction. "He was here earlier this month, and he has now declared that he has had his absolute fill of the sublime Theodore, whilst conceding how strenuous, vigorous and, yes, let us acknowledge it, *supple*, our sovereign is, the sun at the center of the sky, with us as . . . as . . ."

"Clouds," Caroline volunteered.

James frowned. "I once was obliged to let go an excellent typewriter-operator because whenever I paused for a word, she would offer me one, and always not simply the wrong word, but the very worst word."

"I'm sorry. But I quite like us as clouds."

"Why," asked James, "with the delicious exception of yourself, are there no beautiful women at court?"

"Well, there is Mrs. Cameron—if not Martha."

"Alas, not Martha. But Mrs. Cameron's a visitor. What I take to be the local ladies here are plainer than what one would find at a comparable—if anything in poor shabby London could be compared to this incomparability—reception."

Caroline repeated the Washington adage that the capital was filled with ambitious energetic men and the faded women that they had married in their green youth. James was amused. "The same doubtless applies to diplomats . . ."

They were joined by Jules Jusserand, the resplendent French ambassador, and the three lapsed into French, a language James spoke quite as melodiously as his own. "What did the President say to you?" asked Jusserand. "We were all watching the two of you, with fascination."

"He expressed his delight—the very word he used, as, apparently, he always does—at my—and his—election to something called the National Institute of Arts and Letters, which has, parthenogenetically, given birth to an American Academy, a rustic version of your august French Academy, some half a hundred members whose souls if not achievements are held to be immortal."

"What," said Jusserand, "will you wear?"

"Ah, that vexes us tremendously. As the President and I tend to corpulence, I have proposed togas, on the Roman model, but our leader John Hay favors some sort of uniform like—Admiral Dewey's." James bowed low, as the hero passed by them. "He is my new friend. We have exchanged cards. I know," James swept the air with an extended arm, "*everyone* at last."

"You are a lion," said Caroline.

Supper was served in the new dining room, where a number of tables for ten had been set. Henry James was placed at the President's table, a Cabinet lady between them. Saint-Gaudens was also at the monarch's table, with Caroline to his right. Edith Roosevelt had come to depend upon Caroline for those occasions where the ability to talk French was necessary, not that the great American Dublin-born sculptor, despite his name, spoke much French. He lived in New Hampshire, not France. Of Lizzie Cameron, who had posed for the figure of Victory in Saint-Gaudens's equestrienne monument to her uncle General Sherman, he said, "She has the finest profile of any woman in the world."

"How satisfactory, to have such a thing, and to have *you* acknowledge it."

Unfortunately, a table of ten was, for the President, no place for the ritual dinner-party conversation: first course, partner to right; second course, partner to left; and so on. The table for ten was Theodore's pulpit, and they his congregation. "We must see more of Mr. James in his own country." Theodore's pince-nez glittered. As James opened his mouth to launch what would be a long but beautifully shaped response, the President spoke through him, and James, slowly, comically, shut his mouth as the torrent of sound, broken only by the clicking of teeth, swept over the table. "I cannot say that I very much like the idea of Mark Twain in our Academy." He looked at James, but spoke to the table. "Howells, yes. He's sound, much of the time. But Twain is like an old woman, ranting about imperialism. I've found there's usually a physical reason for such people. They are congenitally weak in the body, and this makes them weak in nerves, in courage, makes them fearful of war . . ."

"Surely," began James.

The President's shrill voice kept on. "Everyone knows that Twain ran away from the Civil War, a shameful thing to do . . ."

To Caroline's astonishment, James's deep baritone continued under the presidential tirade. The result was disconcerting but fascinating, a cello and a flute, simultaneously, playing separate melodies.

". . . Mr. Twain, or Clemens, as I prefer to call him . . ."

". . . testing of character and manhood. A forge . . ."

". . . much strength of arm as well as, let us say . . ."

". . . cannot flourish without the martial arts, or any civilization . . ."

". . . distinguished and peculiarly American genius . . ."

". . . desertion of the United States for a life abroad . . ."

". . . when Mr. Hay telephoned Mr. Clemens from the Century Club to . . ."

". . . without which the white race can no longer flourish, and prevail." The President paused to drink soup. The table watched, and listened, as Henry James, master of so many millions of words, had the last. "And though I say—ah, tentatively, of course," the

President glared at him over his soup spoon, "the sublimity of the greatest art may be beyond his method, his—what other word?" The entire table leaned forward, what *would* the word be? and on what, Caroline wondered, was James's astonishing self-confidence and authority, even majesty, based? "*Drollery,* that so often tires, and yet never entirely obscures for us the vision of that mighty river, so peculiarly august and ah—yes, yes? Yes! *American.*"

Before the President could again dominate the table, James turned to his post-soup partner, and Caroline turned to Saint-Gaudens, who said, "I can't wait to tell Henry. The reason he won't set foot ever again in this house is that he's never allowed to finish a sentence and no Adams likes to be interrupted."

"Mr. James is indeed a master."

"Of an art considerably higher than mere politics." Saint-Gaudens reminded Caroline of a bearded Puritan satyr, if such a creature was possible; he seemed very old in a way that the lively Adams, or the boyish if ill Hay, did not. "I wish I had read more in my life," he said, as a fish was offered up to them.

"You have time."

"No time." He smiled. "Hay was furious at Mark Twain, who wouldn't answer the telephone. We knew he was home, of course, but he didn't want to join us at the Century Club. What bees are swarming in that bonnet! Twain's latest bogey is Christian Science. He told me quite seriously, after only one Scotch sour, that in thirty years Christian Scientists will have taken over the government of the United States, and that they would then establish an absolute religious tyranny."

"Why are Americans so mad for religion?"

"In the absence of a civilization," Saint-Gaudens was direct, "what else have they?"

"Absence?" Caroline indicated James, who was smiling abstractedly at the President, who was again in the conversational saddle, but only at his end of the table. "And you. And Mr. Adams. And even the Sun King there."

"Mr. James is truly absent. Gone from us for good. Mr. Adams writes of Virgins and dynamos in France. I am nothing. The President—well . . ."

"So Christ Scientist . . ."

"Or Christ Dentist . . ."

"Sets the tone." Caroline never ceased to be amazed at the number of religious sects and societies the country spawned each year. Jim had told her that if he were to miss a Sunday service at the Methodist church in American City, he would not be reelected, while Kitty taught Sunday school, with true belief. If for nothing else, Caroline was grateful to Mlle. Souvestre for having dealt God so absolute a death blow that she had never again felt the slightest need for that highly American—or Americanized—commodity.

The voice of Theodore was again heard at table. "I stood in the Red Room, I remember, on election night, and I told the press that I would not be a candidate again. Two terms is enough for anyone, I said, and say again." Henry James stared dreamily at the President, as if by closely scrutinizing him he might distil his essence. "Politicians always stay on too long. Better to go at the top of your form, and give someone else a chance to measure up, which is what it is all about."

"Measure up," James murmured, with mysterious, to Caroline, approval. "Yes, yes, yes," he added to no one, as Theodore told them how he had invented, first, Panama, and then the canal. He did not lack for self-esteem. James kept repeating, softly, "*Measure up. Measure up*. Yes. Yes."

– 3 –

Blaise delivered William Randolph Hearst into the eager presence of Mrs. Bingham. "I can never thank you enough," said Frederika, as she and Blaise stood at one end of the Bingham drawing room and together watched Mrs. Bingham's perfect ecstasy at so great a catch. The Chief could now talk and smile at the same time, a valuable political asset that he had finally acquired.

"I hope Mr. Sullivan has not been invited." Blaise looked at Frederika with a sudden fondness, the result of having got to know, at last, someone well. The experience of furnishing a house with another person was, he decided, the ultimate intimacy: each comes to know the other through and through until the very mention of Louis XVI sets off endless reverberations in each.

"Mr. Sullivan has been warned away. Did you hear Mr. Hearst's speech yesterday?"

Blaise nodded. "He was remarkably good." Sullivan, an iconoclastic Democrat, had seen fit to attack Hearst on the floor of the House. Until that moment, Hearst had never made a speech; he also left to others the presentation of his own bills, of which the latest, to control railroad rates, had distressed Sullivan. The attack on Hearst as an absentee congressman was answered with an attack on Sullivan in the *New York American*. Sullivan again rose in the House, and this time he inserted into the record a libellous attack on Hearst, made years earlier in California. Hearst was depicted as a diseased voluptuary, a blackmailer, and bribe-taker, to the delight of the nation's non-Hearstian press. Sullivan described Hearst as "the Nero of modern politics."

The Chief then rose to make his maiden speech to the House. He spoke more in sorrow than in anger, a style he had become remarkably good at. The California attack had been made by a man who was once indicted for forgery in New York State; and fled to California, under another name. As for Sullivan, Hearst shook his head sadly. He remembered Sullivan altogether too well from his Harvard days. Sullivan and his father were proprietors of a saloon that Hearst had never visited, as he was temperance. But the saloon was known to everyone in Boston after a drunken customer was beaten to death by Sullivan and his father.

Blaise was seated with Brisbane in the crowded press gallery when the House exploded with joy and fury. Various friends of Sullivan shouted at the Speaker to stop Hearst, but Mr. Cannon, a Republican, was delighted by this battle between two Democrats, and Hearst was allowed to end his attack with the pious hope that he would always be considered the enemy by the criminal classes.

Later, the Chief had been in an exuberant but odd mood. "I won that," he said, "but I can't win the party. I've got to start a third party. That's the only way. Or knock off half the politicians in the country, which I could do, if I really wanted to get even." When Blaise asked how this might be done, the Chief had looked very mysterious indeed. "I've got a lot of research on everybody." Meanwhile, he was preparing to run for governor of New York in 1906; and from Albany, he would try again for the presidency in 1908.

James Burden Day introduced Blaise to a recently elected Texas congressman. "John Nance Garner," said James Burden Day. "Blaise Sanford." Once again, Blaise felt somehow nude without the third all-defining name so valued by his countrymen. Garner was a cheerful young man with quick bright eyes.

"We were talking about Mr. Hearst," said Frederika. "And Mr. Sullivan."

"Sullivan's a polecat," observed Garner. "I'm for Hearst. We all are in my neck of the woods, now Bryan's drifted off."

Blaise looked at Jim, who seemed tired and distracted. The previous fall, he had failed to be elected to the Senate; and he was restive in the House. Kitty was a good political partner, but nothing more. Blaise suspected that Jim had another woman. But Blaise did not ask; and the prudent Jim did not volunteer. On the other hand, Jim had been delighted to go with Blaise to New York's most elegant bordello, in Fifth Avenue. Here Jim had performed heroically, and surpassed in popularity Blaise, who was never more contented than when he could play sultan in his rented harem, with a friend like Jim. "I like our colleague," said Jim, indicating Hearst's back, "but those who don't really don't."

"A third party?" Blaise repeated not only the phrase but imitated the Chief's tone of voice.

"They don't work, ever," said Garner. "Look at the Populists. They're going nowhere like a bat through hell."

"So are we." Jim was grim. "The country's Republican now, and we can't change it. TR's pulled it off. He talks just like us and acts just the way the people who pay for him want him to act. Hard to beat."

Mrs. Bingham drew Blaise into her orbit where Hearst now moved, larger than life. "He is my ideal!" she exclaimed.

"Mine, too." Blaise winked at Hearst, who blinked, and smiled, and said, "I'm running for mayor of New York. This year."

Mrs. Bingham emitted a tragic cry. "You're not going to leave us? Not now. We need you. Here. You are excitement."

"Oh, he'll be back." But Blaise wondered how anyone with the Chief's curious personality could prevail in politics. Then he thought of those cheering delegates in St. Louis; and of the sizeable majorities Hearst obtained in his congressional district. "What about Tammany?" asked Blaise. The Democratic candidate for mayor was almost always a Tammany creature.

"I'm running on a third-party ticket." The Chief looked suddenly mischievous, and happy. "Tammany's going to run McClellan again. I'm going to beat him."

Blaise was amused by the Chief's confidence. George B. McClellan, Jr., son of the Civil War general, had been a New York City congressman; now he was the city's major. Despite the support of "Silent" Charlie Murphy, the head of Tammany, McClellan was honest and civilized and, Blaise thought, impregnable. "But I'll beat him. I'm putting together my own machine."

"Like Professor Langley." Mrs. Bingham could be tactless.

"This won't crash." Hearst was serene. "I'm coming out for the public ownership of all utilities."

"Isn't that socialism?" Mrs. Bingham's eyes widened, and her lips narrowed.

"Oh, not really. Your cows are safe," he added.

"*Mr.* Bingham's cows. I've never met them."

"Have you done 'research' on McClellan?" Blaise was still intrigued by the Chief's reference to what sounded like police dossiers on his enemies.

"'Research'?" The Chief stared blankly. "Oh, yes. That. Maybe. I know a lot now. But I can't say how, or what."

As it turned out, two weeks later, Blaise knew what the Chief knew. The *Tribune* was now housed in a new building in Eleventh Street, just opposite the department store of Woodward and Lothrop. Blaise's office was on the first floor, in one corner; Caroline was installed in the opposite corner; between them, Trimble; above them, the newsroom; below them, the printing presses.

In front of Blaise stood a well-dressed young Negro, who had been admitted, after considerable discussion, by Blaise's disapproving stenographer. In Washington even well-dressed Negroes were not encouraged to pay calls on publishers. The fact that the young man was from New York City had, apparently, tipped the scale, and Mr. Willie Winfield was admitted. "I'm a friend of Mr. Fred Eldridge," Winfield sat down without invitation; he gave Blaise a big smile; he wore canary-yellow spats over orange shoes.

"Who," asked Blaise, perplexed, "is Mr. Fred Eldridge?"

"He said you might not remember him, but even so I was to come to see you, anyways. He's an editor at the *New York American*."

Blaise recalled, vaguely, such a person. "What does Mr. Eldridge want?"

"Well, it's not what he wants, it's maybe, what you want." The young man stared at a painting of the gardens of Saint-Cloud-le-Duc.

"So what do I—want?"

"Information about people, you know, bigwigs. Like senators and that stuff. You know John D. Archbold?"

"Standard Oil?"

"Yeah. The same. He looks after politicians for Mr. John D. Rockefeller. Well, my stepfather is his butler in the big house in Tarrytown, and Mr. Archbold, a very fine man, by the way, got me this job as office boy at 28 Broadway, where the Standard Oil is."

Blaise tried not to look interested. "I'm afraid we've no openings here for an office boy," he began.

"Oh, I'm out of that business now. Me and my partner, we're opening up a saloon on a Hundred Thirty-fourth Street. Anyways, me and my partner, we went through Mr. Archbold's files, where he has all these letters from the bigwigs in politics who he pays money to so they'll help Standard Oil do different things. Anyways, I happened to come across Mr. Eldridge about that time, last December it was, and he asked me to bring the letters round to the *American* where he could photograph them, and then I could put them back in the files, so nobody'd know they was ever missing."

Hearst had the letters. That was plain. But how would he use them? More to the point, how would—or could—Blaise make use of them? "I assume Mr. Eldridge told you that I might be a customer for the letters . . ."

"That's about the size of it. Mr. Hearst paid us pretty good for the first batch. Then, a couple weeks ago, Mr. Archbold fired us, my partner and me. I guess we didn't always put things back in the right order, or something."

"Does he know which letters you photographed?"

Winfield shook his head. "How could he? He doesn't even know that *any* of them was photographed. Because that was something only somebody like Mr. Eldridge could do, at a newspaper office— like this."

There was a long silence, as Blaise stared at the window, which now framed a most convincing rainstorm. "What have you got to sell?" he asked.

"Well, when we was fired, I'd taken out this big letterbook for the first half of 1904. I've still got it . . ."

"Then you'll go to jail when Mr. Archbold reports the theft . . ."

Winfield's smile was huge. "He won't report nothing. There's letters in there from *everybody*. How much he paid this judge, how much he paid that senator, and other things, too. I offered to sell it to Mr. Eldridge, but he says the price is too high, and Mr. Hearst's got enough already."

"Did you bring the letterbook?"

"You think I'm crazy, Mr. Sanford? No. But I made out a list for you of some of the people who wrote Mr. Archbold thanking him for money paid, and so on."

"Could I see that list?"

"That's why I'm here, Mr. Sanford." Two sheets of paper were produced; each filled with neatly typewritten names. Blaise put them on his desk. Where once railroads had bought and sold politicians, now the oil magnates did the same; and Mr. Archbold was Mr. Rockefeller's principal disperser of bribes and corrupter-in-chief. The names, by and large, did not surprise Blaise. One could tell by the way certain members of Congress habitually voted who paid for them. But it was startling to see so many letters from Senator Joseph Benson Foraker of Ohio, the man most likely to be the Republican candidate for president in 1908. Blaise was relieved not to find Jim's name on the first page. He picked up the second page. The first name at the head of the column was "Theodore Roosevelt."

Blaise put down the page. "I think," he said, "we can do business."

15

— I —

On March 3, 1905, John Hay wrote a letter to the President, whose inauguration was to take place the next day. Adee stood attentively by, combing his whiskers with a curious oriental ivory comb. "Dear Theodore," Hay wrote. "The hair in this ring is from the head of Abraham Lincoln. Dr. Taft cut it off the night of the assassination, and I got it from his son—a brief pedigree. Please wear it tomorrow; you are one of the men who most thoroughly understand and appreciate Lincoln. I have had your monogram and Lincoln's engraved on the ring." Hay affixed one of his favorite tags from Horace to the letter, and hoped that he had got the Latin right. He sealed the letter and gave it to Adee, with the small velvet box containing the ring. "It is the laying on of hands," he said, and Adee, who was staring at him, nodded. "You are the last link." Once Adee had left the room, Hay walked over to the window and looked out at the gleaming White House, where, as usual, visitors were coming and going at a fast rate. The sky was cloudy, he noted; wind from the northeast. There would be rain tomorrow. But there was almost always bad weather at inaugurations. Hadn't there been snow at Lincoln's second? Or was that Garfield's? He found it hard to concentrate on anything except the pain in his chest, which came and went as always, but now, each time it came, stayed longer. One day it would not go; and he would.

Clara and Adams entered, unannounced. "We have seen the ring-bearer, on his joyous errand." Adams was sardonic. Despite Hay's best efforts, Adams had discovered the gift of the ring with Washington's hair to McKinley. "You will be known to posterity, dear John, as the barber of presidents."

"You are jealous that you have no hair suitable for enclosing in a ring."

"We are booked," said Clara, "on the *Cretic*, sailing March eighteenth."

Hay coughed an acknowledgment. Each January he was host to a bronchial infection, and this January's was still in residence.

"We land at Genoa on April third, by which time you should be dancing the tarantella on the deck." Adams gazed thoughtfully up at his grandfather's eyes, which stared down at them from the room's fireplace. Except that each was entirely bald, there was no great likeness.

"I've made arrangements at Nervi. With the heart specialist," Clara declaimed idly.

"Then on to Bad Nauheim and Dr. Groedel, but not with me," said Adams. "As I am totally valid, I have no desire to join the invalid . . ."

"Bad No Harm, Mark Twain calls it." Hay was beginning to feel better. "Then on to Berlin. The Kaiser beckons."

"*You won't see him.*" Clara was firm.

"I must. He hungers to know me. And I him. Anyway, the President says I must."

"You are," said Clara, "too ill, and he is far, far too noisy."

"That is the nature of kaisers," said Adams, "and of at least one president . . ."

"Henry, not on this day of days." Hay held up a hand, as if in benediction.

"All is energy," said Adams abruptly. "The leader of the world at any given moment is simply the outlet for all the *Zeitgeist*'s energy, all concentrated in him."

"Major McKinley was much quieter," said Clara, thoughtfully.

"Less energy flashing about in those days." Hay indicated that Clara could help him up. "I have a feeling that it will rain tomorrow."

But though there was rain in the early morning, by the time of the parade down Pennsylvania Avenue and the first inauguration of Theodore Roosevelt at the Capitol, the sky was clear, and a strong wind made it impossible to hear the President's speech, which was just as well, thought Hay, for the speech was cautious and undistinguished. Theodore had made too many promises to too many magnates for him to sound a bugle note of any kind. For the moment, the square deal was in abeyance, and the progressive President retrogressive. Later, Hay was certain that Theodore would exuberantly betray his rich supporters. He could not *not* be himself for long.

Hay sat with the Cabinet in the front row of the platform which had been built over the steps of the Capitol's east front. Hay was grateful to have Taft's huge bulk next to him, shielding him from the icy wind. Directly in front of him, Theodore Rex addressed his subjects, and, as always, Hay marvelled at the way neck became head without any widening at all.

The President was not going to have an easy time of it. Now that Mark Hanna was dead, he would have difficulty getting so obvious a bill as the one regarding the inspection of meat through a Senate where nearly everyone had been bought or was himself, like Aldrich of Rhode Island, a millionaire buyer of votes, while in the House, Speaker Cannon was wedded to the rich, no bad thing in Hay's eyes, himself a millionaire not only through marriage but his own efforts. Even more than Adams, he had always had a golden touch, a source of some surprise to one who had begun life as a poet.

Although Hay deeply believed in oligarchy's "iron law," as Madison put it, he saw, as Roosevelt saw, the possibility of revolution if reforms were not made in the way that the new rich conducted their business at the expense of a powerless public. The Supreme Court and the police together ensured not only the protection of property but the right of any vigorous man to bankrupt the nation, while the Congress was, for the most part, bought. The occasional honest man, like the loud young Beveridge, was, literally, eccentric: too far from power's center to do anything but make the public love him—and the all-powerful Steering Committee of the Senate ignore him.

As for Cabot . . . Hay shuddered; and not from cold. Cabot's vanity and bad faith were one of the constants of Washington life. Cabot will be the rock, Adams had once observed, on which Theodore wrecks himself. So far, Theodore's barque had sailed the republic's high seas without incident; yet Cabot was always there to try and block every one of Hay's treaties. Cabot's *my* rock, Hay murmured to himself, happy he would soon be sailing not on the republic's viscous sea but on the Mediterranean.

There was loud, long applause, as Theodore finished. In the north a black cloud appeared. Taft helped Hay up. To Hay's surprise, Taft asked, "Was it here Lincoln gave his last inaugural address?"

Hay nodded. "Yes. Right here. I remember *now*. There was rain at first. Mr. Johnson, the vice-president, was drunk. Then the rain stopped, and the President read his speech."

Taft looked thoughtful. "I know that speech by heart."

"We never suspected, then, that we were all so—historical. We just saw ourselves caught up in this terrible mess, trying to get through the day. I remember there was applause *before* he had finished one sentence." Hay had the odd sense that he was now, if not in two places at once, in the same place at two different times, simultaneously, and he heard, again, the President's voice rise over the applause, and say with great simplicity the four terrible words "And the war came."

"We lost a generation." Taft was oddly flat.

534

"We lost a world," said Hay, amazed that he himself had survived so long in what was now, to him, so strange a country.

– 2 –

The day after the Inaugural Ball, Caroline celebrated her twenty-seventh birthday with Blaise, and two lawyers, one her husband, John, the other Mr. Houghteling. The celebration began in her office at the *Tribune*, where various documents of transfer were signed and witnessed and countersigned and notarized. John asked pointed questions. Houghteling's answers were as to the point as his innumeracy allowed. Blaise stared into space, as if he were not there. Caroline now had what was hers; while Blaise, in possession of half of what was hers, was marginally better off. To be a half-publisher of a successful paper was better than being a non-publisher, or the custodian of the *Baltimore Examiner*.

"Now," said Houghteling, as the last set of signatures had been affixed, and Caroline had become a number of times a millionaire, "in the matter of the Saint-Cloud-le-Duc property, the will of your late father neglects to make clear which of you inherits. In law then, a court would doubtless find that you own it jointly as you do the rest of the estate, and should the property be sold, you would divide, evenly, the money from the sale. Is that agreeable?" He looked at John, who looked at Caroline, who said, "Yes," and looked at Blaise, who shrugged and said, "Okay."

"I want it for May and June," said Caroline. "I miss the place."

"I'll come in July and August," said Blaise. "For my honeymoon."

"Good," said Houghteling, who never listened to anyone except when specifically paid to.

Caroline looked intently at Blaise, who was now wiping ink off his middle finger. "Frederika?"

"Yes. We're getting married in May."

"Then you must have Saint-Cloud. For May, that is."

"We can all stay there." Blaise was equable.

"Congratulations," said John, and formally shook Blaise's hand. Houghteling had now put away his documents in a leather case and, still unaware of his client's approaching marriage, bade them all good-by with the sentiment that, after nearly seven years, all must be well that had ended so well.

Blaise suggested that Caroline join him and Frederika for dinner that night at Harvey's Oyster House. "And you, too, John," he added; and left the room.

In recent years, Caroline and John seldom looked at each other directly; nor very often aslant, either. "Well, it's over." John took out his pipe; filled and lit it. Caroline studied a mock-up of the Sunday Ladies' Page. Princess Alice was featured yet again; and there were hints that she might marry Nicholas Longworth; and then, again, she might not. "How is Emma?" Caroline had been touched to find that John had taken to the child and she to him.

"She flourishes. She asks for you. I've talked to Riggs Bank. They will start making monthly payments into your account, as we agreed."

John stood up and stretched himself. He looked years older than he was; and the face was now of the same gray as the hair. "I suppose you'll want a divorce." He played with the heavy gold watch chain, to which were attached emblems of exclusive clubs and societies. He, too, was Porcellian, a gentleman.

"I suppose so. Would you like one?" Caroline was amazed at the tone that each had managed to strike, a mutual lassitude, like guests at a dinner party that would never get off the ground.

"Well, it's for you, really, to decide. You see, I have no future."

"What makes you think *I* have one?"

John gave a wan smile; and exhaled pale blue pipe-smoke with the words: "Heiresses cannot avoid having a future. It's your fate. You will remarry."

"To whom?"

"Emma's father."

"Out of reach. For good."

"Kitty might die . . ."

For the first and last time in their marriage John astonished her. "How did you know?"

"I have eyes, and Emma has *his* eyes, and Emma can talk now, and she speaks of his Sunday visits, with pleasure, too."

"You haven't spied on me?" Caroline's face felt unnaturally warm.

"Why should I? It's no business of mine. What business I ever had with you is concluded, and yours with me."

"I trust," said Caroline, rising from behind her rolltop desk, "you will always be a—lawyer to me."

"And you a client to me." John smiled, and shook her hand, formally. "You know I did want to marry you, when you first came over. I mean *really* marry you."

Caroline felt a sudden strong emotion, which she could not identify. Was it loss? "I'm afraid that wasn't meant to be, no fault of yours—though, perhaps, of mine. You see, I wanted to be all myself, but had no real self to be all, or even part of. I think I make no sense." Caroline was suddenly flustered. It was not her way to speak so personally to anyone, even Jim.

"Well, the key to your—brief," John was dry, "was that it wasn't meant to be, and that certainly proved to be the case. I helped you, and, God knows, you helped me. Shall I divorce you, or you me?"

"Oh, divorce *me!*" Caroline had regained her poise. "For desertion, that's fashionable now. In the Dakotas, which should be lovely in the summer."

"I shall notify you legally. Here." To her amazement, he gave her his handkerchief; then he left. To her amazement, she found that she was weeping.

Blaise sat at the edge of an artificial lake, and watched the swans sail back and forth, greedy eyes alert for food, predatory beaks ready to strike at any land-creature that moved within range. A perspective had been carefully arranged by an eighteenth-century gardener who believed that nature could only be revealed in its essential natural-ness through total artifice. Trees of various sizes gave an odd sense of a huge park that extended to what looked to be a second larger lake, which was, actually, smaller than the first. Roses in full bloom made bonfires of color in the dim greenness. Blaise was content. If he had no inherent talent for marriage, Frederika had more than enough for two. With every show of amiability, she and Caroline had each taken over a wing of the chateau, and each kept to her wing unless unvited by the other for a visit.

The state rooms were held in common, under the jurisdiction of the butler, who was also, in effect, the estate manager. M. Brissac had been at the chateau for thirty years; it was he who hired and fired and stole discreetly; it was he who had known both Mrs. Sanfords, and never had a word of the slightest interest to say about either. Now the old man approached Blaise from the central part of the chateau, an astonishing creation of rose-red brick, high mansard windows, gilded ironwork, and chimneys like so many monuments to Saint-Simon's beloved peers of France.

Brissac bowed low, and presented Blaise with a telegram, which he opened: "Millicent and I and four others will come to lunch May 30. Hearst."

It was typical of the Chief to give only a day's notice. As Blaise gave orders to M. Brissac, Caroline and Emma appeared from the woods. They looked like figures on a Watteau fan, thought Blaise, once again thinking not only in French but with French malice, as he noted to himself that *this* fan could not be shut.

Emma ran forward to her uncle, who picked her up, and listened to her chatter in a combination of French and English. She had her grandmother's complexion, hair.

"The Chief arrives tomorrow. For lunch. With four lords-in-waiting."

"He does us honor." Caroline sat in one of the curious carved sandstone thrones that the builder of the chateau, in a frenzy of premature pharaonism, had sculpted beside the lake. "With the beautiful Millicent?"

Blaise nodded. "He's very respectable now. He expects to be elected mayor of New York in the fall."

"Poor man. But I suppose it will give him something to do. Frederika fits in very well."

Blaise was mildly disappointed that wife and half-sister got on so well. But then Caroline had known Frederika longer than he. "She has discouraged Mrs. Bingham," he said, giving pleasure.

"*She* would not fit in." Caroline put out her hand. "The key."

"To what?"

"Father's desk. I want to read Grandfather Schuyler's memoirs, or whatever they are."

"The desk's open. They are in two leather-bound boxes."

"Have you read them?"

"I don't like the past."

"That's where *the* key is. If there's one, of course. Come on, Emma."

As Caroline collected her child, Blaise said, "Why are you getting a divorce?"

"Why not?"

"It's very American of you."

"I am very American. Anyway, I wasn't married in the church. It doesn't count, really—for us, anyway. It's just a legal convenience. Just another key, to just another lock."

Blaise was still mystified by the whole affair. "Was John with . . . someone else?"

Caroline's laugh dispelled any suspicion along that line. "I wish he were."

"Are you?" Blaise was convinced that Caroline had, for some

time, been having an affair, but she was even more guarded than he about her life. He assumed that the man was married; otherwise, now that she was divorced, she would have been free at least to mention if not marry him. Blaise did not rule out a passionate liaison with a lady: Mlle. Souvestre's powerful example was a fact of their world. But Washington seemed hardly the setting for so Parisian an activity.

"I wish I were." Caroline echoed herself and was gone.

Blaise found the Chief rather less phlegmatic than usual. He had gained so much weight that had he been shorter he might have presented to the world a comforting McKinley-esque rotundity. But because of his height, the result was more ursine-menacing than McKinley-majestic. The two couples with the Hearsts were part of his publishing life. "I've just bought *Cosmopolitan* magazine," he said, as Blaise showed him through the suite of state apartments.

The Chief stopped at every painting, sculpture, tapestry, console. Blaise was pleased at the Chief's awe. "I've never seen anything like this," Hearst said, as they entered the grand salon, where windows opened onto the vista of lakes and forests, "outside of a royal palace or something. Those tapestries Gobelins?"

"Early Aubusson. It was my father's hobby, fixing up this place. When he bought it, in the seventies, it was a ruin." Behind them Frederika was hostess to Millicent, whose moon face shone with pleasure, as she said in her tough New York Irish accent, "Don't sell a stick of furniture to Willy, or he'll buy it all and put us in the poorhouse."

"Warehouse is more like it." Hearst enjoyed talk of his mania for acquiring everything on earth—including Saint-Cloud-le-Duc. "You're not thinking about selling, are you?"

"Never," said Caroline, making a grand entrance on Plon's arm. "We're home at last."

After lunch, Blaise and Hearst walked together by the lake. "I want to know about Willie Winfield." Blaise was direct.

Hearst stopped in mid-stride. For an instant, Blaise was struck by the incongruity of the splendid seventeenth-century façade behind them, the swans and topiary and pale statues before them, and the American political squalor that was their all-consuming subject. Of course, the great duke who had built the chateau had been a notorious thief; on the other hand, he had spent his stolen money with a splendor yet to be rivalled on Fifth Avenue or even Newport's Ochre Point. "How do you know him?"

Blaise was cool. "He came to me, at the *Tribune*. He said he had been stealing letters from Mr. Archbold and that he'd taken them round to one of your editors at the *American*, and the editor would photograph them. Then you paid, he said."

Hearst scowled down at Blaise. "You paid, too." A statement not a question.

Blaise smiled. "Not for the same letters, unfortunately. I bought a part of the first half of the 1904 letterbook."

"I didn't buy that one." Hearst sat in one of the sandstone thrones. In the distance Caroline and Frederika were playing croquet with the guests, the ladies' clothes almost as bright as the tall roses, all around them. Emma had been borne off to her nap.

"I thought we had enough. We got Foraker for good. You know, I've been pushing him for the Republican nomination. Then, just before the election, if he's nominated, of course, I'll spring the stuff. Now," the Chief looked at Blaise sadly, "you can do the same thing, tomorrow morning, and someone else will get the nomination . . ."

"Someone who won't have written Archbold any letters?"

Hearst nodded. "Like Root or Taft. Neither one's in the file, so far's I can tell. But all the small fry and a lot of the big-time politicals are being paid off. So what are you going to do?" Although Hearst's physiognomy did not allow for displays of indecision or apprehension, the weak voice was suddenly, oddly tremulous. Apparently, Hearst was basing a considerable political strategy on the release—or withholding at a price—of the letters in 1908.

"We could work something out." Blaise was by no means certain what, if anything, he himself could do with them. Hearst was capable of anything: he was Hearst. But a Sanford, though not so well-defined, could hardly publish stolen letters unless they were used as background, say, to an investigation of one of Rockefeller's judges. Standard Oil had the same proprietary feeling about judges that Blaise's mother-in-law had about members of Congress, only Standard Oil paid large sums of money to make sure that the judges would always rule in their favor. In fact, most of the letters from politicians dealt not so much with pro-Standard Oil legislation as with judicial appointments. From the look of one letterbook, Archbold's web of bought officials ranged from city halls to governors' mansions to Congress and the appropriate courts and, finally, to the White House. But Blaise had been disappointed in the one letter to Archbold from Theodore Roosevelt. The letter could have meant anything, or everything, or nothing.

"I don't think I have any use for the letters."

Hearst's physiognomy could not betray relief either; he stared blankly at Blaise, who said, "I don't think that the *Tribune*, as a Washington paper, should get too mixed up in these things. If there's a crusade for good government again, we might join in. Or Caroline might. I'm happy with bad government."

"You're in, like it or not. There's no alternative." Hearst was flat. "You'll sit on the letters?"

"I think so." But Blaise intended to keep Hearst in suspense as long as possible. "I'm only interested in one letter, one politician . . ."

"Roosevelt?"

Blaise nodded. "The letter I bought can only be interpreted in its proper context. Well, I don't know the context. Do you?"

Hearst hummed, in his usual high off-key voice, a few bars of "Everybody Works but Father," the year's popular song. Blaise was grateful there was no banjo to accompany that chilling voice. "I'll tell you what I *guess* the context is. Hanna was in deep with Rockefeller. So was Quay. My letters are full of them. But then everyone knows about them, anyway. They got money from Rockefeller, from everybody, for the Republican Party, for Roosevelt, for themselves."

"For him, personally?"

Hearst shrugged. "I don't think he's that big a fool. But he's got to have money so he can go round the country at election time, attacking the trusts that are paying for his train. When was your letter dated?"

"Last summer. After he was nominated."

"Well, that makes no sense. But then, Hanna and Quay are dead. So he's got nobody with the nerve to go to old Rockefeller, or even Archbold, and say, 'Give me half a million for the campaign, and I'll go easy on you.' I expect that when he wrote Archbold, he was fishing."

"Did he catch anything?"

Hearst's thin smile was slow and genuine. "It doesn't make any difference if he did or didn't, does it? I mean, it's the way the thing *looks* that matters. You could make the case as to how Roosevelt's managers have always been on the take from Standard Oil, then, by the time you get around to *his* being in touch with Archbold, when he was desperate, trying to raise money from Morgan and Frick and Harriman, everyone will believe Teddy's on the take, too, which, I suspect, he is."

Ignobly, Blaise wondered how he could put together this story before Hearst did. Obviously, he could not unless he knew the contents of Hearst's letters, all written before 1904. "I suppose you'll use this when Roosevelt does something that favors Standard Oil, if he does."

Hearst shook his head. "I'll use what I've got—or not use it—in connection with my own campaign in 1908."

Blaise did not use to himself the word "blackmail," but that was indeed the Chief's intention. As the owner of eight popular newspapers *and* the Archbold letters, he could make the leaders of the republic leap through any hoop of his choice. "There's one more detail you should know," said Hearst. "John D. Archbold is an old personal friend of Theodore Roosevelt."

"That is something."

"That is something."

"If," said Blaise, doing his best not to sound eager, "you were to publish these letters, what excuse would you give, for having stolen them . . . ?"

Hearst attempted another chorus of "Everyone Works," with invented words. "Well, I certainly wouldn't say *I'd* stolen them. They came to my attention, that's all. *Then* I'd also say that I do not consider that letters written to public men on matters affecting the public interest and threatening the public welfare are ever private letters." At that moment, Blaise realized that Hearst might yet become president and, if he did, he might surprise everyone; in what way, of course, it was hard to tell.

- 4 -

Caroline sat at the large marquetry table, said to have been the very one that the Duke had used when he was the controller of the royal revenues, and opened the two letter-boxes. The first contained fragments of Aaron Burr's autobiography, with a commentary by his law-clerk Charles Schemerhorn Schuyler. She glanced through the pages, and decided that Henry Adams, if no one else, would be fascinated. She skipped to the end of the book, written years after Burr's death, and read what she already knew, of her grandfather's accidental discovery that he was one of Burr's numerous illegitimate children.

The second leather box was a final journal by her grandfather, covering the year 1876. He had returned to New York for the first time since 1836, with his daughter, Emma, the Princess d'Agrigente. This was the volume that she intended to read carefully.

Once the Hearst party had left, Caroline spent every moment that she could reading her grandfather's journal. She was charmed by his amusement at the strange American world, fascinated by his description of her mother's campaign to find a wealthy husband, the object of the visit, appalled at her grandfather's cynical complaisance. But then father and daughter were broke, and he was just able to support the two of them by writing for the magazines. Fortunately, Mrs. Astor took them up; and they were in demand socially, thanks to Emma's beauty, and her father's charm. Briefly, like Caroline, she had become involved with an Apgar cousin.

As Caroline read on, she began to see something alter in Emma's character—alter or be revealed to the reader, Caroline, but not to the narrator, who seemed unable to understand the thrust of his own narrative. Sanford made his entrance, with wife Denise, who could not give birth without danger. As Denise and Emma became closer and closer friends, Caroline found that her fingers were suddenly so cold that she could hardly, clumsily, turn the pages. Caroline knew the end before the end. Emma persuaded Denise to give birth to Blaise. In effect, Emma murdered Denise in order to marry Sanford.

Emma's expiation was the long painful time she took to die after Caroline's birth. But did Emma feel guilt? Did she atone? Confess?

Caroline sent for Plon. It was late afternoon. She wanted to talk to Emma's oldest son while the—crime was still vivid in her mind. Plon sprawled handsomely on a sofa. Caroline told him what their mother had done. At the end, somewhat dramatically, she held up the journal and waved it in the air; told him of the murder. "*Brûlez*," Plon read from the cover. "That's what you should have done, you idiot! Burn it. What difference does any of this make now?"

"You knew all along, didn't you?"

Plon shrugged. "I thought something had happened."

"Did she say anything?"

"Of course not."

"Did she seem tragic or sad or—dark?"

"She was adorable, as always, even at the end, when there was pain."

"Did she make confession, to a priest?"

"She was given the last rites. She was conscious. I suppose she did."

Plon lit a cigarette from a new gold case. "You know, when someone becomes emperor of the French, and conquers all Europe, he doesn't brood much about the people he killed."

"But she was a woman, and a mother, not emperor of the French . . ."

"You don't know how—*I* don't know how—she saw herself. She had to survive, and if the sad lady, her friend, Blaise's mother, must die, naturally, in childbirth, then die she must."

The next morning, Caroline invited Blaise to breakfast in her wing of the chateau. He knew why. Plon had told him. They sat in an oval breakfast room, with du Barry dove-gray walls. "Now you know," he said, casually, "that your mother killed my mother for our father's money. I'm sure it happens all the time."

"Don't be—don't make a joke of it. Now I know why your grandmother was so insistent with me. I am to expiate . . ."

"You? Don't exaggerate your importance. You weren't even there. I, at least, was the direct cause of my mother's death."

"I think these things go on, into the next generation, and further, maybe."

"*You!* The atheist from Mlle. Souvestre's stable." Blaise laughed into his omelette.

"Atheists believe in character, and I certainly believe in cause and effect, and consequence."

"The consequence is that you and I are still fairly young by the standards of our world and very rich by any standard. This isn't the house of Artois."

"Atreus." She corrected him from force of habit. "Plon sounded as if he would have done the same."

"I doubt it. Men are never as cruel as women when it comes to this sort of thing. Look at your dismissal of John. That was very Emma-esque. I couldn't have done that."

Caroline felt a chill in the room, which turned out to be not a ghost but a sudden cold wind from the lake; a summer storm was on its way. Blaise closed the window. "You prove my point then," she said. "The old crime."

"Don't be carried away. Think of all the new crimes we can commit. Let poor Emma rest in peace. I have never, once, thought of Denise. Why should you think of Emma, who, according to

Plon, except for one nicely executed murder, was delightful, as a woman, and admirable as a mother?"

"You are immoral, Blaise." Caroline wanted to be shocked; but felt nothing at all.

"I never said I wasn't. I'm indifferent. You remember our last night in New York, at Rector's? when you were so shocked by the way the whole room sang that song?—well, I was thrilled because I was just like the singers of that song."

Caroline shuddered at the memory. The latest Victor Herbert musical contained a highly minatory song called "I Want What I Want When I Want It." On the night that she and Blaise came, as it were, full circle, in their knowledge of each other, they had dined at Rector's, and when the singer from the musical comedy entered the restaurant, he boomed out, "I want . . ." and the entire restaurant took up the chorus, and on the word "want" everyone banged a fist on the table. It was like a war being conducted by very fat people against—the waiters? or everyone on earth who was not as fat or as rich as they? "So Emma was right, to want what she wanted?"

"You have only one chance sometimes. Anyway, what she wanted," Blaise brought down his fist on the table, and Caroline jumped in her chair, "she got, and that's what counts, and because she did, you're here."

So, in the end, Caroline, the successful American publisher, was not the acclimatized American that her brother, her appendage, was. She wished Mr. Adams was on hand, to delight in the irony.

But the next day, when Mr. Adams was indeed on hand, with John and Clara Hay, there was no opportunity to discuss anything in private except the fading away of John Hay, whose hair was now as white as his beard, the result, he said, still capable of his old humor, "of the waters of Bad Nauheim, which etiolate—my favorite word that I never get a chance to use—all things dark, not to mention false. Clara's henna is all gone."

While Hay sat with Caroline in the sandstone thrones, Blaise and Frederika showed off the chateau, and even Henry Adams affected to be overwhelmed.

Caroline had not had much experience with the dying. But one of her aunts had been something of a devotee of death-beds, and if she so much as heard of someone moribund within a hundred miles, she was on her way, in somber black with Bibles and prayer-books, with medicines to speed the terminal to terminus, and with cordials to assuage the survivors' grief. "You can always tell when they're about to pass on by a certain strong light in their eyes, just toward the end. Well, that's the glory coming." Late for a highly significant death-bed, the Sanford aunt had hurried down a flight of stairs, fallen, broken her neck; and so was robbed of her shining glory, so long awaited by her friends.

But John Hay's eyes were not in the least glorious. Rather, they were dull and glassy; he was also thinner and paler than he had been before the cure; but he had not lost interest in life, rather the reverse. He looked about him curiously. "I couldn't imagine living in a poky house in Georgetown when you have all this. It even beats Cleveland."

"Well, the house is splendid but the company's poky. So I stay on in Washington. Besides, we didn't sort out the estate till this spring."

"Satisfactorily?" Hay gave her a shrewd look.

Caroline nodded. "As satisfactory as anything ever is. Anyway, I like my new sister-in-law."

"I suppose you'll get married again."

"You sound disapproving." Caroline laughed. "But then I'm a divorcée. I'm told if I go to Cleveland, I shall be stoned to death . . ."

"Only when taken, publicly, in adultery, by Mrs. Rutherford B. Hayes. Oh, I shall miss this," he said, with all sorts of resonance that tact required her not to explore.

"You go on to London?"

"Then Washington, then New Hampshire."

"Why Washington in the heat?"

Hay sighed. "Theodore is there. Theodore is busy. When Theodore is busy, I feel constitutionally obliged to be on hand."

"The Russians?" Caroline could no longer forget, even in the company of the dying, that she was a journalist.

"The Japanese, I should say. I'm so far removed from things. I have to read the foreign press with a sort of mental cypher-code to figure out what's happening. Apparently, Theodore has been asked by the Japanese to arbitrate a peace treaty between them and Russia. But what is actually happening—if anything—I don't know. Spencer Eddy—"

"Surrenden Dering?"

"The same. He's posted in Petersburg. He came all the way to Bad Nauheim to tell me that Russia's falling apart. It seems that the Tsar is a religious maniac, and so the thirty-five grand dukes are running the country, which is to say they create endless confusion. The workers are on strike. The students are on strike. Maybe Brooks is right, after all. They'll have their French Revolution at last. Meanwhile, what government they have has instructed Eddy to tell me that they'd like a convention with us, and I had to tell him that, thanks to the Senate and dear Cabot, there is no way of getting such a treaty as long as any senator has one constituent who might object."

Adams joined them. He seemed immeasurably old to Caroline; yet, paradoxically, he never aged. He simply became more himself; the last embodiment of the original American republic. "I like your sister-in-law. She knows what *not* to show you on a tour of the house."

"There's so much *not* to be seen. There is dry-rot . . ."

"I think that's what I've got." Hay sighed. "I was finally examined by an austere Bavarian doctor who assured me, with touching Teutonic modesty, that he was the greatest expert on the heart in the world. As I believe everything I'm told, I said, 'So what's wrong?' He said, 'You have a hole—or a bump,' he was not consistent, 'in your heart.' When I asked why all the other great heart specialists had not noticed this hole or bump, he said, 'Maybe they didn't see it, or maybe they didn't want to worry you.' 'Is it fatal?' I asked. 'Everything's fatal,' he said, with a confident smile. I must say he sort of grew on me. Anyway, he said he could delay the final rites, which, apparently, is a cinch for him."

"I hate doctors. I never go to one." Adams was firm. "They make you sick. Anyway, you look no worse—and no better—for all the waters that have flowed through you . . ."

". . . and over me." Hay stretched his arms. "I can't wait to see Theodore, and tell him that I've been right all along about the Kaiser. Theodore thinks that because the Kaiser is, as Henry James says of Theodore, 'the embodiment of noise,' that he is mindless . . ."

"Like Theodore himself?"

"Now, Henry. Theodore has a mind that is chock-a-block with notions . . ."

"Thoughts, too?"

"Splendid thoughts. Anyway, the latest information is that the Kaiser, after pushing his stupid cousin, the Tsar, into declaring war on Japan, now realizes that Russia is *too* weak, even for his purposes, so he now is making frantic love to Japan, and to Theodore, too."

"They are made for each other."

"Not yet. But the Kaiser has a plan. Would to God I could go to Berlin to see him. He may be a reckless orator but he is a cold-calculator."

Two menservants appeared, pushing a tea-table; and the croquet players joined them. Frederika did the honors, while Caroline and Clara walked beside the lake, keeping a careful distance from the swans. "He *seems* better." Caroline could think of nothing else to say on that subject.

Clara was now huge, even monumental; her manner, as always, secure, declamatory. "He could live another year. Maybe more, if only he would leave Washington."

"He won't?"

"Not yet. We go to London, incognito, June second. Then we sail on the *Baltic*. Then he insists on going back to the State Department before we go on to New Hampshire. He does not trust Theodore." Clara exhorted a willow tree's reflection in the lake.

"Perhaps it's best, to keep on, till . . ." Caroline did not finish.

"I wonder about you and Del." Clara spoke for the first time to Caroline about her son. "I'm not sure—now—it would've been for the best."

"We'll never know, will we?"

"No. We never will. It's when I see all this, I realize you are foreign. He was not."

"I'm both. Or, maybe, neither." Caroline was amused that Clara was still making censorious divisions between what was foreign, and probably bad, and what was American and entirely good. "At least I don't publish the *Tribune* in French."

Clara smiled, as she always did when she suspected that someone had made a joke. "Do you and Blaise get on?"

"We do now. We probably won't in the future." Caroline was surprised, as always, when she said what she actually thought.

"That's my impression, too. The girl's nice. But he does want to be like Mr. Hearst . . ."

"No more than I do . . ."

"Caroline! You are a lady."

"But foreign."

"Even so, you could never want to be like that dreadful man. Henry James returned our latch-key." Clara's mind was so constituted that she could make the leap from Yellow Journalism to the fact that Henry James, who had gone off with the key to the front door of the Hay house, had returned it; and make the non sequitur seem part of some significant whole, which perhaps it was, ungrasped by Caroline, who suddenly recalled her discussion of keys with Blaise, both real and metaphysical.

"Will you see Mr. James in London?"

"If we have the chance. I don't want John to see anyone except old friends. But the King insists. So we go to Buckingham Palace."

"The King is political."

"He likes John. I said, *no food!* The King eats for hours. We shall stay exactly one half hour, I said, no longer." The two women sat on a bench, and watched the others at tea. Adams was walking up and down excitedly, a good sign. Hay sat huddled in his throne, a study in gray and white. Blaise sat on the edge of his chair like an attentive schoolboy. "Divorce still shocks me." Clara hurled the commandment down the length of her figure, which even seated suggested Mount Sinai.

"We were never really married." Caroline started to tell the truth, but then, not wanting to spend the rest of her life in France, she told not the truth but something true. "I was alone, after Del died. So I married a cousin for—protection." Caroline hoped that she could successfully portray herself as helpless.

She could not, to Clara, at least. "I know." She was peremptory. "Rebound. From grief. Even so, one might have waited until there was not a cousin but a true husband."

"That's all past. I'm alone now, and quite content. There's Emma. What," asked Caroline, imitating the manner of Clara, the non sequitur without ellipsis, "ever became of Clarence King's children by the Negress?"

Clara blushed. Caroline knew victory. "They are still in Canada, I think. John and Henry help out. They tell me nothing, and I never ask." Clara rose, ending the subject. Attended by Caroline, the mountain returned to the tea-table.

Hay was describing his meeting with the French foreign minister. "I was expressly forbidden by the President to speak to him, since I hadn't first seen the Kaiser. But I, too, must be allowed my diplomacy. All the troubles in Morocco—no, not Perdicaris, not Raisuli . . ."

"Spare us your high drama." Adams ceased pacing and sat in a chair too large for him. The two tiny glittering black patent-leather shoes were an inch from the ground.

". . . are coming to a head, and the Kaiser is imposing himself on the French, and threatens to go to Morocco himself to take it away from them. Poor Delcassé is filled with gloom. With Russia on the verge of a revolution, the Kaiser has the only important army in Europe. The French don't breed enough, he complained, and the English army is too small, so the Kaiser can do as he pleases, unless Theodore puts down his great boot . . ."

"Stick, isn't it?" Adams interjected. "The one he says he carries when he speaks with a soft voice. The reverse, of course, is the case. He bellows, and there is no stick at all."

"A large navy, Henry, is a big stick . . ."

"When war comes in Europe, it will be on land, and it will be won by land armies, and that will be Germany's last chance to be king of the mountain."

"We," Clara said the last word, "will stay out."

As the perfect day ended with a golden light breaking through the leaves of the west park, Caroline and Blaise and Frederika saw the last of the Hearts into their motor cars. Adams was off to join the Lodges, "part of my secret diplomacy to keep Cabot from John's throat." Caroline remembered too late that she had not mentioned to Adams the fragments of Aaron Burr's memoirs. Fortunately, from the healthy look of him, there would be time during the winter in Washington.

"You must come see us at Sunapee." Hay took Caroline's hand; she almost recoiled from the coldness of his touch.

"I'll come in July."

"Come for the Fourth. We will all be there." Clara kissed Caroline's cheek. Then they were gone.

The young trio regarded the departure of the old trio with, on Caroline's side, considerable regret. "They are the last," she said.

"Last of what?" Frederika gazed bemusedly at her, hair suddenly dark gold in the slanting light.

"Last—believers."

"In what?" Blaise turned to go inside.

"In . . . Hearts."

"I believe in hearts." Frederika had misunderstood. 'Don't you, Caroline?"

"I meant something else by Hearts, and what *they* were, and tried to be, made them different from us."

"They aren't different from us." Blaise was final. "Except that they are old, and we aren't. Yet."

John Hay sat in a rocking chair on the verandah of The Fells and stared across the green New Hampshire lawn to the gray New Hampshire mountains with Lake Winnepesaukee between, so much flat shining water that reflected the deep clear blue summer sky. Exhaustion did not describe his condition. He had returned on June 15, and after a day at Manhassett with Helen, he had gone on to Washington, despite firm instructions from the President to go home. For a week in the damp heat of the tropical capital, he had done the business of his department, and plotted with Theodore on how—and where—to get the Japanese and the Russians to sign a peace treaty. He had found Theodore more than ever regnant, and the mammoth Taft apparently indispensable. The last bit of business that they had set in motion was to put an end to the Chinese Exclusion Act, which earlier administrations had used to keep the Chinese from immigrating to the United States. With the rise of Japan, paradoxically, the Yellow Peril must be put to rest as a means for politicians to frighten the people.

The house in Washington was depressing, with white sheets over everything, closed shutters and windows, and a musty smell. Clarence, now grown and amiable if not brilliant, kept him company, and together they had left the city on June 24 for Newbury, on the overnight sleeper, where Hay had caught his inevitable sleeper-cold. Today he was better; but mortally tired. He had also developed a habit of falling asleep in the middle of a sentence, and dreaming vividly; then he'd wake up, disoriented, with the sensation, yet again, of being, simultaneously, in two places, even two epochs of time. But now Clarence sat beside him in a noisy rocker, made noisier by the instinct of the young to rock vigorously, while that of the old is to be rocked gently.

"Of course, I've been lucky." Hay stared at the sky. "There must be a kind of law. For every bit of bad luck Clarence King—

for whom we named you—had, I got a prize. He wanted to make a fortune, and lost everything ten times over. I didn't care one way or another, and everything I did, just about, made me rich, even if I hadn't married an heiress." Hay wondered if this was entirely true. When he had worked for Amasa Stone, he had been drilled thoroughly in business. Of course, he had been an apt student, but without Stone's coaching he might have ended up as just another newspaper editor, earning extra money on the lecture-circuit.

"I've never really been sick till now, or, as old Shylock says, 'never felt it till now.' The family's turned out better than I ever had any right to hope." He turned and gazed at the attentive Clarence. "I'd go to law school, if I were you. Also, don't marry young. It's a mistake for a boy to tie himself up—or down—too young."

"I've no intention," said Clarence.

"Good boy. Poor Del." Hay's chest seemed to constrict a moment; and his breath stopped. But, for once, there was no sense of panic. Either he would breathe again, or he would not, and that was that. He breathed; he sighed. "But Del's life was splendid for someone so young. We got used to that, my generation, to dying young. Just about everybody I knew my age was killed in that terrible trouble. Name me a battle, and I can tell you which of my friends fell there, some never to rise again. Say Fredericksburg and I see Johnny Curtis of Springfield, his face blown away. Say . . ." But already Hay was beginning to forget both battles and youths. Things had begun to fade; past, present mingled.

"I thought I'd die young, and here I am. I thought I wouldn't amount to much and . . . I really believe that in all history, I never read of a man who has had so much—and such varied—success as I have had, with so little ability and so little power of sustained industry. Nothing to be proud of. Something to be grateful for." Hay looked at Clarence, thoughtfully, and was somewhat surprised—and mildly irritated—to find him reading a stack of letters.

"You're busy, I see." Hay struck the sardonic note.

"You should be, too." Clarence did not look up. As he finished reading a letter, he would let it fall to the floor of the verandah, in two piles. Obviously one pile was to be answered; the other not. Who used to do that? Hay wondered. Then he thought of himself again, soon to be no self at all, and he wondered why he had been he and not another, why he had been at all and not simply nothing. "I have had success beyond all the dreams of my boyhood," he proclaimed. But that was not true. The poet John Hay, heir to Milton and Poe, had come to nothing but a pair of very "Little Breeches." "My name is printed in the journals of the world without descriptive qualifications." Who had said that that was the only proof of fame, as opposed to notoriety? It sounded like Root, but Hay had forgotten.

Hay turned to Clarence, who was now on his feet. For the first time Hay noticed that the boy had grown a long pointed beard, not the style of the young these days. He must tell him, tactfully, that when the summer was over he must face the world clean-shaven.

"The President wants to see you," said Clarence.

Hay leapt—to his own amazement—to his feet, and crossed the crowded corridor to the President's office. Obviously he had been dreaming of New Hampshire while napping in the White House, awaiting Theodore's summons. The Japanese . . .

In the office, Hay found the President staring out the window at the Potomac, and blue Virginia beyond. The President was hunched over, and was unlike his usual exuberant noisy self. Over the fireplace, the portrait of Jackson glowered at the world.

"Sit down, John." The familiar high voice sounded deathly tired. "I'm sorry you've been sick."

"Thank you, Mr. President," and Hay realized that he had made a mistake in hurrying so quickly across the corridor. Exhausted, he sat in the special visitor's chair with all the maps of battle in full view, and a yellow curtain ready to cover them up, if the visitor was not to be trusted.

Abraham Lincoln turned from the window, and smiled. "You look pretty seedy, Johnny."

"You don't look too good yourself, if I may say so, sir."

"When did I ever?" Lincoln went to his pigeon-holed desk, and took out two letters. "I've got a couple of letters for you to answer. Nothing important." Lincoln gave Hay the letters; then he sat very low in the chair opposite, so that the small of his back would press against hard wood, while one long leg was slung over the chair's arm. Hay realized with some excitement that he had, at last, after so many years, been able to remember Lincoln's face from life as opposed to ubiquitous effigy. But what was he thinking? This *was* the President, he realized, on a Sunday afternoon, in summer. "I can't sleep," the Ancient was saying. "I *think* I'm sleeping but then I find I'm only day-dreaming and I wake up, and by the time it's morning, I am plumb worn out, or as the preacher said to his wife . . ."

Hay felt, suddenly, at one with the President, as the melancholy dark green walls, picked out with tiny golden stars, swirled all about the two of them like the first attack of sleep which always starts, no matter how restless one has been, with a nothingness out of which emerges, first, one image, then another, and, finally, mad narratives unfold which take the place of the real world stolen now by sleep, unless sleep be the real world stolen by the day, for life.

16

Caroline had promised to look in on Adams before the White House dinner in celebration, for once, of nothing; and true to her word, she arrived, wearing in her hair the diamonds that she had inherited that autumn from Mrs. Delacroix, who had proved, after all, not to be immortal; who had proved, above all, to be grateful for whatever "expiation" that Caroline might have made in her coming to terms with Blaise, and their common past.

Adams sat beside his Mexican onyx fireplace, looking more small and isolated than usual. "I see no one. Except nieces. I am no one. Except an uncle. You *are* beautiful as nieces go . . ."

"You should be happy." Caroline settled before the fire; and refused William's offer of sherry. "You have Mrs. Cameron in the Square. What more can you want?"

"Yes, La Dona makes a difference." The previous year, Mrs. Cameron had reinstalled herself and Martha at 21 Lafayette Square. She was, again, queen of Washington, for what that might be worth: to Adams, apparently, nothing. Although a year had passed, he was still not reconciled to John Hay's death on July 1, 1905. Adams had been in France when the news came; and so had not been able to go to Cleveland, where Hay was buried, beside Del, in the presence of all the great of the land. Ironically, Adams had been with Cabot and Sister Anne Lodge when the news came; and it was said that the Benevolent Porcupine had, one by one, shot each of his poisoned quills into the fragile senatorial hide, blaming, not entirely unfairly, Lodge for Hay's death.

"Anyway, I'm bored. I'm mouldy. I'm breaking fast. I've nothing, nothing to live for . . ."

"Us. The nieces. Your twelfth-century book, which you must have finished for the twelfth time now. And, best of all, as you said yourself, you will never again have to see, in this life, Theodore Roosevelt."

Adams's eyes were suddenly bright. "You do know how to cheer me up! You're absolutely right. I shall never set foot in that house again. The relief is enormous. I have also quarantined Cabot, and if it weren't for Sister Anne, I'd relieve myself of all Lodges. Why are *you* going tonight?"

"I am still a publisher. I'm also the only publisher of the *Tribune* who's welcome. The President is furious with Blaise, for helping out in the Hearst campaign."

"Hearst." Adams managed to hiss the "s"; thus the serpent in Eden celebrated evil. "If he is elected governor of New York, he'll be living over there in two years' time."

Caroline tended to agree. Although Hearst had lost the election for mayor of New York, in a three-way race, he had come within a handful of votes of winning it. Only a last-minute burning of ballots by Murphy of Tammany Hall had secured the election for McClellan. Hearst was now behaving like a Shakespearean tragic hero, in search of a fifth act.

With remarkable skill, Hearst had created his own political machine within New York State, and now he was prepared to seize the governorship, with Blaise's help. Caroline was not certain quite why her apolitical brother had decided to come to the aid of a publishing rival, unless *that* was the reason. If Hearst were to become governor, president—Cawdor, Scotland—he might be obliged to sell off his newspapers, and Blaise would want them. So, for that matter, would Caroline.

"I've always hoped that in my senility I wouldn't, like the first three Adamses, turn against democracy. But I detect the signs. Racing pulse, elevated temperature; horror of immigrants—oh, the revelation in Heidegg! Even John was horrified to what an extent we've lost our country. Roman Catholics are bad enough. Yes, my child, I know you're one, and even I tend, at times, to the untrue True Church, but the refuse of the Mediterranean, the detritus of *Mitteleuropa*, and the Jews, the Jews . . ."

"You will have a stroke, Uncle Henry." Caroline was firm. "One day your hobby-horse will throw you."

"I can't wait to be thrown. But I'm always astride. That's because I'm nobody. Power is poison, you know."

"I don't know. But I'd like to taste it."

"The problem is what I call Bostonitis. The habit of the double standard, which can be an inspiration for a man of letters, but fatal to a politician." Adams picked up a folder beside his chair. "Letters to John Hay. Letters by John Hay. Clara's been collecting them. She wants to publish."

Caroline had, from time to time, received a note from Hay. He was a marvelous letter-writer, which meant that he was always indiscreet. "Is that a good idea?"

"Probably not. I'm sure Theodore will think not. Hay liked him, but saw all his faults. Worse, his absurdities. Great men cannot bear to be thought, ever, absurd."

"Publish! And be praised."

"I think I *will* edit them."

"Why not write his life?"

Adams shook his head. "It would be my life, too."

"Write that, then."

"After St. Augustine, I'd look more than usually inept. He did best what cannot be done at all—mix narrative and didactic purpose and style. Rousseau couldn't do it at all. At least Augustine had an idea of a literary form—a notion of writing a story with an end and object, not for the sake of the object, but for the form, like a romance. I come at the wrong time."

"But you occupy the right space," said Caroline. "Anyway, I don't believe in time . . ."

"Are you content?" Adams looked at her closely.

"I think so. I wanted to be—myself, not just a wife or mother or . . ."

"Niece?"

"That I wanted most of all." Caroline was entirely serious. "But then I have never confessed to you just how ambitious I am. You see," she took the great plunge, "I wanted to be a Heart."

"Oh, my child!" Adams struck a note that she had never heard before. There was no irony, no edge to that beautiful voice. "You *are* one. Didn't you know?"

"I wanted to—know." She was tentative.

"That is it. That is all there is, to want to know . . ."

Elizabeth Cameron and Martha entered; each was dressed appropriately for the White House dinner.

"We've heard from Whitelaw Reid," said Lizzie, after her usual warm but not too warm greeting of Caroline. "Martha's to be presented at court, June the first, and you know what Martha said?"

" 'I'd rather stay in Paris' is what Martha said," said Martha.

"You must give pleasure to Whitelaw. He has so many presentations to make and so few presentables." Adams had greeted Whitelaw Reid's appointment as ambassador to the Court of St. James's with exuberant derision. Reid's pursuit of office and its attendant pomp had, finally, been rewarded by the President, who had required that all ambassadors and ministers resign after the election. Everyone had now been moved round—or out.

"I do it for Mother." Martha would never be beautiful, Caroline decided, but she might yet cease to be plain.

The clocks were carefully checked, and it was agreed that the three ladies share the same carriage to get them across the perilous wintry waste of Pennsylvania Avenue, a matter of so many icy yards.

Adams rose and showed them to the door of his study; he kissed each on the cheek.

"I hope Cabot won't be there," said Lizzie. "I have a permanent grudge against him, since John died."

"Be forgiving, Dona." Adams smiled his secret smile. "Life is far too long to hold a grudge."

The Lodges were not present; the dinner was relatively small; and there was no theme, which Caroline enjoyed. Of the Cabinet, only Hay's successor, Elihu Root, was present. He and Caroline gravitated toward each other in the Red Room, where the company was gathered before dinner. The Roosevelts never made their regal entrance until everyone was present.

"What *is* your brother doing?" was Root's less than ceremonious greeting.

"He is travelling through New York State, enjoying the scenery."

"I am alarmed. We're all alarmed. You know, Hearst was really elected mayor of New York. Then Tammany destroyed the ballots."

"Then why are you alarmed? When he's elected governor, Tammany will just burn the ballots all over again. Fraud is the principal check—or is it balance?—of your—sorry, *our*—Constitution."

Root's mock alarm was replaced by, if not real alarm, unease. "We can't rely on our most ancient check this time. Hearst has made a deal. He's going to be Tammany's candidate."

"Is this possible?" Caroline was startled.

"Everything's possible with those terrible people. Warn your brother away."

As Caroline was explaining why Blaise accepted no warnings from her, Alice Roosevelt and her new husband, Nicholas Longworth, made their entrance. Root looked at his watch. "Amazing! She's arriving before her father. Nick's influence, obviously."

Alice looked, if not blooming, as in a rose, bronze, as in a chrysanthemum, while her husband's bald head was scarlet from sunburn. They had been married in mid-February, with great pomp, in the East Room; then they had gone to Cuba for their honeymoon. This was their first White House function, as man and wife. Alice joined Root and Caroline. "Well, I've been to the top of San Juan Hill, and it's absolutely nothing. I looked for the jungle—remember the famous jungle? where Father stood among the flying bullets, ricocheting off trees, and parrots and flamingos— I always added them to every description—sailed about? Well, the place couldn't be duller. The hill's a bump, and there is no jungle. All that fuss about so little. But they gave us something called a daiquiri, made with rum. After that, I remember nothing."

The President and Mrs. Theodore Roosevelt were announced, rather as if they were the Second Coming, and Theodore conducted himself rather as if he were God, surveying, with quiet satisfaction, His Creation. Edith Roosevelt looked tired, as befitted God's conscientious consort.

The President greeted Caroline with his usual amiability, usual because the *Tribune* usually supported him. As a reward, he would occasionally ask her to the White House, where he would give her a story—usually minor—that no one else had yet printed. He was even stouter and redder this season, she noted; apparently, the vigorous, strenuous life he advocated for others and practiced himself was not, of itself, thinning. "You must come to lunch, and tell me about France. I envy you last summer. If I ever get away from here . . ."

"Come to us, Mr. President."

"Delighted!"

"What, if I may cease to be a lady at court for an instant, is going to happen to the Hepburn Bill?" This was a commanding work of legislation which the House of Representatives had passed the previous year. The regulation of railroad rates was, somehow, at the center of the national psyche. The progressive saw it as a necessary means of controlling the buccaneer railroad operators, while the conservative courts and Senate saw it as the first fine cutting edge of socialism, the one thing that all Americans were taught from birth to abhor. Characteristically, Roosevelt was vacillating. When he had needed money for his presidential campaign he had asked the railway magnate E. H. Harriman to dinner at the White House; no one knew what promises were exchanged. Yet Caroline had taken heed of one of Adams's truisms which was so true as to be ungraspable by minds shaped from birth by an American education: "He who can make prices for necessaries commands the whole wealth of all the nation, precisely as he who can tax." That said it all. But the ownership of the country controlled both Supreme Court and Senate, and so they need not give up anything, ever. "I shall stand fast, of course. I always do. To Principle. I'm sure I can bring Senator Aldrich around. One thing I *won't* accept will be an amended bill."

"How curious to see you allied with the populists, like Tillman . . ."

"Terrible man! But when the end is just, grievances are forgotten. We must make do. If we don't, Brooks fears a revolution on the left or a coup d'état on the right. I tell him we are stronger-fibered than that. Even so . . ."

An aide, roped in gold, moved the President through the room to greet the other guests. "It was in this very room, on election night," observed Root, "that Theodore told the press that he would not run for a second term of his own."

"He must have been—temporarily—deranged," observed Caroline, admiring Edith Roosevelt's inevitable look of interest in the presence of even the most ruthless bore.

"I think he got the mad notion from mad Brooks, whom he was just quoting. In order to be profoundly helpful, Brooks went through several million unpublished Adams's papers and found that both of the Adams presidents had thought that one term was quite enough, and despised what they called 'the second-term business.'"

"On the sensible ground that since each had been defeated for a second term, the principle was despicable."

"Exactly. Anyway, Theodore, in a vainglorious mood, said that there would be no second election for him."

The fat little president was now showing off a new ju-jitsu hold to the German Ambassador, while Edith's lips moved to form the three dread syllables "Thee-oh-dore." "He'll be bored. But then he will keep on governing through his successor—you, Mr. Root."

"Never, Mrs. Sanford. First, I'd not allow it. Second, I won't be his successor." Root's dark eyes glittered. "I'm not presidential. But if I was, I'd tell my predecessor to go home to Oyster Bay, and write a book. You do this job alone, or not at all. Anyway, he can bask in glory. He loved war, and gave us the canal. He loved peace, and got the Japanese and the Russians to sign a peace treaty. He will be, forever—which in politics is four years—known as Theodore the Great."

"Great," murmured Caroline, "what?"

"Politician," said Root. "It's a craft, if not an art."

"Like acting."

"Or newspaper publishing."

"No, Mr. Root. We create, like the true artist. News is what we invent . . ."

"But you must describe the principal actors. . ."

"We do, but only as *we* see you . . ."

"You make me feel," said Root, "like Little Nell."

"*I* feel," said Caroline, "like the author of *Freckles*."

On the way into dinner, Alice told her of the great advantage of matronhood. "You can have your own motor car, and Father has nothing more to say."

"This means that you're a socialist."

For once Alice was stopped in her own flow. "A socialist, why?"

"You missed the story. You were in Cuba. The new president of Princeton said that nothing has spread socialistic feeling in this country more than the use of the automobile."

"He sounds mad. What's his name?"

"I don't remember. But Colonel Harvey at *Harper's Weekly* says that he will be president."

". . . of Princeton?"

"The United States."

"Fat," said Alice, "chance. *We've* got it."

Blaise was filled with admiration for Hearst, who had managed to make himself the candidate of the independent lovers of good government forever hostile to the political bosses, while simultaneously picking up the support of Murphy of Tammany Hall, and a half-dozen equally unsavory princes of darkness around the country who, should he be elected governor of New York in November, would make him the party's candidate against Roosevelt's replacement. Hearst had adopted the Roosevelt formula: with the support of the bosses, you run against them. Hearst had even announced, with his best more-in-sorrow-than-in-anger compassion, "Murphy may be for me, but I'm not for Murphy." Thus, the alliance was made and the tomahawks in the Tammany wigwam currently buried.

In due course, Hearst became the Democratic candidate for governor as well as the nominee of his own now potent machine, the Municipal Ownership League. The Republican candidate was a distinguished if dim lawyer, Charles Evans Hughes, known as the scourge of the corrupt insurance companies. He was considered no match for Hearst, whose fame was now total.

When, in April, San Francisco had been levelled by earthquake and fire, Hearst had taken over the rescue work; had fed people; sent out relief trains; raised money through Congress and his newspapers. Had anyone but Hearst been so awesomely the good managing angel, he would have been a national hero and the next president. As it was, he was forever associated not only with Yellow Journalism, to which most people were indifferent, but with socialism (he favored an eight-hour work day), the nemesis of all good Americans, eager to maintain their masters in luxury and themselves in the hope of someday winning a lottery. Yet despite so many handicaps, Blaise could not see how Hearst was to be stopped.

566

At the end of October, on a bright cold morning, Blaise boarded Hearst's private car, *Reva*, on a railroad siding at Albany. He was greeted by the inevitable George, now grown to Taft-like proportions. "It never stops, Mr. Blaise. The Chief's in the parlor. Mrs. Hearst won't get out of bed, and little George won't go to bed. I can't wait till this is over."

To Blaise's relief, Hearst was alone, going through a stack of newspapers. The blond hair was turning, with age, not gray but a curious brown. He looked up at Blaise, and smiled briefly. "Seven in the morning's the only time I've got to myself. Look what Bennett's done to me in the *Herald*." Hearst held up a picture, with the headline "Hearst's California Palace" and the sub-head "Built with coolie labor."

"You don't have a house in California, with or without coolies."

Hearst dropped the newspaper. "Of course I don't. It's Mother's house. Built by the Irish, I think, years ago. Well, it's in the bag."

Blaise settled in an armchair, and a steward served them coffee. "The animated feather-duster," Hearst's name for Charles Evans Hughes, "is getting nowhere. No organization. No popular support." Hearst gave Blaise a general impression of the campaign thus far. The entire Democratic ticket seemed to be winning; and Hughes could not ignite popular opinion despite the anti-Hearst press (the entire press not owned by Hearst), which was outdoing even Hearst himself when it came to inventions and libels. But the voters appeared unimpressed. "I've never seen such crowds." Hearst's pale eyes glittered. "And they'll be back in two years' time."

"What about the Archbold letters?" For Blaise, the letters were the essential proof of the rottenness of a system that could not survive much longer. Either the people would overthrow the government or, more likely, the government would overthrow the people, and set up some sort of dictatorship or junta. Blaise suspected that if it came to the latter, Roosevelt would do a better job than Hearst.

"I don't need the letters. I'm winning. The letters are for 1908.

In case I have problems. You see, I'll be the reform candidate then."

"If I were you, I'd use them now. Hit Roosevelt before he hits you."

"Why bother?" Hearst chewed on a lump of sugar. "There's nothing Four Eyes can do to me, in this state, anyway."

The following Sunday, Blaise arrived at Caroline's Georgetown house; on the first of the year she would move into her new house in Dupont Circle, close by the Pattersons.

Blaise knocked on the door; there was no answer. He tried the door handle; it turned. As he stepped inside the entrance foyer, Jim Day appeared on the staircase, tying his tie.

For an instant they stared, frozen, at each other. Then Jim finished his tie, as coolly as he could; the face was attractively flushed, the way it had been on the river-boat in St. Louis. "Caroline's upstairs," he said. "I have to go." They met on the stairs; but did not shake hands. As Jim passed him, Blaise smelled the familiar warm scent.

Caroline was in her bed, wearing a dressing gown, trimmed with white feathers. "Now," she greeted Blaise, in a high tragic Olga Nethersole voice, "you know."

"Yes." Blaise sat opposite her, in a love-seat, and tried to look for signs of love-making. Except for a large crumpled towel on the floor, there were no clues to what had taken place—how many times? and why had he never suspected?

"It is all quite respectable. Since Jim is Emma's father, we must keep this in the family. Don't you agree?"

"Yes." Blaise saw the whole thing clearly at last, including the otherwise meaningless marriage to John. He did his best not to imagine Jim's body on the bed, all brown skin and smooth muscles. "It would be the end of him, if Kitty knew," he added, gratuitously.

"Or the beginning." Caroline was airy. "The world doesn't end any more with an affair."

"It does in politics, in his state."

"If she were to divorce him, I'd fill the breach, as best I could. That's not the worst fate, is it?"

"For him, probably." Blaise was, obscurely, furious.

But what might have been obscure to him was blazingly plain to Caroline. "You're jealous," she teased. "You want him, too. Again."

Blaise thought that he might, like some human volcano, erupt with—blood? "What are you talking about?" He could do no better, aware that he had given himself away.

"I said—I repeat we should keep all this in the family as," she smiled mischievously, "we seem to have done, anyway. We have the same tastes, in men, anyway . . ."

"You bitch!"

"*Comme tu est drôle, enfin, Cette orage . . .*" Then Caroline shifted to English, the language of business. "If you try to make trouble between Jim and Kitty, or Jim and me, your night of passion aboard the river-boat, with poor Jim, doing his innocent best to give you pleasure, will be as ruinous for you as anything you can do to him or to me or to poor blind Kitty." Caroline swung her legs over the side of the bed, and put on her slippers. "Control yourself. You'll have a stroke one of these days, and Frederika will be a widow, as well as my best friend."

In the back of Blaise's mind, there had always been the thought—hope—that he and Jim might one day reenact what had happened aboard the river-boat. But, ever since, the embarrassed Jim had kept his distance; and once again, Caroline was triumphant. From *Tribune* to Jim, Caroline had got everything that *he* had wanted. In the presence of so much good fortune, Blaise was conscious of a certain amount of sulphur in the air. But for now at least, he must be cool, serene, alert.

"The White House thinks that Hearst will win." Caroline was at her dressing table, rebuilding her hair.

"So do I. So does he. So does the animated feather-duster."

"Mr. Root is going to Utica." Caroline pulled her hair straight back and stared into the mirror, without apparent pleasure.

"What does that mean?"

"The President is sending him. To Hearst."

"Too late."

"Mr. Root carries great weight in New York. As the President's emissary . . . I would be nervous if I were Mr. Hearst."

But all Blaise wanted to speak of was Jim, and that, of course, was the only subject that he and Caroline could never again mention to each other.

Blaise was with the Chief in New York City when the Secretary of State spoke in Utica. It was the first of November. The weather was peculiarly dismal, even for New York, and a drizzle that was neither snow nor rain made muddy the streets.

Hearst had his own news-wire in his study, set up between busts of Alexander the Great and—why?—Tiberius. Blaise was at his side as the message from Utica came through, even as Root was speaking. Elsewhere in the room, Brisbane kept a number of politicians in a good mood, an easy task since none doubted that soon they would all be going to Albany in the train of the conquering Hearst.

As read, line by line, the speech was lapidary. Root's style was Roman, school of Caesar rather than Cicero. The short sentences were hurled like so many knives at a target; and none missed. Absentee congressman. Hypocrite-capitalist. False friend of labor. Creature of the bosses. Demagogue in the press and in politics, pitting class against class.

"Well," said the Chief, with a small smile, "I've heard worse."

But Blaise suspected that he was indeed about to hear worse; and he did, toward the end. Root read Ambrose Bierce's quatrain, calling for McKinley's murder. Hearst stiffened as the familiar words stuttered past them on the wire. Root quoted other Hearstian indictments of McKinley, inciting the mad anarchist to murder. Then Root quoted Roosevelt's original attack on the "exploiter of sensationalism" who must share, equally, in the murder of the beloved-by-all President McKinley.

Hearst was now very pale, as the thin ribbon of text passed through his fingers to Blaise's. "I say, by the President's authority, that in penning these words, with the horror of President McKinley's murder fresh before him, he had Mr. Hearst specifically in mind."

"The son of a bitch," whispered Hearst. "When I finish with him . . ."

The message went on: "And I say, by his authority, that what he thought of Mr. Hearst then he thinks of Mr. Hearst now."

So it would be on the charge of regicide that Hearst was to be brought down at last. Blaise marvelled at the exactness with which Roosevelt, using Root for knife, struck the lethal blow.

"Champagne?" Brisbane approached with a bottle in hand.

"Why not?" The Chief, who never swore, having just sworn, who never drank, now drank. Then he turned to Blaise. "I want you to go over the Archbold letters with me."

"With pleasure, if I can publish first."

"Simultaneously, anyway, with me."

– 3 –

Caroline was shown into the Red Room, forever referred to by Roosevelt loyalists as the Room of the Great Error. She had received a last-minute invitation to a "family" dinner, which could well mean, considering the Roosevelt family, fifty people. But it was indeed, for the most part, family. Alice and her husband, Nick Longworth, were already there, with, to Caroline's surprise, the sovereign himself, who sprang to his feet, rather like a Jack-in-the-box, and said, just like his music-hall imitators, "Dee-lighted, Mrs. Sanford. Come sit here. By me."

"Why not by us?" asked Alice.

"Because I want to talk to her and not to you."

"There is no reason," said Alice, "to be rude, simply because I'm the wife of a mere member of the House . . ."

But the President had turned his back on daughter and son-in-law, and led Caroline to a settee near the door, so situated that if the door was open, as now, the settee was invisible. Roosevelt practiced several unpleasant grimaces on Caroline, before he began. "You know about the Archbold letters?"

571

Caroline nodded. Trimble had received copies of a number but not the entire set. "I gather your brother Blaise has seen the lot."

"We're not speaking at the moment."

"But if he decides to publish, they will appear in the *Tribune*."

"If *I* decide to publish, they will appear in the *Tribune*."

Roosevelt clicked his teeth three times, as if sending out a coded message to a ship in distress at sea. Then he removed his pince-nez and polished it thoroughly with a scrap of chamois. Caroline noticed how dull the eyes were without the enhancement of shining magnifying glass. "You are the majority shareholder?"

"Mr. Trimble and I are, and he does what I want him to do."

"Good." The pince-nez was again in its glittering place. "I *hope* good. Would you publish?"

"I would have to have a motive. Senator Foraker would have to introduce some legislation, favorable, let us say, to Standard Oil. Then I would publish, of course."

"Of course! As you know, I have done—the Administration has done—nothing for Standard Oil. Quite the contrary."

"But," said Caroline boldly, "there are your letters to Archbold."

"Which I don't even recall. He was a friend, from years ago. He is a gentleman. I am certain there is nothing in anything that I ever wrote him that I would not be happy to see on the front page of every newspaper in the country."

Caroline arranged the spray of hot-house lilies that Marguerite had persuaded her, against her better judgment, to wear on a cold November night. "I'm afraid, Mr. President, that you will probably read those letters on every front page except mine, unless they prove—relevant." Caroline liked the vagueness of the word.

"You mean that Hearst will publish?"

"Exactly. He wants revenge. Mr. Root—and you—lost him the election."

"What did he expect? It is hardly usual for a republic to allow its own overthrow." This was said with such swift savagery that Caroline was taken aback.

"You think Hearst would do that?"

"I put nothing past him. He is outside our law, our conventions, our republic. He believes in class war. That is why I would do anything to finish him off . . ."

"You did do everything, and he has said that *he* will never run for office again." The rage of Hearst had been something to behold. From a commanding lead he had, yet again, because of outside intervention, lost an election that was his: this time to the egregious Hughes. Of one and a half million votes cast, Hearst lost by fifty-eight thousand. Except for Hearst, every Democrat on the ticket had been elected, and the entirely unheard-of was at least heard of: the candidate for *lieutenant governor*, dimmest of posts, was won by an upstate Democrat, an aristocratic Chanler, hardly known for his appeal to the masses, or anything else. Roosevelt had finished Hearst; would Hearst return the compliment? "I gather," said Caroline, "that as many Democrats are involved in Standard Oil payoffs as Republicans?"

"Which explains why this noble citizen, with his so-called proofs of corruption, has been delaying publication for what could be years, to help not justice but his own career." Roosevelt was now speaking for eternity, and Edith, not one to abide too much eternity on an empty stomach, signalled that it was time to go in to dinner.

17

"I will never again be a candidate. But I shall continue to live in New York and educate and support the principles of reform which I have always stood for." Thus, William Randolph Hearst withdrew from politics, as a candidate. But Blaise knew that the Chief would now be even more formidable than before. Free of the wheeling-and-dealing required of a man canvassing votes, Hearst could not only do as he pleased but, if he chose, transform the republic itself. He now knew more than anyone else about the internal workings (for the most part, corrupt) of the republic; he also knew that, with time and money spent, he could decide, through his Independent League, the outcome of numerous elections.

Bryan, on the other hand, was obliged to shift his position according to the prevailing wind. Where, today, was sixteen-to-one silver? Once the only means whereby the American worker, tacked with three nails to his cross of gold, might one day descend—or ascend?—silver had become a non-subject. Yet, unlike Bryan,

Hearst had never wavered in his own program. But now he was finished as a politician. Of course, in the press, he could continue to be the working-man's full-time tribune. Precisely why the working-man had been selected for this distinction, Blaise could never fathom, but he could not fault Hearst for consistency, unlike Bryan and Roosevelt, who tacked this way and that. What, after all, *did* Roosevelt think of that solid rock upon which his party was based, the tariff?—which he used to sigh over in private, and refer to as "expediency," a price he must pay to his supporters for the empire that he was assembling for their descendants. Bryan was at least consistent in his hatred for war and the conquest of far-off places and the mindless acquisition of other races. Hearst was genuinely ambivalent about Roosevelt's tempting vision of empire. Sometimes he approved; sometimes not.

Blaise put this down to Hearst's hatred of the British empire; after all, much of his support was Irish. In fact, whenever Hearst could think of nothing to say to an Irish audience, he would announce, as though the thought were new to him, "You know, if I ever get to be president, the first thing I'm going to do is send an Irish-American to the Court of St. James's. That'll wake them up." The cheering would be deafening. He still used the same line, adding, "I offer the suggestion to some future president, and hope ardently he'll do it."

For Theodore Roosevelt, Hearst had only contempt. "He sold himself to the devil in order to get elected, and you've got to hand it to him—for once, he's kept his side of the bargain." Blaise knew that the first part was true. Roosevelt, in his famous pre-election panic, had promised the rich everything. Then, as he would never again run for president, he double-crossed the lot, or as Frick not so dryly put it, "We bought him but he isn't staying bought."

Somehow, whenever Blaise thought of Hearst—no longer, remotely, the Chief to him—he thought of unopened crates. He had acquired everything, tangible and intangible, and then never got around to unpacking what was his; and making sense of it. Currently, literally, unopened crates provided the only furniture in Hearst's new home, the Clarendon Apartment Building at the

575

corner of Riverside Drive and Eighty-sixth Street. Hearst had taken over the top three floors, some thirty rooms.

At the very top—the twelfth floor—Hearst and Blaise went over the Archbold letters, spread across the width of a huge refectory table from Spain, pitted with newly drilled wormholes, as guarantee of antiquity. Over the years, at Saint-Cloud-le-Duc, Blaise had learned a good deal about furniture. Over the years, Hearst had learned almost nothing. But the law of averages was, eventually, on his side. If one bought everything, sooner or later one might really buy something, and the lost Giorgione would be his. Blaise wondered if the something might not also apply to politics. If one kept on long enough, spending money, organizing voters, one might end up with the lost—what? Crown, no doubt, in Hearst's case.

"What happens if Archbold brings charges against you, for theft?"

"I didn't steal anything. I just copied some letters offered me *pro bona publica*."

"*Pro bono publico*."

"That's what I said. I wish I could make more out of Theodore's letters." Hearst looked wistfully at the short enigmatic letters from the White House to Archbold. Within the "right" context, they could send the President to jail. But there was no context at all to these anodyne texts. "Of course, one could cook something up."

"I wouldn't," said Blaise firmly.

"I won't. Until I have something to go on. I have detectives at work, going over his bank accounts. Also, the Republican Party's accounts, which are almost as bad . . ."

". . . as the Democrats'."

Hearst looked at Blaise gloomily. From the floor beneath them, they could hear Millicent's voice, loud and harsh enough to be heard at the back of the third balcony of the Palace Theater. She was at work with her designer, creating if not a pleasure dome, the largest apartment in New York, filled with what was, by now, the largest collection of old and new antiques in the Western world. "I'm going to start off with Hanna and Quay. They're dead. I'm going to show how much they collected for Roosevelt's campaign. Then I'm going to show what TR has done for Standard Oil . . ."

"He hasn't done a thing. We ran that story. Of course, the real story is hard to write. The fact that he's actually done nothing at all is the only thing against him."

"I can work that one out," said Hearst. "And still stay with the facts. He's done nothing because they helped finance him. At least in 1904. Oh, I've got him. He's terrified. Next Sunday, I'm dropping some hints in all the papers that we have his letters to Archbold, compromising letters."

Blaise was beginning to feel that the impossible was about to happen; Hearst was actually going to go too far. Unless the detectives turned up something new, Hearst was about to find himself in the dangerous position of one who has accused of corruption a popular president in office. This was not quite like going after Murphy of Tammany Hall. Blaise said as much. Hearst was offhand.

"All I've got to do is smoke him out. I do think he's corrupt, by the way. I mean, everyone in this business is—to raise money to run—but because he's a hypocrite, he's worse than the others. That's why I want to keep him guessing. My ace is this, he doesn't know how much or what we know, and he'd give anything to find out."

Hearst wandered over to the French window that opened onto a terrace, with a view of the Hudson, and the high Palisades. "When I quote from his two cronies Hanna and Quay—and Foraker, too—everyone knows I mean Roosevelt, too. So we may as well throw him to the wolves right now. Otherwise, people will say we only mention dead people who can't fight back, or dead ducks like Foraker. Then we say, next week we'll publish the Roosevelt letters. Oh, there'll be a hot time in the old town *that* night."

Hearst had agreed that Blaise might use certain letters that he himself had no immediate use for. The powerful Senator Penrose was given to Blaise; and a half-dozen members of the House. In exchange, Blaise would use the *Tribune* files to back up the Hearst "investigation," if that was not too lofty a word for what Hearst was doing. Since most of the country's politicians were paid for by the rich and since most of the electorate knew this and did not care, Blaise kept urging Hearst to make some useful point instead, simply, of listing names, with prices attached. Hearst disagreed. Yes, he admitted to a desire for revenge. Roosevelt had accused him, yet again, of McKinley's murder and for that low blow Hearst was whetting his journalistic ax. But as for true reform, Hearst looked, mournfully, at Blaise. "I guess," he said at last, "if you don't like it here you can go back to France." All in all, Hearst took for granted his country; and Blaise did not.

Blaise was at his desk in Washington when Caroline made an unannounced entrance, the first, in fact, since each had seen fit to confide to the other more truth than was necessary for everyday life in the American republic.

"Look," said Caroline, who seldom said anything so obvious.

Blaise spread out the *New York Journal American* on his desk, and read the headline. "W. R. Hearst Proves the Rule of Oil Trust in Politics." He read the story quickly. Someone, probably Brisbane, had put together a highly damning account of Standard Oil's promiscuous dealing with the politicians of both parties. With some subtlety, the story never got far from Roosevelt and the Republican Party, but, thus far, no line of Roosevelt was quoted. That was, the story concluded, to come.

"I suspect that this will not be a happy morning at the White House." Caroline sat down; she stared off into space, no doubt, at headlines as yet unset in type.

"Well, he's done one thing I didn't think he could. He's proved that Standard Oil gave a lot of money to Roosevelt's campaign, and Roosevelt, so far, hasn't really gone after any of the oil trusts. Well, that's cause and effect, isn't it?"

"But," said Caroline, "Archbold also contributed to Judge Parker and the Democrats. So the two cancel out."

"I wonder." Blaise turned to Caroline. "Do you—and Mr. Trimble—agree to breaking the Penrose story?"

Caroline nodded. "Mr. Trimble's running it tomorrow, front page."

"That puts us one ahead of the *Post*." Blaise was pleased. "Hearst wants to do the best of Sibley's letters. But we can have the rest of him, the part that doesn't concern the President."

Joseph C. Sibley was a Republican congressman from Pennsylvania, who had never tried to disguise his loyalty to the Rockefeller oil interest. Sibley wrote Archbold: "For the first time in my life I told the President some plain if unpalatable truths as to the situation politically, and that no man should win or deserve to win who depended upon the rabble rather than upon the conservative men of affairs ..." This could have been, thought Blaise, the beginning of Roosevelt's abrupt shift to the rich—and to Standard Oil—in order to raise money for the 1904 campaign.

"Have you ever thought of going home?" Caroline was sudden.

"Home? To Connecticut Avenue?"

"To France."

Baise laughed. "That's where Hearst told me to go—instead of hell, I suppose, when I was making heavy weather about some of his crazier tactics. No. I like it here, more than ever. Besides, do you know anything about *French* politics? Look what they did to your friend Captain Dreyfus."

Caroline seemed uncharacteristically disconsolate. "In France, I—you—we wouldn't be publishers. We wouldn't have to know such people, or care."

Blaise shook his head. "Sell me your share, and go back. I'm in my element now."

Caroline smiled without pleasure. "That famous shoe keeps shifting, first to one, then to the other foot. Oh, I stay. I'm in too deep. I have my—expiations."

"You and that mother of yours!" Blaise disliked the subject intensely. "You don't need expiation. What you need is an exorcist."

"I want to publish my grandfather's journal, about her."

"Go ahead. It's none of my business," said Blaise; and meant it. Then Mr. Trimble joined them, a note in hand, a gleam in his eye. "From the White House. From the President."

"Never explain," sighed Caroline, "never complain."

579

"He's done both." Trimble gave them the short message, for publication. The President had no specific recollection of the conversation as reported by Mr. Sibley. "The President would like to see you tomorrow at noon." This was addressed to Blaise. Then Trimble was gone, and Blaise said to Caroline, "We have drawn blood."

"Whose, I wonder?" asked Caroline.

The President was receiving a delegation from the new state of Oklahoma when Blaise was announced. "Bully!" the President shouted, and Blaise's entrance was a signal for the Oklahomans to withdraw. Blaise did get a good look at the state's first governor, who was also treasurer of the Democratic Party. This gentleman, C. N. Haskell, had that day been named by Hearst as yet another employee of Standard Oil, guilty of serving not the people but the Rockefellers. Bryan, once again the party's peerless leader, was said to have ordered Haskell to resign as treasurer. As the Oklahomans withdrew, each with a firm handshake from the President, there was no sign that anything was awry other than, as the door shut on the officialdom of the latest state, a sudden explosion: "Taft—the procrastinator—really let us down out there. We could have had all seven of Oklahoma's electoral votes. But then they came up with this constitution which was mad—pure socialism, and Taft said, wait and write a new one, as if anyone gives a damn about a state constitution, so while he's dithering, Bryan comes in, praises the constitution, and now they've elected nothing but Democrats, including that crook Haskell. They have also, in their infinite Western wisdom, sent us a blind boy for one senator, and an Indian—an Indian!—for another."

"I know, sir," said Blaise, "your views on the virtues of the dead Indian, but I didn't know you took so powerful a line against blind men."

"I do against this one." The Roosevelt teeth clicked twice. "A populist demagogue . . . You've read about Haskell?"

"I've read everything."

"What does Hearst want to do? Wreck our political system?"

"If you put it like that, sir, yes, he does."

Roosevelt did not acknowledge so truthful if radical a response. "What letters of mine has he got?" This was sudden. The President, whose back was to Blaise, turned round. The bright red and yellow leaves of autumn as seen through the window back of him made him look as if he were incongruously trapped in a stained-glass window.

"In themselves, as far as I know, nothing much. But if *interpreted . . .*"

"Oh, he'll interpret! Here." Roosevelt gave Blaise a typed statement. "Can you run this tomorrow? I'm afraid it's not exclusive. I'm releasing it to the whole country. But you'll have it before McLean at the *Post*."

Blaise read the short statement and marvelled at the easy even flow of political hypocrisy at its fullest tide. "Mr. Hearst has published much interesting and important correspondence of the Standard Oil people, especially that of Mr. Archbold with various public men. I have in times past criticized Mr. Hearst but in this matter he has rendered a public service of high importance and I hope he will publish all the letters dealing with the matter which he has in his possession. If Mr. Hearst or anybody else has any letter from me dealing with Standard Oil affairs I shall be delighted to have it published."

Thus, Roosevelt made the best of a bad business by praising the enemy and trying to regain for himself the high ground in what looked more and more like a swamp filled with quicksand. What, Blaise wondered, for the first time, *were* the President's relations with Standard Oil? Obviously, there was something that he did not want known; and it probably had to do with the gathering of money for the 1904 election. Although the President had struck a jaunty pose, he looked unnaturally ill-at-ease.

"I shall publish your statement tomorrow."

"Good. I gather you're in communication with Hearst?" Blaise nodded. "When next you talk to him, say that I'd like a word with him here, in the White House, soon. Tell him there are other . . . forces at work, that he should know about." The President's smile

was as bright and artificial as his pince-nez; he showed Blaise to
the door.

– 2 –

Although William Randolph Hearst had been requested to enter
the White House from the south side, where private visitors came
and went, the great man ordered his chauffeur to drive up the
main driveway to the north portico, to the general consternation of
the police. Then, slowly, like some huge bear of the sort that the
President liked to shoot in quantity while roaring about the
necessity of the preservation of wildlife, Hearst entered the main
hall of the house which he would never, short of an armed
revolution, occupy. Apprehensively, the chief usher received him.

"Tell the President that I am here." Hearst did not bother to
identify himself. He took off his coat, and let it fall, quite aware
that someone would catch it before it touched the floor; and an
usher did.

"Come this way, Mr. Hearst." The chief usher led Hearst to the
west wing. When told to wait in the secretary's office, Hearst
opened the door to the empty Cabinet room, and took his place at
the head of the table. The secretary's shock was silent; but
profound.

Hearst sat back in the chair of state, and shut his eyes, like a
man exhausted in a noble cause. He was home. But not for long.
As usual, noise preceded the Chief Magistrate. "Delighted you're
here! Bully!" The President was now at the door to the Cabinet
room. Hearst opened his eyes, and gravely nodded his head in
greeting. For a moment, Roosevelt appeared uncertain what next
to do. Then he shut the door behind him. There would be no
witnesses to what might follow.

Slowly, majestically, Hearst got to his feet. As the two men
shook hands, Hearst deliberately pulled Roosevelt toward him so
that the President was obliged to stare straight up into the air at

582

the taller man. "You wanted to see me?" Hearst inquired, as if bestowing a huge favor on a junior editor.

"Indeed. Indeed. We have so much to talk about." Although Hearst stood between the President and the presidential chair, the tubby but sturdy Roosevelt simply charged the chair, knocking Hearst to one side in the process. Most royally, Roosevelt seated himself; and said, with smooth condescension, "Sit there. On my right. Mr. Root's chair."

Hearst's smile was thinner than usual. "I'd fear some terrible contagion if I were to sit in the chair of so notorious a liar."

Roosevelt's face was now dark red; and the smile a snarl. "I've never known Mr. Root to lie."

"Then you've had a lot less experience with lawyers than I'd suspected." Hearst pulled an armchair from its place at center table, putting a considerable distance between himself and the President.

"Root spoke for me in Utica." Roosevelt was flat.

"Well, I didn't think he was speaking on oath to God. Of course, he spoke for you when he accused me of McKinley's murder."

The conversation was, plainly, not going where Roosevelt had intended. "Your press incited—incites—violence and class hatred. Do you deny that?"

"I don't deny or affirm anything. Do you understand that? I'm here at *your* request, Roosevelt. Personally, I have no wish to see you at all, anywhere, ever—unless, of course, we share the same quarters in hell. So I must warn you, no one says 'Do you deny' to me, in my country."

"*Your* country, is it?" Roosevelt's falsetto had deepened to a mellifluous alto. "When did you buy it?"

"In 1898, when I made war with Spain, and won it. All my doing, that was, and none of yours. Ever since then, the country's gone pretty much the way I've wanted it to go, and you've gone right along, too, because you had to."

"You exaggerate your importance, Mr. Hearst."

"You understand nothing, Mr. Roosevelt."

"I understand this much. You, the owner—no, no, the *father* of

583

the country, couldn't get the Democrats to nominate you for president even in a year when there was no chance of their winning. How do you explain that?"

Hearst's pale close-set eyes were now directed straight at Roosevelt; the effect was cyclopean, intimidating. "First, I'd say it makes no difference at all who sits in that chair of yours. The country is run by the trusts, as you like to remind us. They've bought everything and everyone, including you. They can't buy me. I'm rich. So I'm free to do as I please, and you're not. In general, I go along with them, simply to keep the people docile, for now. I do that through the press. Now you're just an office-holder. Soon you'll move out of here, and that's the end of you. But I go on and on, describing the world we live in, which then becomes what I say it is. Long after no one knows the difference between you and Chester A. Arthur, I'll still be here." Hearst's smile was frosty. "But if they *do* remember who you are, it'll be because I've decided to remind them, by telling them, maybe, how I made you up in the first place, in Cuba."

"You have raised, Mr. Hearst, the Fourth Estate to a level quite unheard of in any time . . ."

"I know I have. And for once you've got it right. I have placed the press above everything else, except maybe money, and even when it comes to money, I can usually make the market rise or fall. When I made—invented, I should say—the war with Spain, all of it fiction to begin with, I saw to it that the war would be a real one at the end, and it was. For better or worse, we took over a real empire from the Caribbean to the shores of China. Now, in the process, a lot of small fry like you and Dewey benefited. I'm afraid I couldn't control the thing once I set it in motion. No one could. I was also stuck with the fact that once you start a war you have to have heroes. So you—of all people—came bustling along, and I told the editors, 'All right. Build him up.' So that's how a second-rate New York politician, wandering around Kettle Hill, blind as a bat and just about as effective, got turned into a war hero. But you sure knew how to cash in. I'll hand you that. Of all my inventions you certainly leapt off the page of the *Journal*, and into the White House. Not like poor dumb Dewey, who just stayed there in cold print until he ended up wrapped around the fish at Fulton's Market."

Hearst sat back in his chair, hands clasped behind his head. Eyes on the ceiling fan. "When I saw what my invention could do, I decided to get elected, too. I wanted to show how I could take on the people who own the country that I—yes, that I helped invent— and win. Well, I was obliged to pay the inventor's price. I was—I am—resented and feared by the rich, who love you. I could never get money out of Standard Oil the way you could. So in the long— no, short—run it's who pays the most who wins these silly elections. But you and your sort won't hold on forever. The future's with the common man, and there are a whole lot more of him than there are of you . . ."

"Or you." Roosevelt stared at the painting of Lincoln on the opposite wall, the melancholy face looking at something outside the frame. "Well, Mr. Hearst, I was aware of your pretensions as a publisher, but I never realized that you are the sole inventor of us all."

"Oh, I wouldn't put it so grandly." Hearst was mild. "I just make up this country pretty much as it happens to be at the moment. That's hardly major work, though *you* should thank me, since you're the principal beneficiary of what I've been doing."

Roosevelt arranged several statute books on the table. "What do you know about me and Mr. Archbold?"

"Standard Oil helped finance your last campaign. Everyone knows that."

"Have you any proof that *I* asked for the money?"

"The asking was done by Hanna, Quay, Penrose. You only hint."

"Mr. Archbold is an old friend of mine." Roosevelt started to say more; but then did not.

Hearst's voice was dreamy. "I am going to drive many men from public life. I am also going to expose you as the hypocrite you are."

Roosevelt's smile was gone; the high color had returned to

normal; the voice was matter-of-fact. "You will have an easy time with the Sibleys and Haskells. You will have an impossible time with me."

"You fight the trusts?"

"As best I can."

"Have you ever objected to Standard Oil's numerous crimes against individuals, not to mention the public?"

"I have spoken out against them many times as malefactors of great wealth."

"But what," Hearst's voice was soft, "have you *done* to bring Standard Oil to heel? You've been here six years. What have you done, except rant in public, and take their money in secret?"

"You will see." Roosevelt was very calm indeed. "Next year, we bring suit against them in Indiana . . ."

"*Next* year!" Hearst slapped the table gleefully. "Who says this is not my country? I've forced *you*, of all people, to act against your own kind. Because of what I've revealed this year, you'll do something next year. But you don't ever really lead. You follow *my* lead, Roosevelt." Hearst was on his feet, but Roosevelt, not to be outdone, had done his special Jack-in-the-box rapid leap to the perpendicular so that, technically, the President had risen first, as protocol required, ending the audience.

At the door to the Cabinet room, Hearst got his hand on the doorknob first. "You're pretty safe, for now."

"I wonder," said Roosevelt, softly, "if you are."

"It's my story, isn't it? This country. The author's always safe. It's his characters who better watch out. Of course, there are surprises. Here's one. When you're out of a job, and need money to feed that family of yours, I'll hire you to write for me, the way Bryan does. I'll pay you whatever you want."

Roosevelt produced his most dazzling smile. "I may be a hypocrite, Mr. Hearst, but I'm not a scoundrel."

"I know," said Hearst, with mock sadness. "After all, I made you up, didn't I?"

"Mr. Hearst," said the President, "history invented me, not you."

"Well, if you really want to be highfalutin, then at this time and in this place, I am history—or at least the creator of the record."

"True history comes long after us. That's when it will be decided whether or not we measured up, and our greatness—or its lack—will be defined."

"True history," said Hearst, with a smile that was, for once, almost charming, "is the final fiction. I thought even you knew that." Then Hearst was gone, leaving the President alone in the Cabinet room, with its great table, leather armchairs, and the full-length painting of Abraham Lincoln, eyes fixed on some far distance beyond the viewer's range, a prospect unknown and unknowable to the mere observer, at sea in present time.